Bombing Trilogy

Bombing

The Business of Killing

The Weak and The Strong

Prologue   **Passage**

Thursday, January 27, 1983

He awoke from a fitful sleep.   For weeks his bloated, ascitic belly had compromised his breathing and he could sleep only when sitting in a chair.   But tonight was different, he felt well enough to try sleeping in bed next to his wife.   Propped on three pillows, he chatted with her in the dark until she fell asleep.   Soon he dozed, too.

An hour or so later, he awakened and struggled to his feet, trying hard not to disturb his sleeping wife.   He slipped into his bathrobe.   It hung loose on his cancer-ridden body.   He could not resist an ironic reflection that the long, painful course of radiation treatments and chemotherapy had prolonged his life sufficiently to allow him to slowly suffocate.   He looked down at his beloved and long-suffering wife, studied the gentle rise and fall of her chest. Holding the headboard for balance, he leaned over and, saying goodbye, kissed her cheek.

He went to the kitchen for a can of beer.   He took great delight in the knowledge that this would have given his oncologist apoplexy.   He thought the doctor was, deep down, a reasonable man and would understand.   Sipping the drink, he went to the front door and stepped outside.   It was bitterly cold and the night was as still, dark and clear as any he had ever seen, yet his state of mind made him impervious to the cold.   His breath made large clouds of steam which evaporated slowly into nothingness.   A fresh snow had fallen that afternoon making the scene peaceful and idyllic.   He recalled the neighbor kids digging out his sidewalk that afternoon and smiled. He looked up at the stars, spotting Orion, the Hunter.   It was his favorite constellation.   How many times in his life had he gazed intently at those particular stars?   He thanked God for this night.   It was how he wished to remember earth in his last moments.

He returned to the house and went to his study.   In a room crammed with pictures, mementos, medals and books on shelves from floor to ceiling he sought out a single, small, faded snapshot resting in a plain black frame.   The photograph was of a group of ten men kneeling and standing beneath the nose of an old army bomber.   Each man had long ago scribbled his name beneath his face.   All ten men grinned widely.   It was the grin of camaraderie, youth and innocence.   They were the finest; the very best America had to offer.   Ten stories, ten paths converging on one instant in time caught forever in a faded black and white photograph.   If America and democracy needed defending, it was fitting that these ten should be among the ones chosen to defend them.

He held it in his hand while he looked at the other pictures on the wall.   They were of his four daughters, their husbands and his grandchildren.   He sat on a leather couch and carefully placed the photograph on the coffee table.   He got up and went to a cupboard and pulled out an old wooden ammo box filled with brittle, ancient 78 rpm phonograph records. The box was heavy and it took nearly all of his remaining energy to move it.   He carefully placed the box beside the photograph and returned to the couch.   He picked up the picture, studying every face in the soft light.   He knew every name without reading the signature.   He had pictures of their children and grandchildren on his wall, too.

He struggled back to his feet and returned to the wall and took down a recent picture of the same pose in front of a shiny, restored Flying Fortress in a museum.   It had been their last reunion before he had gotten sick.   Some spaces in the pose were missing, left empty by passage.   They grinned broadly as before, now silver-haired, heavier and bespectacled.   One was in a wheelchair.   His smile was a little feeble, but no less genuine.

He sipped his beer and looked at the pictures for a long time.   His mind brimmed with thoughts and emotion.   He studied the outline of the old B-17, sleek and dark, beautiful and sinister; the new one pristine, and cleansed innocent by restoration and fading remembrance.

Revisionists with selective memories, he knew, would have him wear the mantle of an unrepentant destroyer, the murderer of innocent women and children, totally devoid of morality, particular in the abject brutality of his method.   He rejected this.   He did the job he had been asked to do in good faith, choosing instead to leave the morality questions to the collective wisdom of a higher authority.   Maybe it hadn't been a "good war", but it had been a righteous one.   If he had been required to do penance, he had done none.   If he should feel guilt or remorse, he was unmoved.   He smiled to himself.   It was too late anyway.   Judgment was a few breaths away.

Finally, he laid back and rested the older photograph on his chest.   Contented with a life well-lived, he closed his eyes and fell asleep, sure in the knowledge that the grass in Europe grows especially green over the bodies of the missing and dead airmen who were his friends. No one was there to mark the last beats of his proud, tired heart as he left this earth to join them.

Killing the Cow

Wednesday, June 3, 1942

The instructor stood still and erect, perfect in his military bearing. He might have been a model on a recruiting poster for Air Corps pilots were it not for the black patch over his right eye and the tight, leathery scars blanched white on the side of his face. He had been burned while being shot down in the Philippines during the first days of the war. He was too smart and brave to be dismissed from the service because of disability. His contribution to the war effort as a bloodied hero standing before a room full of Aviation Cadets far exceeded any residual value he might have as a pilot or a warrior.

What stood before the students was a man whose fighting spirit had been broiled away with the flesh of his cheek and his eye. He spoke from a distance in a place few of these young men could yet imagine. He spoke in monotones without making contact between his remaining eye and the eyes of his students.

Before them was a genuine hero, proven in battle, tested by fire. They stared at him in awe. He had been there already. They could not know that he loathed his life, his survival and his betrayal of the dead by living, because he had been deprived of the necessary faculties and could not now exact his revenge on the savage yellow race. Perhaps these young men might be infused with the same insatiable rage that consumed him and, through them he might yet obtain vicarious retribution. Perhaps not. Rage like this came from being seared and searing left few survivors. Besides, youngsters resisted such rage as aberration. Rage like this was acquired not taught.

The student to Hollis's left leaned over to him and whispered, "Jesus, would you look at this guy. What is this, some sort of circus freak show? Bombing 101?"

The instructor looked down and turned his head slightly to bring his good eye over the words on the slip of paper. He spoke softly, there was a small droplet of spit glistened at the scarred angle of his mouth. It was distracting and Hollis wished he would wipe it away with his finger.

"There are two kinds of bombing. Tactical and strategic. Tactical bombing is used against military targets usually, but not invariably, in direct support of troops on the ground.

"Strategic bombing, on the other hand, is the large scale application of area and/or precision bombing to targets designed to break the enemy's will and fundamental capacity to wage war. Such targets include vital industrial complexes where the instruments of war are produced, key military installations and population centers where the workers and their families reside. We will explore the various facets of each of these forms of bombing and show how they can be used to win the war. But, in its simplest terms, with tactical bombing you kick over the pail of milk. In strategic bombing, you kill the cow."

Hollis stared at the patch and the clinging droplet of spittle in disbelief and foreboding. He understood for the very first time what a monumental mistake he had made.

Rizzo   Reese   Dodge   Hulse   Quinn   Mollica

Sullivan   Hollis   Wychulis   Smith

Book I

The Big League

It can't happen to me.   I'm too handsome, intelligent, in love...

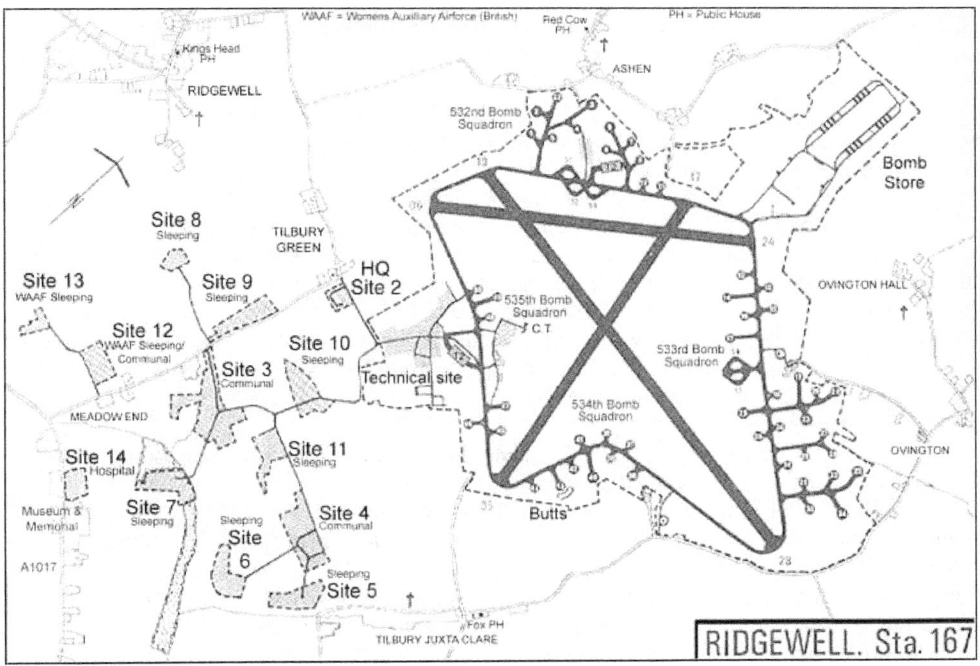

Chapter One   **The Big Mistake**

Thursday, August 12, 1943

  It was an ignoble, even anticlimactic, arrival. They rode to their assigned airfield in the back of a GMC truck named **Chantilly**, smelling of damp, weathered canvas and gasoline, ten men seated on long wooden benches which ran along each side, their baggage, all they brought with them, piled in a huge jumble of foot lockers, Val-packs and B-4 bags, on the floor. The second crew, Cahill's, rode in the truck behind them. It was a warm, sunny day, not what they had been told to expect in England where they would find drenching rain and impenetrable fog.

  Hollis watched his crew on their journey. He tried to gauge their mood. He expected excitement, but they seemed somber. He expected curiosity, even; perhaps, eager anticipation that the long journey from peace to war each had made was finally over. Instead, they seemed quietly absorbed in their own thoughts.

  Everybody except Augie, the back-woods bumpkin from Mississippi. He kept yapping like an annoying little dog, chattering things about which no one cared, flicking cigarette butts like tracers from the front of the truck out over the tailgate. Perhaps this was his way of dealing with the uncertainty.

"Hey Lieutenant," he said, meaning Hollis because he invariably addressed the other officers by adding their surnames, "I heard the whores in London will fuck you standing up.   I didn't think y'all could do that.   Jesus, this is gonna be great.   I ain't never done anything like that before."

Sully, the bombardier, also a Southerner, replied, "What's the matter, Augie, couldn't talk your sister into doing it that way?" that caused everyone to laugh.   Even Augie.

Leo, their copilot, said, "How'd you ever manage to get out of Dogpatch, Augie?"

"I was drafted."   This caused more nervous laughter.

Hollis drifted back behind a veil of thoughts as another ember zipped past, a foot from his nose.   He turned to look back at Augie who rocked back and forth with the shifting of gears, still smiling, his slow mind trying to sift through the insult to his sister. Hollis found himself on the fine edge of panic and despair, each moment carrying him closer to his destiny such that if one more butt flew past his head he was going to kill the annoying bastard with his bare hands.

"Wow, Augie," Sully said, "this must be quite a thrill for you.   Here you are in Merry Ol' England.   Y'all have to be sure and write your Maw and Paw and tell 'em about all the interestin' things you seen."

Leo, sitting beside Hollis, muttered quietly into his ear, "Now why would he want to go and do that?   They probably can't even read."

Hollis smiled back at him.   Augie was one of those people God placed on earth to challenge the patience of the righteous, educated man.   A Darwinian anomaly.   Nurture versus nature is the biological argument.   Augie just happened.   A random mutation like a square Mendelian pea.   His hillbilly way and mannerisms were a curiosity and slightly amusing at first. Like a precocious, if unruly, child.   More undomesticated than precocious.   His profligate use of the word 'nigger' and his distrust of personal hygiene made him almost intolerable. H-y, the navigator, couldn't stand him from the moment he laid eyes on him.   Hollis had heard about guys like Augie but he had never actually seen one.   "Betcha he was a problem child."

Leo replied his agreement by snorting a laugh through his nose.

Sully, staring out the back of the truck, whispered just loud enough for Leo and Hollis to hear, "Happy the nose that cannot smell a barbarian."

Leo nodded.

Hollis was perhaps the only person who knew Sully was referring to the Roman take on Anglo-Saxon hygiene.

Finally, the grinding of gears and bouncing along washboard roads came to a merciful end as the two trucks approached the main gate of the airfield.   The MP at the gate must have recognized the drivers because they were waved through without stopping.   The two corporals who had come to fetch the two crews from the Replacement Center could be spiriting a platoon of *Waffen SS* killers or two truckloads of prostitutes for all the guard knew or cared.   Delivering more lambs to the slaughter.   They had not been told their destination and the driver refused to disclose it despite their efforts to pry it out of him.   "Station 167" is all they were told.   For all they knew that could be in outskirts of Copenhagen.

They rumbled down a narrow lane, their journey punctuated by the frequent splash of a mud puddle. All eyes peered out the back of the truck as they pulled up to a cluster of single-story brick buildings and Nissen huts all connected to each other.   The truck screeched to a halt and the driver dropped the tailgate with a loud clang.   "Headquarters Block, Gentlemen. Unload you gear and report to the duty officer inside."

"Where the hell are we?" Augie asked.

"Ridgewell."   He returned to the cab of the truck and gunned the engine to speed the unloading along.   The pile on the floor of the truck became a pile on the grass in front of the large Nissen hut.

The crew started looking around, but mostly up into the sky.   On such a nice day, surely they were up, bombing something.

He glanced over at Cahill's crew as the second truck roared off behind the first.   They were looking up, too.   The reflex action of any airmen on any airfield.

"Everybody wait here.   Come on, Leo."   Cahill followed them in and they stepped up to the counter and said to the sergeant, "Hollis and Cahill crews reporting in."

Without looking up he said, Welcome to the 381st, sirs," and he pointed around the corner where there was another counter behind which, on the wall, stood a large blackboard with rows of names and numbers listed by squadrons.   There was a lot of chalk dust and names partially erased and written over.   The names, Hollis figured, were crews each named for the pilot and their assigned aircraft number.   It was a busy blackboard.

"Lieutenants Hollis and Cahill.   We're here from the Replacement Center."

The Captain replied, matter-of-factly, "Welcome, glad you're here."   He turned to look at the board.   "Uh, I don't have squadron assignments for you yet, but go grab some chow and come back in--" he glanced at his watch--"say, an hour and I will get you settled."

Leo whispered in his ear, "Probably waiting to see who didn't make it back."

Hollis and Cahill exchanged glances.   "They out now?" Cahill asked.

"Yeah," he said, bringing his eyes up to look at Cahill, "they should be back in an hour. When you get done eating, why don't you go out to the flight line and watch 'em come back."

Cahill nodded and smiled at Hollis.

Word passed quickly: They were on the way in.   Hollis and Leo scanned the empty sky. The rest of the crew was waiting elsewhere.   In the distance, on the infield beyond a cluster of empty hardstands, Hollis could see the control tower.   The brass was lined up on top, leaning against the railing, their pant legs fluttering in the breeze.   After a few moments, he heard the far-off drone of approaching engines, like the low roll of distant thunder and saw a formation of planes, a cluster of slowly moving gray dots above the horizon.   Some seemed not to notice. Others turned to look but quickly turned away.   They, apparently, were not Them.

Soon the droning diminished.   The sky was empty and silent again.

This, no doubt, was the quietest time on a bomber field: when the planes were gone. Today they had gone to Gelsenkirchen, Germany, the officers had been told.   Hollis thought the identity of the target was a secret, but then he realized the Germans already knew where the target was.   And soon they would return.

The tingle of anticipation gathered in his loins, made the hair rise on his neck.   He had waited a long time for this moment.   A tremendous and unpredictable history was playing out around him, mankind's greatest calamity, and, irresistibly, he had become part of it.   For a moment, he felt detached, unreal and remote, the viewer of an historic chronicle enacted on a giant motion picture screen. The War. Everything up to this moment had been preliminary, anticipatory. This peculiar reverie was eclipsed by the realization that from here on there was no going back. Coincident with an arrival had been a departure, each with its own increasing gravity, centripetal pull. His participation in this fantastic adventure was not without a price: his scrawny little neck. This ambivalence had not escaped him. It took the form of an ugly word: fear. For the moment, however, the scales were unbalanced; the image of the black eye patch and glistening droplet of saliva compartmentalized below his awareness. He was excited and he was, strangely, happy; his terror from a few hours back sequestered, unheard in a remote part of his brain.

Yes sir, he thought as he scanned the sky, *this is it.* *The real thing.* *The Big League.* He had passed every test, done everything he was supposed to, weathered the cold scrutiny of his peers, survived the process of elimination that thinned the field of potential Army aviators down to an elite group and graduated into the left seat of a bomber flying with the Eighth Air Force out of England. They called it The Big Leagues for a reason. He considered himself lucky to be here. He could have been sent to the South Pacific where living conditions were more arduous, the medals came quicker and the missions were all escorted. His crew was known by *his* name. If there had to be a war and he had to fight in it, this was where he wanted most to be. Strategic, geopolitical or patriotic issues did not concern him. He fervently hoped that this had not been some monumental mistake, that now, facing the supreme challenge, responsible not just for the mission and the aircraft, but for nine other lives, he would not fail. He had, after all, volunteered, seduced by the glamour and romance of being an Army pilot.

Someone in the crowd gathered outside headquarters yelled, "Here they come!" and a half dozen binoculars rose as one to a half dozen pairs of eyes all looking eastward. Hollis heard them, but he could not see them. The distant, rolling thunder returned. Someone pointed.

There they were. Hollis strained his eyes for his first glimpse: dark specks arranged in a loose formation which grew into a gaggle of Fortresses, not unlike geese returning to a pond. The droning of the engines increased in intensity as the Group began a long, wheeling turn around the field, orbiting as each squadron broke off, plane by plane, for landing. A single Fort broke from the pack, popped two red flares from the roof of the cockpit, and entered a steep bank bringing itself quickly over the end of the runway, engulfed in priority. The sun glinted briefly off the propellers flashing four bright silver disks as it leveled off and descended. Two more red flares arced up as the plane settled toward earth, flaps down, wheels extended groping for the ground, hanging on its broad wings in a picture-perfect glide onto the runway. The big bomber flared and touched the concrete, two small blue puffs blossomed from the tires, the tail remained in the air briefly and settled gently to the runway.

He could hear someone from the gathering count slowly until the formation passed overhead and drowned out the voice.

A tech sergeant walked past and climbed into a jeep and started the engine. Leo yelled to him, "Hey Sarge, where you goin'?"

He pointed at the Fortress finishing its roll out. "Can we ride along?"

The sergeant jerked his thumb at the back of the jeep.

Leo said, "Come on, let's see what's going on." They ran over to the jeep and got in just ahead of a major wearing the Caduceus on his collar. The sergeant gunned the engine and they tore off down the perimeter strip.   By the time they arrived at the B-17 it had pulled off the runway onto a nearby vacant hardstand and the engines were shut down. A crowd had gathered around the waist and two ambulances stood by.   A major leaped from a jeep as it screeched to a stop and the crowd parted as he quickly entered the bomber.

Hollis surveyed the damage to the plane which appeared concentrated around the right waist and trailing edge of the wing.   Hollis felt a wave of nausea rise in his stomach, his excitement canceled out by dread.   There was a large, jagged hole in the thin metal skin near the waist gunner's window.   It was big enough for a man to climb through.   Behind the tail, a gunner was hunched over, vomiting.   Two medics passed a flexible litter up through the waist window.

The next plane finished its roll out and taxied by, the roar of engines rose and fell and brakes squealed in protest as it maneuvered onto the perimeter strip.   The rest followed.   Some of the bombers appeared unscathed; a few had feathered props and blackened engines.   One was missing its rudder and the tip of the vertical fin was gone.   Hollis could see the faces in the passing bombers as they rubbernecked to get a glimpse of the damaged plane.   A jeep weaved between the passing planes and pulled up beside the parked bomber.   A captain hopped out and walked past.   Someone shouted 'how many?'   "Three," was the terse reply.

Hollis watched the formation as it passed overhead again, and one by one, more bombers peeled off and turned into the downwind leg forming a single file.   There was some shouting from inside the bomber and soon the litter was gently handed out the waist window to waiting hands on the ground.   A bottle of blood and a bottle of water clinked against each other as they followed the litter out.   Small tubes ran down to the body held tightly in the embrace of a splint stretcher.   Hollis caught his first glimpse of the blood that covered the man's face and the brown leather of his jacket.   It had matted into the shearling collar and his hair.   Hollis felt queasy again, but he could not look away for, while the sight was grotesque, it was also irresistible. The injured man moved his arm as if reaching for something only he could see.   They carefully lifted him into the ambulance.

Another bomber pulled up and stopped, the waist door fell open and a man stepped down onto the perimeter strip, walking toward the ambulance.   He held his right shoulder which was slick with bright red blood, his torn leather jacket flapped in the breeze created by the engines as the copilot gave a wave and the plane pulled away.   A medic walked over and guided him to a waiting stretcher and he, too, was conveyed to the ambulance which drove away.

A short time later, a second litter was handed into the plane and, after a few minutes, another body was passed out through the window shrouded in a blanket which was tucked carefully around the head.   The flying boots stuck out from beneath the blanket.   The major stepped out of the plane as the dead man was placed on the ground.   He was followed by a flying officer wearing a New York Yankee's baseball cap.   The major spoke to him and he was escorted to the second ambulance.   He was bloodied also, but did not seem injured.

Another bomber stopped and the nose hatch dropped open.   Its Plexiglas nose was shattered.   An officer holding a bloody bandage to his face lowered himself to the taxiway and stepped out in front of the plane, waved back at the pilots and trotted over to the medics.   The plane roared off.

When the last of the planes had landed, they loaded the body into the second ambulance and it, too, drove away.   A few men looked into the bomber, shook their heads and walked away.   The crowd thinned.   Hollis felt drawn to the damaged B-17 by a grim, obscene fascination.   He and Leo walked over to the gaping hole in the waist, its aluminum skin ripped open and peeled back by the impact of whatever explosive had detonated against it.   He stepped to the waist door and leaned in for a better look.   In the dim light of the waist compartment, he could see that the interior of the fuselage was spattered with gore.   Large pools of dark, dirty blood covered the black rubber mat pulled along by gravity in broad crimson rivulets on the sloping floor flowing over and around the hundreds of brass shell casings which littered the floor. Always analytical, Hollis realized that a few inches either way and the bomber would have been missed completely or torn in half.

"Good God Almighty.   It looks like they've been slaughtering cattle in here," Leo said.

Hollis placed his hand on the inside of the doorway, bending his body to get a better look. His palm and fingers touched something cold, wet and sticky.   It felt like cherry pie.   He quickly jerked his hand away and looked to see what he had touched.   It was a grayish-white piece of meat which Hollis recognized as brain matter.   He pulled the flesh off the metal to which it clung. Attached was a fragment of skull and overlying skin.   He noticed the eyebrow, an upper eyelid and part of the bridge of a nose.   He wiped his hand off on the grass and walked away.   Leo, who up until that moment had a comment for just about everything, was quiet. They flagged down a passing truck and rode back to the Headquarters.

Before now death had been abstract.   A cold stiff aunt sleeping serenely in a casket.   A rising black pyre at the end of the runway, a training accident for someone else to clean up.   Or they simply vanished, disappearing over the ocean known but to God.   Hollis did not expect this.   He felt foolishly self-aware of his naiveté.   What did he think they were up to over here? He looked at his fingers.   They had not come clean on the grass.

Blood. In abstract terms of biology, blood is nothing more than a liquid.   A complex solution composed of billions of teeming red and white corpuscles, chemicals and lots of salt water.   It was a symbol of a body's integrity or lack thereof.   But blood can be deceptive. Enormous amounts can be spilled from a relatively innocuous and unthreatening laceration of the scalp and yet a man could suffer an instantaneously lethal wound to a vital organ and not shed more than a thimbleful.   It was a matter of how big the hole was and how long the heart pushed blood out of that hole before there was none left to pump.   Somewhere between a pin prick and complete evisceration and dismemberment most combat injuries could be found.   It didn't matter.   A waist gunner in a B-17, an infantryman in a foxhole in the Kasserine or a gun tub on a battleship.   They said the blood was so thick on the Somme that it created a swamp.   It is the tearing of the flesh that elicited pain.   Blood loss is itself painless.   Countless millions of blood donors could attest to that.   It was also a simple fact of biology that the brain can think faster than blood can spurt from a broken heart.

He wondered what happened when you died instantly.   One second you are looking at the airspeed indicator or staring into an empty patch of sky then poof!   Whammo!   What? Vapor?   Heat?   Blinding light?   Unspeakable, unimaginable pain?   Ecstasy?   Relief? *What?*

They stepped into the Operations Room again and stood at the counter.   Cahill was already there waiting. "I'll be with you in a moment, Gentlemen," the officer behind the desk said.

The captain they had seen drive up in the jeep earlier walked in and spoke to the officer behind the desk.   The officer took an eraser and brushed the name 'Cody' off the board and wrote in 'Hollis'.   He then erased 'Gruver' and wrote in 'Cahill'.   Hollis read the other names on the list: Ransahoff, Eisenberg, Selkirk, Cassidy.   They had been assigned to the 532nd Bomb Squadron.   There should have been nine names on the list.   Nine crews to fill in a squadron's compliment.   With the exchange of these two names there were six.   Hollis could not help but think that, with a scrawling of chalk his fate had been sealed.

The captain looked at the two pilots and, without changing his business-like expression, walked away.

"Gentleman, a truck will take you to the 532nd Squadron office.   Report in and they will get you billeted."

Hollis gathered up his stuff, all his worldly possessions.   Except for his book collection and civilian clothes at home everything he owned was contained in that B-4 bag and foot locker. The only things not Government Issue he had brought from home were a picture of his parents, a couple pictures of Jessie and a cherished, battered old copy of Gray's Anatomy given to him by Jessie's father on the day he told him of his desire to become a doctor.

On the blackboard in the Squadron headquarters, Hollis's and Cahill's names were already chalked in.

"Cahill," the billeting officer said, "you're with Selkirk.   Hollis you're with Eisenberg. Welcome to the Squadron.   We only have six combat crews in the squadron and our minimum strength is supposed to be nine.   You'll need a Class B pass to go certain distances from the field.   You will have a separate combat mess because your hours and diet will be so different from everybody else's.   A supply truck makes a daily run to Cambridge and there is train service from Great Yeldham, down the road a piece."

Hollis hauled his stuff to his assigned barracks.   Over the door was a hand-painted sign:

PILOT'S HOUSE
ENTRY RESTRICTED
SERGEANTS WILL BE SHOT ON SIGHT

The barracks was a one level wood and cinderblock building with ill-fitting doors at both ends.   It contained three rooms on each side of a central, dimly lit hall.   The floor was concrete.   It sat alongside a similar building.   They faced a road across which was a large cluster of Nissen huts, half-barrel-shaped structures of corrugated metal with brick ends sitting on a concrete pad all connected by a cinder path.   Hollis had stayed in one with other officers at the Replacement Center at Bovingdon and he felt glad about the slightly improved quarters. The enlisted men stayed in Nissens further down the road.   The communal site for the squadron was nestled in a small wood.   Squadron headquarters consisted of two Nissen huts not far up the road.   The latrine facilities for the officers, he found out, consisted of a large Nissen hut on its own little cinder path about twenty yards away.   There was a hot water source for showers. But, he also found out, fuel was in short supply and the availability of a truly hot shower was limited.

Sergeant Beamis, the Charge of Quarters, introduced himself to Hollis and explained that he had a deal worked out with the squadron high command such that if he hoarded enough coke and could guarantee a hot shower at least once a week for the officers, he could use the facility for his own ablutions before the hot water ran out.   He also got to quarter himself in a small anteroom in the other cinderblock hut as long as he also kept the hot-water heater that supplied heat to the two buildings up and running.   Beamis pointed to the complex system of pipes and a tiny furnace that provided the heat.   He had converted the system from coal to waste engine oil to keep the twelve radiators in the two buildings primed with hot water.   He was obviously proud of his improvisational engineering, but he was sorry to admit that he had not been able to convert the shower to waste oil because he had been unable to scrounge up the necessary equipment.   Beamis reminded Hollis of a convict who maintained his status and improved his lifestyle by currying favor with the prisoner hierarchy. Or his jailers.

"Explain to me," Hollis asked, "how I ended up in better quarters than my copilot and the other officers?"

"You guys are the envy of the squadron, even the whole base," Beamis said.   "Only the Group staff live better.   When the Group moved in this site was assigned to the 532nd.   These two buildings were supposed to be torn down as they were not part of the original construction specifications by the Eighth Bomber Command.   The base was intended for use by the RAF. In fact, Stirlings with 90 Squadron were here for a week when we moved in, but was reassigned to the Eighth and we were only supposed to get those metal shithouses.   So don't complain about it.   It'll just piss people off even more.

"Now, to answer your question, Entwhistle, the CO, I guess you ain't met him yet, wanted all the first pilots together.   He never said why, but everybody figured it had something to do with cohesion between the pilots.   Entwhistle," Beamis went on, "has a dim view of copilots, navigators and bombardiers.   Navigators could live in grass shacks for all he cared," Beamis added.

Beamis betrayed his contempt for Entwhistle by never once addressing him as 'Major.'

Beamis directed Hollis to his room, but made no effort to help him with his stuff.   Hollis dropped his footlocker to the floor with a loud clump.   He looked around.   One side of the room was empty, the bed linens carefully folded in a small stack on the thin, bare mattress.   The locker at the foot of the bed, its door open, was also empty except for a few metal coat-hangers. A small desk, nothing more than a wooden table really, stood by the window which was covered by a blackout curtain.   The desk was cluttered on one side, but had obviously been swept clean on the other.   The wall above the empty bed was covered with pinups in various stages of undress.   Vargas, Pettys, nudes in artistic poses clipped from photographic magazines, cheesecake and the usual assortment of pretty faces, some familiar, most not.   The other side of the room was well lived-in.   The bed was unmade, dirty socks and underwear were stuffed under the bed.   Gray towels were suspended on hooks nailed into the occupied locker. Various personal items were strewn about, a tooth brush, a pair of sneakers, a baseball mitt, a beat up garrison cap.   The wall above the bed was naked except for a calendar from a New York delicatessen.

The floor was crusted by clots of dried mud.   There was the unmistakable odor of sweat, stale cigarette smoke and aviation gas.

"Nice, huh?" Beamis asked.

Hollis stared at the empty bed.

"Who slept there?"

"Nobody."

Hollis turned to look at the sergeant.

"Besides, it's probably bad luck to ask."

They exchanged glances in silence.

"One other thing, Lieutenant.   Whenever you leave the hut, you have to carry your gas mask."   He pointed to the small musette bag hanging on a nail over the desk.   Another was hung beside it.

"Base regulations."   Beamis tapped the back of the door with his fingernail.   There was posted the base regulations as well as what to do in case of fire, air raid, gas attack, invasion...

"Slit trenches are out back. Don't go pissin' in 'em in the middle of the night.

"Oh, and one other thing.   You may be called upon to help me steal coke from the bin over at the 533rd.   For reasons I cannot explain, they seem to have a constant and reliable source of it.   I think they're stealin' it from somebody else.   They keep it hidden, but I know where.   You want hot water, you gotta help me steal the coal.   That applies to all the officers but Entwhistle, who don't know nothin' about it."   Beamis turned to leave.   "Welcome, Lieutenant.   I hope you enjoy your stay with us"

Hollis looked at the stark, vacant bed.   It probably wasn't even cold yet.   Wonder where the poor bastard is who slept there last night?   *Fuck.*

Suppressing the thought that he was violating some hallowed ground, Hollis began to unpack his belongings.   He opened his footlocker and took out the picture of Jessie and placed it self-consciously, almost reverentially, on the empty space on the table.   It was a portrait she had taken a few years back.   She was radiant in the photograph, beaming a beautiful, perfect smile, a string of pearls around her neck.   It was not done in color but had been shaded in by the photographer.   Her lips were red and her hair flowing blond onto her shoulders.   He took out the other photographs of his parents and a small leatherette folder which contained pictures of him in his uniform standing with his arm around Jessie and her arm around him.   It had been taken a few days before his furlough ended.   She was beaming in that photo, too.   His heart ached as he looked at the snapshot and rubbed its leather case with his thumb.   He wondered if she truly loved him.   Or was he a pity fuck for the war effort?   He should write telling her he had arrived at his final destination safely.   If the censors allowed it. He wondered what had happened to the third crew.   If their wives, girlfriends and parents had been told yet that they were missing and presumed lost over the ocean.

He spread his B-4 bag onto the bed and unpacked his uniforms, hanging them in the locker.   He took out his flying clothes, two summer weight flight suits, boots, leather jacket and helmet.   He had been issued a .45 automatic.   He took the holster and hung it on a nail in the locker.   He hadn't quite figured out what the gun was for or why he and the other members of the crew had been given them.   Maybe he was supposed to fight his way out if downed. Maybe he was part of base defense, shoot anybody that looked German or had an accent. Maybe they were all supposed to take turns shooting the Norden if they had to crash land in enemy territory.

When he was finished he made the bed and sat on it smoking a cigarette trying to make sense out of his predicament.   He smoked another.   He looked at the pinups taped to the wall behind him.   He recognized Jinx Falkenberg, Betty Grable, Chili Williams, and Ann Sheridan. Rita Hayworth kneeling on a bed regaled in her black lace and satin nightgown.   And Jane

Russell with her thirty-eight inch tits, stretched out seductively on that haystack saying to all the world "Come fuck me" with those dreamy eyes.   He thought of Jessie.

Chapter Two   **Stan**

He stared at the empty, unmade bed, speculating on the fate of its occupant.   Was he still alive?   Hurt?   The last plane had landed over two hours ago.   Surely by now everyone had cleared interrogation.

The door of the hut flew open with a loud, wooden bang followed by the unmistakable clumping of flying boots on the floor.   Hollis was startled to see a brown leather blur enter the room, fling a Yankee's baseball cap against the wall, slamming the door behind him.   He threw himself onto the bed making the metal frame rattle and clank against the wall.   The man coiled himself into the fetal position facing the wall and did not move.   Hollis noticed blood on the shearling cuff of the man's jacket and along the collar of his dirty, yellow Mae West, his muddy, booted feet tucked up against his rear end.

Hollis felt awkward again as if his presence violated a moment of private anguish.   He contemplated leaving, but wasn't sure where he might go or what he might do when he got there.

Suddenly, he felt very sad.   He wanted to go to him, whoever he was, and say something, perhaps try to comfort him.   But he had no moral authority to do so.   Anything he might say would be inappropriate, patronizing.   Uncomfortable and perplexed by the whole situation, he would keep his mouth shut and wait for something to happen.

A soft knock shattered the stillness like a pistol shot.   Hollis leapt to his feet to answer the door before there were more knocks, but the door flew open before he could reach the knob. A tall lieutenant took a step inside turning to the man on the bed, "Hey Stan, want to get something to eat?"

The body did not move.   The tall man paused for a moment and left without closing the door or giving any indication that he had seen or was even aware of Hollis's presence.

Leo appeared at the door and looked at Stan.   Leo had the kind of face, round, cherubic, animated and predominately cheerful, that could give silent expression to every human emotion. He seemed unmoved by what he saw. "Let's go eat. I'm hungry."

Hollis dropped his cap onto his head and walked with Leo into the late afternoon air. The evening was warm, but it was starting to cloud up.   In the distance, they could hear the approach of a truck.

"What gives?" Leo asked as he nodded back in the direction of the hut.

"Don't know.   I think he was the guy from the plane we went to see.   The one wearing the ball cap.   He came in and threw himself down and didn't say a word.   I couldn't even tell if he was still breathing.   He was giving me the willies."

"One of the guys in my hut said the other gunner died."

They got on the truck and proceeded to ride the circuit to the Combat Mess.   Passing through the door, they saw an expansive room filled with men seated at long tables in various combinations of uniform eating quietly.   Above the door was the ubiquitous sign which read: "Where the elite meet to eat.   Take what you want but eat what you take."

Hollis and Leo took their trays filled with mutton, boiled potatoes and beets and walked over to a pair of empty seats.   Hollis placed his tray across the table from a man who ate hunched over his food.   Without looking up he said, "Don't sit there.   That's Lonnie's seat."

"You can sit there," a captain sitting nearby said softly.

"No," the Hollis said, "that's OK."

"It's alright, really."

"That's Lonnie's seat I said.   Sit somewhere else."

"I'm sorry, is Lonnie coming?"   Hollis turned to look for Lonnie, who was probably on his way that very moment to claim his seat.

"No, Lonnie won't be needing it," the captain said.

"Don't sit there I said!" and he picked up his tray of food and heaved it at the place where Lonnie was supposed to sit.

The captain motioned to the empty seat in front of him and told Hollis he could sit there instead.

"Where's Lonnie?" Hollis asked, shaken.

"Gone," the captain said simply.

No one seemed to notice the commotion caused by the tossed food tray and Leo said nothing as he sat beside the captain who shortly got up and left.

"Jesus, Leo. What have we gotten ourselves into?"

"I don't know, but it's put me right off my mutton."

Hollis returned to the room expecting to find Stan still curled up on his bed, but it was vacant.   He sat at the desk and took out some writing paper.   When he first arrived in England, because of censorship, he realized he didn't have much to say.   He had written letters while at the Replacement Center. All of it small stuff. They were specifically admonished about keeping a diary for reasons not made clear. The mail from home had not yet caught up with him.   He couldn't tell Jessie where he was or what he had seen.   He couldn't tell her what brains felt like to the touch.   Or how uncertain his future looked.   Or that he was completely scared shitless. What had started out as high adventure had grown ominous and uncertain.   What not long ago seemed so glamorous had become grotesque and terrifying.   He did the best he could.

Dear Jessie,

I arrived safely at our new station, 'somewhere in England'.   They went out today and had a rough time of it.   I must admit to some apprehension about this.   Which he knew to be an extraordinary understatement.   *But, God willing, I should get through this.   I know I am a good pilot and I have a good crew.   We have a few oddballs perhaps, but they are good at their jobs.   And when the chips are down I know they will pull together and get the job done.*

I hope you are well.   I think of you always.   I think of the night we spent together before I left and I am restored.   I take solace in you; the thought of you in my arms makes me want to return home to you

He read what he had written and tore it up.   It was not what he wanted to say.

He was about to start another when there was a knock at the door.   Another strange face stepped into the room

"You the new guy?"

Hollis stood up and shook the man's hand, "Yeah, John Hollis."

"Hi, I'm Mickey Selkirk.   Put you in with Stan, eh?   Where is the little bagel-snapper?"

"He was here earlier.   He looked pretty shook."

"Yeah.   He should be getting a package with some victuals from his folks.   He's due. I really like that filter fish in a jar.   Tasty."

"You mean gefilte fish?"

"Yeah, that's it.   Where is he?"

"Don't know."

"I came over to tell you Entwhistle wants you to report to the squadron office at oh-eight o'clock. Tell your crew."

"OK."

"Wanna go over to the Club and get a beer?"

"Sure."   Hollis grabbed his gas mask and noticed that Stan's still hung on the hook in the wall.

As they walked along the gravel path Selkirk said, "They put you in with Stan, eh? They must be hoping some of his wisdom rubs off on you."

"Did Stan's wisdom help the guy who slept in my bed last night?"

Selkirk turned to look at Hollis as they walked, but said nothing.   "What happened to him?"

"Who?"

"The guy in my bed?"

"Whatcha carrying there?" Selkirk asked as he tugged at the musette bag.

"My gas mask.   Beamis told me to carry it at all times.   Base regulation."

"And you believed him?"

"Well, yeah."

"You seen anybody else carrying one?"

"Now that you mention it, no."

Selkirk grabbed the canvas bag from his shoulder and said, "Here let me show you what to do with that."   He nonchalantly hurled it over his shoulder into a clump of bushes.

Hollis laughed aloud.   Leo, he knew, would have climbed into the bushes to retrieve it. "Where are you from?   What the hell kind of accent is that?"

"I'm from Vermont.   West Paulet, to be exact.   Had a nice dairy farm going when the war started."

"You grew cows?"

"Yeah, big ones.   Holsteins.   Best dairy cows in the state.   Wife and a kid, too."

"What the hell are you doing here?"

"I've asked myself that question a million times."

"Being a farmer with a family you must have been able to get out of it."

"The Selkirk's have been patriots who have fought in every war since Lexington.   I am my father's only son.   Somebody had to do it.   Tradition."

"You're out of your mind."

"If I'm nuts what are you doing here?"

"I wanted wings."   Mickey laughed.   "So what's up with Stan?"

"Got shot up today.   Both waist gunners were killed by a flak burst."

"That was his plane?   My copilot and I went out to see it.   It was a mess."

"Stan took it hard.   He's a great pilot, best natural pilot in the Group and he's the most experienced man in the Group.   He was with the 91st until he was wounded.   While he was still in the hospital his crew went down.   When he recovered they didn't want him back so they sent him here as a replacement pilot.   He's two or three trips away from a full tour and a ticket home.   Lately, he's been takin' to brooding about his imminent demise."

"Poor Stan."

"Stan actually likes this stuff.   He considers himself an avenging angel for every aggrieved Jew since the Diaspora.   Not long after I joined the Group we went to Hamburg and the lead bombardier froze up on the bomb run and by the time the navigator realized what was going on we passed the release point and the whole Group toggled late.   The entire bomb train went over.   Everyone was upset about the wasted mission.   But not Stan.   He said no bomb dropped on a German is ever wasted.

"You know those Negroes in the Ordinance company wash off the bombs before they load 'em so they're clean and they'll fall true.   Not Stan.   Before they take off Stan puts a wad of gum onto the nose of one of the bombs.   He wants one to not drop true so it will either fall short or long and hit a hospital or an orphanage so he can kill more Germans.   None of this pickle barrel shit for ol' Stan. He says that God's true measure of a man is not by the big things he did with his life, but by the small things, the little evil things he did when he thought no one was watching.

"He believes the only way to prevent future wars is to eliminate every German from the face of the earth.   They have been a war-like race since ancient, Teutonic tribes, Goths and Vandals defeated the Romans. Germans are racially and genetically a savage and remorseless people, noted throughout history for their brutality dating back to the Neanderthals.   Get rid of them.   Blow 'em all up.   Kill 'em all.   Every last one of 'em. At least that's what he says."

"Interesting."   Hollis lit a cigarette and offered Selkirk one.   They continued walking, their embers glowing in the dark.

"Stan doesn't want me hanging around him anymore.   In China, the custom is that when you save somebody's life you are responsible for them for the rest of *their* life.   Ol' Stan saved me on my second mission and I wanted to show my gratitude, my being his friend because he ain't got many.   He keeps telling me to beat it, this isn't China. So don't pet him. He might bite."

"What's *that* mean?"

"He got into a fight in Cambridge right after Hamburg.   Some infantry captain said something anti-Jewish with which our esteemed Lieutenant Eisenberg took exception.   Stan broke his nose and tried to bite off his ear when Mattson and Watanabe pulled him off.   They thought he was gonna kill the guy.   Stan's got some sort of runt's complex.   Tries to be tougher than anybody else.   So don't make him mad."

"Great..."   Hollis could hear music coming from the Officer's Club up ahead.   He turned to Selkirk, "How many did the Group lose today?"

"Three.   They never tell us, but we can count.   The Squadron lost two plus Stan's gunners."

"What happened to the guy in my bed?"

"Who?"

"The guy I replaced."

"Cody?   Gone."

"Yeah, I gathered that. What happened to him?"

"We rolled off the target and the fighters jumped him.   He lost an engine, but kept up pretty good for a while.   Then he lost a second engine.   Stan and I closed in to cover him. Gleason slowed the group down, but the fighters saw us getting strung out as we 's'ed along and they hit us with a vengeance and we had to leave him.   The FWs went to finish him off.   He tried to make a run for the clouds, but he couldn't get away.   That was the last we saw him."

"Hanging around Stan didn't help him, did it?"

"Guess not.   But it didn't hurt either."

They entered the Officer's Club, a big room containing a piano in the corner and a fireplace, a long bar and clusters of lounge chairs and couches, a few card tables and a record player and radio near the bar.   The room was filled with music from the BBC and a great blue haze of cigarette, cigar and pipe tobacco.   Selkirk sidled up to the bar and Hollis followed.   He found Leo already sipping a beer.

"Mickey, this is Leo Wychulis, my copilot."

"Yeah, we met," Leo said. "He was talking to us earlier.   Came by and told us not to unpack, we won't be here long.   He say the same thing to you?"

Selkirk put his arm around Hollis' shoulder, handed him a beer and said, "Ol' Hollis here don't need to be flakked up, he saw the inside of Stan's plane."

"So did I," Leo said.

"So tell me about the Group," Hollis asked.

"Been here since early June, flew their first raid on June 22nd.   They been losing planes ever since," Selkirk replied.   "Bomber Command has been rearranging things trying to get it right."

"What do you mean?"

"The original air exec, a guy by the name of Holt got sick and had to go back home. TB, I think.   That's when Van Patten showed up.   Couple weeks later Garrett, the CO since the Group was formed back in January, was relieved and Van Patten took over.   No one knows what became of Garrett or why he was axed, but he was well liked apparently and they thought he got a raw deal bein' canned like that.   Then along comes that crazy Texan Gleason as air exec.   Turns out Gleason was with the 305th as a squadron CO until he got hurt.   He's loony as they come.   Dust ain't settled yet since that son of a bitch showed up.

"Whitewater Begay, Horace Duckworth, Buckley Bonner and Deke Cavanarro were all the original squadron commanders.   The Group ops officer, some guy I never heard of, left to become air exec at another group and they promoted Begay out of the squadron and brought in Entwhistle.

"They're supposed to lead the Group on a rotating basis, Van Patten, Gleason, Begay, and the four squadron COs, but it seems like Van Patten and Gleason have been doing it all.   Maybe the Squadron COs are weak.   I know Entwhistle is.   Bombs on the target is all he ever talks about, but he's only flown one pissant little milk run since he got here.   Ransahoff hates him."

"Somebody told me he's been here longer than anybody."

"Yeah, maybe that's his problem.   He came over with the 97th, they were the very first Group.   They left for Africa with TORCH and he got shot up there and sent back here.   People at Wing sent him here when they pushed Begay upstairs.   He musta seen a lot of combat. Maybe he's got combat fatigue."

"Maybe he's just tired."

"Yeah, he's been here a year.   But you gotta remember: only combat crews rotate home. Squadron COs and above are supposed to be here for the duration."

"Tough luck."

"That's why they get the extra pay.   Besides, at the rate they fly it might take 'em a year to accumulate 25 missions. My advice, don't become a squadron commander."

Hollis said nothing.

Selkirk continued, "With Cody and Gruver gone Ransahoff and Cassidy are the only original members of the Squadron.   The rest of 'em have all been lost.   We're supposed to have nine crews.   We've been working with six for almost two weeks now.   Then we lost those two and they only replaced 'em they didn't get us up to full strength yet.   The other squadrons are in better shape than us.   Or so I'm told.   I'm just a pilot.   They don't consult me on command matters."   He smiled at Hollis and added, "But if they did I'd let 'em know what for.   Tell 'em where they could stick their bombs and their targets."

Hollis had heard rumors that each bomb wing had its hard luck group and each group had its hard luck squadron.   It looked to him as if the 532nd was it.

"How many missions you flown?" Hollis asked.

"Five.   They say the odds of you gettin' to five is one in three, but if you do your chances improve a lot.   They figure if you get through five missions you've figured out enough to survive so they give you the Air Medal.   But they've been a tough five missions.   I been to Hamburg twice, Hannover, Kassel and Gelsenkirchen.   Or actually Bochum since Gelsenkirchen was socked in.   And actually the trip to Kassel was recalled over Holland and we brought the bombs back but we still got credit.   I ain't had a God-damned milk run yet.

"Keep your wits about you and fly in tight," Selkirk continued.   "Green pilots can't stay in tight and they throttle back and forth.   Jerrie can spot you a mile away.   Those tracers hit the 190s and 109s and bounce right off.   They keep coming no matter what you throw at 'em.   The big thing is an engine fire.   When you see that fire you got maybe thirty, forty seconds at the most before the explosion."   Selkirk lifted his beer in salute and downed it.   He dropped the empty pint to the bar, slapped down some coins, and walked away.

The Club was crowded, but the level of conversation was subdued.   No one wanted to talk to Leo or Hollis.   He also noted Cahill and his officers sitting by themselves in the corner near the piano.   They were being ignored, too.   Except for Selkirk, no one seemed to notice or care that they were here.   As he sipped his beer he began to understand.   They were officially members of the Group, but they were not yet members of the fraternity.   They had not yet been shot at and anyone who hadn't yet stared down the muzzle of a gun was not worthy of acknowledgment.   Certainly not admission to the club.   They were strange faces, untested newcomers.   There was nothing subtle about this.   He felt like an interloper.

Leo, of course, was nonplused by the reception and happily lapped up several glasses of the warm, strange-tasting beer oblivious to the somber faces around him.

"You know," he said just before they left, "we've got to get ourselves some bikes.   It's too God-damned far to walk around here."

Chapter Three   **Jessie**

When Hollis returned to his room he expected to find Stan sulking but he was gone. He made sure the blackout curtain was closed and flipped on the light, little more than a naked bulb suspended on its wire.   The Mae West and blood-spattered shearling jacket were lying in a pile on the floor.

His first day at the Group had been a brutal revelation.   He had expected he would not have an easy time of it.   Even so, he was not been prepared for what he had seen.   His thoughts of high adventure and daring-do had been wiped off on the grass; the Group's aura of loss pervasive and menacing.

He sat at the desk and wrote a long letter to Jessie.   He was guarded in what he said. He wanted her to know how much he missed her without becoming maudlin; he wanted her to know he was homesick without seeming to wallow in self-pity.   He tried to concentrate on what he was saying, but was repeatedly distracted by what he had seen and heard and touched since arriving this morning.   He also wrote a letter to his parents.   He was a bit more frank with them, but not so blunt as to unnecessarily frighten them.   He had been cautioned not to reveal anything of military significance; names, places, organizations.   Officers were responsible for censoring the mail sent home by the enlisted personnel.   Officers were expected to self-censor what they wrote home.   He measured his words carefully.   He wanted to conceal his intent in code, hoping that, with a liberal reading his meaning could be discerned.

The Air Force did not officially acknowledge losses to the men in the groups, Hollis knew, but no one could deny the growing number of bombers that failed to return.   They saw how many bombers left each morning and how many came back.   Who were they kidding? Their deception was counterfeit and incomprehensible.   Each successive increase in the size of the striking force was met with an ever increasing number of German fighters. And with each deeper penetration the reaction of the *Luftwaffe* had been incrementally more violent.   He had heard about the mounting losses before he ever left the States.   How could he convey this? Why should he?   After thinking it over, he decided to keep this to himself.   Besides, this was war.   His mother, perhaps, and father, most certainly, didn't lack the imagination to know what this entailed and what their son's role was in it.

Jessie, on the other hand, he would try to protect from the unpleasant realties of the predicament in which he now found himself.   If he lived through it he would come clean with her as if she could not discern the facts promulgated by a free press.

Jesus, he missed her.   She lived next door their entire lives and he had always loved her if only from afar.   Their rooms were separated by no more than fifty feet, he guessed, over a grass covered yard, but it might have been a thousand miles over a deep, blue ocean for all it mattered.   To her, he was just the neighbor kid who seemed to spend every waking moment pining after her.   He carried his unrequited love for her like a badge of honor, if not also a weight around his heart.   It seemed destined never to be.   She was polite, of course, tolerant, even conciliatory and, on rare occasions, playfully affectionate, engaging even but never serious. Then something wonderful and unexpected happened.   The War.   When he returned home for his ten day furlough after phase training she was there.   She was at his home to greet him the minute he arrived.   They were inseparable, much to the delight of his mother and consternation of his father.   For reasons he could not fathom things had changed. They went to the movies, soda fountain, took long walks, met with friends, although their ranks had been significantly depleted by the war, ate dinner at each other's houses and finally, on the last night, *The Night*, made love.   It was the defining moment in his life.   An epiphany.   In his heart everything had changed for he knew that he would love this woman, and only this woman, forever.   The nagging doubt about the validity of it all based on his prior history with her had eroded his confidence and he was not at all sure, with the passage of time, that she felt for him as he did for her.   *Maybe you were just a pity fuck*, Leo had said.   *You know, for the good of the war effort. We want you to give up nylon stockings, not use the car, save your waste fats and fuck a soldier. And, in the end, the Forces of Evil will be defeated.   Besides*, Augie said, *'ain't fornicatin' one of the Four Freedoms?'*

His uncertainty over the mutuality of their love left him bewildered and sad.   He could die tomorrow and never know for sure.   So he analyzed that night, dissected it over and over trying to glean some degree of resolve or commitment, something definitive that he could carry with him to his death, a notion which was becoming a paralyzing obsession.   There was no rationalizing it away.   *Timor mortis conturbat me*--the thought of dying scares me to death.

He had Jessie on the one hand and a demonizing fear of his capricious demise on the other.   In between was the business of flying and the war.

He wrote the salutation on the second letter, perused it once again for occult military secrets, neatly folded both letters and placed them in envelopes.   He turned out the light and went to bed.

He thought he would fall asleep immediately for he felt physically and emotionally exhausted.   But he could not, staring instead into dark empty space, the only light a small sliver coming under the door.   He lay awake for what seemed like hours.   His last conscious thought was of the front of that man's face under his hand, cold and wet, stuck to the aluminum.   How many times had that man's mother kissed that forehead or touched it with her cheek to see if he was running a fever?

When they got to their assigned spot on the flight line, a big concrete apron with two dozen new B-17Fs in two rows facing each other, they found nothing.   A big gap of concrete spotted by oil and rubber tread marks.   The crew turned to Hollis as if he knew the answer to their latest mystery: where was our plane?

Relax, the line chief told them, it'll be here any minute.

The Nebraska sun was hot, made worse by a total lack of wind.   Dressed in flight clothes, they started sweating and bitching. Stripped down to tee shirts and bitched.   Hollis told them to knock it off.   He tried to be good-natured about it, but they were getting on his nerves.

They watched as a B-17 fired up and taxied past, then another and yet another.   Three quarters of an hour had elapsed.   No plane.   If they were out here much longer, Hollis figured, they might be ready for basting.

He looked at the crew and wondered yet again how they would behave in combat.   Who would be the weak link?   Who would fail?   *Might it be me?*   They had gotten high marks in phase training which had been the source of some amazement to Hollis.   But they hadn't been tested yet.   H-y had gotten them lost twice, once at night and once during a detour around a thunderstorm.   They had lost an engine a couple of times and on one occasion had lost two. They had a small fire when something shortened out in the radio room, but it had been quickly extinguished.

The closest they came, Hollis remembered, was H-y's lost night flight. After a long cross-country flight, they found themselves getting perilously low on fuel, wandering around for two hours trying to find their way over the dark, flatlands of Oklahoma. Most of the crew were asleep in the waist or on the floor in the radio room, oblivious to their predicament. Sully was perched in the Plexiglas nose looking for something familiar; H-y, totally befuddled, kept pleading with Quinn for a radio fix; Poole and Leo staring at the fuel gauge as if that alone might help. Finally, Leo said, 'I think you better find a flat spot to put this down on.'

The number one engine sputtered to a stop and Leo dutifully feathered the prop. They were about to lose a second when Quinn came on the intercom telling them he had picked up a commercial radio station in Wichita. They were playing Lionel Hampton's 'Flying Home,' which caused him to chuckle, and he had a good fix on it, but they better hurry, it was close to midnight and most stations signed off then. Hollis brought the bomber around hoping they would have enough gas to land. Hollis set the mixture as lean as he dared and told Sully to keep his eyes open. The loss of the engine must have caused the sleeping gunners to stir because when Quinn got off the intercom Augie said, 'What happened to the engine?'

'Outta gas.' Quinn answered.

'And we're lost,' Sully added.

'Stay off the intercom, Bombardier, unless you find that airfield.'

Hollis felt a tap on his shoulder, Poole pointed to the rotating beacon of an airport, alternating white and green--a civilian field. Hollis turned the plane in that direction, made a low pass at the tower and they came up on the radio giving them permission to land. When they finished their roll out only one engine was still running.

H-y was apologetic, but Hollis would have none of it. He figured his silence would speak for itself. Hollis phoned in to headquarters and told them they were safe. He was instructed to set a plane guard, sleep in the aircraft, gas up at first light and get their sorry asses back to Ardmore as fast as they could. He turned to H-y, 'You better make sure we get back on time, you dumb fuck, or we're all AWOL.'

Hollis gave H-y the opportunity to redeem himself. He and Hollis took a taxi into town and bought back sandwiches and beer for the crew. He made H-y pay for the cab.

Now, on the line in Grand Island, Nebraska, that particular incident, only two months ago, seemed like ancient history. H-y never got them lost again and they never had another close call.

A jeep pulled up and the line chief handed them ten cold Cokes. He said the B-17 was due in from the Douglas plant in Long Beach any second. Having finished B-17 Combat Crew Training and a ten day furlough, they had all reconvened here to break in a new Fortress and take it to England.

Hollis looked over at Poole who had not touched his Coke. "You don't look so good, Virgil," Hollis said. Poole was laying on his back, perspiring even more than the others. He was pale and still.

"I don't feel as good as I look."

"What's the matter?" Leo asked.

"Bellyache."

"Virg had too much Spam sandwiches and beer last night. I tried tellin' him. Slow down, pace yourself," Augie said.

"But he wouldn't listen," Mollica added.

"Drink your Coke," Leo said, "maybe it will settle your stomach."

Hollis watched a B-17 make a gentle approach and landing. It taxied smartly up to the vacant spot and, using the outboard engines and squealing brakes, turned into it, causing the somnolent crew to scatter from the approaching propellers. Hollis watched as the engines shut down, the line chief dropped chocks under the wheels and the copilot put on some lipstick.

The nose hatch fell open and three women in flight suits dropped to the ground. The pilot, wearing a St. Louis Cardinal's ball cap, sunglasses, throat mike and headphones cocked on her temples, handed a clipboard to the line chief and ducked under the wing running her hand under the nacelle of the number two engine. The third one out looked about eighteen years old. She carried three duffle bags to the jeep and walked back to the pilot. She had her hair tucked under a bandanna and her pant legs rolled up revealing some shapely calf above her bobby socks. The tall blond with the Victory Red lips, Hollis supposed the copilot, lifted her gunner's cap off allowing her beautiful, auburn tresses to fall to her shoulders, causing the crew to start howling and whistling. Even the ailing Poole rose to his elbows to take in the sight. She flipped off her sunglasses, smiled at the appreciative crew and said in a husky, sensuous voice, "She's all yours, fellas."

"Come with us, please, please, please, pretty please..." Augie begged, as Mollica, Rizzo and Hulse continued to whistle and clap. Quinn, Hollis noted, just stared in awe at the fetching, fair-haired amazon. And, of course, any woman who could heft around a B-17 certainly had Hollis's respect. Bombshell or not.

"She's almost as pretty as your wife, Miss Christie, Lieutenant Wychulis," Rizzo added.

"Not even close," Leo said as he waved cheerfully at the blond. The ferry crew got into the jeep and sped off.

They climbed into the plane after it was refueled and took off for a two hour orientation flight. When Hollis dropped into the pilot's seat he could still smell the lingering aroma of perfume mingled with the smell of the new plane. Leo pointed to a message scrawled in red lipstick on the copilot's side window, "Angel, Sepulvada-6771."

That night Virgil Poole had his appendix removed. The next morning Noah Dodge joined the crew.

Two days later, they sat under the wing waiting for a passing thunderstorm to clear away and talked about naming the plane. Leo said he could see it as **Christie's Crusaders**. Hollis overheard Augie say only loud enough for those around him to hear, "Hell, I'd like to call it **Christie's Crotch**." Dodge kicked him in the foot and said, "Hey, that's that man's wife you're talking about." This prompted Augie to fire back a fearsome glance at Dodge. Hollis said, "No, let's not name it. It will probably end up belonging to somebody else, but if we do get to keep it, we'll name it then. We've got time to think it over, come up with a good name."

They spent three more days flying 'Angel's Plane', as Leo called it, testing systems, feathering engines, and were ready to depart for England. Before they left they drew winter flying gear, side arms, filled out forms for war bonds and insurance, named beneficiaries and made out their wills.

The next morning, they departed for the ETO convinced to a man that they were as ready as they were ever going to be. Certain of their invincibility and, for better or worse, that they were about to have the time of their lives. When they delivered the plane in Prestwick, it still had the   name and phone number in lipstick on the window.

The door opened with a sudden crash and the room was filled with blinding light.   A dark amorphous mass bounced around the room breathing heavily as he swore, banging against the desk and chair.   Two other figures entered the room their shadows coalescing in the light from the hall.   Hollis, startled awake, rose to his elbows.   The man bouncing around the room like a pinball was Stan.

Hollis recognized the tall man trying to guide Stan into bed as the navigator who had been by earlier.   The other was an oriental-looking fellow with pilot's wings on his chest. They grunted as they guided their pilot into his bed.   Stan was drunk beyond the capacity for purposeful activity.

"Need any help?" Hollis asked.

"No, I think we're OK," the navigator said.

Hollis got up from his bed, stepping in some mud tracked into the room on Stan's shoe. He helped the two undress Stan who had conveniently passed out and quit resisting.   When he was between the sheets the two thanked Hollis, turned and left.   Hollis flicked the mud off his foot and climbed into bed wondering if any of Stan would rub off on him.

Everyone saw the flares.   Red-red.   The Fortress heeled slowly in a shallow bank and settled down for a flawless landing.   Everyone watched the bomber complete its roll-out and pull onto the infield.   The engines shut off and the propellers slowly spun to a stop yet no one moved toward the plane.   There was silence except for the crackling of the hot manifolds.

At least a dozen doctors, medics and orderlies stood by the three ambulances, a long neat row of ten stretchers at their feet. They were motionless as statue rigidly staring at the Fortress. The nose of the bomber had **The Butchershop** painted on it. It did not display any outward signs of significant damage. In fact, it appeared un-touched, without so much as a bullet hole, standing motionless, as motionless as the medics and the litters and the ambulances.

"For Christ's sake what's going on," Hollis heard himself say.

"Maybe we better find out," Leo said and walked toward the still, ghostly airplane.   A feeling of dread overwhelmed him as he followed Leo. They got to the waist door and, for a moment, contemplated whether they should open it.   Hollis looked back at the medics who stared passively at them.   They displayed no movement, no emotion, no sense of recognition.

Leo looked at the ground.   He was standing in a pool of blood. It made a dripping sound as it hit the toe of his shoe. Hollis looked for the source.   It oozed out from beneath the closed waist door.   Hollis felt nauseated.   He started to gag.

Leo unlatched the door before Hollis could beg him not to.   The opened door released a cascade of bright, red, sweet-smelling blood onto their pants and around their feet.   When the red flood stopped Leo leaned into the doorway for a look.   He turned back to Hollis with a fiendish grin, his face drained of color, his lips and eyebrows beaded with perspiration.

Hollis could suppress his morbid curiosity no longer and leaned in to see two dead men laying side by side in the waist compartment.   They had been gutted, their entrails dangling from the stringers that ran the length of the fuselage.   Long ribbons of sinews were draped grotesquely over the machine guns.   Their throats had been sliced open and he could see the empty, severed ends of the blood vessels.   The smell of rotting flesh and rancid blood filled his nostrils. It was pungent and sickeningly sweet. And it was everywhere.   It was as if the inside of the bomber had been sprayed with it.

Hollis turned away.   He could feel a cool breeze cross his face.   He could sense the droplets of perspiration slide down his back and beneath his armpits. It ran down his forehead and stung his eyes.   His stomach was a teeming cauldron.   The spit pooled in his mouth, a harbinger of his lunch returning.

Leo ran around the horizontal stabilizer to the tail gunner's position.   Hollis followed. Their shoes, saturated with blood, squished when they walked.   The dead gunner's head was all he could see. He ran around to the front of the plane.   The dead pilot's head was pressed against the window his face pale and exsanguinated, his mouth open in some primal scream.   Blood dripped from beneath the nose hatch and collected in a pool in the grass.   Through the Plexiglas nose Hollis could see the bombardier hunched over the bombsight, his body charred, his hands held by the flesh of his fingers welded to the knobs, his face melted down over the eyepiece of the bombsight like wax dripping from a candle.

What had happened to these men?   Who flew the plane?

Hollis looked around. There were no medics, no ambulances, no control tower in the distance, no runways.   No droning engines or squealing brakes.   No circling Fortresses, no rustling leaves, no chirping birds, no men shouting.   Only silence.   Absolute unfathomable silence, the silence inside a buried coffin.   Hollis spun around seeking some explanation. **The Butchershop** loaded with ten dead men had vanished.   Leo was gone.   Hollis was alone, standing in the middle of a field.   He could feel the cold, wet fabric of his pants against the skin of his legs. They were dark. The red stained the olive drab gabardine.   His socks were wet and sticky.   He blinked and he was naked.   The only thing left was the smell.

Hollis bolted up. The room was dark. He looked over at Stan, a lump beneath the blankets. Stan was snoring softly, the sound of a drunk. The room was cool. He shivered with perspiration as he lit a cigarette and reached for his flashlight. He shown the beam of light onto his shoes in the corner of the room. They were, as he had left them, not covered with blood. He felt both relieved and ridiculous.   He finished the cigarette and tried to go back to sleep.

Chapter Four   **Freitag**

Hollis pulled his pants down and looked at the insides of his knees.   They were covered with purple bruises and they ached terribly.

Hollis stood with three other students at their assigned spot on the flight line.   They waited nervously for their Primary Flight instructor.   They didn't have long to wait.   A short, stocky man in a flight suit walked briskly up to them and threw out his hand, gave a big smile and said, "My name is Gayle Freitag.   I'm your instructor."   He introduced himself to the four students and he seemed pleasant, cheerful enough.   He explained the plan of the day which was to take each of the students up for a ten or fifteen minute orientation flight and then tomorrow they would start flying in earnest.   So, he said, sit back and enjoy the ride.

Hollis was third up.   Each of the students before him had climbed out of the Stearman biplane in a state of unbridled euphoria, caught up in the exhilarating experience of what, for each of them, was their first ride in an airplane.   Now it was his turn.   He climbed up eagerly into the narrow cockpit and placed the helmet over his head setting the earpieces carefully over his ears.   They were at the end of a voice tube which originated in a funnel in Freitag's cockpit behind him.

"Strap in, Mr. Hollis.   Can you hear me OK?"

Hollis responded by flashing the 'okay' sign with his fingers.

"Good.   You ever fly before, Mr. Hollis?"

Hollis shook his head 'no'.

"OK.   Just sit back, relax and enjoy the ride."

Freitag gunned the engine and they were off.

It took only a few moments for Hollis to realize that he wanted to fly more than anything and he would do whatever it would take to do so.   He climbed down out of the cockpit as excited and enraptured as he had ever been.

The next morning, they were up early and out to the flight line while the dew still speckled the grass.   Freitag was there, all smiles again.   "Hollis, you go first this time."

Hollis climbed eagerly into the Stearman.   He put the Gosport on his head and Freitag began his one way conversation about the preflight checklist.   Hollis tried to follow closely, but he was too excited.   Soon the engine fired up and they were in the air.

Hollis was overwhelmed by the thrill of it all, looking at the other planes in the pattern, watching as the ground receded behind them.

"Mr. Hollis, we are going to make some elementary maneuvers, first a turn to the right and a turn to the left.   Place your hands lightly on the controls and follow my actions."

Hollis complied.

They turned gently one way, then the other.   It was easy.

"OK, now you do it."

Hollis looked out at the fluffy white clouds, cumulus he had recently learned, and was taken aback by the realization that he had never seen the top of a cloud before.

Suddenly, the stick slammed back and forth rapidly between his knees like a clapper inside a dinner bell.   Freitag cut the engine, pulled back on the stick and the plane shuddered in the beginnings of a stall.   Freitag kicked the right rudder pedal and the plane dropped off on its right wing and plummeted into a tight spin.

The movement was so abrupt Hollis could not react.   He saw the earth spin in front of him, instantly aware that it was rising up to greet him.

Why would he want to kill us both?   Hollis asked himself as he realized death was seconds away.

"Now, put your hands on the fucking stick!"

Hollis was so dizzy and terrified he could barely bring his hand up to the stick, but he did. Freitag pushed full left rudder and allowed the stick to return to neutral.   He added power and pulled back on the stick bringing the plane out straight and level.

For what seemed an eternity, Freitag said nothing.   It was during this silence that he first noted how much his knees hurt from the pummeling they had just received.

"You know how to get a mule to do what you want him to do, Mr. Hollis?"

Hollis shook his head.

"You first have to smack him in the head with a two-by-four so you can have his undivided attention."

Hollis flashed a shaken 'OK.'

"Shall we try this again?"

Hollis gave the thumbs up and promptly vomited over the side of the cockpit, the slip stream splashing the slurry back onto the windshield and coated Freitag's goggles.

Now he sat on his bed rubbing his aching knees while he looked at Freitag's vomit-stained flight suit on the floor.   He needed to clean them and return it in the morning, lightly starched, pressed and folded with precision.   Precision, Mr. Hollis.

Chapter Five   **Geese**

Friday, August 13, 1943

At precisely eight o'clock, the Hollis and Cahill crews were assembled in the Group's briefing room, a large half-barrel-shaped Quonset hut filled with benches and folding chairs and an elevated stage at the front.   The room was empty except for the two crews and two men, a major and a captain, the latter Hollis recognized from the bomber the afternoon before.

"Gentlemen, my name is Major Entwhistle and I want to welcome you to the 532nd Bomb Squadron.   This is Captain Ransahoff, the squadron ops officer.   He would like to welcome you to the Squadron, also."   Hollis could sense people around him shift in their seats.

Entwhistle was a tall, thin man with a Gable-like moustache and dark, deep-set eyes. He spoke softly.   What little he had heard about Entwhistle up to that point suggested to Hollis that few people liked him.   Entwhistle, they said, was chickenshit.

"We've had a fairly high turnover in crews recently--" an ugly euphemism for losses, Hollis thought--"and we need to get you into the scheme of things, Squadron and Group procedures, quickly.   You will be seeing a lot of flying soon so pay attention and fly in close. The name of the game here is formation flying."   There was more shifting in seats.   "I've been around long enough to testify to that.   You stay tucked in close, concentrating the firepower of the Squadron and you'll have something to tell your grandchildren.   The closer in you fly, the better luck you'll have against the fighters and the closer in you fly the more likely you will be of putting the bombs on the target which is what you're here for in the first place.   Bombs on the target.   First, last and always.   That's why we're paying you this generous salary.   Fly 'em 'till the wings fall off.   I want pilots who won't deny a target and I got no room for no momma's boys.

"We are the Hammer of God, gentlemen, sent forth to rid the world of a loathsome evil. Bombs on the target will win the war.   And you are here to do precisely that.   All else is superfluous.   Do it twenty-five times and you get to go home a hero.   Just keep it in close and place your trust in the Lord.

"Behave yourselves.   We are guests in this country.   Conduct yourselves accordingly." He turned to Ransahoff and nodded.

Ransahoff called the two crews to attention and Entwhistle strode from the room.   He waited until Entwhistle was gone and said, "As you were.   Smoke 'em if you got 'em."   He then spent two hours explaining procedural matters from taxiing to assembly to bomb runs, radio doctrine, mission credit, passes and, inevitably, venereal disease.   All without the use of notes. Hollis hoped he would remember everything for who knew what item, what particle of information might mean the difference between life and death?

At the Combat Crew Replacement Center at Bovingdon, they had been told the quickest way out of a dying bomber, how long you could expect to last in the North Sea if you ditched, what happened if you became disconnected from your oxygen supply, but no one was there, like the Wizard of Oz, to bestow courage by edict or example.   That was something you had to figure out on your own.   Luckily for America, Hollis thought as he listened to Ransahoff, most of 'em figured it out.

He recalled the lecture they had received on Escape and Evasion.   Dutch, Belgian and

French underground risked their lives to help Allied aircrew avoid falling into the clutches of the Nazis.   Hollis recalled wondering what his father, a Francophobe of legendary proportions, would think of the French if they managed to save his son from capture.   There are dozens, perhaps hundreds of partisans risking their lives to get you back, they said, facing swift, certain and lethal punishment for helping you.   Never betray the network, these people are your only hope, your only means of escape--it was then Sully leaned forward and said, "You know, I don't think I'm going to like this nearly as much as I thought I would"-- and if you give up your protectors to save your hide you will be costing the lives of countless people and destroy the means of escape for all the airmen who will follow you down in the future. It is their way of fighting the war.

"Lastly," Ransahoff concluded, "I would like to comment on our policy about abortions. If you experience mechanical trouble or personnel failure and cannot reasonably be expected to complete the mission without jeopardizing unnecessarily the lives of your crew and your airplane you should return to base by the quickest means available.   It has been our experience that ninety percent of all abortions are legitimate.   Ten percent are not and we know which is which."   Hollis thought Ransahoff was looking at him when he said that.

"Bombs on the target *is* what this is all about.   It's the bombing.   That's why you're here.   Do your jobs, work as a team and you'll all get to go home.

"We're not supposed to discuss losses with the crews, but I think it is important that you know what you are up against.   This is the Big Leagues, boys.   One out of every three men finish a tour and about half never make it through the first five missions.   Work as a team. Never forget the lives of the other people in your crew, your Squadron and this Group are in your hands.   Pay attention.   Get the first five missions past you and the odds of finishing your tour improve.   But take nothing for granted.

"Each of you is responsible for checking the alert list every day on the bulletin board outside Squadron HQ.   This list contains those crews alerted to fly the next day's mission. You may not actually go, but if you're name is on the list you are restricted to base and should be ready to go on a mission the next day.   The Charge-of-Quarters will wake you in the morning with the poop on chow and briefing.   If you are not alerted you can, with permission, go off base.   We're still short some crews so it's a safe bet everybody in the Squadron will be on the alert list.

"You will need to check in with the quartermaster to draw flying equipment which you will store in a locker in the Equipment Room.

"Any questions?"

There were none.

"There will be an aircraft recognition class at thirteen thirty.   If no mission is posted for tomorrow we will hold a practice mission at ten hundred."   Augie raised his hand.

"Yes, sergeant?"

"Yes sir, I was wonderin' about when we might get to go to London?"

Ransahoff was silent for a moment and smiled broadly at Augie, "Anything else?"

Nothing.

"You're dismissed."

Hollis returned to his room after the lecture.   Stan sat on his bed in his Class A uniform.

Mattson, his navigator, Watanabe, his copilot and Selkirk were there in Class As, also. Whatever conversation had been going on before he arrived stopped when Hollis entered the room.   Selkirk turned to Hollis and placed his arm around him and said, "Let's go to the Club. I'll buy you a Coke and we can throw some darts."

Outside on the gravel path Selkirk started to talk. "We just buried Stan's two gunners in Cambridge.   One of 'em was a Jew and since we couldn't find a rabbi on such short notice Stan had to say the Kaddish or prayers or something.   He said it in Hebrew.   The chaplain said they were brothers in combat, brothers in life, and brothers in death, their blood mingling together on the floor of their plane.   It was a nice eulogy.   Stan's pretty shook up, though."

They walked for a long time without saying anything.

"You get the inside dope from Dutch yet?"

"You mean Ransahoff?"

"Yeah, one and the same."

"Yeah, he lectured us on procedure after Entwhistle welcomed us to the Squadron."

"Entwhistle may be in charge, but Ransahoff is running things.   He's mean as a snake. Him, Cassidy and Van Patten, the Group CO, are the only West Point men in the Group and Ransahoff and Van Patten are both tough as nails.   Even Entwhistle is scared of Dutch.

"Entwhistle chewed Stan's ass when he left the formation to cover me, but it was Dutch that told Entwhistle to do it.

"Did he give you the spiel about the importance of the formation, all those guns amassed to defend the Group?"

"Yeah."

"Did he tell you how every gun counts and if you straggle you're good as dead?"

"Yes, he did."

"He means it."

"I figured as much."

"He's right, you know."

Selkirk walked on for a while quiet, pensive.

"We were over Hamburg.   The primary, some U-boat yard or something, was covered over by smoke and clouds by the time we got there so we went on to the secondary, some truck tire place or engine factory or some such.   Between the primary and secondary we were hit.   I was on Stan's left wing in the second element.   We took a cannon hit in the nacelle of number one.   It tore the cowling off and it started throwing oil.   It started smoking and when it started heating up I feathered it.   We fell back a little, but we weren't in serious trouble until we took another hit which set number three on fire.   I got the fire out and feathered, but we fell back and were alone.   We could see the FWs lining up to finish us off.   They were just sitting out there takin' their time.   Not in any hurry.   I knew we had it.   So did they.   Jesus, I was scared. I was never so scared in my whole life."

Selkirk's voice trembled with emotion.

"At about that time, we were over the target and I toggled the bombs figuring we might be able to catch up, but when they picked up speed at the Rally we were good as finished.   We fell back and when the flak eased the FWs started back at us.   Two made a pass and killed our top turret gunner.   Before he died he was screaming into the intercom.   He was hanging in his sling with his right leg blown off at the hip.   Blood was everywhere.   The ball turret gunner kept yelling if it was time to bail out yet.   One more pass like that and we were done.   I looked up and they broke off to the right. I couldn't understand why they did that until I looked over and saw Stan nuzzling up on our right wing.   They came back a couple of times and Stan threw that big, old bomber out in front, guns blazin', winking his landing lights at 'em like he was flying a P-38.   They broke off probably thinkin' this idiot's gonna get 'em killed.   Stan broke formation and dropped back to save the new guy.   They musta lost some of their nerve.   They mighta figured I wasn't gonna make it back anyway.   He stayed with us all the way home.   We dumped everything that wasn't bolted down, but we made it.

"At interrogation, Ransahoff was beside himself.   He told Entwhistle to tear Stan a new asshole, yelling at him about how he was compromising squadron integrity.   Then the colonel yelled at him about group integrity...I'm surprised the general didn't drive down from Wing and have a long talk with Stan about jeopardizing *his* Wing.   In the same fix though, I'm sure they'd all want Stan to do the same for them.   Tough to argue with a hero.   Strange business this bombing.

"I'm not sure Ransahoff would do that for anybody.   You know how those professional pre-war Army assholes are.   Especially some chickenshit from West Point.   But he'd sure as hell want somebody to do it for him.   If Ransahoff keeps pissin' people off they just might let him auger in.

"Problem is Stan never told Ransahoff about the geese."

"Geese?"

"Geese are interesting birds.   The further they fly away from home the closer they fly in formation.   The new birds always fly with older birds and each generation guides the next on migration.   When geese migrate, if one becomes ill or injured two of his fellow geese follow him down and stay with him until he either recovers and can go on or he is dead."

"Why do they do that, do you think?"

"Because that's the way they are."   Selkirk wiped the tears from his cheeks and said, "We used to see a lot of geese on the farm, you know, flyin' south."

By the time they arrived at the Officer's Club, Selkirk had regained his composure.   He walked up to the bar and said 'fuck the cokes let's have a beer.'   It was a little early in the day for that sort of thing, but Hollis joined him.   They started throwing darts, a game Selkirk had obviously mastered to a fault because he won five bucks from Hollis without any demonstrable effort.

As Hollis pulled the bill from his wallet, a voice spoke from behind him, "Mickey beat you at darts?"

He turned.   It was Ransahoff.

"Yeah, he's pretty good at it."

"Shameless Irishman would take money from his own sainted grandmother.   Somebody should have warned you."   Ransahoff turned and walked over to a group of high-ranking officers seated in the corner of the room, and took a chair.

"Who are they?" he asked Selkirk.

"Red-faced guy is Major Begay, some friggin' Navajo Indian chief or something, Group ops; the bald-headed guy is Colonel Gleason, Air Exec; the other guy, the smart looking one, is Van Patten, the Group CO.   Ransahoff is brown-nosing the brass.   I figure he's trying to get rid of Ol' Stan."

"Or Entwhistle."   Hollis turned, it was Mattson.

"Some sort of palace *coup d' etat*," Watanabe added.

Hollis introduced himself, but they ignored him, took their drinks and walked away.

"Maybe Ransahoff is reminiscing about old times at the Point with the Colonel," Mickey said, leaving to join Mattson.

Rather than stand at the bar alone, Hollis finished his beer and left.

On his way back to the Squadron communal site, he ran into Leo and H-y.

"We were over at Squadron ops after chow and found out which plane they assigned us to for the practice mission tomorrow.   We were on our way out there, wanna go?"

"Sure."

"I borrowed us some bikes," H-y added.   "But they told us to be careful of these English bicycles.   They got hand brakes and if you brake too fast over the handle bars you go."

"Considering all the bullshit I've had to listen to since we got here I thought it was right nice of them to warn us, but it also makes me a little suspicious," Leo said.

"Yeah, with all the horror stories they been spouting Hulse and Rizzo are so scared I don't think we'll be able to get them in the plane," H-y said.

"Naw," Hollis said, without any real basis for saying so, "they'll be fine, you watch."

They picked up the bikes at Leo's Nissen hut and, as they pedaled down the tree-lined road to the dispersal area, Hollis once again thought of his crew.   Leo seemed to know where he was going so they followed him.

Hollis could not dispel his nagging doubts about the crew.   They never struck him as a cohesive unit, a crew.   It seemed like ten guys flying a plane.   They had none of the easy confidence or coolness that other crews seemed to possess even in phase training.   They were good men, with the possible exception of Augie Reese, and they seemed to know their jobs, it was just that a crew was more than the sum of its individual members and something here just didn't add up.

Leo and H-y engaged in light banter as they rode. Hollis wondered again if maybe he was being premature in judging them.   Maybe he should wait until they were under fire before coming to any conclusions.   But he had been with these men for almost three months and he thought he knew them pretty well.   Perhaps it was a matter of perspective.   To him they seemed like ten individuals, or nine individuals and one aberration, Augie.   To an outsider they might appear just fine, no better or worse than any other crew thrown together by their government to fly a bomber.

Maybe *he* was the problem.   Maybe *he* was the one who lacked the confidence.   This thought had preoccupied him, also.   He was disappointed that he didn't get to be a fighter pilot; most bomber pilots were at first.   Then he realized, without being told, that he was responsible for nine other lives, not just his own, and the people running this air force would not trust him with that if there was even a speck of doubt that he could handle it.   He had, after all, been tested and evaluated at every step along the way.   Poked and prodded, humiliated and degraded. Often by people of lesser stuff than he, people he could not like and certainly could not respect. So if he had survived the selection process, this variation on Darwin, passing muster, perhaps he was exactly what they wanted and he should quit worrying and start acting like the pilot and officer they figured him to be.

Of course, then there was Leo. If they could make a bomber pilot out of Leo Wychulis, the cherubic, easy-going math teacher from Los Angeles, the selection process had its flaws, cracks through which the untalented could slip un-noticed.

When he was about to solo for the first time, Freitag had yelled over the engine noise, "Relax, Hollis!   One take off, one landing.   Don't worry, I'll notify your next of kin!"   He wondered what were they thinking when they let Leo fly alone for the first time?   A biological as well as technological moment of truth.   A blind act of faith for all concerned.

Leo was supposed to go to B-24s.   He actually spent a couple of weeks at B-24 transition school before he was redirected as a copilot to B-17s.   This was a curious thing for which no one, least of all Leo, had any explanation.   Leo said the B-24 was an interesting plane to pilot.   You could turn the wheel and a couple minutes or so later the plane would start to turn. If you turned into a dead engine you would die.   He hated it.   Called them 'Big Uglies'.   This led to speculation about why they had yanked Leo out of B-24s.   H-y said it was because the powers that be thought a nose wheel and the Davis Wing might be too confusing for him. Hollis thought that perhaps the B-24 was too demanding for Leo for it was not an easy plane to fly.   It took a lot of getting used to, Leo said.   So they put him in the '17, which was a much more forgiving airplane to pilot.   That being the case, H-y replied, why didn't they put him in a C-47.   That was the easiest thing there was to fly, you know, limit the number of engines to two so he wouldn't get confused.

Leo was good-natured about the ribbing he took.   He had something they would never have: Christie, the most beautiful woman any of them had ever seen or would likely ever see. Not only his wife, but a *bona fide* Hollywood movie star.

They pedaled the bikes past the technical site and control tower onto the perimeter strip. The Fortress they had drawn was parked on hardstand number 10 at the far end of the field near the bomb dump.   It started to mist lightly and everything was instantly wet.   The tires on the bikes made a hissing noise on the wet concrete taxiway.   It had grown increasingly overcast during the afternoon and now low, scudding clouds moved quickly overhead.   H-y started griping about the rain and turned back, saying he wasn't *that* interested in seeing the damned thing.

They approached the area where the 532nd's bombers were quartered.   There were two long side branches off the perimeter strip each containing several hardstands where B-17s were nested among a large grove of trees. On the infield side of the perimeter strip sat a lone Fortress. Hollis examined it as they rode past.   It looked dark and sinister in the mist.   Flaps up, bomb bay doors closed it was clean and sleek, strangely beautiful if also menacing.   On the nose was painted **The Flying Dutchman** in large red script.   This must be Ransahoff's plane.

They came to the last two hardstands belonging to the 532nd, number 10 and 11. Runway 17-35 came to an abrupt end nearby and beyond that was the gentle sloping Stour Valley.   Two Fortresses sat side by side on the outside of the strip as if they had been paired and intentionally separated from the rest.   The nearer of the two sat on hardstand number 10.

Chapter Six   **Cleopatra's Asp**

The Flying Fortress was an early model B-17F.   Its olive drab paint was more drab than olive having been faded by weather and long hours spent closer to the sun, bleached of some of its green hue.   The light undersurface was dirty gray.   The bomber looked old and tired.

They laid their bikes down on the grass.   Behind the hardstand sat two packing-crate shanties one of which had a stove-pipe chimney belching dark, oily smoke.   Three men walked around or beneath plane.   One of them was Noah Dodge.

The two officers walked over to the Fortress.   Her nose was smooth and sleek lacking the wart-like astrodome on the roof of the nose compartment that identified newer models.   A single .50 caliber machine gun poked out through the Plexiglas nose.   It was supported by a framework behind the plastic shell which detracted from its clean lines making the nose look cluttered.   It was a field modification for Hollis had never seen a gun rigged like this before.

On the side of the nose, below the navigator's windows was the plane's name, **Cleopatra's Asp**.   It had been bestowed by a previous owner for it, like the bomber bearing its name, was weathered and faded. Cleopatra was a nude in high heels bending over at the waist, her hands resting on her knees, her full breasts hung down in excess of anatomic proportionality, her robust ass pushed way out.   She wore a semblance of an Egyptian headdress, but nothing else.   Not far from her generous behind was a coiled cobra ready to strike.   The snake's forked tongue was excessive, his fangs drawn, his eyebrows (on a snake, no less) pursed, his smile lurid and comical.   The reptile's target was obvious.   The artwork was rather elaborate and explained why it had not been reproduced on the opposite side of the nose.   Hollis decided the best part of the painting was the smile on the snake.   He wasn't sure whether the asp was a species of cobra.   Nor could he decide if he liked the picture.   It didn't matter.   The plane had her name and far be it for him to change it.   It was probably bad luck or something anyway.

There was tremendous wear and tear exacted on these planes by combat operations; taking off with war loads that far exceeded the limits on the plane set by the designer and manufacturer.   Carting two or more tons of bombs up to a chilling 25,000 feet with enough gasoline to take off, assemble and fly five or six hundred miles, constantly jockeying the throttles, through flak and fighters placed enormous stress on the machines.   After a month or so of operations any surviving Fort looked old and tired.   **Cleopatra's Asp** had seen a lot of flying, probably one of the Group's original aircraft..

Up by the pilot's window was a row of yellow bombs signifying the number of effective missions the plane had flown.   There were fourteen bombs.   Beneath the bombs were three yellow swastikas, each signifying a German fighter confirmed as destroyed by the crew flying this plane.

There were dark, recently painted patches of sheet metal where bullet and flak punctures and tears in the aluminum skin had been repaired.   A few were close to the pilot's window. The faded paint on the leading edges of the engine cowls was chipped and worn revealing bare metal.   The big, paddle-blade propellers were flat black and tipped, as all propellers were, in yellow with bare metal hubs.   The black rubber de-icer boots on the leading edges of the wings and tail surfaces had been removed and replaced with aluminum.   This was done to reduce weight and cut down on drag created by rubber torn, pitted and pocked by the debris and detritus of aerial combat, or worse, if torn loose, they might jam the control surfaces.

Hollis walked under the broad left wing and followed it out to the wing tip.   The engine nacelles were smeared and streaked with oil and exhaust soot.   The B-17 was notorious for throwing and consuming prodigious quantities of engine oil and this particular Fortress appeared to be no exception.

Hollis looked at Leo and winked.   Leo returned a smile, but it was half-hearted and as forlorn as the bomber he stood under.

There were flak patches on the under surfaces of the wings.   The left aileron had been recently replaced and it was a different shade of olive-drab.   He walked to the left waist.   The gunner's window was pulled shut and a large tarpaulin was draped over the open radio operator's roof hatch.   A large panel of the fuselage had been recently replaced also, betrayed by more fresh paint in rectangular fashion.   The star and bars of the national insignia had a red surround, a motif since outmoded.   The new bombers had a blue surround.   The large white letters 'VE' and 'B' appeared on the side of the fuselage.   The 'E' was slightly crooked.   The tail fin had a large white triangle on it and a black 'L' in its center.   Below that was the aircraft serial number. The broad panel of the fin was painted green.   More flak patches.   Hollis looked back upon the upper surfaces of the wings.   They were smeared with engine exhaust, too.   The trailing edges of the wings and tail surfaces were painted with green crow's feet, a hasty sort of camouflage. He finished his walk-around saddened by the fact that this once proud, beautiful B-17F, Queen of the Skies, had been slowly transformed into a beaten up, battered old maid.

Dodge walked up to them.   "She ain't pretty but she's sound."

"Boy, you said something there," Leo replied.

A tech sergeant walked up behind Dodge and threw out his hand, "Lieutenant Hollis, my name is Moe Jablonski, the crew chief."   He turned and pointed to a corporal who followed behind, "And this is Tommy Drake, assistant crew chief."

"This is Leo Wychulis, my copilot."   Everyone exchanged handshakes.

"I've been taking care of this plane since it was assigned to the Group in March.   She's one of the original aircraft.   Fourteen missions and never aborted for mechanical problems. Ain't another plane in this Group can say that."   Moe exuded pride in his charge.   Many crew chiefs only left their aircraft in order to eat and sleep.   Such devotion did not go unobserved or unacknowledged by the fliers, Hollis knew.   "She doesn't have Tokyos and we've rigged a 50 caliber in the nose which works out pretty well.   We kept crackin' the nose Plexiglas by the recoil until we braced it.   All four engines have less than a hundred hours.   She's had some sheet metal work as you can see, but she's never had any major damage."

Hollis looked at Dodge who nodded.   If it was okay with Dodge, it would be OK with Hollis.

"Thanks, Moe.   I guess I'll see you in the morning.   Tommy.   Noah."

The two pilots walked back to their bikes in the light rain and left the hardstand. Neither said anything as they rode back.

Hollis reflected on the harsh realities of his current station.   He thought he would be inundated with patriotic fervor when he arrived in England, 'why we fight' crap, but he wasn't. He thought he would be assimilated warmly into the Squadron, but he wasn't.   He thought, at the least, he might get a new B-17, but he didn't.   The odds of finishing the first five missions were only one in two.   The odds of completing a full tour of twenty-five missions was only one in three.

Nobody, except for Mickey Selkirk, wanted to invest the emotional energy to be his friend or even speak to him in anything more than a single sentance.   Two, at most.   He was flying one of the oldest, most dilapidated planes in the Group and, being the new guy, would be placed in the worst, most vulnerable position in the squadron formation.   Could it get any worse?

Yeah, he thought, he still hadn't heard from Jessie.   Either the mail hadn't caught up with him or, he worried, she hadn't given him another thought once he had disappeared from her sight on the train platform four weeks ago.

Saturday, August 14, 1943

The Group had not been alerted for a mission by the time Hollis had gone to bed. Besides, the Hollis and Cahill crews had not been placed on combat status, their names would not have appeared on the operations list even if a mission had been posted.   Ransahoff had told them they would fly a practice mission so he was not surprised when Beamis came around at 0730 and woke him.

"Lieutenant Hollis, Lieutenant Eisenberg, practice mission posted for ten hundred. Briefing at oh-nine hundred."

When it was apparent to Beamis that Stan was not moving he walked over to the sleeping pilot and shook his shoulder.   "Lieutenant Eisenberg, c'mon, you need to get up."

From under the covers a muffled voice, "I heard you, Beamis.   Tell Ransahoff to go fuck himself.   I've only got three missions left and I ain't taking no chances on a practice mission with these yokels."

"Aw, c'mon, sir, I can't tell him that.   You know how upset that'll make him."

"Beamis, don't make me bite you."

"OK, I'll tell him."   He turned to make sure Hollis was up and he left.

"Dress warm," came the voice from under the blankets, "He's gonna take you high."

At breakfast, Hollis ate with Leo, H-y and Sully.   Smith and Sullivan seemed genuinely happy to be going on the practice mission for it meant one more step closer to what they had come here to do, destroy things and kill people.   Leo looked as if he could care less what they did.   He just smiled and cheerfully consumed his powdered eggs, fried Spam, and coffee.

At precisely nine o'clock, the officers of the six crews, less Eisenberg, were gathered in the briefing room.   Ransahoff stood on the stage before a large map of Northwestern Europe. Red yarn marked off a course that would take them out over the North Sea, up toward Northern Ireland and back.   A chalk board was marked with the positions each plane would fly.   Major Begay sat to one side.   He was in flying clothes.

Ransahoff outlined the general plan.   They would take off at 1100 and climb to 5,000 feet where they would orbit the field using Ridgewell's buncher beacon for assembly.   They would then head northeast climbing to 25,000 feet, proceeding to Scarbourough on the east coast of England. They would then turn, after making several dog-legs, to a course almost due west which would take them over the narrow waist of England to a bombing range in the Irish Sea.

Once the bombs were released, they would reverse the course and come home.   Off Kingston-Upon-Hull they were to be intercepted by a flight of P-47s who would act as escort. The fighter pilots, Ransahoff said, needed the practice, too.   They would meet several target tows over the North Sea on the return leg.   The gunners, he said, would obviously be carrying live rounds.   That was in case a German intruder was encountered, something which was known to happen for they were, after all, in a war zone.   More importantly, it would give them an opportunity to fire at moving targets while in tight formation, something they may not have done before.

Ransahoff talked about the weather and told the navigators to stay behind for discussions of routes and timings.

"Hollis and Cahill, I want you on VHF.   Watanabe, you will be pilot.   Lieutenant Eisenberg is feeling a bit under the weather and will not be flying with us so Major Begay has been kind enough to act as your copilot.   I want you on the command channel, too.   Cassidy, I want Slagle flying this one.

"Ok, then.   Engine start at 1045, taxi at 1055.   Questions?"

There were none.

Cahill and Hollis walked up to the blackboard and studied their position.   Ransahoff would be lead in number one position, Watanabe in number two off his right wing, Cassidy off his left in number three.   The second element would be led by Selkirk in number four, Hollis off his right wing in number five and Cahill off Mickey's left in number six.

As they left, Selkirk told Cahill and Hollis that the Group was short of crews and that if they made a decent showing they would be placed on combat status right away.   They walked over to the equipment room and drew their gear, placing it in large canvass bags to carry out to the plane.

The truck pulled up to the hardstand where **Cleopatra's Asp** sat waiting.   The gunners had already arrived and were conducting their own survey of the plane.   They seemed to be arguing about the artwork as Moe and Dodge approached Hollis.

"She's all set to go, Lieutenant," Moe said.

"Good.   Okay Leo, let's have a look."   Hollis dropped his bag near the nose, said good morning to the crew and started inspecting the aircraft.   It was a ritual drilled into him from the first day he entered Primary.   *Check the airplane*, Freitag said.   *If the wings fall off, it's your fault.*   So Hollis, with Leo in tow, followed by Moe and Dodge walked around and through the big bomber testing control surfaces, checking for fluid leaks, tugging on the props, kicking the tires, spinning the turbo wheels until there was virtually nothing left to check.   He overlooked nothing.   Butch Mullen, his B-17 transition instructor, would have been pleased.

"Yep, she's ready," Hollis said to Moe.

Moe was about to hand him the clip board with the Forms One and One-A on them when he said quietly to Hollis, "May I speak with you, sir?"   They walked far enough away to avoid being overheard and Moe handed him the clipboard.

"Sir," Moe said tersely, "when I say she's ready to fly she's ready to fly.   Do you understand that?"

Hollis was startled by Moe's indignation, restrained as it was.   "Yes, of course, I meant no--"

"Fine, sir."

"--disrespect.   I wanted to...uh..." Hollis muttered, signing the forms.

Moe took the clipboard and walked away.

Hollis saw Dodge casting a sympathetic eye towards his pilot, but said nothing.

Stung by the rebuke, Hollis walked over to the crew.   "Gather 'round."   The crew turned to Hollis as he began to lecture them on details of the practice mission.   He finished, "Today is practice.   If we do a good job and nobody screws up, we get to go on the real thing soon.   Like it or not, we're here.   We all need to do our best.   Function as a team, look out for one another.   Anyone drops the ball drops it for all of us.   I want discipline on the interphone and I want everybody to concentrate on their jobs.   Regular oxygen checks, too. OK? Anybody got anything to say?"

Nothing.   He glanced at his watch--1020.   "OK, stations."

The crew gathered up their equipment and climbed into **Cleopatra's Asp**.

Hollis pulled his silk scarf up around his neck and tucked the woolen muffler inside his leather jacket.   He pulled the Mae West over his head, setting it onto his shoulders passing the straps beneath his crotch.   He checked the seal on each CO_2 cartridge, slipped into his parachute harness and placed the throat mike against his voice box.   He rested his headphones on his temples and gathered up his bag.   He looked out beyond the end of the plane where he saw the crew standing shoulder to shoulder urinating into the grass.

Good idea, Hollis thought, and walked behind the wing beyond the concrete apron and pulled down the zipper of his flight suit, then his pants, fished through his long johns and then his shorts until he clasped his penis by the skin.   He finally worked it out into the daylight, but it came out reluctantly, shriveled by apprehension, barely enough to hold with confidence.   He waited for a moment until his stream started.   It was a pathetic little pee.   Like wringing the water out of a damp washcloth.

He adjusted the silk scarf and returned to the plane.   Jessie had made the scarf out of the silk slip she wore their last night together.   She had handed him the package, neatly wrapped in lavender tissue paper, tied with a white ribbon, while they stood with his folks on the train platform.   *What's this?* he asked.   *A little something to keep you warm and remind you of me.* He opened the package and saw the scarf.   She whispered in his ear what it was.   She had cut up the slip and stitched a hem while he was eating breakfast with his folks.   He could feel his face flush red and she laughed at his reaction.   *Well*, she said, *you couldn't wear my panties around your neck now, could you?* He wore it every time he had gone flying since. He smelled it for any lingering aroma of her, but it was long gone. The fabric felt good against his skin and kept his neck from being chaffed by the woolen muffler as he rubbernecked. He never put it on without thinking of her. The scarf had done exactly what she had intended it to do.

Chapter Seven   **Practice**

He never touched it or placed it around his neck without imagining it against her bare legs or clinging to her perfect bottom.   He was transported back to that moment on the platform when he said goodbye.   The details were fresh and precise in his mind.

There was a Boy Scout selling cartons of cigarettes from a wicker picnic basket.   Odd, he thought, the boy in his uniform made an image on his brain as indelible as his memory of Jessie.

It was a picture-perfect July day, barely a month ago.   If the weather could have been construed as an omen, he took it to be a good one.   There was not a cloud in the sky and the gentle breeze blew warm against his face, lifting Jessie's blond hair away from her beautiful face.

She smiled and held him by the arm, letting go only long enough for him to hug and kiss his hopelessly tearful mother and shake his father's hand. It was apparent his father was fighting back tears as well. Probably pushed back by the man's pride in his son.

He hugged his mother one last time, holding her tightly, feeling her tremble under his arms.   Her tears made dark spots on his tan tunic, the mucus from her nose leaving a thin, silvery tendril on his lapel.   He sensed her fear that this would be the last time she would hold her son, the last time she would ever touch him, her only child.   He held her tightly, not wanting to make her come to the point of having to let him go.   He took his father's hand, a grip strong enough to crush rock, his face beaming.   His son, an Officer and Gentleman by Act of the Congress of the United States in the glorious service of his country, a pilot, a leader of men, the hope of a civilization.   His father smiled easily, but Hollis could see a wet rim at the bottom of each eye.   Hollis understood the relationship, the balance between them.   If his mother was crying he could not.   Besides, it was not in the man's nature to show such feelings.

He turned to Jessie.   She was radiant in her light yellow cotton dress and white heels. He took her in his arms and kissed her long hoping by some miracle that this might never end. He could still feel the touch of her hands on the skin of his neck, the taste of her lips, the smell of her perfume, the sensation of her firm body against his.   He wanted this moment frozen in his memory.   He whispered in her ear, "I love you.   I'll be back."   When he finally released her she was crying, too.   This he did not expect.   Maybe he meant something to her after all.

The conductor shouted "Booo-oard!" and Hollis stepped up into the rail car. He found a seat before the train lurched into motion, leaning out the window for one last look. He never took his eyes off Jessie until the train rounded a turn and she disappeared from his sight. He wondered if they could see his tears.

There was so much unfinished business with this woman. He had found it too late, left too soon.

Yes, the silk slip had done exactly what she had intended.

Hollis walked over to the nose hatch and was about to step up into the plane when he caught sight of Ransahoff walking briskly across the perimeter strip toward him. He was carrying something and he looked angry, almost livid.

"Oh shit, here he comes," Tommy clucked.

Hollis looked over at Moe who was laughing.

"Now what?" Hollis said aloud.

"Come here, Hollis!" Ransahoff shouted, holding in his hand a bucket of red paint. "Ladder!"

Tommy, barely able to contain his glee, lifted the pre-positioned stepladder and erected it beneath the left wing tip where Ransahoff, without breaking stride, climbed up to the wing. He took the brush and slapped the red paint onto the wing tip. It looked as if he had performed this odd ritual before as there was already an existing coat of red paint on the aluminum.

When he was finished, he stepped down, looking Hollis in the eye. "You listen to me, Hollis. You wanna live long enough to fuck your wife again you better fly tight formation. I ain't shittin' ya. You're flying the five spot. I better see red paint scraped onto Selkirk's waist gunner's shirt. I mean it."

Hollis watched Ransahoff turn and walk with equal ferocity over to the right wing of Cahill's plane where the crew chief also had a ladder waiting. Hollis heard Ransahoff yell for Cahill and watched him repeat the act.

Moe walked away shaking his head. His task completed, Ransahoff strode briskly back down the perimeter strip to **The Flying Dutchman** and his chuckling crew. Leo stepped under the wingtip and surveyed the paint-job. "You're not married. You think you oughta tell him?"

They climbed into the plane settled into the cockpit and ran through the checklist. Dodge stood between them, as he always did, and watched as Leo carefully checked each item, each lever and switch, with a light touch. The pre-flight completed, Hollis looked at his watch. Another five minutes to engine start. He looked at Dodge who returned his glance with a nod. Hollis wondered if the engineer could perceive his apprehension. He was eager to make a good showing today. He didn't come all of this way, be this close, and then not be ready, found wanting. The entire crew would be judged, but the person who would be responsible for them making the list would be him. He was anxious for his crew to feel confident in his ability to pilot them around, take them into combat and bring them back alive. He glanced at Leo who was fiddling with his seat.

Watch my ailerons, Selkirk had told him. *They'll tell you what I'm doing. Pick a spot on my plane and fly off it. Go easy on the engines, keep an eye on the manifold pressure and try and stay a step ahead of what's actually happening. Set the inboards and jockey the outboards.   Relax and think.*

Flying good formation in the Big Leagues is the down payment on your ticket home, they said and they said it over and over again.

Hollis, You wouldn't make a boil on a good pilot's ass, Freitag told him.   It was his favorite expression.

"OK," Leo said.

Hollis glanced up and saw the first puff of blue smoke leave Ransahoff's left outboard engine as the prop slowly turned over.

"Clear!" Hollis yelled out the window.   He turned to Leo, "Start one" while he held his left index finger out the window for Moe to see.

Leo leaned forward and held down the toggle for the energizer of the left outboard, number one, engine with his left index finger while he pumped the primer at his right foot with his right hand.   Hollis counted the seconds in his head.   He could hear the inertial starter grind in protest.   "Mesh one."

Leo depressed the other toggle to the engine, engaging the clutch of the starter.   The blades turned one revolution and the engine caught.   The first tentative explosions in the cylinders caused the big plane to shudder as the engine came alive with a cloud of blue smoke and a throaty rumble.   Leo pushed the mixture control to auto-rich.   He watched the cowling rattle and vibrate from the irregular combustion until the roar of the thundering engine became steady and strong.   Hollis eased the throttle forward slightly.

"Oil pressure," Leo said.

Hollis checked the gauge, "Coming up."

Hollis knew in an instant these were good engines and this was a good plane.   Once again the bond between man and machine was reestablished as the big, metallic beast came to life.   He looked down at Moe and held two fingers out the window. "Start two."

They waited while the squadron taxied past and when Selkirk went by Hollis eased off the brakes and the ungainly bomber lurched forward.   Moe give him a quick thumbs-up which Hollis returned.   Hollis guided **Cleopatra's Asp** onto the perimeter strip with squealing brakes and surging engines, joining the procession passing the waiting Cahill who dutifully fell in behind.

By the time they arrived at the threshold of the runway, Ransahoff was already miles ahead.   Hollis turned the airplane smartly onto the runway and had Leo lock the tail wheel.   He set the gyros and called the tower.   Given permission to takeoff, he advanced the throttles to 1500 rpm and turned on the generators.   He could sense Dodge brace himself.   Hollis pushed down hard on the brakes and advanced the throttles full to the stops.   The bomber roared and shook with the burgeoning power.   He watched the needles twitch on the rpm and manifold pressure gauges.   Satisfied, he set the friction lock on the throttles and let up on the brakes. **Cleopatra's Asp** seemed to leap forward like a wild animal released from its cage.   The familiar acceleration pressed him against his seat.

The rubber-streaked runway sped in a gray-black blur under the nose of the plane as it lifted effortlessly from the runway.   It felt good to be airborne again, exhilarating and, as it had always been for him, liberating.

As they started their timed climb, Hollis turned the plane over to his copilot.   It gave

Leo a chance to get some stick time and allowed Hollis to rest until they joined the formation and the real work would begin.   Hollis glanced at the instruments and watched as Dodge stepped behind Leo's seat and begin his post-takeoff ritual.   The engineer removed his earphones and ball cap setting them aside.   He slipped his leather helmet over his head, placing his RAF fighter pilot's goggles on his forehead.   Hollis had never seen them before today.   They had a flip shield of darkened lenses which he could snap down to protect his eyes from the harsh glare of the sun while looking for fighters.   He placed his oxygen mask around his neck and adjusted the leg straps of his chute harness under his groin.   He stood up and climbed into the top turret, fixing the seat strap under his bottom, connecting his microphone and headset to their jacks. When the turret started to spin Hollis returned his gaze to the instruments.   Leo had them right on course as H-y called for the first turn in a steady upward spiral.

There were a few broken clouds and squadron assembly could have been easily accomplished using visual means, but Ransahoff had insisted that they use the Group's buncher beacon to fix their ascent geographically.   So, conforming to Ransahoff's wishes, Hollis tried to avoid looking for the plane ahead until he reached assembly altitude, ten thousand feet.

As they passed nine thousand feet, Hollis took the controls from Leo.   At ten thousand, he announced that the crew should go on oxygen and check in.   Hollis adjusted his mask, smelling strongly of rubber, aftershave and spit, and checked his flow meter which blinked at him with each inhalation, "Three OK."   He then glanced out the side window and was pleasantly surprised to see Selkirk ahead and slightly above.   It worked just like it was supposed to.   He had made timed climbs before using a radio beacon as a reference point but, somehow, this was different.

Selkirk continued his climb to bring himself, as the leader of the second element of three planes, above and behind Ransahoff.   Hollis's position in the formation was below, behind and to the right of Selkirk.   He would climb above his final position and settle back down into it. This prevented the planes from mushing when they went into level flight directly from a climb.

Red paint or not, he didn't want to get too close to Selkirk so he placed the plane about a Fortress-length behind **Vermont Revenge**, below and about a wingspan to Selkirk's starboard side.   Selkirk reached altitude and leveled off with Hollis, and then Cahill, in tow until he was slightly higher than Ransahoff's three planes.   This was the configuration of the high squadron in a group combat box.   Hollis was surprised at how close Ransahoff's wingmen were and how close in trail Selkirk was to Ransahoff.   It was apparent to him that he was sticking out like a sore thumb revealing his timidity in the process.   Even Cahill was tucked in tighter.   Hollis could feel his palms sweat inside his leather gloves, soaking the rayon liners.   He lined up Selkirk's ball turret with the left outboard engine nacelle to fix the position on Selkirk's wing. He glued his eyes to Selkirk's starboard aileron and tried to bring **Cleopatra's Asp** in a little closer.   Then he thought better of it and would wait until they were at altitude which, for today's exercise, would be twenty-five thousand feet.

It dawned on him that the position he was given, on the outside of a formation was also the most vulnerable.   In fact, the outer-most aircraft or the very highest or very lowest always were at greatest risk.   They were also hardest to fly being on the very inside or farthest outside of any turn and hence staying in formation required either racing ahead as it wheeled one way or back way off, coming close to stalling, to keep from getting too far ahead when it wheeled the other way.   It depended on the guy flying the lead plane.   If he knew his business everybody stood a pretty good chance of keeping proper position.   It was a crucial hierarchy.   The wing lead, the group lead, and the squadron lead and the leading plane of the second element.

If the turns were sharp and erratic, the formation could get strung out in a matter of moments in a massive chain reaction with potentially catastrophic consequences, and, once scattered, was difficult to get back in place.   Occasionally, it never did, becoming an inviting target for predation.

If the turns were smooth, wide and well-executed, everyone could hang on and survive a change in direction more or less intact.

Selkirk said that Ransahoff was the best in the business and throughout the Group's history it was the widely held opinion that everyone would rather have Ransahoff lead than just about anybody except Rager or Hightower.   They had acquired the skill to handle a large flock of planes and, at least in Ransahoff's case and despite his other shortcomings, were good leaders in the air.

Leo tapped Hollis's arm and pointed to his earphones, the signal to switch from the command channel to the intercom.   "Navigator to pilot, passing seventeen thousand feet. We'll be making a ninety degree turn in about two minutes and head for Splasher number 5 at Mundesley."

"Pilot to navigator, OK.   Two minutes."   Hollis glanced at the clock on a little panel above the windshield then reached down and switched back to command.   They would continue to climb to twenty-five thousand feet on the way to the Splasher and from Mundseley they would turn out over the water and head for Scarborough.

Hollis became aware of the cold.   He turned up the cabin heat, but is was close to worthless.   The bomber hit a bubble of air and bounced up, then down again.   It was growing increasingly turbulent outside and the roughness of the air forced Hollis to concentrate even harder on keeping position.

Right on time, almost to the second, Hollis could see Ransahoff wheel his plane to the right, the two wingman followed in perfect unison.   Hollis marveled at the precision they displayed.   It was as if the three planes were connected by rigid members.   Selkirk kept his place behind Ransahoff, the six planes seeming to move as one.   This won't be so hard, Hollis thought.

Hollis was startled by Ransahoff's voice booming into his headphones, "Good, Hollis. That's about the right position for the climb.   At twenty thousand feet close it in."

Jesus, Hollis thought, *where is he that he can see me and how much closer does he expect me to be?*   Ransahoff had to be riding in the top turret.

"You too, Cahill."

Hollis snapped a glance over at Cahill who seemed even further away from Selkirk.   He looked at the altimeter.   Nineteen thousand feet.   *Might as well start closing in now.*   Hollis swallowed hard and pulled in tighter beside Selkirk until they were about three quarters of a wingspan separated them.   The closer he allowed the two planes to get the rougher the air seemed to become as disturbed air spilled off Selkirk's wingtip like a huge horizontal whirlpool. He was satisfied with his position although he was working harder to keep it.

At twenty thousand, the headphones crackled again, "I told you to close it in Hollis.   I meant it."

Christ, if I get in any closer we might actually scrape the goddamned red paint after all.

So, for safety's sake he stayed where he was and waited to see what happened.

"Close it up a little more Cahill...That's it.   Hollis I'm not gonna tell you again.   Bring that thing in tight."

Ransahoff's voice was irritatingly matter-of-fact, as if he were discussing the arrangement of living room furniture instead of thirty-ton bombers bouncing around thin air loaded with tons of fuel and ten souls.

Hollis could feel sweat gather on his lip and armpits.   He wasn't cold anymore.

Passing through twenty-two thousand feet, the engines started to give off condensation trails.   They were short, wispy and spun white as snow.

"Navigator to pilot, Splasher in two minutes."

Hollis shot a glance at the altimeter, twenty-three thousand, five hundred feet.

"Hollis...Hollis!" Ransahoff screamed.

He pulled the big bomber in even further.   It had gone beyond risky to dangerous and now, suicidal.   The turn would be in a minute and it would be to the left.   Anticipating it, Hollis waited until what he thought was the precise moment and inched the throttles forward and made a slight bank to the left.

It was too much too soon and the wing tips vertically overlapped, almost touching. Selkirk's waist gunner's eyes were big as china saucers above his oxygen mask and the gunner pointed his weapon at Hollis.

Fuck, I'm gonna kill us all!   Heart pounding, his palms soaking his glove liners, Hollis moved the plane away.   This was the closest he had ever come to colliding with another aircraft.   Probably the closest he had ever come to death.

Someone must have been shouting into the interphone for Leo started bouncing around in his seat to get a better look at Selkirk.

"Nice way to anticipate a turn, Hollis, but it's better if you wait until we actually make it." At that precise instant Ransahoff's plane suddenly veered to the left, causing even Cassidy and Watanabe to get out of place.   Selkirk held on for dear life while Cahill dropped from view and, in the span of a few heart beats, Hollis found himself two hundred yards to the right of the formation in a giant game of crack-the-whip.   Reflexly, he poured on the coal jacking up the manifold pressure while Leo adjusted the rpm to increase the propeller's bite in the air.   Poor Cahill was probably plummeting to his death in a high-speed stall, turning away abruptly as he did to avoid running into Selkirk.

Leo tapped his arm.   "Navigator to pilot, you gotta hand it to that Ransahoff we made that turn within twenty seconds of the flight plan.   By the way, are you trying to kill us?"

Hollis looked over at Leo.   Leo's skin, what he could see of it, was pale, drained of blood.

On the command channel again, "Hollis, if there's enough room for a Focke-Wulf to fly between you and Selkirk one surely will.   Now get back in formation."

He watched as Cahill regained his place, climbing back up, flogging his engines in the process.   His hands trembling, Hollis pushed the throttles forward and banked in toward the formation.   When he was again where he figured he should be, he eased the plane in as close as he dared, about half a wing span.   He did not take his eyes off Selkirk or his fucking aileron.

"I want you to fly the son of a bitch, not aim it," Ransahoff admonished him.

Where'd you get those wings, Hollis, his transition instructor, Butch Mullen, had asked,

Woolworth's?

Butch Mullen was a natural pilot.   He had flown some of the early big ones, St. Nazaire, Brest.   He started out a second lieutenant in the dummy seat and ended up a first pilot after only two missions.   He, among others, had been culled from the combat groups in a harvest of experienced pilots to fill transition instructor slots.

Butch could fly a tight formation with consummate, effortless skill.   He would sit in the right seat with one hand on the wheel, the other on the throttle, squinting through smoke from a cigarette perched between his lips.

Hollis felt shaken.   He was an imposter, not competent to pilot a bomber and was demonstrably risking the lives of everyone. He would finish flying the practice mission, but it was apparent that he would never fly a bomber in the Big Leagues again.   He stole a glance at Leo who stared out the window at the **Vermont Revenge**.   He appeared to be hyperventilating. Being on the interphone, he could not hear the haranguing that Hollis was receiving but that didn't matter.   Every time he lapsed, for even a moment, Ransahoff would start in on him. Cahill caught some of it too, but not like Hollis.   Ransahoff's words scalded his heart, rendering him puny and pathetic.

At Scarborough, they made another erratic turn and he was thrown out of position yet again with resultant screaming.

When he recovered, Ransahoff told Hollis and Cahill to let their copilots take over for a while.   Good, Hollis thought, now Ransahoff is going to see what really bad is like.

To Hollis's surprise, Leo kept them fairly close, not as close as he had, Hollis quickly noted, but still a respectable showing.   Ransahoff took the squadron through a series of dog-legs as they crossed England.   They were gentle and easy turns and Leo handled them well.

Over the Irish Sea, Hollis resumed control and they made a run at the bombing range. Sully did okay; his bombs were dropped at precisely the right moment and on target.   By now Hollis was ready for almost anything, even so the sharp diving turn after bomb release, as if going for the Rally Point, took him by surprise and he was out of place before he knew it. Another tongue lashing.

The bombers orbited above Kingston-upon-Hull for fifteen minutes.   H-y asked where their fighter escort was, but that was the least of Hollis's worries.   Nonetheless, the fact that the P-47s didn't show up was not reassuring.

Back over the North Sea, the target tows arrived.   Two RAF Vultee Vengences flew past dragging long yellow sleeves behind them.   Hollis switched to intercom, "OK, clear your guns and fire at will.   And remember, aim at the sleeves."

Hollis watched them circle back and make a head-on pass with a closing speed near 400 miles an hour, the yellow sleeves whizzing by in a blur.   **Cleopatra's Asp** shook as the guns opened up, all firing at once, making it seem as if the plane might shake apart under his seat.   It was sobering to see the tows fly back and forth.   It was not difficult to imagine them bearing black crosses, shooting at the little formation, trying to kill him.   Hollis swallowed hard in an effort to rid himself of the choking lump in his throat.   The smell of burnt cordite wafted through the cabin, the smoke stung his eyes.

But none of it mattered.   As soon as they returned to Ridgewell he would be sent packing.

The two Vultees made two more passes, **Cleopatra's Asp** shook and, as quickly as they came, they were gone, the whole exercise lasting no more than a few minutes.

Ransahoff made a couple more nasty turns, seemingly in an effort to shake Hollis and Cahill one last time.   Hollis tried to stay as close to Selkirk as he dared, but it seemed futile. The harder he tried, staring at Selkirk's right aileron until his eyes hurt, the worse his performance.   His incompetence was now public knowledge, beyond serious dispute.

Formation flying should be easy for a smart guy like you, Butch said, *it's just an exaggerated game of follow the leader.   Don't make it harder than it oughta be.*

They were behind schedule, thrown off by the stooging around waiting for the P-47s. Finally, Ransahoff turned the squadron one last time and set a course toward Ridgewell.

Ransahoff brought them over the field and, one by one, they peeled off and landed. Hollis placed **Cleopatra's Asp** back on the hardstand and Jablonski and his partners were demonstrative in their inspection of the left wing tip, checking to see if any of the red paint had been scraped off.   Hollis filled out his forms while Leo and Dodge left the flight deck.   He unplugged his cords, gathered his stuff and climbed down to the nose hatch.   He expected to see Ransahoff's angry countenance staring up at him as he lowered himself to the ground, but he did not.   He gave Ransahoff silent credit for being leader enough not to humiliate him in front of his crew.   He loosened his clothing and found that he was drenched in sweat.   His hair was damp and matted as he removed his helmet.   His arms were so fatigued they were rubbery and ached from his chest to his hands.   So tight had he gripped the wheel that only now did it seem that blood was returning to his fingertips.   He could not remember when he had worked harder at flying an airplane.   He tried to collect his wits when Moe walked over.

"Well, sir.   How'd we make out?"

Hollis gave Moe a long look and said, "She was fine."

"That's not what I meant, sir."

"I know what you meant."   He handed Moe the forms and turned away.

The crew finished deplaning and gathering their guns and equipment.   They seemed pleased with themselves and chatted amiably with the ground crew, not the least aware of how close he had come to killing them.

He looked over at Cahill who was walking across the grass clutching his mask and helmet.   Hollis looked back in the direction of **The Flying Dutchman**, expecting to see Ransahoff charging down the perimeter strip as he had earlier, but he was not to be seen.   Hollis ambled over to Cahill.

"Well," Cahill said, "I must say that was an interesting experience, wasn't it?"

"Ransahoff was trying to get us killed."

Cahill cocked his head at Hollis and said, "I didn't take notice that Ransahoff was flying my plane today.   Was he flying yours?"

"You scrape off any red paint?"

"No.   But I sure as hell tried.   You?"

He turned and walked away from Cahill.   He wasn't interested in dissecting the experience with him either.   He returned to his crew, taking consolation in the fact that no one on board had heard Ransahoff's harangue. Looking at them, they could not truly appreciate how deeply despondent he was.   Quinn walked up to him and smiled broadly, "That Cap'n Ransahoff was really somthin', 'eh, Lieutenant?   He tried to ream you a new asshole up there today."

"I thought we told you to monitor the intercom on today's flight."

"Well, sir," Quinn continued, not giving up his smile, "I came out to the plane yesterday and rewired my headphones so's I could keep one ear on the interphone and the other one on the VHF.   That ways I could stay in touch with everybody."

"So you heard every word Ransahoff said?"

"Yes sir.   Every word.   I figure Ol' Cap'n Ransahoff was just tryin' to figure out a way to keep us all alive."

"Yeah, that's my guess, too."

Dodge walked over saying, "Wow, that turbulence ran us all over the place.   Almost banged us into Lieutenant Selkirk.   I thought that waist gunner was gonna shoot us.   You did a fine job of getting us out of trouble there, sir."

Hollis snapped a glance at Quinn who, not losing his smile, nodded agreement.

They climbed onto the truck sent to fetch them.   The crew babbled incessantly.   Hollis figured they had endured some sort of ritualized test of virginal bomber crews and had passed. When they returned to Squadron Headquarters he expected them to be given a new pilot.   He knew he was going to have trouble explaining what had happened.   To his folks.   To Jessie. To his crew.   They deserved better than him.   How could he explain his utter failure as a bomber pilot and their caretaker?   He had been found incompetent, incapable of looking after the safety and welfare of his crew.   Bad enough the Germans were going to try to kill them all, they didn't need the handicap of a pilot unprepared for the challenge.   He could not recall ever feeling quite so low.   He, after all, had told *them* not to fuck up.

Chapter Eight   **The List**

When Hollis returned to his room he found Stan napping, a *Stars and Stripes* on the floor beside him.   An exploding bomb might not have disturbed his slumber so Hollis was not particularly careful about avoiding the noise.   He threw his hat onto the table and stripped naked to his dog tags.   He was going to shower even if today was not the day for heated water. If he froze to death or caught pneumonia and died, so be it.

The water, held in some sort of holding tank, actually warmed slightly in the afternoon August sun so that the shower was not nearly as brutally cold as expected.   Even so, one could have struck a match on the goose bumps.

The debriefing had been a relatively benign affair.   Ransahoff said nothing to the pilots. Hollis figured they all knew where they stood and Ransahoff did not need to point this out. Instead, he was more interested in discussing the situation the navigators found themselves in, being jerked, as they were, all over England by a formation which did not follow a predetermined course, going first one way then another seemingly at random.   Making a rendezvous precisely could be a difficult task.   Arrive too soon and you had to stooge around waiting, all the while burning gas.   Too late and you had to figure out a way to make a new rendezvous burning gas trying to catch up.   Unexpected course changes were the norm.   If you want to know how to find your way back home, first you need to know where you are and in which direction home could be found.   Navigators were to stay behind and go over their logs with Ransahoff's navigator.   They were joined by Sudbury, the Group navigator.

Bombardiers did okay.   They dropped on the leader and the pattern was a good one. Where the bombs end up depends as much on where the pilot places his plane in the formation at the time of bomb release as it did on the bombardier aiming from the lead ship.   *And if you don't put the bombs where they are supposed to go you've wasted the taxpayer's money and risked your life for nothing.*   Pilaccio, the Group bombardier joined them, too.

When the meeting broke up, Hollis expected to be taken aside by Ransahoff and told to report directly to Entwhistle's office to be cashiered into obscurity.   But Dutch ignored him. He ignored Cahill, too.

After his shower, during which he mused about the similarity between ablution and absolution, Hollis dressed for dinner.   He wanted to get over there and eat before Leo showed up.   Leo clearly understood what had transpired today, having had a ring-side seat for the whole ordeal.   Even though he had been monitoring the interphone during the ride, he could, and surely did, watch his pilot struggle.   Little imagination was required.   He had borne witness to the near-collision.   Hollis had managed to scare the pants off him and Leo, no doubt, heard the crew's panic on the intercom.   So Leo was the last person he wanted to be around.   He couldn't bear the thought of being consoled by someone who couldn't fly his finger into his own nose.

"Chow time," Leo said, standing in the door.

Avoiding Lonnie's seat, Hollis and Leo ate without conversing.   Leo might have been impervious to those around him, but Hollis was not.   A few minutes after they sat down, Stan and Mickey walked by carrying their trays.   They chatted quietly, for Hollis could see their mouths move.   He wondered what they were talking about.   The hapless rookies perhaps.   A moment later, they were joined by Watanabe and the tall, lanky Mattson, both still in their flight suits.

Hollis's mind raced.   He figured there was no way they were going to send him into combat now.   And he had no idea how to redeem himself even if offered the chance.   How could he explain what had happened to him?   To Jessie?   To his father?   *Gee, dad, I just couldn't keep the wing tucked in.   The harder I tried the harder it got.   They told me they didn't need me.*

He looked over at the four men sitting quietly eating their dinner.   They had been shot at.   Every time they strapped themselves into a B-17 they demonstrated their heroism.   Their grit.   They always went.   There must be something they had which he lacked.   Some inner strength or moral imperative.   Some reactive synapse.   Some circulating hormone.   It wasn't willingness.   Hollis, blighted by fear and doubt and even self-loathing, knew to the very root of his soul that he would go.   He really didn't want to, but he would.   How could he not?   They were no better or worse than he.   So what was the difference?   Eisenberg had the reputation as the finest natural pilot in the Group.   But Selkirk?   All he knew were cows.   What was it?

They were proven.   But it was more than the courage of the collective.   These were brave men.   They could be counted on to mount up and ride to the sound of the guns.

Hollis again realized how much his arms and hands ached as he moved his food around his tray with his fork.   He felt as though someone was watching him.   He looked up at Leo who smiled.   He had cleaned his tray.

"That was the worst formation flying I ever saw," Hollis said.   "I can't imagine what Begay must've thought."

"I think you missed the point," Leo replied.

"What do you mean?"

"Dutch wasn't interested in showing us how easy it could be, but how hard.   He wasn't trying to be a good leader today.   He wanted to be a bad one."

Hollis stared at Leo who added, "If it were easy anybody could do it."

Good old Leo, his copilot.   Leo, as did all copilots, came to phase training without the benefit of the three to four months of specialized B-17 transition instruction.   His mastery of the B-17 was to be acquired as on the job training.   Hollis understood this and did his best to teach Leo everything he knew or heard or experienced about flying the plane.

Even so, Hollis had his doubts.   Hollis would explain the function of some instrument or elaborate some procedure and Leo would smile, as he did now, and nod unprepossessingly.   A copilot was more than an extension of the pilot.   He had to take over for the pilot should he be disabled, the official term for killed.   In a pinch, or if disaster struck, Hollis harbored deep concern about Leo's ability to bring his plane back and save his crew.   If he could not, if Leo failed, it would be his failure, too.   Even in death, Hollis would have left a legacy of failure, betraying not only his copilot, but his crew.   Hollis understood this from the very beginning and spent long hours out on the ramp sitting in a quiet cockpit patiently going over things again and again.   Every chance he got.   One more time.   Leo would just smile and nod and occasionally say 'OK' or "Right, I got it.'   Hollis just wasn't sure he really did.

As he contemplated the day's events, he continued his introspection asking how could they knowingly imperil his crew by leaving him in charge of it?

"I was talking to Watanabe, Eisenberg's Jap copilot," Leo said.

"And?"

"He was telling me about Stan.   You know what he did before the war?"

"Some piano player, or something."

"No, he was a graduate of the Julliard Institute of Musical Art in New York and was working on his PhD in musicology at NYU when he got drafted."

Hollis turned and looked at Stan across the room and thought of Stan throwing himself into his bed, dabbled with the blood of his waist gunners emitting the pungent aroma of sweat, fear and cigarettes, who looked and acted more like a teamster than a PhD candidate.

"Jessie went to college at Columbia."

"Yeah, I know."

"Her father's nurse went to work at the Navy Hospital in Philadelphia and Jessie might have to work for her father."

"That's tough.   Well, there *is* a war on.   Better she work for her old man than in some defense plant stitching combat boots."

"I guess.   I wonder when our mail will catch up to us?   We've been over here almost two weeks, for Christ's sake."

"There you are."   Hollis looked up at the voice which he had instantly recognized as Selkirk's.   "You musta really impressed 'em today, Old Boy."

"Not Ransahoff, that's for sure.   Why?"

"You're on the mission list for tomorrow."

Hollis's heart was still pounding when he strode into the Squadron operations room. Entwhistle and Ransahoff were standing before a chalk board silently staring at it.

He looked at the names on the list: Ransahoff, Eisenberg, Cassidy, Selkirk, Cahill and Hollis.

Entwhistle said, "What's Hollis's name doing here?   He and that Cahill just came from the Replacement Center and he isn't ready.   We've got to take him off the first pilot list and put him in the dummy seat for a while.   Jesus, we're gonna get him bumped off just like the last one."

"Nope, we don't have a first pilot to replace him so he stays on the list.   Same with Cahill."

"We're gonna get 'em killed."

"We're still down three full crews.   We can't put up a squadron without them."

"OK, Ransahoff.   You can wet nurse a bunch of rookies, if you want.   It's your decision.   You live with it."   Entwhistle turned and looked at Hollis.   "Who are you?"

"I'm Hollis."

Without another word, Entwhistle walked away.

"Wet nurse?" Hollis asked.

"Listen, Hollis.   You stay tucked in and use your head.   You'll be alright."   Ransahoff turned to the blackboard, his fingers white with chalk dust, and started writing again.

As Hollis turned to leave he bumped into Cahill who had heard part of the exchange. "What, exactly, is a 'wet nurse'?" Cahill asked as they walked out into the night.

They ran into H-y and Leo.

"I heard we're alerted for tomorrow and we've been made operational," H-y said, much too cheerfully.

"You heard right," Hollis said.   "Where's Sully?   Does he know?"

"Back at the hut studying."

"Studying what?"

"Doctorin'."

"What?"

"He's back at the hut brushing up on his first aid.   He heard we were on the list and he got out his books."

"I don't understand."

"Sure, you remember," Leo said.   "Back at Ardmore you told Sully that as bombardier he was to be in charge of administering first aid.   Kind of like the ship's doctor.   Don't you remember?   He argued with you saying 'you're the one going to medical school, you do it.' And you said, 'I'm the one in charge of flying the airplane.'   Well, Sully took you very seriously and took it upon himself to read up on doctor stuff.   He got a hold of a book on surgery and a manual on high altitude medicine and started readin'.   He even borrowed your copy of <u>Gray's Anatomy</u>.   Stan gave it to him."

"He skipped dinner and started boning up on dislocations.   You know, just in case," H-y added.

Hollis talked to Leo and H-y for a time then returned to his room. It was empty.   He sat on his bed and chain smoked four cigarettes trying to collect his wits.   He was terrified, so much so that clear thoughts had trouble forming in his head and the ones that did were fleeting.

For months he had known this day would come filling him with dread each time he thought of it.   He tried to reassure himself that his fear was well-founded and probably no more or less than anyone else on the eve of their initiation into combat.   Apprehensive as he was, he was also relieved.   The wait was over.   And, he was excited for the same reason. Momentarily, the flood of self-doubt that choked his heart disappeared.   Still, there were questions.

How would he behave in combat?   Would he measure up?   How would his crew behave?   Who was the weak link?   Who would fail?   Might it be him?   Such thoughts had filled his head on the flight over from the Atlantic.

He had spent hours staring into the night, hunched down in his seat while the autopilot flew the plane and Leo slept, Leo's head resting against the window where Angel had scrawled her phone number with lipstick.   Hollis could see the stars through the window panel above his head, contemplating what was in store for him seeking Divine guidance.   Some sign.   Maybe this had been a big mistake.   *The* Big Mistake.

He felt a soft tap on his shoulder.   He turned to see Salvatore Mollica, the tail gunner from Chicago.   Mollica leaned in close to his ear yelling above the engine noise, "Look what I found."   He handed a folded piece of paper to Hollis.   Mollica shone his flashlight on it while Hollis unfolded the note.

Good luck, it said.   *God protect all who fly in this ship.   Mary Spezio, Airframe Inspector #37.*

"Where'd you find it?"

"It was tucked behind the tail wheel housing."   Mollica paused for a moment, "Shame we probably won't get to keep this one."

"Yeah, shame."

"She's a good aeroplane."

"Yep, best there is."

Hollis stared at the note for a few moments and carefully refolded it.   "Put it back where you found it."

In the glow from the flashlight, he could see Mollica's boyish face and his wistful, brown Italian eyes.   "I'm scared," he said.

Hollis smiled reassuringly at Mollica, patting him on the arm.   "You'll be fine.   I promise."

"I promise," he said aloud as he sat on the bed.

It was all counterfeit.   All he knew of bravery was read from books.   Melville.   Crane. Stan walked through the door.

"We're alerted for tomorrow."

"I know," Stan said.

He would have given anything to be Stan at that moment--dead gunners and all--just to be that close to being finished.   Proven.   Leaving no doubt with anyone.   He'd have given anything.   Jessie.   His first born son.   His career in medicine.   Anything.

"Any advice?"

Stan started undressing and said, "When I was with the 91st we went to Hamm one day. First time we ever went there.   Hetrick was the Deputy lead and took over just before the IP. That made Klett the lead bombardier.   Rumor had it that Klett was blind in one eye and couldn't see out of the other causing conjecture about which eye he put on the eyepiece.   If there was a river near the target the bombs fell into the river.   If there was an important structure or landmark close to the aiming point it was the landmark or the structure which would feel the weight of Klett's bombs.   Everyone understood this to mean if you wanted your bombs to count, placement depended on each individual bombardier in the squadron sightin' his own bombs.

"Up front, there was Klett, who didn't know which end of the bombsight to peer into and Sumner, the navigator who couldn't find his dick with both hands.   The Germans could not have helped themselves more if they had put those two in that ship themselves.

"So there was Klett hunched over the bombsight spinning his knobs when a shard of flak ripped into his boot scattering his toes around the nose seconds before bomb release.   He didn't move until the plane shuddered with the precise separation of the bombs.   Then he grabbed his torn boot with a squeal you could hear without the interphone.   He forgot to say 'bombs away,' but his bombs were right on the money.   Does that answer your question?"   He feigned interest.   "What, exactly, was the question?"

Hollis watched as Stan finished undressing and climbed into bed, his back to Hollis.

Chapter Nine   **The War**

Hollis smoked another cigarette then turned out the light.   He lowered himself into bed contemplating the probability that this might be his last night on earth.   The butterflies zooming around in his stomach would not give him rest.   He tried to distract himself with pleasant thoughts.   He could only think of one thing: Jessie.

Jessie Snowden.

There were so many things he wanted to tell her but, to his eternal regret, never seemed to have gotten the chance and this made him sad.   He thought about flipping the light on and writing a letter to her.   But he had not yet received any correspondence and hoped it was because the mail simply had not caught up to him, not because she chose not to correspond.

He had last spoken to her from a phone booth at Grand Island the day they left to fly east. Her parting words to him were that she loved him and he should finish up what he needs to do and hurry back.

This was encouraging.   He distinctly remembered her saying that: she loved him.   Can you say such a thing and not really mean it?   Of course, he answered his own question, it happened all the time and to better men than him.

Hollis and Jessie were the same age, born within a few months of each other.   She was the fabled girl next door.   Two parallel lives now hopefully convergent.   He would forever wonder how a girl so beautiful and perfect in every way could find love in a man like him. Same with Leo and Christie, perhaps even more so.   But that was another story. Theirs was an indecipherable biological attraction.

Jessie grew up a tomboy.   She always wore a red baseball cap that had long ago faded to pink.   She would bound out her front door and leap off the porch, baseball glove in hand.   He could never hear the unmistakable slam of a screen door without thinking of the little blond girl who dashed out the moment before that noise.

At first, they wouldn't let her play baseball in the field across the way.   No girls could play baseball and no respectable sandlot team would allow one to be a member.   So she tucked her curly, blond locks under her faded, red ball cap and spit into her glove, massaging the saliva into the leather.   She wound up and fired a fastball so hard it stung the hand of the boy who caught it.   The boys soon realized she was the only one who could throw a brush back pitch without plunking the batter.   She threw a wicked inside curve that was un-hittable, was a switch-hitter and made some sort of contact with the ball whenever the bat left her shoulder. When they divied-up sides she was always the first player chosen.   Who said girls couldn't play baseball?

One summer day, they were in the back yard hitting fungos and she smacked a hard line drive striking Hollis in the middle of his forehead, knocking him out cold.   When he came to, the first thing he remembered seeing was Jessie's head blocking out the sun.   He remembered the look of concern on her sweet face.   The sun made her blond hair glow around her face like the halo of a Renaissance angel.   As his eyes refocused on her he knew that he had seen a vision and that he loved her.   Dr. Snowden attended his concussion with bed rest, a piece of steak to the forehead and frequent convalescent visits by his daughter.   *Jessie, run over there and see how the boy is doing.*

Then, after she turned fourteen, she didn't come to the field any more.   One day she didn't show up and never came back.   Speculation was rampant that it was in some way related to the observation that she was sprouting breasts.

Looking back, it was inevitable that such a pretty girl would get noticed resulting in a constant string of boyfriends that would come to visit.   Carry her books home from school, they would, until Hollis seemed to fade into the background.   It wasn't just an unrequited crush, he told his mother, it was genuine love.   *Stop pining after the girl*, his father would say.   *There are other fish in the sea.   Dad*, he would say, *you don't understand.*   Her preoccupation with other boys saved him the embarrassment of having her endure his squeaky voice and the pimples on his face.   It also meant that when his high school senior promenade came around someone else beat him to the draw so he boycotted the event rather than see her dance in the arms of another man.   It had been an on-again, off-again relationship that was mostly off.

Hollis greatly admired Jessie's father.   A physician, and intellectual who read Mark Twain and Sinclair Lewis for fun, he was also a practical man much like his own father.   Hollis always found him a fascinating blend of these characteristics as if the two traits were somehow mutually exclusive.   Dr. Snowden once had a tryout at spring training with the Philadelphia Phillies as a short stop.   They wanted to send him to the minors.   Instead, he went to medical school.   Jessie's affinity for baseball was genetically endowed.   He possessed great wit and charm and Hollis wanted to emulate the man who would leave his warm home in the middle of a snowy night to come to the aid of his fellow man, bringing honor to himself and his profession with each selfless act.   It was noble, redeeming and perhaps then Jessie would notice.

Hollis remembered being awakened one night for no apparent reason.   Perhaps it was the sound of a phone ringing somewhere.   It came from next door and a few moments later the screen door slammed and Jessie's father walked out into the darkness with his black bag in one hand and his car keys in the other.   It was probably then that he decided to become a doctor.   It would please his father for young John to become a physician because it was his father who preached morning, noon and night about the value of a college education, something he would never have, but always longed for and something that might make his son 'Depression-proof'.

But, more importantly, Hollis hoped it would please Jessie.

Then, after they graduated high school, she went off to Columbia in New York City, where her father had gone, to study the liberal arts.   He left for Swarthmore to study pre-medicine.   He figured he would never see her again, but if he did, it would never be the same. So he cursed a God who could be so cruel and tried to think of something, or someone, else. He concentrated on his studies, sublimating his burgeoning sexual urges by studying the reproductive cycle of sea urchins.   He would write her and occasionally she would write back, but it meant nothing.   There was no substance.   No curiosity.   He would see her from time to time.   Holidays and such, and during the summer when he wasn't working in his father's hardware store.   But it was never the same.   Now her boyfriends were serious business.   One even came home with her one Christmas and Hollis figured it was all over.   He would read the announcement of their forthcoming nuptials and that would, indeed, be the end.

Then something happened.   The War.   The War changed everything.

Hollis had graduated Phi Beta Kappa from Swarthmore in June of 1941 with a degree in biology.   He had been accepted to Jefferson Medical College but had failed to obtain a scholarship so he asked for, and received, a deferment from matriculation for a year so he could work and save enough money to start in the fall of 1942.   He was disappointed by Pearl Harbor for it meant his dream of becoming a doctor might now be nothing more than that. And he knew, in his quaintly naive way, that regardless of the outcome, no one would arrive at the end of the war the same as when it started.

His father, who had friends at the local draft board, had been warned that his son, John, would be receiving his notice any day. Forewarned, the next day, December 15, 1941, Hollis walked into the Army Recruiting Office and signed up for Aviation Cadets. *Everybody wants to be a flyboy*, he was told. *Especially you smart college boys. Fill out an application and we'll be in touch.* On the 16th, his induction notice arrived so he went to the draft board advising them of his application for the Cadets. *Okay, but if you don't hear from them within a month drag your scrawny ass down here with your bags packed.*

It was a long month. Eventually, he received deliverance in the form of a telegram ordering him to report to Fort Dix, New Jersey for written qualifying tests and physical and mental examinations for the Cadet program.

Found eminently qualified, he was sent to preflight school in Texas. There, out of loneliness and his frustration with petty hazing, he wrote to Jessie. And, much to his surprise, she wrote back. There ensued a sporadic, attenuated correspondence. His inclination was to assume that it was part of the overall war effort. Like pen pals, rationing and women's service clubs. Keep up the morale of the troops by writing them from time to time, that sort of thing. Remind them what they're fighting for. And who. As before, there was never any substance to her letters. It was mostly light banter about home, his folks, her folks, mutual friends, her volunteer work. He made no presumptions about her intentions and was always oblique in his references to the two of them.

Then came the ten day furlough between advanced and transition. He spent it at home. She wasn't there. He was not surprised. He didn't expect her to be there and was therefore not disappointed.

The letters he received during the four months of B-17 transition training were different. She apologized about not being home to spend his furlough with him. She was not expecting him and, truthfully, the furlough had come as a sudden development about which he had little warning. She was in Pittsburgh visiting her dying grandmother. He would have gladly spent the time off in Pittsburgh had she told him. It was after that exchange of letters that things seemed to take on a different tone. Perhaps even a purpose.

His next, and last, leave came after combat crew training and before he picked up a B-17 at Grand Island. It was during those ten days that he found out how she really felt, acknowledged his lifelong passion for her and the first hint of a future together. They made love. It seemed the answer to all of his prayers. It seemed surreal. A dream. He made love to a woman he had worshiped and adored since before puberty and just that quickly it was gone. Like his career as a doctor, his dreams of Jessie had been abruptly, perhaps irretrievably, terminated by the God-damned war.

Stan's bed springs creaked under his shifting weight, "Old Klett's sittin' out the duration in a Stalag somewhere, poor bastard."

To Hollis, the war had been a distant abstraction. Until now. Even the practice mission today, with live ammunition and real bombs, had been only another exercise. Tomorrow he was actually going to fight in it. Tomorrow. A matter of hours.

He couldn't think of the war without also thinking of his father. By mid-1941 his father had perceived the inevitable.   He turned over management of the hardware store to his mother and took a job as a master carpenter with the Sun Shipbuilding and Drydock Company on the Delaware River in Chester.   The orders for ships poured in from England and then the Navy. He made more money in a week than he did in a month from the store.

His father was not the studied intellectual that Jessie's dad was, but he read the paper and listened to the radio.   He formed opinions. He was a Republican and, as such, a bit of a cynic who felt FDR was a socialist whose policies would eventually lead the country to ruin.

Hollis and his father would talk about politics and world events.   They would read the newspapers together then discuss what they had read.   His father thought the initial phase of the war, The Phoney War, as it was called, was nothing more than a territorial dispute between the Germans and the Poles.   He continued to feel that way until the invasion of France.

The America Firsters and Isolationists were frightening in their rhetoric, but, even so, he did not feel it was the United States' role to intervene in what was basically a European conflict and then one day the bombs started falling on England.   The Blitz caused him to change his mind completely because he thought innocent men, women and children were dying at the hands of unchecked evil.   The innocent men, women and children of Poland and the Benelux countries notwithstanding, Hollis noted.

Hollis's father was sympathetic to England, but cared nothing for France.   No Francophile, he took morbid delight that France had been over run and was disappointed that England appeared not to be able to handle the Germans.   He was not surprised the French folded their tent so quickly and was bewildered by Dunkirk and the battering of England by the *Luftwaffe*.   His father expressed the sentiment that he knew they would have to defeat Germany, but it was a shame that they would probably have to liberate France in order to do it.

He remembered the speeches of his high school history teacher who said that trouble was coming soon and the world would be forever changed.   He spoke of Weimar, Bolshevism and civil war in sentences filled with foreboding.   This was Hollis's first inkling that there was real trouble in the world.

In college, Hollis stood somewhere between apathy and enthusiasm and he did not know what to think except that it was chic to be intellectual and isolationist, but he wasn't sure why or if this was morally correct.

Hollis became interested in international affairs, read lots of newspapers, the <u>Bulletin</u> and the <u>Philadelphia Inquirer,</u> and worried about the destruction of civilization if another war came. He did not understand why the League of Nations was so ineffectual and why Hitler, increasingly demonstrating himself to be an obvious despot, could rise to power so easily.   The Germans loved him, it was said, because he made the trains run on time.   He restored their dignity.   He revived their self-esteem. How could he be faulted for that?   Mussolini's growing strength concerned him too, although at first he was thought of as a clown.   Or maybe it was Mussolini that made the trains run on time… Hollis asked his history professor how this could have happened and the professor simply said, "Nationalism."   He said it as if it were a dirty word.

Hollis also recalled a not impartial witness named Werner Kalmbacher, a German exchange student in 1938.   Werner seemed like a very nice fellow.   Good looking, athletic, affable.   Poster model for the Aryan ideal who spoke excellent English, almost without accent. Werner.   He could be facing Werner in the morning.   Probably an ardent Nazi spy, the cur.

An SS henchman.   Hollis remembered that Werner avoided Jewish kids and even kids who looked Jewish, but were not.   Now he was going to drop bombs on Werner and his folks. They were the unchecked evil.

Kalmbacher made a point of saying that Adolf Hitler was the Savior of the Germanic race and the Nation of Germany, doing more than just making the trains adhere to their schedules, he had restored pride and prosperity to Germany and demanded a redress of the rape of the Fatherland by the punishing, immoral Versailles Treaty.   Nationalism was just another name for patriotism.   Zionism and communism were the real threats to civilization. And homosexuals.

Yet, Hollis was told by others that Hitler was the greatest danger to human life and the community of man since the Black Plague.   He was not sure where the pacifists and isolationists stood in all this rhetoric and propaganda.   Their rallies did tend to attract a lot of young woman, he noted.   Nothing was ever *all* good or *all* bad.   Hollis found the cynicism and sarcasm of his professors toward the war naive and repugnant and without explanation.   People, innocent people, who had no cause to suffer, were dying by the thousands.   These were important issues, a threat to the very fabric of the structured, law-abiding civilization they took for granted.   They seemed to conveniently forget that the first thing the Nazis did was burn the books and openly persecute the Jews.   *Krystallnacht* was not some neighborhood misunderstanding.   If one did not take a public stand against the corruption it would be allowed to flourish. The only thing required for evil to triumph is for good men to do nothing. He had forgotten to say that.

It outraged Hollis when one of his professors said that US soldiers should refuse to fight because they had no specific ideological purpose and should not be forced to shed their blood in a war they could not explain.   Draftees and their captains would just do what they were told without thinking about it much, if at all, confirming their immorality.   If their fighting served no higher motive and if the average soldier could not articulate that motive then he should not be forced to fight.   It was all very confusing.

The same professor after the Christmas, 1940, Fireside Chat, ("no American boys will set foot on foreign soil...I hate war, Eleanor hates war" *and so, presumably does Fala*) said with unabashed, righteous indignation that, "American involvement in the European war is now inevitable. If this doesn't work, Roosevelt will concoct some other way of getting us sucked into it.   Ladies and Gentlemen, we have taken the first, irrevocable step toward catastrophe and it was taken by a democratically-elected president.   The war has started, it just hasn't been declared yet.   May God help us."

"Peace in Our Time" signs popped up around campus.

Now, America *was* in the war and Hollis found himself lying on his back staring into space, overseen by a wall full of pretty, naked women in seductive poses, wondering if he would live through it.   But, he told himself, American had never lost a war and he found it inconceivable that they could lose this one.   An irresistible, undeniable spirit existed in his country ignited by the flames of Pearl Harbor, that he felt convinced, in a simplistic and, perhaps naively patriotic way, existed in no other.   It dated back in an unbroken string of successes beginning with the Revolution when the right side won and the Civil War when again the correct side prevailed.   The correct side would win this time. He knew they would win. He had seen signs...

The train lurched to a stop waking him.   They had pulled off on a siding.   He heard it before he saw it and felt it before he heard it.   Like the first ripple of an earthquake.   Hollis turned to look into the night and saw the approaching headlight as it rounded the bend.   Two Big Boys thundered by in tandem pulling a hundred flat cars each with a self-propelled gun, a big rifle on a tank chassis, lashed to it, shapeless hulks rolling past the window in the dark.   He flew over the Mississippi and saw two spanking new fleet subs heading for the Gulf.   During his last furlough he went down to the Delaware River with his father, as he had so many times as a young boy, and watched four escort destroyers, gray, weathered, rusty and proud, sprint down the channel to pick up a convoy.   He could see sailors scampering around on the deck, in their pale blue shirts and dungarees, and ensign snapping smartly in the breeze.   Victory was inevitable.   He just hoped he'd live to see it.

It was funny, though, when he went into the service the war, its causes and progress, slipped into the background.   Sure there was the constant "Four Freedoms versus Lebensraum" and the "Slavery of the Jap Greater East Asia Co-prosperity Sphere" clatter which he suspected was nothing more than unabashed propaganda.   "Why We Fight."   It seemed endless to the point of becoming numbing.   He and all his colleagues were totally absorbed by the process of elimination they found themselves in on their way to becoming pilots and they paid little attention to the day to day prosecution of the war.   They all knew, without saying, that they would all get to see it soon enough.

Hollis was homesick.   He realized for the first time that it was the simple things, the mundane daily stuff of life which is taken for granted that he missed the most.   The smell of the summer air after a heavy downpour.   The aromatic sizzle of bacon and eggs on a Sunday morning, the smell and the sound wafting into his bedroom like a siren song.   Sitting in the cool shade of the two big oak trees in the front yards of his and Jessie's house.   The careless summers and weekends working as a stock boy in the hardware store arranging the hammers and paint cans just so.

He could hear the soft snore of Stan's breathing in the dark.   As a child, he had always tried to keep contact with the outside world at night because he loathed the darkness.   He would listen for the ghostly whistle of the two AM milk train as it passed through Chester.   Sometimes, when he went to bed, he left the radio on until they signed off and would listen to the static so it would ward off the demons of the night.   Then each morning he would awaken to the start of a new broadcast day.   Hope and spirit reborn.

His thoughts of home and his choking homesickness made him think of the bedtime prayer his mother taught him, which he would recite every night after he pulled the covers up to his chin, "Now I lay me down to sleep, I pray the Lord my soul to keep.   If I should die before I wake, I pray the Lord my soul to take."

He wondered what Jessie was doing at that moment half a world away.   He imagined her soft face on her satin pillow and his heart ached with longing and sadness...

Chapter Ten   **"If I should die..."**

"Lieutenant..."

Hollis felt the gentle tap on his shoulder and snapped awake.

"Lieutenant, breakfast at oh-three-thirty, briefing at oh-four-thirty."

The sound of Beamis's voice was like a clap of thunder against his brain.   It seemed as if he hadn't been asleep long, certainly not more than a few minutes.   He flipped his legs out of bed and sat up.   Stan was already up, a glowing ember betraying his cigarette in the dark. "Where to today, Beamis?" Stan asked.

Beamis turned his flashlight on and said, "Hell, sir.   Right directly, I suppose."

"And?"

"Twenty-four hundred pound demos, two thousand gallons.   Milk run."   He turned and left, thumping down the hall in his boots to continue his rounds.

The words were like a reprieve.   If true, his first mission would be an easy one.   But men die on milk runs, too.   Hollis wondered how a lowly Charge-of-Quarters like Beamis could come by such information and how reliable was it?   Hollis scratched his head and asked, "How does he know that?"

"Don't know.   I'm sure he has his ways.   He's almost always right," he replied as he turned on the light and crushed the cigarette in an ashtray.   Stan dropped his feet into his fur-lined flying boots, put on his A-2 jacket and tossed a towel over his shoulder.   He picked up his kit and walked out the door.   Hollis imitated his every move.   They stepped out into the night, the cool air raising goose-bumps on his legs, and joined the growing procession of shadowy figures, similarly clad, in a ritualized pre-mission pilgrimage to the latrine.

He tried to read the mood in the conversation that surrounded him in the dark.   There was some light laughter.   Some cigarette coughs.   Mostly low gravel voices of the recently awakened.   Somehow they seemed to know, or believed what Beamis said.

Hollis found a vacant spot at the wash trough beside Sully.   "Looks like a milk run."

Sully stopped brushing his teeth and turned to look at Hollis, "Now how in the hell do you know that?"

"Beamis told me."

"He's a buck sergeant in charge of wakin' us up.   How the hell should he know?"

"Guess somebody tells him."

"And you believe him?"

Hollis felt the abrupt return of the gnawing anxiety which had so recently left him.   *How would Beamis know?*   "Stan told me he's pretty reliable."

"And you believed him, too?   You know, Jack, in another time and place I might find your gullibility endearing.   Now, it is one of the reasons I worry about you."

Hollis ignored Sully and washed his face.   He shaved close.   The meticulous removal of all whisker stubble would make the oxygen mask fit better, with less chafing of the skin and more efficiency.   If he died today at least he would die clean shaven.   He quickly brushed his teeth and when he saw Eisenberg turn to leave he followed him out, a few paces behind him trying not to be obvious.

Back in the room Hollis watched Stan very closely.   He had, after all, survived twenty-two missions and whatever he was doing he was doing right.

Stan dressed slowly, methodically.   He stripped naked and powdered his groin, hairy chest and armpits. Then he reached into his footlocker and pulled out fresh underwear.   Hollis remembered the talk at Bovingdon.   *If you had clean underwear on when you were hit, the theory went, it might help reduce the risk of infection.*   Clean underwear, driven into the flesh by shell or fragment, made for less infection than dirty underwear.

Stan dropped to his bunk with a metallic clank and powdered his feet.   He pulled on a pair of long silk socks and a set of GI long johns, then a heavy pair of wool socks over that.   He put on his ODs, slipped a pre-knotted tie over his head and cinched it up under his collar.   They were officers and expected to wear ties even in combat.   He dropped his feet into his flying boots, pulled on his shearling jacket, wiped clean of the blood stains, placed his sunglasses in his breast pocket, his wallet in his hip pocket.   He walked over and pulled the holster containing his .45 from its nail and placed it around his waist.

Hollis asked, "I thought they told us not to carry a side arm."   Lest the Germans shoot first and ask questions later.   Or be thought of as a saboteur and hanged.

"You fight the war your way and I'll fight it mine."

There were seven rounds in a clip.   He might have a hard time shooting his way out of Germany with that.   Hollis figured he was probably saving the last round for himself, him being a Jew and all.   He picked up the Mae West from the place it had come to rest three days before and slung if over his arm.   He dropped a woolen muffler around his neck, his cap on his head and stuffed his beat-up Yankees cap into his pocket and let out a soft chuckle.

"What's so funny?"

"You know, they patched up old Klett's foot and wanted to send him home.   They said he couldn't fly anymore because if he got shot down he couldn't escape and evade with only half a left foot.

"He said no.   He didn't want to go home.   He was having too much fun.

"So next mission he gets shot down.   I guess they were right.   We later got word he was captured."   Stan was quiet for a moment.

"He got a Silver Star for that Hamm deal."   He turned to walk out.   "Don't make your bed.   Leave it the way you left it."   And he was gone.

Hollis finished dressing and found himself alone with his thoughts.   The dread he felt, based on the unknown future and fueled by what he already knew, influenced each move he made and every thought that formed in his head.   He had to learn quickly for it was on these early missions that he was most likely to be lost.   In fact, the risk of being shot down was greatest on the very first mission than at any other time.   Milk run or not.   Why give a new plane to an inexperienced crew?   First combat would be the moment of truth for him and his crew.   Never underestimate the enemy.   Pay attention.   Stay in close and keep your wits about you.   And for God's sake fly the plane. He knew his innocence and naiveté would offer no protection.   How much of a liability they would be he could not gauge.   He had to start sometime.   Perhaps he would have been better off waiting until tomorrow to start.   One more day to collect his wits so that he could keep them .

When he was finished he pulled out the pocket New Testament from his foot locker and placed it carefully into his left breast pocket of his shirt, without realizing it, over his heart.   The small book had a steel jacket with the legend "May this keep you safe from harm." It had been a gift from his mother.   He finally pulled Jessie's silk slip scarf around his neck.

He could not understand why Jessie's parents had not embraced him.   Perhaps this was a laissez-faire attitude to let Jessie pick and choose a qualified suitor; trust her to use her own judgment in discerning the man best qualified to attend to her future.   He was a bright, energetic and good-looking young man.   Demonstrably brave, at least up until now.   An excellent choice for their daughter.   Maybe it was because they were Presbyters and he was a papist.   Tolerant as Presbyterians were, perhaps this was the reason they could not whip up much enthusiasm for the boy.   He looked back at his unmade bed and turned out the light.   What if Beamis was wrong?   At least he would die clean and well-dressed, having spent his last night in a warm, dry bed.

He joined the irregular procession to the officer's Combat Mess, climbing into the back of the shuttle truck.   He did not recognize anyone with which to share the ride so he made the journey accompanied by his fear.

Leo was waiting for him at the door to the Mess.   "Ah, there you are.   I've been waiting for you," he said, failing to grasp the incongruity of his cheerfulness with both time and circumstance.

They entered the large room and were greeted by the smell of burnt grease, cigarettes, brewing coffee, body odor and aftershave.   Breakfast consisted of powdered eggs reconstituted in some bacon grease, creamed chipped beef on toast, shit on a shingle as they preferred to call it, pineapple juice and coffee. They took their trays and found H-y and Sully in the crowded room joining them.   H-y ate with abandon while Sully sat back and marveled.   They said there were signs at breakfast.   Fresh eggs, mission eggs they were called, were a sure indication a bad mission was in store.   This morning's fair could be taken as favorable.   If the brass were dressed in flight clothes it might be a rough one.   The only ranking officer he saw was Entwhistle and he wasn't in a flight suit.   Perhaps another good sign.   There was light talk and an occasional laugh in the crowded room of men in brown leather hunched over breakfast. Perhaps another sign.

Everything in combination, however, had taken his appetite from him.   He drank the juice and the coffee and nibbled at the periphery of his chipped beef on toast.   The eggs remained untouched by his fork.

"I just love these creamed foreskins," H-y said between noisy bites.   "Whatsamatter, Jack, not hungry?"

"How can you eat this stuff?   You realize we haven't had a truly decent meal since we left Grand Island?   This absence of edible food has ruined my stomach.   My entire digestive tract is in revolt."

"Be glad you aren't eating K-rations in some foxhole somewhere," Sully said.

At least he would die well fed.   Hollis ate what he could and they departed for the briefing room.

They met up with Selkirk outside the large Quonset hut.   "Top o' the mornin' to you John, boy-o."

"Hiya, Mickey."

"What are you so cheery about?" H-y asked.

Selkirk took a deep breath through his nose and looked up at the predawn sky and said in an exaggerated Irish brogue, "Sure it's a great day to be bombin' tootins."

"Who?"

"Teutons.   That ugly race what started this and took me away from me beloved Mary Catherine Selkirk."

As they approached the entrance Hollis saw a group of twenty or so men in flight clothes, cigarettes dangling from their lips, pipes and cigars in clenched jaws, watching as the officers entered the room.

"Who are they?" Hollis asked Selkirk who turned to see.

"They're the lookouts.   They wait to hear the reaction after the curtain is pulled. They can tell by the sound we make what kind of target we're going after.   Then they find their crews and tell them what they heard.   Around here the gunner's don't get a briefing.   Besides, they're not all that interested in what we're bombing, just whether it's gonna be hard or easy."

Hollis recognized Hulse who smiled and gave a little wave.   Hollis returned the gesture.

Two MPs, clad in white helmets, leggings, web belts and sidearms checked AGO cards at the door.   Chaplain Brown and three Red Cross girls, their faces fresh, boasting large, warm smiles, their hair perfect and their lips red with precisely applied lipstick, stood just inside greeting each officer with a 'good morning,' handing out coffee and donuts.   No one, Hollis figured, should look so irrepressibly lovely at four-thirty in the morning.

Hollis, Leo, H-y and Sully found seats with the rest of their squadron-mates.   The room was already filled with a haze of tobacco smoke and the murmur of conversation.   And the smells.   Leather, sweat, smoke.   And fear for no one really knew for sure what was in store.

The big, half-barrel shaped room was bright and the big map at the front of the room, on the raised stage was covered by a black curtain.   To one side was the large chalk board with group's formation written onto it.   Each plane silhouette had the pilot's last name and serial number of the aircraft he was assigned.   There was a big 'C' beside each plane assigned to carry a strike camera.   The 532nd was flying low squadron, Hollis in the number five slot. Minor adjustments were made to the squadron formation from the practice mission the day before. Dutch would lead, Mickey on his left, Cassidy on his right, Stan leading the second element with Cahill on his left and Hollis on his right.

The Group adjutant, a small man with spectacles, took the stage and called out the roll of aircraft commanders.   When he was done he stepped off the stage and went to the back of the room.   The room became quiet.   It was exactly four-thirty.

"Atten-hut!"

The collection of officers rose as one to their feet, chairs and benches scraping the floor. It was not a rigid military formation, more a seventh-inning stretch.

Down the center aisle came the Group brass, Van Patten, the CO, first, followed by Gleason, Begay and the four squadron commanders.   They stepped to one side at the front and Buckley Bonner, CO of the 534th, took the stage.   He was in flight clothes as was Princep Cavanarro, CO of the 533rd.

"Seats, Gentlemen!" he said.

Everyone sat down, a murmur filled the room.   More signs.   The Group brass were all in pinks and greens or leather jackets, not flying today.   Clevenger, the Group flight surgeon, Saul Gorton, the S-2, the weather, flak, ordinance, communications, flying control, security officers, and Sudbury and Pilaccio sat against the wall on the left.   Entwhistle and Duckworth sat beside Begay.   They looked bored.

"I'm the Bangmaster for today's sortee."   And, with great theatrical flourish, Bonner pulled back the black curtain.   All eyes went to the eastern most point of red yarn which marked a course from East Anglia across the Channel to the target.   Loud hoots and cheers went up as they all saw the line describe a dogleg path to Brussels.   A milk run!   That son of a bitch was right!   Bonner waited for calm to return.   "Our target for today is the Evere airdrome at Brussels, Belgium.   We will be high group of the 101st Combat Wing.   The 351st will lead, the 91st will be low.   Our route will be over water most of the way and we will have fighter escort all the way from RAF Spitfires and Thunderbolts."

There was scattered applause.

Bonner looked over at Gorton.   "Major."

The diminutive major climbed the step up onto the stage and took the pointer from Bonner and started talking about the target, a fairly large airdrome near Brussels.   H-y leaned over to Hollis and whispered, "And here I was hopin' it would be Berlin."   The compelling need to inject humor at times like this baffled Hollis.   Maybe because it was still an adventure, a rude game.   To see if one lived or died.

Other combat wings from both divisions would be attacking other *Luftwaffe* airfields in the Low Countries and Northern France.   He discussed in very business-like fashion, the details of the mission, the primary target, secondary target which for today would be another airfield in Flushing, Holland, tertiary target, a railroad yard and any last resort target.   He told them about the routes in and out, checkpoints en route and locations for rendezvous with escorts and anticipated fighter reaction.   There were about a hundred GAF day fighters within striking distance of the expected routes of penetration and withdrawal and he pointed to the airfields on the map identifying where they were based.   While the escort was expected to be more than adequate, some fighters may break through to the bombers so be alert.   Stay on your toes and beware of German fighters in twos and fours behaving like escorts.   These guys are particularly good.   They've had plenty of experience opposing daylight raids before and they will come at you from all sides but mostly the standard head on attack.   While the German fighter pilots are hesitant to fight out over open water they may not be counted on to behave that way.

On cue, an assistant lowered the projection screen in front of the map while another maneuvered the large Bell Optican overhead projector into position down the narrow aisle.   The lights went out and the machine clicked on.   Its fan was noisy and the shaft of light emanating from it was clouded by drifting smoke.   He showed detailed maps of the target, the aiming point, terrain features, enemy camouflage, important landmarks along the bomb run, and, finally, aerial photos of the target.   He did the same for the secondary.

Hollis looked over at Stan, his face illuminated by the reflected light.   He had a blank stare, his eyes glazed over as if he were watching a movie he had already seen a dozen times.

A hundred German fighters.   He hoped the P-47s would make a better accounting of themselves today than they had yesterday when they failed to show up for their practice rendezvous.   Men die on milk runs.

Gorton finished and the lights came up.   The flak officer got up and quickly pointed out the known flak battery concentrations along the routes and at the target.   He pointed to the overlapping circles in various shades of red from pink, denoting light flak concentration, to scarlet red, denoting heavy.   Flak was expected to be moderate, but accurate.

Next came the group ordinance officer who told them that most of the Fortresses would be carrying twenty-four 100 pound general purpose demolition bombs and the rest would be carting incendiary clusters.

The weather officer followed.   Hollis wasn't sure, but doubted, whether or not he was a trained meteorologist or just some lackey repeating somebody else's prognostication and didn't know an isobar from a Hershey Bar.   Ceiling absolute, visibility unlimited over the primary and secondary targets, five-tenths cloud cover for takeoff and assembly which was expected to increase to seven- to eight-tenths cloud on landing.   Freezing level 11,000 feet.   Icing was not expected to be a problem during the climb.

The communications officer got up and briefed them on call signs for bomber and fighter communications and radio frequencies.   He reminded them, although for most present there was no need to, that the radio operators were attending separate briefings and would be furnished with flimsies containing all the necessary information.

The flight control officer gave detailed instructions on the schedule and order of taxi, takeoff, assembly and the position of each plane in the formation.   He went over to the formation diagram and ticked off one by one each plane, the pilot and his position.   Stations will be at 0630, engine start at 0640, taxi at 0650 and takeoff at 0710.   Since conditions should be good, thirty second interval for takeoff.   Assembly over the field at 5000 feet, climb to 10,000 feet to wing rendezvous over Splasher 16.   A copy of the formation diagram would be given to each pilot at the conclusion of the briefing.

The security officer got up and spoke in very sincere fashion, "Do not talk about the target once you leave this room.   Report at once to the S-2 office any person having knowledge of the target whose duty does not require that knowledge.   This applies even more to a scrubbed mission.   Hollis thought he would have to turn in Beamis. Anyone flying this mission who has not had   POW instructions is to report to an S-2 officer after this briefing.   Be sure you wear your dog tags, GI shoes and do not-repeat-do not wear squadron insignia.   Carry your name, rank and serial number only.   No one will leave this room until dismissed.   If you get shot down give your name, rank and serial number only.   That's all.   Destroy all secret papers and documents.   Destroy the bombsight and, if necessary, the plane itself.   He briefly described the best routes for evasion and known border check points.   The Belgian and Dutch underground are very effective and will see to it that you are well taken care of, but be wary.   Even though, he thought, not all civilians can be counted on to be sympathetic or helpful.

Finally, Begay took the stage.   He reiterated the routes and times and gave the time hack.

Then Van Patten took the stage and in so doing cast a spell over those in the room.   He stood ram-rod straight, dressed in his tailor-made tan pants and olive drab tunic, the crease in his pants defining a razor's edge.   West Point down to the last corpuscle.   He looked the type who, when handed a frag order, would say *'we're going to bomb such and such target today'* and with a dismissive wave of his hand to his minions add, *'attend to it.'*

He surveyed the room, all eyes on him.   "This should be an easy one, gentlemen.   Hold those planes in tight formation, especially on the bomb run.   I want a tight, compact bomb pattern.   But remember: we're bombing Occupied Countries today.   These people are on our side.   If you cannot be absolutely certain about your target, do not drop your bombs.   Bring them back.   We're trying to liberate these people not bury them.

"Bombardiers and navigator will stay for their respective briefings.   Copilots pick up escape kits.   Any questions?"

There were none.

"Good luck and good bombing.   Protestants to the front.   Catholics to the rear. Dismissed."

"Ten-hut!" the adjutant called.   The men rose to their feet, but by the time they were erect Van Patten had bounded down from the stage and his entourage had fallen in behind him.

Unlike a GI in a foxhole, whose view of the war was limited to what he could see, hear, touch and smell with little thought given to the bigger picture, Hollis had the entire day's campaign explained to him, in exquisite detail.   If he were to die today, at least he would die informed.

H-y and Sully got up and sought out their separate briefings.   Hollis walked over to the large formation blackboard and Leo followed him.   There, with several other pilots, they studied the formation and, at least in Hollis's case, committed it to memory.   They turned to leave.   Leo said nothing.

"Better go get ready," he said to his copilot.   As each pilot left the briefing room, he was handed rice-paper flimsies with the formation and the day's bomber code and colors, mission route in and out and times.   Hollis folded them carefully and placed them into his pocket.

He walked out into the pre-dawn light and headed, with the others, for the nearby equipment hut, a cinder block building, not nearly large enough to accommodate all those bodies trying to suit up, like knights of old, for combat.   The room bore the same strong scents of the briefing room, but in a much more compact space.   For the uninitiated it was nearly overpowering.   Hollis was whelmed by a sense of dread, hoping it would never start, but here he was butt-cheek to butt-cheek trying to slip his F3 electrically-heated coveralls over his ODs. His pride and his desire to impress girls had caused him to get into this fix and he had reached the point of no return.   He had slipped off his boots and placed his feet into heated shoe inserts and plugged in the wires to the tab connections at his ankles to complete the circuits.   He pulled on his summer-weight flight suit and zipped it up, slipping his feet back into the heavy fleece-lined boots.   He pulled on his leather jacket after he wrapped Jessie's scarf and a woolen muffler around his neck.   Over his head he pulled on his yellow Mae West and passed the strap between his legs and secured it.   He checked each inflation cartridge of the Mae West to make sure the pin had not punctured it.   He slipped on his parachute harness passed the leg straps beneath his crotch and pulled the straps snug.   He reached into his locker and pulled out his canvas B-3 bag and placed his B-8 goggles, A-11 leather helmet, bulbous dark rubber A-10 oxygen mask, throat mike, an old pair of GI shoes, rayon glove inserts, electrically heated gauntlets and a light weight pair of leather gloves, into it.   Lastly, he picked up the steel helmet and his survival knife from the bottom of the locker and put it into the bag.

He turned to head for the personal effects line when he spied Ransahoff sitting on the bench, cigarette perched between his lips, casually reading a piece of paper, seemingly oblivious to the turmoil around him.   He hadn't even dressed, his cap still sitting jauntily on the back of his head, like the hot rock he was or perceived himself to be.   It was as if he was reading a race form at the track, trying to handicap some horse instead of getting ready for war.   Hollis was in awe of such clinical detachment.   Unlike he who now found himself sweating from head to foot, stomach churning in rebellion, his anxiety rising to his throat, afraid that his burgeoning fear would betray him to those in whose company he now found himself.   Terror was such an unmanly indulgence.

Hollis reached the front of the line and placed his wallet on the counter. A quartermaster officer sitting behind a wire screen like the post office took it and smiled. He placed the wallet into a brown paper sack, recorded the name and number, and handed it to a private behind him who then placed it on a shelf with dozens of other small paper bags, neatly arranged, row by row. Admonished not to carry any personal effects into combat lest it reveal some useful information to the enemy, Hollis nonetheless kept a small photo of Jessie in his breast pocket beside the New Testament. It would be his link to her in case his memory faded and he might forget what she looked like should he find himself in a Stalag for the next five years. He wanted it to be the last thing he saw as he bobbed alone in the ocean waiting to drown or freeze to death. Besides, what useful information could be gleaned from Jessie's sweet face on a photograph?

Lastly, he was issued a chest-type parachute. He checked the inspection flap to make sure the seal was unbroken on the wire to the ripcord. He had heard rumors that the silk parachutes had been removed on occasion to be given to the girlfriend of the packer and replaced with old GI blankets.

He stepped out into the dawn and waited for Leo. Other officers milled about talking while trucks waited to carry them down to the dispersals.

Shortly, Leo approached with a ditty bag filled with escape kits and they headed to a truck, threw their stuff over the tail gate and climbed in. He sat down on the bench beside Watanabe and Mattson who both nodded to Hollis. He realized he was at a complete loss for words. What topic of conversation could they have any possible interest in at such a time? He had assumed Watanabe had done well yesterday because Hollis had not heard Ransahoff haranguing him. This realization only made him feel even more the rookie.

Watanabe reached into his pocket and pulled out a pack of Luckies and offered one to Hollis. He eased one from the pack and thanked him. Hollis assumed this was a gesture on Watanabe's part to calm the obviously rattled neophyte.

Mikasa Watanabe, everyone called him Mike, he had learned, was a second generation Nisei. He was born in California and was attending Cal Tech when he joined the California National Guard in 1940. He had been commissioned a second lieutenant before Pearl Harbor and transferred to the Air Corps not long after the bombs fell on that place. He was in flight school when his parents, who ran an importing business in San Francisco, were rounded up and placed in internment. It had been over an insult to Watanabe by an infantry captain in a public house in Cambridge that had led to the legendary ear-biting incident. 'Who let this Jap in here?' 'He's with me you red-necked mother fucker,' Eisenberg had responded, 'and he's seen more combat than you have, you big asshole.' 'No little Jew-boy's gonna talk to me like that.' The next sound, according to the legend, was the muffled crunch of the captain's nasal bones after they made contact with Eisenberg's knuckles. Legend also has it that Watanabe and Mattson saved the infantry captain's life, but not before Stan had crunched his molars onto the captain's left ear.

The truck lurched down the road toward the perimeter strip, turned onto it and started the rounds at each hardstand of the 532nd. When they pulled up to **Ain't Miss Behavin'** Watanabe got up, patted Hollis on the back and got out.

When they stopped in front of **Cleopatra's Asp**, Hollis and Leo gathered their stuff, dropped down to the concrete and walked toward their plane.

Chapter Eleven   **Mutiny**

Hollis stepped across the perimeter strip as the truck roared off, gears grinding.   He looked at **Cleopatra's Asp**, dark and sinister in the half light of early morning.   Tommy and an assistant pulled through the number four propeller while Moe and Dodge talked beneath her. Her bomb bay doors hung open.   She appeared as some ancient, fabulous bird of prey being preened for the hunt by man-servants in some Greek mythology.

As he neared the beast, the smell of oil and gas filled his nostrils.   He could see Sully and Hulse, the left waist gunner who was also the assistant armorer, peering into the open bomb bay. He noticed Augie lying serenely on the ground, his head propped on his folded shearling jacket, the top of his blue bunny suit visible above his leather bib pants.   Everyone else was in or under the plane, checking their stations, preparing the plane in some newly acquired preflight ritual. They spoke quietly, the greater silence broken only by the rhythmic putt-putt of the auxiliary power unit on the ground beneath the nose supplying the bomber with juice.

He placed his bag beneath the nose hatch and turned to see Dodge and Moe approach. "She's ready, Lieutenant," Moe said.   Dodge agreed with an almost imperceptible grin.   Hollis thanked them and made a cursory inspection of the plane, looking up at the engines, running his hands along the control surfaces, kicking the tires.   Satisfied the wings would not fall off, he signed the form and handed it back to Jablonski who smiled and nodded.   Hollis turned and walked back across the perimeter strip to the infield.   He sat on the tall grass and looked back at the plane.   He lit a cigarette, taking a long pull on the tobacco before exhaling a huge cloud of smoke admixed with the damp steam of his breath.

He knew this was a seminal moment in his life, waiting for the adventure to finally begin. He found himself shaking, shaking with the fear of a wicked and violent death.   But also shaking with the fear of failing.   He wanted to be a good pilot.   This was his debut.

He shared the fatalistic and universal viewpoint that held: *if a bullet has your name on it there isn't much you can do about it.*   There was no controlling that, even though, somehow, some way they all knew it was going to happen to the other guy.   His skill as a pilot, so crucial to everyone's survival, *was* under his control.   He sat and steeled himself against the possibility of failing, haunted by the previous day's embarrassment, he assured himself against recent experience that they had made the important assessment and he was found capable.   He was in the vaunted left seat of a Flying Fortress in the Big Leagues.   Probably no more prestigious a place for a second lieutenant to be in the whole war.   He had stood the test and he should have faith in the wisdom of their judgment.

Hollis felt himself growing increasingly nauseated.   He started to salivate, each swallowed bolus of hot spit heaped into the boiling caldron of his stomach.   He reasoned it was his insistence that he eat some of that wretched breakfast that now caused his innards to seek release.   He lit another cigarette, hoping this might calm his stomach.   It didn't.

He remembered from the Officer's Guide that fear was inevitable and acceptable, but demonstrations of it were not.   So he turned his back to the plane, got down on all fours, and heaved his breakfast onto the grass.   He retched a few times and straightened up, spitting the bitter residue from his mouth, scraping his tongue against his teeth to free clinging particles of chipped beef.   Drenched with sweat, the perspiration was cool on his face and he felt relieved. As he wiped his chin he looked over at **The Flying Dutchman** and saw Ransahoff looking at him.

He glanced at his watch.   Still fifteen minutes before stations.   He watched as the bomb bay doors closed slowly under the deadly cargo.   His crew slowly descended from the plane and gathered near Augie.   Dodge looked over at him and walked toward the place where he sat.

Noah Dodge was a remarkable guy.   At twenty-nine, he was the oldest member of the crew.   He had his fill of life's adventures.   He was from Jacksonville, Florida.   He flunked out of Florida State after two semesters of what he called impractical ruminations.   He purchased a 1938 Indian motorcycle and set out to find his fortune.   He harvested wheat in Iowa, lumber-jacked in Montana, fought forest fires with the Forestry Service in Idaho, labored as a stevedore in Seattle and shipped out on a tramp steamer as an ordinary seaman that plied the route from Seattle to Vancouver to Juneau to Valdez to Anchorage to Kodiak and back.   He later worked for Boeing in Seattle, making B-17Cs.

He was a study in contrast with Virgil Poole who had been a good man, but of opposite disposition.   That is, a bit of a hell-raiser.   Whereas Poole had been the ringleader for the crew's debauchery in Ardmore and Grand Island, Dodge was taciturn, confident, smoked but didn't drink, rarely swore and was deeply spiritual in a non-ecumenical kind of way. The senior enlisted man both by rank and position, the crew looked up to Dodge in a way they did not view Poole, with the notable exception of Augie who resented everything and everybody and whose dark soul kept him the malcontent in an otherwise cohesive unit.

"You need to come talk to them, Lieutenant.   Give 'em some sort of pep talk.   You're their pilot and they're looking to you to help them through this."

Hollis looked up at Dodge from his place in the grass, "I feel silly, Noah.   What am I going to say to these guys?"

"Say anything.   They could all be dead before the afternoon is over.   What you say is not important.   They won't actually remember what it is you've said, just that you said something.   Give them some encouragement..." he paused, "they're just as scared as you are."

Hollis shook his head, the taste of vomit fresh in his mouth.   He knew Dodge was right. He had to get hold of himself.   If he couldn't act cool and collected and fearless, for Christ's sake, try to impersonate someone who is.

Dodge sat on the grass beside him.   "I think there is something you should know.   I hesitated telling you this, but I think now is a good time to get this off my chest.

"I went to see Poole after he had his appendix out to, you know, get the low-down on things.   He told me that during the middle of phase training the crew decided they no longer wanted to fly with you."

"A mutiny?"

"They met in the squadron day room, all nine of them.   They talked for a while but, basically, they wanted to go to the squadron CO and tell him that either they have you removed or break up the crew.   Poole said they had a legitimate beef.   You were riding them pretty hard.   But he said if they did that your career as a pilot would be finished. So he insisted that they have a unanimous vote.   They talked some more then voted.   H-y and Augie started the whole thing and were adamant.   Sully and Quinn abstained.   Leo and Virgil voted to keep you. The rest voted to can you.   They talked for another hour and it was clear they would not reach a unanimous vote so they decided, at Poole's insistence, to give you one more week.   They would meet again in a week's time.   If they all still felt that way, he would change his vote to get rid of you."

It had been hammered into Hollis's skull repeatedly that teamwork was essential for the success of the mission and survival of the aircraft and its crew.   A crew was more than the sum of its individual members.   One poorly trained gunner or one man not on the alert can be the weak link that can kill everyone.   Hollis swallowed, "I pushed them hard, I know, but I never pushed them harder than I did myself."

"They knew that.   That's part of what had them worried.   They figured you were wound so tight, one of these days you might crash and end up killing them all.   Or worse, do something stupid in combat."

"A mistake by any of them could kill us all."

"They know that, too.   You have no sense of humor.   Ease up on them."

"Why are you telling me this?"

"You need to go over there and start acting like they expect you to.   You're the aircraft commander.   They're counting on you to keep them alive.   All of them."

Hollis rose to his feet and the two started walking toward the bomber.   "What happened?"

"Poole said something about making a three-point landing out of gas in the middle of the night.   Then you sprung for sandwiches and beer.   And when you got back you didn't rat on Lieutenant Smith that he got you lost."

"I was surprised they didn't can me on the spot for getting us in that fix in the first place."

"So was Poole."

His mind was a blank as he groped for something to say, some wisdom to impart some encouragement.   What could he say that would sound sincere, honest and not patronizing?   So he just started talking, "OK, everybody, gather 'round."   The crew stood up and moved as one to meet him as he approached.   "Well, here we are.   We volunteered for this and here we are...We're going after a *Luftwaffe* airfield in Brussels.   It should be a short run.   We're told they have a hundred fighters close enough to hit us.   Moderate flak, but should be accurate. Fighter escort all the way.   Ought not be too bad..."   His mind went blank again.   He saw that all eyes were on him, waiting for his every word.   He looked at Quinn whose parachute harness was loosely buckled.   He reached over and tugged at it.   "Tighten these parachute harnesses now because your hands will be too cold to do it later.   Don't forget the knife to cut loose from it in case you hit the drink."   The drink.   Thoughts still would not form in his head so he started to recite the instructions he had memorized a long time ago.   "If we have to bail out, I'll hit the alarm bell three rings, then call each station to make sure you've heard the alarm. Remember the delayed jump.   Wait until you're below the formation to pull the ripcord.   Fight the temptation to pull it as you leave the plane or you'll catch on the tail.   If we have to bail out over water, inflate your Mae West as soon as the chute opens.   Remember you must get out of the chute the minute you hit the water, preferably slipping out of your harness six or eight feet above the surface.   Dive and swim underwater toward the wind as long as you can before you come up.   The wind the will blow the collapsing canopy the other way.   You're sure to be out from under the chute if you come out upwind from it.   The canopy will be wet and air cannot get through it.   If you come up under the chute or get caught in the shroud lines you will drown.

"If we have to ditch, jettison everything and secure loose items.   Everyone go to the radio room immediately.   Get your flying boots off.   Brace for impact against the forward bulkhead.   I will warn you before we hit.   Two impacts will be felt.   The first soft jolt when the tail hits, the second hard impact when the nose hits.   Do not pull the life raft releases until the plane has come to a stop.   Do not inflate your life vests until you leave the plane.   First consideration should be given to any injured men when leaving the plane.   Beware of puncturing the rafts on the wing during launching.   And lash the dinghies together as quickly as possible.   Don't forget the Very pistol and use flares sparingly and only when there is a reasonable chance they will be seen by a ship or aircraft.

"If we have to crash land, destroy all classified information," he turned to Quinn and tugged on his parachute harness again, "Quinn start eating your flimsies and detonate your radios, and get clear of the plane as quickly as possible.   Get as far away from the crash site as fast as you can."

Rizzo smiled and said, "If we have to bail out, I'm gonna get a crack at anyone who leaves without telling me."

Quinn patted Rizzo's head paternally and said, "Don't worry, I won't leave without you."

"One last thing," Hollis said.   Dodge looked at him expectantly and Hollis exchanged the glance, "I want you all to maintain intercom discipline and oxygen discipline.   Call out fighters, but don't bother calling out flak 'cause there's nothing we can do about it anyway.   By the time you see it, it doesn't matter it'll just clutter up the interphone.   Be clear and precise over the interphone.   I don't want any idle chatter.   Don't yell.   Talk clearly and slowly.   Make sure you check your oxygen regulators one last time."   He looked at each face, "We've come a long way.   Now everything is for real.   I want everybody to do his job and help, whenever necessary, everybody else do theirs.   We have to function as a team.   If we encounter any fighters keep your bursts short."   He checked his watch.   Time for stations.   "Any questions or anybody have anything to say?"

Nothing.

"OK.   Leo hand out the bailout kits and let's climb in and get ready to go."

Leo reached into his ditty bag and started passing out the little plastic kits to each member of the crew, saying each time one left his hand, "I want it back".   Hollis took his and shoved it into his left knee pocket.

The pocket-sized escape kit contained a few squares of concentrated candy, two concentrated chocolate bars, a pack of gum, a cloth escape map of the territory they were to fly over, Benzedrine tablets which were to be taken to recover from the shock of being shot down, a tiny button compass which could be concealed in the rectum, a hacksaw blade encased in rubber also for insertion into the anus, a rubber water container and water purification tablets, some French and Belgian francs, and Dutch guilders, a message card from FDR in French, Belgian and Dutch, identifying the bearer as a member of the United States Armed Forces offering a reward if the bearer is 'guarded from harm' and 'returned to the nearest Allied Forces'.   There was a phony ID and some photographs in civilian clothes.

Hollis remembered the photographs being taken at Bovingdon.   Each member of the crew would sit down in front of the camera, under harsh lighting to make them look haggard, and reflexly smile to which the photographer would say, "Look grim.   Pretend you've been under Nazi occupation for three years and they're fucking your sister."   He said it over and over, Hollis was sure, without thinking.   They kept putting on one of three different shabby-looking civilian outfits.   He recalled wondering if the Germans would be amused by dozens of young men all wearing more or less the same thread-bare clothes and the same grim expression.

If an airman was fortunate enough to get picked up by the Underground or Resistance, as occasionally happened, he would need an identification picture for forged identity papers. Never force a conversation with a civilian because you had no way of knowing if it was safe for him to speak or recognize you for what you are and turn you in.   Any family caught aiding an escaping American or English airman was, they had been told, summarily executed.

After each mission, the escape kits had to be turned in and accounted for.   Since Leo had signed for them, he was responsible for returning them.

Dodge handed out sticks of gum to help popping ears during the climb.   Then, in unison, they walked to the edge of the hardstand behind **Cleopatra's Asp** and, standing shoulder to shoulder, urinated.

Hollis watched Augie finish suiting up.   As Hollis turned to walk toward the nose hatch, Augie said, "Whatsamatter, Lieutenant?   Toss your cookies?"

"Climb in, Augie, and close the hatch behind you."

"Yes sir," he said making an exaggerated salute.

Hollis gave Moe a wave, tossed his flight bag up into the nose and climbed aboard.   He pulled the hatch shut and made his way up onto the flight deck.   He opened the bag and removed his equipment.   He took out his parachute and placed it carefully on the floor beneath his seat where he could grab it at a moment's notice.   He did the same with his oversized steel flak helmet.   He stuffed his gloves inside his jacket and stowed the bag.   He sat down in the left seat and placed the throat microphone around his neck and adjusted it against his Adam's apple, inserting it and his headphone cords into their jacks.   He connected his heated suit plug to the outlet on the side wall but left the rheostat off.   He adjusted the seat and rudder pedals to suit.   He felt the return of the fear.   His heart started to pound against his ribs, his throat became dry.   Just below the surface, percolating, was a sense of panic.   Fight or flight, his psychology professors had called it.   The instinctive desire for an individual, confronted with imminent, lethal danger, to remove himself from that danger, allowing the opportunity to survive, in conflict with the visceral compulsion to engage the threat and overcome it.   He removed the locking pin from the control column, releasing the aileron and disengaged the rudder and elevator lock, placing his feet against the rudder pedals and his hands on the wheel.

Before today it was just a four-engined airplane.   Now, when he placed his hands on the control column, he took control of an engine of destruction which dated back to antiquity in an unbroken line of mechanical evolution from battering ram, catapult, cross-bow and slingshot.

He moved the controls full one way then the other checking visually the full range of unrestricted movement and proper direction of operation.   He checked his watch.   Five minutes before engine start.   "OK, Leo."

Leo pulled the laminated card from the pocket behind his seat and started reading from the checklist, holding his left thumb beside each item to prevent losing his place, "Controls unlocked..."

Hollis instinctively repeated the range of motion maneuvers on the controls, with he and Leo looking out their windows, "Unlocked."

Butch had been adamant that the checklist was the most critical thing you could do before flying and that Hollis place his hand on every lever, touch every switch, finger every toggle. Take nothing for granted.   This was the way he had been taught and a few months later he had been equally compulsive that Leo do the same as he taught him to be a copilot.

"Parking brake..."   Leo pushed on the brake pedals and released the knob on the parking brake in front of him.   He then reset the brakes.   Hollis felt the brake pedals move obediently beneath his feet.

"Hydraulic pressure 750 pounds."

"Set.   Fuel transfer valves off and switches neutral..."

Dodge checked the valves and the pump switch on the aft bulkhead and responded, "Fuel transfer valves and switches all off."

"Fire extinguisher..."   Leo turned the selector switch to left outboard, "set for number one.   Intercoolers...cold.   Gyros..."

"Uncaged."

"Fuel shut off switches..."

"Open."

"Hydraulic pump switch...on.   Primer...locked.   Cowl flaps...."

Hollis leaned forward and snapped each of the four cowl flap switches to 'open' then snapped each back to 'locked.' He looked at the engines on his side.   "Open and locked, left."

Leo checked his.   "Open and locked, right.   Turbos..."

"Off."

"Mixture idle cut off..."

"Off."

"Throttles..."

"Closed."   Hollis closed the four throttles all the way back then advanced them forward 'cracking' them to about a thousand RPM.

"Propeller controls full up..."

"Full up.   High RPM."

"Autopilot..."

Hollis reached down on the control pedestal and checked the position of the bar on the autopilot. "Off."

"Carburetor filters on..."

"On."

"Cabin heat..."

"Off."

"Generators..."

"Off."

"Uncage flight indicator and gyro."

"Gyros okayed."

"Landing gear switch..."

"Landing gear switch is down."

This was as far as they could go until they got the signal from the tower.

They waited.   Hollis could sense Dodge fiddling with his gear behind him.   He looked over at Leo who stared out the window.   He glanced over at Cahill and then over at Ransahoff. They waited, too.   He felt the churning in his stomach return.   He also ached for a cigarette. He checked his watch again and matched the time against the clock on the little panel above the windshield.

Hollis looked at Leo again who smiled. *Poor dumb Leo. You're just too dumb or simple-minded to be terrified, aren't you, pal? Something to tell the grandchildren, eh Leo?*

Hollis imagined Van Patten and Entwhistle and Clevenger standing shoulder to shoulder on the balcony of the control tower waiting to start the war for the day.

Suddenly, green-green flares arced up from the control tower like two incandescent pop flies. *Now.*

Hollis yelled out his window, "Clear left!"

Leo yelled, "Clear right!   Battery switches..."

Hollis reached down to his left and toggled the three battery switches.   "On."

"Master ignition switch..."

"On."   Hollis pushed the bar switch on and set all the magnetos to 'both.'

"Inverter..."

"Main."

"Booster pumps..."

"On and pressure OK."

Hollis checked to make sure the fire guard had been set.   He saw Tommy standing in front of the left outboard engine with a large red fire extinguisher.   Tommy flashed a thumbs-up.   Hollis held out the index finger of his left hand and made a circular motion.

"Start one," Hollis commanded.

Leo placed the middle finger of his left hand on the 'start' toggle and depressed it.   The low whine of the fuel booster pump was drowned out by the higher pitched whine of the electrical inertial starter as the flywheel built up speed.   Hollis started counting seconds. *One...two...*   Hollis felt the need to guard against superstition.   It was inappropriate to depend on talismans or ritual.   *Three...*   They could be forgotten or overlooked or missed in the heat of the moment.   To do so would tempt Fate to exert Herself on the unsuspecting, careless or forgetful.   *Four...five...*   Besides it was a mortal sin to believe in superstition.   *Six...seven...* Superstition might prove unreliable when what was called for was skill, guile and wits.   *Eight...* Perhaps prayer might help.   *Holy Mary, Mother of God, pray for us sinners now and in the hour of our death and please don't let me fuck up.   Nine.*   "Mesh one!"

Leo reached down to the floor beside his right foot and unlocked the primer handle and started pumping it with all his might.   Raw 100 octane fuel was injected into the cylinders of the engine.   Then, while holding down the starter switch, he placed his index finger on the 'mesh' toggle and depressed it.   The quarter-ton propeller jerked to life, turning in slow motion under the strain of the starter.   With a cough and a large belch of gray exhaust from the first tentative explosions, Hollis pulled the mixture control to 'auto-rich,' the engine caught then roared to life, the smoke whisked away by the blast of the propeller as it was transformed into a twelve-foot diameter silver blur, the vibrations of the awakening engine transmitted through Hollis's seat into his skeleton.   The cowling rattled briefly until the initial roughness of the engine became steady and strong.

Winded by his ordeal with the primer pump, Leo said over the engine noise, "Oil pressure..."

Hollis watched the gauge for a moment, "Coming up."   He then eased the throttle back to about eight hundred RPM.   He saw Moe run under the nose to disconnect the electric lead of the putt-putt APU from beneath the nose.   It was no longer needed for now the bomber could generate its own electricity.

Satisfied, Hollis said, "Start two." continuing the process sequentially until all four engines were running, the beast awakened from its slumber. Alive, throbbing and angry.

When the engines were warmed and the gauges all gave proper indication of satisfactory function, Hollis and Leo exercised the turbo superchargers and propeller pitch controls. Each time the throttles moved back and forth or the blades rotated in their housings the roar of the engine would build to a crescendo and then, after a few moments, suddenly fall off.

They ran up each engine to twenty-eight inches of manifold pressure and then checked each magneto. Hollis watched for vibration of the engine that would indicate roughness and improper ignition as the magnetos were switched from 'both' to 'right', then 'left' then 'both' again. He then ran the engine up to thirty-six inches and held it there for a few moments.

All across the field, engines roared loudly and throttled back and roared again in a random symphony of whirling propellers and thundering engines as each pilot checked his power plants.

Hollis then reached up to the radio panel situated on the ceiling and turned on the command set, placed the selector switch on the filter box to 'voice' and the switch on the jack box to 'command' to communicate with the tower or other aircraft knowing full well that absolute radio silence was expected. He then set the altimeter to the height Ridgewell rose above sea level. He checked the vacuum pump to the gauges. It was registering the proper four inches of suction.

Hollis switched to the interphone, "Close all hatches. Ball turret position check."

Rizzo came over the intercom, "Ball turret OK."

Again they waited.

Green-green flares.

The taxi and takeoff sequence was a carefully orchestrated plan that would place the lead squadron, the 534th, at the end of the runway first followed by the high, 533rd and lastly, the low, 532nd. This would mean that Hollis would be one of the last planes off the ground followed by Cahill. The two supernumeraries, spares, would follow Cahill to fill in if anyone aborted. Few abortions were expected. No one wants to abort a milk run. Easy ones count just as much as the hard ones.

They would be using runway 28 as the wind direction was from the west. Bonner would bring his bombers to the threshold of the runway first, Cavanarro would follow and Ransahoff would lead his squadron down the long narrow perimeter strip, falling in behind. From where he would be sitting in cab rank waiting, Hollis would be able to see just about every plane take off.

Hollis watched Ransahoff pull **The Flying Dutchman** off his hardstand and taxi past, followed by Cassidy in an unnamed Fortress, Selkirk in **Vermont Revenge**, Eisenberg in **Ain't Miss Beahavin'**. He could see the face of each pilot as they taxied past. Stan was wearing his Yankee's cap, his earphones and sunglasses in place.

By some miracle of metallurgy, **Ain't Miss Beahavin'** had been restored to flying condition. Some sheet metal work, some fresh paint, and a mop was all she needed. Back in business.

At last, it was their turn. Hollis stuck both hands out the window and jerked his thumbs in opposite directions, the signal to remove the chocks and waited until Moe give him the 'OK' signal.   Leo released the brakes and reached down to the floor unlocking the tail wheel.   Hollis pulled the inboard throttles back to about eight hundred rpm and pushed the outboards to twelve hundred.   Using the two outboard engines and judicious braking, Hollis guided the big Fortress off the hardstand.   He touched the brakes gently to assure their function.   With squealing brakes and surging engines, the little hairs erect on the back of his neck, Hollis jockeyed the throttles more expertly than he ever had before.   He gave a wave out the window to Moe and Tommy.   This, he knew, might be the last time they would ever see their charge.   They waved back.

He fell in line behind Eisenberg joining the long, Indian-file of bombers as they snaked their way at a walking pace toward the end of runway 28.   They taxied past Cahill.   The chocks were out and Cahill was already moving.   Hollis had a microsecond of dread that his wing would clip Cahill's nose if he came out much further.   *Now whose fault would that be? Sorry, Colonel, I can't help it if that asshole can't watch what he's doing.*

The Fortresses trundled along slowly like giant prehistoric winged insects, awkward and ungainly.   Small, barely noticeable rises and valleys in the course of the perimeter strip were transmitted up through the big main gear into the wings making the B-17s appear from behind as if they were waddling, tail guns protruding aft like delicate stingers.

The process of taxiing a thirty-ton Flying Fortress compelled the copilot to set and release the brakes and lock and unlock the tail wheel repeatedly.   Whenever they sat for a few minutes Hollis would run the engines up to fifteen hundred rpm to prevent soot from fouling the spark plugs.

Because of the nose-high stance of the Fortress on the ground, it was impossible for a pilot to look straight ahead to see where he was going.   Instead, he had to look out the side and guess, more or less, where the center of the perimeter strip was by where the edges were.   It took consummate skill.   Going off the perimeter strip would fuck up the whole works, for, once a loaded Fortress dropped a wheel into the soft turf or mud, it could not be moved, trapping on the narrow perimeter strip, in bottle-neck fashion, every plane behind it.

They passed the dispersal area of the 535th which was standing down today.   The ground crews working on their Fortresses stopped their tasks to watch the takeoff.   A few waved at each bomber as it paraded past.

They stopped.   Hollis could see the procession waiting, Bonner's big Fortress poised at the end of the runway.   He got the signal to go.   Hollis could not hear the thunder of the engines as the bomber moved at first slowly then gained speed rapidly until it was up on its two main wheels racing down the concrete, its broad wings pulling it gently into the air.

Hollis knew this moment would come when the excitement of the event eclipsed his terror.   He could feel a thrill rise from his arms, his hands on his lap trembling, his breathing a little faster.

They inched forward, one by one, as the bombers took off.   Approaching the threshold of the runway, Hollis could see two jeeps parked off to one side, a large black and white checkered banner on the back of one of the jeeps snapped in the breeze.   The other had a bank of radios in the back and three whip antennae mounted on the bumper that swayed to and fro in the wind.   They were Flying Control.   A man with an Aldis lamp flashed the 'go' signal to each Fortress.

Finally, Ransahoff thundered into the air.   Then Cassidy, Selkirk and Eisenberg in rapid order.   Before Stan took off, Hollis parked **Cleopatra's Asp** at an angle and ran up the engines one last time.   He watched Stan's control surfaces move full one way then the other.   Stan gunned his engines and **Cleopatra's Asp** was rocked by the blast of wind.   The last few seconds before the war started ticked away relentlessly.

Hollis, tramping on the brake pedals and jockeying the throttles, lined up **Cleopatra's Asp** with the centerline of the runway.   He and Leo closed their side windows and moved the controls again one last time.

"Take off check...tabs," Leo said.

Hollis checked that the trim tabs to the rudder, ailerons and elevators were all set at zero. "Tabs zero."

"Flaps up."

"Up.   Lock tail wheel," Hollis said.

Leo reached down and dropped the lever back into its slot in the floor.   "Tail wheel locked, light out.   Gyros..."

"Gyros set."

"Generators..."

Hollis pressed hard on the brakes and advanced the throttles to 1500 rpm and reached down turning on the generators with his left hand.   "On."

"Fuel booster pumps..."

"On."

"Mixture auto rich..."

"Auto rich."

"Turbo boost on...."

"Boost on."

"Props high rpm..."

"Props high rpm."

"Ready to go."   Leo placed the card in the pocket behind him and settled forward again.

One last glance down the runway.   Stan was almost off.   A few more seconds...

No matter how scared Hollis was, this was the stuff of heroes, selfless courage and gallantry.   The last moment before the cavalry charge, the horses nervous and restless before the bugle call.   He was experiencing that moment relived by countless warriors since man took up weapons against his fellow man.   How could any patriotic human being not be moved by this?   His spine tingled.   He was anxious to get started.   For a brief moment he felt invincible.

The lamp flashed.   A quick glance down the runway.   Stan was in his climb.   He sensed Dodge hunker down between them.

Hollis pushed the throttles forward full to the stops, the Cyclones roaring to a earth-shaking crescendo.   Hollis stood on the brakes.   He set his right hand on the throttle and held the wheel with his left.   He watched as the manifold pressure rose to just below 50 inches and the rpm touched 2700.   When he felt he could hold it no longer, he released the brakes and **Cleopatra's Asp** leaped forward, eager to get on with it.   Hollis felt the inertia push him into his seat as the big plane gained speed and momentum, the roar reverberating against his chest, penetrating his muscles.   Leo and Dodge watched the instruments.   The runway began to race beneath the nose, the thousands of rubber scuffs a blur.   The imperfections in its surface were transmitted through the main gear in a pounding vibration giving a true sense of the plane's weight.

Runway 28 was the big one, 6000 feet.   There was little crosswind with which to contend today.   Since the Forts were not carrying maximum loads 6000 feet should be plenty. But all the runway in England wouldn't compensate for a sudden engine failure, a runaway prop or turbo that might prevent the plane from flying or make it quit flying shortly after it became airborne.   A loaded Fortress made a big, smoking hole in the ground.

Hollis gently nudged the brakes and applied slight differential power with the outside throttles to keep the accelerating bomber running straight down the runway by watching the edge until the tail rose and the nose dropped.   He must be careful; too much pressure on the brakes or too much power and the Fort would start weaving from side to side.   Hollis was sensitive as he had never been before to the tremors and feel of the machine in his hands.

"Fifty," Dodge called.

"Lock throttles," Hollis called.

Leo reached over and performed the task, "Throttles locked."

Hollis moved his right hand to the wheel and was instantly replaced on the throttles by Leo's left hand as he watched the rpm and manifold pressure.

Now Hollis could apply a gentle push to the rudder pedals to keep the plane flying straight and in so doing he could feel the force of the wind against the rudder.   Below that speed the big tail is useless for directional control as there is not enough air passing the rudder or the elevator for them to be effective.   Faster.

"Seventy-five."

Hollis eased the control column forward ever slightly lifting the tail wheel off the runway.   Now he could see the end of the runway.   Some of the pounding vibration of the runway lessened as the first tentative signs of lift tugged at the wings.   The B-17 ran on her main gear now, the angle of attack of the big broad wings changed with the change in the plane's attitude.   They would create less lift, but would drag less through the air, allowing more speed. Runway intersections sped past beneath them.

"Ninety."

The point of no return.   At this speed they did not have enough runway remaining to stop the bomber.   Even if the wings fell off, it was fly or die.   They passed over the yellow line indicating one third of the runway left.

"Yellow," Leo said.

Cleopatra's Asp trembled in Hollis's hands as the lift on the wings surpassed the weight of the plane.   The run became smoother as the weight eased off the wheels.   Faster.

"One-oh-five," Dodge said.

Stalling speed.   The speed above which the plane will fly and below which it will not. Still faster.

"One ten."

Not yet.   The margin between stalling speed and take off speed must be as great as possible.   Sometimes no more than five or ten miles an hour.   When a plane leaves the ground the energy it expends in lifting robs it of speed.   If that theft is too much, even only a few miles an hour, the bomber will stall and return to the ground.   The trick is to gain as much speed as possible before running out of runway and still get high enough to clear whatever obstacles lie in your path.

Cleopatra's Asp begged to fly.

"One twenty."

Hollis eased the yoke back and the plane left the ground effortlessly, the pounding was replaced by the smooth reassuring throb of the four Cyclones. The sound of the engines, while still deafening, lessened as the reflection off the ground disappeared. Dodge bobbed from side to side behind the pilots to look at the wings, Hollis knew, to check the gas tank vents to make sure no fuel was being venturied out.

Hollis looked down as they passed well above the end of the runway. They had plenty left. For the moment, Hollis kept the climb shallow to allow more airspeed to build.

"Gear up," Hollis called.

Leo reached for the toggle and touched the brakes. The electric motors powered the screw rods causing the landing gear to fold forward up into each nacelle with a reassuring thump. Dodge leaned behind Hollis, "Left up."

Leo said, "Right up."

Dodge left his position for a moment and returned. "Tail wheel up."

Hollis did not want to abuse his engines unnecessarily so, as they passed one hundred and forty miles an hour, he reduced the manifold pressure to 35 inches and the rpm to 2300. As they climbed above two thousand feet, he turned the booster pumps off, adjusted the cowl flaps to lessen drag and reduced the turbo boost as the atmospheric pressure decreased with the increase in altitude.

The flight plan called for a straight course for two minutes, then a left turn into an ascending spiral around the field. The climb was at 300 feet per minute at 150 miles per hour indicated air speed. The five tenths cloud cover predicted at takeoff had coalesced into a solid overcast. Hollis could make out Stan's speck in the distance.

"Navigator to pilot, one minute, thirty."

He could see Stan's left wing drop as he entered a left turn and vanished into the cloud.

"Two minutes."

Hollis pushed left rudder and while he turned the wheel into a shallow left bank. He looked back over the wing and saw Cahill and the two spares in train. When the turn was made everything went white as they slipped up into the cloud.

Chapter Twelve   **Flushing**

Hollis brought **Cleopatra's Asp** into a gentle counter-clockwise, ascending orbit over the field, guided by the radio direction finder, keeping the turn and bank indicator one needle width to the left of center, the rate of climb at 300 feet per minute and airspeed at precisely 150 mph.   The plane seemed a little tail heavy so he adjusted the trim.

Dodge and Leo dutifully watched the cylinder head temps and fuel pressure.   Satisfied everything was in order, Dodge left his place behind them and began his after-takeoff ritual.

Hollis reached into his pocket, pulled out his sunglasses and placed them on as the inside of the cloud grew brighter.   Suddenly they burst into the blue, the rising sun in the east dazzling bright and warm against his face.   Four thousand feet.   Up ahead, Hollis could see the planes circling, following the same climbing corkscrew in which he guided his bomber.   The lead squadron had already formated and the high squadron was coming together easily in the clear morning sky.

Group assembly was set at five thousand feet and that placed the low squadron altitude a few hundred feet below, to the left and slightly behind.   The group lead had slowed to allow the planes behind to catch up and find their place.   Every few minutes a two pronged flare, one red and one yellow arced into the sky from Bonner's plane denoting the lead ship of the 381st, but it was unnecessary as the cloud was below and everybody was right where they were supposed to be.   *This might not be so hard after all*, Hollis thought to himself.

Several minutes elapsed by the time Ransahoff took up his position as lead of the low squadron. Mickey and Cassidy easily latched on.   Then Stan found his position.   Hollis eased the throttles forward a little in an effort to get into place quickly, unable to cope with the nagging fear of being left behind, as he and Cahill would be bringing up the rear.   The lead ship of the low squadron flew slightly behind the left wing man of the lead element of the lead squadron, the lead ship of the high squadron slightly behind the right wing man of the same lead ship. Everybody had his place in the hierarchy and he was expected to find it and stay there.

As he closed in on his proper place off Stan's right wing, he felt **Cleopatra's Asp** jostled by the lingering wake of the planes that had so recently churned up the air ahead.

No doubt the copilot, riding as tail gunner of the lead ship, whose job it was to advise the leader about the condition of the group behind him, told Bonner when everyone had arrived, each in his place.   After another set of flares, he increased speed and resumed the ascent, dragging the group behind him in a gigantic game of follow the leader, all twenty planes shifting into high gear to get up to ten thousand feet.   From there they would, at the appointed time, depart for combat wing assembly.

Passing through eight thousand feet, Hollis let Leo take over hoping he could keep their station.   Suddenly, Sully appeared in the hatchway leading to the nose.   He smiled at Hollis as he climbed onto the flight deck and ducked past the turret on his way to the bomb bay.   He was going to turn on the rack switches, pull the arming pins from the bombs and retrieve the cardboard tags from the nose fuses.   Removing the pins would allow the arming vanes on the impeller, each about the size of a propeller on a kid's beanie, to quickly spin off in the wind when the bombs fell out leaving the striker pins free to hit on impact and detonate the explosives.   He had to do this before they had climbed too high.   Moisture might freeze them in place making them impossible to extract later on.   If that happened. they would then fall unarmed and harmless rendering the trip, with all its attendant risks, worthless.   It also saved him the encumbrance of having to perform the task carting around a portable oxygen bottle.

Sully would take the pins, place them in his pocket to be turned in after interrogation proving that his bombs had fallen armed or he would have to place them back into the nose of each bomb in order to return them to base, if, for some reason they were not released on a target. Initially, Sully tried to get Dodge to do this task, but Dodge refused, saying Sully was the bombardier, they were *his* bombs *he* should pull the pins.

Sully returned and took a seat on the ledge of the hatchway.   Hollis watched him reach inside his flight suit and pull out a pack of Chesterfields.   "Here," he yelled above the engine noise, "it might be the last one you ever smoke."

They both lit up taking long drags, filling the cockpit with smoke.   Sully yelled into Hollis's ear.   "H-y's as nervous as a New Orleans whore at a Baptist revival.   He's built himself a little fortress with flak vests down there.   He lined the floor and walls with them.   He's even sitting on one to keep his balls from getting shot off."

Sully noticed Hollis was sitting on a flak vest, also.   He laughed.   He finished his cigarette and, with a perfunctory wave and a 'see ya!' descended into the nose.

At ten thousand feet, Hollis called for the crew to go on oxygen and report in.   He took the controls while Leo placed his helmet on and connected his mask.   When he was finished, Leo resumed flying.   Hollis listened as each crew position checked in.   Their voices seemed matter-of-fact, as if they had done this a hundred times before, as if this were not their first trip into combat, but just another high-altitude hop over the amber fields of Oklahoma.

Satisfied, he took off his headphones and cap and reached down to the floor behind his seat, retrieving his leather helmet and mask.   He pulled it onto his head and placed the goggles onto his forehead.   He latched the oxygen mask to the clasp at his left cheek and connected the tubing to the receptacle.   He glanced at the flow indicator which blinked at him from the instrument panel opening and closing its shutters with each breath in.   Leo's flow indicator was beside his and it, too, blinked at Hollis with each breath his copilot took.   He clipped the redundant loop of corrugated rubber hose to his harness so there would be plenty of slack.   He reached down and slipped the small, cylindrical bail-out oxygen bottle into the canvas pocket stitched to his harness and connected the tubing to the fitting on his mask.   He fingered the wooden 'green apple' knob which he would yank to start the flow of oxygen should he need to bail out.   With the leather helmet on, goggles perched above his eyes, bulbous oxygen mask with long, coiled, proboscis-like hose protruding from its center, Leo looked like some giant insect in some atlas of jungle entomology.   Hollis was sure he looked the same.

He tapped Leo's arm and pointed to the altimeter.   Leo understood and turned off the carburetor air filters and turned on the fuel booster pumps, notifying Hollis by interphone that he had done so.   Hollis took control of the plane.   At ten thousand feet, about five minutes early, Bonner leveled them off and made one extra orbit before departing for the combat wing assembly point.   Anticipating possible interference by overcast the plan called for this to be over the radio beacon at Brampton Grange, 'Splasher 16'.   To get there, the route took them to Cambridge where they were to make a shallow dog-legged turn to the Splasher whilst climbing to 12,000 feet.   Few courses were ever straight lines during the tedious assembly process. There were always orbits or doglegged routes built into the plan to allow stragglers to catch up by cutting the corner or for the whole formation to make up time or waste it, as needed, by modifying the course, 's'ing back and forth across the direction of flight.   The timings were critical.   So, precisely at the appointed time, Bonner wheeled the formation and headed for Cambridge.

When they arrived at Splasher 16 the lead, 351st, and low, 91st, groups having the least distance to fly were already there, circling patiently.   Bonner had it just right.   As the big formation wheeled in its turn, Bonner slid them in above and behind the lead group effortlessly. He continued the climb a few hundred feet higher than the designated altitude to let the bombers settle back down in a shallow dive to their assigned position.   This allowed the planes to arrive at cruising altitude with some momentum built up.   Climbing and then settling straight into level flight would cause the heavily loaded bombers to mush in the thin air and this was dangerous in a tight formation.   Bonner knew his stuff.

Hollis had never seen so many planes.   The 101st Combat Bomb Wing consisted of the three groups each supplying 18 bombers in three six-plane squadrons.   Fifty-four planes, Hollis had been told, was found to be the biggest formation that could be maneuvered practically. Anything larger was simply too unwieldy.   Anything smaller would have less concentrated firepower and be more vulnerable to enemy attack.

It became an even more massive game of follow the leader.   The low and high group leads kept position off the lead group, the squadron leaders flew off the group lead and the individual planes flew off the element leader.   It was a pyramidal hierarchy and all Hollis really had to worry about was keeping position off Stan's right wing and rely on people up ahead to know where they were going.   The only guy who didn't need to worry about his place in formation was the guy flying the lead ship of the lead group of the whole wing and he was told where to go by the lead navigator.   Everybody else had to sweat out his position for the duration of the trip spending most of their time looking at the plane next to them instead of straight ahead, a very unnatural situation for a pilot, especially an inexperienced one.

Hollis was mightily impressed.   From his perch high and on the inside he could see the whole formation.   He knew that elsewhere there were planes forming squadrons and groups and combat wings all over southeastern England, all coming together to deliver bombs on the target. If they were smart they should invite some neutral observer, like the Swiss ambassador to Cuba, to witness this display of air power and let him convince the Germans that there was no hope of sustaining themselves against such a massive show of destructive force and advise them to call off the war before it was too late.   But, Hollis knew, it was already too late.   At   the appointed, time the Combat Wing rendezvoused with the other two Combat Wings, the 102nd and 103rd, to form the bomber stream of the entire First Bombardment Wing, nine groups all formed up, heading for war.

"Jesus, look at all those '17s.   The sky behind us is full of 'em," Hollis heard Mollica announce from his perch in the tail.   "All these planes just to bomb a couple of airfields."

They made a series of doglegs, climbing to 15,000 feet, on their way to Splasher 7 at Braintree.   Hollis felt Leo nudge his arm and he pointed to the oil temperature gauges.   The climb had caused the temperature to rise to an alarming level.   Hollis's first instinct was to open the cowl flaps to allow more air to pass through the engines, cooling them, but he knew the big gills would act as speed brakes increasing the drag, slowing the bomber, causing them to fall behind.   Once they started falling behind there might be no catching up.   He made the mental calculation.   He could jack up the manifold pressure and the rpm to overcome the slowing effect of the open cowl flaps, but that would drive the engine temperature even higher, negating the effect.   Dodge must have sensed something was wrong because he appeared between the pilots.

"The oil temp is climbing, but I don't want to open the cowls," he yelled.

Dodge studied the gauges for a few moments and instinctively looked at both sets of engines.   "Let 'em run a little hot.   The gauges are set low.   I think you still got a little margin left. They'll be fine"

Hollis checked the cylinder head temps which were still OK.   He decided to follow Dodge's advice and run the engines until the cylinder heads started to get hot.   Then he would have no choice but to either slow down the climb, fall irretrievably out of formation and likely abort, or open the cowls and try to keep up.   Nonetheless, he felt disinclined to whip Moe's engines with reckless disregard.   Besides, he was likely not the only one experiencing hot oil on the climb and everybody else seemed to be keeping up.   He also knew that to abort his very first mission would probably be perceived as cowardice, and on a milk run at that.   He would be quickly removed and everybody's doubts and suspicions would be confirmed.

He kept a watchful eye on the cylinder heads for a few minutes, resisting the temptation to start fiddling with the cowls and power, and finally convinced himself that they seemed to be holding steady.   Dodge returned to his turret.

At Braintree, they headed for Clacton-on-Sea where the bomber stream would depart the coast.   The coast-out was Checkpoint Able where the extras would drop out and turn for home. The long column of bombers would turn over the Flemish Bight and head for the Continent, again following an indirect path to prevent the Germans who had, no doubt, been following the formations on radar since the individual planes first started climbing up through the clouds, from drawing inferences as to the probable target.   Keep them guessing so they couldn't husband their fighters in one spot was the general idea.   Hollis wondered if such deceptions really worked or whether the German air defense controllers sat in their bunkers and laughed at the back and forth progress of the crazy Americans as if they had not yet decided where they wanted to go.

They left the clouds behind and the sun had risen high in the morning sky, casting a blinding reflection off the dark water of the North Sea.   Now beyond the coast, Hollis noted that the 381st planes started to tighten up the formation and Hollis followed suit by tucking a little closer onto Stan's right.

"We're feet wet, fellas, OK to test fire the guns," H-y said.   Suddenly **Cleopatra's Asp** shuttered with the recoil of its machine guns all firing at once.   The noise and vibration of the twin fifties of the upper turret going off just a foot or two above his head made Hollis jump in his seat.   He knew he would never grow used to those guns.   He watched as the rest of the guns in the formation gave short bursts, leaving puffs of quickly disappearing smoke and hosing ribbons of tracers, yellow and red glowing dots, into the empty patches of sky between the planes.

The guns fell silent almost simultaneously and after a few minutes one of the planes in the lead squadron of the group started leaving a thin trail of gray smoke from an engine.   He watched as the plane, Hollis could not tell who it was, threaded his way out of formation with a feathered prop and turn for home.   After a few moments one of the spares, who Hollis thought had long since high-tailed it back, drifted down through the formation and filled in the empty spot.   He guessed the spares didn't want to miss a shot at a milk run either.   He checked his engines.   Everything was fine.

"Simmons aborted," Leo said.

Hollis imagined H-y seated at his little desk in the nose, pencils, rulers, Weems plotter and stop watch in disarray, diligently jotting this fact into his log so he could later report to the world precisely when Simmons experienced his failing engine.

"Ten minutes from the coast.   Our escort should be here.   Anybody see 'em?"   H-y asked.

Hollis looked around, up and over without seeing anything which looked like an escort.

The knot tightened in his stomach and the drool started to collect under his chin inside his mask despite the fact that his mouth felt parched.   He could sense his rising heart rate as they approached the enemy coast.

"Coast-in in five minutes," H-y announced.

Leo tapped Hollis's arm and pointed to his mask.

Hollis nodded and came on the intercom.   "Bombardier, oxygen check."

Sully came on the intercom and called each position.

Each crewman answered in turn.   Hollis listened to the tone of each response for some weakness, giddiness or irritability which might indicate possible early oxygen deprivation, anoxia.   But he heard none.   Everyone sounded normal.

Up ahead, Hollis could make out the estuary of the Westerschelde.   The formation would wheel right and head up the body of water to Terneuzen where they would again turn right and make a bee-line toward Brussels keeping the flight time over land to a minimum and hopefully keeping the Germans guessing.

Hollis pulled **Cleopatra's Asp** in even closer.   Dutch would be proud.   Twenty-three thousand feet.   The bombers started leaving condensation trails, cottony, white streaks of steam from each engine which would serve as perfect goals for climbing German fighters.   It would not be unheard of for the Germans to climb up and intercept the arriving formations before they crossed into enemy air space, so he started scanning the sky as much as he dared and still keep position on Eisenberg's right wing, certain beyond any doubt that no matter where Stan was going he'd be right there with him.

Hollis leaned forward and looked down at the approaching Netherlands peninsula; the crossing into enemy territory was just moments away.   He felt a chill and realized he had failed to turn on his electric suit.   He glanced at the outside temperature: twenty below.   He reached down and turned up the rheostat and felt the bomber buffet under his hands.   He snapped his gaze at Stan who was also wobbling slightly from the turbulence they had all just encountered. He glanced over at Cahill who had gotten way out of position.   An FW could easily find its way between him and Stan.   *And if it could, it would.*

Hollis adjusted the boost and checked his engines for the hundredth time.   Any second...

The flak vest he was sitting on was growing increasingly uncomfortable.

He listened to every sound, sensing every vibration in the controls and in his rear end and back, watching and waiting for the first indication of catastrophe, the first ugly encounter with Fate.   Would he know it when he saw it?   Would it be over before the recognition could register in conscious thought?   Would it be over in a flash of heat and light or would the agony drag out for seconds or minutes?   Or a lifetime?   Would he be silent when it came or would he scream? Would he shit his pants?   There were many different ways for a man to die in a B-17.

Men die on milk runs.

"Flak!"   The words hit his brain like a thunderclap.   "Twelve o'clock level," Sully said. Hollis saw the first black smudges of smoke dead ahead.

"Here we go!" yelled Augie into the interphone.

"Virgins no more," Rizzo added.

"Knock it off," Hollis said.   "Keep off the intercom and pay attention."

Mercifully, the contrails his group were leaving disappeared.   They came and went without warning as the formation passed through air of different temperature and humidity. The next round of flak bursts were low and meant for the lead group.   They were poorly aimed, without conviction, almost as an afterthought.

"OK, boys, we just passed into Occupied Europe," H-y said.

"Waa-hoo!" Augie yelled, "Bring 'em on!" Hollis felt the ship vibrate with a short burst of machine gun fire, most certainly from Augie's gun.

"Pilot to right waist, knock it off.   Anybody see our escort?"

"Ball to pilot, no sir.   All I been lookin' at is water," Rizzo replied.

"Pilot to tail, anything?"

"Empty sky, Lieutenant."

"Pilot to navigator, make a note."   He looked over at Leo who smiled broadly at him from behind his mask.   Hollis took off his sunglasses and pulled his goggles down over his eyes.   If the windshield should suddenly smash or the cockpit fill with smoke he still had to see. He noted Leo did the same.

"More flak, three o'clock," Augie said.

Flak.   Looked harmless enough.   Little puffs of roiling black smoke.   Hollis remembered the facts.   The 88's and bigger 105's were set to go off at a specified time after the shell left the barrel, or at a specified altitude or on contact with something.   Each round traveled at a thousand feet per second and was effective up to thirty thousand feet.   When a flak round exploded it sent thousands of shards of white hot steel, sharp as razor blades, in all directions, but predominantly upward, hence the rationale for sitting on the lead-lined canvas vests, or as in Dodge's case standing on it.   Might as well sit on it, Hollis thought, it was too heavy and cumbersome to wear while flying and when bailing out, seconds count.   He didn't want to have to get the thing off in order to hook on his chest chute. Annoying as it was to sit on.

Each burst had a killing radius estimated to be about thirty feet.   A direct hit was not required.   Just ask Stan.

They commenced a big right-handed turn toward Brussels and the IP when Sully came over the intercom, "Bombardier to pilot.   Cloudin' up down there.   Hope we can hit the primary."   Hollis withdrew his gaze at Stan long enough to note the puffy, white cumulus clouds, initially scattered, start to gather into a thick, solid layer.   He was cold and his arms ached.

"Navigator to pilot, turn for the run to the IP in two minutes."

"OK, navigator."

"Flak... Hey, more flak," Augie announced again.

"Knock it off, right waist," Hollis responded, now not just scared, but also annoyed. They droned on.

"Navigator to crew, IP in ten minutes.   Flak vests, boys.   Wear 'em if you got 'em."

They droned on.

Down below Hollis imagined the interceptor pilots scrambling to their fighters.   In just a few moments he would get his first real taste of war.   They would try to kill him.   People he didn't even know.   Werner and his buddies.   They were preparing to defend with their life's blood their national interest, no matter what they perceived that to be, with little or no thought to the bigger picture.   Just like Hollis.

"Bombardier to pilot.   I can't see how we're gonna be able to bomb through this stuff."

"Navigator to pilot, IP five minutes.   Be ready for a fifty degree turn to the right."

Maybe there would be a fortuitous break in the clouds.   Anyway, the weather prediction for the target was a bust, the escort never showed up and he was still cold. Maybe the damned electrical suit was busted, too.   His butt hurt.

They droned on.   Down below the clouds had scattered a bit exposing small patches of green, verdant Belgian farmland, but it might not be enough to allow adequate visualization of the target. They were bombing a friendly country; precision was imperative.

"IP."

Hollis shot a glance at Bonner's ship and saw a red-red flares arc into the air followed a few seconds later by another warning of the IP and the commitment to attack the primary target. Simultaneously, his bomb bay doors slowly came open.   Immediately, the lead group turned toward the right, two pairs of flares drifting down behind them, all eighteen planes turning as one.   The low and high groups continued straight ahead.   Twenty seconds later, with stop watch precision, Bonner wheeled the group to the right and fell in behind the lead group.   The low group passed underneath the 381st as it continued a straight path and twenty seconds later it too turned to the right falling in trail behind.   The disassembly from combat wing formation to line of groups was completed. The three groups made their run at the target, one behind the other, each separated by roughly twenty seconds.   One group with eighteen planes was considered the maximum number of bombers over target at one time for the best bomb pattern. Each lead bombardier would sight his own bombs on the target and the rest of the bombardiers in the group would toggle theirs the instant they saw the bombs depart the belly of the lead ship. Fifty-four bombers would release on the same piece of earth in just forty seconds followed three to five minutes later by another line of three groups and then another until the whole Bombardment wing had bombed.   The target would then be, theoretically, annihilated in just a little over ten minutes. Give or take.

The run to the target would take just five minutes.   It was a straight and unswerving flight.   Evasive action was forbidden no matter how rough the flak or fighters.   The formation and, therefore, the bomb pattern was to be as compact as possible.

There was a sudden grinding rumble which Hollis could hear above the roar of the engines as the bomb bay doors started open.   Hollis felt a chill run up his spine.   There was a sudden drop in the airspeed as the drag of the open bomb bay took effect.   The speed fell to 145mph and Hollis pushed the throttles forward to bring it back up to 150.   He eased in closer to Stan and felt the bomber buffeted by the turbulence.

"Bomb bay doors open," Sully said.

"All clear below, bomb bay doors open," Rizzo said from the ball turret.

Suddenly, inexplicably, Hollis felt possessed.   His grip on the wheel tightened and he involuntarily drew himself erect in his seat.   He fixed his gaze on Stan and would not allow himself or **Cleopatra's Asp** to be displaced or diverted.   He started breathing rapidly.   His already pounding heart beat even faster.   This was what they were paying him for, what he had come all this way to do.   Stan and Dutch and Bonner would lead the way.

"Yellow flares!" Sully yelled.   "They're calling off the bomb run."

Leo leaned over to him and yelled into his mask, "Task force commander just announced diversion to the secondary and released the other wings to seek targets of opportunity."

Hollis imagined the other groups peeling off and meandering across Northwestern Europe looking for something to bomb.

The grinding of the bomb bay door motors returned and the thrill was gone as suddenly as it occurred.   He didn't know whether to be disappointed or relieved.

"Bomb bay doors closed."

The light on Hollis's instrument panel blinked out.

Up ahead, the lead group commenced a big turn to the left and Bonner turned almost immediately to fall into position as the wing reformated.   The turn caught Hollis off guard and he fell behind and wide of Stan.   The turn must have caught a lot of other pilots off guard because the low group got all strung out, too.

Leo tapped Hollis's arm and then his left headphone.   Hollis switched to the command channel which was filled with anonymous swearing.   The guy in the lead ship of the lead group had fucked up and made the turn unannounced surprising everybody.   He quickly switched back to the interphone.

"They called for CAVU this morning.   How could they have been so wrong about the target weather?" Sully asked.

"Bad batch of tea leaves," H-y responded.   "Jesus, that dumb fuck better change his course or he's gonna fly us right over Antwerp.   There's a lot of flak at Antwerp."

"OK, navigator," Hollis said, trying to keep what he considered superfluous chatter off the interphone.

"Damn," Augie said.

"No swearing over the interphone," Hollis said.   He was getting pissed again.

The secondary target was an airdrome at Flushing, Holland on the peninsula of Walcheren, guarding the entrance to the Westerschelde.   They had practically flown right over it on the route in.

"Bombardier to pilot, flak up ahead."   Must be Antwerp.

The lead group wheeled to the left in a shallow turn to skirt the flak.

"Navigator to pilot, finally.   IP in ten minutes."

In ten minutes, the ponderous ballet of aircraft was played out again as the groups uncovered and took interval.

The grinding rumble of the bomb bay doors again and Hollis felt himself tense up once more, but not like he had a few minutes earlier.   Bombing the secondary seemed somehow anticlimactic.

The target was clear.   As the bombs emerged from the belly of Bonner's B-17, Hollis felt **Cleopatra's Asp** shudder and lurch upward as the bombs left her.

"Bombs away," Sully said.

The wings waggled a little as he settled the bomber back down to level flight.   He adjusted the trim.   The group suddenly made a diving turn to the left toward the Rally Point.

"Die fuckers," Augie said.

"All bombs are gone," Quinn said after checking the bomb bay for hung-up bombs.

He noticed Leo laughing behind his mask.

"What's so funny?" Hollis yelled above the engine noise.

"Ransahoff just yelled something into the VHF at the Germans."

"What'd he say?"

"'Alles ka-poot, eh, Fritz?'"

"Bomb bay doors closed," Sully said.

"Ball to bombardier, bomb bay doors closed."

"Radio to pilot," Quinn said.

"OK, radio."

"Sir, the lead ship reported the secondary hit at oh-nine- forty-seven.   Results good. Opposition nil.   Other wings released to alternates."

"OK, radio.   You don't need to tell me."

At the Rally Point, the formations, lightened of their bomb loads and not quite half their fuel, gained considerable speed over the North Sea on their way back to England.   The reassembly, like the turn at Brussels did not go well.   The reshuffling of the groups was confused and disordered.   The wing lead must have realized this and he released the groups to make their own way back to England.   Like many decisions in war, he made the mental calculation that the risk of disbanding the defensive positions of the groups was less than the risk of mid-air collisions and mayhem that would accompany any effort at reassembly for the dash back home.

Hollis watched as the groups took separate paths, his own group formation loosened.

"Thirty minutes from the coast, Radio," H-y said.

"Roger, navigator, IFF on."

Hollis let Leo take over.   It had all been very anticlimactic.   He knew there was a war on today, otherwise why all the fuss?   But, except for a few scattered and ineffectual flak bursts, the closest probably not more than a hundred yards away, he had seen none of it.   As they inched closer to home on the map, Hollis still felt a little uneasy.   He had heard stories of German fighters jumping retiring and unsuspecting bomber formations, wreaking havoc.

"Gunners keep a look out.   We aren't safe until the rubber hits the runway."

No Luftwaffe today, boys.   Maybe, Hollis thought, the shallow penetration wasn't worth the effort it would take to oppose it.   Maybe the Germans knew what they were going to hit and whatever it was was not worth protecting.   Perhaps they didn't have the stomach or the patience to tangle with the escort, if there had been any.   Maybe it was raining down there and they just decided to sleep in.   *We can rise up and destroy you any time we chose.   Today was just not the day.*   He wondered what they had done, what contribution they had made to bring an end to the war.   He thought about the damaged airfields which amounted to nothing more than large grass fields, a concrete apron and a few scattered hangers.   A team of forced laborers would, with pick and shovel, have the craters in the grass filled in by the time they landed back at Ridgewell.   At this rate, they would never destroy Germany.

Hollis saw Stan's plane bob a bit as the airspeed passed one seventy-five.   He worried that they might be going too fast for Leo to think and fly at the same time.   He could amuse himself all day thinking about Leo.

Ten thousand feet.

"Pilot to crew.   OK to go off oxygen."   Hollis unclipped his mask and wiped the sweat and saliva from around his lips and chin.   He turned off his heated suit.   "Carburetor air filters on, fuel booster pumps off."

Leo complied and announced that he had done so.

Hollis reached down into a pocket of his flight suit and pulled out a deformed pack of Lucky Strikes.   He delivered one to his lips and lit it, sucking in a large lung-full of smoke with great satisfaction.

"Somebody want to help me up?" Rizzo asked.

"Keep your pants on, Bobby.   I'll come getcha," Hulse said.

"Hey, Ball to Pilot.   Look down below."

Hollis leaned his face against the side window.   Beneath them, flying nearly parallel at perhaps a thousand feet off the water was a group of Marauders.   Twenty, maybe twenty five of them.   Probably heading for Boxted.   One of the Marauders was trailing a long ribbon of white-gray smoke from its right engine.   It looked like it was having trouble keeping up. Nestled around it on either side was an escorting B-26.   Like geese.

"Pilot to tail.   Watch that B-26 at nine o'clock low.   If he ditches let Radio know so he can call it in to Air-Sea Rescue."

Nothing.

"Mollica, did you hear me?"

"Yes, Lieutenant.   I see him."

Somebody had visited the war today.

"His buddies are staying with him."

"Pilot to navigator, how far to the coast?"

"Five or six minutes."

The overcast they had climbed through had broken up somewhat and he could begin to make out the first thin line of the coast in the haze.

Two thousand feet.

Hollis wondered how those guys in the Marauder were making out.

Bonner followed the southern finger of the estuary, the River Stour, until it ended at Manningtree and then turned northwest slightly toward Ridgewell.   Ridgewell was the furthest east of the cluster of airdromes belonging to the First Bombardment Wing.   That meant that on approaches from due east they had the least to go to get home.

Bonner throttled them back to about one forty and lowered his undercarriage.   When Stan lowered his, Hollis did the same.   The Twelve Acre Wood passed beneath them.   The runways were straight ahead.   He glanced down at the wheel on his side.   It slowly turned in the breeze assuring him that the brake was off.   "Left down."

Leo said, "Right down."

Dodge checked in the back, "Tail wheel down, ball turret stowed."

One thousand feet.

The formation passed over the corner of the field, parallel to runway two eight, the one they had lifted from earlier.   None of the planes fired any red flares, no one called the tower to report battle damage or declare an emergency for which they may require a different set of landing instructions.   The low squadron, by convention, would land first.   Cahill, then Stan, then Hollis followed by Selkirk, Ransahoff and Cassidy.   All the while, the lead and high squadrons would continue to orbit the field.

"Pilot to crew, landing positions."

Leo began the checklist, "Autopilot..."

"Off."

"Booster pumps..."

"On."

"Intercoolers...cold.   Carburetor air filters...on.   Mixture..."

"Auto rich."

"Tail wheel locked.   Brakes..."

Hollis pushed down on the brakes while Dodge checked the pressure.   "OK, he said.

"Cowl flaps..."

"Locked."

Hollis looked out the window and saw Stan bank into a steep turn to the left on a shortened downwind leg.   After ten seconds or so he did the same.   He moved the supercharger controls to full on, setting the manifold pressure at 38 inches and the rpm to twenty three hundred.   They had to be prepared to go to full power if, for some reason, they had to abort the landing and go around.   He checked his airspeed.   One forty.

"One third flaps."

"One third flaps," Leo responded.

The nose rose slightly as the descending flaps made **Cleopatra's Asp** tail heavy.   Hollis reset the trim.   Up ahead Stan turned off a short base leg, leveling out just beyond the threshold of the runway.   As Hollis turned off the base leg onto final, he called for full flaps and Leo started calling out airspeed as the plane slowed noticeably.

"One twenty."

Hollis set the bomber in a perfect glide.   He had to kick a little left rudder as they were touched by a slight crosswind.   He also dropped the wing to offset the slight crab into the crosswind.

Lower...lower.

"One ten."

They passed over the fence beyond the end of the runway, nothing more than three strands of barbed wire to deter the cows from wandering onto the field.   A quick glance down the runway, Stan was well into his roll out.   The end of the long concrete ribbon passed beneath them, the rubber streaks a familiar and reassuring sight.

Hollis closed the throttles back and yelled for Leo to move the pitch controls to high rpm. The engine noise died down.   He flared **Cleopatra's Asp** out by pulling back on the wheel. He felt the bomber hang for a moment as if suspended a few feet from the runway.   Lower...

THUMP-THUMP as the main wheels smacked satisfyingly against the runway.   They were down.   Hollis eased the wheel back a little further settling the tail wheel to the runway. Hollis always judged his landings.   This one was one of his best.   *You got a lot of natural talent, Hollis, but flying ain't one of 'em,* Frietag had said.   *Flying is the second greatest experience a man can have, landing is the first.*

As they finished their roll out, Leo reached up and opened the cowl flaps and then pulled the turbo levers back.   Hollis let the B-17 run out all the way without touching the brakes.   Up ahead he could see Eisenberg already turning onto the perimeter strip for the long crawl back to his hardstand.   Leo turned off the booster pumps while Hollis shut off the turbos and generators.

As they neared the end of the runway, with speed at just below twenty-five mph, Hollis applied gentle brake which caused them to squeal loudly, again a reassuring sensation, and told Leo to unlock the tail wheel.

"Tail wheel unlocked."

Hollis ran up the throttle on number four and applied left brake turning **Cleopatra's Asp** onto the perimeter strip.   "Flaps up."

Leo raised the flaps.   Hollis then set the rpm of the two inboards at twelve hundred and waited fifteen seconds as they taxied then moved their mixture controls to idle cut off, shutting them down.   When the engines were dead he pushed their throttles all the way forward to purge the lines of any residual gas, the propellers continued to spin under their own momentum until they finally came to a stop.   As they taxied he watched Ransahoff and then Cassidy touch down as the rest of the group passed overhead.

At last, Hollis delivered them to their hardstand.   Moe and Tommy were standing like two expectant parents waiting for their daughter to return from her first date with a boy they didn't like.   Tommy put up both hands and stepped in front of **Cleopatra's Asp** guiding Hollis onto the concrete pad.   Tommy waved his right arm vigorously and, walking backward, directed Hollis to swing the plane around one hundred and eighty degrees until she was parked in the same exact place he found her, sitting squat on the concrete, facing the perimeter strip.

Leo stood on the brakes and set the two outboards to idle cut off, killing the engines.

There was silence for the first time in over five hours as the blades continued their silent spin.   The vibration of the engines was gone and his buttocks tingled.   He watched as Moe and Tommy set the chocks and Leo released the brakes and locked the tail wheel.

Hollis turned off the electrical switches, then the master and battery switches.   He set the rudder pedals in neutral, pushed the control column full forward and reached down and pulled the lever locking them.   He removed the locking pin from the control column and locked the ailerons.

He then sat silently for a moment collecting his thoughts.   He glanced over at Cahill. They were already on the ground back- slapping in a frenzy of self-congratulation. It seemed foolish in its exuberance.

He unclasped his lap belt and took the bail-out bottle from its sleeve, placing it on the floor behind his seat.   He unplugged his lines and climbed out of his seat.   He gathered up his gear and placed his sweaty helmet and mask into the canvas bag, put on his cap and lowered himself down through the crawlway to the hatch and the ground surprised at the stiffness of his muscles and joints.

Moe was smiling as Hollis performed the pilot's ritual rubbing of his buttocks.   He could hear the now-silent engines crackle with dissipating heat muffled only by the sound of planes flying overhead waiting their turn to land.

"Well, Lieutenant, how'd it go?"

"Milk run, Moe.   She did OK.   The only problem was oil temps during the climb."

"Yeah, they all do that.   Just watch the cylinder heads."

"We did.   Otherwise she was perfect."

Moe grinned even more broadly and handed the clipboard to the pilot.   He signed off on the plane and said, "No battle damage, Moe.   A perfect flight, thanks."   He could have added, but did not, that there was no blood to clean up, no bowels to gather into a bag or burned flesh to scrape off.

"Yes sir."

Hollis looked out over the grass at the approaching Cahill.   The rest of the squadron taxied past one by one.   He watched Dutch swing his bomber around and stop his engines. Hollis could hear his crew laughing and talking loudly beneath the wing like high school kids after a football victory.   They didn't quite understand yet.

"Well, that wasn't so bad, was it?   Kinda easy, don't you think?" Cahill asked.

"I don't think we've seen anything yet."

Cahill scowled at Hollis and walked away.   The gunners returned to the plane and brought out their guns and set them on a tarp to be gathered up by the armorers who were already coming around the hardstand to pick them up.   The gunners would clean them at the squadron armory after interrogation.   Sully and H-y handed down their guns to Hulse and Dodge and then Dodge climbed back in to retrieve his own.

Leo collected the escape kits and placed them back in his ditty bag.   After a few minutes, a six-by-six pulled up and everybody tossed in their gear and climbed aboard.   Augie and Mollica draped their legs over the open tailgate and joked with each other as they smoked, acting as if this was their hundredth mission instead of their first.   As they pulled away, Hollis gave Moe a quick wave.

Augie turned to Hollis and said, "Well, I guess we ain't virgins, n'more, eh Lieutenant?"

No, you stupid fuck, you ain't no virgin n'more.   You wait, you fuckin' cracker, you're gonna see things that will make you wish you were back behind the wood shed jerkin' off.

"Nope."

They arrived in front of the equipment hut and dropped off their gear. They picked up their personal items and walked to the briefing room which was now serving the purpose of interrogation of the returning crews.

Hollis and Leo went into the briefing room first and checked in with a clerk.   They passed a table with the sign REPORT HOT NEWS over it where an RAF officer and a lieutenant from intelligence sat.

Hollis reported the burning Marauder.   They thanked him for the information and said they had already turned it into Air Sea Rescue.   They then passed a large table stacked high with sandwiches and donuts, behind which stood the same Red Cross girls with their same fresh, irrepressible smiles handing out steaming mugs of coffee.   There was another table with combat rations, a generous shot of whiskey, for each crewman, manned by a sergeant from the medics. Behind him, looking at the faces that entered the room was Clevenger.   Over in the corner stood Van Patten, Gleason and the Chief surveying the same scene.

Leo lifted the double shot to his mouth and handed the empty glass to the sergeant. Hollis did not want his.   He had done nothing that deserved the theoretical relief afforded by a shot of whiskey.   It was intended to ease nerves and the shock of combat allowing the words to flow easier at debriefing.   H-y took his as did the rest of the crew.   Sully and Dodge did not.

Hollis munched on a corned-beef sandwich and drank a glass of grapefruit juice while he waited for his crew to gather around him.   The briefing room had been rearranged with eight tables set up around the room.

"Lieutenant, we're ready for you," one of the interrogating officers said.

Hollis and his crew took up seats around the table and the lieutenant started asking his standard list of questions about the target, the opposition, fighter claims, tactics, escorts, weather, *ad nauseam*.   It was over quickly.   H-y seemed genuinely disappointed that he was not asked to show his log.

The navigators and bombardiers had their separate debriefings, but today it was a formality.   Hollis saw Ransahoff, Bonner and Van Patten in an intense, animated discussion. Gleason and Begay joined in and it was fairly obvious, even from a distance, that Ransahoff and Bonner were pretty mad.   Hollis assumed the anger was over the screwed up aborted bomb run at the primary and then again the confusion after they came off the secondary.

Hollis drifted toward the discussion in an effort to find out what was going on when he felt a slap on the back and turned to see Selkirk with a donut stuffed in his mouth and a glass of whiskey in his hand.

"Well, Jack-me-boy," he began, "what'd'ya think of the war so far?"

"Not much.   Where are all them Nazzies you guys keep talking so much about?"

"Oh, Jack, ol' buddy, you just wait.   They let you off easy today.   See they know when a new crew is flyin' and they let you have a free one to boost your confidence before they whack your balls off.   You watch," he said through a mouth packed with moist, disintegrating donut.

"Hey Selkirk!" somebody yelled.   "We're on."

Selkirk winked at Hollis and walked over to a table to join his crew.

Leo said, "Let's go grab some lunch."

Hollis was tired, his arms hurt, he wanted to wash his face and go to bed.   "No thanks. I'm gonna sack out for a while."

Hollis turned and left, grabbing a shuttle to the squadron area.

Before he fell asleep he reflected on the events of the day and wondered if perhaps he had been nearly crippled by a vivid imagination.

Chapter Thirteen   **Mail**

When Hollis returned to his room he could concentrate on only one sequence of events: stripping down to clean skivvies, washing his face and going to bed.   If he woke up and ate supper, fine, if not, so be it.

So he was surprised when he finally got up from his nap to see several envelopes tossed onto the desk.   The thought that one or more surely came from Jessie stirred his heart, filling it with raw expectation for, except for the pre-departure phone call, this was the first communication with her in nearly a month. They were not there when he lay down. Beamis.

He picked the letters up as if they were some fragile, ancient parchment and sat on the bed, staring at them.   One was from his father, another from his parents and three were from Jessie.   As was the custom, each of her letters was numbered.   Jessie's letters were numbered #1, #3, and #4.   There was no #2.   With his luck that would be the one extolling her undying devotion to him and revealing the lateness of her period.   The letter from his dad was not numbered, nor was that from the two of them.

He ripped into Jessie's #1, his hands trembling as they did in combat:

My Dearest John,
You left only hours ago and already my heart is breaking.   I cannot sit in my room now in front of this piece of paper and not think of the night we spent together, here, last night, locked in each other's arms.   I hold my satin pillowcase to my nose and I can still make out the aroma of your cologne.   If I close my eyes, I can feel your warm gentle touch on my breast, your soft lips on mine.

I watched the train until it passed from my sight and I could no longer see you.   But, while my eyes filled with tears, there was a smile on my lips as I knew, somehow, we will see each other again and the future will be ours to share.

Hollis felt a surge of affection as the rush of words registered in his brain.   She had cleverly avoided the emotional ambiguity inherent in the greeting 'Dear John.'   He read each sentence twice before moving onto the next to make sure his eyes did not deceive him.

I rode home with your folks.   They invited me to lunch.   We drank lemonade, sat on the porch and talked about you for hours.   They confirmed for me something I had always suspected, but for some odd reason, had always denied, or worse, taken for granted.   That you loved me and always had.   This was a revelation.   I knew we liked each other, but I had no idea that you cared for me so much for so long.   I must apologize for my obtuseness. Sometimes we don't see or hear the bee until he stings us.

Then your dad left for the shipyard and I came home to write to you.   He is proud of you.   We all are.

I hope you are well.   I hope your adjustment to life away in a foreign land will be easy. I know you must be homesick.   Sitting here in my own home, I am homesick: homesick for you.

Think of me often in the quiet moments when you can steal yourself away from the war. And know that I love you.   I must close for now for my tears get in the way.   I shall write again soon.

Love,
Jessie

Hollis smelled the paper for some sign of perfume or other tell-tale aroma, but found none.   He was overcome by a sense of disbelief.   He had never read anything like this before and he was astonished at the sentiments that now quaked in his heart from a few words on two sheets of paper.

He flipped the envelope over and looked at the glued leaf.   On it were the letters: S.W.A.K.   SWAK.   What the hell was *SWAK*?   *Single Women Against Killing?   SouthWest Athletic Klan?*   Now *he* felt obtuse.

The letter was almost too good to be true spoiled only by its brevity.   As time would pass, he worried, the intensity of her new-found, professed love for him would mellow and they would become just friends again.   Two people caught up in the emotional whirlwind created by the war, who, for one brief, urgent moment, found a sexual attraction and passion that would never have occurred under any other circumstance.   Love like this happened every minute of every hour of every day since the war started why should he or Jessie be immune?   Yet, he refused to accept the notion that she was just another cuddle bunny overly accommodating to an acquaintance about to go get his ass shot off.   Even so, the feeling in the letter was just too good to be true, a mistake made in warm, post-coital euphoria, and for that reason he hesitated opening the other letters because one of them might really start, "Dear John."

This one, too, was marked with S.W.A.K.   It was some kind of sign.   He just knew it.

His conflicted reverie was disrupted when Stan burst into the room and saw the letters on his bed.   "Well," he muttered to himself, "what have we here?"   Stan sniffed the letters, practically wiping his nose with them, and smiled, muttering, "Oo-la-la."   He stuffed the letters into his pocket and charged out as quickly as he came.

A moment later, Selkirk appeared at the door, already out of his flight clothes.   "Where's Stan?"

"He just got mail from home and I suspect he's in the latrine spanking his carrot."

"What?"

"Wanking his Winston."   He made a brisk stroking gesture with his fist.   "He said, 'oo-la-la' and left smiling.   What other conclusion am I to draw?"

"Hey, you don't think he's a faggot do you?"

Hollis felt his testicles twitch nervously in response to the question.

"No, why?"

"Well, as long as I've known him he never mentioned a girlfriend or nothing."

"Really, Mickey.   Just because he chooses not to discuss his sex life with the likes of you doesn't, by logical extension, automatically mean he's a queer."

"Little bastard suffers from such a 'runt's complex' I figured no woman alive could endure the fucker."

"The man was a piano player on Tin Pan Alley.   He's probably been fucked by each of Ziegfield's individual Follies at one time or another."

"Wanna eat?"

"No thanks, I'm gonna wash up, take a shower if Beamis has the coke burner going and go to bed."

"Combat wore you out?"

"Yeah."

"Twenty-four more to go, old chap.   Then you'll be a war hero jus' like your momma been tellin' the neighbors."   Selkirk turned and left, "Tell the little shit I was lookin' for him."

So there he was: a veteran.   A veteran of what he wasn't exactly sure.   He belonged to their fraternity now.   He had survived their initiation and become one of them.   Now the differences were only by matter of degree.   He felt transformed, carried himself in a peculiar way, even the words left his mouth differently.

Yet, except for the shudder at bomb release and the dozen or so AA bursts sent his way by some hapless flak gunners, he hadn't seen anything worthy of the word 'combat'.   The rule for mission credit was that the formation must do one of three things: It can fly the course all the way and drop on the target, drop on an alternate target, or engage the enemy in combat.   That included encountering flak.   A few scattered bursts, in the scheme of things, counted just as much as a whole sky-full.   Men die on milk runs, too.

Hollis ripped open #3.   It was a chatty letter, longer than #1, written a day later, in which she talked about her volunteer work, how she was busy working in her dad's office, that friends they had gone out with during his furlough had shipped out also.   One to the South Pacific, another to a training command in Kansas.   She mentioned at the end that she loved him and hoped he would write soon.   There was no mention of her menstrual cycle.   Number four was similar, but talked about his folks and how they seemed to be coping without him as if, he thought to himself, the previous year he had been away didn't count.   She found herself spending more time with them.   She hoped he didn't mind.   He was certain they didn't know what to make of that.   This made him smile for the joke was on her.

Stan walked back into the room and pulled the rest of his clothes off and laid down on his bed to read the other letters.   He laughed once.

Hollis asked, "I hate to sound stupid, but what does SWAK mean?"

"What?"

"What does-" he spelled the letters S-W-A-K, "-mean?"

"Sealed with a kiss.   Christ, Hollis, you worry me."

Hollis smiled again.

"By the way, Selkirk was looking for you."   The fatigue caught up with him and he decided to shower first and read the letters from his folks later.   Besides, he didn't want to spoil his happy mood by news from home, instead choosing to savor her letters like an afterglow.   He climbed out of his clothes, leaving them in a pile on the floor, and walked out into the warm afternoon sun in his shorts and flying boots, a towel around his shoulder and a bar of soap in his hand.

The heater was not functioning and the shower was cold but satisfying, removing the film of sweat which clung to him like oil around a cylinder.   He mulled Jessie's letters, especially the first one, over and over in his head searching for some ambiguity, but he drew a blank, withstanding the test of skepticism.   It had been a thrill to read.   He hoped it was real, that she meant every word of it.   How could he know?   She had broken his heart before.   He thought of that night, too.   If the water were not so cold and his penis not so contracted he might have stroked himself to completion, also.

He realized as he toweled off that he was still scared.   The novelty of the day's mission and the mail had obscured his fear, now as he thought about what he had done today, it returned to the surface.   What if the flak had been closer or the *Luftwaffe* had decided today was the day for the final showdown?   There was no assurance that tomorrow would be as easy or if he'd even be alive this time tomorrow.   And all of this emotional turmoil Jessie caused in his heart would be so much wasted energy.   He'd have spent his last moments thinking about her when he should be thinking about the important things like God and eternity and not letting your friends down.

He read the letter from his folks.   They talked about Jessie and things around the house, at the hardware store and at the shipyard.   Things were changing as more and more commodities became harder and harder to find.   The government was making business difficult to conduct.   Wage and price controls were all the more insufferable by their arbitrariness.   But the war news, items they could read about in the papers or see on the Movietone reels, was generally good and they took heart in that.   They hoped he would not be traveling anywhere near a place called Ploesti anytime soon.   He looked at the date on the letter.   It was written just ten days ago.   He was obviously missing more than Jessie's #2.

They thought of him often.   They missed him and hoped he was well and that he would write soon.

Then he read the letter from his father.   His dad was a master carpenter at the shipyard and practically from the moment he started working there he was in trouble with the union shop steward sometimes for the most petty of reasons.   Mostly, his father suspected, it was because he was hired at a job level that had passed over many employees in the shop with greater seniority.   There was a job to do and he was unapologetic.   Men were dying and it was his patriotic duty to help out.   Maybe, he stated in the letter, he felt that way because he had a son in the war.   The people who groused the most seemed not to have a loved one on active duty. They bitched the loudest about the shortages of gasoline and coffee, butter, meat, and sugar. The rationing of these items, especially gasoline, caused the most resentment in an otherwise loyal public.   The fact that his father was awarded a 'B' gas rationing coupon for his position as a war worker drove the shop steward to distraction as he, for some inexplicable reason, did not qualify.   Perhaps the dispersal of rationing coupons served some ulterior purpose, a system of rewards which in this case was designed to punish the union management as unions had become increasingly unpopular and, in some cases, counterproductive to the war effort.   By logical extension, this being the case, John L. Lewis and his coal miners were entitled to none.

His father took the bus to the shipyard and his mother the bus to the store which enabled them to save the gas.   Anyway, he dared not drive the car for fear of a blow out in a tire he could not replace.   So he would fill the tank, drive home and siphon the gas into two fifty-five gallon drums buried in the back yard, 'just in case.'   In case of what, he did not say.   While this was not strictly illegal it was still considered hoarding and the shop steward got wind of it and told his father that he had a choice, either sell him some of the gas or he would turn him in to the rationing board and he would lose his 'B' coupon.

As luck would have it, a short time later he found the shop steward *in flagrante delicto*, sitting on a piece of machinery down in the steering gear compartment of a Liberty ship with a woman, his pants down around his ankles and her head buried in his lap.   She was, aptly he thought, a pipe fitter.   His father recognized her and knew her husband, too.   They had been regular customers at the hardware store.   Her husband had a job at the Baldwin Locomotive Works as some sort of boilermaker.

His problems with the shop steward, he related in the letter, abruptly ended.   He made sure he was seen by the shop steward in protracted conversation with the plant matron.

Deliverance in the guise of workplace fellatio.

His father also related that some clown from the Office of Price Administration came into the hardware store and ordered his mother to change the prices on most everything in the store made with metal. Everything, it seemed, except fish hooks and galvanized wash tubs. Damned OPA. Bunch of Communists. Everybody had plenty of money, what with all the war work, but fewer and fewer things to spend it on. Hardly seemed fair. This was a mixed blessing.

He told him that his mother had started drinking her coffee without sugar. As long as Hollis had known his mother she had two cups of dark, rich coffee in the morning each filled to saturation with sugar. She knew Hollis liked his coffee and ice tea sweet so in deference to him she stopped her consumption of sugar as soon as she found out he was coming home on furlough. She continued to save her weekly ration in a large jar just in case he popped in unannounced.

He wasn't sure what to expect when he went home for the first time, but he was sure it wasn't what he found. He walked up to the front door, his new silver pilot's wings proudly pinned over his left breast, expecting to find Jessie waiting for him. But, she was gone, of course. Pittsburgh.

A white, silken banner emblazoned with a blue star hung in the front window like a Christmas ornament. That was *him* hanging there. What had started out as high adventure and an effort to avoid the uncertainty of the draft had been symbolically abbreviated which he resented. His mother was behind the blue star. The great sugar hoarder wanted everyone to know her only begotten son was serving his country and that his place in the home would be remembered and preserved. Now that his father told him of her sacrifice he didn't resent the public display. She was entitled.

It was the first time he had been home since he left for Aviation Cadets and he wasn't sure what to expect. Quiet, somber determination. Collective resolve and mutual commitment to the larger war effort. Instead, everyone seemed to be having the time of their lives. He found a gay, almost carefree home front where people were practically dancing in the streets. People had money they never had before. Morals were relaxed. Willing females abounded. Going out 'sparking' nowadays carried a good likelihood of getting laid, something absolutely unheard of prior to Pearl Harbor.

On a short taxicab ride from one train station to another as he passed through Louisville in his new second Lieutenant's uniform, grommet removed from his garrison cap assuming a rakish "50-mission crush" appearance, pilot's wings pinned to his chest, the female cab driver, not more than eighteen years old, offered to fuck him in the backseat. The selfless donation of poon for the war effort. He declined her gracious offer choosing not to go head to head with unrepentant, and perhaps less patriotic, microbes, a duel which he harbored no illusion he would win.

He had no doubt that the war was the best thing that ever happened to some of these people. Take Augie.

Going from camp to camp, one dull, isolated training base after another, he thought the fact that small towns and their inhabitants were open and entertaining reflected the uninhibited youthful exuberance of the young soldiers who passed through not the other way around. The reality, he admitted, was that there was money to be made and fun to be had all lubricated by prodigious quantities of alcohol and whoever started the revelry was irrelevant. It was as if the war was taking place on another planet.

When he arrived home he found Victory Speed, 35 miles an hour to save gas and rubber, Victory Gardens to make up for shortfalls in vegetables at the local market and Victory Red lipstick, the reason for which he never understood but perhaps serving as a beacon for instant gratification and Victory girls willing to provide it. Sometimes for a small fee. Pure patriotism only goes so far.

He was willing to defend with his very life and treasure, his great country, the last best hope of man on earth, fighting to liberate people who did not deserve liberation and perpetuate empires which did not deserve perpetuation, allied with a dictator as scurrilous, despicable and murderous as any they were trying to overthrow, all the while noting the disquieting race riots in Detroit, the incongruity of work strikes and black marketeering during a time of great, shared sacrifice and the relaxation of the most basic of moral codes of behavior in the name of a good time.

Did Augie struggle with these moral dilemmas or was he satisfied with just shooting up things? Did it matter? If he could not articulate the higher purposes of the war should he be compelled to participate in it? Or was it sufficient that he arrive at the plane each morning and fire his gun as the need arose?

When it was apparent that Jessie was not there and he would spend his first furlough alone, he found himself doing the unthreateningly familiar things he had done as a boy. He found himself drawn to the Pennsy tracks, connecting New York and Philadelphia with Baltimore and Washington like a great artery, that passed not a quarter mile from his house and sat on the embankment while the trains roared by, one after the other. He sat for hours, like a solitary fisherman impervious to the fish, and contemplated his situation, wishing he had some clue as to what the future held, regretting that he had not announced his return to Chester soon enough to allow Miss Jessie the opportunity to make herself available for visitation. He left that furlough convinced he would never see her again, that he should grow accustomed to the idea of a life without her in it.

He watched the huge, black locomotives which he so loved rumble past under his watchful eye looking for a familiar face at the throttle, a friendly wave, some acknowledgment from the powerful, smelly monsters that there would be no change in his absence and things would be the same when he got back. All the while knowing deep down inside they would never be the same.

Everyone eighteen or older who wasn't 4-F or a conscientious objector knew that eventually soldiering would be his lot and he had chosen his role wisely. Or so he thought. As he sat on the berm by the tracks, preparing himself for B-17 transition school, the first nebulous thought formed in the recesses of his skull that he might have made a big mistake.

His dreams of whores and locomotives was disrupted by the accented voice of Mickey Selkirk. He started awake finding his father's letter still held in his hands which had come to rest on his chest.

"There you are," he said. Hollis watched as Selkirk walked over to Stan and grabbed his hand. He checked his palm, "Yeah that hair's startin' to come in real nice."

Stan jerked his hand away, but Mickey persisted, "Understand you got some correspondence from home today. Word has it it caused you to retire to the lay-treen to wank your crank. Don't you know that'll make you go blind, you dumb hebe?"

"Fuck off, Selkirk, you stupid mick or I'll chew *your* face off."

Selkirk turned to Hollis and said, "I wasn't there, but Mattson said it was a fair fight. The poor infantry captain was only twice his size.   Hey Stan, wanna get something to eat?"

Hollis was awakened by the most incredible sound.   It took him a few moments to orient its source.   It seemed to originate down the hall.   Just as the eyes require a second or two to focus upon being reopened so did his ears require a fleeting pause for recognition.   Music.   It was loud and crystal clear.   No radio could produce such perfect sound.   He thought his heart might stop when he realized he was listening to Artie Shaw's "Moonglow."   Perhaps he was still dreaming.   He pulled himself out of bed to investigate.   He walked into Cassidy's room and saw Stan and Cassidy sitting on the beds in their skivvies, their backs against the wall the room filled with the blue haze of cigarette smoke.   The music emanated from a phonograph on the table in the middle of the room.   Beside it was a stack of records in their brown paper sleeves. Hollis picked one up and read the label, "Beat Me Daddy (Eight to the Bar)" by Will Bradley and his Orchestra.

"Be careful Hollis, those aren't V-discs," Cassidy said.   Victory discs.   They were sold as an expedient to get around the musician's strike so servicemen the world over could truck their favorite music along with them.   These were original recordings, not the hastily reproduced V-discs.   Many were probably irreplaceable.   There was a large wooden .50 caliber cartridge box on the floor packed with even more records.

"Jesus, this is quite a collection.   Mind if I listen?"

"No, just be quiet," Stan said.   "No singing."

Hollis took his place on the bed, the three of them, dressed in only their underwear, locked in thought, transfixed by the sound.   When "Moonglow" was over Hollis asked if he could play it again.

"Sure," was all Cassidy said.

Hollis returned the needle to the beginning of the record and closed his eyes, and, as if by magic, was transported through time and space to that moment, that night.

When it was over, Hollis lit a cigarette and Cassidy placed another record on the turntable.   Benny Goodman.

"I was at Goodman's 1938 concert at Carnegie Hall.   It was the greatest moment of my life," said Stan, turning a sly, knowing gaze at Cassidy, "up to that point, I mean.   You'll never guess who was there, too."

"Fats Waller," Cassidy replied.

"Not even close.   Our illustrious Colonel."

"Van Patten?"

"Yeah. After he dressed me down for that little misunderstanding with that captain he asks me what I did when I was a civilian.   So I tells him and wouldn't you know he says he was there, too.   His old man got him the tickets.   I got my ticket from the friend of the drummer in Goodman's band."   He smiled broadly, "I had a better seat."

Hollis turned to him and asked, "What exactly *did* you do in civilian life?"

"I was a torpedo for the mob."

Hollis stared at Eisenberg for a moment unable to tell if he was kidding or not, but saddened that the conversation was being conducted exclusively with Cassidy.

"Van Patten, Ransahoff and I all went to the Academy, did you know that, Hollis?" Cassidy asked.

"Yeah, I knew--"

"As luck would have it, of all the places I could'a been sent to fight this stinking war, the bastards sent me to a squadron in Pyote, Texas, with Ransahoff in it."

"So?"

"I was in the Class of 1941. Ransahoff was a yearling. He took particular delight in hazing plebes. That whole group hazed the bejesus out of us, but Ransahoff was the worst of the lot. At one time or another he had every plebe in the outfit swimming to Newburgh. He had half the class ready to quit by the end of Beast Barracks. Mean as a snake he was. He didn't want no momma's boys in his army. 'What do plebes outrank, you maggot?' 'Sir, Plebes outrank the Superintendent's dog, the Commandant's cat, the waiters in the mess hall, the Hell Cats, and all the Admirals in the whole damned Navy.' You can only take so much of that shit. He had one of the most popular members of our class turned out for cheating. An allegation, I might add, which was never proven. A real martinet, that Ransahoff." Cassidy smiled in the direction of the door and Hollis turned to see Ransahoff standing there.

Ransahoff said without emotion, "You guys better get some sleep, we're alerted for tomorrow." He turned and walked away.

Hollis stood up and thanked Cassidy for allowing him to partake in the music and made tracks for the latrine. Outside it was cooling off and, even though it was late, after nine at night, it was still fairly light outside, what with England's northern latitude and British Double Daylight Time. He had slept for nearly six hours with his mail lying on his desk. He was hungry and he needed to pee.

Hollis returned to his room and found Cassidy and Eisenberg still listening to records. He didn't stop to hear what they were talking about. He could hear them laughing and could only assume they were still getting on Ransahoff.

He dressed quickly and resolved that after he found something to eat he was going to come back to the room and write a letter to his father, one to his mother and one to Jessie. The letter to his mother was short, but reassuring. He told her he had no intention of going anywhere near a place called Ploesti, wherever the hell that was. He told her that he had worked today, a code word he established to mean he had flown a mission, and it was not all that bad. His crew had performed well and everyone seemed to be adjusting to life 'here in England' without problem. He was homesick and suspected they all were. With time, however, maybe that would pass. He hadn't seen much of England outside the airfield and what he had seen had been glances stolen from the cockpit. He told her a little bird had advised him about her stockpiling sugar. Go ahead and use it, he said, as he would not be home any time soon. He wrote that he loved her, he thought of her often and she should look after his dad.

He then wrote a letter to his father. Tell the Great Sugar Hoarder to go ahead and use the stuff, as he figured by the time he got home there would be no further need for rationing. He congratulated him on his success at the shipyard. Tell mom not to worry. Things over here are rough and despite his first uneventful round-trip he figured he hadn't seen anything yet. He would be careful, though, figuring as he wrote the words that if he was at least careful, everything else would be OK. He would write again soon, as soon as he had more to say. In the meantime, look after Mom.

When he had both letters placed in envelopes he took out another sheet of paper and wrote to Jessie:

My Darling Jessie,

I am fine.   I got 1, 3 and 4.   I have no idea where #2 is.   Hope it's not at the bottom of the Atlantic somewhere.   We lost a crew on the way over.   I suspect they're at the bottom of the ocean in eternal rest, known but to God.

We had our first outing today.   It was OK.   The rest is yet to come.   More later.

Gus and David headed out, you said.   Gus should like B-25s.   They are a great plane to fly.   It should be interesting out West.   He should have a nice tan when he gets back!   No chance for a tan here.   Whenever there's enough sun to tan we're up.   I'll probably be back pale as a ghost and thin as a rail.   I wasn't all that beefy to begin with and what with my sporadic eating habits I have lost several pounds.

I am glad to see you are keeping busy and spending time with my folks.   You will provide another link to me and they will appreciate that.   Tell them what you want from my letters.   But don't worry them unnecessarily, my mom thinks I will be able to pick and choose my targets as I see fit.   If that's what she thinks that'll be OK.   Someday I may explain it to her. Then again, maybe I won't.

I enjoyed your first letter. It brought all those memories of our last night together back in a hot rush.   I love you.   I only hope your love for me is as deep and eternal as my love is for you.

I think often of that satin pillow. Your soft golden hair splayed out on it as you slept. Watching you sleep.   Trying hard not to wake you as you rested in my arms.   I hold that memory of you in my heart.   It keeps me warm at night.   Protects me against my loneliness. It will keep me from harm and return me to you.   Of this I have no doubt.

I will write tomorrow and the tomorrow after that and the tomorrow after that...   I love you.

John

He folded the letter and placed it in an envelope.   He wrote SWAK on the flyleaf, addressed but did not sealed it.   He set all three letters aside and climbed into bed.

As he waited to fall asleep, he thought of his flight over and the crew who never made it.

They had been alerted for the morning and he needed his rest.   His arms and shoulders still ached.

Chapter Fourteen   **Presumed Lost**

Three had left and only two arrived.   He wondered what had happened to them.   Did they simply leave the face of the earth never to be seen or heard from again?   Were they dead? Surely they were.   Long since decayed, eaten and discarded by the forces of marine biology. Gone.   Ten mothers did not know what had happened to their sons.   "Overdue and presumed lost" was the military expression for such occurrences.

They had left Grand Island Army Air Field in Nebraska with Angel's Fortress in the company of another B-17 piloted by someone named Murphy.   They were to fly independently, but the general course would take them to the same destinations only a few minutes apart. Before they left, Hollis and Murphy shared notes.   Hollis would go first and report any weather changes or other potential concerns back to Murphy.   In turn, Murphy would keep tabs on Hollis.   Their final destination would be Prestwick, Scotland.   Their orders were sealed and they could not discuss them with each other, but nor were they stupid.   Hollis and Murphy both knew where they were headed.

The night before they left the crew met out underneath the nose of Angel's Fortress and they talked.   They again debated whether they should name the plane and again Dodge told them it was not theirs to name.   They were responsible for making sure everything worked and then deliver the thing, nothing more.

For the second time Augie wanted to name it after Leo's wife who had recently departed for Hollywood.   **Christie's Crusaders** Hulse said.   **Mighty Aphrodite** was Quinn's suggestion.   **Christie's Crotch**, Augie again said under his breath.   Dodge warned him that if he said that one more time he was going to wring his little hillbilly neck.   Augie never discussed naming the plane again.

As they left the plane to go to bed, Leo turned to Hollis and said, "You know, Jack, you and I are participating in something we'll all be proud to tell our grandchildren."

They kept asking him, as if he was prescient and would know, what England would be like even though none of them had yet been officially told that that was where they were headed. They were issued cold weather gear.   They assumed this was not intended for use in the South Pacific.   He was about to go to war with people whose entire experience of the world had been through what they had seen and read in the <u>National Geographic</u> or <u>Life</u> magazine.   If that. Himself included.

For the thousandth time, Hollis told Leo not to call him Jack.   My father's name is Jack and I hate it.   So please call me John.   Leo would call him John for a few times and then revert to calling him Jack again.

They left Grand Island early the next morning and flew all day to Grenier Field in Manchester, New Hampshire.   They sent telegrams home and ate a late supper.   From there they flew to Goose Bay, Labrador arriving the next morning.   After spending the day and night resting they went out with Murphy's crew to the flight line to leave.   At the weather briefing they were warned of a passing low pressure area that might interfere with their planned departure.   Sure enough, when they arrived at the plane shortly after dawn it was raining steadily and the departure was postponed twenty-four hours.   When they showed up at weather briefing the next morning there were now three crews.   Murphy's, Hollis's and another piloted by a swarthy, little guy with a strong Brooklyn accent and an Italian-sounding name.

The low had moved on and it was time for them to do likewise.

Ten hours later, they arrived at Meeks Field at Reykjavik, Iceland. Murphy arrived twenty minutes behind Hollis, but the swarthy, Italian guy never showed. No one had heard a distress call. No one saw anything. Poof. Vanished without a trace. As if lifted from the face of the earth by some mysterious hand. The people at the operations office sent out the proper notification. A convoy passing along the route was told to be on the lookout and two PBYs were dispatched to look for them but nothing was found.

The next day the two crews, now joined by three more, left one after the other and flew on to Prestwick without hearing anything about the missing crew.

H-y's navigation, always suspect since the incident in the middle of an Oklahoma night two months previously, was flawless. They had been warned repeatedly about a ghost beam on the same frequency used by Prestwick which had been responsible for the loss of numerous planes and crews being ferried over. The ghost beam was a very strong signal set up by the Germans to lead the bombers far to the north of their expected landfall and when they ran out of gas they were forced to ditch. Few of these crews were ever found. The Prestwick beacon was also loud and using H-y's navigation as a check they were guided without trouble right into Scotland.

As they approached Prestwick, they were amazed at what they saw. More varieties of planes than any of them had ever seen before. There were dozens of heavies, 17s and 24s, transports, C-47s and '54s, PBY's, mediums and a few Coastal Command Liberators.

No sooner had they arrived, all five planes landing within twenty minutes of each other, when Angel's Plane was taken from them. They were packed into a train to Bovingdon. They were each given a copy of a "Short Guide to Great Britain" and a brief lecture on their expected conduct while guests of the British. After about three hours on the train Augie tossed the pamphlet out the window saying he didn't see what was so great about it.

Hollis wondered what mystery was left forever untold by the disappearance of the swarthy guy with the Italian-sounding name and his crew. Were they treated as casualties of war on the rosters at headquarters? Or did they fall between the cracks? Not a training accident, but not yet an operational loss. Non-operational casualties. Meager legacy for ten lives. Two hundred years or more of combined living gone without so much as an asterisk at the bottom of a page. Ten mothers with the greatest question of their lives unanswerable.

Chapter Fifteen   **Hollywood and the War of Northern Aggression**

"Gooood mornin', Gen'lemen," Gleason said cheerfully, much too cheerfully for Hollis's liking, "Seats!"   The air exec waited for the room full of officers to sit down before he resumed, "I'm the Bangmaster for today's sortee."

Beamis promised them another milk run.   Twelve three-hundred pounders.   Hollis watched as Gleason walked to the curtain and pulled it back with a flourish, "Our target for today is Le Bourget airdrome outside Paris."   There were hoots and cheers.   Hollis noted that Gleason pronounced it 'Lah Boor-jay' with a very strong Texas drawl.

"This is the same place Lindbergh landed a few years ago.   We have reason to believe the Germans have concentrated a large number of newly-minted Mezzersmitts at the air dee-pot there prior to distribution to *Gruppen* stationed in Northern France.   We got a chance to catch 'em on the ground, today, boys.   So let's hit 'em good.

"The First Bomb Wing will hit Le Bourget while the Fourth Wing will hit Poix and Abbeville airdromes.   The 103rd Combat wing will lead, we will be next and the 102nd will bring up the rear.   We will lead, the 91st will be high and the 351st will be low group.   We should have fighter escort for the whole trip.   Major--"

Beamis was right again.   Hollis had hoped to see Paris one day, but not from twenty-five thousand feet above a column of smoke.

Take off was scheduled for just before seven.   Briefing was short and the crew gathered under **Cleopatra's Asp** well before stations.   The crew sprawled out in the grass under the left wing.   In the half light of the predawn, Hollis could tell it promised to be a perfect day for flying.

Hollis wondered if today would be the day he would die and if such a thought constituted a premonition.   He had not eaten much at breakfast, keeping his coffee intake to a minimum and already his stomach was starting to churn.   He lit another cigarette and listened to the idle banter of his crew.

Sully said, "Hey H-y, what's that name doing up by your gun?"

The crew stopped what they were doing and, as one, looked up at the navigator's station where they could plainly see the freshly painted name 'Belinda' beneath the .50 caliber machine gun poking out from the window above H-y's desk.

"Hey, H-y, ain't that the name of your girlfriend?" Leo asked.

"Yep, I came out yesterday and Tommy painted it on for me.   He took a picture of me standing beside it so I could send it home to Belinda."

Leo asked, "You think she'll like a gun named after her?"

"Son, if she wouldn't let you fuck her before, I'm sure she will now," Sully said which caused the rest of the crew to laugh.

Hollis remembered the Lovely Belinda, a nineteen year old coed H-y met while he was attending business school at the University of Chicago.   He kept a large photo of her near his bed.   The picture was taken from below and slightly behind.   Her shapely figure, especially her round bottom and soft, slender thighs, was accented nicely by the lighting and camera angle.   Real Cheesecake.   She wore a white bathing suit and had a large broad-brimmed white hat which partly shaded her pretty face, her shoulder-length brunette hair framed her coquettish expression as she looked back down at the camera.   The picture was taken with her standing on the deck of a sailboat on Lake Michigan.   It was a popular photograph among the crew. Almost as popular as Christie's.

H-y fashioned himself as something of a polished lady's man.   He was, in fact, very handsome, Hollis thought, and was probably as effortlessly popular with women as he claimed. While maintaining steadfast commitment to the Lovely Belinda waiting patiently in Chicago, he also claimed a girlfriend at every airfield and jerkwater town he was ever stationed at or near. And he was probably right.   He cut a dashing figure in Class A's, his fifty-mission crush hat cocked on his head, smiling a big, toothy grin, as if the outcome of the war and the success of every USO dance hinged on his every move.   Sully said he got more mail than the rest of the crew combined.   He also said that he saw H-y walking down the street in Ardmore and Grand Island with a pretty girl on each arm on more occasions than he could remember.

Sully took Hollis aside just before they left Grand Island for New Hampshire and told him that H-y would turn in his seat in the nose and face forward braced for takeoff, holding onto his desk for dear life.   As soon as the plane left the ground, he would snap the stopwatch and begin his timing of the mission, but he would not stop cowering.   H-y, Sully said, was never convinced the plane could actually fly.   Even when the principles of lift and aerodynamics were carefully explained to him, he refused to believe it.

"Hey, Lieutenant Leo, tell us a Hollywood story," Quinn asked.

"I've told you guys all my Hollywood stories," he said.

"Come on, Leo, tell 'em a story," H-y said.

Leo raised himself to his elbows and said, "Ok, Christie and I were eating in the Bamboo Room at the Brown Derby on Wilshire one night when George Burns and Gracie Allen sat down at the table beside us and ate dinner."

"Wow," Quinn said, "you actually met 'em?"

"Well, I didn't actually meet them.   But I smiled at him and they said hello."

"How come," Hulse asked, "they're George *Burns* and Gracie *Allen*?   How come it ain't George Burns and Gracie Burns?"

"Show Biz," Hollis said.

"Maybe they ain't married," Mollica added.

"You mean they been livin' in perpetual sin?" Augie asked.

"Perpetual?   That's a mighty big word for you, Augie," Sully said.

"Now what exactly do you mean by that, Lieutenant?" Augie asked.

"Oh, nothing, really, Augie.   Jus' flappin' my jaw."

"Leo, did Errol Flynn rape them two girls?" H-y asked.

"How should I know?   But you heard the expression 'In Like Flynn'?"

"Why *did* Christie give up being a movie star to become a secretary?" Hollis asked.

"More money."

"How could you leave that beautiful wife out there all by herself?" H-y asked.   "I mean that's like Sodom and Gomorrah.   Look at all the big movie stars who get to fuck anybody they want.   Like Tyrone Power."

"He's on active duty," Sully said.

"Or Clark Gable."

"Active duty."

"Cary Grant."

"Sissy."

"Will you shut up.   I'm trying to make a point here," H-y said.

"Yeah, what is it?" Leo asked.

"I ain't never seen a woman as beautiful as your wife, Lieutenant Wychulis." Augie said.

Everyone turned to look at Augie, surprised by what he had just said.   They were even more surprised when he said, "Jesus, would you look at this?"

Everyone turned to see the source of Augie's comment.   Two Negro ordinance sergeants walked toward the open bomb bay of **Cleopatra's Asp**.   One of them was walking on a set of crutches, his leg housed in a white, plaster cast that went to his knee.

"What happen to your foot, there, boy?" Augie asked.

The limping black man turned to Augie and said, "A five hundred pounder rolled on it."

Augie snickered and said in a loud voice, "Guess you won't be doing the buck and wing tonight, eh, Sunshine?"

"You betta watch your mouth, Sergeant," the one on crutches said.

"Com'ere, nigger and I'll knock your black off," Augie yelled, pulling himself erect posturing like a threatening dog.

"Knock it off, Augie." Leo said forcefully.

"Fuck off, white boy," the other black sergeant said.

"We lynch niggers for talk like that where I come from," Augie said.

"You been missin' a lot of opportunities to keep youwah mout' shut," the second one replied.

Augie started to his feet when Dodge grabbed him and put him back on his rear end. "Leave it be, Augie, before he breaks those crutches over your thick skull," he added, although Hollis knew in his heart of hearts Dodge would just as soon let them pound the shit out of Augie even if just for the hell of it.

"I'll blow torch the both of you, you motherfuckers!"

"Augie, damnit, he said knock it off," Hollis yelled.

"Stupid nigger, I'll fix his ass," Augie said trying to get in the last word.

"What the hell's the matter with you, Augie?" H-y asked.

Hollis watched as the two black ordinance sergeants walked over to the open bomb bay and, with Moe, poked their heads up into the belly of the plane.

"I think we've just solved the riddle of Southern Exceptionalism," Sully said.

Augie snapped at him, "What do you mean by *that*, Lieutenant?"

Unthreatened, Sully just leaned back on his elbows and said, "Nothing, Augie.   Jus' flappin' my jaws."

Hollis was growing to like Sully more and more with each passing day.   He remembered vividly the day Sully joined the crew in Ardmore.   Nathan Bedford Forrest Sullivan, he said, from Front Royal, Virginia.   But everybody calls me Sully, he added.

"When did you flunk out of pilot school?" H-y asked him as they stood around in the squadron day room introducing each other.

"How'd you know I washed out?"

"Well, nobody sets out to be a bombardier," H-y said.

Sully claimed to have the highest bombing accuracy at bombardier school in New

Mexico.   To which H-y responded after several practice bombing missions that Sully couldn't piss into a pickle barrel if he was standing in it let alone drop a thousand pounder into one from twenty-five thousand feet. Even on a bright sunny day over an empty desert. With no wind. Or flak.

Leo said those two were perfect for each other cooped up in the nose like that. Tweedle-dum and Tweedle-dee, he called them.

Sully kept saying that if H-y hits him in the back of the head with a pencil one more time as they approached an IP he was gonna shove that pencil up his ass. Sideways.

No one knew much about Sully.   The only one he really spoke to was Hollis.   Sully had graduated from the University of Virginia in 1940 determined to be the next Faulkner.   A Virginian, he claimed he understood the mentality of the South and was determined to explain the core of the Southern Soul.   To understand that, he said, required an understanding of the effect of the Civil War on the South.   And, quoting his beloved Faulkner, in order to understand that you would have to be born there.

The War of Northern Aggression, he called it.

Why do you people call it that? H-y had asked.

You people?

Because it's not who fires the first shot.   It's who causes the first shot to be fired, Leo had responded, to the astonishment of everyone listening to the conversation.

Vulgar, cheating, fanatical Yankees, he called them.   You didn't think the war was just about slavery did you? Sully asked rhetorically.   He pointed out that the South suffered a higher percentage of casualties and deaths among its populace than any other combatant in any war in recorded history.

So lemme get this straight, H-y had said, feigning a genuine desire to understand.   You thought slave owning and secession by an unhappy and irritable minority was justifiable?

No, my family were neither slave owners nor were they particularly enamored with secession, but they refused to allow heavy-handed Yankees raping our fine state of Virginia. We, suh, were Virginians.   Besides, you ever hear of the Tea Party?

H-y looked dumbfounded and was never sure whether Sully was serious or not.   And, Hollis thought, he had just enunciated what was perhaps the crux of the Civil War after all.

Talking about the war caused Hollis to remember his great grandfather, a gray, frail, bearded old gentleman, though still of very sharp mind, who had lost a foot with Grant during the last assault at Cold Harbor which he said was neither cold nor a harbor.   He lost it and forever was making a joke that he spent the rest of his life trying to find the damned thing. Couldn't seem to remember where he had misplaced it.   Hollis remembered the stump which he kept sheathed in a muslin sleeve.   He recalled it being repulsive yet the source of constant morbid fascination.   The skin was smooth and the severed end of the bone firm and rigid under it.   Minie' ball through the ankle, he said.   Clean through.   I can still hear them bones a'snappin'.   It had been, he said, a hasty amputation.   Hollis recalled asking him a short time before he passed away why he had fought in the Civil War, the Great War of the Rebellion, the old man called it.

He said that he had never seen Virginia before.   He never really understood what he had meant by that until now.   Hollis wondered how so many young men could willingly go off to such inconceivable slaughter.   Seven thousand men had died in just sixty minutes on that hot day in June.   And, because they were young, they all thought they would live through it.

One day when he was in Primary, while marching to class, two silver P-38s screamed by in a high-speed pass and made a graceful, arcing turn.   The whistle and roar of the four powerful Allison engines reverberated against the ribs of the students as forty-odd faces, so typical of every pilot who ever lived whose gaze turned skyward at the sound of an airplane, turned and watched the twin-boomed fighters rise away from view.   He remembered the thrill that ran up his spine, the little hairs on the back of his neck erect.   Virginia roared up into the sky that day, the sun flashing off its wings.

Augie cooled off and the two Negro sergeants left without further shouting although Hollis knew the matter between them was far from settled.   He heard Augie say under his breath, "Stupid jigaboo dropped a bomb on his foot.   Can you imagine?   Bet he'll be limping for life.   Trouble stealin' watermelons now, eh Sunshine?"

Leo turned to Hollis and whispered, "Must of really been something to be a nigger in the South, you know?"

"Leo, don't use that word in my presence again."

Hollis stood up and yelled, "Stations!"

"Where'd you say we were going today, Lieutenant?" Rizzo asked.

"Paris...France."

Just before he entered the plane Hollis emptied his stomach onto the grass, wiped his chin and climbed in.

Chapter Sixteen   **Paris...France**

Assembly and the flight to the target were uneventful.   The escort, P-47s, something until today he had heard about but had not seen, buzzed around the formation like flies around a fresh cow turd, being careful not to approach the formation nose first or from any other threatening angle for fear of provoking a hailstorm of fire from anxious gunners.

It was easy.   They crossed the gray-green English Channel with Ransahoff leading the squadron again, keeping a tight formation as they neared the target.   Hollis let Leo do most of the flying during assembly and up to the turn at the IP.   They were low squadron of the lead group of the wing and from this spot Hollis could see the lead combat wing break down into groups line-astern and turn toward the run at the airfield.   The sky was cloudless and Hollis thought he could see for eternity.

He strained to catch a glimpse of the city of Paris down below.   Le Bourget was on the outskirts of town and sure enough there it was.   Paris...France.   The spot where Lindbergh landed.   Now they were dropping bombs on the place.   He wondered what the French were thinking down there as they saw the approach of this huge column of returning Americans. Were they as excited to see them this time as they were to see Lindbergh's little silver monoplane 16 years earlier?   Then, as he thought of it, he realized he really didn't care.

At the appointed time and place, Gleason wheeled the formation onto the bomb run as the other two groups of the wing took interval behind.   The bomb bay doors swing open and Hollis felt himself once again involuntarily stiffen upright in his seat as the sound of their motors filled the air above the engine noise and the rush of the wind into the open chamber caused **Cleopatra's Asp** to slow.   He switched to the Command channel and listened.

He could feel the bombs separate from their shackles and in his ears he could hear Ransahoff's unmistakable voice, "Stick that in your lederhoosen, you fuckin' Nazi cur!"

He and Leo exchanged grins behind their masks and Hollis quickly switched back to the intercom.   "--away," he heard Sully say.   Leo resumed singing into his oxygen mask.

A moment later, Quinn announced that the bomb bay was clear.   The doors came shut and **Cleopatra's Asp** was restored to clean aerodynamic contour.

He looked around for enemy fighters and had been since they passed over the Channel. Some scattered flak.   Perhaps they didn't think France was worth defending either.   His father could understand that.

They rolled off the target and made a big descending turn to the right heading for the Rally Point.   Gleason dragged the turn out a little to allow the 91st, flying high group to catch up and cut the inside of the turn.   In short order, they reestablished the formation and Gleason took the wing due west, south of Paris.

Hollis craned to look back at the target and he could see a large column of smoke rising in the distance.

"Pilot to ball, how'd we do?"

"Ball to pilot.   We clobbered the place."

They made a dogleg turn to the northwest passing over the Normandy region of France before heading due north over the Channel.

The second half of the mission was as uneventful as the first and the Group landed without incident, nobody hurt, all accounted for.   Two easy missions.   Maybe Cahill was right.

No.   The Germans were not fools.   They were just biding their time.   Soon there would be hell to pay.   Maybe not tomorrow or the next day, but plenty soon.

After interrogation, which was short as there was little to say, Hulse took Hollis aside and said, "Sir, I mean not to make any trouble for anybody, but Augie slept on practically the whole mission."

Hollis could scarcely believe what he had just been told.   "He slept?"

"Yes, sir.   I tried to wake him up.   He told me to fuck off."

Hollis felt the blood rush into his temples and thought his brain might explode with rage. With a blindness brought on by his fury he ran out of the briefing room after the departing crew and found Augie walking behind Dodge and Rizzo.   He grabbed him by his fur collar and pulled him several feet around the corner into the alley and said through clenched teeth, "Let me get this straight, you slept during the mission?   Is this true?"

"Well, yes sir."

"God-dammit, your job is to watch out for and protect our plane and your fellow crew members against enemy fighters."

"Seen any today, sir?"

"No."

"Me neither."

"You do your job, you little son of a bitch or I'll have you shot."

"Take it easy, sir.   Nobody got hurt."

"You don't get it do you, you little fuck?   Smart off at me again and I'll shoot you myself.   I'll send you right to fuckin' hillbillie heaven.   You got that?"

For the first time since he met the man, Hollis thought Augie looked genuinely rattled. "Yes sir.   Sure."

Hollis turned and walked away trying to let his seething anger subside.   He noticed as he walked away that Dodge had witnessed the entire exchange.

When Hollis took his shower he noted that Beamis had fixed the coke stove that served to heat the water.   Unfortunately, word of the successful repair had traveled fast and he found a line at the shower room beside the ablutions hut.   Entwhistle who didn't deserve a shower and probably hadn't done anything more strenuous than lift his feet onto his desk stood at the head of the line.   Ransahoff joined the line behind him, but no one seemed to notice.   Hollis thought about striking a conversation with Ransahoff, ask about the lederhosen business, but, recalling what Cassidy had said the night before, chose instead to avoid talking to him.   Perhaps the Academy had infused Ransahoff with an aura of moral righteousness from which he never recovered, making him the martinet Cassidy said he was.   In any case, Hollis decided to keep to himself.   He wasn't sure there was anything Ransahoff might say that Hollis was interested in hearing.

Hollis glanced up at the sky.   Low stratus clouds had rolled in since landing and if the line didn't move along soon they would be forced to wait for their shower in the rain.

Beamis spotted Hollis in the line and said, "By the way, Lieutenant, it's your turn to help me acquire some coke for the stove tonight.   I'll be by around twenty three hundred.   Don't wear rank or squadron insignia."

"What if we're alerted?"

"Have a nice shower."

After showering and lunch, Hollis retired to his room to write more letters.   He now had two missions accounted for, had survived both without a scratch and wrote home about it in code to skirt the censor.

He dispatched the mail, read a comic book Stan had laying around and took a nap.

Hollis was rousted out of bed by Leo and H-y to join them for supper for which he was ravenously hungry.   It mattered not at all what they were serving.   He was famished and would have eaten anything.

After a satisfying if uninspiring dinner, he retired to the Officer's Club to read whatever he could get his hands on.   He had heard they were alerted for the morning, but later in the evening the alert had been canceled so the bar was open.   He was surprised to find few flying personnel and even fewer groundlings in the Club.   With the alert called off, he figured the place would be full.   Perhaps somebody knew something or read some sign he was not privy to or could not discern and decided to stay close to the bed.   It was raining out, however, usually a sure sign, he had been led to believe, of a stand-down for the 'morrow.

He found an old <u>Stars and Stripes</u> and pitched into it.   As he sipped his Coca-Cola, Hollis wondered how he had gotten to this point.   He realized that all of his education had been worthless, serving no purpose, for it had yielded him nothing but a pair of wings, no matter how coveted, and a pair of gold second lieutenant's bars.

He often wondered why pilots needed to be officers and why officers needed to have all or part of a college education.   Maybe, the logic went, it provided enough cumulative knowledge to allow them to get from point A to point B without infarcting something or it assumed acquisition of wisdom which in turn conferred leadership skills transforming the uninitiated into men capable of ordering other men to their deaths.

He couldn't resist using a little of his "high-falutin' book learnin'" as he surveyed the room.   He paused and peered into the faces of the other combat flyers.   Suddenly, he understood the bond these men felt for each other.   The bond that held them together was deeper than politics, deeper than religion.   It was visceral.   Biological.   Tribal.

Stan entered the Club, walked over to the bar and purchased a beer.   He took the drink and sat down at the piano in the corner.   Quite mysteriously, Hollis thought, he stared at the keyboard and did not move.   He appeared not to notice anyone else in the room and certainly made no acknowledgment of Hollis who was seated on a couch not ten feet away.

Early on, somebody had decided to send Stan over here in an effort to infuse some experience into the fledgling Group, Selkirk said.   They were hoping he would assume a leadership role in the squadron, like ops officer or maybe even CO, but he would have none of it.   They didn't know Stan, he said.   Eisenberg refused any gesture which could even remotely be confused with leadership at any level other than first pilot or element leader.   Except for the incident with Selkirk where Stan had saved them from a novice's death, he seemed to want nothing more than fly his missions and be left alone to listen to Cassidy's records and avenge European Jewry.

Selkirk went on to tell him the story of the day the base was officially turned over to the US Army Air Corps from the RAF.   Some ceremony was planned and the squadron officers were to march in a parade.   Entwhistle came around to Pilot's House and told Milo Cody to wake Stan up and tell him to get dressed so he could march in the parade.

'Hey Stan,' he says, 'wake up, you gotta march in the parade.'

Stan says, 'Tell him I ain't marching in no damned parade.'

Cody says, 'He says he ain't marchin' in no parade.'

Entwhistle by now is beside himself and says to Old Milo, as if Stan wasn't right there laying on his bed lightin' a cigarette, 'Tell him it's an order.'

As he told the story, Selkirk started laughing and had trouble completing it. Cody says, 'He says it's an order.'

Stan looks at Entwhistle and says 'Tell him' and then he said directly to Entwhistle as if he just now sees him, 'Look, I'll drop bombs on whomever you want.   I'll fly a plane anywhere you want me to, but I ain't marching in no parade.   I ain't here for the amusement of the locals.   Arrest me if you want.   Make me walk company punishment, do KP, send me home in leg irons, but I ain't marching.'   And that, Selkirk related, was the end of that.   Even so, he said, it was awful nice to be able to look up there and see Stan holding his position for everyone to see.

Hollis heard the piano ring out, resonating clear, sharp tones through the room.   Stan was in a trance-like, fugue state, detached from the world and all his troubles.   He might still be brooding over his imminent demise were it not for the rapid movement of the keys beneath his long, slender fingers.   The music controlled him instead of the other way around.   His eyes were closed and his body rocked back and forth to the tempo of a rhythm only he could hear.   His fingers flicked across the keyboard with the precision and grace of a studied virtuoso.   Hollis did not recognize the music because the piano playing was disjointed.   After a few moments, he recognized Gershwin's "Rhapsody in Blue."   Stan was playing the piano parts while an orchestra reverberating deep within his skull played the rest.   Occasionally, Stan was overcome and he would play parts meant for the clarinet.   The intensity of Stan's concentration was almost overpowering and Hollis felt self-conscious, as if he were eavesdropping on a private moment of grief.

Hollis felt his chest swell with emotion.   He felt an overwhelming love for this man.   This short, scrappy little Jew who swore like a stevedore and flew a plane better than anyone anyone knew.   He wanted to grab his hands to arrest his playing and tell him.   He suddenly realized that Stan didn't want to be loved.   The emotional currency was too high.   Too costly for Hollis and too costly for Stan.   Stan had endured so much to arrive at this piano on this night that he was clearly at a precipice.   It was a private journey.   Not to be tampered with by a well-meaning, if naive rookie.

Stan had it right.   It was better to draw in, isolate one's self from pain, from feeling.   Crawl into a shell and stay there.   Perhaps this then, was the key to psychiatric survival.   The vital mechanism which kept you from becoming a blathering idiot.   You can't sustain a loss if you do not feel.   This was how they all acted.   Even Selkirk.   It was not dislike or contempt for the newcomer.   It was an emotional Maginot Line.

And here was the paradox: the very person who needed compassion and understanding the most was the very person who wanted it least.   Hollis felt sad.   He could not help his friend.

Soon Stan stopped playing and sat quietly for a few moments, not moving.   He bowed his head slightly and stared at the keyboard.   Perhaps Stan knew he was going to die soon and wanted to play this piece one last time.   Perhaps he was about to cry, cry for his dead gunners or Milo or Gruver or dozens of others long since gone.   Hollis's heart ached.   Stan got up. Hollis feigned reading the Stars and Stripes, but he could not take his eyes off the enigmatic

Eisenberg.

There was clearly something very different about Eisenberg.   Not just in degree, but in kind.   He was a warrior.   So was Ransahoff.   They were different from him.   They had something that he didn't possess or for that matter, neither did Selkirk, Cahill, Cassidy, Entwhistle or so many of the others.   Eisenberg and Ransahoff were warriors and he was not. Hollis also realized that a warrior was not defined by the willingness to stare into the barrel of a gun.   They all did that.   Everybody that went could be defined as a warrior if all that was required was merely going.   No, going was not what made them different.   What set them apart was the fact that somewhere deep down inside, in some dark recess they liked it.   On some deep, visceral plane, rooted near the soul was this ugly, primal yet magnificent quality.   It could not be given dimension or density.   It was just there.   Few of them had it.   Fortunately for the democracy, there were enough, for it counted on them for self-preservation while totalitarian regimes exploited them for their unseemly purpose.   Fortunately for both, it was not a trait which could be enhanced by some eugenics program, not something that could be bred to advantage.   You either had it or you didn't.   It was the difference between self-sacrifice and self-preservation, gallantry and cowardice.   Fight or flight.   Hollis felt small and humble in the presence of such men.   Like he did now.

When he was finished, Stan pulled on his jacket and dropped the hat on his head at a rakish angle, alone with his thoughts, music echoing in his skull, taking no notice that Hollis, or anyone else was in the room.   Hollis sipped his Coke in awe.

Stan was sleeping soundly when he heard it.   Engine noises.   The beasts were stirring. He glanced at the luminescent dial of his watch.   Eleven o'clock.   Beamis should be coming soon.   Having been forewarned, he laid on his bed in an old pair of fatigues.

Sure enough, at precisely 2300 he heard he door of Pilot's House open and steps came down the hall.   The door to the room opened and Beamis whispered, "Come on, Lieutenant. This won't take long."

Hollis got up and followed Beamis into the night.   As they walked in the pitch-black darkness into a light rain, Hollis could hear the rumble of trucks off by the field.   He handed Hollis a bucket and said softly, "This doesn't look good."

"What do you mean?" Hollis whispered back.

"I think you guys are going out again tomorrow."

"You heard anything, you know, official?"

"No.   Now be real quiet."   Beamis stepped under some trees Hollis had no inkling of and around some bushes that scraped loudly against his pail.   They passed stealthily around a fence, over a small stream and up a small rise.   Hollis had no earthly idea where he was.   He could be half way to London and he would not know it.   He suddenly had a twinge of fear that if he lost contact with Beamis he might wander around these woods for the rest of the night and not be where he was supposed to be if the wake up came.   That would be AWOL or desertion. They shoot people for that.

Finally, after what seemed an interminable meandering in the misty dark they arrived.

"Now be real quiet," Beamis admonished.   "Fill your bucket and come back here."

"Aren't you coming?"   Hollis suddenly realized Beamis wasn't carrying a bucket.

"No, I can't afford to get caught.   Now just go," and Beamis pushed him into the opening in front of a huge pile of coal.   A whole dump truck's worth.   Hollis drifted quietly to the open edge of the coal bin and quietly started placing coal, piece by piece, into the bucket. He paused for a moment and realized where he was.   He was in back of the hospital.   He was stealing coal from the base hospital, for Christ's sake.   The bucket was half full when the handle started squeaking under the weight.   He heard someone coming, not from the direction where Beamis was squatting under a tree.   These coal bins, and there were several large caches around the base, were each guarded by an armed sentry.   His heart skipped a beat with the distinct possibility that he was about to get shot, mistaken for a saboteur or Nazi infiltrator.   Jesus, what the hell was he doing here?

"Dammit Beamis," he heard in a very loud whisper.   "If you can't be more quiet than this one of these days I'm gonna *have* to shoot you."

Dead silence.

"OK," Beamis whispered from the bushes.   "Thanks, Red."   And then a little louder, "Thanks again for not shootin' me."

Hollis spent a second debating whether to vacate pronto or continue.   He decided to finish filling the bucket with the loose coal. When he finished, he quietly backed away and found Beamis still sitting under the trees.

"Nice work," he said.

"Beamis, you're crazy."

"Them hot showers sure do feel good, don't they?"

Hollis climbed into bed.   It seemed as if their little foray had taken hours, but they had only been gone about thirty minutes.

Hollis sat by the rails one warm, summer evening with two friends.   They sat on the embankment just at the edge of the ballast on the outside curve of the broad bend.   Hollis had never sat so close to the tracks before.   He was doing so now on a dare.   It was not long before a huge black locomotive pulling what seemed like a hundred freight cars thundering around the bend.   It grew closer and closer and more ominous with each second.   None of his friends seemed to notice.   Hollis did not budge for fear of betraying his fright.   Soon the ground started vibrating under the weight of the approaching locomotive.   His dad had warned him about standing too close to the tracks because sometimes wires and boards protruded from the freight cars or the trucks beneath them.   They could cut off an arm or leg if they struck someone.   At least that was what his dad said and he respected his dad's admonitions.   Don't bother the train, he had said, and the train won't bother you.   Now his fear could no longer be contained or ignored.   The thunderous locomotive passed by just inches away and Hollis leaped back involuntarily, his muscles displaying the common sense his mind tried to suppress.   He couldn't hear his friends laughing at him, but he could sense it and felt their contempt in their little game.   Hollis stirred without waking.

Chapter Seventeen   **Schweinfurt**

Tuesday, August 17, 1943

The light entered the room with blinding suddenness and Hollis realized he had completely missed the approach of Beamis's feet on the gravel outside.

"Lieutenant Eisenberg. Lieutenant Hollis.   Breakfast at oh-two-thirty, briefing at oh-three-hundred."

"Where to today, Beamis?" Stan asked from beneath the blankets pulled over his head.

"Six five hundred pounders and bomb bay tanks.   Sir, I do believe you'll be flying to the crotch of the very Devil hisself."   He paused as Stan stirred, "This is number 25 for you, ain't, Lieutenant?"

Stan mumbled something which sounded like 'truck assembly'.

"Well, good luck, sir."

Stan grunted.   Beamis turned to Hollis and said, "Breakfast at oh-two-thirty, briefing at oh-three-hundred.   Dress warm, sir, you're going for a long ride today."

Hollis waved acknowledgment wondering what Beamis could have meant by the Devil's Crotch.   Beamis left for the next room.

Someone, Hollis did not recognize the voice, yelled out, "Beamis, what's the weather like?"

"Clouds scrapin' the roof," Beamis yelled back.

"Doesn't matter," someone added, "we'll just climb up through it anyway."

Hollis turned on the light, slipped on an old pair of pants and slid his bare feet into his flying boots.   He gathered up his shaving gear and headed for the latrine.   As he left, he noticed that Stan had not moved beneath the covers.

"Stan."

"I heard him," came the muffled response.   Hollis walked out the door into the misty pre-dawn wondering again what Beamis had meant by the Devil's Crotch and the import of the 'long ride.'   Such comments did not bode well even if Beamis might actually know where the target was which, of course, he did not.

While he walked down the lane to the latrine, Hollis met Sully and Cahill.   Leo ran up behind Hollis.   "Mornin'."

"Good morning," Hollis replied with something less than enthusiasm.

"Where to today?"

"I don't know, but I bet it ain't good."

Selkirk's voice came to them from behind, "Hollis, me thinks thou dost worry too much.   Probably another milk run.   Some nice fat airdrome in France.   Betcha."

"Maybe."

Leo turned to Hollis, "You know after this is all over I might become a movie star.   I got connections, you know.   What do you think? 'Fragly my darlin', I don't give a dab.'"   It was a poor imitation of Clark Gable and not amusing at that hour of the morning.   If he hadn't been aware of the line in the movie he could not possibly have known what Leo was talking about.

"I think you should stick with math, Leo.   You got no future as a pilot or an actor," Selkirk said making them laugh softly in the dark, their booted feet crunching against the gravel path.

They shaved and washed as best they could in cold water and returned to dress. So much for the stolen coal.

Hollis returned to the room and found Stan sitting on his bed, a cigarette held between his lips, a two inch ash clinging precariously to its end, his eyes squinting against the smoke. He was scratching the bottom of his foot, seemingly unaware that Hollis had returned and uncaring that he had only another ten minutes to get to the mess. Hollis dressed in silence. Hollis turned to Stan and said, "See you at briefing."

Stan squinted up at Hollis, but said nothing.

He walked alone, his hands deep in his pockets. He looked up at the clouds and, even at this early hour, it was light enough to see the low, scudding cloud drifting by rapidly, dizzying by their movement. He felt moisture on his face. A fine mist. He couldn't imagine the weather clearing up sufficiently to allow them to fly. He remembered being told at the CCRC that the Devil hisself could not have picked a worse place to fly bombers from than England. Three months of uninterrupted, decent flying weather and we could bomb the Germans into oblivion and be home by Christmas.

He could smell the aroma as he approached the mess hall. Eggs, real eggs. 'Mission eggs.' Milk runs called for nothing more special than powdered eggs. Another bad sign.

The combat mess was packed. More men were eating breakfast than on the other two missions. The whole Group. Everyone was flying. It was a good breakfast. Besides the eggs which the cooks were willing to prepare as one wished, bacon, pancakes, syrup, grapefruit juice and coffee.

But the eggs and the crowd cast a pall over breakfast causing conversation to be limited and subdued. All except Cahill whose banter was loud and light-hearted. It was annoying. Clearly something hadn't clicked inside Cahill's brain.

Hollis rapidly lost his appetite as he took in the faces around him. He ate half a piece of toast and handed his eggs over to Leo who, oblivious to the somber tone of breakfast, wolfed them down without a moment's hesitation. He glanced over at Cassidy who had barely touched his eggs, either. Selkirk looked spooked, too. Entwhistle was sitting by himself. He was in flying clothes. And he was eating. Perhaps this was a good sign. The Milk Run Major. If he was going, especially if he was to be the Bangmaster, then perhaps Selkirk was right. Just a 'drome in France or maybe the Low Countries. Ransahoff sat with the other officers of his crew. They were animated and as incongruous as the spirited Cahill. How, Hollis wondered, could they be so calm when all around them, Leo and Cahill excepted, were manifesting such uncertainty and naked fear? Maybe that was a good sign. Then he realized that there were crews from all four squadrons eating breakfast. No airfield the Germans owned warranted this much fuss. Five hundred pounders and bomb bay tanks. A long ride. He felt nausea start to well up in the pit of his stomach.

He forced himself to drink the coffee. Two cups, but no more. He did not want to deal with a full, angry bladder at twenty-five thousand feet and it was a cold, cumbersome journey back to the relief tube in the bomb bay.

It was the fresh eggs. They were a bad sign.

The two cups of coffee, half a fried egg and a fragment of toast sat heavily on his stomach, as if he'd managed to swallow a brick. He rose to go to the briefing.

The trucks were lined up in front of the combat mess, their engines filling the air with steamy exhaust.   There was a lot of milling about, the officers gathering in small clusters, gravitating toward the trucks.   Hollis met up with the sated Leo, H-y and Sully, they climbed into the back of a truck along with the officers of several other crews, the dark void under the canvas alight with tell-tale embers of half a dozen cigarettes.   There was little conversation.   Someone in the front said the mission would be scrubbed because of the weather.   How he knew this he did not say.

The gears started grinding and the truck waddled from side to side as it lurched onto the uneven road leading to the headquarters block.   Hollis looked at the truck behind them, rumbling along, peering into the mist with little cat's eye headlights.

Outside the briefing room, the gunners had gathered.   When he saw Hulse, Hollis shook his head.   An MP, his white helmet, web belt and leggings brightly visible in the murk dutifully checked each man's AGO card and allowed him to enter.   He knew most of their faces and they knew his, but he checked each with the same deliberation anyway and no one seemed to mind.

The two pretty, perfectly-coiffed and -lipsticked Red Cross girls handed out coffee and donuts just in case somebody didn't quite get enough to eat or they had the bladder capacity of a fifty-five gallon drum.   These may well be the last American women many of these men would ever see.   The chaplain was there, too, trying to be cheerful, hopeful, but becoming strangely aggravating in the process.

Inside, the Intelligence major paced back and forth on the stage, guarding the dreadful news, which Hollis had no doubt it would be.

The room filled rapidly with a blue haze of cigarette smoke, the pungent aroma of dozens of perspiring bodies and the definite air of premonition.   There were a few nervous laughs.   Hollis looked around and saw Eisenberg who had never appeared at breakfast.   His face was expressionless.   This being his twenty-fifth mission, Hollis expected him to be wringing his hands or pissed off that Entwhistle had not, by all indications, given him a milk run for his last mission.   Perhaps this was his revenge or maybe Entwhistle didn't have the crews to spare to give Stan a pass.

Equally ominous, Barney Rager and Wesley 'Bud' Hightower, the two lead pilots, were present.   They had been conspicuous by their absence for the past two weeks.   Sudbury and Pillacio were suited up, too.   Wherever they were being sent today, the cream of the crop was going to lead them there.

"Betcha we're going to Berlin," Cassidy said loud enough for three full rows of officers to hear.

Begay took the stage, "Alright everybody, pipe down."   He proceeded to call the roll, each pilot accounting for his crew.

Selkirk leaned over to Stan and, perhaps in response to what Cassidy had said, chimed out quite loudly, "Maybe we can get the Chief to do a fucking rain dance and get the deal called off."   This generated a few chuckles.   "Come on, you go with me.   It'll be fun."

Hollis was sweating fiercely.   He couldn't imagine what Stan must be thinking by now.

"Ten-hut!"

The assembled rose to their feet, attention being nothing more than a shuffling to an erect posture.   The steady march of feet up the aisle caused Hollis to turn to see.   Van Patten was in flying clothes.   Fuck, he was the Bangmaster!   This indeed, did not bode well.   Gleason and the four squadron COs trumped along behind him in a perfectly orchestrated show of authority. Bonner and Entwhistle were suited up, too.   They stepped to one side and took their seats at the front while Van Patten stepped up onto the stage.

"Good morning, Gentlemen, at ease and be seated."   He paused while the shuffling and the grousing died down.   Everyone knew of the significance of Van Patten in flight clothes.

"Today we have a mission of some importance.   If we are successful and our bombing results are good, this will be the vindication of precision, daylight bombing.   It is fitting that this is also the anniversary of the first mission of the Eighth Air Force." The cadence of his voice was slow and deliberate as if he were not just trying to convince his audience but himself.

Van Patten turned and with flourish pulled the white sheet from in front of the huge map of northwestern Europe.   The howls and groans erupted before the eastern most terminus of the red yarn could register on Hollis' brain.   Sweet Jesus, the red yarn went deep into Germany. The crotch of the very Devil hisself.

Van Patten waited for the grumbling to die down.   "The target for today is the ball bearing plants at Schweinfurt."   More grumbling.   Strangely, Hollis thought of the gunners on watch outside in the mist.   What must they be thinking as they took their leave?   He glanced over at Stan who sat motionless, his jaw clenched, unblinking, revealing nothing.   What fury raged inside this man who displayed only a blank stare?   Hollis's mind receded into itself, like a turtle into its shell, as he calculated the odds of his seeing another day.   He strained hard to listen, but he was afraid nothing registered as the Colonel continued his briefing.

"Everyone is flying today.   All four squadrons. Today's mission will be a maximum effort.   No spares.   All available planes and crews will be going on this one."   Van Patten halted and, for a split second, cast a forlorn look at Eisenberg.   Hollis wondered if anybody else noticed.

"Nearly half of all anti-friction bearings used by the Germans are milled and manufactured in the Bavarian town of Schweinfurt.   Intelligence estimates indicate that this supply is hand to mouth and that there is little reserve.   Destroying this target will seriously cripple the armaments industries.   Fewer tanks on the Eastern Front, fewer U-boats in the Atlantic and fewer fighters facing us."

"Facing 'you' he means.   That dumb sonuvabitch wouldn't recognize a German fighter if it shot him in the ass," Sully whispered.   "What are they telling us this shit for anyway?   Just tell us where to put the bombs and cut the crap."

"What are you talking about Sully?   You ain't seen one yet either," Selkirk whispered.

The Colonel continued, although Hollis barely heard, lost in the fog of his own burgeoning terror, convinced at last of the terrible mistake he had made.   "This strike will be a coordinated effort by both Bombardment wings.   The Fourth Bombardment Wing, the First Air Task Force, will depart the coast 15 minutes ahead of us and draw enemy reaction.   They will continue on to Regensburg, here," touching the map with his pointer, "to hit the Messerschmitt aircraft assembly plant.   Theirs will be a diversionary effort.   We will follow the same route and catch the fighter force in the process of rearming and refueling, limiting their ability to react. Utilizing the extra range afforded by their Tokyo tanks, the Fourth Wing will continue on to bases in North Africa while our force, consisting of two task forces of two Combat Wings each, separated by 12 minutes will turn here, at Oppenheim," he touched the pool cue to the angle in the yarn, "and continue on to Schweinfurt.   They will fight the battle on the way in, we will fight it on withdrawal.   That is the plan.   It is designed to confuse the enemy, keep him in the dark as to our true intentions and keep our losses down.   If all goes according to plan we will strike the war manufacturing capacity of the Nazi regime a fearsome and perhaps, crippling blow."

"And pigs might fly," Sully added just loud enough for those nearby to hear.

Hollis noted H-y scribbling away on a pad, taking down everything as if his life depended on it.   Leo watched the presentation detached as someone might watch a tennis match on a lazy, summer afternoon.

"Major."   Van Patten turned to Gorton and handed him the pointer.   The major stepped forward.

"Lights."   The room went dim.   The opaque projector fired up and displayed a reconnaissance photo of the target.   "Here is the Main River.   Here is the Kugelfischer A. G. plant which is the primary target.   The Vereignte Kugellager Fabrik, Plants One and, here Number Two, are subsidiary targets as are the Deutsche Star Kugelhalter, here, and the Fischel and Sachs plants, here, both located in the city of Schweinfurt.   Landmarks are the village of Sennfeld east of the River, south of the targets, the River itself and the city to the north.   These buildings of the Kugelfischer plant, here, are the intended aiming points for the Group.   These buildings right here.   There is a bend in the Main River here and a large island in the river, here. These rail lines run through the target area, here.   For reference, there is a railway station here, south of town and two large army barracks, the Adolph Hitler Kaserne and the Hindenburg Kaserne, located on the western edge of the city, to the north.   The Initial Point is this village here.   The run to the target will be nearly due east to west to take advantage of the position of the sun at time over target and last five minutes.   Bombing altitude for the group will be 24,500 feet.   Time over target should be exactly ten-twelve hours and our bombs should strike Schweinfurt nearly simultaneously with the bomb strike at Regensburg.

"The secondary target is the engineering works at Frankfurt.   Tertiary target is the marshaling yards at Aachen and the target of last resort is this instrument factory in Bonn.

"I cannot stress the importance of this target more.   It is crucial that these targets be destroyed.   These are ripe targets, gentlemen, and the ball bearing industry forms a chokepoint for industrial activities directly related to the war effort.   The Germans are particularly lavish in their use of bearings in their designs of everything from aircraft engines to howitzers.   *Lavish. What the hell is he talking about?*   It might take six months or a year to redesign their armaments to require fewer bearings and we believe the savings thus realized might not be that great.   The pipelines are already short.   We destroy these targets today and we shorten the war. It's that simple.

"Lights.   Fighter opposition should be heavy.   There are four *Jagdgeschweders*, JG-1, -2, and -3 and JG-26, within easy flying distance all along the route of penetration and withdrawal.   The potential total number of enemy fighter aircraft and bomber destroyers is approximately three hundred."   This caused an audible collective gasp.   "But most of the opposition is expected in the coastal fighter belt and your planned route should take you through this directly by the shortest distance possible.   The toughest fighter reaction should be between the coast and a point about halfway to the target.   Hopefully, the maximum danger for fighter interception will be covered, at least in part, by your fighter escort.   The Fourth Fighter Group will rendezvous with you, the two combat wings of Second Air Task Force, at Antwerp and escort you as far as Eupen, the limits of their range.   The Seventy-eighth Fighter Group will escort the two combat wings of the Third Task force.   We expect most of the fighter opposition to be expended against the Fourth Wing and, for that reason, they have been assigned two full groups of fighter escort, so by the time you follow on they should be rearming and refueling. Withdrawal is when you should receive the strongest fighter reaction and we anticipate your escort to be refueled and replenished to rendezvous with you at Eupen on the way out.   We expect night fighters to be pressed into day work today.

"To distract some of the fighter reaction numerous diversions are planned with Marauders and RAF Mitchells and Typhoons going after airfields in France and Holland and marshaling yards in Calais and Dunkirk.   You will also receive penetration and withdrawal support by eight squadrons of Spitfires so be alert to them.

"There will be at least eleven batteries of heavy flak in and around the target consisting of fifty-six flak cannon within the target area, but they cannot all be brought to bear at the same time and flak opposition in the target area should be light.   The route in and out should avoid most flak concentrations.   Major."   He turned to Begay who took the stage.   Hollis figured Selkirk was not alone in his hope that Begay would launch into a ritual dance invoking the sacred Navajo gods of inclement weather.

"We will be low group of the lead wing.   The 533rd will lead, 535th will be low squadron, the 532nd high.   Colonel Van Patten will be the Bangmaster flying with Captain Rager.   Major Bonner will be deputy with Captain Hightower.   The 91st will lead.   The 534th Squadron will join the 401st of the 91st and the 511th of the 351st to form a composite high group in the lead wing."

"Jesus," Selkirk said in a whisper, "low squadron of the low group of the lead wing. Notify the next of kin."

"Boy, they'll be floggin' the old fans today," H-y added.

"Stations will be at 0540, engine start at 0550 and taxi at 0605.   Takeoff will be at 0620. And takeoff should be clear.   Climb out as usual for clear conditions and assemble over our field.   If weather should not cooperate, assembly will be over the buncher at ten thousand feet. The 91st with their squadron for the composite group will join us here, at Brandon. The 511th Squadron should join us at Bury St. Edmunds to complete the high group we will proceed to Splasher Seven for task force rendezvous with the composite combat wing.   We will proceed to Chelmsford and thence to Orfordness reaching combat altitude and speed by the time we reach the Dutch coast.   The third task force will depart Clacton-on-Sea twelve minutes later. Interval between combat wings will be five minutes.   The Order of Battle is here," he stepped over to the large chalkboard with the aircraft dispositions.   Each plane number had a name beneath it.   Hollis could see that he was in the high squadron, position number five in the second element behind Ransahoff.   Cahill would be across from him in number six.   They would be in **Cleopatra's Asp**.   There was a 'C' beside his name.   They would be carrying a strike camera.   Beside that was a smaller chalkboard with the disposition of the fourth squadron, the 534th.

"We will depart the coast at Orfordness and proceed to Schouwen.   Zero hour will be 0845.   Thence to Eupen then to the IP.   The target, rally here," he pointed to the map, "to Eupen to landfall at Felixstowe.

"Navigators and bombardiers will have their separate briefings at the end of the briefing.

Also watch for returning RAF Stirlings returning from a mission.   Pilots should keep your mixture at automatic lean, cut down on your RPM and lower your manifold pressure in order to conserve fuel.   Weather."

The weather officer got up, but before he said anything Begay said, "And I don't want to here anymore of this rain dance bullshit either."   This elicited some nervous laughter.

The weather officer proceeded to tell them that he was sure the warm front would pass and the weather would clear by takeoff and the target and the route in and out should be CAVU. The concern was on return which might pose problems with some low clouds and scattered showers.   He then placed a drawing full of clouds and thermopiles and arrows with prevailing winds and the like on the projector.

When the lights went on Hollis was afraid he might not have heard everything having been lost in his private fog of war.   He felt a sudden surge of panic with the realization that he might have missed some particle of information, some sliver of data with which he might arm himself and prevent disaster.   He turned to Leo, "You gettin' all this?"

Leo looked back at him blankly and said, "Sure.   I got it."

The Intelligence major got up again and told them the usual spiel about not discussing the target with anyone whose job did not require that knowledge and anyone not having been briefed on escape and evasion procedures should come to the front at the end of the briefing, and so on and so forth.

Finally, Van Patten returned to the podium.   "Gentlemen, until now we've been pecking at the edges, infield hits.   Today we're going for the long ball, the home run.   This is it, the linchpin.   We knock out these ball bearing plants and we should deal a critical blow to the war-making capacity of the enemy and shorten the war. It is uniquely German for them to put all their bearing production in one place. Stupid, actually. But very convenient for us.   The importance of these targets is further emphasized by the fact that the RAF is planning a follow on raid tonight, guided by the fires we start today."

Hollis was suddenly aware of what a grave violation of secrecy Van Patten had just committed, imagining an airman, face bloodied by the Gestapo, saying, "If you gimme a cigarette, I'll tell you a little surprise."

"Keep it in tight and keep the lead in their eyes.   Let's do it right the first time so we won't have to do it again.   Any questions?"

Someone in the back yelled, "Is this trip necessary?"

Van Patten's stony face cracked a tiny smile, but it was enough.   The room filled with nervous laughter.

"Anything else?"   A pause.   "Good luck and good bombing.   Protestants to the front, Catholics to the rear.   Let's break some German balls out there today.   Dismissed."

"Ten-hut!"

Van Patten bounded down off the stage and strode briskly down the aisle.   The entourage fell in behind him, trying to keep up.

The cursing started immediately.   No one could truly relieve themselves of the shock. But no one should have been surprised. They all knew before long they would be going deep. Everyone expected it to be Berlin first.   There would be some symbolism to that.   Not this cockamamie plan to divide the forces and trick the enemy *ad nauseum*, striking a target that he suspected the Germans would defend with every pilot and plane and flak cannon at their disposal.

"Low group of the lead wing," Selkirk said. "The Fourth should have 'em really worked up. They should be good and mad by the time we get there."

Cassidy turned to them as he passed and said, "Just be glad you aren't flying in that composite group with a bunch of strangers."

Stan walked by without comment chewing an enormous wad of gum no doubt to be placed on the nose of a bomb to fall errantly into the residential area which encircled the Kugelfischer plant, punishing the Germans foolish enough to live near such an important place. It was his last mission. He might not get the chance to kill Germans again anytime soon.

Ransahoff grabbed Cahill and Hollis by their collars as they made their way toward the exit. "I want you two to stay in real close today, you hear. You watch me. You do what I do and you'll be alright. Keep your formation as you near the coast on the way out, they tend to relax and loosen up and the bastards will jump you in a flash if they see you loosen up."

Hollis and Cahill exchanged glances. Cahill looked shook, his exuberance from earlier vanished. Hollis wondered if his face bore the same look of disbelief and fear. He suspected Ransahoff had seen this expression and thought some fatherly advice was in order. There was none of the ringing authority in Ransahoff's voice. Not like before. Spoken not as an admonition but a plea. This time Ransahoff clearly meant it. This was a different Ransahoff and it only fueled his mounting anxiety. Cahill turned and walked to the front of the room. Hollis walked past the cluster of men taking communion.

The equipment room was bedlam, packed with bodies struggling for space, filled with smoke, the stagnant air was nearly choking.

Hollis grabbed his gear and carried it in a bag to the outside. He looked up. If they really expected the weather to clear it had better start soon. The dawn had arrived and the murk was just easier to see.

They rode the truck to the dispersal in silence. Hollis tucked Jessie's scarf into his jacket to ward off the chill he felt.

When the truck pulled up to **Cleopatra's Asp** they dropped their equipment over the tail gate and dumped themselves out to the perimeter track. Cahill gave him a slight wave and said, "See ya later."

H-y responded over his shoulder as he leapt to the pavement, "Yeah, don't wait up."

The gunners walked over to greet them. Dodge looked at Hollis, his face etched with concern.

"Rough one today, Noah."

"I heard. The guns are in and she's ready, Lieutenant."

"OK." Moe walked over as the rest of the ground crew pulled the big blades of number four through one more time.

"She's all set, Lieutenant." He handed Hollis the clipboard with the Form 1A on it and he allowed his eyes, glazed over, to run over the paper without really seeing any of it. Fear would not allow him to concentrate, permit his eyes to focus on the page. If the words and numbers registered in his subconscious, serving as a safety net for the information, he did not know. He was totally in Moe's and Dodge's hands. If he made some oversight and they died today as a direct result he would be guilty of complicity in the murder of nine people who had trusted him without question. He signed it.

"Good, Moe.   Gather 'round everybody."   It was time again to be the aircraft commander when all he really wanted to do was run and hide.   It was obvious that the gunners had heard.   Not the particulars, of course, but they knew.

"We got ourselves a big one today.   The place is named Schweinfurt and they make ball bearings there.   The Colonel says if we do it and do it right we may be home by Christmas." He had a tell.   They could read his face just like Ransahoff.   "We're in the high squadron of the low group of the lead wing.   We should have plenty of planes around us to keep us company and keep us covered.   Entwhistle is in the squadron lead flying with Cassidy.   Eisenberg is on his left and Selkirk on his right.   We're second element with Ransahoff and Cahill.   I want everybody on their toes today."   He looked at Augie when he said it.   I want the interphone kept clear of any chatter, don't yell and I don't want to hear about any flak.   Telling me about it won't do us any good.   Remember?   I don't want to see one round of ammunition wasted. Not one round.   We're in for a long fight, we've got to make the ammo last.   Don't waste it. Fire only when they're within range and only when they're attacking our plane.   Questions?"

Leo handed out the escape kits which each tucked into a pant leg pocket.

Rizzo came up to Hollis and asked in a low voice, "Is it really gonna be that bad, sir?"

Flushed with a sufficient amount of sympathy to permit lying, Hollis said, "No, we should be alright.   You just stay on your toes and keep your eyes peeled."

"Yes sir."

Hollis climbed into **Cleopatra's Asp** and placed his gear behind his seat where it would be when he needed it.

He looked at his watch.   Five-fifteen.   He had enough time for a cigarette before stations.   He walked across the perimeter track and sat down in the damp grass.   He sucked the tobacco smoke deeply into his lungs trying to steel himself against the distinct probability that he would not live through the afternoon.   He wondered if prayer might help.   The fog had failed to lift.   Somebody's prayers were being answered.

He heard the approach of an engine.   In the mist, he could see a jeep stop briefly at Ransahoff's hardstand and then moved on to **Cleopatra's Asp**.   Hollis flicked the cigarette into the grass and strode over to see what was going on.   It was a Lieutenant from Operations announcing that stations had been moved back an hour.

Another hour's tortured reprieve.   Hollis followed the progress of the jeep as it stopped next at Cahill's hardstand and then disappear into the gently swirling mist.   He crushed an empty pack in his fist as he lit what seemed his thousandth cigarette of the day.   All of the cigarettes were making his already parched throat raw, painful.   With this news the crew seemed to grow less anxious as they took this as a sign the mission was going to be scrubbed. What did it matter? If not today the target would still be there tomorrow or the next day.   They stretched out under the wing and dozed or chatted idly.   Hollis watched as Buster, Moe's ragged little mongrel, walked over and sniffed at Augie.   Augie kicked the dog with his booted-foot when he thought nobody was looking.

Hollis was disturbed with himself that he had sat through an entire briefing and could remember almost none of it.   The gunner's didn't need to hear it, they had a simple job: shoot at the enemy planes and don't shoot at ours.   Smith and Sully, Dopey and Grumpy according to Leo, sat up front along for the ride, reacting to cues delivered by someone else.   His was the job with all the responsibility.   He had a mission and nine other lives to take care of.   There would be a special place in hell for him if he caused them to die today as a result of some snippet he missed because he was transfixed by the horrible implications of the path of a piece of red yarn. He was starting to dwell on it.

"Leo, come here."

Leo raised his head and turned to look at him much as Buster might.

"Yeah?" he said as he sat down on the grass beside him.

"Tell me everything you heard at briefing."

"What's the matter weren't you paying attention?"

"Of course I was, I wanna know that you were."

"We're going to this place called Schweinfurt. We hit it and the Colonel says we can expect the Nazi surrender by the time we land."

"OK, and?"

Leo proceeded to repeat the entire briefing. When he was finished Hollis was convinced Leo had recited it essentially *verbatim*. Leo got up, his displeasure apparent, and said, "Next time pay attention."

After a while, another jeep came around stopping at each hardstand just like the first one. It pulled under the nose of **Cleopatra's Asp**. H-y muttered, "Sky pilot making the rounds."

The group's chaplain called the crew together and said a short prayer. Everyone bowed their heads out of respect. Hollis noted the unique perversity that found a humble servant of God ministering to the spiritual needs of men about to journey to the brink of eternity under the noses of bombers, instruments of death, emblazoned and regaled with portraits of naked women of lewd intent and thinly veiled salacious comment and double *entendre*.

Dodge whispered into Hollis's ear, "We pray for deliverance, we pray for salvation, we pray for justice, we pray that someone is listening to our prayers."

Hollis looked at Dodge, "Aren't you ever afraid that God might not see you when it really counts or that God might just be too busy to notice?"

"Nope. Never."

He was about to climb into a plane and kill people and likely be killed in the process. It seemed only natural to beseech the Lord for deliverance, as hypocritical and selfish as that seemed. He hoped God might overlook his hypocrisy. They all did, he suspected.

"If God will deliver me from this today I promise to conduct myself a true and generous life," Hollis whispered knowing Dodge could hear him.

"God is not in the business of making bargains, Lieutenant," he whispered back.

After the jeep carrying the chaplain drove on another came around and told them stations was pushed back once again. The crew interpreted this to mean that they were going to go sooner or later and they became edgy almost before the second jeep had left the hardstand.

He sat back on the grass across the perimeter strip and wondered what Jessie was doing at that moment. Asleep with her head on that satin pillow case probably. It was still the middle of the night in Pennsylvania. What was she dreaming? Did he stand any chance at all of surviving the day? He had no business being an aircraft commander if he couldn't think straight. He was a menace to his plane, his crew and his mission. *What was she dreaming? What could the Air Corps have been thinking to put me in this position? I hope they scrub this thing. Where's the Chief? If they scrub it it will just mean they'll put it on for tomorrow. Or the day after. Or the day after that. Jesus, I miss her. Does she miss me? Do I pass through her mind at least once a day?   What was she dreaming?*

His attention was again diverted by the sound of an approaching vehicle.   A truck pulled up to Ransahoff's plane and stopped.   He was ambivalent about his hope that the crew would climb on and be done for the day.   Instead, they were unloading something.   Ransahoff's crew gathered for a few minutes and then the truck pulled away and headed up the appendage of the perimeter track that contained the hardstands of the rest of the squadron aircraft.   Shortly thereafter, three more trucks appeared and rumbled past without stopping.   Finally, the truck emerged from the perimeter extension and pulled up to **Cleopatra's Asp**.   Hollis went to investigate.

In the back of the truck stood the Negro Ordinance sergeant and a white lieutenant. "Call your crew over, Sir.   We've got some hot tea and sandwiches and some extra fifty caliber."

"Any word on scrubbing?"

"No," the lieutenant said as he handed Hollis a mug of steaming black tea, "rumor has it we're delayed again.   But it's still on, far as I know."

The gunners took the ammunition and, with the help of Moe and Tommy, loaded the cases into the waist of **Cleopatra's Asp** and returned for their tea.   Moe and Tommy declined the tea.   Hollis knew the ground crews always resented aircrew who were hanging around the flight line mooching in when their coffee wagon made its rounds.   This time the tea and sandwiches were meant for the flyers and they respected that.   Even so, Moe looked tired and could've used the tea.

"No one is supposed to know about the extra ammo.   It's against regulation to carry more than the issued amount.   We got to thinking a little more for the good of the order wasn't gonna hurt nothin'."   Hollis noticed that he was still wearing the cast on his leg.

Dodge said, "I won't tell if you won't."

Hollis sipped the tea.   It was strong, hot and delicious soothing his smoke-raw throat and fear-dried mouth.   He held the mug up to the Negro sergeant and thanked him on both accounts.   "Hey Noah, make sure they stow that extra ammo forward."

Hollis, the lingering warmth and taste of the tea on his palate, sat down with his crew and watched as still another jeep made the rounds.   The same lieutenant from Ops pulled up to the hardstand and shouted, "Stations in one hour!   And this time I mean it!"

Hollis waved perfunctorily.   The wait was allowing them to sense their lives ticking away minute by minute.

A few moments later, a captain from Group ops pulled up in yet another Jeep and told the four officers about a change in the run to the target.   Since they would be taking off so late the axis of approach would be one hundred and eighty degrees from the original bomb run.   The approach to Schweinfurt would be from west to east to take advantage of the position of the sun over the target, since the attack would occur in the afternoon instead of mid-morning as planned. The new IP was the small town of Gemunden am Main situated in a wide loop in the Main River at the junction of four roads.   He drew a path with his index finger on a map.

Now they would not have to fly beyond Schweinfurt to the east before beginning the bomb run westward.   Instead, they would approach the target directly, but over featureless terrain rather than over the built up areas with easily identifiable landmarks.   It also meant a downwind bomb run.   It would save seventeen minutes flying time.   He showed them where the Rally Point would be, wished them luck and roared off into the fog, wheels spinning against the wet pavement.

After a time, Hollis noticed a gathering of men in front of **The Flying Dutchman**. He could make out Selkirk and Stan, again wearing his ragged Yankee's cap, and Cassidy. They talked in animated gestures and then broke up their little meeting. Selkirk trotted down the perimeter strip toward him, clomping along in his boots and flying gear. Great, they were scrubbed. He would live to see another day. He noted the half-smile on Selkirk's face and rose to meet him half way.

"Entwhistle ain't going."

"Entwhistle not going?"

"Yeah, he's out. Quit."

"You must be joking."

"Nope, delay musta let him stew for a little too long. Ransahoff's reshuffled the deck. He's lead. Stan is running the second element."

"He just up and quit?"

"Yeah," he said as he trotted back down the perimeter strip. He yelled back over his shoulder, "They've also changed the bomb run. It's now west to east. Just hang on they'll get you through it."

"Yeah, we heard."

Leo walked over. "What gives?"

"Entwhistle quit. He's not going. Ransahoff is taking over and Stan is leading our element."

Leo grinned, "So Entwhistle's taken a powder. How about that. What'd'ya think they'll do to him?"

"Good question. Dereliction of duty, maybe. Since the trip's already on and going, I guess it'll be desertion in the face of the enemy."

"Jesus, so what do you think will happen?"

"Hopefully, they'll shoot him." Hollis realized it was a terrible thing to have said. Entwhistle, after all, had seen his share of combat, felt the cold metal of the barrel against his temple.

Nobody liked Entwhistle. He was a martinet and, people suspected, a coward. But Hollis still could not suppress a pang of sympathy for the man. The disgrace he must be feeling. The dishonor. What must have been going through his mind as he sat around waiting? Hollis figured he knew. It seemed like such a simple choice. You were supposed to choose death before dishonor. They were soldiers. For Entwhistle it came down to self-preservation. Who was he to judge? His entire combat experience consisted of a few scattered puffs of flak, deadly to a radius of fifty feet.

From his seat in the grass he could look across the way and see Ransahoff and his crew. He watched them. Ransahoff was holding court over his crew. They were seated on the ground in a small circle beside the tail, all faces looking up at him. Ransahoff pointed down at one of them, then another. He appeared to be haranguing them. Two of the crew rolled onto the grass obviously laughing. Two more jumped up and one started chasing the other around the group. Their unzipped leather jackets and pants flapped around giving them the appearance of flayed bears playing tag. Ransahoff bent down and slapped one of them on top of the head and they all seemed to laugh again.   So cool.   So relaxed.   Moments away from a date with doom and they were laughing and frolicking like kids duck-duck-goose.   A good bomber crew was more than the sum of its parts.   Hollis turned and looked at his crew in little unconnected clusters of two and three.   Their faces were somber, frightened, transfixed by their fear like butterflies on a corkboard.   Hollis envied Ransahoff yet again.   His coolness, his *elan*. Maybe he was witnessing the difference between a professional and an amateur.   Their crews already understood the difference.

Entwhistle was chickenshit, but not Ransahoff.   On the surface they seemed cut from the same cloth.   Just below, however, where insight applied, there were serious motives to what Ransahoff did no matter how seemingly purposeless, even ridiculous.   The red paint. Screaming into the command channel to keep their formation tight.   Entwhistle couldn't help himself.   Cassidy was wrong about Ransahoff.   It became apparent to him now.   Ransahoff was interested in seeing to it that everyone survived the war.

He lit another cigarette.   *They need to get this God-damned show on the road,* he thought. *If I sit here and stew much longer* I *might quit.*

His mind started to wander again.   *How did I ever manage to get myself into this fix? Like Stan and Oliver, this is another fine mess you've gotten us into.*   In fact, there was a bomber on the base named **Another Fine Mess**.   Today, he found himself sitting in a grassy field, a former cow pasture, in a strange, foreign place, waiting to engage in an activity he didn't really like or possess a desire to do, with people he didn't really know.   And it could very well cost him his life.   Most likely this afternoon.

He glanced at his watch and wondered how Stan was holding up.   The Fourth Wing needed to get going if they wanted to make Africa before dark.   Surely they were going to call this off.   If only Entwhistle could have held out a little longer he might not have lost his nerve.

There were loud voices and commotion from under the wing.   Quinn and Augie were on their feet and Dodge was between them.   Hollis leapt to his feet and went quickly to see what was going on, extremely agitated by the disruption.   They had been growing restless, talking louder and louder, and becoming increasingly irritating.

Augie saw Hollis's approach and shouted, "Hey Lieutenant, Little Quinn here ain't ever been laid.   Jesus Christ, he could die today and he ain't ever been laid!   We gotta get this boy fucked.   I even caught him jerkin' off in the lay-trine yest--"

Beyond edgy, Hollis had had enough.   Bad enough they carried on like this, humiliating Quinn was too much. Infuriated, Hollis took several large steps up to Augie, grabbed the collar of his shearling jacket and said through clenched teeth, "Augie, shut the fuck up, you stupid little hillbilly.   You better pay attention to what is about to happen to you. Quit picking on people or I'll knock your fucking block off. "

Reese, the blood drained from his face muttered "Yes Sir, never again."

A pall came over the crew.   He could see Moe and Tommy shaking their heads.   They had no idea.   The joshing stopped.   Quinn seemed as much humiliated by the excess of Hollis's response as by the original insult.   Hollis became embarrassed by his sudden loss of control. This was a Hollis no one had seen before.   Perhaps they were thinking their pilot could not be trusted to take care of them.   Dodge showed no emotion.   Perhaps another mutiny was in the offing.

Silently, everyone crushed out their cigarettes and finished dressing; the ground crew went about their business leaning their shoulders into the propellers pulling the engines through yet again.

Composed, as stations drew near without the approach of another jeep, Hollis said, "Let's get going, everybody.   Stations in ten minutes."   Everybody rose to their feet in silence and walked into the grass behind the Fortress and urinated.   Hollis wanted one more cigarette so he walked across the perimeter strip to his spot.   He looked down the strip for any sign of approaching deliverance.   The fog had thinned somewhat, but he could not see much beyond **The Flying Dutchman**, not more than a hundred yards away.   His stomach started to spasm in revolt.   He turned his back to his crew and vomited violently.   He wretched several times then wiped his chin.   He looked up and noticed Ransahoff staring at him as Dutch relieved himself in the weeds at the edge of his hardstand.

Hollis walked back to the plane and finished dressing.   He looked at the tires.   The sidewalls bulged under the weight of the bombs, gas, extra ammo and men.   He hoped they wouldn't pop as they thumped their way down the runway.   A blow out would be fatal.

He hauled himself up into the nose.   Settling into their seats, Leo turned to Hollis and said, "You know Jack, they're just kids."

Hollis adjusted his seat and said, "This is not high school football, Leo.   I don't want to talk to you about this again.   They need to understand that each breakfast could be their last. They could be dead before their food's digested.   This is not a children's war."

"They know that."

"I'm not sure they do, Leo.   They need to understand."

"No they don't, Jack.   It's not our place to sort things out for them."

"Leo, they act like it's a big game.   High adventure.   And it's not.   For Christ's sake, Augie slept over the target on our last mission."

"There's nothing you or I can do about it.   They look up to you, Jack.   Puking, sitting alone in the grass and all.   They trust you with their lives.   We've been together for months now and, given the choice, there's not one of them who would fly with anybody else.   As long as you are okay, they'll be okay."

Hollis fell silent for a moment uncertain if this vote of confidence was genuine.   "Let's start the check list."

Dodge settled behind them and pretended not to notice the conversation.

They strapped on their throat mikes, resting them just so against their Adam's Apples, plugging them in and adjusted the headphones over their ears until the rubber cups sat just right.

Each pressed his interphone button in turn and said 'OK' assuring the interphone worked. Leo picked up the checklist but did not read it continuing the aggravating habit of reciting it from memory.

"Emergency Ignition."

"On."

"Master battery switches."

Hollis checked each battery switch. "On."

"Hydraulic pump."

"On."   Hollis turned on the hydraulic pump which started up with a whine.

"Landing gear..."   Leo answered his own item by leaning forward and checking the landing gear toggle, "Neutral."   He did the same with the flaps.   He then set the parking brake and said so as he did.

Hollis moved the control column, wheel and rudder pedals to the limits of their motion. He then checked his watch.   It was close.

Leo continued, "Cabin heat."

"Off."

"Hydraulic pressure...okay.   Cowl flaps...open and locked.   Turbos."

"Off."

"Fuel transfer valves and pump switches."

Dodge said, "Off."

"Fire extinguisher...set for number one.   Fuel shut off valves."

"Open."

"Intercoolers...cold."

Hollis cracked the throttles.

"Carburetor air filters...on.   Mixture...engine off.   RPM...high.   Primer...off. Magneto."

Hollis reached over turning the magneto switch to number one engine.   "Both."

They stopped and the cockpit fell silent except for the whine of the hydraulic pump. This was as far as they could go.   All eyes everywhere focused in the direction of the control tower although no one could actually see it through the fog, they all knew where it was.   Hollis checked his watch again.   Any second.   He realized to his dismay that he hadn't thrown up enough.   Some hot bilious slurry had found its way back into his stomach and layered there waiting to be liberated.

Two incandescent green points of light arced upward, each surrounded by a pale green halo of mist.   Hollis glanced at his watch again.   It was after eleven.   They had waited over four hours.

Hollis stared at the flares as they disappeared back into the fog.   He thought of Jessie. He wanted so much to see her again.   Maybe God might be willing to strike a bargain even if He was disinclined to do so.   Anyone so covetous of another must be worthy of some divine consideration.   He felt a tap on his arm.

"Shall we start the engines now?" Leo asked gently.

Hollis brought his face to the open window and shouted, "Clear!"   He noticed Cahill already had an engine running.

Slowly, methodically, he and Leo started each engine.

Soon all four power plants were up and running smoothly.   When they were warmed up, Hollis and Leo checked the magnetos and exercised the turbos. As usual, all was in perfect order. They waited.

Hollis glanced over at Cahill and could barely make out the figures in the cockpit though the fog.   He wondered about Cahill, could he be this scared?   Hollis recalled how pale Cahill had appeared after briefing and that it had been Cahill who had prompted Ransahoff's words of encouragement.   But Ransahoff had felt the need to talk to him, too.   Hollis felt another tap on his arm.   Leo pointed to the green flares and shook his head.

Hollis stuck his fists out through the open window and, thumbs extended, jerked them apart.   Moe bent down and made a safe at the plate gesture then gave Hollis a 'thumbs up.' The chocks had been pulled.   Automatically, Leo released the parking brake and Hollis eased the bomber forward several feet and tested the brakes.   All eyes turned to the right.   Soon they appeared out of the mist and passed by, one by one as if on parade, Ransahoff's **The Flying Dutchman**.   Selkirk's **Vermont Revenge**, Cassidy's unnamed Fortress and Stan in **Ain't Missbeahavin'**.   They had to go ahead of Cahill so Hollis set and locked the inboards and, hands on the throttle, jockeyed the outboards.   With squealing brakes, he turned **Cleopatra's Asp** onto the perimeter strip falling in behind Stan.   He could make out Cahill's **Izavailable II** leaving its hardstand.   The great trundling march had begun.   They had to taxi all the way around the perimeter strip to the opposite end of the field.

They fell in behind the 533rd on their way to the end of runway 28.   The 534th Squadron would be up first, Hollis remembered. They had the furthest to climb to rendezvous with other squadrons to make up the high composite box.

As they approached the end of the taxiway, passing other planes waiting patiently on their hardstands, through the mist and fog Hollis could see the lead plane of the 533rd start its takeoff roll.   He could not hear the roar of its pounding engines over the noise of his own.   The sight of all of this: twenty-four heavily loaded B-17s, ninety-six roaring engines spinning ninety-six propellers, carrying two hundred and forty brave men into God knows what.   Two hundred and thirty-nine brave men.   It was the stuff of goose bumps and butterflies.   Ready to do battle with the epitome of evil.   Christ, it was stirring.   To be a part of such a noble endeavor blunted his terror.   Courage of the collective.   Each man telling himself that if two hundred thirty-nine other men could face such uncertainty without leaping from his airplane and running away who am I to feel I was not a part of it?   Only the most quivering coward could not be moved. Perhaps Entwhistle.

Finally, the 534th was off.   The lead squadron followed suit.   One by one, each plane roared away, disappearing into the mist, the visibility not more than a few hundred yards.

Hollis could barely make out Ransahoff's plane as he turned onto the runway, but he could see it start its takeoff roll.   They each stepped up to the threshold of runway 28. **Cleopatra's Asp** was rocked by the blast of Stan's engines as he got the light and started off.

Hollis, by differential braking and throttling, turned **Cleopatra's Asp** onto the runway, lining up the centerline.   He quickly ran through the remaining items on the preflight checklist. Setting the throttles at fifteen hundred rpm, he checked the gauges one last time.   He adjusted the gyro compass, turned on the generators and trim tabs to zero.   Leo locked the tailwheel and Hollis waited for the Aldis light to blink at him.   Stan disappeared into the mist.

"Leo, you keep me on the runway."   Hollis was going to make an instrument take off. It would be up to Leo to keep them running straight down the runway while Hollis watched the airspeed and flight instruments and Dodge watched the engines.

Hollis quickly let his eyes run across the engine gauges.   All looked in order.   His final act was to slide the window closed.

God, please don't let me fuck up.

The minute's wait seemed to take an eternity.   Then the Aldis lamp winked at him.

Hollis pushed down hard on the brakes, his calves and thighs trembling.   The tension in his legs transmitting the throbbing of the Cyclone engines up into his torso.   He walked the throttles forward and the four engines roared and shook the bomber as if it might come apart in a final suicidal convulsion.   He watched the rpm and manifold pressure rise knowing he would not release the brakes and unleash the plane until it felt right.   He held her just a little longer than he really needed before he let his legs release the pressure on the brakes. The bomber seemed to leap forward, pushing him abruptly into his seat with the sudden burst of acceleration. He kept his left hand gently on the wheel, light pressure on the rudder pedals. Leo would be flying the takeoff and he did not want to resist any directional corrections his copilot might make.

Leo, leaning forward, his face pressed against the side glass to watch the edge of the runway, held his left hand on the throttle and his right hand on the wheel.

Hollis watched the airspeed indicator start to climb. *Forty...fifty*...he could feel the rudder pedals move slightly under his feet as Leo gently straightened them out...*sixty*...the over-loaded bomber thumped heavily on its fat, bulging tires against the unevenness of the runway...if they were going to blow out the tires it would happen now...the distended sidewalls giving way in bloated defeat...*seventy*...he dared not look out the window and divert his attention away from the flight instruments, though he wanted desperately and instinctively to do so, the moment or two it might take to readjust his vision back to the instruments from outside could, and occasionally did, prove fatal during an instrument take off...*ninety*...*Christ, we should be lifting soon*...the bomber gave no indication of wanting to fly...*one hundred*..."Come on, you sonuvabitch," he heard himself say aloud...he felt the relentless thumping ease as the first indication of lift tugged at the wings...

"Red lights!" Leo yelled into the interphone. It wouldn't be long now...they would either lift off the runway or all die in an instant--a spectacular fiery detonation of gasoline, bombs, aluminum and bodies.

Hollis placed his hand onto Leo's and pushed the throttles harder against the stops, knowing they could go no further, in a desperate effort to squeeze out even one last, untapped rpm from the engines. He hoped Dodge had told them to stow the extra ammo forward close to the bomber's center of gravity. Maybe they hadn't and that's why she wouldn't fly. He should have checked himself. Shit.

It was a matter of physics. A bet. Made, after all, by someone, not him, that the plane hefting this load with these engines and this wing surface area, under these conditions of air temperature and humidity, wind and barometric pressure would fly. The slightest miscalculation, engine misfire or runaway turbo and...it would be over in the time it would take the calamity to register in the brain.

One hundred and five...

Hollis felt the plane exert some gentle forward pressure on the control column. He let it go. The tail rose. What they gained in speed by the loss of aerodynamic drag with the tail up they would lose in aerodynamic lift by the change in the angle of attack of the wings in the onrushing air. By now it didn't matter...

"Grass!"

The pounding of the pavement became less. She wanted to fly.

Just another moment. She was begging.

Now.

He pulled back gently on the wheel. The pounding stopped.

"Gear up."

Leo's hand went to the landing gear toggle. If they were to crash back to earth better to do so on the belly than onto the extended undercarriage.

The rate of climb indicator did not budge, but the airspeed indicator did...*one fifteen...one twenty...*

Hollis allowed himself to look out.   He knew they were over the fields beyond runway 28 which mercifully was free of any major obstacles.   He could keep the trajectory flat while they gained more speed.   All he saw was fog.   They weren't high enough to call it clouds.

The altitude indicator started to twitch as did the rate of climb needle.

"Jesus," Leo said, collapsing back into his seat.   Dodge shook his head.

Hollis smiled to himself and noted that his legs had quit trembling.

Jesus Christ, Mister, Frietag had said, *you have absolutely no aptitude for this at all. You wouldn't make a boil on a good pilot's ass.   You might as well wash yourself out and take up something you can handle like navigatin' of bombardierin'.*

Augie came on the intercom, "That sonuvabitch is gonna get us killed.   I knew it.   I told you."

Dodge spoke calmly into the interphone, "Shut the fuck up, Reese, before I come back there and toss you out.   Not one more word."

"But--"

"I mean it."

One forty.

Hollis adjusted the superchargers and throttled back a little while Leo moved the propeller pitch to climb settings.

Dodge leaned to look out one side window and then the other then turned around to look down the interior length of the plane looking for the thumbs up.   "Wheels up," he said.

They had won the wager.

Hollis imagined, with a wry smile, H-y resuming the act of breathing, the grip of his hand on his table vice-like, the stopwatch crushed to little pieces in his other hand.

Airspeed reached one hundred fifty and Hollis set the rate of climb to three hundred feet per minute.   At the appropriate moment, on cue from H-y, he banked into a ninety degree turn and, guided by the radio direction finder, started a counter-clockwise orbit around the buncher. The needle on the dial turned around to two seventy degrees keeping the field off their left wingtip.   Hollis held it rigidly as if the needle was glued there.   The heavily loaded **Cleopatra's Asp** felt sluggish under his hands.   He looked at his watch.   It was 1150.   They had taken off over five hours late.

"Radio to pilot."

"Pilot to radio," Hollis replied.

"Sir, I just picked up the strike report from the Fourth Wing.   It says, 'Primary bombed at 1148.   Results excellent.   Opposition severe.'"

Chapter Eighteen   **Baptism**

The outside suddenly became brighter and they burst through the clouds into the blinding sunlight.   They were at 3000 feet.   The overcast had been predicted to end at 2000.   Hollis put on his sunglasses and sensed Dodge arranging himself and his gear.   He must have been pleased with the climb for he turned and stepped up into the turret to take his station looking out for other planes.

Hollis scanned the sky and spotted Ransahoff.   They weren't supposed to formate until 10,000 feet but up ahead he could see Cassidy and Selkirk had already latched on and Eisenberg was dead astern, continuing to climb.   In the gentle orbit, Hollis wrenched himself around in his seat and, looking back, saw Cahill pop up out of the under cast dragging wisps of stratocumulus behind him like a flying fish leaping out of the surf.

Ransahoff had slowed to allow the others to catch up.   Cahill must have really been pouring on the coal for when Hollis turned to look again Cahill had cut the inside corner of the orbit, closing the gap.   He was almost beside Hollis.   Hollis figured the fear of being left behind again fueled Cahill's thinking.

Van Patten was firing flares, but the pyrotechnics were unnecessary.   He was right where he was supposed to be and nobody seemed to be having trouble finding him.   Ransahoff easily slid above and behind, forming the high squadron.   The flares were popping up as fast as the top turret gunner could fire them, red and green arcing into the bright sky like glowing pop-flies.

As they passed through eight thousand feet, Sully climbed up through the passageway and smiled, winking at Hollis.   His oxygen mask dangled from his leather helmet, resting against the side of his face as he started to talk.   Hollis turned the controls over to Leo as they smoked cigarettes in what had become, over the course of their first two missions, something of a ritual.

"Nice clear day," Sully yelled into his ear above the engine noise.

"Yeah," he yelled back.   "How'd H-y do on takeoff?"

"He found it real exciting.   He couldn't see shit out his window.   I don't think he'd ever been that far down a runway before.   By the time he figured we should be in the air he started crossing himself.   He must've crossed himself a hundred times.   I could see his eyes a-bulging and his lips a-goin' in prayer to the Most Merciful Almighty."

"The prayers worked."

"Must have.   Irony is, the boy's not even Catholic."

"Maybe the way the Lord came through for him will make him want to convert."

Sully patted Hollis on the thigh and continued on to the bomb bay adding, "I don't think he was the only one prayin'."

As they circled, Hollis could see the low squadron in position and Van Patten picked up the pace of the climb to arrive at 8,000 feet prior to departing for Brandon where the four squadrons of the 91st would join up.

He saw the 533rd at high group altitude off to the right.   Soon, from the left, the 24 planes of the 91st approached the formation as it turned around at Brandon.   To reduce the risk of collision, the main collection of their planes came in at an acute angle so that only a slight turn was required to slip into position above and ahead of the 381st.   They headed south toward

Splasher Seven picking up the last squadron from the 351st as they passed over Bury St. Edmunds, the seven Forts high-tailing for their proper place in the wing to form the high composite group.   As the bombers came together above the unbroken layer of clouds, Hollis was struck, once again, by the fact that it seemed so relentless.   The formation, the whole effort, had acquired a dark, deadly inertia.   He also knew that, long after he and Leo were gone, there would be an ever-enlarging mass of bombers stretching for as far as the eye could see, spiraling up through the mist, gathering in the deep blue sky, making order out of chaos to sally forth in a monstrous, punishing game of follow the leader.   Running slightly ahead of schedule, the wing made several wide 's' turns to eat up time to prevent a premature arrival at the next splasher.

In due course, they arrived at Splasher Seven and the second half of the second air task force, joined in trail.   Hollis told the crew to go on oxygen as they passed through 10,000 feet.

The second air task force, now six groups strong, 91st in the van, made the big turn at Chelmsford and headed almost due east for the coast.   But the pace set for the climb was too fast and steep. Hollis could see the planes of all three groups of the lead combat wing getting strung out.   Close to the center of the wing, in the high squadron of the low group, Hollis could keep his place, but he could tell the guys on the outside were falling behind.   Something had to happen soon to recover the situation or the wing would quickly become so loosened as to be untenable.

Fortunately, as he was thinking this, word must have reached the lead ship because they slowed down and shallowed the rate of climb.   Even so, he could see several bombers did not return to their positions, revealing gaps in the squadrons, and, for whatever reason, they fell from view, leaving the formation, joining some other group or, more likely, aborting the mission. Perhaps the climb had uncovered some defect in the mechanics, some failure of man or machine that would not allow them to continue.   Maybe, like Entwhistle, they had had enough. Regardless, their departure would weaken the formation increasing the risk for everybody else, each plane taking ten or twelve guns away, and they would not be around when they were needed most.   It was easy to resent this.   There was the irresistible inclination to believe such acts were fueled by cowardice.   And there were no spares.   Everybody was going.   But one could not be expected to continue when the aircraft was not up to the task.   Certainly they would fall behind and be brought down for sure.   No amount of raw, stupid courage could make up for a faltering engine.   What purpose would be served by needless sacrifice?   Whoever they were, he felt awkward in his envy of them.

At 14,000 feet Hollis plugged in his heating suit and turned up the rheostat.   For every thousand feet they gained, the outside temperature fell two and a half degrees centigrade.

The further east they went the more broken the undercast became until, by the time they reached the North Sea, visibility of the ground and the sea was unobstructed.   He looked south in the direction of Clacton-on-sea looking for the third task force, but the residual haze prevented it.   Besides they were still eight to twelve minutes behind.   They would fall in trail completing the bomber stream of nine groups and three composite groups over the North Sea arriving at their assigned altitude of 21,000 feet at 160 miles an hour by the time they reached Holland.

The coast of England passed behind him, the dark waters of the sea sparkling under the sun.   The time was 1313.   Not a propitious moment.   The crossing would take a little over half an hour.

"Over water, gentlemen, test fire the guns," H-y said over the interphone.

"Short bursts!" Hollis called after him.

In an instant, **Cleopatra's Asp** shook spasmodically with bursts of machine gun fire. The bursts were, as Hollis had ordered, short.   Tracers streaked away from the bomber as they did from the other planes in the formation, each gunner shooting into an empty patch of sky between the bombers.

Hollis noticed another plane leave the low squadron of the lead group, an engine feathered.   Better to drop out now because once the enemy coast was crossed it was better to continue regardless of the disability than turn back for few forced to turn back later survived the lone flight home.

"Dutch coast in ten minutes.   Keep your eyes open boys," H-y said.

The bombers started to spin out fine wisps of white condensation trails behind each engine.   Soon the contrails thickened and became dizzying as they passed by.   Even if every radar screen in Europe went blank all the Germans had to do now was look up.

He was close.   The enemy coast was now only a few minutes flying time away.   Soon all hell would break loose.   He needed to empty his bladder, the organ brimming more with anxiety than sense.   If he did not go now surely he would run the risk of pissing himself once it started.   He tapped Leo's arm and pointed at the wheel then at his crotch.   Leo nodded and took the wheel and throttles from him.   Hollis unclasped his lap belt and methodically disconnected his heater plug, head set and throat mike cables, pulled the plug on his oxygen tubing and plugged it into a blue walk around bottle which would provide him with a dozen or so minutes of precious oxygen.   He turned and climbed out of his seat making his way past Dodge standing in his turret.   He opened the door to the bomb bay and stepped onto the narrow catwalk into the dark, freezing, drafty chamber, the pregnant bowel of the beast.   The relief tube was on the back bulkhead on the port side.   He had no trouble finding it.   He had clipped the bottle to his chute harness and braced himself against the bucking and vibration as the bomber bounced around in the turbulence.   He pulled his cumbersome gloves off but left his glove liners on.   He unzipped three layers of clothing and fished his contracted member out into the frigid air, the draft like a knife against his exposed flesh. He tried to be quick but careful. How would he explain a frostbitten dick to Jessie?   Remembering the admonition to aim carefully to prevent a stray urine stream from fouling the bomb bay door limit switches, Hollis took great care to direct his feeble little squirt into the small funnel.   Some ended up on the door to the radio room, some on the catwalk where it froze immediately and some onto his pant leg and boot, but the switches were untouched by the warm, steamy liquid.   Pleased with his puny but satisfying triumph, Hollis reversed his actions and returned to the cockpit.

"Pilot to bombardier, how about an oxygen check?"

Sully counted off the crew.   All reported in.   Their voices betrayed their anxiety but not hypoxia.   This, they all knew, was no milk run.

Leo, monitoring the VHF, came on the intercom, "Task force commander wants the interval closed up so he's gonna 's' a couple of times to let the wings behind us catch up."

"Navigator to pilot, probably hasn't seen his escort.   Neither have I."

The lead wing slowly wheeled to the left and then back across their original path to the right then back again.   They repeated the maneuver which, hopefully, allowed the trailing groups to close the gaps between them.

He caught a glimpse of the wings, the contrails had thinned out and shortened themselves to a few yards behind each engine, and he was surprised at the number of planes stretched out behind him.   Somebody was gonna catch hell today.   All this to make a new and better world. He didn't think the old one was so bad that it need all this changing.

"Navigator to crew, We're crossing the coast."

The estuary of North Beveland between Schouwen and Walcheren passed below. Small scattered flak bursts popped nearby.   Like the flak they had encountered over these very islands only two days earlier, it was sporadic and inaccurate.

Hollis looked down and noticed the straps of his parachute harness than ran under his groin were slack.   Panicked that they would clip his privates like a scissors when his parachute snapped open, he frantically tried to tighten them, but could not.   He pulled his gloves off and tried with his bare hands, but they would not budge.   The metal of the buckles was so cold under his fingertips that it burned the flesh.   Defeated, he resigned himself to the distinct possibility of castration should he bail out.   He wondered if Jessie might love him as much if he had no balls.   While on the subject of his balls, he made sure his flak vest was carefully positioned under his rear end.   A single, destined flak fragment could kill just as assuredly as a sky full of the stuff.

Below, the coast was rapidly receding behind them.   No matter where he looked, no escort. He was filled with a sinking feeling for up ahead he knew that, since the passage of the Fourth Wing, there had been plenty of time for the Germans to regroup, refresh, grab a bite to eat and prepare for more.   Now, as Mickey said, they would be good and mad.   He held his attention on Stan's Fortress, moving in a little closer.   He glanced over at Cahill who, probably thinking the same thing, did likewise.   As he edged nearer, **Cleopatra's Asp** was buffeted by turbulence from Cassidy, dead ahead and Ransahoff.   He felt the wingtip tremble under his hands and reached for the throttle in case he needed to chop them or push them forward quickly. He noted Leo's hand go right to the rpm levers.   It was wake turbulence and wingtip vortices from Cassidy's plane and prop wash from his engines which chewed up the air cascading over **Cleopatra's Asp** like rapids over a rock.   The smooth flow of wind over the wing was gone and the lift with it.

It takes brains, not brawn to fly a four-engine bomber, Hollis, Butch Mullen had said. *Smart boy like you oughta know how to stay out of trouble.   The minute you see that wing start to drop apply full opposite aileron to lift it.*

Most perils of flying were precipitated or aggravated by human fallibility triggered by circumstances which can be largely avoided, Freitag had warned him.

But they were out of it before drastic action was required.   The little event caused a burst of sweat to cover Hollis's body.   Heavily loaded, **Cleopatra's Asp** was mushy and responded poorly.   The margin between continued flight and a stall was razor thin.   It was, after all, a bet.   He felt another burst of sweat.   He had to pay closer attention or he would, through stupidity and inattentiveness, get them all killed.

Leo tapped his arm and yelled, "Bedrock is descending to 17 thousand to go under a cloud bank!"

Bedrock was the code name for Colonel Gross commanding the second task force in the lead 91st ship.   Hollis looked ahead and wasn't sure he saw what it was that caused Bedrock to change the formation's altitude.   Regardless, dropping down four thousand feet put them closer to the guns on the ground and that could not be a good thing.   Then they would have to climb back up to bombing altitude further whipping the engines. Besides the escort, if there was to be any, expected to find the bombers at twenty-one thousand.

"Navigator to pilot, Antwerp, first checkpoint, coming up in four minutes."

"Pilot to crew, keep your eyes peeled.   It's not going to stay quiet like this forever."

They leveled off after the descent and had gained some airspeed in the process.   Hollis wondered if this reopened the gap between wings that Bedrock had 's'-ed around trying to close.

Hollis's heart was pounding inside his chest--

"Sweet Jesus, here they come!"   It was Hulse.

"Where?   How many?   Damn it call them out!" It was Dodge and he sounded annoyed.

"N-n-n-nine o'clock level!   Must be fifty of 'em!"

Hollis snapped his head around just in time to catch sight of several dozen single-engine fighters a mile or more to the left of the bomber stream flying parallel and rising as if on an escalator.   Their appearance was made all the more terrifying for this was the first time he could recall hearing Noah swear.

"I don't think that's our escort," H-y said.

"Get us out of here!" Hulse yelled and Hollis could feel **Cleopatra's Asp** tremble with machine gun fire.

"Knock it off, Hulse!   Wait until they're in range!" Augie yelled.

Hollis watched with dreadful fascination as the fighters flew unmolested into the open space ahead of the bombers.   How, he wondered, could his palms be so wet and his mouth so dry?

"Pilot to crew, don't yell into the intercom.   Call them out clearly."

Leo tapped his arm and then his earphones, the signal to switch to VHF.

"Achtung!   Achtung!   Achtung!   Hitlerites ten o'clock level!"   "Kommen-zie clooza, Fritz.   So we can shootenzie uppen der fucken azzen-holen, bitte."   It was Ransahoff taking advantage of the anonymity of the command channel.   Hollis recognized the voice.   So did everybody in the Group.   Probably the Wing.   "Close it up, we're gonna get hit," somebody else said.   Hollis switched back to interphone and could make out Leo smiling behind his mask. Poor, stupid, innocent Leo.

"Here they come," Sully announced to anyone whose eyes were not already glued to the German planes.

One by one the fighters, Me-109s Hollis thought, peeled off in a steep bank and turned, line astern, toward the oncoming bombers. Sunlight glinted off the shiny parts as they leveled off and bored in head-on at the bombers.   Hollis felt his own azzen-holen tighten as they presented themselves nose-first to the bombers.   He could feel the adrenalin discharge into his blood like hot steam under his skin as their wings and noses winked lights at him.   They had opened fire, squirting lines of tracers.

Cleopatra's Asp shook violently with the simultaneous firing of Sully's gun in the nose and Dodge in the top turret.   *When they come*, Selkirk had said, *tuck in real tight and pray*.

The fighters, one a split second ahead of the next, ripped through the lead and low squadron, snap-rolling onto their backs, diving away eager to put as much distance between them and the bombers as quickly as possible.   As they passed by in rapid succession, he could see hits scored on the bombers below him, each   cannon shell denotation a little flash bulb against aluminum.   Cahill's ball turret turned to follow the fighters as they rocketed down and out of harm's way.   They had come right through the formation, brazenly daring the gunners to fire at them, knowing they would not for fear of hitting neighboring ships.   The time from their turn until the first string of fighters had completed their pass was not more than fifteen seconds, maybe less.

Keeping station against Stan as best he could, Hollis looked at the planes of the low squadron.   One was trailing a plume of smoke from its number four engine.   He could plainly see tongues of flame lapping back on the upper surface of the wing.

"Here they come again!" Sully screamed.

Hollis snapped his head back in time to see five FW-190s wing tip to wing-tip coming right at him.   The guns above his head thundered as Dodge sent a stream of tracers out to meet them.   They were coming after the high squadron.

In the few fractions of a second necessary to think it through, Hollis weighed the advice he had received on the matter.   One school of thought held that a pilot should keep his plane steady without evasive action in order to give his gunners a stable platform from which to fire at the enemy.   The other held that it didn't matter and that an onrushing German pilot closing with his target at between five and six hundred miles an hour, two hundred yards a second, had but a few moments to line up his target and shoot why give him a stable target to aim at?   The German pilot had only three seconds of time between the instant his 20 millimeter cannon were within range and the time a collision between fighter and bomber was inevitable.   Don't make it easy on him.   Swerve, crab, climb or dive, within limits of your place in formation, and get out of his way.   It was called jinking and the evasive action it represented amounted to no more than movement of a few feet up or down, to one side or the other.   And it was as likely that one might jink into a burst as away from it.

Their noses and wings winking light at him, he involuntarily ducked down behind the instrument panel in a muscular reflex too quick to overcome.   He pulled back on the control column and added throttle then dropped a wing, banking right then left.   The maneuvers, as quick and erratic as he could make them without colliding with Stan or Cahill, suddenly seemed not to have made a difference.   He could feel the crash and explosion of shells against his plane like the blast of a shot gun into a bucket.   It was almost a double sound, the sound of impact followed a microsecond later by the eruption of the explosive.   He did not know how many times they had been hit.

He pulled himself erect in time to see one of the FWs flash past his window, belly toward him, close enough to see the dark rim of exposed rubber of the main undercarriage and oil streaks behind the cowling and Dodge's tracers ricocheting off its armored belly.   He looked over at Leo to make sure he was alright.   Leo's head snapped forward having watched the fighters flash past.   Hollis was reassured by the sound and sensation of Dodge's guns above and behind him and he could feel both guns firing in the nose.   He looked down.   He was covered with small fragments of glass and metal.   Where several instruments had been in the panel in front of him only a moment before there now existed a jagged hole.   On the left wing leading edge, beyond the number one engine there was a hole as big as a baseball, the metal ripped and peeled back like petals of a flower.

His head cleared of the initial shock, he saw that all four engines were running, the five men in the front half of the plane seemed alright and the wings were still on.   He looked for the Fortress with the burning engine, but it was gone.

"Navigator to pilot, you guys alright?   They put a big hole in the middle of your panel."

"We're OK," Hollis replied, worried that the crew might hear his trembling betrayed by his voice.

Hollis lifted the bottom of his mask away from his face to let the chilled pool of breath condensate, sweat and drool escape from the rounded cup beneath his chin.   It formed little frozen puddles on the front of his Mae West and on his lap.   He pulled up the goggles to wipe the stinging sweat from his eyes.

The head-on attack had achieved its intended result.   When he looked around at the squadron Cassidy and Cahill were way out of place and so was he, ripe for an eager fighter pilot to plunge into with cannon and machine gun.   Selkirk held steady against Ransahoff and Eisenberg was right behind him.   None of them had tried squirming out of the way.   They flew as if rigidly attached to each other by large steel members.

The lead squadron had been knocked about, too.   Their number six, Hollis's usually photographic memory failing him for he could not think of who it was, had two feathered engines on his left wing and smoke coming from the fuselage.   He watched as the pilot eased the crippled Fortress out of formation to facilitate the safe escape of his crew free of the hazard of nearby planes but also to remove the threat of explosion he posed to the remaining aircraft of his squadron.   Simultaneously, the hatches popped off and the crew bailed out, one by one, brown amorphous lumps falling away in the slipstream, until all ten had left.   Trailing smoke, still probably under the control of the autopilot, the Fortress held its place in the sky for a few moments until the failure of aerodynamics caused it to enter a flat spin and disappear from view.

"Anybody know who that was?" Hollis asked into the intercom, ashamed he couldn't remember for it was his responsibility to do so.

"Ainsworth," someone said.

"All ten chutes opened," Mollica reported.

The herd of seventeen planes of the 381st, one of the original eighteen had aborted, that had crossed into enemy territory had been thinned by two in the span of a minute.   With the group spread out and showing disorganization, the German fighters were sure to be back to tear into them.   It was not graceful parry and withdrawal as Hollis imagined it would be.   They were being bludgeoned.

Hollis looked out the window to his right.   At two o'clock high, he spotted a lone straggler from the 91st dragging thin contrails behind him.   Otherwise, all four were turning and he looked alright.   He took his eyes off of it for a moment and tried to ease in tighter beside Stan.

An FW whizzed past, then another, their silver wings flashing in the sun, sunlight glinting off their canopies.   Going after the low squadron.   Looking up to check on the straggler, something had changed.   He thought he saw something flicker from the left wing root.   A moment later, the left wing was ablaze and the straggler headed into a shallow dive. The hatches flicked off and bodies tumbled out. The last guy out of the waist door pulled his ripcord too soon and the unfurling chute caught the right horizontal stabilizer, entangling it. The bomber nosed over, a solid sheet of flame enveloping it from the wings back. The gunner, hopelessly ensnared, vanished into the lengthening flames.   The doomed bomber rolled and disappeared, a long trail of smoke marking its plunge.   All the while the crew called out the approach of more fighters and **Cleopatra's Asp** shook with the report of its machine guns.

"Dodge!   There's an FW three o'clock high coming around, watch him," Augie said. Hollis and Leo turned to see the lone fighter flying parallel to the bomber stream, slipping through the gap between the lead and low groups. He weaved back and forth avoiding the streams of tracers sprayed his way.   Dodge did not fire because he knew the German was out of his range.   When he was about a mile ahead he placed his little plane in a vertical bank and turned, heading right at Van Patten, eluding each line of tracer sent out to meet him.

"Boy, would you look at that guy fly.   Have you ever seen such guts?" Leo said.

"I think somebody told him we were coming," Sully replied.

"Knock off the chatter," Hollis said, not taking his eye off the FW.   It was truly a marvelous demonstration of airmanship.   But his luck did not hold.   A deluge of machine gun fire from all of those Fortresses caught up with him and Hollis could see pieces of metal fly off as the shells found their mark.   He made no effort to break away, probably dead at the controls, colliding head-on with a Fortress in the second element behind Van Patten.   The fighter slammed into the nose and disintegrated, the collision causing the Fortress to visibly stagger as it appeared to swallow the plane, like a large fish consuming a smaller one.   The front half of the bomber, everything forward of the wings, was gone in a flash.   Something emerged out of the tail of the bomber like a black egg.   Hollis realized it was the radial engine of the Focke-Wulf which had hurtled through the bomber like a cannon ball down a barrel, eviscerating it, and with it, the crew.   The bomber, all four engines turning, metal fragments, struts and wires, sinews of the mutilated bomber, dangling in the wind in the place where its nose and five men had been, rolled onto its back and plunged toward earth.

There was silence over the intercom and the guns, for a moment, did not fire.

"Pull up!   For Christ's Sake pull up!" Mollica screamed.

Hollis instinctively pulled the wheel into his belly and jammed the throttles forward without hesitation.   Something passed between **Cleopatra's Asp** and **Ain't Missbeahavin'** and continued into the space beyond Ransahoff before it exploded in a red flash many times larger than a flak burst.   The bombers flew right through the center of the roiling black cloud.

"Jesus, what the hell was that?" Sully yelled.   "That was close enough to smell."

Hollis immediately noticed the distinct burnt aroma, different from cordite, in his mask. He tugged the straps a little tighter, unable to figure out how the smell could find its way into his nostrils.

"What the fuck was that, Mollica?" H-y asked.

Mollica, shaken, replied, "Some twin-engined job way back out of range let a couple of these things fly.   Rockets, I think.   He popped a couple into the end of the high group and dropped down to send a couple our way--Oh Jesus! get ready here comes another one!   Pull up! Get her up!"

Hollis yanked back on the wheel again and watched with stunned horror as another thin line of smoke zipped past, exploding harmlessly below and in front of Cassidy.   Neither one of the rockets was close enough to strike **Cleopatra's Asp**, but Mollica had no way of knowing that, Hollis thought.

There was a brief lull, no more than a few minutes, during which Hollis and his squadron mates pulled the scattered formation back together, "Close it up, boys, they'll be back," Ransahoff said.   Augie announced the approach of the second wave of fighters.

Cleopatra's Asp suddenly trembled under the effect of all of its machine guns firing at once.

"Short burst!   Short bursts, you guys!   Do you want to melt your barrels?" Dodge yelled into the interphone and then proceeded to let loose a long burst of his own at a passing Me-110.   "Coming back, Augie, three o'clock level!"

Hollis looked up ahead.   There were columns of smoke rising from the ground every few miles.   He did not comprehend what they were until he remembered that they were following the same path the Fourth Wing had taken hours before.

"We're out of ammo up here,"   Sully said.

"Quinn, bring some up," Hollis ordered.

The guns rattled again as fighters blazed by singly and in groups of two and three.   It was like a wagon train running the gauntlet of marauding Indians.   There was no place to run, nowhere to hide.   They could not circle the wagons and slug it out until the cavalry arrived.

Another Fortress from the low squadron was trailing smoke from a feathered engine.   It started falling back, straggling, its future established.   Hollis marveled at the fact that an engine could burn in air too rarified to smoke a cigarette or a man to live.   More firing.

"Nice shot, you stupid, fucking guinea!" Augie said.

"Which guinea are you talking to?" Rizzo asked.

Hollis glanced at his instrument panel and only then recognized that none of the flight instruments, what was left of them, were functioning.   *Don't worry about the damned instruments*, Butch said, *flying should be instinctive, second nature so you can keep your mind free to grasp the big picture.*   This from a man who had never been to Germany.

Quinn appeared, crawling forward between Dodge's legs, a walk around bottle clipped to his harness, a long belt of ammo over each shoulder, trailing behind him on the floor as he passed.   The tips of some of the bullets were colored red and blue.   Tracer.   He lowered himself into the passageway and then reappeared empty-shouldered.   He yelled into Hollis's ear, "It amazes me they left the defense of the front of this airplane to a couple of officers!"   He climbed up onto the flight deck, but slipped on the jumble of spent cartridges from Dodge's guns that littered the floor and spilled over into the passageway.   Leo reached down to grab Quinn as he fell, steadying him so he could climb back up.

"Pilot to bombardier, how about an oxygen check?"

"You do it, I'm busy."

Hollis called out each position, reflexly glancing down at his oxygen indicator with each position called, but Mollica did not respond.

"Augie, can you see Mollica?"

There was a pause.

"Yeah, I see him.   He looks OK to me."

"Pilot to tail.   Pilot to tail."

"Augie, go back and check on him," Dodge said.

A long minute passed, guns still firing, fighters still attacking.

"He's OK, his interphone plug pulled out."

"Pilot to tail, oxygen check."

"Tail OK."

"I got him!   I got him!" Rizzo screamed.   "Hulse confirm that FW."

"You got him alright, he's bailing out!"

Hollis emptied his mask of the accumulated sluice again and it quickly froze on his lap. He glanced down at the straggler again. It had drifted further back. Hollis knew the German pilots would see the smoke as a sure sign they had hurt one and close in quickly for the kill like frenzied sharks with blood in the water, adding an easy one to their tally. Or else they would leave it for the twin-engine fighters whose job it was to finish off anyone straggling or making a break for home. Either way they had had it. Once they fell back into the gap between wings their time left would be measured in just a few minutes.

Hollis felt sorry for the pilot at the controls of the straggler. He had a difficult decision to make once he left the protection of the formation. If they were lucky and, for some strange reason unnoticed in all the fury, they might have the chance to drift backward into the faster, oncoming wing behind them. Then drift backwards through them and so on, until he might reach the coast on the way out before running out of friendly formations in which to seek refuge. Unlikely, Hollis thought. They still had a long way to go.

He could try for England, dump the load, dive hard and make a run for it. Or head for some neutral country if making England was not possible. But it was a long, lonely trip down to the deck from twenty-one thousand feet. And a long ride home. Few made it.

Or he could bail out his crew while they were still alive and take their chances on the ground, knowing the likelihood of evading capture and finding one's way out were very slim indeed.

It was often a Hobson's Choice. He was on his own. He had neither the time or the ability to seek the advice of others. It was instinctive to make a run for it. Statistically, his chances were better if he hit the silk.

Delay opening the parachute as long as possible over occupied territory so as to conceal your descent from the Germans for as long as possible, they said. *But open your chute early over Germany, especially near built up areas, so the German military can see you coming down and get you in custody before the civilians can get to you. They kill bomber crew as soon as they land. German civilians do not feel constrained by the Geneva convention or the articles of war*.

As they fell back, Hollis could see something moving back and forth against the copilot's side window. It was a hand. The copilot was waving 'good-bye'. Poor bastards, they won't be sleeping in England tonight.

At this rate, there wouldn't be enough bombers left to damage the target and they weren't even into Germany yet.

Hollis watched as more lines of tracer criss-crossed the sky, each a little crimson fireball with four unseen bullets hidden between each flashing blur. The tracers didn't exactly follow the same trajectory as the non-tracer because the weight of each round changed as the magnesium burned off. Why his mind had chosen that moment to recall this obscure fact was a mystery to him. He knew that each fifty caliber machine gun was capable of firing fourteen rounds a second with a destructive range of six hundred yards. Even at a distance of four miles, the two ounce bullet, leaving the air-cooled barrel at a speed of almost two thousand miles an hour was enough to kill a man. Each machine gun was normally issued enough ammunition for about one minute's continuous firing.

"Pilot to crew, let's watch our ammo."

The comment reflected an optimism he did not feel, that if they were careful and paid attention to detail everything would work out alright.   Instead, he was seized by an irresistible sense of hopelessness, resignation and the unfairness of it all.   Death would take him soon.   He could barely concentrate enough to fly the plane.   He was beyond terror.

Two more rows of FWs flashed by turning their white bellies to the guns and diving for the ground.   **Cleopatra's Asp** shook and rattled in her own defense.

"They got Cassidy!"   There was the sudden clatter of debris on the nose of **Cleopatra's Asp**.   Hollis eyes shot to the point in space where he knew Cassidy would be.   He was gone.   He leaned to one side and tried to look down over the nose of the plane and caught a fleeting glimpse of the un-named Fortress.   Smoke poured from both engines on the right wing.   The Fortress had torn pieces of aluminum flapping in the wind like the ripped skin of a crazed, screaming animal.   The right aileron appeared to be disconnected and it flipped up and down in the slipstream.

The big, fatally-wounded bomber started to yaw and roll, a movement which bespoke severed controls or dead pilots.   As if on slow motion film, the B-17 dropped it's right wing and rolled lazily onto its back, dropping into a shallow dive.   The twin columns of smoke and flame described a perfect corkscrew in the sky as the plane spiraled down toward earth.   It fell from view but Hollis could see Leo watch its decent.

Pull up into a vacated slot.   Do it quickly and without hesitation.   Your life depends on it!.   Hollis did not want to pull up and leave Eisenberg and Cahill uncovered.   If he lived he would catch hell from Ransahoff, but he was past caring.

He glanced up at the lead group's low squadron and watched transfixed as another bomber, for reasons unknown, slowly started to climb.   Something was terribly wrong for the nose kept coming upward, its airspeed dropping as it approached the vertical.   The plane seemed to heave a sigh and give up.   Lift gone, the plane wallowed onto its back and plunged downward.   Spinning slowly, hurtling down in a premature return to earth, Hollis found it astounding that the wings were not ripped off.   Reflected sunlight seemed to sparkle from the shiny parts.   No one got out. Probably pinned inside.

The sun glared down on Hollis from the window panel inches above his head.   It hurt his eyes for his goggles did not shade them from its fierce, lancinating intensity.   He was hot and cold.   His chin was bathed in ice water and his mask clasped his face like a cold, damp hand.   His arms hurt.   His heart was pounding and he could not swallow.   He wanted this to end.   Might not death seem welcome compared to this continued torture?

"Navigator to crew.   We just crossed into Germany."

For a brief moment, the sky was empty of fighters.   He looked around at the decimated formations of the three groups.   He had lost count of how many planes he had seen go down.   Then came the soft and warm realization that at some point in the last hour he had shit his pants.   Funny, he thought as he looked down at the glistening, frozen droplets and glass fragments on his lap and Mae West, he didn't think Hell would be so cold.

Suddenly, the formation wheeled to the left in a turn which took Hollis by surprise.   He recovered quickly and kept his place against Stan, but he was annoyed with H-y for not warning him.

"Pilot to navigator, did we miss a turn?"

"What?"

"Dammit H-y, where are we?"

"Uh, wait a second."

"Here they come again," Sully said.   The guns in the nose resumed firing.   It was obvious H-y could not tell him their location.

"Darmstadt."

The fighters returned, angrier and more determined than ever to deny the Americans their target.   Hollis wondered if they knew what it was.   Perhaps they did, realized their vulnerability and were fiercely trying to defend it, pissed beyond rationality.   Perhaps the actual target didn't matter to them.   Just as it likely didn't matter that much to the men sent to bomb it. Just another target.   It was Germany they were defending.   The Fatherland.   Were roles reversed and they were about to lay waste to Jessie's house or the shipyard would he behave differently?   Or perhaps they enjoyed it.   Like a big deadly game.   Hungry wolves around lumbering, stampeding cattle, snapping and growling, stalking and parrying, taking joy in the sheer thrill of the hunt, racing in, lunging to the kill, ready to finish off any strays cut from the herd.

Their defense was magnificent, savage, persistent and courageous.   No sooner would one *Gruppen* of fighters exhaust itself against the bombers when they would retire, to be replaced by another, equally as eager, just as voracious, just as angry.   They were wild. Climbing to attack from below, diving vertically onto the backs of the bombers, rolling, ignoring the torrent of tracer sent out to meet them, closing to point blank range.   Maybe they just did an aileron roll, pressed the trigger, closed their eyes and dove. Javelin up, line abreast, singly and in pairs, sometimes three, four or five at a time.   Sometimes whole squadrons.   Spraying machine gun fire, lobbing cannon and rockets.   When all guns were aimed accurately an FW could hit a bomber with seventy rounds a second.   On average, twenty or so hits from a twenty millimeter cannon were sufficient to bring down a Flying Fortress

Hollis watched a floating piece of detritus fluttering in non- ballistic ways like a leaf in a gale.   An engine cowling or escape hatch flipping over and over in the churned up, turbulent air. He saw it thunk against the wingtip with a silent but palpable impact.

He was surprised at the many things which seemed to materialize in the sky, junk that floated, fell, torn loose or ejected   into and from the bomber formation.   Planes were falling, engines smoking, intermittent contrails, fire, smoke, hatches, canopies, links, cartridge and shell casings, jagged pieces of aluminum, blossoming parachutes, brown and white, bodies alive and dead.

Could it have been any more savage or lethal had they been two tribes of hoplites pitching into each other with nothing more than sandals, shields and loin cloths flailing swords against naked flesh?

He knew, with flak filled skies, fighters hurtling every which way, and men and bombers plummeting in fiery agony, that, live or die, this would be the ultimate experience of his life. The day against which all others would be measured.

"IP in ten minutes."

The fighting continued.   Perhaps they were going to be under attack right through the target.   The next ten minutes seemed to last forever, the battle a tumult around him.

Up ahead, visibility astonishingly clear, he could make out the little town which sat quite distinctively on a wide loop in the River Main at the junction of four roads.   They were now just six minutes flying time from Schweinfurt.

"IP."

Hollis glanced at the clock above the window.   It read 2:53 p.m.   Recalling the fight plan, Hollis realized that they were off, late, by only two minutes.   After all of that only two minutes late.

At the Initial Point over the small town of Gemunden, red-red flare popped from lead ships, signifying the primary was the target.   The huge formation wheeled in a forty-five degree turn to the right.   The groups, what was left of them, separated and took interval, the 91st, then the composite high group, and then the remnants of the 381st.   They would be over the target last.   *The flak gunners ought to have the range figured out real good by the time we get there,* Hollis thought.   He watched as the bomb bay doors of the planes around him slowly ground open.

Chapter Nineteen   **The Devil's Crotch**

"Hey, them doors ain't open!" Rizzo screamed into the interphone.

Hollis hadn't heard the grind of the bomb bay doors coming open, but perhaps in the excitement, he had simply missed it.   He shot a glance at the light on the panel which, when lit, indicated the bomb bay doors were open.   The light remained unlit.   Half his instruments were gone or non-functional maybe it was damaged.

"Pilot to bombardier, try it again."

No light.   Now they were beginning to overshoot their place in formation.   The drag caused by the open bomb bays on the other planes of the group had caused them to slow and for that brief time **Cleopatra's Asp** had advanced on all of them.   Hollis had his plane nearly beside **The Flying Dutchman**.

"I'm not getting a light either."

"Rizzo?" Hollis yelled as he throttled back.

"I'm tellin' ya' them doors are still shut."

"Dodge!" Hollis yelled into the intercom, but as the words were leaving his mouth, he could sense Dodge had already scrambled down out of his perch.

So preoccupied was Hollis by the problem with the recalcitrant bomb bay doors that he took no notice of the flak bursts popping around him until a close one rocked **Cleopatra's Asp** like a leaf in a gust, peppering her with fragments like a fist full of pebbles tossed on a tin roof.

"Who pissed on these doors?" Dodge yelled.   "They're frozen like somebody welded them shut."

A minute passed and the flak grew more intense, concentrated, as the gunners on the ground saw the formations bearing down on them.

"You better hurry," Sully said

Hollis looked at the other planes, their doors hung down in anticipation of bomb release that would come at any second, silently willing that his would open before that moment came. If they did not, the trip they would have been for nothing.

"Bombardier try it now."

Nothing.

"Try it again."

Hollis wondered how much time they had left.   Certainly less than a minute.   Perhaps only a few seconds with which to rectify his stupid mistake.

Nothing.

Now Hollis could hear banging within the bowels of the bomber.   They were being hit. No, it was too rhythmic.

"Pilot, hit the emergency release but don't pull full stroke or you'll toggle the whole load."

Hollis reached down to the toggle on the floor by his left leg and without hesitating pulled it halfway.   He was afraid he might salvo the whole load and the bomb bay tank with it if he pulled too far.

He felt a sudden shudder and the plane slowed precipitously.   The light came on.   Now the planes around him leapt ahead as if horses out of a starting gate and Hollis shoved the throttles forward to make up his lost place in the formation.   He wanted to put his bombs where they were intended and he pulled himself upright in his seat and eased in as close Stan as he dared.

"We're OK below.   Them doors are open," Rizzo said.

Behind him he could sense Dodge return to his turret.

The lead groups of a task force always had the best chance of hitting the target accurately as there was, as yet, no smoke and dust to obscure their aim.   Wing tip to wing tip the group would lay down a deadly swath of bombs eighteen hundred feet wide.   And, traveling at their current airspeed, they covered 100 yards in a second, the release at the aiming point required extraordinary precision.   A moment or two's hesitation or inattention or distraction would send the bombs hurtling downward hundreds even thousands of yards from their intended point of impact.   And today they were trying to hit buildings within the plant, not just the plant itself. The strain poor Pilaccio must be feeling.

So many things, fighters, flak, shaking hands, the simple physics of the act, conspired to prevent the accurate placement of bombs on the target Hollis was amazed it could happen at all.

Another flak burst slammed **Cleopatra's Asp**.   Then another, then another.   This seemed even worse than the fighters.   They could shoot back at them.   He wanted to cringe back down into his seat, take some cover behind the thin aluminum skin as some primitive instinct for self-preservation tried to overpower his musculature.   His mind wildly calculated the likelihood of survival and he didn't like the end result of the math.   He felt himself on the razor's edge of panic.   One more bump, another bang would snap his one remaining nerve.

"Jesus, Cahill's hit!"

Flames streamed back from the fuselage behind the cockpit eating through the upper surface of the wing where it joined the plane.   Cahill swung **Izavailable II** wide of the formation as a precaution against sudden explosion, but continued to fly with the group.   The fire devoured more of the Fortress with each second, advancing until flames filled the cockpit, lapping viciously against the inside of the glass.

"Christ, look at him burn."

"Get outta there you guys!"

Hollis tried to imagine what was happening inside that plane as horrified crewman scrambled for their parachutes, yanking their lines from their connections trying to make their escape before the inevitable conclusion.   The ball turret moved into position, guns down, so the gunner could extract himself from it.

Hollis watched in stunned fascination as the waist gunner reached up and grabbed the window edge and lifted a booted foot onto the rim.   He crouched ready to propel himself out the window when he disappeared behind a large wall of flame that suddenly erupted from the wing.

"Bombs away!" Sully shouted.

Cleopatra's Asp shuttered under the release of its burden.   The first bombs emerged from **Izavailable II** when it vanished in an explosion of fire and metal, thousands of burning fragments arcing smoke through the sky.

Thump! KRUMP!!   A sudden, brutal lurch.   Hollis could feel the concussion pound the top of **Cleopatra's Asp**   as if a mighty fist had slammed down from above.   He shot a glance at both wings and all of the engines to make sure they were still attached.   He looked out over the skin of the nose.   It was peppered with perforations where only an instant before there was smooth, unmolested aluminum.   Dazed, the concern for the fate of Smith and Sullivan started to form in his brain when he heard H-y's unmistakable voice in his ears, "That was close!"

Still stunned by the force of the concussion, Hollis looked over at Leo who turned to face Hollis with a pained expression in his eyes.   He jerked off his mask and yelled, "Toto, I have the feeling we're not in fucking Kansas anymore!"

Hollis inspected the left wing.   Midway between the two engine nacelles the skin of the wing had been peeled up around a large round hole like the pedals of a metallic flower.

"We got something venting out of the left wing," he heard Quinn say.

Hollis plastered his head against the window trying to catch a glimpse of the leaking fluid.   He could see a fine mist siphoning out of little jagged holes in the wing.   He pulled his oxygen mask off and sniffed the atmosphere.   Gasoline.   He replaced his mask and yelled into the interphone, "Pilot to crew, no smoking!"   It was a reflex comment from training and he felt silly after he said it.

It would be just a few more moments before the gas was ignited by the white-hot exhaust collector ring and the wing would catch fire and they would blow up.   He was about to tell them to bail out when Dodge suddenly appeared and practically climbed into his lap surveying the damaged wing.   He leaned against Hollis's ear, "I'm gonna transfer fuel out of number one into number two.   That should take care of it.   Sometimes they self-seal and sometimes they don't."

Hollis could not remove his eyes from the leaking fuel, waiting for the first signs of the coming conflagration.   Soon, they too would vanish in an expanding fireball. Just like Cahill.

Hollis felt a slap on his arm and he turned to look at Leo who pointed at the receding group as it began a diving left turn for the Rally Point.

"Ball to pilot, we really clobbered it."

Quinn came on the intercom, "Radio to Bombardier, all your bombs are gone."

Hollis put the bomber into a shallow turn and picked up speed as it followed the group, but he was still dropping back.   He rolled in more throttle and jacked up the rpm, but they were still losing ground as if the mighty hand which had slapped them so fiercely a moment before now held them by the tail.   Why couldn't they catch up?

Sully screeched into the interphone, "Dodge get those goddamned doors up, they're gonna leave us here!"

Then Hollis understood.   They had used the emergency release to open the bomb bay doors which disengaged them from their motors, they could only be closed by cranking them up by hand.   If they did not soon get rid of the drag caused by the open bomb bay they would never catch up and be left behind for good.

Hollis looked around.   There were other planes straggling, too.   They were cutting the corner as the line of groups turned ninety degrees to the left toward the RP where they would reform the wing by making another long turn to the left for the trip out.

The flak let up as the gunners turned their attention to the groups following behind.   No sense shooting at planes that could no longer hurt them.   There were no fighters.   It was mercifully quiet.   They would be left alone in their struggle to catch up.

Hollis turned more sharply trying to cut the inside corner, too.   Perhaps they would arrive at the Rally Point as the groups realigned and just slip back into formation.   That quickly, however, they found they found themselves alone.   There were a few other bombers around clawing to catch up, but, for practical purposes they were in an empty sky.

What was going through Stan's head as he watched Hollis's plane dropping away?   No helping the new guys today.   It was just too dangerous

Dodge couldn't work on the doors until he had transferred the fuel out of the hemorrhaging tank.   By then the wing would have left the Rally and they would be a straggler. They already were.

The cockpit suddenly filled with dust and howling wind as Dodge yelled into the interphone, "Lieutenant Sullivan come up here and help me with these doors!"

A moment later, Sully emerged from the nose and struggled to gain his footing on the floor littered with spent shells and links much as Quinn had earlier.

Minutes dragged by and Hollis turned in his seat to look back.   The third task force was over the target as smoke and dust roiled skyward from the ground.   The air behind them was filled with smudges of black flak and the smoke that trailed behind some of the bombers.

"Pilot to crew, keep your eyes peeled.   The bastards will be back any second and they'll be madder'n hell.   Pilot to radio, see any more gas coming out of that wing?"

"Radio to Pilot, no, not now."

Hollis breathed a sigh of relief, but his relief was short-lived with the realization that there was probably gasoline still sloshing around inside the wing.

Slowly, Hollis could feel the bomber gain speed as the doors were closed and the drag caused by the wind swirling into the open bomb bay dissipated.   He looked around for the wing as it would be crossing in front of him right to left.   The sky was empty.

He would give them a few more seconds, if he did not see them he would turn east and fly the route home alone.

Sully climbed back down into the nose shaking his head as he passed Hollis. He yelled something, but Hollis could not make out what he said.

Hollis's arm was tapped and Leo pointed out his window.   There they were, little specks reformed into the wing and Hollis was guiding **Cleopatra's Asp** for perfect interception.   Leo tapped his ear and Hollis switched to the command channel.   He could hear desperate voices pleading into the VHF.   Somebody's bombardier was dying.   An hysterical copilot said his pilot was dead and he was down to two engines, what should he do?   *Fly the son of a bitch* came the calm, terse reply.   A voice, Ransahoff's he thought, came on and said, "Slow down, Bangmaster and let some of these stragglers catch up."

Another called for a rendezvous of some of the cripples so they could form their own little formation for the trip home.

The task force leader called, "Tighten up, Boys, Gerrie will be back soon."

Hollis pulled up even with the 381st and throttled back sharply so as not to charge ahead of the group as Van Patten had responded to the call to slow down.   Hollis found Ransahoff and to his left was Selkirk who had a feathered engine and to his right sat Stan where Cassidy had been.   He pulled **Cleopatra's Asp** above and behind Ransahoff.   As he did so, he could make out two Fortresses struggling to keep up.

"Pilot to navigator, how long to Eupen?"   Eupen was where they would again rendezvous with friendly fighter escort.

"Fifty-nine minutes."

Hollis looked around and peered down on the low squadron, what was left of it, and saw a Fortress with a scarlet streak, like red paint, running along the top of the fuselage.   Odd, he thought.   He looked closer.   The top turret was missing and the fuselage was painted with the blood of the top turret gunner.

Still the Germans had not returned.   Maybe their fury had been vetted and they didn't have the stomach for more. Unlikely, he thought.

The formation droned on in a sky empty of enemy aircraft.   They were traveling at a speed far slower than that which they were capable.   Empty of their bomb loads and with half their fuel gone, they could race out of enemy territory at nearly one hundred and eighty miles an hour, but doing so would leave numerous stragglers to an uncertain fate.

Hollis began to worry about their fuel.   He had no way of knowing how much they had lost and he was sure, with all of the jockeying he had done, that he had used up a fair amount of their reserve. He did not want to alarm the crew so he yelled for Leo to check the remaining fuel. There was a single fuel gauge for all the tanks.   Dutifully, Leo selected each tank in turn and they both watched the reading from each tank.   The gauge did not function.

"Navigator to pilot, Rhine River below."

Soon they would be out of Germany and back into the coastal fighter belt.   If the Germans did return, perhaps now they would not be so fierce over an Occupied country. Slowly, imperceptibly, the wing   gained speed as it made for the Rhine.   This struck Hollis as particularly cruel for, by doing so, they would be sacrificing several cripples.   Crossing the river, they resumed the course they had followed on the way in.   Below, Hollis could begin to see the funeral pyres of the Fortresses shot down on the way in rising high into the clear sky. There would be no need for navigation.   It was like flying a light line across a Texas night, all he had to do was follow the fires.

And again, equally inexplicable, they descended to seventeen thousand feet.   This, combined with the faster than expected egress, made Hollis worry that they might again miss the rendezvous with the escort.

As they flew over the Rhine, they would have fifty miles to Eupen.   Each passing minute brought them closer to safety.

"Fighters, twelve o'clock high!" Dodge said.

They were not quite to the rendezvous, but even so, maybe they were the escort. Perhaps they were, perhaps not.   In any case, the cluster of black dots, which appeared as a swarm of gnats over a lake, were going after somebody else for their course took them away. The second and third task forces were supposed to arrive at Eupen abreast and several miles apart.   Perhaps they were going after the other wing.

Hollis continued to scan the sky nervously.   He saw dark dots on the horizon, but none came close to them.

After what seemed like an eternity, "Navigator to pilot.   Eupen in two minutes.   We will be making a thirty degree turn to the right."

Selkirk fell further and further behind.   Hollis hoped they would be able to pick up fighter escort as they approached the coast, but there was still a lot of enemy territory to fly over. He thought about falling back to cover him, but decided against it.   He had no desire to press his luck, fearing he had already used up his allotment for the day, perhaps a lifetime.   Selkirk, for better or worse, was in the unenviable position of being on his own.

Leo tapped his arm and yelled, "Must be a helluva fight going on somewhere.   Pilots are calling for help.   Escort pilots are calling 'Tally-ho'.   Must be something."

Hollis was glad, in a perverse and selfish way, that this misfortune was falling on somebody else.   He had seen his share for the day, perhaps forever.

A few single-engine fighters made passes at the wing, but they were fleeting and lacked the determination and ferocity of earlier.   Selkirk was barely visible over the tail as he drifted further back.   Maybe this was the last for poor Ol' Mickey.

They droned on and after a time Selkirk was no longer seen.   Hollis called Mollica who said they were getting further and further behind, getting lower to the ground.

"Navigator to pilot, coast out in five minutes."

Hollis could make out the rim of land which marked the boundary between sea and continent.   Their path would take them over Noord Beveland on a course identical to the one they had taken hours ago.   There was some scattered flak.

"Pilot to crew, we're crossing the coast.   Keep a sharp eye.   They may ambush us just when we think we're home free.   So keep a look out."

Dodge appeared beside him as the wing began a long decent across the North Sea. Passing through fourteen thousand feet, he pulled off his mask and smiled at Hollis, handing him a chocolate bar.

"It's still a little frozen," he yelled.   He handed one to Leo which was gladly accepted. Hollis pulled his mask from his face and breathed in fresh air.   It was cold on his wet face.   He wiped his chin with the back of his glove and brushed off the shards from the instruments. They were still too high for tobacco to burn.   Sully appeared up through the hatchway with a thawed-out, soggy sandwich which Hollis refused.

"Pilot to tail, see Selkirk?"

"No, Lieutenant.   He was headin' for the deck last I saw him."

"Radio to pilot, one of our birds is ditching.   I wonder if that's him."

"Navigator to pilot, Orfordness in two minutes."

There it was: England.   Hollis never thought he would see that piece of land again.   It was dark and green, the strip of beach and white line of surf visible as they lost altitude more quickly.   Hollis dug down into his flight suit, worried this action might release the aroma of the soft turd nestled between the cheeks of his buttocks, pulled out a cigarette and lit it.   He drew the smoke deeply into his lungs. Below them England unfolded in shades of green, verdant, safe.

As they approached Ridgewell, two planes, Van Patten's was one of them, broke early and made for the runway.   They fired red-red flares and each, one after the other, made a hasty approach and landing.

As the planes started to peel off in the pattern, Hollis felt the strength leave his legs. They felt weightless, empty, devoid of muscle. They started to trembled uncontrollably. This scared Hollis for he feared he would be unable to push on the rudder pedals with the strength needed to control the big bomber. The cold sweat returned.

The low and lead squadrons banked on final approach. Hollis watched Ransahoff and Eisenberg peel off and he followed suit.   The few planes left from the composite group fell in behind them.

Hollis lowered the landing gear and banked the plane into the downwind leg.   Well beyond the field he started a long gentle 90 degree turn over the outer marker. He pushed on the rudder panel with his left foot, but he felt like he had no force in it. Leo lowered the flaps and started calling out airspeed as they passed over the middle marker.   The runway stretched ahead.   Hundreds of black rubber streaks stained the white concrete.   Most of them were concentrated in one area leaving practically no concrete showing. It was the place where most of the Fortresses returned to the ground.   As they passed over the open area just beyond the threshold of the runway, he glanced down its length.   He could see a Fort finishing it's roll out. That would be Stan.   The landing was as gentle as he could make it, nonetheless, Hollis bounced the B-17 once before it settled on the runway.

Leo shut down the two inboard engines, retracted the flaps and when the speed decreased sufficiently be reached down and unlocked the tail wheel.   Hollis pushed on the brakes with all his might. His legs were so weak his effort was not enough.   Leo, aware of his pilot's predicament, pressed on the brakes as well.   Hollis pretending not to notice.   The brakes squealed in protest as Hollis eased the Fortress onto the perimeter strip. He glanced at the clock. It was six-oh-five.

They taxied past Van Patten's plane and the other, parked at nearby hardstands to let out the wounded.   A large crowd had gathered around the nose of Van Patten's Fortress.   He wondered if the Colonel had been hit.

Many of the hardstands they passed were empty, save for the ground crew that continued their pathetic search skyward.   There would be a lot of empty hardstands today.   The anxious ground crews would watch the sky beyond all logical hope of a late returning bomber.   Then, of course, there was always the possibility of them setting down somewhere else.   Maybe they will ring up laughing and embarrassed about not making it home for dinner.   But leave the porch light on we'll be along directly.

Not today.

Then the realization would sink in that they were gone. Truly gone. They won't be back today or any other day.   No patchwork tonight.

As they turned onto their hardstand, Hollis spotted Moe and he guided the bomber onto the concrete circle.   By the expression on Moe's face, he was clearly relieved and probably not a little surprised.   Hollis pushed the left outboard throttle forward and held the right brake spinning the plane back in the direction of the perimeter strip.   He looked to his left and saw Cahill's hardstand which now looked stark, empty and sad.   **Izavailable II**'s ground crew stood motionless except to watch **Cleopatra's Asp** taxi by.

When the engines were silent and Leo finished the cockpit check, Hollis sat still for a moment and tried to regain his composure.   He pulled off this helmet and ran his hand through his damp, sweat-matted hair.   He put his gloves, helmet, goggles and mask in the small parachute bag and rubbed his face firmly with his hands, taking a few deep breaths.   Leo conducted himself as if it were business as usual.   He heard Moe yell up into the open hatch, "Is everybody OK?"   H-y said something Hollis could not make out.

The silence was deafening.   Leo left his seat and went down the passageway to the hatch. Hollis tried to collect his thoughts.   He took the Form 1A and marked it off.   When he felt mentally gathered enough, he lifted himself with weakened muscles out of his seat and down to the ground.   When his feet hit the ground he was glad his legs held his weight.   The crew milled about beneath the nose.   They looked agitated, excited, talking nervously, their voices high-pitched, their sentences cropped.

"Everybody OK, Lieutenant?" Moe asked.

"I think so, Moe."   Moe looked around and seemed to satisfy himself that Hollis's assessment was correct.

"Jesus, look what you did to my plane," Moe said.

It felt wonderful to stand straight up.   Hollis rubbed his neck and bottom and stamped his booted feet, surveying the scene   around him.   With the vibration of the engines gone he felt a numbness through his body.   He was stiff and tired, relieved and surprised to be alive. The crew all turned to look at him.   He forced a smile and turned quickly away lest they see the aftermath of terror etched on his face.

Hollis looked over at Cahill's hardstand and Moe turned to confront him.   Hollis shook his head.   "They got Cassidy, too.   Nobody saw Selkirk before we left Holland."

"Jesus, Lieutenant.   Rough, huh?"

"See for yourself."

The gunners gathered under the nose.   They had brass face, especially the two waist gunners.   It was a reddish-brown stripe on the skin between the top of their mask and their goggles from the brass dust generated by the constant feeding and ejection of cartridges firing from their machine guns.

He and Moe started their inspection for damage to **Cleopatra's Asp**.   Leo and Dodge tagged along behind.   The skin of the nose had numerous flak and machine gun holes.   There was a large hole above one of the windows which likely was the cannon shell strike that tore up the instrument panel.   One of the blades of the number three propeller had a cannon shell hole clean through it.   Hollis and Moe exchanged glances no doubt surprised that the engine had continued to function.   By now the entire crew followed the inspection.

Then they came to the hole.   It was a big enough to pass an arm clean through the wing between the two engines.   Hollis looked up through the wing and saw daylight.   He noticed gasoline dripping down from holes in the wing like rain from an awning.

"Flak shell,"   Moe said.   "Clean through."

"Passed right between number one and two tanks and punctured the feeder tank. Probably tore the lines, too," Dodge said.

"Di-rect hit," Quinn said.

"That musta been that big one that went off on the bomb run,"

"Why didn't it explode when it hit us?" Rizzo asked.

"Timed or altitude fuse," H-y said.

"Good thing it wasn't a contact fuse or you'd be dead," Tommy said.   This comment drew an angry glance from Moe.

Quinn turned to Hollis, "I saw it come up through the wing.   I was gonna tell you about it, but I figured you had enough on your mind."

Hollis could only nod.   He felt like throwing up.   Slowly the crew filed past and gaped up into the hole in the wing as if paying their respects to whatever deity or spirit had kept them alive at the moment of impact.

There was a cannon hit on the leading edge of the wing which had peeled back the aluminum skin where it exploded.   There was also a large gouge where the tumbling hatch hit the wing tip.   There were dozens of other holes, slashes and cuts in the skin of **Cleopatra's Asp**, like a beast caught in a fight to the death with vicious predators.   Hollis was surprised they had made it back.   The gasoline formed puddles on the concrete beneath the wing.

Hollis took the pencil and went to sign the 1A sheet for Moe. His hand shook badly and Moe, Leo and Dodge were all there to see it.   He felt embarrassed for his signature was barely legible.

Dodge turned to Hollis so only he could hear, "Old Quinn must have been pretty excited. He shot off the command set antenna and put a dozen slugs in our tail fin."

Izavailable II's crew chief came over to talk to Hollis, a pained, forlorn look on his face. "What happened?"

Hollis was about to speak although he wasn't sure what he would say when Dodge answered, "They were hit on the bomb run.   Took a flak hit, I think.   Fire in the wing spread to the hydraulics and the oxygen.   He pulled it away from the group and it went up.   It was over quickly.   Nobody made it out."

Hollis could see tears welling up in the sergeant's eyes.

"But they finished the bomb run," he added. "They put their bombs on the target."

The sergeant turned and walked away.

After a few minutes the six-by-six pulled up and everyone climbed in.   The gunners would come back to **Cleopatra's Asp** after interrogation and remove their guns.   Before they pulled away Hollis and the crew could easily hear the driver yell out to Moe, "We lost eleven today."

They had sent out twenty-four.

As the truck pulled away from the hardstand Hollis looked back at **Cleopatra's Asp**. She looked battered and, if Hollis could ascribe a human quality to an inanimate object, proud and undaunted, her prow held high in bloodied defiance.   The old bird had served them well today.   And they had been lucky.   Very lucky.   Lucky beyond comprehending.   The crew settled back for the ride to interrogation when Augie suddenly yelled, "Jesus, what's that smell?" He turned to Rizzo and asked, "Bobbie did you shit your pants?"

Hollis looked quickly over at Rizzo who hung his head in stark humiliation.

"Christ, Bobbie, couldn't you hold it?"

"Knock it off, Augie," Dodge said firmly.

Poor Rizzo, the little ball turret gunner from Brooklyn, slung underneath **Cleopatra's Asp**, suspended outside the plane for nearly six hours, had messed his pants. Hollis looked at the rest of the crew. There was ambivalence in their faces. They felt pity for poor Rizzo who had lost control of his bowels and joy that they hadn't. Hollis understood Rizzo's embarrassment as he kept his own little secret.

Suddenly the truck screeched to a halt, the truck behind them slamming on the brakes also. Outside there was yelling. Hollis lowered himself to the ground. "What's going on?" he asked the private who had been driving. He was outside the truck pointing across the field.

"Here comes one."

A lone B-17 banked sharply over the end of the field and settled into a shallow descent to the ground. Its wheels were up. He was going to put it down on its belly. Hollis wondered who it was. The flaps were down and the plane seemed to drift in slow motion down to the grass infield. Contact with the ground was made and a large cloud of dust, turf and dirt clods flew into the air behind the plane, churned up by the propellers as they gouged the ground. It crossed an intersecting runway and a shower of sparks exploded under the plane for a second as it scraped over the concrete. It was a textbook wheels up landing.

It was Selkirk.

The **Vermont Revenge** came to rest, overtaken and momentarily enveloped by its own cloud of dust, about a hundred yards away. Other trucks had pulled over to witness the landing also and several of the officers, Ransahoff among them, took off across the grass to the Fortress. Hollis, his legs still weak and not entirely trustworthy, instantly followed them. By the time they had arrived at the plane Selkirk was outside the plane standing nonchalantly with a freshly lit cigar clenched between his teeth.

"I guess they didn't want us bombin' their little nut and bolt factory," he said.

Hollis and the crew dropped their gear off at the drying room of the equipment hut and went to the briefing room for interrogation. He stopped by a latrine to scrape the compacted, desiccated turd from the cleft between his buttocks. He entered the big Nissen hut and walked past the 'Hot News' table, but had nothing to report now that Selkirk had shown up. He had heard one ditched, but he had not seen it. He took a steaming mug of coffee from one of the Red Cross girls and sipped it, burning his tongue on the hot liquid. He looked around the room at the men milling about and saw the carnage written on their faces. He picked up a Spam sandwich and took a bite wondering if his stomach would accept it or hurl the morsel back at his mouth. It stayed down and he finished it. He could not recall Spam ever tasting quite so good. A gunner stood by himself staring blankly out the window. His crew called for him, but he did not move. Van Patten, still in his flying clothes walked over and placed his arm around the boy saying something to him. The gunner nodded and Van Patten walked away.

The room was quiet and empty. There were half the crews present that had been there earlier. He had been in this room this morning and it seemed like it was a month ago. A lifetime.   Hulse had a bad case of the of the shakes because he held the glass of whiskey Dodge had offered him with two hands, the liquid vibrating in the glass.   Dodge then handed a shot glass to Hollis who took it, downing it with one gulp.   The whiskey went down sharply, mixing with the coffee and Spam in an amorphous coagulum in his stomach.

While Hollis waited to be called to a table, he listened to one of the other pilots.   The interrogating officer was patiently trying to coax information from the man.   He kept answering, "I don't know" or "I don't remember."   The interrogating officer turned to the copilot for help.   He answered for his pilot.   Perhaps the poor man would never remember and spend the rest of his life wondering what had happened during the seven hours he had sat in the cockpit this day.   And if he never recalled the details of those seven hours of his life what difference would it make?   If his subconscious mind refused to let his conscious mind relive it so much the better for the protection it afforded his sanity.

One pilot said, "A bunch of 'em with red cowls came roaring through hell bent for election.   They didn't shoot at us, but sure as hell somebody back there caught it.   They looked real pissed."

"The bastards had blood in their eye and went after the low squadron trying to wipe it out."

"Would have too, but they kept running out of ammunition."

"I looked at Dunston and saw he was hit," his jaw rippling with emotion and his voice trembled, as he bravely fought back the tears, "when I looked back he wasn't there anymore."

"Rockets?" one interrogator called into the room, "anybody else see 'em firing rockets?"

"Yeah, they fired some our way," Hollis said.

"Next crew," one of the interrogators called.

"Here guys," Hollis said and gathered his crew around the table.

Quinn sat down, pulled out his log and poured another combat ration into a tumbler.   H-y snatched the glass from Quinn's hand and said, "You're not old enough to drink that, son. Give it here."

Quinn pulled the glass back and said, "Fuck you, sir.   I flew the same mission you did."

"Yeah, but I could see what was going on."

"Knock it off, you two," Leo said, annoyed.

The interrogator launched into his list of questions: when did you first encounter enemy activity, what was your bombing altitude, magnetic heading and position in formation?   How many fighters, what types, what kinds of attack, what kinds of weapons, and distinguishing markings?   What about flak, where, what kind, how accurate, how much?

Suddenly, Dodge bolted to his feet.   He had been sitting at the table sipping a mug of coffee, a cigarette dangling from his lips.   Everyone fell silent as Dodge frowned, obviously annoyed, dropping his pants quickly along with his blue bunny suit and long johns exposing his white legs.   He used a fingernail to flick at the edge of a small, bloody gash high on the back of his leg near his buttock.   As everyone watched, he worked a two inch long sliver of metal out from beneath the skin.   He stared at it for a moment as if it were an interesting seashell or something, tossed it onto the table and pulled his pants back up.   He grunted, "I couldn't figure out what was itching me all this time."

"Well, that's a Purple Heart," the S-2 officer said.   "Just when did *that* happen?"

Dodge shrugged, "I honestly don't know.   Sometime today."

Quinn said, "Musta been that big one that went through the wing."

Augie picked up the bloody sliver and handed it to Dodge, "Hey Dodge, you need to save this.   No two shells, like lightnin', ever hits the same place twice.   That one had your name on it.   That was the one that got you.   You should keep it.   They can't get you twice."

Dodge picked up the sliver and studied it for a second and placed it in his pocket, wiping his bloody fingers off on his flight suit.

It was then that the Intelligence officer asked for their location during the rocket attack and turned to H-y for some verification.   H-y sheepishly admitted that for two hours there were no entries made in his log.

"Maggie's drawers on this bomb run," Sully said when it became his turn.   "I don't think we hit what we went after today."

The S-2 officer looked at Sully with astonishment then wrote down what he had said. Nobody else showed any emotion at his comment or spoke up to dispute his assessment.

"Excuse Lieutenant Sully, sir," Augie said to the S-2, "he's just pissed somebody went wee wee on his bomb bay doors and glued 'em shut."

Leo and Hollis exchanged glances.

"Well, is there anything else?"

The crew rose to their feet and turned to make room for the next crew.

"Yeah, don't send us back there," Rizzo said.

Hollis turned to leave when he noticed a short, thin little guy, ball turret gunner probably, from somebody's crew quietly waiting in a corner to tell what he had seen.   He had a baby face and couldn't stand still.   He kept shifting his weight from one foot to the other, his eyes darting around the room, looking, but not seeing.   He held a mug in his hands as if trying to warm his palms in a room that was already warm.   His B-3 gunner's cap sat cocked   on the back of his head.   He could see the brass dust marks on his face.   Hollis realized he cupped the mug in both hands for fear of dropping it.   As he brought the cup to his lips his hands shook uncontrollably and the warm, black liquid lapped over the edge and onto his fingers.   He seemed not to notice.   Hollis knew that the poor gunner with the baby face was still caught in the vice of terror and no one would let him out.   It was the same cold vice from which Hollis was only now starting to wriggle loose.

Hollis knew there was a permanent scar on the boy's brain.   The memory of his terror perversely poised to revisit his consciousness, to recycle fresh in his memory.   His brain would force him to relive his terror all over, again and again at random, until the day he died or it drove him insane.   He might eventually feel safe from it then, without warning, in response to some word, a circumstance or a song he would instantly arrive back at the moment his brain was scarred.   His pilot walked over, placed his arm around him and led him to a seat. There seemed to be a lot of that today.

As they turned to walk out Hollis took Sully to one side and said, "Sully, I don't care if you have both feet out the hatch and your hand is on the ripcord.   If I tell you to do an oxygen check don't ever tell me you're too busy."

Sully was visibly taken aback by a bit of business during an extraordinary day and nodded at his pilot.

Dodge met him as he stepped out of the room.   He handed Hollis a freshly lit cigarette and said, "I always feared Judgment Day and I fear this was it."

"Maybe, Noah.   Not likely we'll ever see that place again."

"I don't know sir. Must have been pretty important.   They were very interested in defending it."

Hollis turned to walk toward the truck that would take him back to the squadron area when he saw Mollica approach him.

"You know, sir," he said softly, "I could tell when we were being hit.   I couldn't see it, but I could feel it.   I could see pieces of our plane fly past me.   But you kept us out of trouble and got us home safe.   You did a good job up there today, Lieutenant.   Thanks."

Hollis watched as Mollica turned and walked away.

The crotch of the very Devil himself.

Chapter Twenty   **Bad Arithmetic**

Hollis returned from the interrogation and was shocked, if he could be any more shocked after the day's events, to find Stan's bed stripped and his stuff packed into his footlocker and B-4 bag which were placed neatly in the center of the room.   Hollis knew that Stan was the Group's first pilot to finish 25 missions even if the majority of them had been flown with another outfit. Even so, custom required he be thrown into a tub of water or hosed down by his compatriots or his ground crew in celebration.   But not today.   The events of the day had so stunned and appalled the Group that there was no appetite to celebrate anything.   After the battle they had endured, it was unclear how or why any of them had survived at all.

That he now found himself sitting on his bed smoking a cigarette staring at Stan's luggage filled him with a sense of disbelief and guilt.   He was convinced that it was by pure luck that he had lived through the day.   He had no claim of experience or extraordinary skill to hold up and say this was how I did it.   His mind, still numbed by the unrelenting terror, was only now starting to clear sufficiently to allow him to form cogent thoughts.   As he stared at the baggage he wondered how Stan had done it.   He took out a piece of paper and jotted a note

Congratulations, Stan
Any advice?
Good luck, Hollis

and placed it on top of the B-4 bag where Stan couldn't miss it.

He stared at the note and felt a sudden rush of nausea.   He needed fresh air quickly in hope of preventing the molten mess from leaving his stomach.   He barely made it out of the barrack when the two shots of scotch, cup of black coffee, a Spam sandwich and the smoky residue of half a dozen cigarettes erupted from his mouth onto the mud.   He wretched twice more, his abdomen tight and convulsing.   Light-headed, he leaned against the side of the building for a moment.   He walked into the patch of woods behind the cluster of Nissens and sat on a log shaking uncontrollably.

He fixed his gaze at middle distance and tried to recall what had transpired only a few hours earlier.   He had trouble bringing things into focus.   His brain was like a movie with the film not quite touching the lens.   The fighters, their wings and noses flashing lights, unleashing ribbons of hot lead, spouting death, passing in a dark blur.   Cahill, poor Cahill, burning fiercely, the fuselage consumed by flames so that only the Plexiglas nose and the vertical fin were visible outside the flames, a blazing comet with wings.   He thought of Cahill, cooking alive inside the cockpit, struggling to swing the flying torch wide of the formation before it exploded, reaching his gloved hand down into the flames for the bailout alarm.   What was it like, inside flames? His mind's eye made him see Cahill's index finger curling slowly, purposefully around the small toggle, determined to warn anybody who didn't already know.   The sudden, horrific smear of flame and cascading, blazing aluminum fragments and bodies a few seconds later.   Mollica speaking calmly into the intercom over and over: 'there goes another one.'   Smoke, parachutes, upending wings, flak, black smears flashing past the windows, escape hatches and canopies floating past, streams of tracer crisscrossing the sky, screams over the command channel.   His hands resumed their shaking.

When his mind cleared, he realized he was still dressed in his flying clothes, the silk scarf and terry cloth muffler still tucked into the collar of his jacket.   He did not know how long he sat on the log.   No more than a few minutes, he thought.   He got up and returned to his room. Eisenberg's stuff was gone and a note rested on his bed.

Keep your nose up in a turn
Stan

Hollis flipped the note onto the desk and stretched out on his unmade bed.   There was a knock on the door.   Startled awake, he wiped the small droplet of drool from the corner of his mouth and swung his feet to the floor, again becoming aware that he was still in his flying clothes, boots and all.   He yelled for whoever it was to come in.

Ransahoff, looking agitated as usual, opened the door and walked into the room.

"I got something for you."

"Unless it's my discharge papers, I don't want it."

Ransahoff stepped back into the hall and bent over picking something up off the floor. "Cassidy was supposed to fly with Entwhistle this morning."   They both knew what had happened to Cassidy.   "This stuff belonged to him."   He placed a large wooden cartridge box and phonograph on Stan's bed.   "He left a will saying he wanted this stuff to go to Stan in the event of his untimely demise.   An' o'course Stan is gone so I figure it goes to you."

It was Cassidy's prized collection of phonograph records, 'these ain't no V-discs'.   They were priceless original recordings, anybody would want them.

"I don't want 'em.   You keep 'em."

"I don't want them.   I hate Swing.   Besides, music is the opium of the people."

"I thought that was religion."

"Yeah, that too.   Look, Hollis, I don't care what you do with them.   Give 'em to the Aero Club, or the Red Cross or some local.   Flick 'em and see how far they fly.   Bury 'em for all I care.   They belong to you now."   Ransahoff appeared to notice for the first time that Hollis was still dressed for flying.

"Well," he said more softly, "you better get changed and get to chow.   It's getting late."

"What happened to Entwhistle?"

"He's gone, too."

"What's gonna happen to him?"

"Dunno."

"Boy, after today, I know how he felt.   Our squadron really took a beating today."

"We fared better than most."

"Who's running the squadron now?"

"I am."   He softened.   "Get dressed.   You should eat."   And he left.

One of the milestones of an Air Corps officer's career was to command a squadron. Hollis wondered how Ransahoff felt having achieved that milestone by default because there was nobody else around to do it.   But Dutch Ransahoff was the least of his worries.

Before today Hollis thought he knew who he was.   The thrill of it all.   Piston engines reverberating through his soul.   Now at least, he had a clear understanding of who he wasn't. Mollica had it wrong.   He had done nothing extraordinary today.   He had steered the plane and ran the engines.   They had survived by luck, Fate, Divine Intervention.   Anything but skill or courage or an indomitable spirit or patriotic zeal.

It was almost nine o'clock when he got undressed and went to the shower hoping Beamis had the water heater going.

He did.   He took a long, warm shower and tried to wash himself clean of more than just the sweat.   He hoped his anguish would rinse off his soul and the sight of Cahill's burning Fortress would leave his mind.

He dressed and stared at Cassidy's stack of records.   He left the room and rode the shuttle to the mess hall.   It was nearly deserted.   Everyone had already eaten or they were not hungry either.   He took a tray of food from a doleful mess attendant and sat to eat alone.   He moved the food around the tray, but it had no taste and he had no appetite for it.   He left.

As he headed for the Officer's Club he thought about the Squadron.   With Cahill and Cassidy gone and Stan on his way home, Ransahoff, Selkirk and he were the only first pilots in the Squadron.   And Ransahoff was now the CO and could no longer be considered a first pilot. That left two.   After only six days in the Squadron he was now its third most senior flying officer.   That was some bad arithmetic.

Everyone could tell Ransahoff had had too much to drink.   He had been holding court with Selkirk and other officers from the squadron, as well as Bonner and Cavannaro.   Stan would certainly have been there, too, Hollis noted.   But Stan was gone.   The O club was, surprisingly, full for such a bad day.   Perhaps, Hollis thought, they came, like him, seeking refuge from the day's events in alcohol and miseried company.   Clearly, there was much to take refuge from.   The loss of half its combat crews had left the Group   decimated and in a state of stunned disbelief.   No one had ever experienced a day like this before.   At evening mess there was virtually no conversation and few had actually eaten their meal.   No one was there to lecture them on how many sailors had risked their lives to transport these victuals from the ZI through U-boat- and shark-infested waters.   'Take what you want but eat what you take.'   No one had much stomach for anything tonight.

Hollis had walked in expecting to find the place empty except for the usual paddle feet instead the place was filled with men all wearing the same expression.   No one played the piano.   The radio, perpetually on, was silent.   Conversation was hushed, barely louder than whispers.   No doubt each man was haunted by the same combination of guilt and good fortune at surviving the day and felt the need to share this with others.

"Hollis!"   Ransahoff yelled when he noticed Hollis step up to the bar, "get yourself a drink and come on over here.   I've got a story to tell you."

Hollis got a double-double and walked over to take a vacant seat nearby.   He watched Ransahoff snap down a scotch.

Ransahoff's voice was forcibly loud, his words slurred by the alcohol.

"You know, boys, I found out how they select targets the other day.   You see this fat, old general and his staff get together around ten o'clock and break open a couple of bottles of bourbon and shoot the shit for a few hours.   You know, 'how's the wife and kids' kinda crap. Well along about two, the lieutenant pipes up, 'shall we send them out today, sir?'

"'What's the weather like out? the general says'

"'That never mattered before, general.'

"'Sure let's send 'em.'"

Hollis noticed that Van Patten, Clevenger, Gleason and Begay, who had been conversing in the far corner of the room, ceased their chat and looked at Ransahoff.   They exchanged glances and comments with what seemed like clinical detachment.   He felt like moving to another part of the room or leaving altogether before hell broke loose.   But he could not bring himself to move nor could he understand why.

Selkirk chuckled self-consciously and said, "Jesus, Dutch, maybe you better pipe down."

"'Sir, shall we select a target?' says the lieutenant.   And by now they're pretty soused, so the general says, 'Where shall we send the boys today?'

"So he goes over and picks up the darts and looks over at a map of Europe and takes careful aim.

"'Beg pardon, sir,' says the colonel, 'but I do believe it is my turn.'

"'No, it's not.'

"'Yes it is, sir.   You got to pick last time.'

"'And what did I get last time, Colonel?'

"'Milk run, sir.'

"'Lieutenant, whose turn is it?'

"'Well, sir, I believe the Colonel is correct, sir.'

"'Oh, he is?   What exactly is your assignment on my staff, Lieutenant?'

"'I'm your aide-de-camp, sir.   I'm also your son-in-law, sir.'

"'Well maybe your memory needs a little work, Lieutenant.   Major, reassign this little pissant to a bomber group.   The extra oxygen might do him some good.   Bring in a brand new Lieutenant.   Well, go ahead, Colonel, if you must.'

"'Thank you, sir' and he takes a red dart and throws it at the primary and then takes a blue one for the secondary.   And then he takes a fist full of black darts and tosses them at the map for TO's just for good measure.

"'Ooooh, that looks like a good one.   Bloody good show, Colonel.'

"'Thank you, sir' and the general gets out his glasses and walks across the room to the map.

"'Shreveport.   Shreveport.   That sounds like a good one.'

"'Yes, sir.   Thank you, sir'

"'Lieutenant, see if you can find out what they make in Shreveport.'

"'I believe the Colonel has selected Schweinfurt, sir.'"

Hollis saw Begay rise to his feet.

"'Shreveport, Swinefoot, whatever.   I asked you to find out what they make there.'

"There's a shuffle of papers.   'Ah, yes.   Here it is, sir.   Let's see...a nice Bavarian cheese, potatoes...a delicate white wine unique to the region...pork sausage...ball bear--'

"'That's it.   Good show, Colonel.   Swinefoot it is.'

"'Thank you, sir.'

"Then the new lieutenant says, 'But sir, beg pardon but that's awfully far, sir.   How will they get there and back, sir?'

"'How the hell should I know?   Ask Operations.   I'm Planning.'

"They all chuckle at the new Lieutenant   'But sir, they will be going well beyond escort range, sir.'

"'We can't be expected to molly-coddle those boys, you know.   Major, send this little pissant with them.'

"'Yes sir.   And how many shall we send today, General?'

"'Aah, send all of 'em.'

"'Very good, sir.'

"'The boys will be cooking a little sausage today, eh, Colonel?'

"'Oh, yes, sir.'

"'Cut the field order, Colonel.   One more round then let's get to bed.'"

Finally, Begay walked over and said calmly, even sympathetically, "That's enough, Captain."

Like a lightning bolt, Ransahoff fired back, "Fuck off, Chief, you didn't go today."

Everyone cringed as they waited for the unbridled wrath of the Great Navaho Warrior, to bring down a mighty fist on Ransahoff's skull and crush it like an egg. Begay, his veins stretching the collar of his shirt, spoke evenly, "Ransahoff, go home and sleep it off."

Ransahoff stood up and said, "'Yes sir, General, that sounds like a splendid idea.   Good night, sir.'"   He snapped off an exaggerated salute and walked out, his cheeks wet with tears.

Hollis lay back and stared into blank space.   He felt a shiver come over him, but he was not cold.   He had never felt so lonely or scared in his whole life.   How could he go on?   He didn't bargain on this.   He might actually be killed.   Tomorrow.   Maybe the next day.   How close had he come today?   Inches?   Seconds?   What force moved the hand that selected the fuse for that particular flak shell?

He would never see his parents again.   Jessie would be waiting for him on the station platform and he would never come back.   She would grow old waiting for him to step off the train and he never would.

All the things that were so familiar to him would be gone forever.   The mundane items of life that were so comforting by their continuity, their ordinariness, that provided the guideposts by which he could steer his mind and his life, he would never see again.   He would die in this strange place in a very unnatural way with people not of his choosing.   Would he die in an instant like a bug on a windshield or would he fall slowly through space, dismembered but conscious, aware of his approaching death?   Or would he roast as he sat strapped into his seat, like Cahill, the smell of his own burning flesh filling his mask, breathing it in?

God, he missed Jessie.   If he could spend only five minutes with her again.   Five measly, fucking minutes.   If she could miraculously be transported here and now from wherever she was he might be happy enough, reassured enough to endure this.   He didn't need to touch her or even speak.   Just stand before him so he could see her eyes, her soft face and know that she was real.   Not some cruel joke played by God to make him mad before He killed him.   The memory of her made his heart ache and filled his eyes with tears.   The memory of her.   The last time her saw her.   The last time his eyes fell on her.   As the train pulled away, he leaned out the window and waved like a million GIs before him.   She stood erect,   a foot or two from his mom and dad, in her smart yellow dress.   The sun made her hair shine like spun gold.   She waved back gently, almost self-consciously.   She didn't leave the spot until he could no longer see her.

He couldn't do it.   Whatever the others possessed he lacked.   Something was missing from his being.   Some nerve fiber or piece of sinew that would permit self-sacrifice to be a choice, a rational alternative to the animal instinct for self-preservation.   It separated him from his peers.   They could look at him and tell.

He was a danger to his crew.   The next time he went up and forever after he would be so paralyzed by his personal terror that he could only think of himself.   Not a higher cause or the welfare of his crew.   It was an unnatural act to strap oneself into the seat of a bomber and fly into the mist.   It defied human nature.   Biology.   And it was all a matter of biology.

He thought of his crew.   For Quinn and Augie, it was high adventure.   Besides, that bumpkin Augie was too stupid to truly understand what was going on.   For Leo it was like a summer job.   Bombing was something to do until classes resumed.   No, Augie couldn't understand the rationale for not marrying your cousin let alone the preservation of democratic institutions, the liberation of enslaved peoples and the eradication of genocidal maniacs.

Tomorrow, he would go to Ransahoff and tell him he could no longer fly.   Combat had ruined more than one good man.   Combat failure.   Lack of Moral Fiber was what it was officially called.

Tomorrow, he would screw up his courage and admit he was a coward and remove, once and for all, any doubt.

Of one thing he was certain, he had seen his Cold Harbor.

Tomorrow.

Chapter Twenty-one   **The Night**

The bomb crashed through the lofty ceiling of the factory.   Hollis took great satisfaction that the bomb he had helped deliver, the bomb that came from the belly of his Fortress, had indeed, found its intended target.   From inception, through target selection to delivery, it had been a perfect execution.   There was a loud crash as glass fragments showered down on the workers like ice crystals.   The bomb struck the concrete floor and exploded blowing out the sides of the building with an ear shattering whomp.   The concussion bounced hundreds of thousands of ball bearings into the air, flecks of green paint blowing away.   The corner of the machine came down squarely on a worker crushing him flat like a bug under a hammer.   His eyeballs popped from their sockets and skittered across the floor like dice in a crapshoot.   The ball bearings came down like hail and bounced up off the floor in ever decreasing heights, each making a clicking sound against the concrete, a noise repeated by the tens of thousands amidst the smoke and the dust.   After the raid, the workers went around picking up the ball bearings which, for the most part, were undamaged and salvageable.   Two of the little spheres were moist and stared back at the unsuspecting worker when he held them in his hand.

Hollis lay awake in his bed for a minute staring into dark space.   There was little light in the room except for the sliver coming under the door.   With Stan gone, he felt alone, isolated in the dark.   He gave thought to getting up to smoke a cigarette, but it was too cold and he was too wet with perspiration.   He became aware of his erection.   He reached down and collared it with his fist.   The turgid organ was warm and damp to the touch. He gave some thought to masturbating, but deferred for the same reasons he declined the cigarette.

Then he thought of Jessie.   The thought of her combined with the stiffness he held in his hand made him think of only one thing: the one and only time he had ever made love to her.   He had recalled the memory countless times since it happened.   He had long since committed the details to memory.   It was something of home that made him feel sad and even more isolated. His heart ached at the thought of her.   It was a sweet torture.

Jessie.

On his last furlough he had stopped by her house almost as soon as he had arrived.   His parents made a big fuss over him, but his mind was clearly on the pretty, young blond next door. Despite his chokehold, he began to soften and retract to a less threatening size.

He recalled how she looked the night they made love, how she behaved.   He tried to think of it in its most romantic terms, a special moment shared between two people.   To H-y it would be fucking, pure and simple.   Maybe it had been fucking to Jessie.   It seemed silly, even now, for him to think of it in any way except as an act of love, not a random, inconsequential event. To think of it in any other light made it seem much less important than he wished it to be, diminishing it to a transaction.

You fuck a whore.   You make love to a woman whose feet barely touched the earth when she walks, who could speak French and hit a high, outside fastball over the fence, a woman whose mere touch could cause the heart to race to its physiologic limits.   The language one used to explain the act depended solely on the amount of emotional investment one was willing to make in it.

By any measure, Jessie was very pretty.   She was not   extraordinarily beautiful, not quite in the same league as Christie Wychulis. But she had a fresh, young face that was difficult not to stare at.   Her hair was blonde and she had worn it longer when she was younger.   For the past several years she kept it shorter so that it rested in long curls upon her shoulders.   It was wavy and soft and parted to one side in the fashion of the day.   Hollis thought she might have put something in it because it always smelled good. Jessie's face was set off by soft, round cheekbones and a smooth, unblemished complexion.   She had dimples on either side of her mouth that would appear whenever she smiled, straight white teeth and blue eyes that seemed to light up at the same time her dimples appeared.

Jessie wasn't perfect.   Her breasts were too small and her hips a tiny bit too broad. Hollis had always thought big hips were a biological indicator of the capacity for having lots of big, healthy babies.   She was slightly taller than Hollis, something he did not mind.   Her laugh was a little too loud at times and she had the charming and arresting tendency toward being slightly obtuse.   This, despite the fact that Jessie was very bright, well read and a cum laude college graduate.   Columbia University.

Her faults aside, and they were minor, almost trivial ones at that, Jessie had never suffered from a lack of suitors.   There was always some boy hanging around her, following her like a little puppy, something Hollis would have loved to do had she let him.

Surely, she must have perceived very early that Hollis liked her.   A crush of that magnitude was not easily concealed.   Jessie might have acted obtuse at times but she wasn't stupid.   Whenever she walked down the sidewalk Hollis would stop in his tracks and stare at her or watch her from the window.   She could not help but notice the disappointment in his voice whenever she declined his offer of a date.   How many times had she made him feel like a jerk by making a point of saying hello to him when she left on a date with somebody else?   It bordered on cruel and unusual punishment for someone whose hormones were pounding in his veins like superheated steam, something, he recalled, the Constitution was supposed to protect him against.

The pretty girl next door left Hollis filled with enormous ambivalence.   He loved her truly, like he would love no other for the rest of his life, someone he would think about in old age and be overtaken by a warm flush of regret for what might have been.   Yet, she seemed determined to keep him at arm's length.   He knew with equal certainty that any other woman he might ever fall in love with would be measured against her.

And then there was that night.   *The Night.*   Hollis thought about it as he lay on his back, his penis flaccid and withdrawn, the covers pulled up around his throat to ward off the cold. Outside in the dead of the night far away he could hear an aircraft engine catch and rev up.

That night.

It was his last night at home.   The next morning he would have to catch the train to Chicago and thence to Grand Island, Nebraska, to re-join the crew and pick up a new bomber. His Mom and Dad prepared a nice dinner, his favorite: fried chicken, dumplings, mashed potatoes and corn-on-the-cob. Naturally, they invited Jessie.   The invitation was a formality. She had barely left Hollis's side since he arrived home a week earlier.   They had gone to the movies, sailed a kite, picnicked, gone to several parties with friends from high school, and necked, necked and necked.   This was absolute paradise for Hollis.   If she was going to behave like this, screw the army; he was going to desert and stay right here.   Except for a feel or two of her breast on a date a few years earlier, she had never let him touch her beyond a kiss.   And, now that he thought of it, the feel was through a sweater, a blouse and a bra, in the back of his father's car and so unassuming that when it happened he figured she probably failed to notice the placement of his hand on her left tit.   Now, they discreetly engaged in some heavy necking, but no named organs were touched, no erogenous zones visited.   It had all been very polite lest he be thought of as some sex-starved GI.   He had calculated, as things went along, that frustrated discretion was better than the unknown consequences of the loss of restraint.   He was no gambler.

She seemed cool, almost embarrassed, at dinner.   Maybe she was uncomfortable in the presence of his parents.   Hollis knew they had not been particularly enamored with the girl and, he suspected, she knew it.   Hollis's parents had always been skeptical of the girl's real intention. They thought she had ruthlessly toyed with his emotions and not-so-subtly teased his infatuation. He was sure they felt that way now, skeptical of this beautiful, witty and charming young lady. On more than one occasion, they had told him to grow up, get over her and find somebody who cared.   Someone who mattered. His mom and dad had suffered long and hard in support of their love struck son, so they must have been surprised when, in plain view, she took his hand and held it while they talked.   She behaved as if she and Hollis had already made the assumption and pronouncement that they were a couple and in love.   They had made no such declaration. The word *love* had never come up.   He was terrified to even think about the word as if the mere mention of it would jinx the whole business and he would be out in the cold again.   He wanted them to be in love so badly he ached, but he was afraid the word would rear its ugly head with all its profound implications and ruin everything.

Then, during dessert, apple pie and ice cream of course, he found himself trying to analyze her behavior, dissect it for some meaning, some indication of her true feelings.   He felt silly.   It was like his first tentative efforts at flying.   He should relax and let things come to him naturally, a smart college kid like him.

After dinner, Hollis and his father went to the living room while Jessie and his mother cleared the table.   Hollis and his father talked for about half an hour while they finished the dishes.   He could hear light conversation and her distinctive laugh.

When Jessie came into the living room and sat down beside him, he realized for the first time how genuinely beautiful she was. Pretty, sure. But not beautiful; not until that very instant. If he had the guts and if there was even an infinitesimal chance that she would accept he'd have asked her to marry him.   Despite what had happened between them during the week, their apparent closeness and burgeoning romance, he figured there was a greater chance of personally accepting Hitler's unconditional surrender than there was of having Jessie agree to anything like that.

After their chat, Jessie suggested that she and Hollis go for a walk.   It was a warm, summer night so, after she thanked Hollis's parents for a pleasant evening, they left.   They walked for twenty minutes, her arm around his, without saying very much.   He could see lightning bugs making little random streaks of yellow light in the dark.   The sing-song of crickets filled the night.   Finally, she stopped and kissed him. It was a soft, delicate kiss-- different than the others.   She asked if he would like to go back to her house.   He said yes, although somewhat reluctantly since he really did not care to visit with her folks on his last night. She sensed this, winked at Hollis and told him her parents had gone to the Jersey Shore for the weekend.   Hollis's heart started to thump.   He thought she might be able to hear it above the sounds of crickets and rustling leaves.

So by design or Providence they were alone when they entered the house.   It was dark and she left it that way.

They sat quietly side by side on the couch.   He placed his arm around her, wondering when the kissing would begin.   They sat for a while listening to the radio.   They benignly exchanged smiles.   He felt like he was searching for something.   Or waiting.   He wasn't sure what it was or if he would know it when he found it.   A sign perhaps.   She turned a little to face him.   She reached over and straightened the knot of his tie with a gentle tug and she let her flat palm linger on the front of his chest before slowly dragging it off. The soft music filled the room, but did not disturb the silence.   The street light shown through the window.   The easy, evening breeze causing the curtains to furl.

"Are you scared?"

"Yes, of course, I'm scared. We've never really been alone like this before."

She laughed softly, "No, I mean the war.   Flying and all ... you know."

"Yes, a lot of things scare me.   But the thing I fear the most is that I might never get to see you again."

Their eyes met.   He tried to read them in the low light for some sign, perhaps *the* sign.

The tension changed.   He desperately wished she would say something.   Anything. This was a pivotal moment in his life and he knew it.   He wanted to ask her to marry him.   He was terrified of her answer regardless of what it might be.   So instead, he said the only thing he could think of, "Want to dance?"

Artie Shaw on the radio filled the room with his sensuous clarinet.   The song was "Moonglow".

She said nothing, just smiled and nodded.   She slipped into his arms, a perfect fit, and followed him lightly as they made little circles over the living room carpet.

They were close--closer than he had ever been to her.   He could feel the front of her strong thighs against his.   Her lower abdomen against his.   Her soft breasts against his chest. Her right hand on his neck, her fingers on the skin above his collar.   Her left hand resting gently in his palm.   He could feel the electricity passing between them where their flesh touched. This close, he was sure she could feel his heart banging around inside his chest.

He tried to mentally keep things in control, afraid he might be so consumed by the warm fog of passion that he might not be able to remember the details of his most precious moment. His senses were hyper acute.   He forced himself to be aware of every sound, every smell, every touch.

"Moonglow" seemed to last forever.   He knew that that song would always be connected with this moment and whenever he heard it he would be transported in an instant to this place and time.

He wondered if she could feel him stir.   Since she was not dead and not clad in a suit of armor she had to sense his arousal.   He made no effort to conceal it or diminish its impact. She made no effort to pull away.   In fact, he thought, she might actually have pulled herself even closer to him.   They swayed gently to the music, but he no longer recognized it as such so entranced was he by her and the moment. There might have been no sound at all and neither would have noticed.

After a while, she stopped. He thought she might return to the couch, emotionally exhausted by the episode.

She quickly stepped out of her shoes which made them virtually the same height.   She placed her arms around his neck and kissed him again.   He held her very tightly, tightly enough to feel her chest rise and fall with each breath.   He pulled her away for a moment and told her very calmly that for as long as he had known her he had always wanted to hold her like this, kiss her like this, and make love to her.   For at least as long as he could remember.   It had been the single most compelling desire of his life.   Even more than his desire to be a doctor.

She looked into his eyes, his face lit by the streetlight shining in through the window. Her hand never left his and she guided him up the stairs.

When they entered her bedroom she kissed him yet again, this time more passionately than ever before.   She kissed like she used to pitch.   Pleasant girl smell permeated the room. He had been here before.   The circumstances were far different then.   He had lost a bet and painted her bedroom as payment.   Once he had helped her carry a footlocker down to the basement.   And once she had hid there on a rainy afternoon playing hide and seek.   It was that day some ten years earlier that he had first kissed her right in this very room.   Tonight was the second.   In the faint light, he could tell that it hadn't changed much in those ten years.   It looked very familiar as he had been here countless times in his fantasies. Different paint. He was stunned to see his picture on her makeup table.   It was his graduation picture from flight school that he had sent to her.   He recalled wondering what she would do with it when she received it. In the standard issue photo, he was smiling broadly with a sense of accomplishment she could not have imagined.   He was wearing his helmet and goggles, his shearling jacket and a silk scarf.   He also recalled his sadness at the time for there had been no one present at his graduation to pin his silver wings onto his chest.

She undid his tie and pulled it from his collar and slowly, deftly unbuttoned his shirt. As they undressed, he grew firm and proud.   He felt no embarrassment even though, when he imagined this moment happening, he had expected that he would be.   She seemed totally at ease as she took off her blouse and let it drop to the floor.   In the subdued light, Hollis marveled at the small dark indentation of her navel.   It was perfectly round and discrete.   This was the first time he could remember ever seeing her navel or anything else for that matter.   But, for all the jumping around in the garden hose on a hot summer afternoon, tree climbing, and occasional swims at the communal pool, this was the first time he had seen this exquisite landmark and the promise of discovery its appearance heralded.   She finished undressing him without a hint of modesty.   He stood before her, naked, except for the Gruen GI watch on his wrist, his erection like steel.   He watched her continue.   She reached around, undid her bra, and let her round breasts fall free.   He wished the light could be a little better, but, even so, he could see her pale, pink nipples stand out like perfect round islands against her creamy skin.   He reached out to caress her   causing her to moan with contentment.   She took his hands and cupped them against her face kissing his palms.

She stepped back from him and took off her skirt.   Beneath that was a silk slip.   The garter belt and stockings were next. Lastly, she slid her panties to her feet and stepped out of them. She was naked, and, Hollis thought, exquisite, perfect.   Beyond any right of expectation.

He studied her in the dim light.   The triangle of dark blond hair was small, much smaller than he thought it would be.   Even though he had seen it like this in his dreams a thousand times, this was the first time he had actually laid eyes on it, this sacred forest.   This must have been how Columbus felt, a combination of awe and relief.   She led him to the bed.

He pulled the covers back and she kissed him long and deeply, their nude bodies touching full length.   Her body was firm yet lithe. Her skin was creamy smooth and supple.   Her touch seemed expert and deliberate.   Never, not ever, had he known a moment as exquisite as this.

Their muscles fueled by passion, they were soon writhing uncontrollably against each other until he could contain himself no longer.   She resisted with the smallest of effort.   It was her last obligatory act of surrender. She was every man's idea of perfect.   This was rapture beyond his most erotic adolescent fantasies.

Jessie was a nice girl and nice girls don't fuck.   He had some knowledge of these things. Some, even if limited, clinical experience with the virginal state and the terminal breakthrough. Jessie was no virgin.   Someone had been there before he had arrived at the entrance to the cave that night.   Reflecting on the revelation, he was ambivalent about his feelings on the matter. Mostly he felt lucky and privileged to be among the chosen.

He held very still for a moment trying to memorized the sensation of what it was like to finally be here.   Then he muttered, "Oh, Jessie," and started.

She reached the epitome before he did.   Had it not been for the grinding teeth and moaning he might have missed it for he was driven relentlessly and with single strength of purpose to his own release.   This had become, and would remain, the single most deliriously pleasurable moment of his life.   Their hearts beat fiercely as if in unison pounding against each other separated only by some bone and a thin layer of skin.

Spent, he stayed as long as he could, her arms clasped around his neck, her soft warm breath on his neck.   At last, he lowered himself to the bed.   He placed his head on her shoulder and put his arm around her waist.   They lay silently for nearly an hour, not moving except to breathe.

He brought his head up to look at her, their heads resting on the same satin-covered pillow.

"You've always meant so much to me.   There were times when you were all I could think about."

"I've always known that, John. You've   always been my very best friend.   But I never realized until these past few months while you were away, how much a part of my life you were. And I know that must sound crazy.   You were always around.   Someone I could always count on, someone who would always be there.   When you left I suddenly realized that I missed you. Absence does make the heart, my heart, grow fonder.   I didn't want you to go without letting you know how I felt and that I cared."

"I love you."

"I know that, too.   You always have."   She smiled, "For as long as I can remember." They laughed softly in the dark.   "I love you, John. And I never knew it until now."

"Better late than never, I guess."

"Each in his own good time."

"There is so much to talk about."

She smiled and cocked her head the way she always did when he got too close.   "No. Not now.   We'll have time."

Calmly, he said, "Sure. I guess you're right."   The only thing he didn't have was time. Nobody had much time.

They slept in each other's arms.   It was close to six when he woke up.   The sun had reappeared for yet one more day and the birds were making a terribly inconsiderate racket in the trees between the houses.   Jessie slept quietly.   He gently extricated himself from her grasp trying not to disturb her and padded into the bathroom.   When he returned, she was awake stretching contented muscles and patting the bed beside her.   She lifted the sheet and he resumed his place beside her.   It was still warm with their heat.   Yes, he had to reassure himself, this really did happen.

He glanced at his watch.   He had to catch the 10:05 as it stopped briefly in Chester on its way to Philadelphia.   He would just as soon stay here until he had to leave for the train station, but she insisted that he get up and spend the morning with his folks.   She would rejoin him when they went to the station.

Regrettably, she was right.   He kissed her again wanting to tell her how much he loved her, but he didn't want to touch the word again, choosing to leave things as they had left them before they fell asleep.   Maybe she had time to reconsider her declaration while he was in the bathroom and, in the light of day, withdraw it.

She kissed him back.   He could still sense the soft feel of her lips on his.   The feel of her nude body against him.   It was the kiss he remembered best.   Would he ever know another morning, another moment, like this?

He dressed and left, sorry he had not made love to her a second time.   He made no pretense of having spent the night anywhere else than where he had.   Besides, they were up already, the sound and smell of sizzling bacon wafted over him as soon as he stepped onto the porch.

They said very little which was just as well.   They could, no doubt, sense his thoughts were elsewhere.   He showered and packed.   She came to the porch dressed in a bright yellow dress.   She had a small package wrapped in lilac-colored tissue paper under her arm.   On the porch, with the sunlight behind her, she seemed angelic again.   Like the time she beaned him. She took his breath away; she was stunningly beautiful.

Everyone cordially exchanged greetings.   She acted without even a hint of embarrassment at what had clearly transpired the night before between her and their son. Perhaps, he suspected, they might now think her guilty of the most flagrant form of emotional abuse.   His mother probably thought she had been thoroughly reckless with her son's feelings. If they did, they gave no indication and he cared not a whit.   He had achieved an independence last night that no parent could rescind.   They left for the station, her arm hooked around his.

This was the stuff, he told himself, of a truly historic love. He knew that no other man would ever love this woman as he did.   No one.

He lay in his cold bed, dreaming of that night that seemed so long ago, certain of that. As he stared into the dark, he told himself that, as long as she lived, she would never find a man who cared for her more.   He felt very sad and alone.   He wanted to hold her just one more time.   Just once more.

He pulled himself from bed and turned on the light.   He retrieved a piece of stationary and wrote

Dear Jessie,
Will you marry me?

John.

He folded the letter, placed it in an envelope, numbered it and set it to one side.   Mailing it would be his first order of business.

He turned out the light and went back to sleep.

Book II

Targets of Opportunity

It can happen to me.   I need to be more careful...

Chapter Twenty-two   **Beef**

Wednesday, August 18, 1943

It was raining and had been all night, something Hollis was dimly aware of as he wrote his short note to Jessie.   He slipped on his trench coat and dashed to the latrine to urinate and shave.

When he returned, he finished dressing, placed the envelope in his pocket and went searching for Leo.   He would mail the letter to Jessie and then eat breakfast.   Afterwards, he would march into Ransahoff's office and finish things.

Leo was particularly talkative at breakfast.   His apparent short memory did not break the somber mood of those who had also chosen to eat.   Conversation was subdued.   People spoke in whispers as one might at a wake.

As Leo talked, it became apparent that he either was unaware of how close they had come to eternity yesterday or he chose, in his own incurably optimistic way, to ignore that fact. Hollis thought he knew and understood Leo Wychulis pretty well but he could not discern which it was, stupidity or hopeless, irrational optimism.   *'Toto, I get the feeling we're not in Kansas anymore'* after a flak burst made a *di-rect* hit on them?

They had an aircraft recognition lecture after lunch.   He would tell Ransahoff then.

When Hollis returned from breakfast he found a stranger had visited his room. Whoever it was had moved the phonograph and cartridge box onto the desk and placing his stuff on Stan's bed.   His first inclination was to feel violated by the invasion of his and Stan's room by a stranger.   But then, he had to remind himself that the room did not belong to him and, in fact, it did not even belong to his country.   It was just borrowed space from the British.   It was obvious he needed to surrender himself to the fact that he had a new roommate.   There was nothing he could do about it.   The war had to continue no matter how much he sulked.

"Oh, hi."

Hollis turned toward the origin of the voice and saw a short, stocky lieutenant with a grinning face and an extended right hand.

"My name is Boeuf Salayhan.   I guess I'm your new roommate."

Hollis shook his hand, which was more than Stan had ever done, "Hi, John Hollis."

"What happened to the guy who used to sleep here?"

"Gone home."

"Not in a box, I hope."

"No.   He finished his 25 and left."

Salayhan looked down at the bed.   "Maybe it's a lucky bed."

Hollis lit a cigarette hoping the small talk would soon end.   He needed to find his courage for the inevitable confrontation he would have with Ransahoff today.   Light banter with the new guy was distracting.

"You first pilot?"

"Yeah."

"We just got in from the replacement center.   Seen much combat?" he asked as casually as if he had asked, 'Do you golf?'   He was much too cheerful for his own good.

"Yeah."

"I understand the CO's new."

"You mean Ransahoff?"

"Yeah, he wants to meet with me and the other officers in about an hour.   The sergeant at the squadron office said we may have a practice mission later today."

"Yeah, sounds about right.   Ransahoff's regular army.   He's pretty tough and I'd do exactly as he says.   When he tells you to fly in close, do it."   *And wipe that silly, naive grin off your fucking face, Rookie, I saw men die yesterday.*

"Really."

Salayhan must have gotten the message that Hollis was in no mood to chat so he quietly started putting his cloths away.   That was fine with Hollis.   He had been with the Group less than a week and survived one of the deadliest air battles in history.   Two crews from his squadron, people he had just met, had been blown out of the sky and his own prospects did not look that good.

He wanted Stan back.   Stan may have been mentally unfit, as some people seemed to think, but he was still Stan: hero, survivor, carnivore.   Hollis had no basis for making a judgment about sanity or the lack thereof, but he knew Stan was as sane as anybody on the base, perhaps the planet.   Hollis also knew that rooming with Stan for just five days had not afforded great insight into the complexities of his mind.   Eisenberg was tired, used up.   His withdrawal from casual, daily human intercourse was a defense mechanism.   He simply couldn't handle death anymore.   Maybe it was not death, but the loss.   Stan was the only person Stan knew who had gotten as far as he did.   Maybe, too, Stan felt he was living on borrowed time, walking around as if on the proverbial thin ice.   Disintegrate on impact, burned alive like Cahill. Struck by a bolt out of the blue. And then Entwhistle had to send him to Schweinfurt for his last mission, instead of some milk run which, Hollis was led to believe, was unofficial standard practice for the last mission of a tour.

Anyway, Hollis viewed his departure with mixed emotions.   He lamented his absence, but was glad for him.   Hollis knew that if he ever got into trouble like that clown Selkirk had, Stan would be there to save him.   Yet, it was curious that yesterday, when he fell back after the bomb run, Stan had made no effort to cover him.   Or when Selkirk straggled with a feathered engine Stan did not leave the formation to look after him.   Perhaps Stan, so close to finishing, was unwilling to risk his neck to save anybody else's.   On this particular day the odds were just too long.   Heroics aside, Stan still had nine other lives to look after and in the calculus of risk he chose to abide by the rules of engagement and cover his crew and his squadron first.

Maybe it was for Stan's own good that he got hustled off the base so quickly after he landed.   The last time Hollis saw him was at interrogation when he was standing against the wall talking softly to Gleason.   Meanwhile, Beamis was dutifully packing his stuff.

Somebody, he wondered if it might even be Van Patten himself, wanted Stan removed as quickly and with as little notice as possible.   Stan had nothing left to contribute and keeping him here would only exacerbate his guilt at surviving and his sense of separation from those around him whose fortunes were yet to be determined.

Hollis smiled because he figured it out.   A move he felt was mean-spirited and hasty was, in fact, merciful.   Van Patten did exactly what needed to be done.   Get Stan out of here as fast as humanly possible and without fanfare.   This made him feel good for the first time about Van Patten.   Maybe the Colonel understood this bombing business better than anybody thought.

The call came down from on high: If he comes back, get him off the base.   Gladly, was Ransahoff's reply.   Hollis hoped one day they might be as thoughtful for him.

Hollis looked over at Salayhan with pity.   Poor guy had no idea what he was getting into.   Here he was moving in with a strange guy, needing, as he himself had needed only a few days earlier, someone to talk to, guidance, professional help, maybe only just a friendly face. And Hollis lay there blowing smoke rings feeling sorry for himself.

"Alright, you can finish that later.   Listen up, I've got some things you need to know."

"What the hell kind of name is 'Beef'?" Selkirk asked, a glass of beer in his hand.   "And how do you spell it?"

"It's French.   You spell it B-O-U-E-F."

"Boof?"

"Beef."

"Interesting.   So how'd you like the practice mission?   You keep it in tight like he told you?"

Salayhan smiled.

Selkirk continued, "You better keep it in tight or you won't be here long.   They'll be scraping you up with a putty knife."

Salayhan's expression changed.   He knew Selkirk was serious.   Salayhan turned to Hollis for some sign, some reassurance that Selkirk was just exaggerating.   Hollis just shook his head.   Maybe Selkirk was laying it on a little too thick.

"That little romp with Ransahoff this afternoon didn't give you any great insight into survival techniques in aerial combat over occupied Europe?   Remember Cahill yesterday, Jack? He cooked up real good."

Salayhan's face drained of blood.

"Listen, Boof, you better keep your ass in tight on these missions and you keep your head up and your eye on the ball or the Hun will pick you off and spit you out just for fun.   They look for a plane out of place or a squadron that's strung out and pick 'em off one by one until there ain't nothin' left.   They catch you stragglin' and you better kiss your sorry ass goodbye." He turned to Hollis, "You tell him, Jack.   You're his roommate."

"We already had this conversation."

"Well, maybe you need to have this conversation with him again."

Ransahoff walked over and said, "You guys better turn in we've been alerted for tomorrow."

Hollis watched Ransahoff leave.   He would tell him in the morning before the mission.

Salayhan turned to Hollis, beseeching, "They won't send us, will they?   We haven't been here long enough, have we?"

"You better turn in," Hollis said.

As Salayhan walked away, Selkirk asked, "You make out a will, Boof?"

Chapter Twenty-three   **Stuff**

Thursday, August 19, 1943

Hollis heard the barrack's door open and the approaching footsteps and was instantly filled with a sense of dread. The footsteps stopped at his door.   The door opened filling the room with a shaft of light and Beamis walked in.   Hollis turned his head in anticipation. Instead, Beamis ignored him and stepped over to Salayhan who was sleeping soundly.

"Lieutenant," he said softly, "Get up, sir.   They're putting up a squadron today and you're going with them.   My guess is a milk run."

"Huh?"

"Get up, sir, breakfast at oh-four-thirty, briefing at oh-five-thirty."

Beamis departed when he was sure Salayhan was awake and left the door open to keep light in the room.   Hollis turned over and felt smugly satisfied.   They were sending the new guy on a milk run.   Good for him.

He could hear Salayhan struggling in the shadows, banging things around trying to dress himself.   Finally, he whispered, "Sorry," and turned on the light.   Hollis pulled the covers up over his head, but knew this simple act would not allow him to return to sleep until Salayhan was gone.   Even concealed, cocoon-like, beneath his warm blankets, he could tell Salayhan was fumbling and if he was fumbling he was probably terrified.   Hollis remembered with some humility that it had been less than a week since he had flown his first mission and he was being treated with the deference afforded veterans of much greater repute that he. Stan had been there to imitate.   Salayhan had no one.   Hollis could remain indifferent or he could help him. Heroics were sometimes measured in small increments so he flipped the covers back and sat up. He lit a cigarette and remembered the last words Stan had ever said to him.   Good ol' Stan. After the Schweinfurt briefing he walked over and grabbed Hollis by the arm and said, *"Listen, Hollis, you do exactly what I do and stay in tight.   You hear?"*   He vaguely remembered nodding.

"You better dress warm."

Salayhan snapped around unaware that Hollis had arisen.   "What did you say?"

"I said to dress warm.   If your crate is like mine that heater isn't worth a damn.   And your feet are gonna get pretty cold."   He took a long, luxurious drag on his cigarette and continued, "Put on clean underwear.   It'll cut down on the chances of infection if you're hit.

Salayhan lifted the lid of his footlocker and pulled out fresh shorts and t-shirt.   He then climbed into his long johns.

"You got any silk socks?"

"No."

Hollis placed his feet on the cold gritty floor and stood up, "Jesus, didn't they tell you guys anything?"   He reached into his locker and pulled out his third, and last, pair of silk socks. "Here, put these on."   He tossed them over.   "But powder your feet first."

Salayhan looked perplexed.   "I don't have any powder."

"For God-sakes.   Here."   Hollis took the small can of talc and tossed it to Salayhan. The lid was not on tightly and the white powder puffed out in a small layer onto his hands.

"Thanks."

Hollis watched Salayhan finish dressing and told him to place a muffler around his neck and tuck it into the collar of his shearling jacket for added warmth.   He slipped his feet into the large, clumsy flying boots and stood up for Hollis's inspection.   He seemed ready to go.   Hollis had done all he could.   He crushed out his second cigarette, brushing the grit off the bottom of his feet and slid under the sheets.   The place where he had laid was already cold.   Salayhan reached down to pull the sheets and blanket up with military compulsion to make his bed.

"Don't make your bed.   Leave it.   That way it will be ready for when you get back."

"Yeah, thanks.   See ya' later."

"Right."

Salayhan turned off the lights and quietly, deferentially closed the door behind him. Hollis wondered if Salayhan would remember to shave and brush his teeth.

Hollis ran into Ransahoff at breakfast.   "Where'd you send Bouef?"

"Wing wanted us to put up a squadron today to some airfield in Brussels.   Group sent the 535th.   Should be an easy one so I sent Salayhan along to blood him.   Should be back in time for lunch."   He walked away upset with himself that, for whatever reason, he missed another opportunity to tell Ransahoff he quit.

Around lunchtime, because they had nothing better to do, Hollis walked out to the flightline with Leo and Sully to watch the dispatched squadron return.   Almost right on schedule the dull rumble of the returning bombers filled the air.   There were six bombers.

"How many'd we put up?" Hollis asked to no one in particular.

"Seven."

"Jesus, we lost one?" Leo asked.

"Dunno."

"--on a god-damned milk run?"

They watched the bombers peel away from each other, land one after another uneventfully and taxi to their places.   No one taxied over to the 532nd dispersal area.

"Where's Salayhan?"

Hollis could feel his heart sink.

Leo turned to Hollis and said, "I don't know.   Maybe we better go over to interrogation and find out."

The three men hitched a ride over to the big briefing hut and watched the returning crews climb down off the trucks, their flying gear draped over their arms, cigarettes dangling from their mouths, 'just another day at the office' expressions on their faces.

Suddenly, Ransahoff emerged from the briefing room.   Hollis called after him, "Where's Salayhan?"

Ransahoff yelled over his shoulder, "Didn't make it.   Flak."

"What happened?"

"The first bomb run got fucked up and they went around again.   By then the flak gunners, both of them, had the range pretty good and Salayhan got it."

"Christ," Leo said.   "Too bad.   First mission and he buys it."

Sully said, "Poor sumbitches were here less'n 24 hours."

Hollis returned to his room and flung himself onto his bed.   Salayhan was dead.   Gone. Poof.   His personal effects were still in the room partially unpacked awaiting his return.   The GI inclination was to riffle through the stuff looking for some item or items worth keeping. Their presence made Hollis suddenly uncomfortable as if the stuff was contaminated by some death virus. Hollis left it alone   feeling silly about imparting inanimate objects with some mysterious life and death power, as if only touching it might yield an irreversible hex, and he was happy with his decision.

He wondered if he had done enough to help Salayhan, but realized that all the advice in the world would not protect you from flak.   You could be tucked in so tight your wing tips overlapped, it wouldn't stop a lucky hit.   If it had your name on it, too bad.   It was God's will. Di-rect hit.   Hollis remembered Salayhan had died wearing his silk socks.   His mind reeled with the permutations of superstition.   Maybe they had been cursed and it was Hollis's good fortune someone else had worn them into combat.   Somehow he had survived another close call, a brush with the cold, Fickle Finger of Fate.

A short time later, Selkirk sailed through the door and casually said, "Ol' Beef's gone west.   Shame.   They didn't clear out his stuff yet.   Go through it?"

"No.   Leave it alone."

"Come on, Jack there might be some good stuff here.   If you don't take it someone else will.   Better you than Beamis."   Where upon Selkirk opened the footlocker.   Hollis half expected a provoked, vengeful Moses to rise out of the box and smite Selkirk for his transgression of the Stuff of the Dead. Besides, Hollis thought, he doubted Beamis would pilfer anything. Coal maybe…

Instead, Selkirk gasped with delight.   "Well, that blows that theory."

"What theory?"

"That only the good die young.   Look at these silk panties.   Stick with me honey, and before the night's over you'll be farting through silk.   Nylon stockings?   Jesus Christ, what was he planning to do fuck half of England?   I wonder if the War Materials Board knows about this. This guy was gonna be a big hit in Piccadilly."

"Come on, Mickey, leave that alone.   The CQ will take care of it."

Selkirk made noises with Boeuf's possessions and it was an obscene sound.   "Look, Hollis.   Tomorrow could be my turn.   Or yours.   You want any of my stuff when I'm gone, you're welcome to it. This is total war, the rules of polite etiquette don't apply any more. What's Beamis gonna do, send these rubbers home to his mother?   Or his wife?"   He took the nylons and panties, curled them into a ball and shoved them and the condoms into his pocket. He tucked a carton of cigarettes under his arm and tossed Hollis a Zippo.   Hollis rubbed it's shiny, steel case and wondered how unlucky an inanimate object might be or why Salayhan hadn't had it with him when he perished.   Maybe he forgot it.   Just like he had forgotten to shave or brush his teeth. He wasn't thinking clearly this morning, after all.   Maybe today was the day he quit smoking.   It was such an unhealthy habit.   He looked at it for a minute and placed it into his pocket where it came to rest heavy and ominous against his thigh.

"Huh, another Jew."   Selkirk lifted a small neck chain on which hung a mezuzah. "Poor guy shoulda had it with him."

"Come on, Mickey, stop."

When Selkirk was done looting, he took his stolen treasures and left saying something about Salayhan leading a cloistered life.   The stockings or panties being the only thing of genuine worth.   Or perhaps also the lighter.   Hollis could still feel it against the skin of his thigh, heavy out of all proportion to its size.   He took it out and placed it on the desk and looked at it half expecting it to spontaneously ignite from silent, violated outrage.

A short time later, Beamis sauntered in and looked around the room.   "I gotta clear out poor Lieutenant Salayhan's stuff.   You go through any of it?"

Hollis felt a sudden pang if guilt.   "No," he said truthfully as he glanced at the cigarette lighter, mute witness to the recent pilferage.

"OK, well let me get it out of here so I can send it back where it came from."   Beamis proceeded to gather up the articles belonging to the late, departed Beef.

Hollis noted with some warmth and reassurance how carefully and respectfully Beamis performed his care-taking.   Like some priestly duty to the Dead.   He folded the pants and blouse and packed them away.   He closed the small picture frame, photos Hollis had never looked at, and placed them gently into the footlocker.   Hollis felt sadness and resignation as he watched Beamis complete his task wondering if and when he might do the same after him.

"Well," he finally said, lifting the footlocker and the B-4 bag with a grunt, "maybe Selkirk will want some of this stuff."

Selkirk, the grave robber.

The boy walked silently between the snow-covered rails.   He was preoccupied with stepping on the ties instead of the ballast, making the walk home a sort of game.   The ties were raised in the snow which crunched softly with each step.   The air was cold and crisp in the early evening.   It was almost dark and the phosphorescent light given off by the snow allowed him to watch his steamy breath as he exhaled.   It was very still and quiet.   The snow was so fresh that passing trains had not yet blackened it with soot and dirty steam. The stillness and quiet was tranquilizing, the steady crunching of the shoes in the snow hypnotic.   As he looked down, stepping carefully on each tie as the rails led around a bend, he suddenly became aware of his shadow as if daylight had returned.   Eventually, he could see the shadow of the top of his head as it crossed the next tie then the next.   This, while odd, became mesmerizing as well.   Steadily, his shadow grew darker, more sharply defined and the snow blindingly intense.   As he wheeled around the locomotive headlight, as large as the sun was the last thing he saw.

Hollis bolted up in bed, the sheets soaked, the cold, wet t- shirt made him shiver in the dark.   Salyahan was gone.   His bed was empty, his belongings cleared out.   There was no living person on the other side of the room to provide reference, differentiate nightmare from reality.   No soft breathing, no snoring, no flatus, no grunts or rustle of sheets to confirm the presence of another living soul.   Hollis felt desperately alone, like when he was a boy, waking up in the middle of the night, in the dark, not being able to separate dream or nightmare from reality.   He dropped his legs over the side of the bed, lit a cigarette and stared at the glowing ember until his hand stopped shaking.

Hollis tried hard to regain mental equilibrium.   The events of the past three days had compressed the emotions of a lifetime into a matter of hours.   His baptism of fire had been wrenching.   He started shaking again.   He knew he didn't want to die.   But then, no one did.

Not this way.   The fear he had felt before Schweinfurt began to rise again in his chest, constricting his breathing.   How could they expect anybody to keep going day after day?   Was it raw courage?   The sense of high adventure, like his great-grandfather trudging through hot, dusty Virginia?   Or was the fear and shame of not going worse than dying?   If the guy, a total stranger, sitting across from me at chow was willing to go who was I not to join him?

Had Entwhistle shown more courage by *not* going?   Who was the judge, ultimately? Hollis again toyed with the idea of going to Ransahoff to tell him he couldn't do it anymore.   He just didn't have the guts.

He smiled in the dark.   *Jesus*, he thought, *Ransahoff will kill me.   Yeah, he'd be pretty mad alright*, but Cassidy and Eisenberg and Cahill and Salayhan and the rest, names and faces he could not recall or did not know, would be betrayed.   Which was worse?   Fifty years from now when he had his great-grandchildren on his knee would it matter what he did?   Would Schweinfurt mean as much to people as Cold Harbor? Would it mean anything at all?

One thing they weren't going to do was put another rookie in that bed.

Friday, August 20,1943

Hollis heard the approach of footsteps and knew it was Beamis.   When the door came Beamis shown his flashlight onto Hollis and said, "Oh good, you're up.   Breakfast at oh-six hundred.   Briefing at oh-six-thirty."   Instead of leaving, Beamis stood in the doorway, a shadow against the light from the hall.

"What?" Hollis asked.

"Lieutenant Eisenberg always asked 'where to, today?'"

"OK.   Where to today, Beamis?"

"I don't know, sir.   Briefing at oh-six-thirty."   Beamis turned and left.

If they were going to another tough one, and Hollis was not sure they had enough replacements yet to send up a full group, he would tell Ransahoff that he would not be going.   If it was a milk run he would fly it.   It seemed like a reasonable compromise with his terror.

At briefing, they announced a milk run.   Hollis looked around the room and noticed many new faces.   They seemed eager, as Salayhan had, to join the Big Leagues.   The veterans, and he was one of them, seemed unmoved by the news.   Their reaction would have been the same regardless of how severe the announced target.   He had overheard Clevenger say at the Officer's Club that morale had hit rock bottom after the loss of just one more crew, Salayhan's, on a God-damned milk run.   A God-damned airfield in Holland.   And there were still a lot of empty beds in the Squadron.

Ransahoff had promoted Watanabe to the left seat of Stan's crew and given him a replacement copilot.   The Squadron could put up four planes and two more would be added from another squadron making the full complement of six planes.   Hopefully, today they might get the replacements they needed to bring the Squadron up to full strength, although Hollis was puzzled that such things would even matter to him.

Hollis would fly number three beside Ransahoff and Selkirk would lead the second element.

After taking stations, the rain grew in intensity, drumming steadily on the metal skin of the freshly-restored **Cleopatra's Asp**.   A jeep came around and announced that the mission had been scrubbed.   As Hollis deplaned he wondered how many people would be alive today in France because it was raining in England.

Without removing his flight clothes, Hollis walked directly to squadron headquarters. He strode into the duty office and found the squadron adjutant.

"Who's in charge of billeting assignments?"

"I am, why?"

"Now that Salayhan is gone, I want somebody else besides a rookie in my room."

"I don't know.   Entwhistle wanted new crews integrated into veteran crews.   Thought it would help bring new crews into the scheme of things better and--"

"Entwhistle isn't here anymore.   Put somebody else in there."

"I don't know.   Major Entwhistle didn't want copilots in that building."

"Slagle was in that building."

"Yes, I know but--"

"Entwhistle's gone.   Make a decision."

"Who did you have in mind?"

"Wychulis, my copilot.   Him I can deal with."

"Fine.   Done."

Hollis strode into the Nissen hut where Leo was quartered along with H-y and Sullivan and four other flying officers.   They were undressing from the mission and were surprised to see Hollis still suited up for flying.   Leo was sitting on the end of his bed.   He was smiling.

"What the hell you smiling for, Leo?" Hollis said.

"I heard they gave Rizzo credit for the kill and I just found out the four of us have been promoted to First Lieutenant."

"Boy, I'm sure that has the Nazzis quakin' in their boots knowing that you and that bunch are climbin' up the chain of command," Watanabe said as he pulled the covers up over his shoulder turning his back to them.

Hollis went over to the shelf where Leo kept his pictures of Christie and picked them up, "Come on, Leo.   Let's go."

"Where we goin'?"

"You're moving to the Taj Mahal with me."

"Oh, OK."

Leo had his stuff packed up in no time and they were carting it over to Pilot's House when they were intercepted by Selkirk.

"Hey, where you guy's going with that stuff?"

"Leo's moving in with me."

"Great, you guy's hear the news?"

"Yeah, we were promoted."

"No, that's not what I heard.   We got a new ops officer."

"Who?" Hollis asked.

"Some guy from the 534th by the name of Otho Barbieri."

"Otho, huh?   Does he outrank us?"

"Yeah, he's a captain.   They say he's another Dutch Ransahoff without the great sense of humor."

As Hollis struggled in the rain with the overloaded B-4 bag, he asked Selkirk, "What else have you heard?"

"Barney Rager's getting out of the hospital.   Won't lose his eye after all.   Probably be back on flying duty lickety-split."

"That's great, Mickey.   You keep us informed," Hollis added, unable to conceal his sarcasm.   Rager, the group's best lead pilot had been wounded in the face over Schweinfurt. He was the reason Van Patten landed first.   He had been wounded by the FW pilot who was killed and collided head-on with the following B-17.   He had flown practically the rest of the mission using one eye, the blood he shed freezing as it dripped down the front of his mask onto his Mae West.

There was concern that he would lose his eye and never fly again.   Since, with Eisenberg gone, he was the finest pilot in the group, that would have been especially regrettable. For the Nazis that would be as good as if they had killed him.

When Leo settled into the room, he methodically put his stuff away, placing each item precisely, deliberately.   He took a group of photographs of his wife and positioned them carefully on the desk forming a shrine of sorts before which he could sit and write to her.   His gallery made Hollis's few photos of Jessie seem puny.

He laid back on his bed and stared at the ceiling wondering where his fateful letter to Jessie was and what reaction it would generate when she read it.   He had indeed crossed another Rubicon with so many Rubicons yet to cross.

He looked at his watch and speculated if now would be a good time to quit.   He had been able to participate in this morning's mission by only the slimmest margin of emotional reserve.   Had it not been a milk run he would have done as Entwhistle had, announce his decision not to fly anymore and walk off the field.   And in doing so acknowledge to all the world his assessment that any kind of life, no matter how humiliating, was better than any kind of death no matter how noble.   But he knew the mission would likely be scrubbed allowing him to delay the confrontation.   The rain, varying from a barely perceptible drizzle--a maddeningly deceptive form of mist which left everything soaked without any visible precipitation--to a steady downpour, had started a day and a half ago and had not stopped.   No one really expected it to cooperate and clear out in time for bombing, the Gods of Weather once again thumbing their noses at the Gods of War.

Some were glad for it, a reprieve, but others were less sanguine, viewing each day a mission was not flown as another damp, miserable day away from hearth and kin.   Especially a milk run.

He looked over at Leo who was singing quietly to himself fiddling with his shaving kit, totally oblivious to the tempest of conflict and indecision raging between Hollis's heart and brain not a dozen feet away.   He couldn't tell him.   This was not something that could be easily discussed for it was not a rational act.   It was visceral, instinctive, not some logical conclusion derived from careful and thoughtful reflection of fact and risk.   The decision to participate in an activity than ran counter to the inherent biological need for self-preservation did not lend itself to deductive reasoning.

He couldn't climb into the plane without first heaving his breakfast onto the grass.   He had not the stomach, literally, for this bombing business.   His hands trembled as he dressed this morning.   He had not the strength to pull himself up into the nose and made some excuse to climb in the waist and enter the flight deck from behind.   His mind, overwhelmed by the possibilities, prevented him from concentrating on the cockpit checklist.   The order scrubbing came just in time.   The one person who probably could sense his turmoil was Leo sitting two feet away in the cockpit and he was not about to confirm his copilot's suspicions and casually admit he was yellow, as if he were mentioning a leg cramp or a toothache.

He feared what Dodge might think.   He had enough guts for the whole crew.   Banging on the bomb bay doors with a crowbar inches away from two tons of high explosive, as bullets punctured the chamber.   He was straddling the catwalk when the doors fell away with nothing between him and Mother Earth, but a good grip.   The confines of the narrow catwalk and full bomb bay prevented anyone from conducting business encumbered by the bulk of a parachute. He imagined Dodge leaping back and forth between bomb bay, the turret, transferring fuel and manhandling the bomb bay doors closed as the bitterly cold hurricane swirled inside the empty, cavernous bomb bay, threatening to blow him and Sully out into space.

All the while, Hollis was standing on the sharp precipice of panic, convinced the next vibration or shudder or burble of disturbed air would be the catastrophe he expected--

The door burst open without a knock.   It was a sergeant from the Squadron office.

"Sorry to disrupt your reverie, Gentleman, but you got these letters to censor."   He dropped a stack of letters from the Squadron enlisted men and non-coms on the desk and left.

Leo got up and picked up a couple of letters and began reading.   Hollis did the same, welcoming the distraction from his odious musings.   He started reading a letter from some gunner.   He deliberately avoided reading the name of the author.

There were rules.   No 'x's or 'o's which could pass for coded espionage.   No stray symbols or numerical pattern or recurring words.   Nothing that mentioned place or missions or losses or anything that might reveal some useful tidbit of intelligence, no matter how seemingly trivial, the enemy, in his devious way, might use to advantage.

But there was none of that.   Instead, it was the sad document of a homesick boy.   He missed his mother and father and his younger sisters and his dog, Buttons.   He talked about his friends and mentioned obliquely that some had gone away recently.   Hollis signed it and returned it to its envelope.

There was one from a mechanic, a sergeant and this time he looked at the name.   It was a name he did not recognize.   The sergeant and his wife were obviously expecting their first child.   There was a list of names.   Hollis, perversely and for his own self-amusement, tried to construct some clandestine message out of the names, three for boys and three for girls.   But hard as he tried, he could deduce neither written or numerical code from which he could infer the name of a target or unit number or personality.   He laughed to himself for there was no Schweinfurtia or Lucretia LeBourget or B. VanPatty.

The door opened after a minimal knock.   "Morning, sirs.   I got bikes for sale which their most recent owners will no longer require," Beamis said.   "Less of a purchase really, more like a lease.   When and if you no longer require the use of said bike it reverts back to the owner."

"And who might that be?" Leo asked.

"Me."

"How much?"

"Two pounds sterling per month, Lieutenant.   An outright purchase from a local or one of the other sharks on the base might cost you ten times that.   Besides they're all in good shape except the one Lieutenant Cody broke.   He ran into a tree one night when him and Lieutenant Eisenberg got drunk at one of the pubs and they tried to ride home in the dark.   Bent the wheel, but I got it straightened out pretty good.   I'll let you have that one at half price."

"Whatever got you involved in bike rentin'?" Leo asked.

"For you guys the war is a duty, I mean you volunteered.   Me, I was drafted.   I see it as an opportunity."

Chapter Twenty-four   **Leo**

After securing a pair of bicycles they returned to their censoring.   Hollis read another letter, took out the names of several sergeants who had been shot down and removed a comment, composed in obvious frustration, about missing the target, which could easily be discerned as Schweinfurt, and the prediction that they would have to go back to this terrible place.   This was followed by a statement, also fueled by frustration, wondering if the brass really knew what they were doing.   That they were losing planes faster than they could be replaced and that if they kept pissing away planes and crews soon there wouldn't be any.

Hollis was not shocked that the author felt the way he did, but he was very surprised that he would be so bold as to write down such information in flagrant violations of the rules. Hollis assumed anybody below the rank of lieutenant was too ignorant to worry about the bigger picture.   He was almost certain that Augie was incapable of conceptual or abstract thought and assumed the same of every other non-com.   Hegemony, *realpolitik* and rationalism and the clash of ideologies were on an intellectual level simply too high for them to reach.

Maybe the author wrote down these words knowing full well that they would be rejected and was trying to get it off his chest since one rarely spoke of such things to one's compatriots. Or perhaps he was trying to spread his concerns in hope that his doubts might take root and spread like a virus just in case the results of the bombing were not already crystal clear to everyone.   The mind revolts against the notion of being sacrificed on the altar of some scheme or pet theory no matter how noble or strategic.   In this age of technological superiority, each gadget engendered its own constituency for its proper use.   What was the content of letters sent home after Cold Harbor?

Hollis knew there would be mistakes made on and by all sides. Nothing this cataclysmic had ever happened in all of human history up to this very moment. The side that would ultimately triumph would be the side that made the fewest mistakes.

It didn't matter.   It was too much for Hollis to try and glean the psychology or intent off a written page.   The author's anger and anguish were wasted on the wrong audience. Dutifully, he excised the paragraph with the razor's edge leaving a big gap in the text.

Hollis laid back and decided the rest of the mail would wait.   Besides, Leo diligently read one letter after the other and, if Hollis procrastinated long enough, his new roommate would have them finished.

He had barely dozed off when his photographic memory, which had so effectively blocked the association of name with each burning plane, returned with terrifying clarity.   His mind saw the chalkboard just as Begay had pointed to it and one by one in rapid succession he saw the image of a falling Fortress and the erasure of the name from the board.   Ainsworth, Bannister, Smedley, Dunston, Oquist whose plane was disemboweled, Cahill who burned at the stake, Cassidy hurtling downward in a death spiral which pinned him to his seat with centrifugal force--*How was Cassidy lost?* the interrogator asked--*The Germans shot him down*, Sully fired back.   Each loss was replayed in his brain like a short strip of newsreel. And those were only the ones he could see.   The squadron with the high, composite group lost four planes he never even saw.   He awakened from his twilight sleep by simply opening his eyes and was restored to his place in time and space by listening to Leo singing in little whistles as he conducted the business of censorship.   He even laughed once.   Hollis pivoted his eyeballs only slightly to see him.   Leo was shaking his head, like the teacher that he was, coming across an answer on a test paper so ridiculously wrong as to announce itself as a protest against the asking of the question.

Good old Leo.   He had been with his copilot for nearly six months.   They had met at the squadron office not long after they arrived at Ardmore.   Leo was fresh from his rejection from B-24 training.   His quiet mannerism and reserved sense of humor was chalked up to shyness until it was clear Leo just didn't have much to say.   He was a math teacher at Los Angeles High School.   He had designs of becoming a great theoretical mathematician, but when he graduated from UCLA he was penniless and needed to find work.   He put off his dreams of graduate school and a PhD and found work instructing the uninterested in trigonometry and simple calculus.   He was a popular teacher and when the Japs bombed Pearl Harbor he was recruited by students who had come to his bungalow late that Sunday afternoon brandishing all manner of firearms intent on repelling the inevitable invasion they swore was about to occur on Malibu's beach.   He tried to allay their fears, he recalled, but they would have none of it and instead he decided to join them as an undeclared chaperon to keep them from getting their hands on some beer and shooting themselves in some orgy of youthful, if drunken, xenophobia.   They sat on the beach well into the night by a bonfire--ignoring the tactical implications of its beacon-- until they got cold and went home.   They made Leo promise that if he got word of the approach of a Jap invasion fleet he would notify all of them immediately.   He promised.

Not long after that Leo reported to a recruiting office and volunteered for the Air Corps. He got sick with the measles halfway through advanced and missed nearly two months of training.   He got bumped back a step, and although he and Hollis had actually entered the service at about the same time, Leo ended up behind him, graduating from pilot training, making a short detour to the abortive attempt as a first pilot of Liberators and ended up in the right seat of a Fortress in Oklahoma.

Leo was a good man.   He was decent and honorable.   He had the kind, forgiving face of a teacher who loved his students and the privilege of bestowing on them the knowledge of that purest of disciplines, mathematics.   All the while, he understood his dream of a higher calling was slipping further and further away with each passing day and each trip to the blackboard.

He had several habits which were at once both endearing and annoying.   He liked to sing under his breath.   He must have been told at an early age how annoying people found this so he learned to keep each little ditty to himself, mouthing the words without singing out loud, reducing them to little whistles and whispers.   He was particularly fond of Disney cartoons, *Dumbo* especially, and the songs by Ukulele Ike.   Hollis had heard him sing the words to the song about elephants flying a hundred times.   He would be performing some task when his enthusiasm for the lyrics overcame him and he would sing 'but I be done seen about everything when I see a elephant fly.'   In fact, he was so enamored by the film he called B-24's 'Dumbbombers for Defense.'

His singing was some sort of release, Hollis figured, an expression of redirected anxiety for he sang the loudest when he was most nervous.   They were caught in a typical prairie thunderstorm one afternoon and as they were rudely bounced around amid the lightning flashes Hollis noticed Leo's jaw moving inside the cup of his oxygen mask, the rebreathing bladder expanding and contracting spasmodically.   He was not communicating by interphone and Hollis could not hear him above the engine noise, assuming he was talking and not chewing his tongue down to a bloody stump.

"Hey!" he yelled, "what are you doing?"

Leo leaned close so Hollis could hear and pulled the mask from his face, "Casey Junior's coming down the track, comin' down the track, with a smoky stack.   Hear him puffin' coming 'round the hill, Casey's here to thrill every Jack and Jill!"   He replaced his mask and returned his gaze to the outside, his face illuminated as if by flashbulb with each bolt of lightning, unable to conceal the fear in his eyes.

But, to everyone far and wide he was best known for his wife, Christie.   A woman of uncommon beauty that far surpassed that which mortal man might deem God capable of fashioning out of mere flesh.   *She needed to be kissed and often, by somebody who knew how.* "Christ, if it ain't Blondie and Dagwood," H-y said, for he had been particularly smitten by this arresting beauty when he finally had the chance to meet her in Grand Island, having confronted, finally, the unattainable.

Hollis slyly wondered if H-y fantasized, as he was sure they all did, what it was like to nestle between the long, silky legs of such a magnificent and stunning woman.

She was an excellent swimmer, one of Olympic quality, and, living in Los Angeles and having exceptional good looks, it was only natural that she find her way into the movies and her first movie was as a swimmer in the Busby Berkeley musical *Footlight Parade* with Cagney and Dick Powell and Ruby Keeler.   She had to be eighteen to play in 'moving pictures' and she was just seventeen in 1933 so she lied and swam her way into cinematic immortality as one of the bathing beauties in the funny caps.   She could tap dance, too.   An added bonus for the casting director.   Christie Sweet was her stage name, although her true surname was Mellon

But alas, her film career was short.   She made only one other film, another mindless musical, again requiring a great deal of treading water.   She was constantly being coerced into sleeping with various studio honchos and cast, a coercion, according to Leo, she successfully resisted, until she found out she was being set up as a blind date for Errol Flynn, a man who would fuck a donut.   At that moment she quit show business.

She couldn't find a job, assumed she was being blackballed by the studios for her unwillingness to defile herself with movie stars and executives, and sat, despondent on the beach near Santa Monica pier when she met Leo.   Finding his dry humor engaging, they married not long thereafter.   He finished college while she finally was able to secure a job as Mervyn LeRoy's secretary at MGM.   She was there for the production of *The Wizard of Oz*, had the chance to meet little Judy Garland and Ray Bolger.   She was invited, along with her star-struck husband, to the premier of the movie at Grauman's Chinese Theater in 1939.

She still works at MGM, Leo told him, and used her Hollywood connections to wangle priority passage on a commercial DC-3 to Grand Island to be with her husband one last time before he shipped out.

She stood by the chain-link fence as they taxied in, parking Angel's Plane on the ramp, and everyone could see her standing erect beside her valise, her hands clasping her purse, her broad-brimmed hat bending in the hot, Nebraska breeze.   Somehow she knew that was the plane with Leo in it because she started waving cheerfully.   Even at this distance, the crew could see the striking blond behind the fence and the plane erupted with whistles, cat calls and declarations of vulgar intent.

Quinn said, "Jesus, Lieutenant. Is *that* your *wife*?"

She beamed as the hatches flew open before the propellers stopped turning and the crew veritably ran to her, restrained only by the chain-link fence and their knowledge that this was their copilot's wife. She exuded pride in her husband, the Air Corps pilot. Never mind that he was a copilot and the closest he would get to the left seat was to brace against it as he climbed into the cockpit, or that he was on a bomber crew and not a Flying Tiger.

Leo could not conceal his annoyance with Hollis as he made him stay in the cockpit and finish the post-flight checklist while the crew dashed across the tarmac like jackrabbits with hard-ons.

Hollis met Christie at the fence after he finally let Leo out of the plane. The crew departed, mouths still agape, and Leo, now conciliatory, asked Hollis if he would join them for dinner.

No, he replied, you haven't seen each other for quite a while and I don't want to impose. I'm sure you want to be alone. Hollis noticed that Christie looked longingly at her husband wishing he would just shut up.

No, Leo said, I insist.

Over dinner, Hollis could not take his eyes off Christie. He was delighted that he could sit with her through dinner and stare at those dreamy eyes and perfect face, knowing that by doing so he might end up embarrassing himself and probably make her uncomfortable in the process. Then again, this was a beautiful woman and he was sure she was used to being stared at and he was equally sure such a delectable moment might not pass his was again anytime soon. Through dinner he kept hoping he wouldn't get drunk, forget himself and beg her to fuck him.

They had a pleasant meal consisting of huge steaks fresh off the prairie and glass after glass of bourbon. Hollis maintained his sense of decorum and behaved himself appropriately despite the fact that their eyes kept meeting causing her to smile sweetly and nod at him as befitting the context of the conversation. When it was time to part, he shook her hand, bidding her and her husband a pleasant evening. He laid on his back later that night imagining Blondie and Dagwood rolling around in bed, sweaty and smelling of musky sex, her long legs locked around the simple, unpretentious purveyor of sines, cosines and tangents.

He raised himself to his elbows and looked over at Leo and the alter of adoration he had created to his wife. There was a pin-up quality picture of her in a colorful sarong, an orchid over her left ear, a demure, come-hither expression on her face. There was another of her smiling exuberantly for the photographer. It was the way he remembered her for she had the same smile through the fence and over dinner, the candlelight seductive, flickering across her face. And a picture of her in her wedding dress separately and another standing beside her smiling, baby-faced groom. She had an innocent grace, a virginal quality that lifted right off the photos and he wondered how she could have possibly maintained her virtue and keep faith with her husband in a city teeming with satyrs on the make, decadent film producers and rotogravure heroes where semen flowed like oil in the motor pool. He wondered how she was faring now.

And there was Leo trying to restore sanity to a group of frenzied high school students, sitting with them on the sand as the sun set in the west, listing for them the quality of character and virtue necessary to protect and maintain a perfect Union against the forces of tyranny. How, Leo asked himself, could he wax so grandiloquent on the spirituality of liberty with his students and then go back to the chalkboard as they opened their draft notices? So there he went, leaving his lovely, adoring wife signing up for Aviation Cadets ready to mow down every

Zero from Honolulu to Tokyo, his skin no more or less sacred than anybody else's.

Leo was about to read yet another letter when Hollis interrupted him, "Leo, how in the hell did you ever land such a gorgeous wife?"

Leo looked up at his pilot and smiled, "I asked her."

"All those handsome movie stars and big shot movie moguls and she picks you.   I don't get it."

This made Leo laugh aloud and he said, "Some catch, ain't I?"

Chapter Twenty-five   **Fresh Meat**

Hollis and Leo took their new bikes and pedaled to an early supper.   Afterward, Leo headed for the Officer's Club to read a magazine and get a beer.   Hollis returned to Pilot's House to write a letter to Jessie.   Upon entering the room, he noted the door was open and a young boy in knee pants, probably no more than ten or twelve, stood in the center of the room. Hollis could not have been more surprised had he seen Hermann Goering in the flesh.   The boy was just as startled.

"I've come to fetch your dirties, suh," he said quickly.

"What?"

"The dirty laundry, suh.   I'm the laundry boy.   Me mum will clean and press it up for you.   She does it for most of the Squadron."   He pointed to a small stack of shirts on Leo's bed, "I've returned Leftenant Eisenberg's shirts."   The little boy's face turned sad.   "Me mum wants me to find out what she should do wif Leftenant Milo's laundry."

"Did you know Lieutenant Milo?"

"Oh yes, suh.   I've known all of them."   He looked at Leo's stuff and the pictures on the table and turned pale.   "This isn't Leftenant Eisenberg's kit.   Has sumfin 'appened to 'im?"

"Well, I'm happy to report he finished up and went home."

"Splendid, suh.   I'm sorry I di'n't get to say good-bye.   He was a very nice man, Leftenant Eisenberg was."   The boy's face, of ruddy complexion and intense green eyes, again looked puzzled.   "What shall I do wif 'is shirts?"

"I guess you should just leave them.   We'll keep them.   I'm sure we can always use the extra shirts?"

The little boy stiffened, "'e di'n't pay me."

"Well, I guess I can take care of that for you.   How much is it?"

"Two and six for Leftenant Eisenberg and four shillings, thrup-pence for Leftenant Milo."

"OK, you need to help me here," Hollis said as he reached into his pocket and pulled out some coins and paper currency the denominations of which he hadn't quite figured out yet. "Take the proper amount," he said as he held out the money in both hands, bending over to show him.   Odd, he thought, that he would find himself paying for the laundry of a dead man.

He felt the little boy's finger move the coins around and the flesh touched.   This was the first English person he had actually had the opportunity to engage in conversation.   As the boy's finger moved around his palm, Hollis could hear him whispering to himself.   He had flown over their land and seen them from the air, he had ridden on their trains and passed over their streets in a truck, but this was the first real contact he had had with any of these people.

The boy finished and straightened.   "That should do it, suh."   The boy took the coins and placed them in his pocket.   He took out a small journal and made a notation.   The little fellow could have stolen almost any combination of monies from Hollis's hand and he wouldn't have been the wiser.   He suspected the kid knew that, too.   This may have been more money than the kid had ever seen, for the Americans were obscenely well-paid compared to their English hosts and, except to purchase a few drinks in the O Club and some cigarettes from the BX, he hadn't spent a dime of it.   Hollis was a little embarrassed, a guest in their country walking around with a pocket full of their currency and he could have been swindled by a little kid. Not showing them the courtesy of learning their monetary denomination.

Still writing in his journal, his face very close to the page for he obviously needed glasses, he said, "Would you like me mum to do your dirties, suh?"

"Uh, sure, why not."

"And your name is?"

"Lieutenant Hollis."

The boy returned pencil to journal, "Leftenant 'ollis.   And yer roommate, suh?"

"Yeah, him, too."

"And 'is name is?"

"Lieutenant Wychulis."

"'ow does one spell it, suh?"

"W-y-c-h-u-l-i-s."

"Very good, suh."

Hollis gathered up his dirty shirts and socks and underwear and placed it in the small bag the little boy held open for him.

"Should be ready in a few days, suh.   Thank you."

The little fellow cast a long glance at Hollis and turned to go when Hollis reached into the drawer of the desk and pulled out two Hershey bars and a pack of Wrigley's gum.   "Here," he said, "for you troubles."

The boy took the candy and said, "Thank you, suh, but it's no trouble."

Hollis felt stupid and insensitive for his apparent patronizing, if innocent, comment.

Great Britain, Augie had said, *I don't see what's so great about it* and "The Short Guide to Great Britain" went sailing out the window of the train.

Read it, remember what you've read and use common sense in your dealings with the British, the major had said after they dropped their gear on the hanger floor.   He stood on a small wooden platform and welcomed the crews to Bovingdon.   There were about six crews assembled.   They were all tired and hungry and put off at the necessity of being subjected to a lecture about etiquette having flown across the Atlantic, sat around a dark, rainy station waiting for a train, then enduring a long trip jammed together in uncomfortable clatter-box coaches from Scotland to Bovingdon with only a brief stop for coal and water during which time they were allowed to stretch their legs, piss and drink some hot, black tea.

The Brits see us as wayward cousins, socially subversive, extroverted, wealthy and materialistic, brash and uncivilized.   We in America are getting richer at the same time the Brits are getting poorer.   They get their ideas about America and Americans through the movies--the cinema--which, if to be believed, made every American a rich gangster or a cowboy. They think we are eternally superficial, unrefined, violent and corrupt.

These are proud people.   A little embarrassed about what has happened to them, but they owe an apology to no one.   They stood alone when all hope was lost and no one else was left standing.   You are not conquerors and this is not a vanquished country.   Treat them with dignity and respect.   They've earned it.

We're guests in their country and they've been fighting this war for almost four years now and they've been through a lot.   Over fifty thousand men, women and children have been killed under the bombs and thousands more have been bombed out of their homes, losing everything they own.   And yet they remain undaunted.   Forty-five million people live on an island not much bigger than Minnesota.   They are glad we're here--Again! someone in the back yelled--

and appreciate your sacrifices better than you know, but through it all they haven't lost their dignity so treat them with respect, respect the differences we share and your stay here will be an enjoyable one.   Get some chow, get some rest.   Things start in earnest tomorrow. Of course, they would not be in this fix if they had dealt with Hitler properly in the beginning and I would not be standing here.

"What's your name?"

"Ian.   Ian Thomas."   The boy moved toward the door when he turned around and said, "I understand Leftenant Cassidy got the chop."

"Yes, I'm afraid so."

"I'm sorry to 'ear that.   I can tell when you leave on a mission because you use the long runway and pass right over our 'ouse.   I count 'ow many leave and I can see you when yer come back.   Bad day Tuesday, what?"

"Yes, Ian.   It was a bad day."

"I'll have your laundry back in few days."

"That will be fine," Hollis said and Ian left.

A short time later Selkirk bounded into the barrack and yelled down the hall, "Hey Jack, the squadron just picked up three new planes, want to go see if we get one of 'em?"

"No, I've got some letters to write.   I really don't care what plane they give me.   You go."

"Come on, fresh meat.   We'll see 'em and then we'll ride to the White Horse for a beer."

"Well, OK."

Hollis followed Selkirk on his newly acquired bike on the mile or so journey down to the squadron dispersal area.   There they found three brand, spanking-new Fortresses all parked on the side branch of the perimeter track.   The crews that had ferried them over from the modification center were also additions to the Squadron.   Now they were only short two crews.

Hollis realized as he approached the gathering that, after only three missions, he was considered a combat veteran and, as such, found it irresistible that he deport himself like one. Then, as he did so, he felt foolish because he was, at heart, chickenshit, a coward who lacked only the opportunity to tell Ransahoff that he was done.   He knew better than anyone that his status as a squadron veteran had been arrived at only by process of elimination and blind luck and any pretense of heroism was counterfeit.   What passed for courage was bluff.

Introductions were made. There was Clinton DeBerg and Conner Robertshaw but, everyone's interest was piqued by the last one, Second Lieutenant Vladimir Andreivich Konstantin Nevtushenko, a relative, he quickly proclaimed, of the late, dearly-departed Tzar.

"But everybody calls me Spats," he said.   Spats Nevtushenko. That required some explanation.

"You an American?" Selkirk asked in his uniquely tactless way.

Spats turned good-naturedly to Selkirk and said, "Born in the Williamsburg section of Brooklyn.   Moved to the Lower East Side when I was three and Central Park West when I was ten.   My father escaped Mother Russia one step ahead of the Bolsheviks and left everything."

"How come they call you Spats?"

"Long story, but I married Daisy Van Hazen, heiress to the Van Hazen peanut oil fortune in a very fancy Fifth Avenue wedding in 1941.   Bluebook all the way.   Real High Society stuff.   Big reception at the Plaza--you know, that sort of thing."

"Oh sure," Selkirk mocked, obviously feeling stupid for not knowing who Daisy Van Hazen was.

"We had to wear these spats with our soup-and-fish.   You should have seen it: tails, top hats, white gloves and spats.   God, I was beautiful.   Daisy's mother, Sabrina, nicknamed me that after her second bottle of champagne which was a definite improvement.   Prior to that she referred to me as the Mad Russian.   I felt like I was the luckiest man alive that day.   So anytime I need a little luck I pull out my spats and wear them."

"Bring 'em with ya?" Selkirk asked.

"Yes, I did."

"Good, you're gonna need 'em around here."   This caused the ebullient smile to depart Nevtushenko's face.

"Don't pay any attention to him," Hollis said unconvincingly.

"So, you rich or something?" Mickey asked.

"Filthy."

"Couldn't buy your way out of coming?"

"But of course I could have, but then stuck all summer in the Hamptons how could I possibly meet such interesting people like you?"

Hollis smiled and winked at Nevtushenko, a little embarrassed at Mickey's irritating attitude.   Perhaps he had jarred his brain when he bellied in the other day and the dislocation of his senses was only now becoming apparent.   Maybe there was something else...

A jeep came tooling up the perimeter strip.   Ransahoff was driving with Barbieri in the right seat.   Otho had a scowl on his face sternly projecting his newly-appointed role as Squadron Ops.   Hollis noticed the gold oak leaves on Ransahoff's shirt.   Maybe that explained why Otho was so torqued.   Ransahoff outranked him.

"Where's DeBerg and Robertshaw?" Ransahoff asked.

"That one there is Robertshaw and DeBerg is there, sir."   Spats pointed to the men gathered around stacks of luggage accumulating under the noses of the planes.

"Don't move," Ransahoff said as they drove further down the strip to the other two pilots.

"Who is that?" Spats asked.

"That's our new Squadron CO.   Lovely man.   Dutch Ransahoff is his name. Of the famous Leather-stocking Ransahoffs. " Hollis said.

"West Point asshole if you tell me.   Not much better than the man he replaced." Selkirk retorted, mildly surprising Hollis who never heard such bitter words from his friend, Mickey Selkirk of the Vermont Selkirks.

"Who is the Group CO?"

"Another West Point asshole by the name of Van Patten."

"Who?" Spats asked pointedly.

"Brock Van Patten," Selkirk replied.   "Why?   You know him?"

"Sure, I know him.   His old man's Colonel Armstrong Van Patten, the only person to make money during the Depression.   Doubled his fortune, I've been told.   They lived a block up Central Park West.   Their shit don't even stink."

Hollis and Selkirk exchanged glances. Oh, *those* Central Park Van Pattens.

The jeep returned with Robertshaw and DeBerg crammed into the back.

"You Nevtushenko?" Ransahoff asked.

"You mean heir to the Van Hazen peanut fortune?" Selkirk said sarcastically. Perhaps he'd already been drinking although Hollis smelled no alcohol on him.

"Yes sir, I'm Nevtushenko."

"Get in."

Spats climbed into the back of the jeep, struggling for room. As the vehicle sped off Nevtushenko yelled out the back of the jeep at Selkirk, "That's oil! Peanut *oil*!"

Selkirk nodded and gave a perfunctory wave. "Another asshole," he muttered.

"What's eating you?"

"Nothing. Let's go," spoken in such a way as to end further conversation. They pedaled over to a gap in the split-rail fence that marked the boundary of the field and turned onto a small road that lead to the village of Ridgewell a half mile away. This was the first time he had left the base. The ground felt different. Ancient. Less threatening. Oddly familiar as if recognized by some internal gene dating back generations in an unbroken pedigree to this place.

Under the overhanging limbs of trees, the remaining light of dusk was blocked out and they relied on the narrow white line painted down the center of the lane to lead them through the dark tunnel. Finally Selkirk produced a flashlight with blue tissue paper taped over it to shield the light from the searching eyes of Nazi intruders. Hollis figured as thick as the trees were they could have illuminated the lane with a search light and no German flying in the night would have spotted them. Selkirk knew where he was going and turned at an intersection with its road signs notably absent from their poles. They pedaled through small hamlets with no names, nothing more than a cluster of two or four houses nestled behind stone or hedge fences, yellow stucco or clay structures with small windows, some thatch-roofed, others not. They were quiet, without light, as if they were asleep for the night, perhaps the duration. Selkirk remained uncharacteristically silent as if he did not want to disturb their slumber.

Finally they came to the White Horse, a public house with nothing more than a placard adorned with a white stallion to signify its presence along the darkened road that bisected the village. They leaned the bikes against the wall of the pub and stepped in through a door and around a blackout curtain. They were greeted by a warm, smoky room containing several large wooden tables that dated back, Hollis thought, to the days of the Norman Conquest. There were several locals, farmers, he suspected, who sat in small groups sipping their pints, smoking pipes and cigarettes and conversing in soft voices. The room was flushed with a coziness that made Hollis feel welcome even though he was an absolute stranger to these people and their country.

Selkirk, fortunately, was not. "Mickey!" was yelled from a corner of the room.

Selkirk turned toward the direction of his name and returned the greeting, "Angus!" Selkirk guided him to the table in the corner where an elderly pensioner sat, a large, tar-encrusted pipe clenched in his teeth. They took seats.

"Jack Hollis, this is Angus McCullen, late of the Black Watch. Angus, this is my good friend Jack, late of **Cleopatra's Asp**."

Hollis took the grip of the man's hand and knew, with little effort, Angus could crush every bone in it. Such were the byproducts of an agrarian existence. Selkirk turned and went to the bar to purchase pints of beer from a fat woman with rosy cheeks and a generous smile gapped by the memory of teeth long-gone.

"Angus here was in the Great War.   A sergeant in the Black Watch.   He likes to buy beers for the combat crews.   I put these on your tab, there, Mr. McCullen.   Mr. Roosevelt and the Air Corps thank you."

"Forgive his sarcasm, Mr. McCullen, my friend here is a bit out of sorts," Hollis said.

"If yer 'andn't told me I'd have never 'ave noticed."

Selkirk fired a sideward glance at Hollis and sipped his beer.   "Drink slow, my friend," he said to Hollis. "This beer's a lot more potent than the stuff they serve us."

"What's eating you, Mickey?" Angus said.

"Now, don't *you* start, Angus."

"See," Hollis replied.

"You boys got it easy.   I'm sorry you had to leave home to fight the Hun wiv us again, but you guys are lucky, up there in the clear, blue sky, bombing the bastards to bloody hell and home by supper, having beers with Angus.   When I was at Passchendale the field was converted to mud by the blood.   Once you get that smell of stale blood in your nostrils it never leaves.   I can close my eyes and smell it still."

"Angus, we've heard this before.   Tell us about all the girls you fucked in Paris."

"Mickey," Hollis said quietly, a little taken aback by his rudeness.   After all, the man was nice enough to purchase a round of drinks for his Allied compatriots.

There was something terribly wrong with Mickey Selkirk.   He noticed for the first time that he was wearing his wedding band.

"How's the wife and kids, Mickey?"   Hollis said.

Selkirk underwent a transition the likes of which Hollis had never seen in a grown man. The gruff, rude, congenitally insolent man he had pedaled over with was transformed into a pitiful, sobbing child.   "I almost didn't make it the other day.   The bastards had me in their sights and I nearly bought it.   That's twice they almost got me."

"And Stanley, your Guardian Angel, went home," Angus smiled at Hollis.   "'e stopped in to say good-bye the over day."

Jesus, Hollis thought, *the poor son of a bitch is coming unraveled.   Two close calls, sure, but Christ, man, get a hold of yourself.*   This from a guy who can't strap himself into the airplane without first puking his guts out.   He didn't expect his innocent question to elicit such a pathetic catharsis.   As the words formed in his head and nearly achieved voice he recalled how close he had come to walking in to Ransahoff's office and declaring himself LMF, Lack of Moral Fiber.   Did Selkirk have such thoughts?   What arrogance was Hollis entitled to that allowed him to pass judgment on a man so nearly and repeatedly shot from the sky?   He could understand if Selkirk had been drinking and he had slipped into some sodden fugue state, but he thought Mickey was stone sober.   Perhaps he had gotten some disturbing news from home, some item of misfortune, that had he been home, wouldn't have generated a second thought, but now, three thousand miles away, assumed extraordinary significance.

Hollis looked to McCullen for some help, but he seemed unmoved.   Perhaps he had seen this all before and they were replaying a ritual release of emotion, an emotion he dared not allow to escape on base in front of his friends.   Regardless, it was unsettling.   Maybe Angus was made of sterner stuff and saw this little display as nothing more than the uncontrolled weeping of another spoiled, homesick American who could not truly understand what real sacrifice meant.

How many missions had Selkirk flown?   Eight?   Was this what Hollis had to look forward to?   By his eighth mission, should he be alive to fly it, would he be reduced to a blubbering wretch by the slightest provocation?

Just as quickly as he had deteriorated, Selkirk regained his composure and lifted the large glass of bitters to Angus and said, "Here's to Passchendaele!"

Angus raised his glass and smiled at Hollis.   Hollis responded by lifting his and the three vessels clinked together.

An hour and a half later it was closing and Selkirk was thoroughly drunk.   He walked out, or rather was guided by Hollis, into the night and they retrieved their bikes, but not before Mickey pulled down his zipper and urinated onto the side of the pub.   Mickey was in no shape to navigate his way home and Hollis hoped his memory of the trip over would allow him to retrace their ride.   He had a difficult time guiding his drunken friend, who, at any moment, might disappear into the woods beside the lane and break some bone, the front wheel wobbling back and forth describing a sine wave on the pavement.

They came upon a familiar section of split-rail fence and walked through the gap, pushing their bicycles along.   Suddenly Mickey's bike rattled onto the ground. Selkirk grunted as he drained his bladder onto some brush.

"Come on, Mickey.   Almost home."

At last, they arrived at Mickey's hut having completed in an hour a trip that had earlier taken them less than twenty minutes.   Mickey banged his bike against the wall and staggered into the room, still guided by Hollis.   He dropped Mickey onto his bed.   He pulled off Selkirk's boots and covered him with a blanket.   This was a scene Hollis had witnessed before.

He left.   He never did find out what was on Mickey's mind. Other than getting shot at.

As he walked his bike across the alley he heard someone whisper his name.

"Rizzo, is that you?"

"Yes, Lieutenant.   I was hoping I could talk to you for a minute."

After what he'd been through tonight what was one more fucking problem?   "Sure, Bobby what is it?"   *Are they still razzing you about shitting your pants?*

"I got a bit of a problem.   I have this friend of mine, his name is Homer, from my neighborhood.   He's just a kid from my neighborhood and I never knew him all that well.   His mom is sick and when she found out he was bein' sent to England she asked me to keep an eye on him for her so I been writin' her, tellin' her I been seein' him every day and that he's doin' fine, you know, to keep her from worryin', her bein' sick and all.   I just mailed a letter saying how I seen him just today and he looks great and all."

"And you haven't seen him have you?"

"No sir.   Not once."

"Well, I think that's OK."

"Sir, my mom just wrote me that Homer was killed over Ploesti."

For the next three days there were no missions.   Ransahoff made them fly a practice mission one day--

"*Practice?*"   *Worked for Stan.*   "*Tell him I'm not going.*"

"*He thought you'd say that, Lt. Hollis, so he*"--holding up a chit of paper--"*made me write it down.   'Tell him he isn't Eisenberg and I'm not Entwhistle.   Tell Hollis to get his ass in gear or he'll have you shot then court-martial your corpse.'*"

-- and then Gleason had them up as a group the next.   The day after that it rained.

Chapter Twenty-six   **Abortion**

Tuesday, August 24, 1943

The rain cleared out by morning, the crews alerted the night before.   When they awakened, no one was sure whether there would be a mission or not.   Then word was passed that a mission was laid on for the afternoon.   A milk run was suspected because they wouldn't put on a big mission so late in the day.   At briefing their suspicions were confirmed.   They were being sent to bomb the air depot and workshop at Villacoublay, south of Paris.   They were to be escorted by the P-47s halfway to the target and opposition was expected.   Villacoublay was a target the Germans were fond of defending and early on it was the scene of some fairly vigorous air battles.   Not only that, Gorton said, the GAF had given them a pass on some the last few short penetrations and they could be expected to contest this one.   The bomb load was four one-thousand pounders which Sully liked better than the five-hundred pounders because they were heavy enough to be counted on to fall free of the shackles when the time came.   Several five-hundred pounders had failed to fall over Schweinfurt and there was hell to pay trying to get rid of them.   A plane was forbidden to land with an unreleased, hung-up bomb in its bay.

Hollis kept his eye on Selkirk expecting him to show signs of mental fragility, but he seemed his old, normal self.   Ransahoff had assigned him to the role of second element leader for the first practice mission and Selkirk acquitted himself without problem.   Ransahoff also placed Watanabe on the number three position and Hollis in the number two.   Otho had lead the Squadron on the second practice and shuffled things around.   The next day, Hollis flew second element lead and Selkirk the Squadron lead with Otho badgering him from the right seat for the entire flight.   Selkirk seemed fine, the new guys hung on for dear life and Otho and Ransahoff seemed pleased.   Perhaps Selkirk was more resilient than Hollis thought and all that blubbering of a few nights earlier had been aberration.

Selkirk had been roundly congratulated for making it home on two engines, unable to extend his landing gear, but was then chewed out for not jettisoning the ball turret before he bellied in as this was standard procedure.   The impact of the turret with the ground sent the thing up into the fuselage as if it had been smacked with a giant bung hammer.   That drove the turret's supporting stanchion up into the main spare which usually broke the plane's back.   When that happened it could never be structurally restored and **Vermont Revenge** went category E.   Today, he was assigned Robertshaw's plane.   Robertshaw would be flying with him as copilot.   Perhaps the chewing out had set him off the other night.   That, combined with alcohol and too much time to think.

Hollis deferred his desire to quit for the moment having regained control of his terror, forcing it back like Jack into his Box.   The visions of burning planes on the ground, however, would not leave him.   All he had to do was close his eyes and he could see them, funeral pyres, one after the other, in a line leading to the sea.

The new guys looked fairly worried by the time they showed up for briefing.   They had spent the few days since arrival   getting flakked up by the veterans, a practice Hollis initially thought was cruel, but, on further reflection, might make them wary enough to give them an edge, force them to pay attention, and any advantage, no matter how seemingly trivial, might mean the difference...   Ransahoff was just as vehement with the three new pilots as he had been with Hollis and Cahill.   Red paint demonstration and all.   Even so, being on the receiving end of a blistering, very public lecture at twenty-five thousand feet, could be tough to take and Hollis took no pleasure in their discomfiture, but was glad, nonetheless, that someone else was getting it.   There was a fine line between giving the new guys that extra bit of skill and needlessly ridiculing, reveling in one's exercise of authority.   Just one more haranguing in a military culture accustomed to using this as a method of instruction.   He wondered if Ransahoff knew of this line.   All it seemed to accomplish was make everybody mad at him and, in Spats's case, nearly overcome with fright.

Otho was even worse.   He had none of the command stature or *bona fides* that Ransahoff had.   He was an ordinary pilot with the 534th of no particular distinction other than the fact that he, also by process of elimination, found himself in the survivor's column at the end of the Schweinfurt mission.

What had been most irritating, however, was the fact that the new guys got to keep the planes they had flown in.   It was not standard practice to assign a particular crew to a particular plane even though a crew frequently became informally associated with one or another aircraft. Ransahoff, however, felt it was important for a pilot and his crew to become accustomed to one particular aircraft since, as every pilot knew, no two airplanes were alike and even this might mean the difference.   They could leave the same production line, one right behind the other, but contain idiosyncrasies which made them different.   That meant the practice of not wanting to waste a new plane on a new crew was over, at least for the 532nd.   So there, upon returning from the second practice mission, sat the three crews trying to arrive at consensus regarding names for their planes.

Perry Solomon, one of the assistant weather officers, had become the Group's unofficial nose *artiste*.   His reputation for applying paint onto aluminum was quite good.   In fact, his contribution to the war effort boosting the morale of the crews by elaborating remarkably accurate pictures of naked women, Disney cartoon characters and such probably exceeded that made by his meteorological prognostications.   Sometimes his services were in such demand and the turnover in aircraft so rapid that a plane frequently flew its first mission or two unadorned. This was unsettling for the crews who believed such heraldry charmed the aircraft which bore it and the more lascivious or irreverent the better.   And recently, business had been brisk.   So he did the best he could, often painting under an umbrella or by floodlight under a tarp.   Solomon's reward was, initially, a bottle of scotch, but scotch was scarce and he already had more than he could drink so finally he did it at no charge finding his reward on the faces of the crew when viewing the finished product for the first time.

After almost no deliberation at all **SPATS** showed up on the Mad Russian's B-17. Robertshaw had two dice, each showing a five, painted on the nose with the words **The Big Dick** under it.   DeBerg's crew offered a more sobering, if thoughtful, statement.   **Celina** appeared under the navigator's window.   It was a name derived from the first initial of every wife or girlfriend of the crew.   No massive, biologically impossible naked breasts.   No coiled snakes. No plagiarized or bastardized cartoon characters.   No clever double *entendre*. And, in a way, they were the envy of everybody in the Squadron.

Hulse had already warned the crew that the mission was probably a milk run and they seemed loose and unconcerned about their fourth mission.   As stations approached, Hollis noted that his hand shook as he lit a cigarette telling himself that it was probably going to be a short, easy one all the while remembering that Salayhan's was supposed to be an easy one, too.   He wondered, as the moment of irretrievable decision approached, whether he would be able to bring himself to climb into the plane and start the fans.

Ransahoff would lead the Squadron and the Group which would assume the high position in the lead wing.   It might be an easy one, Hollis said to the crew, but keep your eyes peeled. The intelligence people are saying the Germans might hammer us despite our escort.   As the words left his mouth he felt the uneasiness return to his belly.   He could name them: Ainsworth, Bannister, Smedley, Dunston, Oquist, Cahill, Cassidy...plus four others he never saw.   *You're getting us out of formation!* he heard someone yell over the VHF.   *We* are *the formation*, came the terse reply.

Hollis was suddenly afraid he might not make it across the perimeter strip before the volcano erupted from his stomach.   He walked as far away as he could, turned his back to the crew and vomited violently.   When he straightened up he saw Spats looking over at him from Cahill's hardstand.   Even at this distance he could see the fear etched on the Mad Russian's face. They exchanged glances and Hollis watched Nevtushenko turn and walk toward his plane. Hollis did the same.

"We all done throwing up, Lieutenant?" he turned to see Augie smiling at him.   Hollis picked up his leather jacket and walked toward the tail to empty his bladder.

Hollis was about to climb into the nose of **Cleopatra's Asp** when H-y caught him by the arm, "We're second element leader, today, Jack. Don't forget we got two rookies on our wings."

Hollis climbed into the cockpit almost hoping the engines wouldn't start.   Bad enough, he thought, that I have to look after my own crew, I got twenty other men to look out after, Spats on one wing and DeBerg on the other.

He settled into his seat and went through the checklist hoping the assumption of a familiar task would allow him to continue.   When they were finished, as they sat waiting for the green flare, Hollis saw Leo fussing with something inside his flight jacket.   "Whatcha doin'?" He recalled how Leo had two ties, one he wore at ordinary times and the other, his mission tie, which was pre-knotted and slipped easily over his head as he readied himself.

Leo looked hesitant, glancing over his shoulder to make sure Dodge wasn't right there, then pulled out a pair of silk panties which he held out for Hollis to see.

"Christie's."   He put them back where he had found them, a look of concern passed fleetingly over his face.

Hollis wondered how many times he had sniffed those panties for any lingering aroma of his wife's crotch.

"Did you hear about Augie?" Dodge said to Hollis.

"No, why?"

"He's turned into a one-man race riot.   Seems he beat the heck out of a black army sergeant in Cambridge the other night.   Seems this guy was walking with a white girl whose father had invited him to dinner because they liked to talk about Shakespeare.   She was escorting him because their house was hard to find."

"Christ, Dodge.   Why are you telling me this?"

"I thought you might want to talk to him.   Flares," Dodge said and the three men in the cockpit watched the forked green flare arc skyward.

Soon they were all up in the afternoon sky.   As they approached 10,000 feet Sully stopped by to pull his pins and share a smoke. They were to climb to 25,000 feet and form the wing then head for the target.   As they crossed 20,000 feet Rizzo said his intercom kept cutting out.

"I can hear you fine, ball turret.   What's the problem?"

"Sir, it's OK until I traverse.   Watch: one, two...fo--...seven...eight...ni--...see?"

"OK, we'll get it fixed when we get back.   Keep your eyes open."

"Yes sir."   Rizzo's voice brimmed with concern.

After they had formed up and started for the coast, Mollica announced his oxygen regulator wasn't working.

"What's wrong with it, tail?"

"I don't know sir, it stopped blinking and I'm getting short of breath."

"Take slow deep breaths, tail and keep an eye on it."

Hollis waited a few minutes and checked with him, "Pilot to tail, how goes it?"

Mollica sounded like he was gasping, "I don't know sir.   I think it ain't workin' right."

The failure of an oxygen system results in giddiness, then a gradual decline of alertness, followed by gradual lapse into coma.   Its symptoms were not manifest as a conscious shortness of breath.   He was pretty sure there was nothing wrong with the regulator in the tail, but he sent Hulse back to check on it anyway.   A few moments later, Hulse reported that it seemed OK, but Mollica was correct, the regulator was not blinking.

Hollis figured it had been ten minutes since Mollica had announced trouble with his regulator, he should have been unconscious by now.

"Well, OK, Hulse return to your position, but you and Augie keep an eye on him."

"Yes sir."

It was cold at 25,000 feet.   Even before they left the coast the bombers were spinning out huge, booming contrails.   The outside temperature was forty degrees below zero.

"Ball to pilot, there must be a short...the...cutting out..."

"Jesus Christ," Hollis said out loud, "Pilot to engineer, Dodge go down and see if you can find out what's wrong with the ball turret."

"Yes sir."

Hollis felt a tap on his arm.   Leo pointed to the manifold pressure on number four engine.   It barely held at thirty inches.

"We've lost the boost on number four," Leo said.   They both glanced at the outboard engine on the right wing.   Simultaneously, Hollis noticed they had fallen back almost a plane's length.   He watched as his two wingmen fell behind also.   Hollis reflexly advanced the other throttles and regained his position, but in so doing, he was demanding more of them.   He had to increase the manifold pressure and the RPM to keep his place.   The wingmen struggled to catch up.

Suddenly, his mind began to race with all of the unpleasant realities.   None of the mechanical difficulties they had individually would have prevented them from continuing on to complete the mission.   Collectively, he wasn't so sure.   What if the ball turret jammed at a crucial moment and they could not defend themselves or get Rizzo out in a hurry?   What if they found Mollica dead in the tail, knowing his oxygen hadn't been quite right?   What if number four quits completely and they lost another engine?   They would be a straggler and ripe for the picking.   Weren't the Germans expected to put up a decent fight today?   He was responsible for the two rookies, what if he lost his position because of his failing power plants and they were stupid enough to follow him down?   It had been known to happen.   His mind began swirling with a litany of dread.

Dodge had reappeared on the flight deck and in an instant had surmised the painful calculus.   He shook his head saying nothing.

They were nearing the mid-point of the Channel, the turnaround point for the spares. Hollis had to make a decision very quickly.   He knew there would be repercussions.

Hollis turned on the command channel and broke radio silence announcing that he was aborting the mission.   Ransahoff's copilot acknowledged the message and Hollis waggled his wings and eased the plane out of formation hoping that a spare would see this and, eager to get credit for an easy mission, would jump into the vacated spot and guide the rookies.   He felt the guilt of abandoning them   for he did not know of the competence of the spare.   Would he look after the neophytes?   If they were lost whose fault would it be?

Hollis reported the situation to the crew and his decision to abort the mission.

"We're aborting?!   A fucking milk run and we're aborting?!" Augie screamed into the intercom.

With all four engines still running he knew he would catch hell.   He felt more guilt. What if the spare died in his place?   *What if he died today because of my poor judgment when he could have gone home and drink at the White Horse tonight?   I lived, he died.*

The crew was pissed.   As they deplaned their frustration with the turn of events was very plain to see. The only person besides Hollis relieved to be on the ground was Mollica. Otho greeted them at the hardstand and was fuming.   Moe was crestfallen.   **Cleopatra's Asp** had never suffered an abortion before, his perfect record ruined by some yellow, pipsqueak lieutenant.   Hobbled or not, maybe facing the Germans today might have been a better choice.

It was not immediately apparent why the manifold pressure in the number four engine could not be maintained.   The Group and Squadron engineering officers were there within minutes peering up into the engine squinting to see into the small places that only they recognize, like doctors conferring about a variation in disease, inspecting a corpse with clinical detachment for some subtle clue as to mode of demise.

Ninety percent of all abortions are legitimate.   Ten percent are not.   And we know which is which.

The only thing missing were the two MPs to arrest Hollis and place him in shackles to await court martial for cowardice in the face of the enemy.   *LMF.*

What if?   What if?   The permutations for disaster went through his head.   He explained in careful detail the course of events to Otho and Moe, who took each item as a personal affront to the quality of his care for her.   It would go to an abort board who would review the evidence of mechanical failure and report their finding as to the legitimacy of their premature return.

It was almost dusk when the planes returned.   All were present although a few had wounded and some of the planes had been damaged, one or two significantly.   At least, Hollis figured, no one had died on his account.

Hollis could not ignore his despondency.   He laid in bed and tried to compose a letter to Jessie in his head.   Leo said nothing.

A short time later, Barbieri came by and told Hollis that Moe had found a crack or separation of a joint in the exhaust stack which prevented the manifold pressure from staying up. It had initially been difficult to find.   Further, he said, they had found a frayed wire in the intercom of the ball turret.   There was nothing wrong with the oxygen system in the tail, nor could they confirm a problem with the ball turret that would explain why it had repeatedly jammed.   They gave him a pass on the abortion, but, Otho said as he left, "I got my eye on you, Hollis."

"I wonder what he meant by that?" Leo asked.

Chapter Twenty-seven   **The Engine**

Wednesday,   August 25, 1943

Hollis awakened in a state of severe melancholia.   He was intensely homesick and had demonstrated himself a coward.   He knew that the engine driving the abortion was his own cowardice.   A better man, a braver man would have ignored the mechanical difficulties and flown the mission.   It was, after all, only a milk run.

He tried to comfort himself with the fact that he was caught in a dilemma more than one good man had faced.   His paralyzing fear pitted against the mission.   The Mission.   *The mission comes first--it's the whole reason you are here* had been hounded into him and every other officer since the day they put on the uniform.   It should be automatic.   Unthinking.   There is no room for personal choice.   This is total war.

Yet again, 'what ifs' swirled around inside his mind, like angry bats startled in a cave. What if he had continued the mission, undaunted in his leadership of the second element, guiding the new guys through their baptism of fire, and today had been the day the *Luftwaffe* wanted the Decisive Battle, the Great Showdown?   What if the engine failed altogether and they straggled? Ransahoff had told him: 'straggle and you're dead.   Straggle and you're guilty of murder. Don't straggle or else.'   They might have been able to keep up.   Probably would have, but if they were to straggle they would be easy pickin's.   The Germans could deal with them as an afterthought, mopping up after the big massacre, the Little Big Horn of the Second World War.

A measly crack in an exhaust pipe had provided him deliverance.   Deliverance from what?

He wanted to go out to **Cleopatra's Asp,** ostensibly to look over the engine, to make amends with Moe.   He did not want Moe to think him yellow.   He wondered if Jessie would think him a coward.   Or his father.   He was certain, regardless of what action he had taken, that his mother would think him prudent.

He was mildly surprised that their investigation had found the abortion justified.   He would not have agreed with them.   He knew Dodge would not.   Neither would Moe.   They could have kept up.   Probably.

It was just the inescapable fear that in the journey from Chester to Schweinfurt he had used up all his God-allotted courage and luck and he would have none left.

He wondered how the crew felt.   He couldn't fathom what Leo's thoughts were.   Leo just smiled and tried to figure out what they might be having for dinner.   It was not his decision to turn around.   There were no consequences for him to suffer.   He was along for the ride, singing and whistling into his oxygen mask, clutching Christie's panties for luck.

Perhaps by now they were gathered in Ransahoff's office to urge him to disband the crew or assign them a new first pilot.   They had seen enough.   And perhaps their mutiny would be justified.   Who could blame them?   He would have quit him, too.   It had been, after all, only a milk run and all four engines were running when they landed.

He was lonely, humiliated and outside it was raining.   This was his lowest point. Lower than after the practice mission.   Lower than after Schweinfurt.

At breakfast, Hollis ran into Sully and H-y.   He was interested in their reaction when he sat down beside them, placing his tray before him on the wooden table.   They greeted him with indifference.

Sully looked up from his powdered eggs and greasy bacon and said, "I understand they accepted your explanation for the abortion."

Hollis waited until he had a mouthful of food and turned to Sully, "The squadron and group engineers found the problem with the turbo, if that's what you mean."

H-y looked at Hollis without revealing any judgment.   Hollis knew that H-y and Rizzo might have been the only others besides Mollica thankful for the abortion.

Hollis always had a difficult time trying to figure out what Sully was thinking.   Sully had abstained from the vote to get rid of him back in Oklahoma.   He skipped dinner so he could study the course of the arteries in case somebody was in need of a tourniquet.   Perhaps he was still smarting over the dressing-down Hollis had given him after Schweinfurt for not doing oxygen checks frequently enough despite the raging gunfire and imminent death.   Regardless, his current attitude demonstrated contempt for Hollis and his decision.

H-y said little during the meal except to ask, rhetorically, when it would stop raining.

Hollis returned to the squadron area and strode into Pilot's House.   He found Leo still asleep, an amorphous lump beneath the covers.   Hollis put on his trench coat and the plastic cover for his hat and got onto his bike.   He rode the mile down to the dispersal area. **Cleopatra's Asp** stood silently in the rain.   Moe and Tommy were nowhere to be seen.   He placed the bike against the tire under the shelter of the right wing and walked over to the outboard engine.   He looked at the exhaust stack as it passed along the underside of the cowling to the supercharger.   He spun the turbo wheel and peered into the end of the stack to look at the waste gate.   Everything seemed in order.   If it were broken, Moe certainly would have it fixed by now.   He followed the course of the pipe back into the engine until it disappeared into the nacelle.   He stepped back into the rain to look into the front of the engine, hoping it might grant him absolution.

"You have to take the cowling off to see where it was cracked."   Moe's voice startled him.

"I came out here to see if I could figure out what was wrong with the engine."

"Well, Lieutenant, if you are really interested I could pull the cowling off and show you. The crack was at the collector ring."   Moe was silent for a moment, *probably taking his measure of me*, Hollis thought.   "I respect your interest, if that's what you came out here for. Most pilots I've known wouldn't give a shit about what happened.   They might be mad something broke.   Or relieved.   But not interested."

Moe remained under the wing out of the rain and Hollis stood before the engine, the rain dripping from the brim of his cap.

"I made the judgment that what was wrong might jeopardize our survival," Hollis said.

"I respect that, too.   I'm down here."   Moe pointed skyward, "And you're up there."

"I was not happy.   Relieved maybe, as you say, but not happy."

Moe turned from him, "It doesn't matter."

Hollis looked up into the engine again, squinting against the rain.   When he looked for Moe he was hunched over, walking toward his ramshackle hut, smoke curling from its makeshift stovepipe.

He wanted to talk to someone, but there was no one he wanted to tell.   He wanted to explain without revealing.   Seek approval where he knew none would be found.   He picked up the bike and pedaled onto the perimeter strip.   Instead of taking the shortest route back to dry land he turned left.   He would pedal the several few miles around the perimeter track until he had completed the circuit, hoping the indifferent rain might rinse away his lamentations, knowing full well it would not.

When he returned to the room, Leo was gone.   It was raining particularly hard, drumming against the window.   He pushed the blackout curtain back and stared out from his seat at the desk.   He looked at Christie's picture.   Sweet, Mellon, Wychulis, whatever her last name was.   He took out some stationary and composed a long letter to Jessie.   He explained what had happened and his moral crisis over the decision to abort the mission. It had been a week since he had mailed the letter requesting her hand in marriage.   Much too soon to expect a reply to have reached him.   A week to get there, a few moments deliberation and a week to return.   Two weeks, tops.   He had another week to sweat out her decision.   Maybe, he thought, she was deliberating things right now.   It would be close to dawn there at this very moment.   Maybe she was awake, having spent a sleepless night trying to compose her tactful rejection.   Then again, she could simply write "No," number an envelope so there would be no confusion about the sequence and mail it.   Maybe that's what he needed most, something, anything, definitive.

A corporal opened the door and told Hollis there was an aircraft recognition class at fourteen hundred.   Attendance was mandatory.   Oh and by the way, he added, here's your mail.   He tossed a handful of envelopes and a package onto Leo's bed.

Hollis retrieved the mail and separated his from Leo's.   Once again, Leo's smelled terrific as if they had made the trip immersed in some exotic perfume.   Some chick, that Christie.   He found two envelopes addressed to him.   One was in his mother's hand and the other unmistakably Jessie's.   To his surprise the package was addressed to him as well.

Trying to maintain order, he decided to finish his letter before opening his mail.   He would make himself wait.   The waiting, he thought, would restore character.   It took him fifteen minutes to complete his letter.   The distraction of the unopened mail and the mysterious package disrupted his stream of thought.   When he finished, his closing sentence was an admission of his undying love for her.   He counted the pages.   Eight.   He folded the letter carefully and placed it in an envelope.   He numbered and addressed it, placed it in his pocket and checked his watch.   One forty-five.   He had just enough time to get to the briefing room for the stupid lecture.   He rode his bike through the rain, driving inadvertently through a large puddle, soaking his left foot and pant leg.   He stopped at Group Headquarters and placed the envelope into the mail bin and ran across the road to the big Nissen hut.

It was an uncomfortable hour.   His shoe and sock failed to dry out in the damp room and the lure of his newly arrived, as yet untouched mail prevented him from paying any attention to the lecture.   They flashed onto the screen from the projector silhouettes at various angles of every stinking plane in the German or Allied inventory.   There was even a biplane or two. And a Corsair which he was certain was only being used in the Pacific. Half the people in the room were asleep the minute the lights went out.   But Hollis diligently tried to focus on the black outlines not particularly worried about how to tell friend from foe.   One would be shooting at him and the other would not. And the Corsair pilot would obviously be quite lost.

When they were dismissed Hollis bolted from the room, retracing his ride back to Pilot's House careful to avoid the puddles and the quagmire of an endless sea of mud.   He sat on his bed and opened the letter from his mother.   His father had been promoted to shift supervisor at the shipyard.   It meant more money and longer hours.   But it did not result in a larger gasoline ration or a bigger sugar allotment.   Overall, she said, the war seemed to be going well.   At least the news was good.   In a flash of rare enlightenment, she admitted that she understood the two were not necessarily synonymous.   She hoped he was well.   The damp climate, she had heard, made people prone to colds.   When she concluded the letter, he realized she hadn't mentioned Jessie once.

He returned the letter to its envelope and ripped into the one from Jessie.   She started off with the usual chattiness.   She told him how much she missed him and hoped he was well and not getting into any danger.   At the end she mentioned their mutual friend, Robert Owens, a Second Lieutenant of Marines, was killed by a sniper on some place called Vella Lavella as he stood in line for chow.   She missed Hollis, she said.   Be careful.

He remembered Robbie.   Tall, lanky, affable.   They were on the high school baseball team together.   Robbie was their ace.   He had excellent control of his pitches, once throwing a no-hitter, the only one ever pitched in the school's history.   This must have made him extremely popular with the Marines.   He could hurl a grenade sixty feet six inches and brush back a Jap with it.

Pop.   A bullet to the head.   One instant standing in line holding out a mess kit.   The next a bleeding heap on the jungle floor, his brains dripping from the leaves of a banyan tree.   Where in the hell was Vella Lavella?

Sadly, he refolded this letter, too and set it to one side.   He turned his focus onto the package.   He studied it as if it was an archeological find.   It was addressed in his mother's hand, wrapped by brown paper and secured with several strands of twine.   He pulled off the twine and tore off the wrapping.   He opened the box and was thrilled by what he found.

His folks sent three bars of Ivory soap, his father, always the utilitarian, included razor blades and shoelaces, a small cardboard box lined with waxed paper in which nested a stack of two dozen oatmeal raisin cookies.   Manna from Heaven.   Candy bars, rolls of Life Savers, stationary, a fountain pen but no ink and most intriguing of all, a package wrapped in several layers of lilac colored tissue paper wrapped with a string tied in a bow.   There was a small note, sealed, slipped beneath the string.   He meticulously unwrapped the package, taking great care not to tear the paper much as the prudent archeologist seeks to preserve the trappings which surround an ancient parchment.   His eyes fell upon a white satin piece of cloth which he gingerly unfolded revealing itself to be a pillow case.   A satin pillow case.   He opened the envelope and took out the note.   He instantly recognized Jessie's handwriting and he could feel his heart accelerate in his chest.   The note was dated August seventeenth.

Hello my love, hope this note finds you well and rested.   I dream of you often and enclose my satin pillow case, the one on which my dreams arise.   It is the one on which we rested our heads so long ago.   I placed a few drops of my perfume on the inside to remind you of me.   If you close your eyes and   breathe deep you might think of me and be transported back to that night we shared. By resting your head where mine has slept maybe you might dream the same dreams that I have and our spirits will be as one once again.

Love Jessie.

That seemed pretty definitive.
His heart swelled with joy and he felt absolved, renewed.
The door burst open rudely and in stepped Selkirk, uninvited as usual.
"I heard you got cookies."
"Well, if it isn't Minnie the Moocher."
"What are you grinning about?" Mickey asked.
"Nothing."

Chapter Twenty-eight   **A Very Special Mission**

Friday, August 27, 1943

Word traveled fast.   By suppertime, all the cookies were gone.   Letting Selkirk know that cookies were to be had was as good as announcing it over the Tannoy.   A steady stream of well-wishers, unsolicited advice-givers and unapologetic panhandlers showed up at his door. Of course, Leo was one of the first to arrive, followed by Robertshaw and his copilot, Spats, Watanabe, Sully, who acted as if all was forgiven, Ransahoff and Barbieri who, as he crammed a second crumbling cookie into his mouth muttered to Hollis that, if he thought this would bring him into his good graces he was mistaken.   Hollis kept mentioning the need for rationing as each new face showed up at his door, shelling out cookies as if they were the Body of Christ. Until, finally they were gone.   He had eaten just two.   He played no favorites.   He parceled out the same number of cookies to Ransahoff who controlled his destiny as he did to Spats, who meant nothing to him.

After supper, Hollis wrote a second letter to Jessie thanking her for the package and its delightful contents telling her not to pay too much attention to the first.

It continued to rain, to the disappointment of some and the joy of others.

By Friday morning, the weather had cleared and when everybody awakened they were surprised a mission hadn't been laid on.   So, with blue skies and warm temperatures it seemed only obvious that they were alerted for an afternoon mission.   After lunch, they reported to the briefing room most sure, again, that it would be an easy one.   Dutifully, Hulse stood outside in the warm sun smiling and waving to Hollis.   Perhaps he had heard of the cookies and hoped, by ingratiating himself to Hollis, he might get a crack at the next batch.   Hollis waved back.

With a milk run predicted the banter in the room was light and there was laughing, which he had rarely heard recently.

"Ten-hut!"

Up the aisle strode Van Patten, dressed for flying.   He was the Bangmaster.   This might mean something serious.   The interesting thing was that Gleason, Begay and all of the squadron commanders were in flying gear, too.   Whatever they were going after today, they wanted to make sure they hit it.

"Seats, gentleman," Van Patten said.

After the rustle and mutterings stopped, Van Patten began.   He stood erect wearing his usual stern, authoritarian countenance which he, no doubt, spent hours practicing before a mirror at West Point.

"Gentlemen, we have a mission of some importance today.   We are going after a special installation at Watten, France."   The curtain was pulled back and a cheer went up, sending Hulse and his comrades scurrying to their planes with the good news.   A quick glance of the map showed the penetration would be shallow, time spent over enemy territory brief.

"I will be leading, flying with the 532nd, Col. Gleason will be flying deputy lead and Major Begay will be flying with the high squadron.   We will be low group in the lead combat wing.   Because of the critical nature of the target, bombing altitude will be 14,000 feet by squadrons."

This caused a great moan to arise from the assembled.   Anything worth hitting that badly would be valuable enough to be heavily defended.   A bombing altitude of 14,000 feet would put them within very easy, accurate reach of anybody with a flak gun.   *At that altitude, Hollis thought as he felt his sphincter tighten, they could hit us with rocks.   Shame Hulse and his pals didn't stick around to hear that reaction.*

"To give you some measure as to the importance of this target we have no assigned secondary or last resort targets and all sixteen groups of B-17s will be bombing.   Each plane will carry two two-thousand pounders.   Each squadron lead bombardier will make his own sighting.

"There is a six-gun eighty-eight battery one mile south of the target and one four-gun battery one quarter mile north of it.   We will be heavily escorted."

"What do you think is so all-fired important we gotta make all this fuss over?" H-y asked as they walked toward the equipment hut.

"I think if they wanted us to know what it was they would have come right out and told us," Sully responded, seemingly annoyed by the obviousness of the answer.

Leo chimed in, "Probably not a secret weapons site at all.   Probably some Gestapo headquarters or something.   Probably holding some beautiful countess suspected of being in the French Resistance."

"Jesus, Leo, that doesn't make any sense.   Why in the hell would they want sixteen groups to drop two-thousand pounders on some jail in order to free some rich French broad?" H-y asked.

"Well, H-y, has any of the rest of this made sense to you so far?"

"I'm thinking maybe they don't want her to survive the attack," Sully said.

"Maybe they're afraid she might talk if they torture her," H-y added.

"For Christ's Sake, will you guys knock it off.   If they wanted to torture her they'd send her here to spend a day with you three," Hollis said. "Trust me, she'd spill her guts."

"Yeah," H-y said.   "I'd have her talking in no time.   She'd probably be telling me things I didn't even want to know."

"O-o-oh-la-la," Sully said as they entered the crowded, smelly equipment shed.

Hollis paid careful attention to the way the crew reacted to him.   This was the first time they had assembled since the abortion three days earlier.   Maybe the passage of time had rendered their ill feelings toward him less focused, softened.   Perhaps this was the case with everyone but Augie who gave Hollis an unnerving stare.   The promise of a milk run and heavy escort could not allay Hollis's fears.   Lunch found its way onto the grass beside the perimeter strip.

As they approached the IP, the Wing broke down to groups and the groups into squadrons in single file.   The route from the IP, to the target, which was to take only three and a half minutes, would take them almost equidistant between the two flak batteries.

Nearing the target, Hollis could see the black puffs erupt out ahead of them.   The preceding groups had given them plenty of time to get the range on those that followed.   As they passed over the target **Cleopatra's Asp** was bounced around.   Those ten barrels must be glowing red hot by now,   Hollis thought, considering all the lead they were throwing up.

Hollis wanted to acquit himself well as leader of the second element of the lead squadron in light of his past performance in that role. He placed himself right behind Ransahoff, who had Van Patten riding shotgun, and held them there. Even so, he could not resist the temptation to look out the window at the ground to see what was so all-fired important. He didn't see much. There was significant haze and middle-level clouds and the target itself had been dusted up pretty good. They just salvoed into the churning earth. The lead group had been jumped by fighters as they turned onto the bomb run, but the escort was particularly effective in driving them away. The 381st was unmolested by anyone except the flak gunners. It turned out to be the milk run everyone had predicted. Bomb release was at 1850 and the last bomber rolled off the target an hour later. Hollis had **Cleopatra's Asp** back on the hardstand just as the last rays of light faded below the horizon. Everyone, including Moe, seemed pleased. They had uneventfully completed their fourth mission.

That evening they were given their orders officially promoting them to First Lieutenants. It was felt by all to represent a major turning point in the war.

The next day no mission was planned. The weather wasn't too bad to fly over England. On the Continent it was another matter. Two squadrons flew practice missions in order not to waste the semi-clear skies. Ransahoff had the 532nd stand down.

Word passed that the Provost Marshall was looking into the incident in Cambridge where Augie had beaten up a Negro. Hollis hoped they would arrest the bastard and throw him in some stockade somewhere and lose the key. He was pretty sure most others on the crew agreed. But nothing happened. Augie was not removed from the field in manacles and things went on as usual.

Hollis received two letters from Jessie, neither one of which addressed the Big Question, leading Hollis to surmise that she either had not yet gotten it or her reply was still forthcoming. He censored some mail, drank some bitters with Mickey and Leo at the White Horse and slept a lot.

Sunday it rained.

Monday they got as far as the Channel when they were recalled due to bad weather. This raised the level of frustration and tempers grew short. The crew started grumbling about a pass to London and beseeched Hollis to make discrete inquiries about the subject. So Hollis went to Ransahoff to clarify the situation and he laughed. "Five mission rule," Ransahoff said.

Hollis was unaware of any such rule and said so.

"Five mission rule" says nobody gets to go to London 'til they've gotten credit for five missions. What he actually said was 'survive five missions.'

Then how 'bout a pass to Cambridge?

No passes, I told you. You deef?

Then how come Augie, my gunner, got to go to Cambridge?

That's under investigation.

Tuesday, August 31, 1943

After breakfast an announcement came over the Tannoy stating that the afternoon's cricket match was on, the coded message that was meant to alert everyone about a mission scheduled for the afternoon.

At briefing, they were told the primary target was the air depot at Romilly-sur-Seine. Weather, they said would be marginal but probably OK. General Gross would lead. The Order of Battle found the 101st CBW at the head of the bomber stream and the 102nd and 103rd in trail. The 381st would be high off the 91st. The 532nd would be low squadron. Hollis would lead the second element, Robertshaw on his right and DeBerg on the left.

This does not promise to be a milk run, Begay said, he was Bangmaster. Romilly has always been well-defended but, we will have an escort for most of the mission.

Hollis felt his heart sink at that news. What did he mean by 'most of the mission?' What was the message behind 'well defended?' Should they expect a big fight or not?

Take off, at 1515 in the afternoon, and assembly were uneventful. Robertshaw demonstrated himself to be a good pilot. He rarely got out of place and when he did he pulled right back in. DeBerg, on the other hand, was a lot like Cahill and *also like me*, Hollis thought, initially anyway, for he was always trying to keep up, get back into place. Maybe he would get the hang of it soon, Hollis hoped. If not he was going to have a rough time. Ransahoff and the Germans do not forgive mistakes.

The formation made a slight dogleg to the right over Beachy Head and flew out over the Channel making a bee-line toward Paris where they would make another dogleg, this time to the left toward Romilly.

Somebody must not have been paying attention. The exact cause will likely never be known. Hollis had his eyes on it as the deadly events unfolded. Down below, in the high squadron of the 91st, the number two Fortress drifted sideways into the number one. As if in slow motion, the left wing of the first ran across the right wing of the other, the engines tangled in an eruption of sparks and hurling metal. Both planes rolled into each other and, joined in an ugly conjunction of aluminum, fire and flesh, fell toward the sea.

"Jesus Christ, did you see that?" Sully said into the interphone.

Hollis stared at the cascading wreckage until it fell from sight to the water below. A third Fortress, an innocent bystander in the whole affair, was battered badly by debris and dropped from the formation, under control, and made a turn back toward Beachy Head. In the matter of just a few seconds, twenty men were gone, their bits and pieces of flesh and bone settling to the bottom of the sea.

They passed over the French coast at twenty-one thousand feet. As Hollis watched in stunned disbelief, the formation below, so recently decimated and scattered by the loss of three planes, resurrected itself, regrouping quickly.

The coastal flak belt fired up some random bursts, none of which appeared to hit anything. The escort did not appear and the clouds coalesced down below. It came as no surprise when, halfway to Paris and a third of the way to the target Leo tapped Hollis on the arm to announce that they were diverting to the target of last resort.

General Gross wheeled the formation around in a huge one hundred and eighty degree turn to retrace their path toward the coast. As they re-crossed the coast, Gross wheeled them around again in the direction of the airdrome at Amiens/Glisy. This back and forth caused the formation to loosen and, without any escort, it also came as no surprise when several Me-109s showed up to protest the wanderings of the American Fortresses. They had seen enough. They pressed home their attacks, fortunately on somebody else, until the target was reached and they faded back into the clouds.

Hollis looked down at 'bombs away' and only saw clouds. If an airdrome was down there he hoped somebody saw it because he didn't. But, he told himself, the ordinance fell on something. The mission counted, Number Five, the collision still fresh in his mind as they landed, again, as the sunlight retreated. Gathering his equipment, he climbed into the truck for the ride to interrogation, speculating on how far they had gone today toward ending the war.

As darkness descended over the field and the truck rocked back and forth over the ruts in the path toward the Headquarters block, Hollis closed his eyes and saw the two B-17s collide as each tried to occupy the same piece of air. Twenty men decaying quickly at the bottom of the sea. Fishes and crabs nibbling at fingers and noses.

Not long after they completed interrogation Hollis was in bed, exhausted. He fell asleep quickly.

There was a long line of men standing patiently with ground fog hanging still around their ankles. They were expressionless, staring ahead apathetically. The man at the head of the line had no left arm but he did not appear to be in pain. Torn bloody flesh protruded from the ragged edge of his leather jacket. The man behind him had been gutted, his torso an empty cavity from his neck to his groin. Behind him stood a man charred black, his eyes vacant, a melted rubber oxygen mask dangled from the side of his face, fused with the scorched flesh of his cheek. Behind him was a man balanced perfectly on one leg, the other a bloody stump at the knee. Behind him a man with no eyes, his arm resting gently on the shoulder of the man with the missing leg. The next man was missing the top of his head, sliced cleanly off at the eyebrows. He was the only one who showed any emotion. He smiled whimsically when he saw Hollis staring at him. He winked. And on and on the line went, single file for as far as the eye could see. He saw Robbie. But Robbie did not see him. The front of his head and most of his face was gone. Hollis turned to see what it was they were waiting for.

God. They were waiting at the Gates of Heaven, confronting God, one by one. At his right hand stood Jesus still wearing His crown of thorns, His forehead traced by rivulets of His Divine Blood. At His left side, seated at a small desk, was a first sergeant, the Divine Bookkeeper, slowly, meticulously writing each name, rank and serial number in a large ledger, each man taking one step forward, giving his name and disappearing into a cloud. Hollis searched to see who was at the far end of the line but he could not tell for the had no end.

Hollis awakened. The only sound was the snoring of his copilot.

The next morning, after breakfast, they were ordered to report to Group Headquarters in their Class A uniforms. There, in a small ceremony, three crews were awarded the Air Medal for completing, or did Van Patten say 'surviving?,' five missions. Technical Sergeant Noah Dodge was awarded the Military Order of the Purple Heart.

Hollis slept so soundly that he failed to hear Beamis enter Pilot's House. They had been alerted the night before but the weather had been so iffy that everyone went to bed fairly convinced nothing was going to happen.

"Where to today, Beamis?" Hollis managed to get out, surprised his night hadn't been ravaged by another nightmare.

"Light load today, Lieutenant. Like milk from a mother's teat. You'll find Hell waiting when you get there, nonetheless."

Hollis was determined to stop asking as long as Beamis kept giving those stupid, cryptic responses, but his curiosity always got the better of him.   "Do you say that to everybody?"

"No."

"Then why do you say it to me?"

"'Cause you're the only one who bothers to ask."

It was indeed a milk run.   They were dispatched to Vannes/Meucon airfield in Northern France but were recalled just as they crossed into France.   They had to endure Augie as he groused in a loud, obnoxious voice, about not receiving credit for the mission.

Otho Barbieri strode over to them, a most agitated look on his face.   Good, Hollis thought, he's going to box Augie's ears, punch that fucking, obnoxious hillbilly right in the mouth.

"Hollis," he said, barely able to contain his disdain, "you and your crew have been issued a three day pass to London.   Pick 'em up in the Squadron office and you can catch the first train in the morning."

The crew gave out a collective hoot.   London.   *Xanadu*.

Chapter Twenty-nine   **Trains**

Friday, September 3, 1943

The night was punctuated by the sound of aircraft engines rising and falling.   Activity. Hollis heard them, but paid them no mind.   They had been promised a seventy-two hour pass to London and he had little fear that they would renege on that promise, although in the army anything was possible.   Besides, the 532nd had been stood down, Otho said.

Leo set the alarm so they could be up, showered and ready to go when the first shuttle left for the station at Great Yeldham, a few miles from the base.

The bombers roared off, one by one, into the mist as Hollis and Leo trudged down the cinder path to the latrine.   No one looked. No one knew where they were going or much cared.

When word passed the evening before that the crew was headed for London, they were deluged with advice about where to go and what to do.   If you were interested in seeing the sights and investigating the culture of the Mother Country there would be plenty to do and see. If you were interested in dancing there was a dance hall or night club on nearly every street.   If you just wanted to have a hot bath, lie around in clean sheets and drink yourself into unconsciousness, London had some of the finest hotels in the world in which to do it.   If you wanted to get laid, you truly had come to the right place.

There was a girl for every taste, many were pretty and they were all anxious to please. A quick fuck costs two pounds sterling.   The highest concentrations were to be found by the Marble Arch and Piccadilly Circus.   The French girls considered Duke Street their own and were willing to defend it.   There was nothing, they said, like a catfight between two whores, one of whom barely spoke English.

They were everywhere.   You can spot 'em in every doorway smoking a cigarette, like a beacon in the night, to let you know they're there.   Once you give 'em the money they'll fuck you right there on the spot, standin' up.   They can service five customers that way in the time it would take to do one in a hotel room.   Time is money.

And be careful, those Piccadilly Commandoes will give you a dose of the clap that will peel your pecker right off.   Just keep those French letters handy and you'll be OK.   Don't worry if you run out.   Rubbers are easier to get in London than soap.   And if you think you got a dose you can perform a rudimentary prophylaxis by pulling the foreskin down over the head of your dick and pissing.   That'll take care of it.

Well, what do you do if you ain't got a foreskin? H-y asked.

Then cut the sumbitch off 'cause it just fucked you, too, came the reply.

Secure lodging quickly, they were told.   There is an increasing influx of regular Army assholes, ground-pounders and the like, who snatch up all the good hotel rooms.   By afternoon, most of the best rooms are gone.   Grosvenor House and the Savoy were the tops.   For about twelve bucks you could get a terrific room and a great breakfast to go with it.

If you get a chance you should go see the Windmill Theater.   The place features this live, nude, girlie show.   They strip down naked and then they have to stay perfectly still, otherwise, it ain't legal.   They say the place never closes.   Even during the bombing.   The star of the show is named Dixie.   Beautiful and the best set of tits in London.

There were great dance halls where the bands played a pretty good imitation of American swing.   The places are always packed with English broads ready and willing to trip the light fantastic.   It's a lot of fun.

Of course, you can always go to the Tower of London or Madame Taussaud's Wax Museum.   Buckingham Palace.   The Changing of the Guard.   Ho-hum.

If worse comes to worse, you can always go to The Rainbow Corner on Shaftsbury off Piccadilly Circus.   It was run by the American Red Cross and open twenty-four hours a day.   It has pinball machines, juke boxes and pool tables.   You can always get a hamburger, donuts, coffee and all the Cokes you can drink.   You can get a bed, a shower, or a haircut.   A patch sewn on or a sympathetic ear.

Eager with anticipation, they found themselves on the same truck headed out.   As the truck approached the gate, the M.P. made each man produce a Pro-kit and prophylactics as a condition for leaving the base.   He didn't particularly care to see their passes as long as they could prove they were alert to the unchecked ravages of venereal disease.   Each Pro-kit consisted of a scrap of soaped paper for washing, a tube of some kind of ointment, Hollis presumed to ward off scabies, and two sulfa tablets to kill the clap.   Hollis wondered what was going through Leo's mind as he held up his Pro-kit.   Would he tell Christie of this exigency of Army life or not?   Would the fore-swearing of lechery have made any difference to an M.P., a lowly corporal whose sole order of the day was to ensure a commitment against VD by all who passed?   Would Leo pledging his undying devotion to his wife make it OK to leave the base without a rubber?

"Flies spread disease," the M.P. shouted into the back of the truck as it roared off. "Keep yours closed."

Armed and forewarned, the truck rolled off the base and headed toward the village of Great Yeldham.   There they would catch the train to Liverpool Street Station and London.

As the truck rattled and ground its way along the tree-lined road it was obvious the driver still hadn't figured out how to shift the gears.   The pungent mixture of aviation gas and aftershave filled the back of the canvas covered compartment where the crew sat shoulder to shoulder on the benches.   It harkened back to the time not long ago when they had ridden onto the base in similar circumstance heading for an uncertain future, Hollis recalled.   Now they were again headed for an uncertain future but on this occasion it appeared highly-likely that they would all live through it.

Perhaps nobody else seemed to notice the strong, almost choking smell.   Hollis turned to Rizzo, "Do you smell that gas?"

"Yeah, we don't have any stuff to dry-clean our uniforms with so we use gas."

Augie turned to Hollis and said, "Hey Lieutenant, we had to stop and see the flight surgeon before we were allowed to leave.   He gave us a lecture on sexual hygiene.   He said he ain't never seen anybody come back from a pass in better shape than when they left.   He told us not to forget before we put our dicks in anything to make sure we put on a rubber.   He said vynereal disease is a court martial offense.   Did you have to get a lecture, Lieutenant, before they'd let you leave?   Naw, I guess not, you bein' officers and all.   They don't need to tell you not to forget to cover your dick.   I mean you bein' officers and all."

Hollis paid no attention to Augie.   He couldn't get over how much he loathed Augustine Reese.   He rested his head back and feigned sleep.

Sully spoke, "Article Twenty-nine states 'Injury incurred as a direct result of improper relations with women, such as an assault by the husband on account of such relations is due to misconduct.   Article Thirty states that venereal disease, in view of the small number of cases contracted innocently, is generally held to be due to misconduct.   Thirty-one and thirty-two go on to say that if you contracted it while in the hospital for another cause or contracted it before enlistment, you must make up the bad time.   Thirty-three and Thirty-four say that if you are quarantined or hospitalized on suspicion and tests prove negative, it is not bad time.   The articles state that drunkenness as a proximate cause of injury will be regarded as due to misconduct.'"

All eyes, including Hollis's, turned toward Sully.   They all laughed, a laugh which exuberantly exceeded the humor of the situation.   It was as much a release and acknowledgment that they were, in fact, finally off the base as it was the result of the content of Sully's brief instruction on the Code of Military Conduct.

Augie turned to Sully, whom Hollis knew Reese disliked intensely, and asked, "Hey, Lieutenant Sully, I heard the nuns in London are all spies.   You heard that?"

"No, Augie, can't say as I have."

"I also heard all the WACS have to strip naked in front of a bunch of officers in order to get in.   Is that true?"

"Augie," Sully replied as if trying to find patience with an annoying child, "can't say as I heard that one either."

"Well, I thought maybe you bein' an officer, you might know these things."

"Can you imagine the history that took place right outside this truck.   Here we are in Merry Ol' England.   This is terrific," H-y said.

Sully replied, "Do you realize the history that is going to be made if we don't get H-y laid?"

"Try real hard not to embarrass us on this trip, H-y," Leo chimed in.   "It could threaten the Alliance."

"My ancestors left this place and landed on Plymouth Rock," H-y continued.

"I guess they couldn't navigate either, H-y.   As I understand it, the pilgrims were originally headed for Miami Beach," Hollis added.   This caused more laughter.   It was good to laugh away from the bombers.

Within a few minutes, the truck rolled to a stop in front of the railway station.   It was a tired looking wooden structure with a large overhang that Hollis figured dated back a century.   They purchased tickets, twelve shillings for a roundtrip to Liverpool Station and back.   Above the ticket window was a sign which read, "IS YOUR JOURNEY REALLY NECESSARY?"   Hollis mentally answered, *You bet it is*.

They went up to the platform to wait.   There, standing at the far end, stood Barney Rager with a white patch still taped over his eye and a small bandage around his right hand.   Hollis viewed him with a combination of awe and envy for Rager, one of the Group's lead pilots, had a reputation as a real stick and rudder man.   With Eisenberg gone, he was far and away the best natural pilot in the Group.   Courageous beyond reproach, he cut a fine figure in his trench coat and fifty-mission crush hat, his musette bag slung over his shoulder, a recruiting poster for the American Airman, exuding *esprit* and confidence.   He seemed to be all the things Hollis was not.   He was painful to look at.

Barney was talking to another officer from the Group, Beck Farrell, he thought, who was assistant Group Ops under Begay.   He noticed Rager turn and look up the tracks.   A moment later, Hollis heard the unmistakable chugging of an approaching steam locomotive.   It was a sound that evoked so many fond memories of his childhood, remote now as the last Ice Age. There was something strong, dependable and reassuring about a steam engine.   At night, back home he could lie in his bed and hear the Pennsy milk train rumble through Chester on its way to Baltimore and Washington, a swift Pacific with a tank car, a boxcar filled with mail and a coach or two.   Hollis would always awaken a few moments in anticipation of it, heralded by its whistle blowing precisely each 2:05 AM.   He would listen to the rumble of the train as it receded into the night as quickly as it came.   He would turn over and fall fast asleep again, assured that life continued even in the dark.   The sound of human endeavor made the night less frightening, less lonely, endurable.   Hollis forever felt gratitude for the trains, leviathans of the ballast.   Big, iron guardians of the night.   K-4s, Pacifics.   They made the earth shake.

The London North East Railway. LNER emblazoned on the side of the tender.

There was a high-pitched whistle.   He could see the steam popping spasmodically above the trees beyond the bend.   He was ill-prepared for the quaint, little engine that rounded the curve.   Back home, Hollis thought, that locomotive wouldn't have made a decent yard switcher. *Jesus, I've got a bigger train under my Christmas tree*, he heard someone say.   It had smoke deflectors, elephant ears, flanking the front of the boiler looking like blinders that had slipped down over the horse's nose and a little cow catcher that looked too frail to brush aside a cat, let alone wayward livestock.   It was sad.   The train made its stop with a flurry of steam, squealing brakes and another toot on the shrill, piercing whistle.   The cars were quaint Victorian coaches with each compartment having its own door opening onto the platform.   Every compartment appeared full.   Hollis quickly located one that contained only two people and grabbed Leo's arm, making a bee-line for it.   He leaped into the compartment and sat next to a woman while Leo planted himself hastily beside an elderly gentleman.

Hollis excused himself as he slightly jostled the woman beside him, realizing only after he sat down that she was pregnant.   Ready to deliver by the looks of it.   She smiled and nodded.

"Hiya, Pop," Leo said cheerfully.   "How are you this fine day?"

"Very well, thank you," came the terse reply, the man not lifting his eyes from the newspaper he held.

"Whatcha readin'?"

"The newspaper."

"I really love your country.   I guess you're not too happy we're back, huh?"

The man finally lifted his gaze from the page and turned to confront Leo, clearly succeeding in his effort to be deliberately annoying, a display Hollis found totally out of character for his easy going, but usually reserved copilot.

"Hey, you're not still pissed about Bunker Hill, are ya?"

"My dear boy, Bunker Hill was *our* victory."

"It was?"

The old man seemed stunned by this ignorance.   Hollis saw Leo wink at the old man and the two laughed at each other.   Leo had achieved his goal, a rapid connection between taciturn Englishman and admiring Anglophile.   The exchange started a spirited and amiable conversation.

Hollis turned to the pregnant woman and asked how long it would take to get to London.

"About three hours, usually.   We change at Chelmsford.   Sometimes there is a delay."

Hollis took his musette bag and placed it on the floor in front of him.   It contained a clean shirt, change of socks, underwear and toiletries.   He also had a small stash of Life Savers which he had successfully hidden from pilferage after the cookies were gone.   He took a roll and opened it, offering one to everybody in the compartment.   There was a sudden shrill toot and the conductor slammed the door shut.   With a sudden lurch the train was rolling.   The station passed from view, the platform now deserted.   Within a few moments, the little train was hurtling along at breakneck speed.   Hollis figured they were doing close to sixty. Much too fast for such antiquated rolling stock.   The door rattled and Hollis expected it to fly open abruptly pitching all four into space.   There was a sign over the door which read: IT IS DANGEROUS FOR PASSENGERS TO PUT THEIR HEADS OUT THE CARRIAGE WINDOW.   Hollis wondered what event had prompted the need for that particular admonition. He watched the verdant green countryside flash past the window.

"I never knew England would be so green," Hollis said.

"Or so wet," Leo added.   "Even the sunshine is rationed."   The old man, sucking noisily on a large pipe, paused to laugh yet again at his new Yankee friend.

Hollis looked at the rolling hills and hedgerows and the occasional thatch-roofed cottage beside a road or solitary church steeple rising above the trees.   The arrow-straight rock walls that separated pastures, some of those stone walls likely dated to the days of the Romans. The England he could see out his window had been untouched by the war.   It was the land of Stonehenge, the Magna Carta, Druid sacrifices, Cromwell, Shakespeare, Richard the Third, and Robin Hood, Europe's first communist.   There was virtually not a speck of this ancient land that had not, at some point in time, felt the weight of a human foot, Hollis suspected.   Whereas, back home, there were probably whole tracts of forests and prairies that had never been seen or touched by a human being.

England had always been remote, an abstraction from high school and college history. The New World view of the place was often jaded by preformed notions of England's negative role in shaping that history, unable to separate the country from its unsavory politics and hegemony.   So here they were for the second time in a quarter of a century, Americans, an occupying army.   Friendly by most accounts but an occupation force none the less.

At the beginning of the war, the British ruled one quarter of the earth's surface, subjugating one quarter of its population, the sun never setting on its colonial empire.   *Awfully noble of us to help them preserve it again, don't you think?* Hollis mused.

The British were ambivalent that they had returned.   Hollis knew there was an irreconcilable dichotomy of opinion of Brits toward Americans.   Happy and relieved to have them here in a time of crisis, but unabashedly resentful at having to endure the haughty, arrogant Americans in their midst, drinking their pubs dry and fucking their woman, acting like a conquering legion of spoiled rich kids.

What was it Sully said?   *God put the Atlantic Ocean there for a reason.*

Hollis noticed them slowing as they neared Chelmsford where they would switch trains. The whistle blew again as the train lurched to a stop.   The old man opened the door and Hollis heard the conductor yell, "Chelmsford, all out!"

The train disgorged itself onto another platform already crowded with civilians and men in uniform.   Hollis noticed some British soldiers and a few RN sailors.   There was a small kiosk, a small NAAFI, station where they could get hot tea and a sandwich.   They would have a long wait in line for there must have been twenty soldiers and sailors crowding its small counter. Hollis and Leo had barely stepped onto the platform when the door slammed behind them and the little train chugged off.

"I wonder how soon the train to London will be by?" he heard H-y ask as he and Sully walked up behind them.

"Not long, I think," Hollis said.

After a few minutes, a train pulled into the station, not much bigger than the one they had just gotten off.   It too, discharged passengers, further jamming the already packed platform. H-y grabbed a man in a railway man's uniform and asked if this was the train for London.

No, he said.   It will be by soon.

A moment later it too chugged off.

Ten minutes passed before a larger train pulled into the station resulting in an ebb and flow of humanity, pushing and shoving impolitely to get on or off.

"Is *this* the train to London?" H-y yelled.

"No, ya bloody yank!" came an anonymous reply.   After a moment, it left.

Twenty minutes later, a third train pulled into the station.   The passengers shifted almost as a single unit toward it before it came to a stop.

"I don't give a fuck whether this is the train to London or not.   I'm getting on the son of a bitch," H-y said.

This many people trying to get onto the same train must be a sure sign that this was the one they wanted, so the four officers joined the throng willing to gamble that everybody knew where they were going.   Should they end up in Glasgow, Hollis was willing to kill H-y for yet another navigational error, his most egregious yet.

By the time they were on the train they could only stand.   There was simply no room on the dingy, threadbare seats for any of them to sit.   Hollis caught a glimpse of the pregnant woman he shared the ride with as she lowered herself into a seat afforded her by an American soldier, who, he recognized, was Quinn.

The train pulled off, but never gained the speed the little one had.   With this many people anxious to get to London the engineer should have taken pity on them and drove like a bat out of hell.   Instead, it slowed and pulled into another station.   Ingatestone.

"Shit," H-y said.   "We got the local."

Hollis looked him in the eye and said, "I blame you."

H-y laughed. Hollis did too.

Brentwood was next.   Then another.   Then another.

Hollis had to bend over to see out the windows.   He did so reluctantly and when he did, he quickly noted the transition from the rural to the industrial.   Green marshy flats gave way to huge rail yards and gray, smoky factories.   Block after block of yellow and red brick row homes passed into view.   Then he saw it.

They slowed through the East End of London, he saw his first bombed out building. They were traveling slow enough for him to study it.   It was not a building.   It had been a block of buildings.   Charred timbers jutting up like blackened ribs, immense piles of bricks and stone filled the bottom of the hulk.   People walked past inured to its presence for no one looked at it.   Even the people on the train paid no notice.

As one block passed from view, another entered his sight.   A storefront stood in stark defiance with nothing behind it but empty space.   He felt a tap on his arm.   Leo motioned out the window.   Hollis nodded his acknowledgment.   He could not take his eyes off of the ruins. He had never seen anything like this before.   Movietone News footage was an abstraction. The uninitiated mind rejected such things as unreal, contrived.   The pictures of flame leaping from windows, falling walls, firemen scurrying for their lives.   When he walked out of the theater the images would cease to exist.   Like Tarzan and his jungle. The crump, crump, crump of bombs exploding in the background as Edward R. Murrow reported the Blitz.   When he turned the radio off it would all be gone.   There it was just a few feet from where he stood.   If they stopped the train he could pick up a broken brick with his own hands and the thing might actually start to weep with sorrow.   Hollis wondered what it must be like under the bombs-- simultaneous detonation of all those bombs striking the earth at the same time.   One continuous roll of ear-shattering thunder magnified a million times.   Who could be so stout-hearted not to sue for peace under such concentrated violence?

He could see the barrage balloons, dozens of them.   Some were high, some rode low, each pointing to its own point on the compass, swinging gently to and fro in the breeze, tethered to earth poised to ensnare some marauding Heinkel or a straying Fortress.

Then he noticed something else.   There were no children.   Not on the train.   Not on the sidewalks they passed.   Nowhere.

The conductor negotiated his way stiffly down the aisle calling, "Liverpool Street Station, tickets, please."

The train slowly entered the station with its high, vaulted ceiling looking much like an oversized hanger.   When Hollis stepped onto the platform he could see pigeons flying around the rafters amidst clouds of roiling steam and smoke.

The crew found itself together again all following the tide of passengers as they headed for the exit.   Up ahead, Hollis could see Barney Rager, his cap jauntily cocked to one side, the trench coat tossed over his shoulder, his bandages white badges of courage.   He seemed on top of the world.

When they stepped onto the sidewalk Hollis saw Rager climb into a little black taxi which miraculously appeared as if from thin air at his feet.   The door popped open and Rager stepped in.   Hollis heard the driver ask, "Where to, Yank?"

"The Savoy."   The door slammed shut and off they sped.

"Last train back Sunday night," he heard Mollica yell.

"Yeah," Hollis yelled back and the four officers watched the enlisted men bolt off in different directions, Quinn, Reese, Rizzo and Mollica in one group, Dodge and Hulse in another.

"How ya gonna keep 'em down on the farm after they seen Paree?" Sully asked.

"Where to, Yanks?" Hollis turned to hear the voice of another cabbie.

"Come on, fellas," Hollis said.   "The Savoy."

Chapter Thirty   **Xanadu**

"Righto," the cabbie said as the four officers wedged themselves into the taxi.   He was obviously proud of his city for he felt obliged to point out everything of even minor significance on their journey.   He took them past St. Paul's Cathedral, onto Fleet Street, past St. Clement Danes Church onto the Strand ending up in front of the Savoy.   The four officers gawked out the windows like the tourists they were.   The streets were bustling as they would in any big city on a Friday afternoon.   London was dark and dingy, Hollis thought, like somebody needed to hose it down to dissolve and wash away the dirty crust.   They saw the bright red double-decker buses pass by, dozens of small, identical, black taxis, pubs, offices, restaurants, shops.   Men wearing bowlers and carrying umbrellas walked by as they stood at a stop light.   Newspaper vendors hawked papers on nearly every street corner.

"The Savoy, mates," the cabbie announced.   The hotel had a huge awning which extended almost to the street.   A gray-haired doorman opened the door and the four officers bounded out of the cab.   Hollis gave the driver his three bob fare and they stood for a moment looking at the front of the hotel.   They turned to see Rager step from his cab.   How they had managed to beat him there was a curiosity.   All four watched as he strode briskly up to a young, gorgeous, statuesque blond waiting patiently beside the entrance, impervious to the people walking by her and the hard glances she engendered.   She beamed when she saw Rager approach an instant before she was swept into his arms.

Leo turned to them, "You guys go on.   I'll catch up with you later."   He turned and walked down the street as if he knew where he was going.   Where that was Hollis hadn't a clue.

Rager and the blond, arm in arm, walked off probably heading for a destination they both knew well.

"Let's see if we can get rooms," H-y said and they strode into the spacious, elegant lobby, the hushed atmosphere a sudden, sharp contrast to the noisy street.   The room was filled with huge, overstuffed chairs and coffee tables.   Officers of every rank walked past or stood talking.   Some were American, others British and several from countries he did not recognize.   Two wore kilts and red berets.

Hollis stepped up to the counter and quickly got a room which came with a large bath and breakfast in the morning.   He stepped to one side after receiving the key while H-y leaned over to Sully saying, "Let's share a room."

"If you think that just because I share the front of that plane with you, I'm going to share a God-damned hotel room with you, you're nuts."

"Sullee, Sullee...I'll make you a deal.   You let me share a room with you and I'll find you a chick that will spend the whole weekend with you for free."

"Deal."   They shook hands and each coughed up his half.   This, Hollis thought, should prove interesting.

They went to their rooms, Hollis uncertain where Leo had headed off to or what arrangements he might make for catching up with them later.

Hollis entered the room, saw the large bed and knew he had, in the midst of a strange city in a strange land, finally reached Paradise.   He threw the musette bag onto the chair and looked into the bathroom and there, as promised, sat a large white porcelain tub.   He couldn't decide what he wanted to do first.   Take a bath.   A nap.   See the sights.   Have a few drinks.

He finally decided to go to the lobby, see if he could find Leo and have a few drinks before dinner.

As he walked toward the bar, he saw H-y and Sully   depart the lobby for the street, H-y clearly in command, navigating for once with an air of self-confidence reserved for such forays.

In the bar, he had a double scotch.   Then another.   He watched people coming and going.   He marveled at how quickly and smoothly the two doubles went down.   He kept a watchful eye in the direction of the lobby.   No Leo.

His head started swimming as he ordered his third drink determined to finish it before ordering the biggest steak they had.   He thought he might go lay down for a quick nap first and returned to his room.   It was well past nine when he awakened, still clothed, on his bed.   He could not recall the journey back from the bar.   A line of drool ran down his chin which he wiped off when he got up.   He washed his face, straightened his uniform and went to the hotel's restaurant.

After a huge steak, mashed potatoes, gravy, corn, biscuits, ice cream and hot apple pie, he had two cups of rich coffee and left the hotel.   London was completely blacked out.   He could see stars in the sky and hear traffic nearby, but, for the most part, things were quiet.   He contemplated going to Piccadilly Circus and stopping by the Rainbow Club, but decided instead to walk down to the Victoria Embankment.   There was a small park nearby and he could make out dark figures fornicating under an elm tree.   He might not have noticed them at all except for the moaning.   At the Embankment he looked out over the Thames.   He could make out the dark outlines of the bridges.   The water lapped softly against the stone wall.   In the distance, he heard the eerie, plaintive wail of a lone, air-raid siren.   Then another joined in.   A couple of searchlights flicked on and scanned back and forth for a minute then extinguished.   False alarm, perhaps.   He smoked a couple of cigarettes careful to shield the burning embers against detection from above.   The last thing he wanted to do was call down a German bomb on himself and the fornicators by the careless display of a glowing cigarette.

He wondered what Leo was up to and why he had become so suddenly distracted.   Then he thought of the crew.   With the possible exception of Noah Dodge, they were all out either in the process of getting laid, trying to get laid or had been laid, perhaps several times by now.   This was the first time any of them had experienced anything like this.   Time was short, they were young, impetuous males and sex was readily available.   Even in the States, they had not encountered anything to compare.   Then, he wondered, why he had placed Dodge above such shenanigans.   Why should Dodge be any different?

Sex.   It was the great engine of the night.   That and booze.   Sex was such a powerful motive.   Sex and love could lead men to do strange things, things they would never dream of doing under any other circumstances.   Was it sex or the fear of bad crops which caused the Druids to sacrifice virgins on an alter?   Why people?   Why not dogs or cats?   Especially cats. Maybe all the different gods they feared and adored would find humans more worthy.   If you were willing to sacrifice your neighbor or your wife, now that was saying something.   Behead your daughter and the gods knew you meant business.   That might strike a resonant or appeasing chord with at least one demi-god and he might then be willing to spare them the Black Plague or famine or body lice.

How did they do it?   Who decides these things?   He wondered if the Druids thought that the method mattered.   Did one whack off the head?   Did they stone someone to a pulp? Did they burn them at the stake?   Did they simply heave them into a chasm somewhere? Perhaps they tended to tailor the method to the god they were trying to impress. One for good crops. Another for an early spring. No more comets or eclipses. They were just too scary.

How did they choose whose turn it was?   Did it represent a form of applied Darwinian selection?   If you were ugly you went.   Or maybe if you were beautiful you knew at some point you would end up baring your neck.   Maybe all you had to be was stupid or slow of foot. Or did the high priests just grab who was closest?   The Entwhistle method.

Even for such a primitive world how could one explain such arbitrary cruelty?   What were these people thinking?   Did they think at all?   Had their brains developed the extra gyri required for insight and reflection?   Or pathos?

He turned and placed his back to the river.   He saw two Negroes walk past the park, one was a corporal and the other a private.   He could hear them talking softly.   He thought of Augie and the KKK and lynching and broiling niggers with blow torches and he figured things might not have evolved as far as he thought. Or hoped.

He slowly developed a ringing headache, a hangover from the three doubles.   He finished his last cigarette and returned to his room, stripped naked and turned in.

The siren awakened him with a start.   It was close.   It sounded as if it might actually be in the room above him.   His heart started pounding.   He didn't want to die.   Not like this. He looked around the room for his pants and grabbed them running down the long hall.   He stopped suddenly by an open door which led into a   darkened hotel room.   There was a sudden, shattering crash and the room was filled with dust and burning embers.   The building had been hit by the first bomb.   It had exploded on the roof.   Why was he standing here when he should be in the basement shelter by now?   He felt a presence.   Something was moving. On the floor across the room he could make out a dark, squirming figure.   He shouted out but all he heard was soft moaning.   What should he do?   Should he stay or should he run for his life?

The dust suddenly obscured his view.   Against all reason, he was drawn irresistibly into the blackened room.   He tripped over some bricks falling to his hands and knees when the next bomb struck, his outstretched palms punctured by glass and splinters.   Then another.   Unless he left this place that instant he would not survive.   A fire started in the corner of the room providing him enough light to see the figure on the floor.   It was a pregnant woman, the same one he had ridden with to Chelmsford.   How did she get here?   She screamed out.   Was she hurt?   No, she was in labor.   She lay on her back, her skirt hiked up around her waist, exposing he large, white, rounded belly.   Her legs were drawn up and her bottom was smeared with blood.   Her hands were tightly clenched and face contorted by the agony of childbirth. She glistened with sweat, flashing red and orange by the flaring of the flames.   She turned her head and saw Hollis, reaching out for him when the next bomb erupted with a shattering bang causing the ceiling to buckle.   The plaster gave way to naked beams which, losing support, came crashing down upon her head and upper torso crushing her to a pulp.   Suddenly, the fetus popped from her womb in a bloody splash, like an erupting boil.   Hollis felt the hot liquid splash onto the skin of his face.

He watched as the baby squirmed on the dirty floor for a moment or two, flailing its arms weakly, but not crying out.   It drew its knees up spasmodically and then stopped moving.   It lay still, eyes open, staring back in the direction from whence it had just come.

Hollis awakened with a start.   No sirens.   The room was cool and he was soaked.   He sat up and looked at his watch.   Four AM.   He got up and smoked a cigarette   going into the bathroom to check.   There was no blood on his face.   He washed it anyway.   The cool water felt good.

He slept in.   No one bothered to wake him and he felt no inclination to get up.   He could hear the traffic on the street below.   He checked the time.   Ten thirty.   He hadn't slept this late since his last furlough.   He thought of his nightmare, but dismissed it as the alchemy of alcohol, the spooky air raid siren in the pitch-black night and the ride with the pregnant woman. He chalked it up to a revolt of the subconscious.   He drew a hot bath immersing himself in it until he was nearly wrinkled. It was the cleanest he'd felt in months.   For breakfast, he had steak and eggs, toast, marmalade and that rarest of all commodities, orange juice.

The concierge gave him a map of central London and Hollis sallied forth into the afternoon to see the sights.   He once again wondered about Leo but dismissed that, too.   Leo was a big boy.   He could find his own way home.   Hollis was just surprised.   He spent the afternoon going from pub to pub for beer searching, he finally admitted to himself, for a familiar face, somebody he could talk to.   He visited the National Gallery and saw the Changing of the Guard.   He returned to the room and laid on the bed daydreaming of home and Jessie until it was time for dinner.

There was a sudden commotion out in the hall followed by an abrupt rap on the door.

"It's open!" Hollis exclaimed.

The door flew open and Hollis saw H-y and Sully grinning from ear to ear.   They stepped into the room each accompanied by a woman.   H-y had an army nurse draped around his arm and Sully had his arm around a WAVE ensign.   Giggling like prom queens, they were young, nubile things, Hollis thought.   Much too sweet and innocent to be consorting with the likes of those two.

"You gonna lay there all weekend and choke your chicken into those clean white sheets or are you going to have some fun?" H-y asked.

"If anything's gonna get choked around here it's going to be your scrawny little neck." Hollis turned to the young ladies and said, "These fellas aren't bothering you are they, ladies?"

The girls exchanged looks and laughed.

"Seen Leo?" Hollis asked.

"No, we thought he was with you."

"Nope, haven't seen him."

"Come on, Jack, old boy.   Grab your coat and hat, we're going to show you a good time in spite of yourself."

"Sure.   Why not?"   Hollis got up, grateful for the human contact, even if it was Smith and Sullivan.   "Where we going?"

"First, we're going to the Grosvenor House Hotel.   They have this place called Willow Run which is this huge restaurant.   Then We're going to Pioneer Hall.   It's this dance club. Supposed to be the best in London," H-y said.

"Play your cards right and ol' H-y here might hook you up with some WAC," Sully added, a newly converted H-y-phile.

This comment caused the two girls to chuckle at each other again. Probably already drunk, they looked like high-school coeds not military officers. What a pity they had fallen under the spell of the likes of H-y Smith, Lady's Man, *Bon-vivant*, erstwhile navigator.

Dinner at Willow Run was fabulous. Hollis had southern-fried chicken, some sort of dumplings, and all the fixin's.

As they headed for Pioneer Hall H-y turned to Hollis and said, "This is a bottle club, Jack--"   he let Hollis peek into the musette bag containing a bottle of Gilbey's Gin and a bottle of rum "--and I got the bottles."

When they entered Pioneer Hall, nothing more than a large dance floor with a fifty foot-long bar at one end of the room and an expansive stage at the other.   On the stage was a medium-sized orchestra and a thin little guy wagging a baton, clad in a shiny tuxedo with a pencil-thin, Gable-like moustache hugging the edge of his lip.

H-y followed Hollis to the bar where they muscled their way through the throng of GIs and woman to the bartender.   Hollis could not figure the necessity for a bartender if you had to provide your own libations.   The top of the bar was packed with bottles of liquor.   Every time someone new stepped up to the bar a new bottle was added.   There was enough alcohol on the bar to make everybody in the room comatose several times over.   Hollis obtained a Coke and H-y poured several finger's worth of rum into it.   "One problem," H-y said. "No ice.   Oh, well, down the hatch."   Hollis and H-y clinked their glasses together in a toast and down they went, the sting of the rum on his palate causing Hollis to involuntarily shiver.

H-y with his nurse disappeared into the crowd while the *maestro* launched the band into a rough facsimile of "Avalon," his arms flailing, baton whirling.   What they lacked in talent they clearly made up for with enthusiasm.

"He thinks he's Glen Gray and that's the Casa Loma Orchestra.   They're not very good, but after a few drinks you won't give a shit."

Hollis turned in the direction of the voice.

"Hi, Lieutenant."   It was Virgil Poole.

"You old son of a bitch.   Virgil, how in the hell are you?"   Hollis slapped him on the back and Poole grabbed his hand and shook it briskly.

"I'm great.   How are you?"

As the band played louder and louder, Hollis raised his voice to be heard.   "Fine.   You made it over.   Where are you at?"

"Thorpe Abbots.   I'm with the Hundredth.   Got assigned as a replacement engineer. Kind of a hard-luck outfit.   They pulled together a lead crew and put me on it."

Hollis looked around, "So how was Africa?"

"Hot and full of sand."

Hollis noticed that Poole was wearing a ribbon   for the Purple Heart.   "They give the Purple Heart for appendicitis?"

Poole chuckled and said, "No.   Bullet blew off my little toe.   Regensburg.   Didn't even know it till we were over the Mediterranean.   Too bad I'm not in the infantry, I'd be out of a job.   Turns out you can operate a top turret just fine with a little toe missing.   War is hell. Let me buy you a drink."

"I heard about the mutiny.   Thanks."

"You saved yourself, Lieutenant.   I was just a better judge of you than they were.

They still with you?"

"Yeah."

"See."

Their attention was drawn to the crowded dance floor.   The dancers parted like the Red Sea as the band lit into an exuberant, if slightly imprecise, rendition of "Claps hands!   Here Comes Charley!"   Front and center was a splendid little English red-head and a sergeant who jitterbugged so quickly to the tempo that the poor girl could not keep up.   She ended up hurtling across the floor into Hollis's arms while the sergeant grabbed another GI to finish the dance. The crowd hooted and cheered with delight.

Breathlessly, the little red-head smiled up at Hollis and said, "Nice catch, Joe."

Virgil Poole grinned broadly and yelled above the cheers, "War is hell, ain't, Lieutenant?"

"Helluva war, Virge.   Helluva war."

"Whatcha drinkin'?" she asked in a cockney accent so strong he could barely understand her.

"The King's rum"

"Think he might part with some for me?"

"I'd bet money on it."   Hollis produced a glass of Coke and poured a jolt of H-y's rum into it.

"Thanks, Yank.   What's your name?"

"John Hollis."

"You pilot?"

"Yeah."

"Do you like to fuck?"

Hollis could see out of the corner of his eye Poole laughing.   He turned to Poole, the red-head still in his arms, and said, "Enchanting little vixen, but has a real mouth on her."

"That ain't the 'alf of it, John 'ollis."

Poole raised his glass to Hollis and walked away.   "Helluva war, helluva war."

Hollis's mind reeled with the possibilities.   Had he longer to think about it he might have chickened out but, as the saying went: If you can't be near the one you love, love the one you're near.

She made Hollis dance and buy her drinks until, a little before ten, the bandleader stepped up to the microphone and said, "Time please, Ladies and Gentlemen."   The band played the National Anthem and "God Save the King" and the place emptied out.

"Where to?" Hollis asked.

"Come wif me, John 'ollis.   You're fun is just beginning."

Hollis's loins tingled as she led him into the crowded street.   They walked hand-in-hand to a flat a few blocks away.   They walked past couples copulating in doorways and under bushes.   She seemed not to notice but their indelicate ministrations were unavoidable.

She lead him up a flight of stairs and into a small room with a bed, an end table and a lamp.   Hollis studied her under the limited light given off by the small bulb.   She was adorable.   Probably not more than eighteen or nineteen.   Shiny red hair.   Perfect white teeth inside a perfect, carefree smile.   She had a lot to drink, but appeared completely sober.   He lay back on the bed as she stripped in front of him.   He noticed how shabbily she was dressed. Her underwear was worn so thin he could see her freckles through the fabric.   Her stockings, held up by a thin black garter belt had runs in them.   She took her yellowed, frayed bra off and let her small, milky-white breasts fall loose.   Naked except for the stockings and garter belt, the little red-head smelled as if she hadn't had a decent bath or been near a bar of soap in a month. It was the fishy smell of stale, dried sex and sweat.   She climbed onto the bed and, with practiced dexterity, undid Hollis's belt buckle and pulled down his pants.   She grabbed his turgid member.   He had heard of fellatio before, but, like Everest, had never actually seen it, let alone experience the noisy, wet enthusiasm he now found swirling around his other head.

He wondered if she was prepared for what she was shortly about to receive.   He watched her bobbing red head, mesmerized. In what could only have been a minute or two, he was brought to the exquisite pinnacle.   Dropping his head back, he decided not to tell her.

She finally got what she wanted, an eruption that would have made Vesuvius proud. Pleased, her little red head stopped bobbing and she purred with delight.   She looked up at him, his molten, pearly lava clinging to the corners of her smile.

"Di' that please you, John 'ollis?   Better than a fuck, what?"

"I ain't ever had anything like that before."

"All of 'em say that.   Well, you just rest 'ere for a minute and we'll see what other tricks I 'ave up me sleeve."

In what could only be described as a biological improbability realized, her lightest touch and whispered exhortations had him ready again in a few minutes.

"Now," she said, admiring her work as any craftsman might, "are you ready for a good fuck?"

He could only nod, the words caught in his throat.

"Give it to me 'ard, yank.   Make me scream like a banshee."

He drilled her for all he was worth, reaching a whole new level of achievement at the hands of this enchanting, little, red-headed Limey slut.   For as long as he lived, sex would never be the same.   He had crossed yet another Rubicon.   There were certain events in life against which all others are measured.   This, he knew, was one of them.

There was no waiting out the afterglow.   Before he stopped panting she was up and dressed.   "That will be five pounds, John 'ollis.   Two for the suck and two for the fuck and one for the room."

He paid her.   She tucked the money into a small, leather purse and turned for the door.

"Hey, what's your name?"

"Penelope.   Penny."   She shook her head, making her red hair fly about.   "Copper-top, like the coin."

In the heat of the moment, he had failed his duty.   No rubber had shielded his penis. Maybe the flight surgeon should have talked to him, too.   *No, that wasn't necessary, him being an officer and all.*   Now he was going to get some big, weeping sore on the end of his dick and he had no foreskin with which to draw on to prevent it.   The only thing Jessie would see when he returned was a scarred nubbin above his balls.   All because of some libidinal indiscretion. But he could be dead tomorrow or next week, gone from earth and life, an ulcerating penis seemed rather inconsequential when compared with dead.   He figured he had reached the apex of rationalization.   It was the same excuse they all used.   It would ring hollow were it not so true.

Hollis lay still, staring at the dingy plaster ceiling while he recovered.   He dressed and stepped back into the night, greeted by some distant laughter and the rumble of passing vehicles. He tried to reorient himself to the direction of the Savoy, figuring he could not have been more than a few blocks away. He wandered down a side street and he could hear masculine singing from the end of the block. He was thirsty and decided to see if he could get a beer even though most drinking establishments had been closed for the night by curfew.

He was drawn to the sound of the singing which came from a small pub a few steps down from the sidewalk. He could make out the distinctively accented "Waltzing Matilda" sung out by booming voices. Curiosity got the better of him and he went in, stepping around the blackout curtain to enter a cozy, smoke-filled room, the song coming from a group of RAF-types sitting and standing around a table in the corner of the room. The few patrons not involved in the singing seemed to ignore them completely although it was hardly possible that anybody could. One of them was swinging a pint of bitters that lapped out onto the floor in step with the beat of his singing. He turned and saw Hollis.

"Hey Yank, this 'ere's an Auzzie club," one of then shouted.

"Relax, you bloomin' fool. Come in chap, we're a friendly lot," the tall one said.

"Well, lookie 'ere, mates, we got one of 'em Yanks 'ere wif us."

Some continued their singing, paying no attention to Hollis. "Come over 'ere, Yank and join us. That is, if you'd be a mind to."

Hollis smiled and walked over. The tall one drew near.

"Me and me mates are wif the Royal Australian Air Force. Bomma Command. You bomma pilot, yank?"

"Yeah."

"I hope the irony 'as not been lost on you that 'ere we are, the Colonies, trying to save the bloody, forkin' Empire, 'as it, Yank?" The words, pronounced close to his face, reeked of cigarette smoke and beer.

Hollis smiled cautiously and nodded, not wanting to agree too little or too much.

"Lookie 'ere, mates, the Yank's got 'imself one of 'em ribbons. Wha's it for?"

"It's the Air Medal."

"'e's got a bleedin' air me'al, mates."

"Wot's it fer?"

"I completed five missions."

One of the Aussies started laughing.

Good naturedly, Hollis asked, "What's so funny?"

"Laddie, that's five missions over 'ostile territry?"

"Yeah."

"Well, I've made 47 trips, Brian's made 52 and Nigel here"--Nigel's eyes were glazed over, staring at middle distance, oblivious to the conversation--"has 63. Johnnie had 81 when he bought it last night."

Hollis felt his face turn red. Without thinking, he pulled the little ribbon from his breast and threw it away. Nigel tracked its trajectory with his glassy, unfocused eyes. He got up as if waking from a coma, and walked over retrieving it. He weaved his way unsteadily back to his seat clutching the little cloth ribbon. For a moment, he studied it in the palm of his hand like some delicate bird's egg and handed it to Hollis. Hollis knew that if he tossed it into the corner a second time poor, drunken Nigel would struggle to his feet and get it again.

Hollis felt the need to apologize, but wasn't sure for what.

"We meant no 'arm, matey.   Put it back on."

Hollis placed the ribbon in his pocket, but couldn't bring himself to look them in the face.

"Wanna beyah?"

Hollis nodded and one of the Aussies went to the bar.

"This is a wake," the Australian said.   "We're celebrating the passage of our friend, Johnnie.   Alistair Johnson of Freeman'le.   One of the finest Lancaster pilots ever to come down the pike.   'andled that thing like it was a bloody Spitfire.   Good man 'e was.   One of Four Sixty Squadron's originals.   We saw a big flash in the sky last night ova Berlin and figured that was Johnnie."

Hollis took the beer in his hand.   "I raise my glass to him."

"'ere, 'ere," the tall Australian said.   "Thanks, Yank.   You're a good man, too."

Hollis sipped his beer in silence and looked at Nigel.   He hadn't spoken a word, but his blank glassy stare and absence of voice spoke volumes.   Maybe a piece of him died when Johnnie did.   *That's Lonnie's seat.*

The Aussies were giving him the creeps despite their hospitality.   He thanked them for the beer and, heavy with the weight of humility, returned to the night.

He finally saw the entrance to the Savoy in the dark distance.   He put his head down against the light mist that began to fall. Maybe it was just a heavy fog.

"Hey Jack, is that you?"

"Leo?   Where in the hell have you been?"

"I've been seeing some interesting sights."

"Where'd you run off to?"

"Thought I'd send a cable to Christie.   Told her I was in London and that I was thinking about her.   She likes me to tell her when I've seen something new or interesting."

Did you send her a telegram when you got back from Schweinfurt?   "Yeah, like what?"

"I went to Westminster Abby.   Saw the Changing of the Guard at Buckingham Palace."

"Yeah, me too."

"Big Ben and the Tower of London.   I saw the spot where Anne Boleyn lost her head."

"No kidding."   He thought of white muslin.   He wondered if she had been looking for it ever since or if she had ever found it.   He laughed at his private joke.   He also thought it was funny the propensity of the English for decapitation.

"She was beheaded for committing adultery.   Have you defiled yourself with some sweet, English lassie this fine night, Jack?"

"Yes, Leo.   I have.   I don't know who defiled whom."

"Why am I not surprised?"

Hollis just shrugged.

"Let me show you the most interesting thing of all.   Let's go for a walk."   Leo took him down the long steps of an Underground station.   It was dark.   Like descending into the bowels of the earth.   He realized it was a motionless escalator.

"Come on, Leo.   It's late and I'm not in the mood to go anywhere."

"Shish.   Be quiet.   Don't worry, this won't take a minute."

Hollis could hear some coughing in the dark and a baby crying briefly.   There was just enough light for him to make out what the hundreds of people sleeping on cots and mattresses on the platform lining both sides of the tracks.

"You know some of these people have been sleeping down here practically every night for the past four years.   Pretty amazing, huh?"

The next morning, he was hoping to see an orderly or a sympathetic doctor.   What he found manning the Pro-station was an old nurse, a captain who, from the outset, seemed in a foul mood.

"Hey flyboy," she said sarcastically to Hollis, "how's the war going?"

No answer.

"Did we get our little dick wet last night?"

"Yeah."

"How long since you've been exposed?"

"Last night.   Eight hours, maybe.   Hey, what are you so pissed off about?"

"I've been an Army nurse for nearly ten years and my life has been reduced to treating a bunch of snot-nosed kids for the clap."

"Well, don't get pissed off at me, I'm the one who got his dick wet last night, remember? And the war's coming along fine, thank you for asking."

"Thank you for asking, what?"

"Thank you for asking, sir."

"Ma'am, Lieutenant."

"Hey, aren't you Florence Nightingale's older sister?"

"See there, son?" she pointed to the bars on her collar.   "Treat me with respect or I'll have you up on charges faster than you can say 'insubordination,' Lieutenant.   This may seem chickenshit to you, but it's still the army and it has rules."

"Yes, ma'am."

"Take your pants down."

Hollis undid his belt buckle and let gravity lower his pants to the floor.   She wiggled her index finger at his boxer shorts and he complied.   He thought he should feel embarrassed, but he did not.   She made him sit, bare-assed, on the cold examination table, his pants gathered at his ankles as she washed her hands in a sink, taking an inordinately long time drying them off. She took a syringe filled with a fluid and grabbed his penis and injected the material into the his little cock-eye.   She did it so adroitly that she was finished before he had an opportunity to absorb what was happening and react.

"What the hell was that?"

"Argelol to kill the clap and syph.   Pull your pants up and go shower with this."   She handed him a bar of medicinal soap and a tube of blue ointment and pointed him toward the shower.   "For the crabs."

He took the soap and left as directed.   In the shower, he had time to reflect on his insolence and how good the hot shower felt, as if it washed away his moral lapse, the indelible blemish he had placed on his life, for surely he could not undo what the little red-head had so masterfully accomplished.

When he was finished, he went out to apologize for his rudeness but the nurse was already busy with another customer.   An orderly handed him two sulfonamide tablets and a paper cup of water without comment.   After he swallowed the contents the orderly handed him a compliance chit proving to anyone who cared to know that Lieutenant John Hollis, serial number 6378464, had done as he had been directed and sick time that might result from his sexual foray into enemy territory could not be charged against him at the end of his time of service.   He stuck the little piece of paper in his pocket and left.

He stepped into the bright morning sun, the melodious change-ringing church bells still echoing through the streets.   He looked up at the sky.   There were a few medium-level broken clouds.   Good flying weather.   They were probably up today.   He walked back toward the hotel and thought about Jessie.   He felt a peculiar absence of guilt about his dalliance last night. He was surprised about this.   It was easy to rationalize his behavior, feeling bad that he didn't feel bad.   He could be dead tomorrow.   One last fuck for old time's sake.   Selkirk had said it would be easy.   It was.

He walked at a leisurely pace down the Mall toward the cluster of trees and big grassy expanse that he assumed was St. James's Park aware that a small crowd had gathered on the sidewalk.   He stopped to see what was going on.   He heard the unmistakable approach of a band.   The bleating, tortured wail of bagpipes echoed closer and closer, the crowd turned toward the approaching sound almost as one.

"What's going on?" he asked a young girl standing beside him.   She was likely dressed for church, but her clothes were faded and dingy, worn thin like her town and everything else.

"I believe it's the King's Own Scottish Borderers.   The regimen'al bands like to parade on Sundays."

Hollis craned his neck to look and soon saw the cluster of flags and banners snapping crisply in the light breeze.   The rat-ta-tat of the snare and the boom-boom thumping of the bass drums filled the air and he could feel some involuntary, martial spirit stir, the little hairs on the back of his neck erect as the Cold Stream Guards marched by in review in an otherwise impromptu-appearing parade.   The irrepressible bagpipes wailed and the white tom-toms twirled in perfect unison as they passed.   A magnificent sight.   There was subdued clapping which Hollis could not interpret.   Was it apathy or polite tradition which limited the enthusiasm?

"The Cold Stream Guards, it would appear."

The girl looked up at Hollis squinting at the sun behind him, "You know, Yank," she said, "I believe you are correct."

Hollis smiled down at her and, as the band marched on toward Buckingham Palace, she turned and walked away.

An obvious effort to keep up the moral of the home folks, these little parades must be. The British were weary of the war and he wondered if this helped.

He returned to the Savoy and checked out.   He met Leo for breakfast, the last good meal anybody expected for a while.   They had ham and eggs and a bucket of the coffee.   When they were done they paid for the meal and wandered around town for a few hours looking in shop windows, buying a newspaper.   They had to be back at Liverpool Street Station by 1700 as per plan.   Anybody that didn't make the last train back would be in serious trouble.

They arrived on the train platform at more or less the same time.   The flight surgeon was right.   Everybody, Hollis included himself in the clinical assessment, looked terrible, far worse than when they had left.

Hollis noticed that Augie stood quietly to one side and was about to say something to him when he noticed the two snowdrops, M.P.s with their white helmets, web belts and leggings, standing nearby with Billy clubs held behind them.   He noticed the forlorn look on Augie's face and he seemed to be favoring one leg.   Rizzo stood to one side, but no one else went near him. A major walked up to Hollis.

"This boy wichu?"

"Yes sir, he's one of my gunners."

"Son, I'm from Waycross, Georgia and we never treated our nigras the way this boy treats 'em.   He's picked a fight with every web-footed brunette in London.   He oughta save some of that fightin' spirit for the Germans.   And to top it off he picks a fight with a WAC colonel.   If he comes into my town again, I'll arrest him."

"I'm not his mother."

"I'll allow the stress of combat and youthful exuberance will occasionally cloud judgment and incite some misbehavior.   I am a generous man, Lieutenant, but I have my limits.   If I find him here again, after I arrest him then I'll find you and arrest you, too."   He tapped the end of his Billy club against Hollis's collarbone causing a sharp twinge of pain, making him wince. "Do we have an understandin'?"

"Yes sir."

"Good, ya'll have a safe trip home.   We'll be here when you come back."

The major and the M.P.s left and the crew gathered around.   Augie hobbled over to them, no doubt some contact had been made between his knee cap and one of those Billy clubs. Augie was uncharacteristically quiet.   His knee must be smarting too much for him to speak, Hollis thought.   Good.

Rizzo said, "Ol' Quinn-boy here launched a maximum effort against the Ten Commandments.   He committed adultery with some poor laddie's wife.   He musta took the Lord's name in vain a hunert times, but who's counting?   He stole a pint of scotch.   What else? Is blasphemin' a Commandment?"

"Yup," Dodge said.

"Then he broke that one, too."

"I didn't know she was married, sir.   Honest."

"Quinn.   I'm surprised.   You seemed like such a nice kid when I first met you," Sully said.

On the train, Hollis turned to Mollica and said, "I can understand Augie getting into fights with Negroes, but how in the hell did he get into a fight with a WAC colonel?"

"He didn't salute her."

"He didn't?"

"No, and then when she dressed him down he got real smart with her.   So finally he salutes and then he asks, 'Hey Colonel, lemme ask you a question.   She says, 'Yes, Sergeant?' 'Did you have to strip naked in front of men officers in order to get in?'   She had the major on top of him before he could take off.   They wanted to throw him in the stockade, but he talked his way out of it."

"A miracle."   One of many he had witnessed in the past seventy-two hours.

"I'll say."

Alas, Hollis reflected, London had not been the spiritually enlightening place he had expected.   Certainly not what he had hoped.   Yet, he felt satisfied he had fucked one of the best looking whores in the entire city.

It was close to eleven when they returned to Pilot's House.   Ransahoff came around as they undressed.
"Oh good, you're back.   You're going out tomorrow."
Hollis felt his stomach start to churn.
Leo looked over at Hollis as he sat on his bed, "Hey Jack, what's a web-footed brunette?"

Chapter Thirty-one   **SNAFU**

Monday, September 6, 1943

It was a stupid plan.   Everybody knew it was a stupid plan down to the guy whose job it was to screw the fins onto the back end of the bombs.   But, as with practically all military decisions, there was an inevitability which rendered it immune to any modification by strength of reason or experience.

So when disaster struck, as all seemed to sense that it would, it would not be because of the skill or cunning of the enemy or that their cause was more holy or deserving of victory.   It would be the result of fiat and incompetence.

Hollis figured he had been asleep for only a matter of a few minutes when he heard the door open at the end of the hall.   After the late visitation by Ransahoff, he and Leo quickly unpacked and turned in.   Even so, it was close to midnight when they did and Hollis found sleep fitful and unrewarding, the knowledge of an impending mission near the surface, nagging the subconscious.   When Beamis entered the room at two-thirty Hollis was more exhausted than when he had climbed into bed.

Hollis heard himself croak as he shielded his eyes from the flashlight, "Where to today, Beamis?"

"Dress warm, bomb bay tanks and incendiaries.   You'll be bombing the *frau und kinder* before lunch."

Leo began to stir and Beamis turned to him gently, "Oh, you're not on the list, sir. Lieutenant Hollis has a rookie riding with him."

Hollis was certain his heart had stopped, that somehow, the routine had been changed, the security of the familiar and predictable disturbed and his hours were numbered.

Leo calmly said, "Oh...OK," pulled the covers back up over his head and fell back asleep.

Everybody had a talisman, an amulet, some item possessing spiritual energy of sufficient power to ward off evil and death.   They were a not-so-subtle concession to mysticism or the metaphysical; a lucky charm or some ritual which served the same purpose.   Leo had Christie's panties, H-y his beloved picture of the beloved Belinda above his desk in the nose, Rizzo had a rabbit's foot beside the whistle attached to the collar of his jacket.   A lucky scarf, a mission tie, a lucky coin, the same pair of underwear or socks, Dodge's piece of shrapnel.   For Hollis it was Leo.   Except for Butch Mullen and some captain who certified Hollis as qualified to pilot a B-17, no one but Leo had ever sat in the right seat beside him.   Singing into his mask when he was scared or inappropriately cheerful, oblivious to looming catastrophe.   Hollis looked at Leo and felt his sphincter tighten up with the power to crush a walnut.

Leo had resumed snoring when Beamis turned to Hollis and said, "No hot water, sir. Someone stole a part from my water heater.   Sorry.   Breakfast at oh-three hundred, briefing at oh-three thirty."

"What's it like outside?"

"Cloudy and cold.   But don't get the idea they might call it off.   Latrinogram has some big muckity-mucks in from Washington to see how we do it.   You're going today even if you have to cross the Channel in a rowboat."   Instead of persisting, perhaps the point would be better made to the big muckity-mucks if the whole mission turned out to be a big recall. How much effort went into such an endeavor only to have it succumb to the vagaries of nature?

Beamis was correct. It was cool outside. He could see his breath rise into the night.

There were some unfamiliar faces in the washroom. H-y saw Hollis and asked if Leo was coming.

No, they gave the little shit the day off.

Hear it's a big one, Robertshaw said, raw apprehension in his voice.

Yeah, Hollis said as he shaved his face with the frigid water, if Beamis is to be believed.

Damn that Beamis, they all muttered. Him and his fucking water heater.

As they approached the combat mess, the smell of burnt grease and eggs wafted into the cool air and hung like a pall around the building. Everybody's fears were confirmed the moment they picked up their trays. Fresh eggs cooked to order, bacon, toast, marmalade and grapefruit juice. Hollis drank only a single cup of coffee. He wanted no revolt from his bladder this trip. The hot liquid felt good going down his throat. It took some of the chill from his bones, a chill as much the result of fear as the temperature. The room was filled with smoke from cigarettes and cooking, a blue haze settled over the subdued conversation like a bad premonition. Everybody knew.

Hollis looked around. He could see Selkirk and Ransahoff. Watanabe. Sully, H-y and Robertshaw. DeBerg and his copilot. Barbieri was not in flying clothes, but sat voraciously consuming a full breakfast as he talked to Ransahoff with white and yellow egg fragments visible around his teeth as he talked. *They should throw the son of a bitch out*, Hollis thought. *If he ain't going he shouldn't be allowed to eat with us.* Hanging on each syllable were three men he had never seen. *Rookies*, Hollis thought. *Listen good, Hell is just beyond that stretch of water over there.*

As they waited for the briefing to begin, Barbieri led the three guys over to him. They looked frightened. It was a familiar look. He, no doubt, was wearing it himself.

"Hollis, this is Ward Brubaker, he's going to be your copilot today." Barbieri turned to the others and said, "And this is Peter Fissano who will be flying with Selkirk and Harry Powell who will be with Watanabe."

Hollis shook hands with the three and pulled Brubaker over to sit with Sully and H-y. After introductions, they talked briefly until the room was called to attention. Hollis turned to look.

Van Patten walked briskly down the aisle followed by Gleason who was dressed for flying. Begay was dressed, so was Ransahoff and Cavanarro.

Gleason took the stage, pushed back the gunner's cap so the light reflected off his pate and smiled broadly.

"Seats, Gen'lemen. I'm the Bangmaster for today's sortee."

Hollis wondered what kind of sick mind would relish such theatrics at a time like this. Gleason should be shot. Hollis looked at Brubaker who hung on every word. He glanced at Selkirk to gauge his reaction when the target was announced.

"Today we will be launching our first large-scale strategic raid against Germany since Schweinfurt." There was the inevitable, collective moan sending the gunners outside scurrying. At that moment, the curtain was pulled back revealing the long, painful route into Germany. Selkirk closed his eyes and lowered his head, his face as white as the sheets in the Savoy.

"Stuttgart.   Our target is the Robert Bosch A.G. plant in the suburb of Feuerbach where ninety percent of the diesel injection nozzles and magnetos are made.   We will be part of a maximum effort.   The primary target for the leading Fourth Wing will be the SKF instrument bearing factory in central Stuttgart.   Over four hundred heavies will take part.   Four groups of the Second Wing will fly a diversion toward the North of Germany.   Eight groups of B-26s from the Third Wing will fly strikes against airfields in Holland and North France.   Four groups of P-47s will fly escort to the limits of their endurance.   Two for the leading Fourth Wing and Two with the leading elements of the First.   The order of battle for the First Wing will be the 103d Combat Bomb Wing followed by the 102d and the 101st.   We will be carrying incendiaries.   The Air Commander will be Brigadier General Travis who recently took command of the First Wing.   Major."

"We trust he knows what he is doing," Sully whispered.

Begay then took the stage.   "We will be high group.   The 533rd will be lead squadron, 532nd high and 535th low."   He pulled the sheet off the formation blackboard.   Hollis found his name quickly.   He would be flying lead of the second element.   DeBerg to his left, Robertshaw to the right.   Ransahoff will lead, Selkirk number two, Watanabe number three to his left.   Number 485-**Cleopatra's Asp**.   There was a 'C' beside the number.   They would be carrying a strike camera.

"We will be departing from our usual routine on today's flight."   When he said it all eyes fell on him.   Any departure from the routine was cause for alarm.   That he now felt compelled to mention it gave said departure all the more gravity and everybody present knew it in a heartbeat.   Even the rookies.   Hollis felt another walnut break apart in his asshole.

"A great deal of fuel is being expended by climbing to altitude with   full tanks.   We will assemble at a lower altitude and climb later in the penetration when the tanks are emptier. This should extend the range and save wear and tear on the engines."   Begay looked down, like a tell in a poker game.   He didn't believe the theory either.

"Jesus, Chief, what idiot thought *that* up?"

All eyes snapped around at the anonymous voice in the back of the room.   There was some nervous laughter.   Van Patten bolted to his feet and turned toward the audience.   With one look he quelled any further discussion of the merits of the plan.   If a turbocharger were to fail, an engine run rough or some other mechanical or human failing were to occur under the stress of the climb or at altitude, better it should take place over England or the Channel, not deep inside France or Germany, halfway to the fucking target. Close enough to the ground the Gerrie pilots wouldn't need oxygen.

Hollis was disappointed with Van Patten for his very visible demonstration of annoyance. A better man would have let the comment pass un-noticed.   The Chief did.

"I can't believe this," Selkirk whispered.

Begay continued, "We will assemble at five thousand feet, join the wing at ten thousand and climb to 17,000 feet by Strasbourg and to 25,000 feet, our bombing altitude, by the time we reach the IP at Tubingen."   Hollis stared at the route again.   Most of the trip in and practically all of the route out would be over France.   Very little of the route would be over Germany proper.   This provided small consolation, though, for, Hollis knew, as they all did, that they would be within easy reach of hundreds of German fighters anywhere along the way.   It was a stupid, stupid plan.

The weather officer took the stage and delivered his carefully rehearsed prognostications. The weather for assembly would be broken clouds, but the target and the return should be OK. There was no conviction in his voice.   He was guessing.   Hollis would have had more respect for the man and his efforts if he would just come clean and admit it.

There was a front draped across the route, he said, it shouldn't interfere.   The odds of them getting all three forecasts right were remote.   Poor Brubaker, who sat beside Hollis making notes on a small pad, probably trusted as truth, every word spoken.

Finally, at the end of the briefing, Van Patten took the stage and looked over the crowd seated before him.   He might have been looking for the culprit who yelled out at the Chief.

"This is no milk run."   *We note you are not going.*   "This will be one of our longest missions to date.   You will be at maximum weight and the limits of your range.   Climb slowly and make slow, shallow turns.   Make gentle changes in your power settings, keep your mixtures lean and your rpm low.   You should have enough fuel to get you home."   He paused.   "Any questions?"

While everyone expected the lone voice of doubt to be raised yet again, wisdom prevailed and there was silence.

"OK, then.   Good luck and good bombing.   Protestants to the front, Catholics to the rear."   *And Jews seek help where you can find it.*   "Dismissed."

Brubaker turned to Hollis, a pained look on his face.

Very little was said on the truck-ride out to **Cleopatra's Asp**.   She sat brooding on the hardstand in the dark, her bomb bay doors hanging down.   The crew sat waiting on the grass. They looked anxious and, as one, rose to approach the four officers as they dropped over the tailgate to the perimeter strip.

Rizzo yelled, "Hey, where's Lieutenant Leo?"

Hollis introduced Brubaker, who, he said, would be taking Lieutenant Wychulis's place for today's mission.   Immediately, he could tell that this departure from the routine did not sit well with the crew either.

Hollis explained the mission.   He told them they were going after some plant in Stuttgart where they made injection nozzles and magnetos.   It was an important target, he said.   As the words left his mouth he wondered if they believed him or if they cared.   We're going to take a slightly different approach to things, though.   We will assemble and head out at ten thousand feet and climb slowly all the way through France and then finish the climb near the target. Hollis figured that, except for Dodge who understood everything, the crew might have trouble grasping the dreadful significance of such an idiotic plan.

Quinn asked, "What are we gonna do if we lose another turbo?"

"Drop the load, hit the deck and run for home," Hollis said, confident they now understood too well, feeling slightly guilty that, once again, he had underestimated the intelligence of his crew.

Brubaker, thumbs hooked around his parachute harness like suspenders, took in everything.   Hollis noticed the crew glancing at him with suspicion and disdain no doubt making him feel like the unwelcome interloper that he was.

Hollis tapped him on the arm and led him toward the bomb bay, his discussion with the crew finished for the time being.   Moe followed them and shone a flashlight up into the cavern illuminating the contents. On one side of the bomb bay was the large auxiliary gas tank, on the other, one suspended above the other, were eight five-hundred pound incendiary clusters. Each, shaped like an overgrown stick of dynamite, was filled with a concoction of rubber and gasoline designed to explode on impact. The cluster of incendiary sticks was held together by metal bands that, at a preset altitude, would release and scatter the sticks of jelly. They seemed innocuous enough, but it meant **Cleopatra's Asp** would go up like a roman candle if hit. As the last planes in the bomber stream, their purpose today was to make the rubble burn.

Moe handed Hollis the clipboard and he began his cursory walk around. Brubaker may have noticed how exceedingly superficial the inspection was, maybe he didn't. Regardless, Hollis made a specific point of looking at the turbo on number four as he had on every flight since the abortion. This was a tacit attempt to either placate or antagonize Moe Jablonski. Hollis couldn't decide which motivation fueled his action. He signed the form, thanked him and returned the clipboard.

Hollis looked at his watch in the dim light. Oh-six-oh-five. Ten minutes to stations. Hollis figured he had time for another cigarette so he walked across the perimeter strip and sat down as he had every time since the beginning. He hoped Brubaker would not follow him, granting him his moment of solitude, but to no avail. Seeing Hollis head for the grass across the strip, Brubaker dutifully followed like a little puppy. Anxious, Hollis thought, not to miss anything.

Hollis kept silent, but offered him a smoke which he took. Perhaps Brubaker got the message that Hollis was in no mood to chat. Hollis looked over at Ransahoff who was pissing into the grass behind **The Flying Dutchman**. Hollis wondered what Ransahoff thought of the scheme. No, Hollis thought, he was pure Army. West Point. The Mission. *Theirs not to reason why, theirs but to do and die.* Duty honor, country and all that insane bullshit. This was not the first time the insanity of it all had occurred to Hollis. As he dragged the smoke deeply into his lungs he again mentally recalculated their expected fuel consumption. He was flying **Cleopatra's Asp** again. That was good. He knew and understood the idiosyncrasies of the thing. She was no gas hog. If he ran her lean and avoided a lot of jockeying around as Van Patten said, he could economize on fuel expenditure and they would probably be alright. Even so, it would be close. No margin for error or miscalculation. Keep an eye on the cylinder heads. He hoped everybody else understood this. If they didn't they were stupid fools. Like the unmitigated shithead who thought up the scheme in the first place.

He looked up at the sky. There was still dense cloud. Ceiling about five thousand feet, Hollis guessed. Hopefully, it was not a thick layer and they could get up through the overcast without too much difficulty. It was getting lighter and Hollis could see a jeep approach. Barbieri. A delay, he yelled to Hollis. Stations pushed back fifteen minutes. Perhaps they had come to their collective senses and called the damned thing off or maybe the mission would be withered away by recurrent delays, the weather accomplishing what reason could not. Still, he found no cause for optimism. Hollis smoked another cigarette and finally walked over to join his crew.

They were stretched out on the grass under the wing.

"Fifteen minute delay," Hollis told them.

"I saw you looking up at the clouds, Lieutenant. Think we'll get scrubbed?" the soft-spoken Hulse asked.

Hollis thought about what Beamis had said.   Knowing Beamis' reliability so far, Hollis could only say, "Doubt it.   I think they're pretty committed to this one."

"You know, I'm getting pretty tired of all these 'bottle-neck industries.'   First, it was ball bearings, now it's magnetos.   You get the idea they really don't know what they're doing?" H-y said.   "You figure if we blow up and burn down this place and wreck every magneto in Europe it will get me home by Christmas?"

Sully laughed at him.   It was a nervous laugh.

Augie, who had been laying on the grass slightly removed from the rest said, "My cock is limp, I cannot fuck.   The nitrate has a-changed my luck, the nitrate has a-changed my luck."

Quinn started laughing while the others just turned in surprise.   Augie raised himself on his elbows.   "Hey Dodge, you been around for a while.   You ever know anybody who actually put saltpeter in the food?"

"Yeah.   There's this corporal whose only job is to put it in the food.   He goes from base to base dumping a load into the powdered eggs or creamed spinach."

"And if I ever catch the son of a bitch, he's a dead man," Rizzo added.   Everybody, even Hollis, laughed, more in appreciation of the distraction than the humor.

Augie turned to Hollis and, jerking his thumb at Mollica, said, "We gotta get this little guinea laid, sir.   All them whores in London and he was too busy seeing the sights.   He went to the damned art museum to look at pitchers of naked ladies when he could a been out there screwin' any damsel he wanted.   It would be such a shame to let this boy die in the virginal state.   If you catch my drift."

"How's the knee, Augie?" Hollis replied.

"Fine, sir.   How's the collarbone?"

Hollis wondered if the pass to London had done them any good at all. With or without the libidinal release.

When no one showed up to tell them the folly was scrubbed he told the crew to mount up. They grumbled, pissed in the grass and gathered their parachutes and gear and headed for the hatches.   Hollis, as always, was the last one to climb inside.   He vomited his breakfast onto the grass, wiped his chin with the back of his hand and lifted himself into the nose.

Brubaker was very efficient and practiced in the cockpit.   No small talk.   He knew his business.   Being a first pilot, Hollis would have expected nothing else, but when he tried to run through the checklist without actually looking at the words on the laminated card, Hollis stopped him, saying sharply, "I don't know you from Adam and I'm not sure I want to trust my life to your memory.   Read it.   Every time."

Properly chastened, Brubaker started over, the laminated page shaking slightly.

"Green flare," Dodge announced.

"Shit," Hollis whispered, "we're going."   He leaned his head to the window and yelled, "Clear!"

Moe gave him a thumbs-up and, for a moment, Hollis was paralyzed by indecision.   He couldn't decide whether he wanted another quick cigarette or to throw up again. "Start one," he said.

Soon he and Brubaker had all four engines running smoothly.   Hollis throttled back the inboards as low as he dared so they wouldn't stall.   At the appointed time, Hollis jerked his thumbs out the window and Moe and Tommy pulled the chocks.   Brubaker released the brakes as soon as Moe appeared in front of the plane and gave them another thumbs up.   Hollis eased the Fortress forward and Tommy guided them off the hardstand.   He turned **Cleopatra's Asp** right onto the perimeter strip and slowly taxied her up to the next hardstand, Ransahoff's, and waited for **The Flying Dutchman** to make its way onto the taxiway.

They patiently waited as **The Flying Dutchman** turned expertly onto the perimeter strip and they followed it up to the entrance of the next dispersal.   Ransahoff continued on while Hollis waited for Watanabe and Selkirk to taxi by.   He recognized Watanabe, but did not see Selkirk.   As they waited Hollis could count each droplet of fuel they were wasting like blood dripping slowly from a severed vein in his arm.   Brubaker tapped Hollis on the arm and pointed over to the dispersal area.   They could make out rising smoke from one of the planes and an ambulance bounded across the infield and onto the perimeter strip.   Suddenly, Brubaker's head jerked around.

"Switch to Command!" he yelled into Hollis's ear.

Hollis switched channels.

"Afghan leader to Afghan B-Baker."   It was Ransahoff.

Hollis pressed the throat mike against his larynx, "Go ahead Afghan leader."

"Afghan F-Fox will be replaced by Afghan A-Able.   A spare will fill number five.   Acknowledge."

"Roger.   A-Able to number two.   Spare to number five."

"Roger, out."

Brubaker and Dodge turned to Hollis to find out what was so important to break radio silence.

"Selkirk's not going.   That must be him."   Hollis pointed in the direction of the smoke. "Robertshaw moves up to number two and a spare will fill in with us."

They watched as Robertshaw hurriedly taxied past in **The Big Dick**.   Hollis gunned the outboards and they slowly moved forward, followed by **Celina**.

Puzzled by what might have happened to Selkirk, Hollis recalled that one of the Group's two spares was Spats Nevtushenko.   Maybe he would be the one to fill in.   Get to fly with his own squadron instead of a bunch of strangers.

As they rode heavily down the perimeter track, Hollis saw a lone figure waving as **Cleopatra's Asp** passed, a bicycle on the ground at his feet.   Hollis instinctively put his hand out the window and waved back at the anonymous well-wisher.   It was Leo.

Ransahoff, Watanabe and Robertshaw all took off in rapid succession.   There was no holding anybody back today.   Despite the cloud layer above, the visibility down on the ground was good enough to allow a thirty second take off interval sparing more fuel.   The flight control officer was releasing the planes at probably closer to twenty seconds for the turbulence of the preceding planes still churned over the runway, buffeting **Cleopatra's Asp** as she made her way.

She was heavy again.   Not quite as heavy as for Schweinfurt, but still loaded and she bounded forcefully on her bulging tires as she slowly gained speed.   Hollis had only scant more confidence in her ability to become airborne this day than he did then.   He kept her straight and Brubaker called out the airspeed as the big plane gained momentum.   Crossing ninety miles an hour, he could feel some of the bounding ease and took small comfort at the sight of Brubaker cringing down in his seat.

"Red lights!" he called

One-oh-five...

He felt the column tug forward in his hands and he let the tail rise.

"One ten."

Hollis pulled the bomber gently from the ground and yelled, "Gear up!"

As if fired from a cannon, Brubaker's hand shot out and toggled the gear.   They made it off the runway with a couple hundred feet to spare.   Brubaker was quite distressed.   Both Dodge and Hollis could plainly see him shaking.   Hollis wondered if he had pissed his pants, perhaps still waiting for the bomber to spin off to the right or left in a stall and fall back to the ground.   No one needed to tell him what happened when a loaded Fortress failed a takeoff.

One fifteen.   One twenty.   They would be OK.   Hollis leaned over to Brubaker's left ear, "You can stop shaking now."

Hollis managed a rare moment of introspection noting that nothing put terror into proper prospective than bearing witness to someone even more terrified than you are.

Brubaker nodded and gave a little wave remembering to look down and confirm the retraction of the right main undercarriage.

"Right up."

"Left and tail wheel up," Dodge added.

"Is it always like that?"

"No.   We're going far today.   She's carrying a heavy load."

"And to think I had my choice of P-38s or '17s.   No.   I wanted the Big Leagues."

At five hundred feet of altitude and one forty indicated air speed, Hollis banked gently into a left handed turn.   He resisted the temptation of slowing his rate of climb to save gas because he knew, just a scant twenty seconds behind him, was DeBerg.   So, reluctantly, Hollis kept their ascent at five hundred feet per minute hoping nothing would go wrong.

The overcast was both lower and thicker than they had been told.   They were in it after only a few minutes.   Hollis dutifully circled the buncher, but this was not what had been expected and by eight thousand feet they were still not above it.

Suddenly, **Cleopatra's Asp** began to lose power.   She was already sluggish and responding poorly but now, quite without warning, she felt even more mushy.   Hollis looked outside.   He could barely make out the outboard engine in the cloud.   His eyes could not confirm what his brain suspected.   They were picking up ice.

"Hey!   You got ice on them wings!" Augie yelled into the intercom.   Just because Hollis could not see it didn't mean it wasn't there.

"Carburetor heat on, close the intercoolers!" Hollis yelled.

He heard one of the engines backfire, their rate of climb now down to a scant hundred feet per minute.   Hollis overcame his concern about fuel economy and pushed the throttles forward and the rpm lower so the propellers would bite more air.   The extra weight of the ice coating the plane, combined with the struggling power plants as ice choked their air supply, brought them, within the span of a few heartbeats, to the brink of disaster.

Hollis switched to VHF and yelled, "Ice at angels eight!   Ice angels eight!" and quickly switched back to intercom.

They had to break out of it soon and get the sun onto the plane to melt the ice or they would cease to fly.   Hollis wondered what an ugly compromise it was to remove the deicer boots from the wings.

After a few moments, the ice must have cleared from the carburetors because the engines began to settle out, but the weight required that he keep the throttles forward just to maintain a hundred feet per minute. **Cleopatra's Asp** was still sluggish. Although the recovered power offered some grace they were still on the razor's edge of catastrophe.

The safe operation of group assembly through clouds is predicated on each pilot adhering to a rigid method and timetable of execution. Air speed, rate of climb and orbit around the buncher had to be precise. Any deviation from it would send the bombers blindly milling about in the soup making a collision inevitable. Hollis's desire to speed things up was counterbalanced by his agonizing need to conserve fuel. He watched the oil and cylinder head temperatures start to rise as the engines struggled to pull **Cleopatra's Asp** higher. He told Brubaker to crack the cowl flaps a little in order to send more cooling air over the engines. The change in the aerodynamics forced the engines to strain even harder. Hollis hoped something would break so he could remove himself from the rising spiral of loaded bombers, descend to warmer temperatures and return to base after everyone had safely departed.

No such luck.

Suddenly, the outside grew bright and they popped up from the clouds into the brilliant sunlight. The warmth of the sun on his face and his bomber melted away his panic with the ice. Hollis looked around and spotted Gleason and then Ransahoff off in the distance. He knew they were trying to form up, but from where he sat it looked as if they were just milling about directionless. Hollis glanced at the altimeter. Just above ten thousand feet.

He watched as Gleason turned in a gentle, flat arc back around in a racetrack orbit. He fired flares as did Ransahoff. It was a waste of pyrotechnics. Hollis looked back over the left wing and could see other planes emerging from the clouds. They would each turn back into the formation as it passed around, climbing slowly to avoid getting run into by the rest of the group as they materialized from the undercast.

Hollis had them into position as they passed, settling in above and behind Ransahoff. Watanabe and Robertshaw were in position and, in short order, DeBerg had himself in place as well. That left the slot empty on Hollis's right wing, the number five position. Hopefully, one of the spares would fill in.

The icing must have become a problem for the other pilots for Brubaker mentioned that there was a lot of bitching on the command channel. That, and the clouds nobody predicted would be there, put some of them on the verge of hysteria.

As the Group turned for wing assembly, a stranger found his way into the vacant slot. Wing assembly, at about ten thousand, five hundred feet was uneventful and Travis guided the bomber stream toward the Channel.

With no pins to pull Hollis wondered if Sully would stop up for his customary smoke. Sure enough, as they prepared to depart the coast Sully sat on the edge of the hatchway and handed Hollis and Brubaker a cigarette.

"How we doing?" he yelled.

Hollis made the 'OK' sign with his thumb and fingers. They finished their cigarettes and Sully   returned to the nose.

They could see the French coast below and sporadic flak burst around them. At the tail end of the bomber stream, a lot of the guess work on the part of the Germans had been removed. The flak was quite accurate and menacing although Hollis saw no one hit.

As they flew deeper into France, the interphone crackled, "Radio to pilot."

"Pilot, go ahead Quinn."

"Sir, it sounds like a pretty good fight going on up ahead."

"Who's winning?"

"Nobody saying."

"Clouds are building up down below, Radio.   Keep an ear out for the recall."

"Roger, Lieutenant."

"Pilot to crew, the lack of enemy fighters might mean they're concentrating for a big fight inland.   Stay alert."

The further they flew, the looser their formation became.   They had yet to see a fighter, friend or foe.   As they slogged along the clouds thickened even more to about five-tenths. Hollis tugged at his mask.   It chafed the bottom of his chin where some errant whiskers remained, made more irritating by the drool and sweat accumulating at the bottom of the rubber cup.

Hollis tapped Brubaker on the arm, the signal for him to take over.   He scanned the sky; empty except for the plodding bombers.   He did some mental calculation.   At normal cruising speed each engine burned about fifty gallons of gas an hour.   Everyone seemed to be of like mind, allowing the formation to play itself out a little, rather than burn up more gas trying to jockey into position and fight to keep in close.   Hollis hoped they would not regret this.

"Navigator to Pilot."

"Go ahead, Navigator."

"Jack, we're over Luxembourg.   We cross into France again in three minutes.   Getting awfully cloudy down there."

"Roger."

Something flashed by the window, instinctively Hollis grabbed the wheel.

"FWs twelve o'clock high!" Dodge yelled.

"Here come two more!" Sully screamed simultaneous with the eruption of tracers from the top turret and the nose.   Hollis jacked up the throttles to close in on Ransahoff, hoping DeBerg and the spare would follow suit.

The two Focke-Wulfs raced past exposing gray bellies as they barrel-rolled away from the fire.

"Two more, Rizzo, coming down!"

Hollis could feel the plane shake and as quickly as they appeared they were gone. Hollis did a check of the plane and his gauges.   Everything seemed fine. He quickly checked his wingmen.

"Navigator to pilot."

"Go ahead, navigator."

"Strasbourg five minutes.   We start our climb to twenty-five thousand feet.   IP in sixty miles."

Flying time about twenty-two to twenty-five minutes.   Hollis again made some rough calculations.   At a climb of five hundred feet per minute, it would take sixteen minutes to reach bombing altitude, just five to seven minutes or so before turning at the IP over Tubingen.   Up ahead was a solid wall of clouds almost perfectly defining the Franco-German border.

Surely, there would be a recall.   The bomber stream started the climb.   If those clouds continued solid like they appeared, there was no way they would see the target. Maybe Travis knew something nobody else did.

Hollis eased the throttles forward and Brubaker adjusted the rpm. The moment of truth had arrived. If a turbo or engine failed now it was a long, lonely ride home. **Cleopatra's Asp** responded. Everything seemed to work as expected. DeBerg lagged behind and silently Hollis admonishing him to catch up.

The formation barely climbed above the front by the time they reached it. Twenty-seven thousand. Two thousand feet higher than planned. The bombers started to leave contrails, adding yet another aggravation.

"Navigator to pilot, IP five minutes."

Hollis looked down. The clouds persisted, but there was enough of a break to see a river curling around below like a snake through dense forests. The Black Forest, in fact. The haunt of Hansel and Gretel and cannibal witches. The dark, hilly forest slipped beneath wispy clouds and he could no longer see the ground.

"Navigator to pilot. IP."

Gleason swung the group to the right and lead them into a long curving turn behind the lead group as they took interval.

Sully crackled into the interphone, "Bomb bay doors open."

Hollis could feel the grinding of the motors and the sudden rush of air, **Cleopatra's Asp** slowed by the drag.

"Bomb bay doors open," Rizzo announced.

"It's ten-ten down there. I know we're close to the target because of all the flak up ahead. But I'll be damned if anybody's going to see it," Sully said.

Three wings, nine groups, bomb bays open were lined up Indian-file to unload on a place nobody could see. That was *two* forecasts fucked up.

They drew closer to the flak and Hollis could see the tell-tale signs of wounded planes, smoke, in thin dark ribbons amidst the white contrails. He saw a straggler or two. One dropped its bomb load and turned for home. He lost sight of the other, disappearing from view into the clouds.

The flak grew more intense and **Cleopatra's Asp** was knocked around rudely by the bursts, the occasional rattle of pebbles on a tin roof as shrapnel hit the plane. Hollis's stomach was knotted to the point he had trouble breathing. He even glanced at the oxygen flow meter to make sure he was still drawing in.

"Jesus, that was close!" Rizzo yelled. "I got a hole punched in my window."

Hollis waited for the clusters of incendiaries to tumble from the bellies of the planes up ahead. The wait seemed interminable.

"We shoulda passed over the target by now, pilot. I think the son of a bitch is going around again."

As quickly as the words registered in his ears, Hollis saw Gleason turn, bomb bay doors still extended, for another go around.

"I told you we wouldn't be able to see it, for Christ's Sake!" Sully yelled.

"Knock it off, Bombardier."

Reluctantly, Hollis pushed the throttles forward yet again, pulling DeBerg and the spare along with him trying to maintain their place to the right and above the lead squadron, like the outside members of a turning line of skaters playing crack-the-whip.

"Jesus Christ, what the hell's he doing, we don't have the gas for this."

"Bombardier, unless you have something important to say, stay off the interphone," Hollis said.   He glanced at the spare to his right and didn't see him.   Hollis tapped Brubaker on the shoulder and jerked his thumb outward.   Brubaker, a terrified look in his eyes, did not at first understand.

"Spare!" Hollis yelled into his mask.

Brubaker nodded and looked out to the right.

"Don't see him," he yelled back.

"Pilot to right waist, do you see the spare?"

"He's back there hanging on for dear life," Augie said.

"Bombardier to pilot.   Here we go again."

Hollis watched the bombers level off and head toward the flak once more, like moths drawn irresistibly to a flame.

Madness.   Absolute madness.

"They hit one of the guys in the low squadron!" Hulse screamed into the interphone.

Hollis snapped his head down to the left but his view was obscured by the wing.

"They're bailing out!   Come on you guys, jump!"   Hulse's voice was seized by fear for he could hardly get the words out.

Hollis hunkered down and waited for the final explosion while trying to keep the **Cleopatra's Asp** level and steady.   He thought he might actually choke on his own vomit.   He glanced at Brubaker who craned his neck out like a turtle trying to catch a glimpse of the ground while firing glances back at the spare.

"No dice, Jack.   The fucker's going around a third time.   Bombardier to pilot, situation normal, all fucked up!"

Hollis could barely comprehend what was happening.   Why would anyone be so reckless with life and treasure as the bastard at the head of the line?   Had Travis, the ignorant neophyte, any idea of what was happening back here?   He gave some thought to toggling the load and dropping out of formation to make a dash for the coast on his own, for clearly, at the rate they were going, nobody was going to make it back.   And an American general will have accomplished what no German force would ever be thought capable of, wiping out an entire bombardment wing.

Hollis grasped at the last tether dangling from his sanity, "I'm not going to tell you again, Bombardier.   Stay off the interphone."

"Spare's gone," he heard Augie say.

Brubaker's head snapped around.

"What happened to him?" Hollis asked.

"Don't know but, he's not back there anymore."

"Pilot to tail, see him?"

"No, sir."

"Smoke? Anything? Who was it?   Anybody know?" Hollis asked.

There was silence.

"Somebody with the 533rd, I think."

They ran the gauntlet of flak a third time and rolled off the target still in possession of two tons of incendiaries.   Hollis watched as Gleason's bomb bay doors slowly closed. **Cleopatra's Asp**'s followed suit.   The leader of the 101st Combat Wing, Hollis didn't know who it was, announced that they were going after a target of opportunity and peeled away from the bomber stream.   H-y notified Hollis that, according to his plot, the wing leader was taking them to the coast by the shortest route possible.

Suddenly, the bomb bay doors came open again and Hollis watched as the clusters of incendiary sticks fell from the bellies and disperse as the timed device released the wires holding each cluster together.

"Pilot to Bombardier, what did we hit?"

"It might have been an alternate."

"Some place called Offenburg, I think," H-y said.

"Pilot to tail, what did we hit?

"As best as I can tell, Lieutenant, it looked like some cow pasture," Mollica said. "Looks like we hit it pretty good, too, sir."

"We'll be cookin' hamburgers tonight, Boss," Augie announced into the interphone.

Lightened of their load and a fair amount of their gas the pace picked up.

Brubaker tapped Hollis's arm, "Somebody just told them to slow it down or some of 'em aren't going to make it on the gas they have left."

Hollis adjusted the mixture to make it even more lean, raising the rpm a little more.

The Wing leader started a gradual descent which would help, too.

Hollis told the crew to stay alert, but be ready to give the heave-ho to anything they could throw out to lighten the weight.

"Navigator to pilot, Switzerland is still closer than England," H-y said.   "But it won't be for long."   This caused the crew to start grumbling into the intercom.

"Knock it off.   Navigator, I'll let you know if I want a new set of directions."

By the time the formation had pulled even with Paris, somewhere near Reims, still over a hundred miles from the French coast by any route, pilots came on the command channel to announce that they had red lights showing on their fuel tanks.   A fuel warning light indicated less than fifty gallons remaining in a tank, enough for about another hour of life from the engine it served, maybe a little more.   By the time they hit the coast bombers would be dropping like flies.   They still had an hour and five, maybe ten, minutes to the British coast, maybe a little less.

With each passing minute, Hollis found his eyes drawn again and again to the fuel gauge, the indicator lever for which Brubaker repeatedly snapped from one tank to the next.   Hollis adjusted the mixture yet again hoping to lean out the gas-air ratio even further until he was sure there was barely enough gasoline entering the engine to ignite let alone push against a cylinder.

Time dragged by.   An occasional German fighter would approach, parry and withdraw. Had the Germans been aware of the vulnerability of the lumbering bombers they would have made an all-out effort to annihilate them.   But, they apparently did not.

"Channel, five minutes, pilot."

"OK, as soon as we're over water dump everything loose except parachutes," Hollis said. Two red lights shone brightly on the panel.

Hollis watched as Gleason took them down to five thousand feet as they passed over the water.   Hollis looked down.   The sea was smooth, mercifully, he thought.

"Calls going out to British Air-Sea Rescue, Lieutenant," Quinn said.   Hollis watched as two planes left the formation and headed for the water.

Brubaker leaned over and looked down.   "There's some poor SOB down on the water.   Smoking.   Might be getting ready to dit--"   Brubaker jerked suddenly in his seat as if trying to poke his head through the side window--"Jesus, there's a Jerry behind him!   A twin-engined job.   A Ju-88.   He's stalking him.   Waiting to finish him off.   Taking his time, the bastard.   Either the tail gunner's out of ammo or he doesn't see him."

"Or he's dead," Augie said.

Brubaker was silent for a moment then shouted, "You gotta do something!"

Suddenly the intercom crackle with excited voices.

"Everybody shut up!" Hollis yelled.   "Christ, the sky could be filled with Ju-88s and you want me to pick a fight with one of them."

"You gotta do something."

"Some Spits or Jugs gotta be in the area, they'll take care of it."

Calmly, Augie announced, "He's gaining on him."

"Jesus, what am I doing?" Hollis muttered to himself.   It was the geese.   Selkirk's fucking geese!   Hollis pushed the throttles forward and pushed the nose over in a banking turn to bring himself over the German.   He could see the plane over the rim of the window, practically straight down, so low on the water it made a wake with its prop wash, slinking along like a cat ready to pounce.

"Rizzo," Hollis said.

"I see him."

Brubaker said, "We're at 3000 feet we can't hit him from up here!"

"Jesus Christ, we don't have the gas for this!" H-y said forcefully.

Hollis said, "Spray some lead his way, even if it just falls on him it might give him second thoughts."

"Get closer!" Augie yelled.

"Jesus, we can't."

"Get closer!...he's gaining on him."

Hollis put **Cleopatra's Asp** into a shallow banking dive to get over the German.   After a few seconds...

Dodge, "Lead him."

"Jesus, Dodge."

Rizzo fired a steady burst shooting his tracers straight down shaking the plane and raising small white spikes of water.   He walked the tracers back onto the top of the Ju-88.

"I hit him!   He's breaking off, smoking from his left engine.   I got him!   I can claim him!"

Dodge, "Did you see him hit the water?"

"No, but he peeled off and--"

"Then you can't claim nothing but a damaged."

"Shit."   Hollis watched while abruptly the left wing dipped and the slender tip caught the water.   The German cartwheeled and disintegrated in an explosion of water with a small flame at its center.   The outer panel of the wing fluttering above the churned-up water like a leaf in a storm.

"I got him!   I fuckin' got him!" Rizzo yelled.   "Confirm *that* Mollica."

"You fuckin' got him."

As the German plane crashed into the sea, the third fuel warning light came on.

Hollis turned to Dodge and said, "Transfer any fuel we have left out of number two and three engines into number one and four, we'll need one engine on each side for landing."

Dodge gave him a thumbs-up and turned back to make the transfer.

As **Cleopatra's Asp** crossed the English coast, the number two engine stopped running. Brubaker feathered the propeller.   Hollis figured they might have enough fuel to reach Ridgewell, but he was not interested in stretching their luck.   He told Quinn to find the nearest field big enough to handle a Fortress and he would set her down there.

In a minute, Quinn had them in touch with an RAF fighter base near Hastings.   It was a grass field but they should have plenty of room, the officer in the tower said cheerfully, apparently delighted to be of assistance.

Hollis easily found the field, an expanse of green with a small cluster of buildings at one end nestled next to a medium-sized hanger.   The officer gave him the speed and direction of the wind and Hollis turned the bomber on final approach wondering if the stupid Brits had any idea how big a Fortress was because he would be dropping it into a field that didn't seem big enough to handle Stearman.   He throttled back as soon as he cleared the perimeter of the field, putting **Cleopatra's Asp** onto the grass in a hurry.   The big bomber bounced twice, each hard contact with the ground absorbing much of its kinetic energy, and settled on the main gear.   Hollis kept the tail up in order to put all of the bomber's weight on the main undercarriage, applying as much brake as he dared to slow the plane before he ran out of grass.

"Clear the runway quickly, old chap," the officer said.   "There's a couple more of your mates right behind you."

Hollis looked back out the window and saw two more Fortresses on short final.   When all but a small amount of forward motion had been expended the tail settled to the ground and two of the engines quit.   With one engine, number four, still turning, he pulled **Cleopatra's Asp** clear of the runway and parked it.

Brubaker, the look of befuddled astonishment on his face, turned to Hollis and said, "Are all of these missions like this?"

"No, not usually."

Dodge laughed out loud.

As they deplaned, an RAF car pulled up and an officer climbed out shaking H-y's hand, "Good show, Old Boy.   Bloody good show."

"I'm not the pilot,"   H-y turned to Hollis and pointed, "he is."

"Smashing good luck, Old Man.   Simply wizard!"

Hollis shook his hand and watched the last Fortress come in a little too hot and ground loop in a shower of grass and dirt clods.

"Bloody good show, Leftenant, everyone's seemed to make it down alright.   Now, shall we have some tea while we top you off?"

"Sure," Hollis said as he lifted a cigarette to his lips trying hard not to tremble.   "H-y, go find a phone and call in.   Tell them we'll be back soon."

Shortly the crew was sipping hot, black tea while the RAF ground crew pumped gas into the four tanks.   It wasn't a cold beer on a warm Kansas night, but it felt just as good to be back on *terra firma*.   Hollis made sure they only put in the minimum amount necessary to fire up the engines and get them back to Ridgewell.   Too much gas would make them too heavy for the short take off run required to get airborne from this little field.

The Brits fawned all over the crews acting as if they had never seen an American up close before and, here on the coast, perhaps they hadn't.

One of the other crews was from the 91st, the other from the 379th.   The last one had some damage to the plane when they ground looped, torqueing the main strut.   They would not be flying it out until they replaced it.   That crew headed for the Officer's Mess for gin and tonics.

When they were finished, Hollis thanked his British hosts for their hospitality, started the engines and took off.   It was an easy, if bouncy, take off run over the grass field.   Hollis hoped they wouldn't blow out a tire on the flinty soil, having been warned at Bovingdon about the risk.

They landed at Ridgewell almost two hours late.   Ransahoff, Barbieri and Leo were there to greet them sitting in a jeep, patiently waiting to hear their story.

Hollis deplaned having completed the necessary paperwork.   Moe looked relieved. Ransahoff, with Barbieri and Leo in tow, walked over to him and handed him a glass.   He then pulled a bottle of Johnnie Walker from his coat and poured.   Hollis didn't really want the drink but sipped it anyway.   He smoked a cigarette while he related what had happened.   As the story was told, Leo beamed.

Report to Group CO's office pronto, Ransahoff told him.   Don't even stop to take a piss.

Still dressed in his flying clothes, Hollis presented himself to Group headquarters, reporting as ordered.   He was nearly as scared as he had been in the flak.

"Hollis, get in here," came the booming command from Van Patten's office.   He walked into the small, spartan office and saluted.

"Lieutenant Hollis, reporting, sir."

Van Patten returned the salute, got up from his desk and stepped around to confront Hollis.   "I got a phone call from another group CO a little while ago thanking me for having one of our planes dispatch a Ju-88.   You saved one of his crews.   They had tossed off all their ammo to save weight and were defenseless when the German found them.   They were barely making it back as it was.   I don't suppose that was *you*, was it?"

"Uh, yes sir.   It was."

"Don't ever leave formation again.   Do you read me?   You ever leave formation again and you won't have to worry about the Germans, I'll shoot you down myself."

Hollis's knees were shaking.   He could feel the beads of sweat collecting on his forehead.   He figured he was about to get a lecture on squadron, group and wing integrity... He began to wonder if these people were capable of being pleased by anything.

"I guess I'll have to give you a medal.   But let me warn you, selfless acts of heroism are not what is going to win this war.   You are dismissed."

Hollis turned quickly and left.   He went by the briefing room to see if they were still holding interrogation, but the place was deserted.   He went to the equipment room and changed. He decided to eat and went over to the combat mess to get a sandwich.   He ate alone.

As he consumed the sandwich and coffee, he was surprised by his ambivalence.   He didn't consider himself a hero and yet they thought he must be, engaged in an activity they could not condone and may, in fact, be counter-productive to the successful prosecution of the war. It was not like he had engaged in a dog-fight. He simply flew the plane over the German fighter and had his ball turret gunner fire a few rounds his way in an effort to discourage him. Now he had been dressed down by the Group CO and yet they were probably going to give him a medal. What would Stan have done?

He finished eating, changed and went to the Officer's Club. A fire burned in the large stone fireplace and the place was crowded. He looked around the room for a familiar face, some approval, but instead stood at the bar and had a second drink.

He felt someone standing beside him and turned to look. "Hollis, right?"

"Yeah."

"Pete Fissano, we met earlier."

"Yeah. You were supposed to fly with Selkirk. What happened?"

Fissano looked around to make sure he was not being overheard. "I've got to tell somebody about this and I don't know what to do."

"What do you mean?"

"We had finished warming up the engines. We did our run-ups and turbo checks. We were about to pull the chocks when Selkirk says he wants to do another mag check on number four. I don't know why he wanted to do that, it was fine. He runs it up to 28 inches and did something to the mixture. He has me check the magnetos and when he thought I wasn't looking he set the turbo to full."

"Jesus, if it backfires it'll blow the turbo apart."

"It did. The turbo disintegrated with a loud bang. It nearly cut the leg clean off the crew chief."

"He did it on purpose?"

"What do you think?"

Hollis couldn't believe his ears. "Why are you telling me this?"

"I thought somebody ought to know. His stupid action nearly killed a man. Cut the damned artery in his leg."

"You should tell Ransahoff."

"No. You do it. I'm telling you he didn't want to go today."

Hollis was stunned. Fissano turned and walked away. Hollis did not see Selkirk in the room.

He felt an arm go around him. A total stranger had walked over and had placed his arm around Hollis's shoulders. "You Hollis?"

"Yes, Captain, I'm Hollis."

"Great, they told me you'd be here."

Hollis quickly studied the man. No wings. No medals. Just a captain in a Class A Air Corps uniform.

"My name is Harley. I'm the PRO from Wing. Boy are they pissed."

"You came all the way down here to tell me that? You could have phoned me with the news."

Harley smiled broadly. "Yeah, but that's not why I'm here. I'm here to write a press release for your hometown newspaper. 'Local Boy Dogfights JU-88 with His B-17. Downs One Nazi and Saves His Mates,'" he said as he formed the banner headline in the air with his hands.   "You know your standard 'Joe Blow' story. The home folks will be real proud."

Or real pissed, maybe they don't want me sticking my neck out like that.   "What's *your* story?" Hollis asked.

"I used to work for an ad agency in New York.   I had the Palmolive account until all this crap started.   The brass at Wing is pissed about this Ju-88 incident because it sets a bad precedent, too much cowboy stuff.   Flies in the face of all this teamwork bullshit, but if it's good for home front morale it's good for Wing so we roll with it.   They don't care how we win the war as long as they look good doing it.   So cheer up.   Lose the long face.   I'm going to make you a hero.   Your folks will love it.   Make all the girls swoon."

"I'm not interested.   What I did was stupid."

"Come on, Lieutenant.   You didn't throw yourself on a grenade or something, for Christ's Sake."

"No thanks."

"You don't get it.   This is an order.   Tell me the damned story.   Now, were you scared?"

"I was scared shitless, you little son of a bitch.   I'm scared shitless every time I go near that airplane.   You ever been on a mission?   You have no idea what it's like, do you?"   Poor Selkirk.

"Aw, come on, Lieutenant.   I'm just trying to do my job."

"Then go find the guy who jumped on the grenade."

Hollis downed his drink searing his gullet with the scotch and walked away.   As he was about to leave the room, he passed Ransahoff who said, "You got balls, Hollis.   You're stupider'n shit, but you got balls.   Don't do that again."

How did it start with Selkirk?   Was it bad dreams?

Hollis did something he never thought he would ever do.   He grabbed Ransahoff by the sleeve and pulled him back out through the door.

"I think Selkirk needs a trip to the flak house."

"How long have you been here, Hollis?"

"Three weeks."

"How many missions have you flown?"

"Six."

"I'll decide who and when anybody goes to the flak house."

"Dutch, he's drunk almost every night.   He has these crying spells.   He's increasingly despondent and he has the look.   Besides, Fissano says he blew up that turbo on purpose.   He's flown enough times to know not to make such a dumb-assed mistake.   He just didn't want to go today and he nearly killed somebody.   He closed the waste gate and did a mag check."

"How do you know this?"

"Fissano told me."

"Everyone is entitled to their opinion, and Lord knows you've been here long enough to have one, but I'll decide how to run things around here."

"Fine, Major.   Fine."   Hollis threw up his hands and walked away.

Ransahoff jerked his thumb in the direction of the Club.   "Is he in here?"

"No.   Haven't seen him."

"We lost forty-five today.   Twelve of them ran out of gas and ditched in the Channel."

Hollis could only shake his head.   "How did *we* do today?"

"We lost one.   Low squadron.   Ten chutes.   Everybody else made it back.   You were the last one."

Chapter Thirty-two   *Luftgangster*

Hollis returned to his room, surprised that he had the strength or the interest in eating or stopping in at the Club.   The drink had precipitated a muscular lethargy that made it difficult for him to walk.   His exhaustion was complete, mental and physical.

Leo sat on his bunk in his underwear and smiled at Hollis when he entered the room.

"I'm proud of you, Jack."

"Not now, Leo.   I am tired and I have a headache."

"You saved those guys in that plane."

"Perhaps."   Hollis stripped down to his underwear and climbed into the bed, his head coming to rest on the satin pillow case.   London one day and Stuttgart the next.   He calculated that, except for a brief catnap on the train from London he had exactly two hours of sleep since Sunday morning and they hadn't been worth much.   If he stayed awake much longer his brain would cease to function.   If they were to lay on a mission tomorrow he might just have to blow up a turbo, too.   Poor, dumb Selkirk.   What was happening to him?   Had the fine line between sanity and insanity been crossed.   Did he know it?   Did anybody else besides Fissano?   There had been rumors of a pilot who began a calculated campaign of peculiar behavior for the benefit of the flight surgeon.   He enlisted the help of some of his crew.   Inevitably, they drew the expected response and to everyone's delight they were pulled off ops and sent to a rest home for a week.   It was only later, when they returned and bragged about the success of their ruse, that it was exposed.   There were no repercussions except that a trip to the rest home became a little harder for those who needed it.   No one, least of all Roscoe Clevenger, the Group's Flight Surgeon and final arbiter of such matters, enjoys being made a fool.   Even so, Clevenger maintained a constant, if unobtrusive, vigilance, eyeing up the crews at briefing and chow, in the Clubs and especially at interrogation.   It was unsettling to be stared at by the Flight Surgeon.   Hollis had caught his eye more than once.   He purged all thought of Selkirk and Clevenger from his mind.   Ransahoff, too.   He could run the Squadron any way he damned well pleased.   It mattered not a whit to Hollis, who buried his cheek into the pillow and sniffed.

Barbieri poked his head into the room, "Hollis, you got more balls than brains.   I never would have thought that about you."

"Fuck off."

He could hear Barbieri laughing as he walked down the hall.

He wondered again how much closer today the war had come to ending.

Hollis felt like he had been asleep for days.   When Beamis walked in he felt refreshed, terrified as usual, but rejuvenated.   It was a unique and unexpected feeling.   When he had climbed into bed he thought a mission unlikely as there were heavy clouds and the rumor of a warm front settling over the British Isles.   Nonetheless, the armorers and bomb-loaders were diligently working through the night in the cold and wet.   When the mission was finally scrubbed, as he felt confident it would, they would begin the whole process in reverse like Sisyphus condemned to their own special Hell.

So he awakened surprised.   Early.   He was pleased they had let him sleep so long.   It was a decent sleep, no dreams, just blank, empty sleep.   For that he was thankful.   He cleaned up, shaved and, with the sleepy Leo in tow, went to breakfast.   Leo, as usual, wolfed down the powdered eggs like a man who hadn't eaten anything in weeks.   Coffee, toast with orange marmalade.   That was about all Hollis's stomach could handle.

Outside the briefing room, they caught up with Sully and H-y, checked in and went inside.   They sat behind Ransahoff and knew he was not leading.   Ten-hut and the entourage strode down the aisle.   Fuck!   Van Patten was in flight clothes. That meant he was the Bangmaster.

"The target for today is potato storage depot in Pfumpfenhaven."

A lackey dressed all in white pulled the curtain back.

Christ, Hollis thought, following the string with his eyes as it angled across the Netherlands into central Germany.   Pfumpfenhaven was smack dab in the middle of the fucking Fatherland.   In the middle of nowhere.   Nonetheless, it was surrounded by large flak circles. Ugly scarlet ones.

"This is an important target.   A successful mission against it will result in a major potato shortage and we all know what that means...We can expect significant fighter opposition...Major."

Saul Gorton, also dressed in white, got up and continued.   "This is the linch-pin, gentleman.   Our bottleneck target.   An army travels on its stomach.   They can't fight if they can't eat."

The logic was flawless.   Suddenly dropping stray bombs into potato fields and cow pastures made perfect sense.   Yep, this is the one.   Home by Christmas.

"The target is a large cluster of one-story buildings here."   He smacked the screen with his billiard cue so it shattered in his hands startling Hollis but no one else seemed to notice. "The First Wing, which we are leading, will drop HE while the follow on wings will drop incendiaries.   Gentleman, we're gonna make a lot of French fries this morning."

Perfect.

"Why do they bother telling us this crap?"   Sully whispered.   "Every target is more important than the last one.   Every industry is *the* bottleneck industry.   Next it will be the pharmaceutical firms that manufacture vitamins or the screwdriver plant, or light bulbs or brake shoes.   How about toothbrushes?   If their teeth fall out, they can't eat.   They'll all starve and die.   I'm no tactical genius but it would make great sense for them to decide once and for all what is *the* most critically important of the critically important industries and blast it over and over.   Bomb it again and again and again and yet again until there was nothing but cratered earth for 50 miles in any direction.   And any time someone looked even interested in rebuilding it bomb *them*.   I hate to say it but I'm beginning to think these guys don't know what they're talking about..."

"We must be precise, however, as there are orphanages and a children's hospital nearby. But if they think that this will make the target off-limits, that this will prevent us from striking this, most important target, they are mistaken."

Clever Nazis.

Hollis could see the target in the distance as they turned onto the IP, plain as day.   The large cluster of one-story buildings in the middle of fucking nowhere.   Just like he said.   The navigation was flawless.   Should be easy to hit.   Real pickle barrel stuff.   This could end the war.

Suddenly, the sky became pocked by flak.

Hollis felt the thud.   He knew in an instant that the hit was fatal.   Unmistakable. Right after bomb release.   The number one engine ignited in a flash.   Fuel lines to it had been ruptured by the impact of the flak explosion spilling gasoline into the engine nacelle behind the firewall starting a huge fire within the wing.   For an instant he stared in disbelief at the blinding light of the blaze as if a fiery comet had attached itself to the wing.   The engine lost power and the left wing started to drop.   Hollis seemed powerless to correct it.   A moment later, the blaze burst through the thin aluminum of the wing and spread back toward the wing root.

Hollis knew, without the need for conscious evaluation, that they were all going to die in a mighty eruption, of the sort he had witnessed time and time again and that the matter was out of his hands.   He was much calmer than he thought he would be when this moment finally came.   He was strangely satisfied.   He reached down and hit the call bell three quick times as he tried to right the plane.   He allowed the bell to ring continuously and put both hands on the wheel trying to bring the plane, against all hope, level.   He thumbed the intercom, "Bail out! Bail out!   Bail out!" he shouted in case there was anybody who hadn't heard or figured things out on their own.

With that, he knew he had done everything he could to save his crew.   The B-17 continued to roll despite his efforts to level it out.   All was lost.   Every man for himself.

Quickly, Hollis released his seat belt, disconnected his lines and dropped down into the crawlway grabbing his chute from beneath his seat as he went.   The nose hatch was gone and there was no one left in the nose as he dropped into space.   When he fell free he was going as fast as the plane, one hundred and fifty-five miles an hour and the wind slammed against him like striking a wall.   He could feel the radiant heat from the blazing wing above him until he slowly fell away from the burning bomber, the propellers from the number two engine just a few feet from his head.   He alerted himself to the imperative of not opening his chute too soon lest it catch on fire.

As he fell away, his mind was so relieved at having escaped the burning bomber that no clear thought came to him except the heat and the need to hold his chute.   He pulled the green apple on the bailout bottle strapped to his chute harness and instinctively reached for the D-ring and wished he had taken the time to cinch up the parachute harness to prevent the scissors action of the leg straps on his genitalia, but it was too late for that.   Perhaps, if he lived, Jessie would understand.

He looked back at **Cleopatra's Asp** and watched it slowly bank away rolling onto its back commencing the long plunge back to earth.   Pity, he thought, she was a good airplane. Now he noticed things.   He watched two Fortresses pass below him and another passed close overhead.   Since his relative speed had not slowed appreciably since he bailed out, the bombers seemed to fly by slowly, very slowly.   He looked back in the direction from which they came and could see the black specks of the following wings turning onto the IP toward him.   All twirling propellers and Plexiglas noses, they seemed to be racing right for him as if he were suspended from a long string.   The Fortress above him flew into the plume of smoke left by **Cleopatra's Asp**.

He looked around for other chutes and didn't see any.   He wondered for the first time whether anybody else got out, feeling a fleeting pang of guilt at his failure to notice what had become of Leo.   He hoped he would fall below the bomber stream before those next wings came along.   He tightened his grip on the D-ring and again admonished himself to delay pulling it.

He was surprised by his clear-headedness during his plunge toward earth.   Everything seemed so remarkably distinct, the details pristine.   When he figured he was below the oncoming bombers he pulled the ripcord and the chute billowed out with a snap.   The open parachute jerked him rudely upright out of his free fall, the harness yanked up tightly around his groin as the resistance of the parachute met the fierce tug of gravity and hurtling momentum. The conjunction of the two forces nearly crushed his testicles.   The pain was excruciating.   In the midst of his physical agony, he saw, sadly, no other chutes.   From so high up he could see a small town where some stray bombs, no doubt Sully's handy-work, had landed.   The little houses were burning.   He turned to see **Cleopatra's Asp** collide with the ground crumbling into a huge ball of flame. He swayed gently back and forth at the end of the risers, marveling at his escape, his good fortune.

It had probably taken no more than a few seconds from the time the bombs had dropped to the time he had fallen out of the hatch.   It seemed like a movie played back in slow motion. He could remember every detail even how adroitly he had left his seat, snapped on his chute, connect his mask tubing to the bailout bottle, pulling the green apple to start the flow of oxygen and negotiated the small passage into the lower compartment.   He also noted how easily he had dropped through the open hatch.   It had been an action he had rehearsed countless times in his head until he knew it would be as he wanted it to be: reflex. Yet he had always thought that when the crucial moment came his fear of falling and fear of height would paralyze him and he would perish along with his plane, gripping the rim of the hatchway, unable to move as the ground came up to greet him.   Imminent death is a great motivator.

He landed with a hard thump.   The wind was knocked out of him and he gasped for air. He tried to calm himself and take a deep breath, but it hurt too much.   His back, his ankle and his genitals all screamed with pain.   The world went black.   Mercifully, a veil of unconsciousness settled over his eyes.

When he regained consciousness the first thing he saw was the empty, blue sky above. He raised to an elbow and surveyed his predicament.   By some stroke of good fortune he had descended into a lush, green meadow filled with the unmistakable aroma of fresh cow shit. The sky really *was* empty, no bombers, no flak.   No metallic torrent of shell casings and links falling down like hail from the tumult above.   No clouds.   CAVU, just like the man said.   No chutes floating down.   Maybe they were all dead.   They had been his responsibility.   He held the dying bomber as steady as he knew how those final seconds.   He tried with all his might to right the plane as it fell off to one side, but it resisted his every effort.   How could they have not known and reacted as he had?   Surely, they knew precisely as he did that the golden moment to leave had come and, recognizing it, made good their own escape.   He could not have done more.   It was a sad and bitter revelation.   The moment arrives when it's every man for himself. What virtue would have been served to die with his ship?   He felt no guilt just relief and he wondered why.

The pain in his back and leg and groin returned, but not so much so that he could not resist a smile and a giggle to himself.   "For you, the war is over."   He sat up and lit a cigarette.

He looked around for a cow but didn't see one.   He glanced at his watch.   Bombs away had been at 1205.   It was now quarter of one.   The grass smelled sweet and the manure pungent.   The collapsed parachute rippled in the same soft breeze that brought the aromas.   He unhooked himself and stood up.   His ankle was very sore, but it could support his weight.

He noticed some German soldiers in field gray uniforms, rifles at port arms, running toward him.   Inexplicably, he felt no apprehension.   The euphoria of standing in the tall grass, smelling the cow shit and feeling the wonderful ache in his ankle was overwhelming.   No more bombing.   He would see Jessie after all.   The voices of the Germans, their field gear clanking with a tinny sound on their belts made him aware of how quiet it was.   There were no other sounds.   No planes, no bombs.

He raised his hands and said, "I quit.   I give up.   Giveupinzee.   No sprechen zee deutsche."

The Germans shouted at him to raise his hands, but they were already up.   They motioned to him to gather up his parachute and march in front of them in the general direction of the rising column of smoke which he assumed was the village Sully had so ruthlessly bombed. They held their rifles nervously in their hands ready to shoot him full of holes if he made a break for it.   This was unnecessary, he thought, where the hell was he gonna run to?   Sweden? It was almost funny, but his musing was short-lived when he saw the burning buildings and homes in the village.   The townspeople would sooner kill him with their bare hands than breathe. This was their chance to pick-axe to death a real *Americanischer Luftgangster*.   The grim expression on the faces of the soldiers provided him no reassurance.

They topped a small rise outside the village.   His ankle really hurt and the Germans seemed not to care at all that he was limping.   There were small cottages on either side of the road.   The center of town was an inferno, the ancient wood crackling and snapping loudly in the conflagration.   There were huge craters scattered in a random pattern all over the place with debris and dirt everywhere.   There was an uprooted tree and lots of yelling in German.

Hollis rubbed his forehead.   There was a crust over his right eye halfway to his hairline. Mud? Cow shit?   He looked at the crimson flakes on his fingers.   Dried blood.   He explored his forehead with his fingers and found a small, but deep gash where a flap of skin had peeled back.   It didn't seem to hurt.   How did he get cut?

The place was rubble.   The acrid smoke obscured everything more than a few feet in front of him.   Someone came out of nowhere and snatched the parachute from his hands and disappeared into the smoke.   He could still hear the shouting but this was joined by a new sound, that of water splashing onto the buildings.   He had to step over rocks and bricks and cobblestones being careful not to trip.   If he fell to the ground the soldiers might lose him in the smoke and the civilians would kill him with pitchforks and shovels or throw a rope around his neck and lynch him.

The smell of burning wood, upholstery and what he figured was animal hair stung his nostrils and he coughed.   Frantic people ran around, into and out of the smoke.   There were two large roaring fires on either side of the road.   He could hear them but they remained obscured by the smoke.   An occasional flare would cast a bright orange glow in his direction.

The smoke cleared slightly and he saw a group of towns*volk* doing something he could not quite make out.   He strained to look.   They were hunched over gathering something, dark objects, into burlap bags.   Looked like coal.   A coal bin must have been hit.   Maybe they were burned potatoes.

Off across the road in the swirling smoke an old man and woman dressed in white smocks were gathering what appeared to be short sections of dark wood, logs maybe. They repeatedly disappeared into the smoke only to return with another piece held carefully with both hands. Odd, Hollis thought, stacking cord wood in neat piles while the town burned down around them. They were so deliberate and careful. Odd, especially, because the wood already looked burned.

Suddenly an enraged man, the town *gaulieter* probably, charged up to the German guards shouting at the top of his lungs, his voice driven with pure rage, foamy spit erupting from his lips as the guttural words exploded from them. Hollis felt a shiver of fear. The *gaulieter* was pointing his finger at Hollis and seemed to be imploring the soldiers to release Hollis to him which they seemed reluctant to do at first. They looked confused. While he was in their custody he was protected by the Articles of the Geneva Convention. Once he left their protection he was good as dead, swinging from the nearest lamp-post, for the civilians felt no such constraints. The *gaulieter* looked like a very pissed off Oliver Hardy.

He had a right to be pissed. Some *Luftgangster*, probably that cretin Sully, had accidentally bombed his poor little town, scattering the winter's supply of coal and firewood. Too bad.

The *gaulieter's* hair was singed as were his eyebrows and his moustache. His face was covered with soot which, moistened by sweat and rage, looked like black grease paint. Oliver Hardy as Jolson.

The German soldiers, exercising judgment over passion, must have decided that they had had enough of the harangue and poked Hollis in the ribs with the muzzles of their rifles motioning him to move on. They passed the old man and the old woman carefully stacking the wood. As he passed close to the wood pile, Hollis could see for the first time that it wasn't wood they were stacking but the charred corpses of infants. They were stacking dead babies.

His eyes were drawn by gruesome fascination to the face of one of the babies. It had not been burned, but probably killed instantly by the blast for there was not a mark on it. It might still be alive because the baby's face appeared to be twitching. He looked closer, maggots were eating the baby's face swirling around the empty eye sockets eagerly anticipating the taste of brain.

Hollis felt pressure on his shoulder and a voice. It was Leo's. "Wake up, Jack. You're having a bad dream."

"What time is it? How long have I been asleep?"

"Ten, fifteen minutes maybe."

"Jesus," he muttered and rolled over turning his back to Leo, the satin wet with perspiration.

Chapter Thirty-three   *ennui*

Tuesday, September 7, 1943

When Hollis next awakened he saw Leo still sitting on his bed in his underwear.

"What time is it?" Hollis asked sleepily.

"The more relevant question is 'what day is it?'"

"Huh?"

"It's Tuesday.   You've been asleep for almost eighteen hours."

"What time is it?"

"Time for lunch."

"I heard the planes.   They go out?"

"Yeah, two squadrons left on some milk run, I think."

"I thought I was dreaming."

"Yeah, I noticed.   You did a lot of talking and carrying on for someone who was supposed to be sleeping."

"I think I'm going crazy."

"Nah, you're just hungry.   Let's eat."

"I gotta piss first."   Hollis pulled the covers from him and lowered his feet to the cold floor.

"I guess Brubaker didn't get much sleep either."

"What are you talking about?"

"He must have mulled it over last night.   He walked into Ransahoff's office this morning and dropped his wings on the desk and said he wasn't going to fly anymore."

"You're shitting me."

"No.   What did you do to the boy?"

"Fuck it, Leo.   I didn't do anything to the guy.   He didn't look too happy to be in that flak yesterday, that's for sure, and the emergency landing might have shaken him up some, but he seemed pretty level headed to me.   He knew his job.   I thought he handled it pretty well."

"It's the quiet ones which you least expect."

"So what happened?"

"Gone."

"What do you mean, 'gone'?"

"Vamoosed.   Ransahoff had him pack his things and get out of town on the first truck. Something about detriment to the morale of a fighting unit."

"Bullshit."

"And other news while you snoozed.   They sent Selkirk and his crew to a rest home. They're gone, too."

"No fooling?" Hollis said, almost as an afterthought.

"No fooling."

"What else happened during my hibernation?"

"We got mail."

"Gimme."

"I thought you had to piss?"

There was a sudden boom shaking the building, rattling the windows.

Leo looked at Hollis and said, "Now what do you suppose that was?"

His first thought was that the bomb dump had blown.   "I dunno, but whatever it was it was close."

Spats ran down the hall yelling, "We're under attack!   They know I'm here!"

"Jesus Christ, what now?" Hollis asked and got dressed quickly and went out to see what was going on.   They could see smoke rising from the latrine.

Leo laughed, "I'll bet Beamis's heater blew up."

Hollis and Leo turned around and saw Spats sitting in the mud at the bottom of the slit trench between the barracks.

"For God's Sake, Spats, get out of there.   Don't you know people piss in there at night?"

"Son of a bitch," Nevtushenko said as he climbed out of the hole.

They walked down the lane toward the smoke and found the back end of the latrine blown off, wooden splinters scattered for yards in every direction.   Beamis ran around emptying an extinguisher onto the smoldering heater.   The fire had been short-lived and partially doused by the erupting water pipes and sewage effluent from the ruptured drains.

"God-damned bastards," Beamis muttered.   "Sons o' bitches."

"What happened?" Leo asked.

Beamis sat the exhausted red cylinder on the ground and said, "I think those guys in the machine shop sold me a bad metering valve.   I was convertin' the heater from coke to sump oil and I think they sold me a busted valve."

"That's a helluva mess you got there," Hollis said and went to a twisted and dented trough to urinate.

Hollis took his mail with him to lunch, reading Jessie's first of three letters.   There was one missing.   Fourteen, fifteen and seventeen.   No sixteen.   This was disturbing.   Perhaps sixteen contained the answer to his proposal.   He was prepared for any answer, yea or nay, but to not know which was mental torture.

Lunch consisted of bologna sandwiches and some mystery soup which they strongly suspected had Brussels sprouts dissolved in it, and, wonder of wonders, a banana for dessert. The cook passed them out making some comment about these being the only bananas in existence in all of the British Isles.   It was a rare treat.

Letter fourteen was fairly routine chat.   Fifteen was much the same, five pages that said very little.   Seventeen was much more interesting.   It was dated just a week ago.

> *Dear John,*
>
> *I hope you are well.   Things around here are pretty much the same.   Not much different than when last I wrote.   I had dinner with your folks and told them the good news. This is wonderful!   I've told all of my friends--our friends--and they are as happy as I am.   So close yet so far away!*

Hollis stopped reading.   What was she talking about?   What happened in sixteen? Did she say yes?   Must have.   He felt himself flush with joy.   But was this true?   He needed confirmation.   Should he reveal his proposal to Leo and have him interpret the letter for its tacit inference like some professor of an ancient language?   Or should he not assume and write back asking obliquely, or even forthrightly, for some sort of confirmation?   He read on.

My war work is coming along nicely.   I hope yours is also.   Three days a week I volunteer at the Naval Hospital to help out however I can.   There was sailor badly burned in an accident at the Navy yard.   He was covered from head to toe in bandages like a mummy.   He was   in constant pain.   I read his mail to him and talked with him.   He has a girlfriend in Milwaukee.   They plan to get married after the war.   He cries before they take him away to change his dressings which they do every afternoon.   It is a very painful process.   I have been reading an anthology of poetry and short stories to him.   He seemed to enjoy   that.   Today when I went in to see him he wasn't there.   I asked if they were changing his dressings but they told me, no, he had passed away.

I think of you and my heart is filled with joy.   My hope renewed.   Everything I do has taken on a new meaning, a new purpose.   I love you with all of my heart and live for the day when we will be reunited--reunited forever.   Please take care of yourself, John, and hurry back to me.

All my love,
Jessie

Hollis folded the letter and watched Leo lapping up the soup which smelled so unseemly that Hollis could not bring himself to taste it.

"All rested up, Hollis?"

Hollis turned around and saw Ransahoff standing behind him.

"Yeah, thanks for asking."

"Be in my office after you're done lunch."

"Are you going to chew me out some more?"

Ransahoff ignored the question and walked away.

"I wonder what he wants?" Leo asked.

"Dunno, but I betcha it ain't good."

"You shouldn't talk to him like that."

"Why not?"

"He outranks you."

"What's he going to do, ground me?"

Leo laughed and peeled back the skin of his banana.   He laughed again as he placed the banana into his mouth and chomped down on it.

"Leo, what the hell's so amusing about eating a banana?"

"Eating this banana made me think of Christie."

Hollis smiled politely, totally uncomprehending what Leo was talking about.

He finished and walked off to the Squadron headquarters.   He rolled over in his mind the many possibilities behind the request for a private audience with the Squadron CO.   Hollis was so weary of it all it seemed liberating to declare to himself that regardless of what it was, he didn't care.

Then it occurred to him and it made him laugh, too.   The banana.   Fellating females and that marvelous thing they do with their mouths.

Hollis stepped into the building and said, "Hi, Otho, what's going on?"

Barbieri looked up from the papers and shrugged in such a way as to give Hollis the impression that Otho was no more interested in conversing with him than he was in sticking pins in his own eyes.

"You know, Otho, you're a hard guy to like."

The sergeant behind the counter turned trying to ignore the exchange.

"Then I'm succeeding."

"Fuck you, Barbieri."

"That's 'Fuck you, *Captain* Barbieri.'"

"Hollis, that you?   Get in here."   It was Ransahoff.

Hollis walked into his office and saluted.

It was a mocking gesture and Ransahoff ignored it.

"Sit down, Hollis.   I know this is chickenshit to you *Phi Beta Kappa*-types but don't fuck with me.   This is war and I've got a job to do.   You're not Eisenberg and I'm not Entwhistle.   I'm not going to put up with crap from you so you better get used to it."   He rubbed his chin and continued, "You were right about Selkirk.   He was in need of a rest.   I'll give you that one.

"As you may know, Brubaker walked in here this morning and quit.   We were finally up to full strength.   Counting my crew,"--he started counting on his fingers--"we had Selkirk, Watanabe, Hollis, DeBerg, Nevtushenko, Robertshaw, Fissano, Powell and Brubaker.   With Brubaker taking a powder I'm short a first pilot.   I want to know your thoughts on promoting Wychulis into Brubaker's seat."

"Why are you asking me?   You're in charge.   If you want to put him in the left seat, just go ahead and do it."

Ransahoff leaned back in his seat and sighed, obviously exasperated by Hollis and his attitude.   After a moment he said, "OK, Hollis you can go.   I don't know why I expected more from you.   What was I thinking?"

It occurred to Hollis that Ransahoff really *was* interested in his opinion.   That it might actually mean something.   Perhaps he should tacitly declare a truce with this guy and help him out.   If Ransahoff were to make his own decision he would be wrong.

He was mad, but he had no real beef with Ransahoff.   It was as if he had no control over his attitude.   The words, as antagonistic as he could make them, just came out of his mouth, the reflex responses to a provocation which had lingered from December 7, 1941.

"I think that would be a mistake."

"Why?"

"He lacks the mental toughness and he's not a very good pilot.   They tried to make him a first pilot once before.   Did you know that?"

"Yeah, I knew that."

"When he's scared he sings into his oxygen mask."

"And you puke your breakfast into the grass.   So?"

"You asked me, I gave you my opinion.   Lord knows, I'm entitled to one."

Ransahoff stared at Hollis for a moment and said, "What's eating you, Hollis?   You're one of the most miserable sons o' bitches I ever saw."

"Does **The Flying Dutchman** have Tokyo tanks?"

"No."

"Neither did mine.   When did it occur to you that the Stuttgart deal was a bad idea? When the Chief refused to look us in the eye or when your warning lights started to come on?"

Hollis knew Ransahoff was compelled by military custom from acknowledging any criticism of his superiors or their plans, regardless of what he felt personally.

Ransahoff only sighed which confirmed what Hollis had already suspected.

"And did the delay getting off on the Schweinfurt deal worry you?   Did you think they might be pretty pissed off by the time we showed up five hours late?"

"Now listen, Hollis--"

"No *you* listen, Dutch.   We're not all as stupid as they suspect.   I'm not convinced this bombing business is doing any good anyway.   I think half the bombs we drop land on nothing more important than a hayfield but, I'll be damned if I'm willing to risk my life to prove somebody's theory or execute some pet project.

"No one gives his life for his country, his life is taken.   I do not plan to go gently into that good night.   I refuse to be sacrificed like some Druid on the altar of incompetence or folly.

"And then you invite me in to ask me what *I* think of Leo becoming a first pilot.   What am I supposed to think?   When they get up and tell us this is the one, the target which, when destroyed, will end the war, who are they trying to convince?   I'm thinking Brubaker may have been the smartest guy on the base.   Not some coward as everyone would like to think because it makes them feel more comfortable.   I think Brubaker put more rational thought into his decision that anybody did over Stuttgart."

Ransahoff came to his feet.   "Thank you for your help.   Remember, Jack, without faith in our leaders and their decisions we are lost.   We will cease to become an army but a rabble where every order is challenged and no one is obeyed.   We might as well pack our bags and go home.   I believe I have the answer I was looking for.   You can go."

Hollis saluted.   His salute this time was not mocking.   Ransahoff returned it and Hollis left.   Ransahoff should have said *blind* faith.   How blind must blind faith be? he wondered. He was glad Ransahoff did not demean himself by a "what we're fighting for" lecture.   Had Ransahoff chosen to do so Hollis would have puked onto the floor.   Perhaps he was a wise man after all.

He ignored Barbieri.   He wasn't sure if their conversation had been overheard or not. Hollis didn't care.   It suddenly occurred to him that he *was* interested in what Ransahoff thought of him.   He had gained some small sliver of respect for his CO for he had revealed himself as human.   Whether unwittingly or not was irrelevant, he had betrayed his doubt, too.   He possessed free will and was capable of rational, critical thought.   Not the arrogant martinet Hollis thought he was.

Hollis understood what kind of unenviable position Ransahoff now found himself in. That, whether he liked it or not, whether he agreed with it or not, Ransahoff was one of the chain of command and had to do what he was told.   He had to follow orders just like everybody else. He couldn't pick and choose which ones he liked and ignore those he didn't.   There was no place for the discussion of moral imperatives or strategic ramifications.

A thoughtful and reflective soldier might legitimately challenge the technical aspects of an order but never its validity or purpose.   Ransahoff was part of the warrior class. Contemptible in peacetime, worshiped in war.

He stepped out into the sunlight and dropped his cap on his head.   He saw Leo standing not ten feet away, obviously waiting.

"What was that all about?"

"Nothing."

"They're due back in a few minutes.   Want to go over to the tower and watch 'em land?"

"Sure, why not?"

They mounted their bikes and pedaled the mile or so to the tower.   Not long after they arrived the two squadrons roared   overhead in a big sweeping turn like geese circling a pond, and disassembled for the approach.   They counted fifteen planes.   They were all back. Landing was uneventful.   No flares.   The bombers just taxied back to their hardstands as if it had all just been practice.   Even the planes looked bored.

They were about to ride away when they heard someone from the tower yell something about somebody needing to make an emergency landing.   Leo and Hollis stopped.   Maybe something interesting was about to happen.

Leo tapped Hollis on the arm and pointed toward the end of the field.   A B-24 was approaching with smoke coming from a feathered number one engine.

"I didn't think it could fly with number one feathered," Leo said.

"Neither did I," Hollis added.

There was a good-natured rivalry between the men who flew or crewed B-24s and B-17s. The B-24 was bigger, faster and could go farther with a slightly heavier bomb-load.   But it was also fragile.   One lucky hit and either would go down but, a B-17 could be banged around all day and still make it home.   A Liberator could only take so much and it was finished.   Less resilient.   A hit in the fuel tank over the shoulders of the wings and it would go up like a roman candle.   A Fortress could climb on two engines and fly on one.   A B-24 had trouble remaining airborne on three.   The newspapers back home constantly featured pictures of B-17s with huge chunks gone, noses blown off, tail surfaces burned through.   It made Boeing proud and gave faith to the home folks that their boys were well protected by the tools of war they were provided.   One rarely saw like pictures of B-24s.   Hollis wondered if that disparity had occurred to anyone.   He wondered how B-24 pilots felt.   Knowing what they knew about their planes and the ruggedness and durability of the Fortress, did they ask themselves, in their moment of travail, if the B-24 was the best their country could afford.   When a B-24 was hit, did its pilot have the same confidence in his machine or the gratitude toward its manufacturer or respect for his government for making him fly in it, selecting him for it?   He thought not.

As way of confirmation, Leo whispered, his voice rife with concern, "I hated those Big Uglies."

"He's coming in hot."

"No flaps."

"Jesus, Leo, he's turning into a dead engine.   I thought you told me they couldn't do that."

"They can't.   Hold your ears."

Hollis willed that the pilot would not be so stupid or distracted as to turn his plane into the defunct engine for if he did the plane would invariably stall, spin off to that side and all aboard would die in a loud smear of fire and metal.   Hollis had never seen a B-24 crash before.

They breathed a loud sigh of relief when the pilot righted the plane and, instead, placed the big bomber in a bank toward the nearest runway.   He expertly flared the bomber onto the runway the instant the wheels cleared the concrete.   They could hear the wheels chirp and see the blue-white puffs of smoke erupt rudely from the tires.   The wings waggled as the plane slewed from one side to the other struggling to stay erect.   The wheels smoked and the squealed as the pilot stood on the brakes.   Suddenly, two parachutes blossomed from the waist windows in an effort to brake the hurtling bomber.   It worked.   In a few hundred feet, the plane stopped dead in the middle of the runway.

Leo turned to Hollis and sang the line from the movie, 'Dumbo,' "I thought I seen 'bout everything when I seen an elephant fly."

The crew deplaned as the fire trucks and ambulances roared up.   The engine continued to smoke, giving the crash crews something to hose down.   The pilot, Hollis presumed it was the pilot, walked funny, like he had shit his pants.

Leo saw this too and laughed.

"What's so funny?"

"Look at the way that guy's walking.   His left leg must hurt pretty bad holding that left rudder for so long.   I'm surprised he can walk at all."   He remounted his bike.   "Come on, Jack.   Maybe we got more mail."

Thursday, September 9, 1943

Hollis felt the nudge against his shoulder and the beam of light strike his retina through his eyelids.

"Get up sir, you're flying.   Breakfast at oh-three thirty, briefing at oh-four hundred."

"Where to today, Beamis?"

"I don't know sir, and I ain't Beamis."

"Where's Beamis?" Hollis asked with surprise.

"MPs came and arrested him."

"For what?"

"Playing with matches, sir.   And the unlawful discharge of an explosive device.   And theft."

"Did they forget tax evasion?"

"Theft of what?" Leo asked.

"Stole parts off a jeep motor to make his water heater."

Leo chuckled.   "Now that's funny."

"Who's jeep?"

"Colonel Van Patten's."

"Where are we going?"

"How should I know, Lieutenant?   Breakfast at oh-three thirty --"

"Briefing at four." Leo finished the sentence for him.

The corporal turned and left.

Joining the pilgrimage to the latrine, or what was left of it, the officers had a good laugh over the fact that Beamis was in trouble for blowing up his water heater.   They cursed him when they realized that the damage had destroyed most of the urine troughs and they had to wait in a line to relieve themselves. A few impatient ones stepped outside and watered the grass. The roughly fashioned sinks in which to wash, shave and brush their teeth had been replaced by steel helmets resting upside down in holes on a board.   This was simply too Spartan for them   They bitched loudly in the cold predawn, the back end of the small wooden structure gone.

Ransahoff got an ear full.   Do something, they said.   Intervene.   Regardless of what Beamis was guilty of, they needed him back.   Combat with flak and the *Luftwaffe* was one thing,   washing one's face in ice-cold water was quite another.

Quit your bitchin', he told them.   Don't you know there's a war on?

Breakfast was standard issue, powdered eggs, fried Spam, toast, coffee, orange juice and an apple.   It predicted a milk run.

When they arrived at briefing and took their seats Hollis saw Otho in flying gear. Wonder of wonders, Hollis thought, and Otho looked none too happy about it.   They were beginning to make bets that Otho didn't even know how to fly.

The staff and squadron officers walked in and Cavannaro was Bangmaster.   He was considered the weakest of the Squadron COs, so whatever it was they were going after today couldn't be that important.

Hollis scanned the formation board and did not see his name.   At the bottom of the board there were always two extra names listed.   They were the supernumeraries, the spares. Hollis found his name there.   A milk run and they were a spare!   He was listed next to an aircraft number he did not recognize.   Number 702, Colby L-Love.

Van Patten got up and started the briefing, a bit out of the ordinary since he was not Bangmaster.   He had a sort of whimsical smile which flooded Hollis with a sense of dread. What were they up to now?

"Gentlemen, we have a mission of some importance. It is important not because of the target, which will be the Lille-Nord airfield, but because of what is happening in conjunction with today's mission."

"I wonder if it's the fucking invasion?" Sully whispered.

Hollis felt a tingle run up his spine.   There had been rumors of the impending invasion for weeks.   Everyone had been at a loss to explain the shallow penetrations against air depots and aerodromes.   Stuttgart and Schweinfurt had been the only big missions in nearly a month.

"I want to warn you that you are not to comment on what you might see when you cross the Channel.   Do not, repeat, do not, discuss anything over the interphone.   We don't want Gerrie to pick up any stray transmissions.   We will have heavy escort in and out.   After landing you will leave your guns at their positions and proceed quickly to interrogation and be ready for a second mission.   You are free to speculate on what you think is going on.   But keep your speculations to yourself.   I want no discussion of what you think was going on until the completion of today's operations," he turned to Cavannaro, "Major."

"Gotta be the invasion," Sully whispered yet again, beseeching.

"Shut up, Sully," Leo whispered forcefully.

Cavannaro broke down the mission.   It would be a short run to the target with another group and return.   This could be the easiest mission we've ever flown, he added, let's do it right."

At the end of briefing, as was the convention, Hollis was to meet with the pilot of the other spare, at the formation board.   Hollis found him, a guy he did not know, and produced a shilling.   They would flip to see who filled in first.

"Call it," Hollis said when the coin left his hand.

"Heads."

Hollis caught the coin and slapped it over onto his wrist.   "Tails it is.   You lose."

The other guy smiled broadly.   The winner of the toss would fill in second.   The loser first.   On a tough mission, the odds both spares would fill in were not great and the winner would probably avoid a rough mission and be home in bed before they were near the target. Today, however, the real winner would be the first spare because he would probably get credit for an easy mission.   Hollis would fill in only if a second plane aborted, an unlikely situation on a milk run. A mission like this might prompt somebody to bomb the target even if only one engine was running.   No one wanted to abort and miss an easy one as had been made painfully obvious to Hollis.   Everybody would continue to fly unless the plane was simply incapable of staying in the air.   Especially on a day which carried the tacit prospect of historical significance.

As part of the ritual, Hollis shook the other guy's hand and said, "Good luck," but there was no warmth to it.   *You lucky bastard.*

He slapped Hollis on the back and said, "Thanks,"   *you poor sonuvabitch.*

Hollis felt despondent.   Today's activities would probably be for naught.   This was all the fault of that fucking Otho.

H-y walked up to Hollis still standing at the front of the room.   He was shaking the mission flimsy in his hand.   "Hey, we're a spare!"   He was incredulous.   "A milk run and we're the damned spare?   What kind of crap is this?"

"Shut up, H-y.   It was our turn."

"Get this changed.   Pull rank or something."

Hollis grabbed H-y by the arm and pointed to Ransahoff standing at the door taking another cup of coffee from the Red Cross girl.   "There's Dutch.   Run over there and tell him how distraught you are.   I'm sure he'll change things."   *You dumb shit.*

The likelihood that they would complete the day's exercise was slim.   Nonetheless, the idea of flying in a formation with a bunch of strangers who lacked a certain predictability, flying in an airplane with which he was unfamiliar was disquieting, milk run or not.   One had to have a certain amount of faith in the people he was flying with.   Even if it was Otho.

It was still well before dawn when the truck dropped them off at the 535th dispersal area. He saw that the crew had already gotten used to the idea of flying in a different plane.   When Hollis broke the news that they were a spare he was greeted with howls of protest.   Augie, who he expected to whine the loudest, was curiously quiet.   He did not refrain from casting a look of contempt at Hollis, though, as if this was Hollis's doing.   Hollis ignored him.

Hollis explained the need for secrecy although he could not reveal his speculations. Stay off the intercom, sometimes through freak electronic transmissions, leaks will occur and the Germans can pick up what we say, so be quiet.

What are you all worried about, Sully said, unable to conceal his displeasure, we aren't going to fly this one anyway.   I don't know why they even bother with spares for a milk run.

Hollis looked at the nose art and saw a lithe young woman, naked, on all fours in front of a backdrop of the Rockies with a huge smile and an exaggerated wink.   The plane's name was **Mount 'n' Ride**.

They sat around in the dark waiting for stations when Augie said, "Hey Lieutenant, Ol' Quinn here was out spoonin' yesterday.   Sowin' some seed with the Lassie, were ya?"

Quinn, provoked, responded, "Augie, do you go to church?"

"Yeah, I go to church.   Every God-damned Sunday.   Why?"

"Just wonderin'.   Do you remember the part where it says to love your fellow man as you love yourself?"

Augie was quiet for a moment then spoke, "Yeah, I recall hearin' something about that. Why?"

"Well, your attitude towards everybody would obviously tend to contradict that. Especially when it comes to Negroes."

"I don't get what you mean."

Everybody cringed.   If Quinn persisted there might be a fight.

Suddenly Sully said, "Why do you people continue to argue with him about this?   It's like discussing Euclidian geometry with an ape."

This Augie understood.   Wisely, he kept quiet.

For the first time, Hollis felt no need to vomit.   The fear of the unknown might have been less, he didn't know.   He had overcome his ambivalence about his current predicament and decided to make the best of the situation, frustrating as it was.

The twin green flares arced into the predawn and shortly Hollis and Leo had the engines running smoothly.   After they were warmed and run-ups were finished, the second green flare was fired.   Hollis pulled them off the hardstand, guided by flashlights in the hands of the crew chief.   The taxi process was slower because of the dark.   Sudden stabs of bright light shot across the field as pilots hit their landing lights briefly to help guide themselves around the perimeter strip or illuminate a turn.   The aircraft finally stood close in line at the end of the runway.   The turbo superchargers glowed blue-white from the heat casting an eerie light beneath the wings.   The Aldis lamp flashed the takeoff signal and, one by one, the bombers roared down the runway, a tongue of blue flame at the end of each exhaust stack.

Hollis and the other spare were the last planes off, Hollis at the very end of the line of bombers.   He could easily follow the planes ahead by the fire from their engines.   They took off almost due west flying out over the two small farms just to the left of the flight path beyond the perimeter of the field, the outlines of the small homes and barns barely discernible in the early light.   They banked over the village of Ridgewell, the buildings gray-brown and amorphous.

Hollis looked down and saw a Fortress low to the ground, wheels extended, flaps down, heading back toward the base. That was one.   The Other Guy would get his easy mission. They continued to climb reaching rendezvous altitude of seventeen thousand feet.   Hollis assumed his place above and behind the Group and saw that the formation was complete.   The first spare had filled in.   He saw the low squadron, led by Otho Barbieri flying with Brubaker's crew.   This was odd as they had no mission experience and were flying lead with Barbieri, also of limited lead experience, in the hardest position in the Group formation.   Flying lead of the low squadron had challenged the skill and acumen of many a good pilot.   The pilot had to constantly lean forward to see the lead squadron and keep his position off its lowest, most leftward-positioned Fortress.   Some had tried to fly the formation from the copilot's seat, but that meant using the left hand for the throttle and the right for the wheel and it never seemed to work out as intended.   The only persons in the Group alleged to have succeeded in flying lead of the low from the right was Rager and Eisenberg either of whom could have flown the formation from any position in the plane.

Cavannaro turned them toward the orbit awaiting the arrival of the 351st flying down from Polebrook.   It was a sharp turn, too sharp, and cast the high squadron off into space causing them loss of position, forcing them to speed up to regain their place.   It was ugly. Otho did a poor job of staying out of their way as they passed over and in front of his low squadron almost resulting in a lethal tangle.   They recovered, but just barely.

Cavannaro had no talent for this.   Maybe it wouldn't be a milk run after all.   He had none of the skill or finesse that Rager or Ransahoff possessed   He would surely kill somebody if he couldn't get it right.   And quickly.   Otho, too.

The plan called for the 351st to meet with them, and the 381st would assume a position in trail all the way to the target.   They would have to follow a narrow corridor of approach because there would be seven different small task forces heading for airfields over Northeastern France all to be hit more or less simultaneously.

When they approached the Channel they saw it.   The object of all the secrecy.   The sea was filled with ships.   For as far as Hollis could see in the haze and fog of the post-dawn sunrise there was ships of all sizes all steaming in the same direction.   Toward France.

"Jesus Christ, would you look at all those ships!   It must be the fucking invasion!" Rizzo yelled into the intercom.

"Naw, they wouldn't do that without telling us,"   Mollica added.

"Knock it off.   Didn't you hear me, for Christ's Sake?" Hollis yelled into the interphone. Sometimes it was like lecturing sheep.

Hollis wondered how did it all get started?   How so many men could spend so much time and effort and life to render dead one madman and a handful of his cronies.   How did war start?   Was it when man acquired his taste for meat?   Or was it when he assumed an erect posture freeing his hands for grasping a weapon?   He had slept through most of anthropology. He had only taken the course as a senior because of a fetching young coed he was particularly enamored with.   Had he paid attention he might be able to answer these questions.   Between the time he had signed up for the course and the time it commenced she had dropped from it and he was stuck in an intellectual pursuit for which he had absolutely zero interest.

It was probably australopithecus africanus, some drooling, slack-jawed beast with a shallow, sloping forehead and no sense of community.   An ancient precursor on the evolutionary chain of events who went from rooting for grubs and seeds on the savannah to crushing the skulls of small rodents.   It was no great leap to go from smashing the head of a squirrel for their meat to smashing the head of your neighbor for his woman.

When would it end?   How does one reverse or suspend evolution?   Man's brain was not yet big enough to figure that out.   It might never be.

Leo tapped Hollis's arm.   He pointed.   Up ahead the number two Fortress beside Cavannaro was trailing smoke from an engine.   As heartbroken as they must have been, desire could not overcome a burning engine and the pilot eased the B-17, still trailing smoke, away from the formation.

Without realizing it, and without any indication from his navigator, Hollis had gone beyond the turn-around point.   H-y must have been about to say something to correct his inattention when they both saw the Fortress drop away.   They waited for the plane flying the number five slot to pull up and fill the vacancy but, perhaps fearing Cavannaro's erratic flying, chose to remain where they were.   Hollis was confronted with a choice of his own.   He could take his fortune where he found it and fly in the diamond, above and between the three planes of the second element.   Or he could do as he was supposed to and assume the vacated position beside Cavannaro.   Doing so would inadvertently make him the *de facto* deputy group leader. If Cavannaro could not proceed to the target that would make Hollis the Bangmaster.   From second spare to Bangmaster.   Wouldn't his mother be proud?   What would Otho think?

Hollis felt terribly stupid as he pushed the throttles forward.   His musings and distraction had cost them the opportunity to turn for home.   Yet by flying past the turn-around point, an imaginary line in the Channel, he had gained for them an easy mission.   Would his crew be happy for his perseverance or pissed they weren't headed back to bed?

Such thoughts were of only passing interest as he flew the bomber wide of the number five and eased **Mount 'n' Ride** into position beside Cavannaro.   This was the furthest forward he had ever flown in a formation.   He liked it.   The only person he needed to worry about was the guy on his left.

"Pilot to Navigator."

"Navigator, go ahead."

"H-y, I hope you know where we are.   If Bangmaster falters, we're it."

"Roger, wilco on that, Pilot."

Hollis scanned the instruments.   All was perfect.   He looked down as they passed over the Belgian coast.   They would fly over a small section of it on the way to the little eastward-jutting portion of France where the airfield was.   Ypres was a control point on the way. Flanders fields.   Lush and green from the moldering bodies of a million men.

"Escort twelve o'clock high," Sully said.

"Right on schedule," H-y added.

Hollis leaned forward to glimpse the sixteen fighters in loose finger-four formation weaving back and forth in a lazy sine wave to stay ahead of the bombers.   No one came up to challenge them.

"Navigator to Pilot.   IP five minutes.   Be prepared for a one hundred and ten degree turn to the right."

"Roger, Navigator."

Hollis anticipated the turn at the Initial Point perfectly and, as he guided the bomber around, he heard and felt the sudden rush of air as the bomb bay doors came open.   A few moments later, the bomber trembled as the twenty-pound fragmentation bombs fell from their shackles and tumbled into the wind below the bomber.

Flak was sporadic and inaccurate.

The rest of the mission was as uneventful as the first part. Hollis made an acceptable landing, parked **Mount 'n' Ride** where it belonged and headed quickly, as directed, for interrogation.   There was little to report and no mention was made of the ships they had seen. They were instructed to get something to eat and return to their quarters for a possible second mission.   The call never came.   They had completed their seventh mission.   No one griped that Hollis had taken them beyond Checkpoint Able.

The next morning, at breakfast, word passed that the headlines in the newspapers reported the invasion rehearsal carried out to confound the enemy as to when and where an invasion might take place.

On Saturday morning, all officers were instructed to report to the briefing room.   It was raining and no alert had been laid on so those who were not curious were annoyed at the disruption of the pervasive and paralyzing ennui that had seized many in the Group.   Combat, some said, was better than this.   Maybe all they longed for, Hollis thought, was a bright, sunny day and a softball game.

Van Patten called the assembled to order.   Hollis noticed that the audience included paddlefeet from administration and weather and the like.   Those who could not squeeze onto a bench or chair, stood against the curving wall two and three deep.   What was so all-fired important? Hollis wondered.

"Gentlemen," Van Patten began, "I have called you together to announce the reorganization of the Eighth Air Force.   There has been a change in command, as well.   As of today, General Spaatz has been relieved of command of the Eighth Air Force and has assumed the command of all Army Air Force organizations in the ETO and MTO.   Major General Eaker will move from Bomber Command to command the Eighth Air Force.   General Fred Anderson will assume command of the Bomber Command.   The First Bombardment Wing will become the First Bombardment Division.   The Second Wing the Second Bomb Division.   The Third will be transferred into the newly-organized Ninth Army Air Force and the Fourth will become the Third Division.   The Provisional Combat Bombardment Wings will be given permanent status.   Our Combat Bomb Wing will be the First.   The 102nd will become the 40th, the 103 will become the 41st--"

"Now why in the hell are they bothering to tell us this?" Sully whispered.   "Is there one person in this room who gives a shit?"

Leo shushed him and added, "This is the army, stupid.   If they don't do this stuff they can't sleep at night."

"--The breakdown of the rest of the Divisions and Combat Wings will be given to you on mimeograph form at the end of this briefing."

It continued for another fifteen minutes, Van Patten using the assembly of his officers as an excuse to give a general pep talk.   It was just so much chickenshit. No one cared.   Or if they did they hid their interest well.

As they left the building Hollis saw Dodge approach him.

"Good morning, sir."

"Hiya, Noah."

"Nice drizzle we're having, Lieutenant."

"You want something, Noah?"

"You know what that God-damned Augie did?"

"No and I really don't want to either."   He looked at Dodge, squinting against the drizzle, "But you're going to tell me anyway, aren't you?"

"Yes sir."

"OK."

"He met this girl who was at a Red Cross dance.   She was taken by his accent and thought he was from the Wild West or something.   Anyway she invites him to dinner at their home in Great Yeldham."

"Yeah, so?   Come to the point, Dodge."

"Well, he takes Quinn with him and Augie proceeds to eat them out of house and home.

Ate their entire month's ration of meat, butter and sugar."

"How'd you find out?"

"Quinn told me.   He was pretty embarrassed.   And a bit taken by the girl, I might add."

"Christ, what a jerk."

"Yes sir.   Just thought you might want to know."

They walked on for a distance, most of the crowd behind them quickly dissipated in the drizzle which had advanced to a steady rain.

"What do you want, Dodge?"

"Well, Quinn tried to liberate some victuals for the folks, you know, to make amends but, no dice."

"Go tell the Chaplain."

"I was hoping maybe you would."

Hollis thought for a moment.   "Where's this family live?"

"Quinn knows."

"I'll see what I can do."   *Stupid limeys*, he thought, *they should have known better than to invite that stupid hillbilly.*

"Augie can be a pretty charming guy when he wants to be."

"OK, Noah."

Hollis turned and walked back to the Headquarters block.   In his entire military career he had never needed the services of a chaplain and he required intervention by the Almighty only rarely, so he felt awkward knocking on his door.

Chaplain Brown, who had a reputation as one of the finest clergymen ever to put on the uniform, opened the door where Hollis stood .   This close to so much concentrated sin must have made the Chaplain's life most interesting.

"Good morning, Lieutenant Hollis.   Come in."

Hollis was stunned by the fact that Brown knew his name.   They had never met.

"Good morning, Sir. Sorry to disturb you on this fine morning but, may I have a moment of your time?"

"Of course, please have a seat."

Hollis took a seat across from the Chaplain's desk and proceeded to tell him of the predicament.

When he was done, the Chaplain leaned forward and folded his arms across the desk.

"Unusual situation, Lieutenant.   Most traffic I get through here is for some moral dilemma or human failing.   This is a situation I have not confronted before."   He fell silent for another moment and said, "I'll see what I can do.   Come back in an hour."

"Yes sir.   Thank you, Sir."

Hollis took his leave.   As he left the building, he saw Dodge standing under the eve of the bulletin board.   Hollis feigned not seeing him and walked, head down against the rain, toward the Officer's Club.

"Hey Lieutenant!   What did you find out?"

"Not much.   You tell that Quinn to stand by in case I need him."

"Thanks."

"Don't thank me yet.   I don't know what's going to happen."

Dodge waved and trotted off into the rain, leaping with a long stride over some puddles.

Hollis couldn't believe those stupid Brits would be dumb enough to invite Augie for dinner.   If he ate all their food, raped their daughter and ravaged the misses, who's fault was that?   How could they be so stupid? Was it even possible for Augie and the word charming to be used in the same sentence?

He drank a Coke and read the <u>Stars and Stripes</u>.   Some nice soul had found a couple of sticks, it would have been too generous to call them logs, and set them afire in the stone fireplace at the end of the Club.   Most of the loose kindling and stray wood had already been burned and there was a strident prohibition against cutting down any of the King's trees, so a fire was rare indeed.   The twigs crackled in the flames.   He felt a sudden warmth out of proportion to the size of the fire.   He thought of his own home in Chester.   Their coal bin was never empty even during the Depression.   In the harshest winter he could ever remember there had always been warmth.   He would help his father shovel coal into the furnace.   It was a dirty chore and he hated it.   Here these people don't even have two sticks to rub together.   They were destitute. They dealt with cold by simply putting on another layer of shabby clothes.

He returned to Chaplain Brown's office precisely one hour later.   As he passed, he saw Dodge and Quinn huddled under the bulletin board overhang.   Quinn smiled and waved, but said nothing.

"Lieutenant, I was able to procure some food from the Combat Mess."   He looked at the list.   "It took some bargaining.   I had to call in a marker or two, but I was able to get a pork loin, two pounds of sugar, a can of pears, and   block of butter.   And two pints of vanilla ice cream."

"Jesus, Sir," Hollis said without realizing his blasphemy, "that's terrific.   Thank you."

"Jesus, did, in fact, have a lot to do with it.   The generosity of decent and God-fearing men knows no bounds.   Faith in Christ Almighty is all the food our souls will ever need.   But ice cream does help."

"Thank you again."

"I admire your coming here to help out, Lieutenant.   You are a good man.   You can pick up the food in fifteen minutes.   Take my jeep.   That way the ice cream won't melt.   Like those ships in the Channel, we don't want anyone to know where this is coming from, so keep it to yourself."

Hollis reached over and shook his hand warmly.

"Oh and you might tell our English friends to be a little more frugal when entertaining our troops."

"Yes Sir, I'll be sure to do that."

Hollis waved to Quinn to join him.   He walked to the Chaplain's jeep, it was clearly marked with a white cross on the bumper, and got in.   Dodge and Quinn ran over and opened the door.   Hollis told Quinn to get in.   He thanked Noah and they drove off to the Squadron area to get passes.   Once procured, they drove to the back of the Combat Mess and found a corporal waiting.   He handed Quinn two musette bags filled with the food and said, "I don't know what you're up to, Lieutenant.   But you have my thanks.   This wipes out a ten dollar debt I owed the Preacher."   He slapped Quinn on the shoulder and said, "Don't ever play poker with the man.   I think he cheats."

In order to deliver the goods with the least opportunity for the ice cream to melt, Hollis drove quickly.   It had been the first time he had been behind the wheel of a vehicle since his last furlough.   Quinn kept yelling, "Hey Lieutenant, don't forget you gotta drive on the wrong side of the road!"   He bounced through huge puddles and rain-filled potholes sending their heads bouncing against the canvas cover of the jeep.   He skidded a little on the wet streets, relying on Quinn for directions, forcing his brain to remember to keep the jeep on the left side of the road so Quinn would stop yelling at him.

Quinn held the bundles tightly on his lap, smiling.

"What's so funny?"

"I love this girl."

"Oh," was all Hollis said.

"And thanks for helpin' out, Lieutenant."

"You're welcome.   You keep Augie away from these people.   It's bad enough *we* have to deal with him."

"Yes sir."

In no time, they pulled up to the row of homes on a street almost too narrow for two cars to pass side-by-side.   "That's it right there, sir."   Quinn pointed to a yellow-gray door very similar to every other door on the block.   Like so much of what he had seen of wartime England, it was a drab row home, on a drab block, in a drab, little town, in a drab country.

After a single knock, the door opened revealing an older Englishman in a train conductor's uniform.   He looked surprised to see an American Lieutenant standing in the rain on his stoop.   He seemed suspicious and who could blame him?   "Hello, Yank.   What can I do for you?"

"One of my men exceeded his welcome and your hospitality.   I apologize for his appetite and his indiscretion."   Hollis held up the musette bags.

The old Brit looked cautiously at the bags.

"You need to eat this ice cream.   It's melting at a fearsome rate."

The man, stunned by the largesse, was suddenly moved to tears.   "This is very kind of you, Leftenant.   Very kind indeed."   He saw Quinn seated in the jeep.   Quinn gave him a cheerful wave.   "Would you and Sergeant Quinn like to join us for a spot of tea?"

"Uh...no thanks, sir.   You have been generous enough as it is.   One yank per month is all we're permitted by treaty."

The old Brit stared blankly at Hollis for a moment then smiled and said, "Fuck the bloody treaty, my good man.   I insist.   Now you come in out of this rain."   He gestured to Quinn as Hollis stepped past him into the tiny living room.

Quinn was beside himself.   He could barely contain his joy at revisiting this place.

Hollis looked around.   The room contained two large, old   stuffed chairs stained by the oils of resting heads.   There was a small davenport and a coffee table crammed tightly into the tiny room, small ceramic bric-a-brac scattered about.   And doilies.   He hadn't seen a doilie since he walked out of his own living room three months ago.

The daughter, Hollis presumed it was the old man's daughter, appeared and smiled warmly at Quinn.   They shook hands, but their touch lingered beyond that of a normal handshake.   They stared at each other for a long moment before Quinn introduced her to Hollis.

She needed no introduction.   It was the redheaded Penelope.   There was no question about it.   Hollis looked at her closely for some sign of recognition but, if she recognized Hollis, she gave no hint.   He felt his loins stir at the sight of her.   He could not withdraw his stare but she ignored him and kept her gaze on Quinn.   They seemed hopelessly enthralled with each other.

The man and his daughter chatted at some length with Quinn and Hollis while they ate the ice cream which had turned to the consistency of thick, cold soup.   They drank tea and the old Brit, Byron Halliday, was his name, explained how his son was off in service to the Army in Burma.   He explained his generosity toward Augie by saying he would hope someone might be as generous to his own son when the time came.   Hollis tried to explain the notion of country bumpkin to Halliday, but he seemed not to grasp the concept.   His wife was with the Land Army, probably out plowing some field or shoveling mud, Hollis supposed.

Penelope worked in London during the week, he explained, as a copy-reader for a newspaper.   She only came home when her travel allowance permitted, he said.   Then he confessed.   His working for the railroad allowed her to come and go as she pleased so she came home frequently.   His job, he explained, did have certain advantages.

She turned to Hollis.   A moment of uncertainty swept over him, did she finally recognize him?

"I see your aeroplanes come and go.   I always say a prayer for all of you when you fly over.   Early in the morning when you start up the darkness is filled with a sound like distant thunder.   It makes me feel happy and sad at the same time.   All the fine young boys."

Yep.   That was her.   He could barely understand her then, he could barely understand her now.   The cockney accent was strong, almost impenetrable.

Hollis grew bored, even the voyeurism he now found himself engaged in as Quinn and Penny whispered and giggled failed to entertain him.   He felt strange also, but mostly bored.

Hollis stood.   "Well, you have been most gracious to us, sir.   Thank you, but we must be going."

Quinn protested, but Hollis reversed this with a glance and he stood up also, still holding Penelope's dainty hand in his, a hand she had wrapped firmly around his cock less than a week earlier.

"Please come back, Leftenant.   You are always welcome here."

So might the rest of the Air Corps, Hollis thought.   *Bring money.*   "Thank you for the tea."   He turned to Penelope for one last chance at recognition.   "You have been most kind."

"You are welcome, Leftenant," she said, smiling at him brightly, her perfect, white teeth shining.   Hollis recalled his   lava on those lips certain she did not know who he was.   He was tempted to ask her if she had ever jitterbugged at the Pioneer Hall, but did not.   If you believe that God has a master plan then there's no such thing as coincidence.

"Thank you for the food," Halliday said as they bounded down the steps into the jeep.

On the ride back no mention of the girl was made by either man.   Quinn did not lose his smile.

Chapter Thirty-four   **Darky**

Hollis understood how life was at once marvelous, mysterious and violent.   War took a lifetime's worth of human emotion and experience and compressed it.   This War was the first mandatory step to a virtuous life.   That Quinn's girlfriend was a London whore and that she had serviced him was almost beyond coincidence.   There were, he supposed, tens of millions of people on the island.   It was supernatural.   Cosmic.

Poor Quinn.   Should he intervene?   Was truth more precious than love?   Was it love?   If so, by whose definition?   If not, by whose sanction?   He doubted she worked for a newspaper at all.   He knew that Penelope Halliday would forever remain a secret he would carry to his grave.

Sunday morning continued the monotonous meteorological trend of overcast and intermittent rain.   He read some mail, censored some, wrote letters and read a book of verse his mother had sent him.   Try as he might, he could not shake the contrasting images of Penelope from his brain.   One, an accomplished prostitute; the other, a sweet and innocent young girl who batted her eyes when she looked at her new beau.

He was glad it rained.

Monday morning they were ordered to the briefing room for another lecture on escape and evasion.   Some navigator from the 306th spent nearly two hours telling how he had eluded the Germans after bailing out over Rennes.   He knew they were hunting for him.   What was probably nothing more than a terrified navigator cowering under a bush had been escalated to the status of legend.   He could hear trucks pass and shouting in German.   For nearly two days he did not move from the spot under a bush.   He sucked the dew from the surfaces of leaves and ate berries from a nearby tree.   They made him sick and he developed diarrhea so bad he became fearful the smell might betray him.

Finally, he was awakened by a rifle barrel poked into his ribs.   A farmer, *perhaps drawn by the odor*, Hollis thought, came over with his rabbit gun to investigate and found him.   He knocked the rifle from the startled man's hand and ran.   He found refuge in a barn, not sure where, exactly, he had come down.   Germany or France?

"Sounds familiar," Sully whispered.

By Day Three, he was thirsty, starving and lost.   Out of despair he thought of turning himself in, but, as a Jew, he knew that could well prove fatal.   So, he explained, he gathered his wits about him and formulated a plan.   He was going to head due west, relying on the silk map in his escape kit, foraging for or stealing whatever he needed.   He got somewhere south of Paris when he was captured by the French.   He was treated like a prisoner and initially thought he was going to be turned over to the Gestapo but, instead, was placed into the hands of the *Maquisards* who kept him hidden in a cellar for two weeks.   He narrowly avoided a sweep of the countryside by German soldiers and was spirited out of danger by an elderly couple in the back of hay wagon.   He reached the border with neutral Spain after a difficult climb over the Pyrenees.   From there he was turned over to American authorities and returned to England.   The ordeal had lasted just over a month.

Hollis thought his story sounded contrived and rehearsed.   The fact that he had probably repeated it before an audience dozens of times did not seem to matter to him.   The wayward navigator said some of the French are not sympathetic to the Allied cause and cannot be trusted, something Hollis's father would understand.   But, the majority of the French were anxious to help him escape even at the risk of their own lives, something his father would have found hard to believe.

At the end of the lecture, Hollis felt bad that he had reduced this man's heroic act of escape with such cynicism and went up to congratulate him.   He smiled broadly and said, "I was scared shitless, pal.   There was no heroics involved on my part.   I just didn't want to get caught."

After the lecture, they held an aircraft recognition class and it was time for dinner.

When they were done eating, Spats, DeBerg and Sully got on their bikes and rode to The White Horse for a few beers.   There were the usual locals, although Angus wasn't there,   a couple of paddlefeet and two Negro sergeants from the Ordinance company.   They sat quietly chatting while the four officers sat down a table away and drank their beer.   Hollis recognized them as the two who had gotten into a shouting match with Augie.

DeBerg and Spats spoke about baseball and the upcoming World Series.   Their conversation was lively and drew the attention of the rest of the people in the bar.   Hollis listened intently when he felt a tap on his arm.   Sully motioned toward the door.   Augie stood beside Rizzo surveying the room.

The two took the only remaining table which was beside the Negroes.

"Boy," Sully said, "I don't like the looks of this."

"What do you suppose happened to him to make him such a despicable character?" Hollis added.

"I do not know.   But being a writer, I admire your use of the choice of 'despicable.'"

DeBerg and Nevtushenko stopped their conversation to see what had so suddenly distracted Hollis and his bombardier.

"The span of human behavior continues to astonish me," Hollis said.   He noticed DeBerg and the Mad Russian exchange glances.

Augie started speaking loudly, 'nigger' this and 'nigger' that.   After a few moments Rizzo slunk down in his seat, obviously upset by what was happening.

Finally, one of the ordinance sergeants turned to Augie and told him to knock it off.

It was like gasoline on a fire, exactly the provocation Augie was looking for.

"Beat it, Niggers!" Augie shouted as he stood.

"We were here first," one of them said.

The larger of the two turned so he could confront Augie without standing up and said, "I'm telling you for the last time to watch your mouth."

Hollis was glad he decided not to stand.   He thought that had he done so it would have been enough to trigger a fight.   Hollis felt Sully's eyes suddenly fall upon him, beseeching him to intervene.   DeBerg and Nevtushenko were speechless.   The room long since hushed. Hollis was ambivalent about getting into the thick of this.   On the one hand, he was the ranking officer in the pub and a public dispute was occurring between subordinates.   On the other hand, he was hoping that he was about to witness Augie get the righteous pounding he so richly deserved.

He was shifting himself to stand when the proprietor walked over and said to Augie, "You better leave.   I don't want no trouble and them Coloreds got as much right to be here as anybody.   Now leave or I'll have you arrested."

Augie rose to his feet, surveyed the situation and wisely decided to depart, but not without flashing a provocative glance at the two black men.   The proprietor followed Augie to the door and told him that he was no longer welcome in his establishment.

Mortified, Rizzo got up and left also.   Hollis figured Augie had begged somebody to accompany him to the pub.   He had become increasingly isolated from the rest of the crew.   Rizzo was the weakest of the bunch.   No doubt, Augie had promised him he would behave if he came along.   No scene, no fighting.   Couple beers, that's all.   And Rizzo, the poor, naive, little ball turret gunner, believed him.

Hollis stood up and walked over to the black sergeants and took a seat uninvited.   He was an officer and he could do as he pleased.   "Why do you guys put up with such crap?"

They ignored him.

"Why do you guys want to fight for a country that treats you like shit?"

"We have our dignity," the tech sergeant said.   "Hitler thinks we're first cousins to the apes.   It isn't a perfect system, but it's better than what he's offering.   Good evening, Lieutenant."

Without finishing their drinks, they got up and walked from the pub.

Hollis returned to his seat, exchanged an exasperated glance with Sully.   He gave thought to explaining things to the other officers, but realized some things were beyond explaining.

The next evening Selkirk and his crew returned.

He looked well-rested, Hollis thought.   But that was about it.

Tuesday afternoon, after supper, Hollis and Leo sat on their beds reading mail when Otho walked in.

"Oh good," he said.   "You two gather up your navigator, flight engineer and your radio operator and report to operations.

"What for?" Hollis asked.

"You guys got to take up 709 and slow time the engines."

"Get somebody else to do it."

"Hollis, you don't get it.   I'm not asking you, I'm telling you.   It's called an 'order.'"

"Why us?" Leo asked.

"'cause you're the first two I found.   You better get going before it starts getting dark.   And Dutch wants Wychulis doing the flying."

It took nearly half an hour before he and Leo were able to round up Quinn, Dodge and H-y.   They all gathered at Squadron Operations, standing in flight gear, all five pissed off that, by random selection, their evening had been so precipitously disrupted.

Seven-oh-nine was **The Flying Dutchman**.   All four engines had been changed and they needed to be slow-timed, broken in, before taking them on operations.   That required two hours of unstressed flying usually in a large orbit at about seven thousand feet away from traffic.

The early evening was clear and Hollis thought they shouldn't have any trouble.   Otho briefed them.   Run a race track pattern over Buntingford that should keep you out of the Raf's way in case they're up tonight.   Don't go gettin' lost over London or they'll bring you down sure as shootin'.   Two hours of flight time, no more, no less.   Hurry up and get going before it gets too dark.

They went to the equipment shed and drew their gear.   No need for oxygen masks or heated suits, Hollis had no intention of taking them above seven thousand.   He wrestled with the idea of having Leo fly from the left seat.   Dutch seemed bound and determined to make a first pilot out of him so he would give him what he wanted.

After they had settled into the cockpit, Leo on the left, Hollis knew they were in trouble. During the preflight checklist Leo kept wanting to do the copilot's part.

"You're the pilot," Hollis said.   "You do the pilot's part."   After saying it a third time he nearly made them change seats.   Even the imperturbable Dodge was losing patience.   Maybe Leo was just nervous.   Maybe Leo really was incapable, physiologically, from assuming the role of pilot.   Either way, it did not bode well and both he and Dodge sensed it.

Finally, all four engines were running and Hollis requested permission to taxi.   It was granted.

Leo pulled the B-17 onto the perimeter strip and Hollis found himself half hoping that somehow Leo might torque the landing strut in the mud or otherwise break something on Dutch's plane to teach Ransahoff a lesson and abort the exercise altogether.

To his surprise, Leo took them down the taxiway without difficulty all the while Hollis's feet just a fraction of an inch off the copilot's rudder pedals, ready in an instant to brake the plane if disaster seemed imminent.   He was still responsible for the plane regardless of which seat he was in or whose hands were on the wheel.

After settling at the end of the runway, Leo requested permission to take off, which was also granted.   Leo ran up the engines to full throttle and released the brakes.   They became airborne easily, Leo expending little effort to get them off the ground.   With no bomb load, half a crew and only enough gas for about four hours' worth of flying the B-17 handled like a fighter. Not a true test of Leo's skills as a pilot, Hollis thought.   H-y kept giving Leo the turns, changing direction at right angles every ten minutes in one direction and twenty minutes in the other.

Assured they would be OK, Hollis began to daydream.   He watched the English countryside lose its color in the fading daylight.   He thought about his conversation with Selkirk the evening he returned from the rest home.

Selkirk seemed to have used the time off to good advantage.   He may have put on a few pounds.   He seemed less gaunt, certainly.   But Hollis could not gauge his mental state.   He seemed ebullient enough, his usual emotional location, but underneath, where the demons live, did the emotional corruption fester?   Hollis could not get over the fact that he deliberately blew up a turbo supercharger, making one of the most fledgling of mistakes, almost mortally wounding a ground crewman in the process.   Hollis began to wonder if anybody was paying attention.

"Radio to cockpit."

"What is it, Quinn?"

"Everything OK up there?"

"Yeah, why?"

"Number three is throwing buckets of oil.   The whole wing is covered."

"Christ Leo, I thought you were watching the god-damned dials."   Hollis failing to realize that, as nominal copilot on this particular trip, the dials were his responsibility.

"You better shut it down," Dodge said.   "Lose any more pressure and it won't feather."

Leo started the feathering routine for the number three engine.   Without prompting, he told Hollis what to do and the propeller spun to a halt, the blades turned into the wind.   The nacelle behind the cowling was slick with shiny, black oil.   Hollis was distressed with himself for not noticing the sequence of events.   As copilot, it was his responsibility.   He instinctively reached to adjust the power of number four to compensate for the loss of the engine and reset the trim, but stopped himself short.   He wanted to see if Leo would do it.   When he failed to do so on his own, Hollis reminded him of this and Leo made the appropriate adjustments bringing the attitude of the plane into proper position and the airspeed back up.   What was Ransahoff thinking?

His preoccupation with the failing engine and the need to correct Leo to make it right, made him fail to appreciate the undercast rolling in under the plane.   The sudden appearance of the clouds made the light diminish quickly and it was almost dark.

"Pilot to navigator, er, I mean copilot to navigator, where are we, H-y?"

"I think we're over Thaxted, BB-31."

"You think?!"

"Yeah."

"Jesus, H-y, you mean we're lost?"

"No, I don't think so."

"What?!"

"Well, I wouldn't exactly say we're lost."

"Well, what exactly are we, you nincompoop?"   Hollis could see Leo start to laugh oblivious to the predicament they now found themselves in.   "And why are we flying around in a circle?   Quinn, call up Darky."

"Darky's on command channel, Lieutenant."

Hollis switched to the command channel, "Hello, Darky, hello Darky.   This is Afghan C for Charlie.   Need steer to Ridgewell."

A few tortured moments passed with empty ear phones.

A calm, English voice came on.   "I hear you Afghan C for Charlie.   Are you declaring an emergency?"

"No, just lost."

"You are to our north.   Grid BB-31.   Throttle up for a moment."

Hollis eased the throttle forward and started a gentle banking climb.

"Roger, Afghan C-Charlie.   We have you.   Watch for the light."

The climbing turn would put them off the right wing.   Hollis tapped Leo's shoulder and pointed to the right.   Hollis looked away so as not to have his night vision shattered by the bright searchlight.   The beam flicked on at about the spot he expected and pointed straight up toward Heaven placing a huge brilliant disc on the undersurface of the overcast which had sneaked in, also unnoticed.   It then dropped north-east flashing through and beneath the undercast and, as quickly, flicked off leaving a shadow on everybody's retinas.

"See," Smith came on, "I told you where we were.   Come to heading zero seven five and we should be over Ridgewell in 15 minutes."

"Thanks, Darky."

Hollis watched the instruments closely.   He made sure Leo kept them on a steady course toward Ridgewell. He looked outside for a moment and could not discern the separation of Heaven and earth. It was dark. Absolute darkness. They were caught in a sandwich between an undercast and an overcast. Not even starlight illuminated the earth. Hollis suddenly became disoriented and panic seized him in its cold grip as his unreferenced senses convinced him they were flying upside down or vertically. He grabbed the wheel from Leo and waggled the wings until he convinced himself that they were flying straight and level, confirming by instruments that which his senses refused to believe. Leo seemed surprised by the sudden relinquishment of control of the aircraft. He did not see the panic which had so recently gripped his pilot. Leo simply hadn't noticed.

Hollis steered the plane as directed and lowered slowly through the undercast. Fortunately, it was thin and **The Flying Dutchman** emerged below it at about four thousand feet, a safe margin of altitude. But, in the blackout, the ground below was as dark and foreboding as the undercast had been.

"Navigator to pilots, Ridgewell dead ahead. We should be over the field in ten minutes."

"Thanks, H-y," Hollis said, his voice under control even if he still remained close to the fine edge of hysteria. He gathered his senses and orientation calming down enough to debate the wisdom of letting Leo land with one engine out. If he did and they all died in a fiery crash he would be guilty of very bad judgment, his death testimony to his own stupidity. If he retained control of the plane and landed himself he would humiliate Leo perhaps beyond the point of no return. It was an easy choice.

He leaned close to Leo's ear and said, "I'll land it. It can be tricky with three out."

Leo nodded. In the dark he couldn't tell if Leo was disappointed or not and really didn't care. He had no faith in Leo's ability to land a bomber on three engines in the pitch black darkness.

Switching to the command channel, Hollis requested permission to land and asked that the landing lights to be turned on. The tower gave him information on the prevailing winds and the runway they were to use. Soon the red runway lights lit up the long east-west runway. Hollis made an orbit of the field and settled the B-17 onto the runway without difficulty. He taxied the Fortress back to its hardstand, a daunting task in the dark, even with flicking the landing lights off and on and shut down the engines.

"Ah, good thing you're back, Lieutenant," the crew chief said. "We've been alerted."

"Sergeant, I had to shut down number three because the oil pressure went to zero. Otherwise, everything went fine." He looked over at a befuddled H-y and signed the Forms 1 and 1A and walked away. A few moments later, Otho came by in a jeep and drove them back to the equipment shed.

Hollis made a point of seeking out Ransahoff who was in his room going over some paperwork.

"I know what you're trying to prove, Major. I don't think Leo Wychulis is capable of commanding a bomber. I didn't think so this morning. I don't feel that way now. Unless you send him through transition training I think to turn a Fortress over to him would be a criminal act. Even if the outcome of the war hangs in the balance, don't do it. By the way, your number three engine is fucked up." He turned and left.

When he returned to the room Leo was quiet, preparing for bed. Nothing was said.

Wednesday, September 15, 1943

They arrived at the planes by mid-afternoon, the mission to bomb some industrial targets near Paris. At the hardstand, they saw that **Cleopatra's Asp** had been rigged with two external bomb racks, one under the root of each wing, each holding a thousand pounder, prompting Augie to declare, "Aw, would you look at this."

Why such things would matter to him escaped Hollis. The planes were off and assembled by five o'clock. The task force, five groups in two wings, turned for the target, passing just east of London, enroute to Beachyhead. Hollis had some problems getting number four engine to fire up delaying his take off until the Group was up and gone putting him about ten minutes behind the formation. Since he was flying the number four slot behind Ransahoff and since the mission promised to be a milk run, he was determined to meet up with the formation as it reached Checkpoint Able, the departure point on the coast. His navigation and intentions proved accurate and he found the 381st exactly as expected. Somebody, the spare, since it was not of their Squadron, had taken his place. This violated the policy that the spare wasn't supposed to fill in until *after* the formation had reached Checkpoint Able. The spare, eager to get in an easy one, too, refused to pull out of formation as Hollis eased up beside him.

Hollis could see the copilot of the spare waving him off. Hollis nudged in closer.

"Look at that son of a bitch," H-y said. "They're in our spot. Fire one across his bow, Dodge."

After a moment, Hollis and everyone on **Cleopatra's Asp** could see the bombardier, navigator, the top turret and waist gunners thumbing their noses at **Cleopatra's Asp**, waving them away. Hollis, defying the freezing air, pulled off his glove and, making sure they could see him, flashed them his middle finger. He simultaneously got on the VHF, radio silence be damned. "Supers don't fill in until Checkpoint Able. You better move, you son of a bitch, or I'll run you over. You're in our spot."

The copilot pulled his own glove off and returned the middle finger salute to Hollis. They poured on the gas and climbed out of Hollis's slot. He moved **Cleopatra's Asp** to the left and took up his proper position, leaving the spare to his own fate.

Everyone seemed pleased. Leo smiled behind his mask.

As they approached the primary target the announcement came for diversion to the last resort target, the airfield at Romilly-sur-seine.

The bombing was uneventful. A few Me-109s flew past. They didn't seem interested in a fight. The escort was good. At bombs away, Sully called down to Rizzo to make sure the external bombs had dropped. Hollis knew Sully liked the thousand pounders. They were heavy enough to reliably release from the shackles and fall free of the bomb racks even if they had frozen up.

They landed after dark. It was past ten o'clock before they returned to their rooms. There was mail, a few letters and a small package. Hollis was disappointed when he found out the package was not for him.

Leo worked the string off the box and opened it. He stared at the contents for a moment and slammed it shut. Leo grinned broadly and turned red. Hollis pointed out a little known tradition of copilots sharing goodies from home with their pilots. Nobody turns red over crumbled cookies and the box was too small for almost anything else.   What in the hell had she sent him?   He had never seen Leo react to anything like that.

"Cookies, pray tell?" Hollis asked trying to conceal his curiosity.

"Nothing really."   Leo got up and, with great deliberation, placed the box in the bottom of his foot locker and closed it.

Jesus, I gotta find out what's in that box.

A short time later he got his chance.   Leo said he was going to the latrine and flipped a towel over his shoulder and left.   Hollis waited until the door at the end of the hall slammed shut and then opened the footlocker.   Unabashed by the blatant invasion of Leo's privacy, he went right to the box and opened it.   The little box contained a pair of silk stockings, garter belt, panties and a lacy bra.   No note, no cookies.   Just Christie.

On his way to the latrine, Hollis heard female laughter.   It was so incongruous that at first he thought he was imagining it.   Then he heard it again.   He went to investigate. Robertshaw walked past, shaking his head.

"What's going on?   I thought I heard women laughing."

Robertshaw said, unable to conceal his annoyance, "Some of those fucking gunners snuck some prostitutes onto the field by hiding them in the back of a truck.   They made them wear caps and overcoats.   They told them to act drunk and nobody noticed."

"Or gave a shit."

"I wish they'd all finish their business and beat it.   I'm tired.   I have a headache and I want to go to sleep."

Hollis wondered if Mr. Halliday knew where his daughter was tonight.

Chapter Thirty-five   **Number Two**

Thursday, September 16, 1943

They had been alerted the night before.   The signs were there almost as soon as they returned from Romilly.   Fuel and oxygen were replenished before the gunners had their weapons out of the planes.   Hollis could feel the familiar sense of dread descend over him. Except for the Stuttgart fiasco, they had nothing but milk runs since Schweinfurt, all with little or no opposition.   Perhaps they had learned some sort of lesson about deep penetrations.   They could rack up missions bombing nothing more challenging than airdromes in France and the Low Countries, which would have suited Hollis, and everybody else he could name, just fine.   The problem was, shallow strikes and milk runs would not win the war.   He understood enough about the concept of precision, daylight, strategic bombing and economics to know that the heart of the Fatherland must be ripped asunder for ultimate victory to be achieved.   Otherwise it would become a war of attrition and Germany just might win.   Perhaps all this activity meant a return to business as designed: deep, unescorted missions with high losses and uncertain results.

The novelty of the excursion to London had worn off becoming a distant, imprecise memory and the oppressive boredom of the past week had left him feeling homesick and sorry for himself.   The incident with H-y and Leo the previous night had done little to reinforce his confidence in ultimate survival.   If he were incapacitated he had no real hope that Leo could guide them home or H-y would show him the way.   No lucky escapes or miraculous reprieves could be counted on.   There is no Darky over Germany.   Despite the comparatively easy time they had recently and the fact that he had eight missions behind him was no reassurance that disaster did not loom the next day, the next time they rolled down a runway.

So, when Beamis came around to tell them that briefing was at oh-eight-hundred and that they should be prepared for a long ride, Hollis was not surprised.

It was the first time they had seen Beamis since the back end of the latrine had blown off. Hollis thought they had seen the last of him, figuring Beamis had been court-martialed and sent to some stockade.

"What are you doing back here?" Hollis asked.

"They figured out that they couldn't run this squadron without me.   They were pretty pissed off about the latrine and I got demoted.   They're gonna make me pay for repairing the latrine but I figure if I get a donation from all of the officers, I can pay off the debt and still have enough cash to rebuild a decent water heater."

Leo looked up as he slipped his socks on, "How much?"

"Five pounds per officer oughta do it."

"You know, I can get laid in London for less than that," Leo replied.

"Yeah, but can she get you hot water?"

"When do you need the money?"

At the latrine, most of which had been rebuilt, Hollis saw Selkirk standing alone, a look of concern on his face.   He looked as if he had been crying.   Hollis had enough on his mind without getting involved in Selkirk's tale of woe, but he could not resist the necessity of addressing him.

"Hiya, Mickey.   I haven't had much chance to talk to you since you been back.   How was the Flak House?"

"Huh?   Oh, it was OK.   The food and company was good.   They did everything they could to take all our troubles away and get our minds off things."

"Yeah?"

"It was a cruel joke, Jack.   It was like a dream, like the war didn't exist.   Like you weren't thousands of miles from home.   It only made coming back to this that much harder. It was like a last meal before they walk you to the gallows."

Hollis was sorry he opened his mouth.   Selkirk's tether was thin, indeed.   Nothing further was said and Hollis started shaving.

At breakfast, the sense that a big mission was on was very pervasive.   The information Beamis used to predict the nature and length of the mission was likely available to everyone else. Fuel and bomb load ratios.   It was like reading astrological charts or the entrails of sacrificial animals.   The fact that Begay was in flying clothes only added to the mystery.

At briefing, the squadron line up was Ransahoff leading, Hollis number two, Fissano number three, Selkirk lead of the second element, with Robertshaw and DeBerg.   Ivan the Terrible was listed as spare.

"Our target today is a ship in the Loire River at Nantes."

The reaction was neither enthusiastic or aggrieved leaving Hollis to wonder what inference Hulse and the other gunners might draw.

Begay took the pointer and continued, "The First Division has been assigned as its target the *Kreigsmarine* refueling and supply ship which is moored here, on the Loire River a few miles up from the Bay of Biscay.   This ship is used to replenish U-boats on North Atlantic patrol. We should have fighter escort most of the way and expect opposition to be brisk.   The Third Division will attack the port facilities in La Pallice as well as airfields nearby.

"We will be the third wing in the First Division task force.   Each aircraft will carry twelve 500-pound GPs.   Secondary targets will be the general port facilities of Nantes and nearby marshaling yards.   The target of last resort will be the airfield at Chateau-Bougon, here.

"This target is of some importance or they wouldn't be sending the whole Division to hit it."   He turned to Gorton and said, "Major."

While Gorton gave them a breakdown of the mission details Hollis studied the map. They would assemble over central England and head almost due south toward the coast-out point east of Portsmouth.   They would turn slightly west and cross the French coast east of Cherbourg.   A direct line across Normandy and Brittany to the IP and a ninety degree turn to the left to Nantes.   Rally to the right then another right toward the Atlantic.   The return flight, over four hundred miles, would take them out over the ocean swinging around the Brittany peninsula back to coast-in at Plymouth.   It amounted to a big trapezoid, most of it over water. It was not lost on anybody that if they got into trouble at the target it would be a long haul above open ocean.   The chances of rescue by anybody was slim.   By friendly forces next to nil.

At the end of the briefing, Hollis heard Ransahoff take Fissano to one side and tell him, "This is your first mission.   You keep it in tight and they won't be able to pick you out as a green crew."   He turned to Hollis, taking him aside, "Not counting your trip as a spare, this is you first mission as second.   I don't trust Selkirk to take over if I cannot continue.   Keep sharp. Tell your navigator to keep sharp, too.   Your bombardier will be carrying a Norden.   He must be ready to sight the target, too.   Don't fuck up."

Jesus, Hollis thought, *I don't like this.*   Flying lead of the second element was bad enough, he had fared okay with that, being second lead of the whole squadron was something else.

They went to the equipment shed and Hollis watched Selkirk carefully, detached, clinical. He looked morose, irritable.   He did not say anything to anybody and nobody approached him. Not even his copilot.

Selkirk handed in his personal effects and left.   Hollis made a point of riding out to the dispersal with him.   Hollis tried to strike up another conversation, but Selkirk did not respond. As scared as Hollis was, he knew the demons inside Selkirk must be on the verge of consuming him.   Hollis worried Selkirk might do something crazy again.   He had no business flying a bomber in combat and he suspected Ransahoff shared that view.   But what choice had he?   It was like falling off a horse. One must get right back on or one might never ride again.   After one too many close calls maybe Selkirk thought his hours were numbered.   They should never have sent him to the rest home.   It had given him too much time to mull over his fate.   Perhaps they should have removed him from operations altogether.   He was finished.   Where was Clevenger's discerning eye?

At the plane, Hollis gathered the crew around and explained the mission.   When he was done he walked across the perimeter and sat, smoking until stations.   It had become ritual and nobody seemed to pay much attention anymore.

A few minutes before stations, he walked behind **Cleopatra's Asp** and vomited.   As he emptied his bladder Dodge joined him saying, "Thanks, Lieutenant."

As Hollis worked his penis back into his pants he said, "For what?"

"Making amends with that English family.   They were so appreciative they're thinking of asking Augie to come back."

"What do you know about those people?"

"Very little.   Just what Quinn told me.   Which isn't much.   He is very smitten with the lassie, for sure, and they seem very taken with him.   Why?"

"Just wondering.   Listen, from your perch up there keep an eye on things.   Especially Selkirk."

"Anything I should know?"

"Uh-uh.   Just keep your eyes peeled." It was a stupid thing to say. His eyes were always peeled.

"OK."   Dodge nodded, returning his member to its nest.

By eleven the engines were running and taxi began a short time later.   Assembly was complete by noon and the bomber stream, with the 41st Combat Wing in the van, turned for the coast.

Almost before they crossed the Channel, the bombers began leaving thick contrails.

Hollis started easing **Cleopatra's Asp** in on Ransahoff's right as the French coast was approached.   Unexpectedly, H-y appeared in the hatchway."

Hollis lowered his mask enough to yell at him, "Where the hell are you going?"

H-y, holding a walk around oxygen bottle in one hand held up a bomb fuse can with the other.   It was filled with feces and toilet paper.   He was going to take it back and set it on the bomb bay doors to go out when they opened.

The odor filled the nostrils.

"Jesus Christ, H-y, couldn't you hold it?"

H-y, smiling behind his mask, shook his head.

"Don't put that in the bomb bay or we'll have to smell it all the way to the target.   Toss it out the waist.   That's an order."   Hollis pushed his mask against his face and inhaled deeply into his lungs.

H-y put the can on the deck and saluted, still smiling.   He passed back around the turret and disappeared.

"Pilot to top turret, how's it going?"

"Top to pilot, OK, Lieutenant.   Everybody's where they oughta be.   I saw the spares turn for home."

"Roger."

After a few minutes H-y reappeared and lowered himself back into the nose.   In so doing, he gave Hollis the 'OK' sign and winked.

Hollis looked up and saw the fighter escort weaving vapor trails back and forth.   As last wing in the Division, most of the escort was somewhere up ahead where the fighting usually started.   The few fighters he could see were most welcome.   The Germans saw them up there, too.

Leo banged his arm yelling, "You know I can still smell that."

Hollis could, too.

"Pilot to navigator, H-y I thought I told you to pitch that shit out the waist window.   Did you stick it in the bomb bay?"

"Roger, pilot.   The waist gunners told me if I pitched it out the back the odds were good it would fly back in my face.   What would *you* do, over?"

Throughout the plane ten men all laughed simultaneously.

The trip was fairly uneventful except for the smell, which after a time, was superseded by the tension and nobody seemed to notice anymore.   The wing up ahead, the 40th, was barely visible in the blue sky, the contrails which marked their passage dissipating by the time the First Bomb Wing reached the same point in space.

"IP, ten minutes."

"Radio to Pilot."

"Go ahead, Radio."

"Escort turned back.   They're in a fight up ahead."

"Roger, Radio."

Hollis felt his sphincter tighten involuntarily.   He looked for the P-47s, hoping they hadn't left yet, but they were gone.

"Bogies nine o'clock level," Hulse announced.

"They're coming around, watch 'em."

Hollis tucked in even closer to Ransahoff hoping Fissano kept his wits about him doing the same and not get buck fever staring helpless as the fighters winged around.   Hollis watched the German fighters, Me-109Gs he thought, perhaps a half dozen in number, fly several thousand yards ahead, bank sharply and hurl themselves at the lead group of the wing, the 91st.

Hollis saw pieces of bomber fly off, but from what he could see, nobody was burning or dropped out.   A few moments later, they climbed up, circled around and went after the lead group, head-on, lining up for seconds.   This time somebody was hit, for smoke emerged from one of the planes, slowing it down.   Hollis watched as the cripple drifted toward the back of the formation.   They were still a long way from home.   He was finished.

Hollis tightened his grip on the wheel.

They came around a third time, going after the 91st yet again.   Each new attack more aggressive than the last waiting a little longer to break off into a dive.

"IP five minutes."

"Pilot to crew, anybody see what happened to that 91st 'seventeen.   He was smoking."

"Pilot, Ball.   They got him.   Spun in.   I didn't see any chutes."

"Pilot to bombardier, warm up your sight and level your bubbles."

"Bombardier, thank you pilot, I *have* done this before."

"Here they come again, twelve o'clock level," Dodge announced.

Suddenly, the cockpit erupted with noise as Dodge fired his machine guns spewing tracers in a flat arc toward the oncoming fighters.   Other lines of tracers from other turrets followed suit.   Hollis could see the wings and noses of the fighters blink like flashbulbs, firing just before they flipped over onto their backs rocketing downward, away from the formation.

Hollis lifted his mask away from his face to let the drool and sweat escape silently praying they weren't next.

"IP."

Hollis watched as the wing took interval.   The lead group, the 91st, made a gentle, banking turn to the left.   Simultaneously, Begay swung the high group to the right for a minute before turning back to the left, rejoining the bomber stream in file.   Flak bursts, roiling black smudges, erupted in and around the formation.   The flak gunners in these U-boat ports had a reputation for accurate, deadly fire.   The bombers hadn't been here in a while, maybe they had grown fat and rusty on French cuisine and French whores.

The bomb bay doors opened with a sudden rush of air, scattering dust and the smell of cordite.   There was a sudden jolt and a bang.

"We're hit," Augie said.   "Right wing has some damage.   Outer panel.   Nothing leaking.   Should be OK, Pilot"

Not wanting to remove his eyes from Ransahoff he banged at Leo, an indication that he wanted his assessment.   A moment later, the OK sign was held up for him to see.   No bombs fell from Begay's bomb bay.

The bomb run seemed to take an inordinately long time.   He watched as the bomb bay doors started to close.   Dammit! Hollis yelled into his mask.

"Radio to bombardier!   Aztec is diverting to the secondary."

Aztec was the wing leader.   Hollis caught a glance at the ground, but could not discern anything.

"Pilot to bombardier, what's going on?"

"Strikes on the target.   The whole area is covered with smoke.   They're not gonna drop on an occupied country if they can't make out the target.   Lord knows, we don't want to hurt the wrong people."

Pity, Hollis thought.   He could sense the tension in Sully's voice.   He was having to work for a living.   He watched as Aztec dragged the three groups toward the alternate, the airfield at Chateau-Bougon.   It was close-by and almost immediately the doors cranked open again with another rush of air and **Cleopatra's Asp** slowed.

Hollis pulled   in close and, again, concentrated on Ransahoff.   As the bombers approached the airfield there were a few sporadic flak bursts, but it seemed more a demonstration of annoyance than a threat.   He stole a glance at the right wing.   There were small areas where the aluminum had been peeled back near the tip but nothing serious.

Cleopatra's Asp shuddered with the sudden release of the bomb load.   Hollis could feel the bomber rise into its wind.   Instinctively, he nosed it back down and reset the trim.

"Radio to bombardier, the bomb bay is clear."

Hollis could feel the doors grind shut once again, restoring aerodynamic purity to the plane.

"Ball. Bomb bay doors closed."

Aztec lead the bomber stream in a descending turn toward the ocean after the rally.   The bombers moved out from the Brittany coast and turned northwest, loosening up as they put France and the threat of fighter interception behind them.   The fighters were reluctant to stray too far out over the water.   If they were forced down, be it through enemy action or mechanical failure, the odds of survival were near zero.   Relaxed, the formation spread out and assumed a line of groups again.   Soon they were down to about a thousand feet so the planes could slide under an overcast.

As they passed Brest, someone made a comment about a U-boat in the water, but Hollis did not see it.   These were bad times for the U-boats.   The air offensive against the sub-pens had been halted several months ago.   It was a war the Navy seemed to be winning without much help from the Air Corps.   Which was just as well.   Everyone's impression was that the bombing campaign against the sub pens had been a big waste of time and treasure. They said you could actually see thousand pounders bouncing off the concrete.

They landed a little after six.   It had been a long tiring mission.   They checked the damage to the right wing.   A flak burst had punctured numerous holes in the outer panel of the wing and the wingtip.   None of the damage was structural.   It was all cosmetic and Moe would have the damage repaired in no time.

The clouds they had flown under were the advance guard of a front which descended over the British Isles by late evening, bringing rain.

Hollis sat at his desk composing a letter.   He was in a self-congratulatory mood both for acquitting himself well as the number two but, more importantly, completing his ninth mission. In his letter he told Jessie that at the rate he was accumulating missions, nine in a little over a month on ops, he would be home by Christmas, maybe even Thanksgiving.

A short time later, just before he climbed into bed, Otho came around to tell everybody that the squadron was being stood down for a week.

Chapter Thirty-six   **Crap**

Leo looked at Hollis and said, "You know every time that man comes in here he craps on us."

"Yeah, I know.   I say we shoot him."

Hollis, suddenly seized by a nebulous fear, replied softly, almost as an afterthought, "He can't help it, it's in his nature."   He looked down.   His hands were shaking.   What was it Otho said that would release such an adrenal surge?   They had been stood down before.   Was it the inflection in his voice?   No, Barbieri was too ornery and obnoxious to be clever or subtle.

No.   Hollis reckoned he had been touched by some metaphysical signal, some deductive logic, arisen within the subconscious perhaps, that calculated in an instant all the good and bad factors in the world and in his life and arrived at an awful sum: that he was probably going to die.   The witless Barbieri had merely triggered the math.   Maybe *this* was the premonition of death he had heard so much about.

The real war was not over some airfield in Belgium or a boat docked at some pier on a river in France.   The real war was over Schweinfurt and Munich and Berlin.   They would be going there soon.   Of that he had no doubt.   He couldn't stop his hands from shaking.   He could feel Leo's analytical stare and it added to his discomfort.

"What's wrong with you?"

"Do you think Selkirk is crazy?"

"Who?"

"Mickey Selkirk.   Do you think he's crazy?"

"I don't really know.   I never paid much attention to him.   I'm a copilot.   We tend to stick with our own kind.   There's pilots and navigators and sergeants and Jews and Negroes. Just like the Math Department didn't spend much time chatting with the English teachers.   I don't mix much with you pilots."

"Cut the crap, Leo."

Hollis could feel the intensity of Leo's eyes upon his flesh, like the heat from a blinding light he dared not look into.   "You think you're going crazy, too, don't you?" he asked.

Hollis did not answer.   He was afraid of it.   If he clasped his hands together their tremor became less visible.   Maybe Leo hadn't noticed.   Hollis broke into a cold sweat as if he had witnessed a Dickensonian apparition, a simultaneous visitation by the Ghost of Bombing Past, and with it the names and the faces, and Bombing Future, with it his own swift, certain and grisly death.

"Stop thinking about it, Jack.   Go have a beer or something.   Write another letter. Jerk off.   Do something.   Just stop thinking about it.   Unless you wanna drop your wings on Ransahoff's desk, too, put it out of your mind.   One day we will all die.   Nobody lives forever. Fly the missions and try to be careful."

That's it, Hollis thought, *I need to be more careful.*

Yet, hard as he tried, the thought would not leave him that tomorrow, or the day after that, held an unspeakable horror.   He did as Leo suggested.   Rather than turn out the lights and seek sanctuary in sleep no matter how potentially tortured, he sat and wrote another letter, a long one, telling Jessie how much he loved her and that she would always be the center of his life. When he read the letter he thought she might think it written by a stranger as it was barely legible.   She was a smart girl.   She would read it and know.   She might even get the letter after she had been dutifully notified by the Office of the Adjutant General of his death.   "The Secretary of War regrets to inform you..."   Then he remembered that, according to the Army, she was nothing to him and that the person opening the telegram would probably be his mother. Jessie would know by the anguished shriek that would echo across the lawn.   He closed his eyes and tore up the letter.   He looked around and saw that Leo was fast asleep, untouched by the terror that gripped him, snuggled safe in the cocoon of his naiveté.

He thought of Jessie, her sweet smile, the perfect symmetry of her face and cried, convinced as never before of his own mental fragility.

Friday, September 17, 1943

Hollis awakened feeling slightly silly that his imagination had gotten the best of him. He had brought his fears under control after the Schweinfurt mission, by consciously ignoring them, and had been lulled into a false sense of optimism by a string of milk runs.   Stuttgart had been too frightening to register.   It was yesterday's trip to Nantes, where the Germans had brought the battle close aboard again, that had reignited his terror, a terror he thought he had under control.   He understood now why Eisenberg and Cassidy and so many others simply lived from one day to the next, one mission to the next, withdrawn, sullen, refusing to think of the future because from where they stood there was none.

Perhaps Selkirk had arrived there, too.   He had undergone a slow, seemingly irresistible, transformation from the happy-go-lucky Vermont farmer he had met a month ago to a depressed, ill-tempered combat pilot with a short fuse.

Hollis thought that maybe what was happening to him was just the normal evolutionary change combat wrought on the psyche.   It was inevitable.   Men like Leo escaped the ugly metamorphosis because they lacked the imagination to visualize their own death.   It was something that happened to the other guy.   The Cahills and Cassidys and Codys of the world. Was Robbie Owens still feeling invincible when the bullet cracked into the back of his skull?

Maybe it was all a matter of dumb luck.   If Robbie'd been wearing his helmet all he'd have to show for the incident was a monstrous headache, a sore neck and the mutilated corpse of a Jap sniper at his feet.

Then again, perhaps he *was* sliding into madness.

Either way, he was hungry and his bladder was full.   He got up, it was unlikely today was the day he would die.

Leo returned to the room with a towel over his shoulder mumbling how he'd donate a month's pay if it would speed up Beamis in his effort to reestablish dependable, running hot water.

"Well, good morning, Sunshine," he said to Hollis.   "Feeling better?"

"What do you mean?"

"You looked like you'd seen a ghost last night.   You feeling better?"

Hollis shook his head uncertain how to answer.   It was so unmanly to admit fear.   Yet he knew Leo better than anyone.   If he was to confide in anybody it would be Leo.   "Naw, I just think I'm catching a cold or something.   That's all."

Leo stared at Hollis for an uncomfortably long few seconds and said, "Oh."

The pregnant moment was broken by a slight tap on the door.   Ian Thomas was standing with a bundle of laundry in his arms.

"Morning suhs," he said and stepped into the room and placed a bundle on each bed.

Hollis looked at the small parcel of clothing bound with twine and said, "Thank you, Ian. How much do I owe you?"

"Three shillings, Mr. 'ollis."

Hollis went to the pants hanging from a hook in the closet to retrieve the money.

"Yer's comes to three shillings also, Leftenant Wychulis."

"Very good, young man."   As Leo fished around for the change he turned to Ian and said, "Say, it's Friday.   How come you're not in school?"

"Feedin' me mum is more important than Latin, suh.   Besides, our teacher is in the Land Army and they have some manner of militree exercise today."

"Isn't that some sort of secret?   Military exercises?   Perhaps you should keep that information to yourself."

Hollis knew Leo was chiding the boy, but Ian turned serious and said, "Not much secret about harvesting beets, now is it, Leftenant?   I 'ardly think the Germans can derive much militree advantage by the knowledge of the bloody beet harvest, whot?"

Now, Hollis wondered who was kidding whom.

"Hey, Ian, how's your math lessons coming along?"

"Long division, suh.   She's a bitch."

Leo chuckled, "'She's a bitch'?   Now where'd you hear an expression like that?"

"Sergeant Snavely said that about one of 'is engines.   'e let me sit in the cockpit while 'e run 'er up.   Backfired, she did.   'e never could get it to run right."

Leo smiled again.   They were contaminating a whole race of people, Hollis thought, unable to contain his own smile.   The New World shitting contemptuously on the Old.

"Well, maybe I can help you.   I'm a math teacher back in the States."

"Really?   Leftenant Sully told me you were a 'ollywood movie mogul, whatever that is. You know any movie stars, Mr. Leo?"

"Yeah, I'm married to one."

"Go on wif, ya," Ian said, failing to conceal his incredulity.

"No, Ian.   It's true," Hollis said.   "Show him Christie's picture."

"Sure, Ian here she is."   Leo handed him the leatherette case with her pictures in it. Hollis watched as Ian's eyes attached themselves to the one in which Christie was wearing the sarong, a coy smile gracing her lovely face, her decolletage bursting forth like ripe melons on a shelf.

"Blimey,"   he muttered.   "She's a real looker, suh.   Oh, excuse me, suh.   I meant no disrespect.   She's very beautiful.   You say she's in the motion pictures?"

"Yeah, a couple of Busby Berkeley musicals."

"Who's Busby Berkeley?"

"It's not important, Ian," Leo said as he returned the picture case to the shrine.   "Now, about the math."

"Is arithmetic the same in America as it is 'ere?"

"Sure.   Even on Mars one and one still equal two."

The boy wrinkled his brow in contemplation.   "In that case, Mr. Wychulis, let's 'ave at it.   In the meantime, you still owe me three shillings."

Leo dropped the money onto the boy's outstretched palm and said, "Bring yer lessons by and we'll see what we can do."

Ian made careful note in his ledger, again bringing the small notebook close to his eyes. "Dirties?"

"No," Hollis replied.

"Me neither," Leo added.

"Very well, suhs.   Thank you."   The boy turned, stepped back into the hall, picked up a fresh satchel of clean clothes in his arms and moved on.

"Little Robber Baron," Leo muttered, still smiling.   "Reason he can't do his long division is because he can't see the bloody blackboard."

"Probably."

"We've got to get that boy some spectacles."

"How do you propose we do that?"

"Maybe you could go talk to the Chaplain again."

The door at the end of the hall opened with a bang and Beamis walked into the room. "Hey, Lieutenant Hollis, Major Ransahoff wants to see you at eleven hundred in his office."

"Now what?"

"Beats me, sir.   Whatever it is, good luck."

Leo buttoned his shirt asking, "What, do you suppose, he meant by that?"

"Christ, who knows, Leo?   You must think I'm clairvoyant."

"Hollis, you don't have to be a mind-reader to be able to figure out that big things are in the offing," Ransahoff said, rocking back in his swivel chair.   "I want you to learn to lead the Squadron."   Hollis started squirming in his seat, but before he could blurt out any sharp retort, Ransahoff continued, "I know you hate this chickenshit.   You'd have been a lot smarter riding out the war in medical school or some supply outfit in New Zealand.   But you violated the first rule of military conduct--you volunteered for a combat assignment.   So here you are."

"Let Otho do it."

"Otho isn't the pilot you are; not that you're all that great.   Believe it or not, you have more combat experience.   Whatever your personal turmoil, you and your crew appear competent and reliable.   I can't trust Selkirk; he's just not up to it.   Watanabe was a copilot until a couple of weeks ago.   Spats, Robertshaw, DeBerg, Fissano and Powell are still wet behind the ears.   That leaves you.   You've flown nine missions and acquitted yourself well.   I can't lead every mission so with no other option in sight, you're it."

"I don't want to do it, Dutch."

"Listen, Hollis, I'm not going to give you much choice here.   Whether you've gotten this far through skill or pure luck does not matter to me.   You're here and you're all I've got and you're it."

"Shit."

"That business with the ice cream, that was a nice thing you did."

"You know that laundry boy, Ian Thomas?"

"The little kid?   Yeah."

"You think we could get him a pair of glasses?"

"No.   Report to Group and meet with Rager and Farrell.   They'll give you the inside poop on what you need to know.   Pay attention.   They're very good."

As ordered, Hollis reported to Group and met with Beck Farrell and Barney Rager. They, along with Bud Hightower, were the lead pilots with the Bangmaster as the copilot. Joining in the instruction, which took the form of a bull session rather than a formal didactic lesson, was 'Scorch' Alexander, a nickname the result of several unexplained engine fires. Hollis, ever the student, took notes, much to the surprise of Farrell and Rager who kept exchanging glances.

When they were done, he stepped out of headquarters, pulled his cap down tight and bowed his head into the driving rain.   He watched for puddles as he walked, his mind filled with conflict.   He was flattered, even if it might be damned by faint praise, that he was somehow good enough to be given the task of leading the Squadron.

By some process of perverse natural selection he had risen to the top of the outfit.   An unenviable position, he thought.   Yet there was some concomitant sense of satisfaction or veiled compliment to be chosen from amongst his peers.   It was both a blessing and a curse.   It was *his* squadron, they were *his* comrades- in-arms.   He belonged to the tribe and they were rewarding him with greater responsibility, something he neither sought or wanted.   If someone, be it Ransahoff or Van Patten or even Chaplain Brown thought he possessed the necessary skill or wit or balls to serve the greater good, who was he to deny them?   Leo was right.   He should quit worrying and get on with it.   He wondered if Oquist or Dunston thought that.

Up until this moment he was responsible for only ten men, one airplane and making sure, to the best of his ability, he delivered his bomb load to the place he was told.   Now he would command sixty men, in six airplanes, charged with placing all of their bombs on a target.   He had only wanted to do his twenty-five and go home.   No heroics, no fanfare.   No more, no less.

His mind swirled with their words.   Rager kept saying over and over again to *make sure your navigator stays on top of this and tell your copilot to do that.   You'll need them now more than ever.   You're not flying for one plane or three but for all six.*   As he walked, the rain dripping steadily from the brim of his cap, he kept thinking of Leo and H-y.   He began to have serious doubts about the wisdom of this whole business.   Maybe they were making a terrible mistake.

Every navigator in this group, Rager said, *should be able to take over at any moment and lead the group home.   But that is especially true for a lead navigator...*   Poor H-y.   He was out of their league.

Hollis thought of Barney Rager, a regular stick and rudder man.   Fearless, he had a dashing persona.   A real Hot Rock; immensely popular and capable.   The scar like a saber slash across the brow of his eye.   Rumor had it that he was shacking up with a woman at the U.S. Embassy who had an apartment on Grosvenor Square, probably that blond bombshell he had seen waiting for him outside the Savoy.   He was held in awe by all who knew him.   Now Hollis had become one of the chosen.   He lit a cigarette, trying to shield it against the downpour, convinced it was all a big mistake.   He wasn't in their league either.   He would tell Ransahoff to find someone else.   For the good of the Squadron, the Group, the war effort.

"What did Ransahoff want?"   Leo asked when he returned to the room.   "He want to make me a first pilot again?"

Hollis was still at a loss about what to say and in no mood to explain himself.   He didn't want to reveal anything.   Besides he had grown tired of talking to Leo whose constant questions and cherubic cheerfulness had grown annoying.   Instead, he kicked off his muddy shoes, mumbled something about the chaplain and laid down on the bed to take a nap, the universal refuge.

Just before he fell asleep Barbieri poked his head through the door and said, "Well, I guess this makes you some sort of hot shit now, eh Hollis?"

Leo looked at Hollis and asked, "What does he mean by that?"

"Dunno."

Hollis figured he had been asleep for about an hour when he heard a woman's voice. His first thought was that somebody had snuck another whore onto the base.   As he swung his legs onto the floor Beamis appeared at the door and said, "That's him" and pointed to Leo.

The woman removed her shawl, glistening with rain and said, "Are you Leftenant Wychulis?"

"Yes."

"My name is Lucretia Thomas.   I'm Ian's mother.

Always the gentleman, Leo came to his feet and waited for her to extend her hand which the woman cautiously did.

"You do a nice job on our laundry, Ma'am," he said.   "Just the right amount of starch."

Hollis studied the woman as she spoke.   She lacked any sophistication, plain, simply dressed.   Not unattractive, but ordinary.   Her cheeks were rosy, the result of the lashing her face had received from the wind-driven rain.

"Leftenant I want to thank you for your offer to tutor Ian wif 'is long division.   I won't be able to pay you.   But I would be 'appy to work out an arrangement for your laundry."

Leo grinned, "That won't be necessary."

"I insist."

"No, really," Leo said, clearly becoming embarrassed by the fuss.

"Then you must come to dinner.   And I will not take no for your answer."

"Well, I ah...   Yeah, sure.   I'd love to."

She turned to Hollis and said, "You must be Leftenant 'ollis."

Hollis stood and, having seen Leo establish the protocol, waited until she offered her hand before shaking it, also.

Perhaps, as an afterthought, she suggested that he join them for dinner.   Hollis envisioned a barren cupboard and said, "No thanks, Mrs. Thomas.   I have other plans."

She returned her attention to Leo and said, "May we expect you tomorrow?   About four?   Ian will come fetch you."

"That would be nice.   Four it is.   Unless of course" he pointed up to the ceiling "you know."

"Of course."   She turned again to Leo and, saying "Good day," took her leave.

Hollis smiled at Leo and said, "Maybe you can go to the Chaplain and see if he can liberate some ice cream for you."   He fell back onto the bed and added. "Call me when it's time for supper."

For the next two days, Hollis kept to himself trying to figure out a way to get out of his new assignment.   Short of punching Van Patten in the mouth or carving his initials in Gleason's bald head, there was nothing he could think of to remedy his predicament.   Going to Ransahoff and simply saying he didn't want to do it would not suffice.   *Don't tell me you aren't going to do it just because you don't feel like it, you little chickenshit!   There's a fuckin' war on!* would be the predictable reply and rather than expose himself to a tirade, one he knew he would rightfully deserve, he just kept to himself and pondered the meaning of it all, the war and his minuscule, inconsequential role in it.   He still knew he was going to die, being in the lead of the squadron just meant they would get to him first.

Leo had dinner with Ian and his mother two evenings in a row.   For reasons known but to him, Leo was very closed mouth about it.   Hollis decided not to inquire.   If there was something Leo wanted him to know he would say so.

Finally, after spending another afternoon with them Leo said, "That boy can't see worth shit.   Somehow we have to get that boy some glasses.   Maybe we can cut the ends off some Coke bottles and wire them together."   He turned to Hollis and added, "You've got to do something."

"Now what makes you think *I've* got to do something?"

"Because you're the first pilot and I'm just a lousy copilot."

Hollis ignored him.   Leo sat on his bed and looked at Hollis, "When were you going to tell me they were making you a lead pilot?"

Slightly flustered, Hollis said, "They want us to fly the squadron lead, Leo.   I didn't think it was newsworthy enough to comment about it."

"Is that what Ransahoff wanted to talk to you about the other day?"

"Yeah, actually it was."

"Look, Jack," Leo said with an emphasis on his words Hollis had rarely heard, "as you so frequently told us in Phase, we're a team.   What one does affects all of us.   You eventually reached the point where we simply ignored you and your bleatings.   This is different.   If you have something you need to tell us, for the good of the order you should say so and stop thinking this war is about you personally."

Hollis mulled over the humiliation he had just been handed.   "You're right.   Tomorrow I'll talk to the Chaplain about some glasses.   In the meantime, I'm going over to the Club."

Hollis stood at the bar and downed a double bourbon.   He drank another quickly.   The alcohol made the blood warm inside his veins.   Regrettably, Leo was right.   The war wasn't just about him.

That night Hollis dreamt he was leading the squadron in a great air battle and by the time they reached the target they were the only ones left.   They were all alone.   He watched as the German fighters flew alongside, licking their chops, waiting to count coup on this one last plane. "We're next," Leo said.   He awakened wishing he could have at least one good dream so he could wake up happy.

The next morning, Dodge rapped on the door and walked in.   It was unusual to see any enlisted man inside their quarters other than Beamis and the occasional corporal from the Squadron office so when he appeared, Leo could not resist the opportunity to chide him.

"Hey Noah, what are you doing here?   This is Officer's Country."

"'Morning, Lieutenants, I was just over at the Office and they told me we've been assigned a brand new Fortress.   I just thought I'd come over and tell you and see if you wanted to go down and see it."

Hollis, his head throbbing from the bourbon, said, "Does it have two wings, four engines and a rudder?"

"Yeah."

"Then I've already seen it."

"Come on, Lieutenant.   The crew is going to meet out there in half an hour and Lieutenant Otho told the crew chief we could take it for a short hop."

Leo and Hollis exchanged glances.   "OK," Leo said.

"Tell you what, Noah," Hollis added, "Anybody who wants to go can meet us out there in an hour.   I've got to get something to eat."

Dodge smiled and agreed.

"Good," Leo said, "a little flying time might do us some good."

An hour later, the crew gathered by the new B-17 which was as yet unnamed.   Hollis had checked with Otho and he had, indeed, told them they could take it for a short transition flight to familiarize themselves with its new features.   *A few touch and goes then park it back where you found it*.

Outwardly, it looked like every other Fortress he had ever seen except for the fact that a large bulbous gun turret had been grafted onto the chin below the bombardier's perch.   The Fortresses had lacked any real protection in the forward area giving rise to the frontal attack and the necessity of field modifying the bombers by placing one or two hand held machine guns through the Plexiglas nosepiece.   Most of them were jury-rigged and not very sturdy.   Recoil would often crack the Plexiglas and to overcome this braces had to be fitted to absorb the shock as they had done with **Cleopatra's Asp**.   This turret, which looked like a cook's kettle with two guns poking out and a faring behind it, was designed to take the place of the hand-held guns.   It was fired by the bombardier using a remotely-controlled gun sight.   In the process they had taken away the two cheek guns which were fired by the navigator.   When H-y saw that his gun had been taken away he bitched loudly.   "How can I defend myself?" he spouted.   Sully told him to *knock it off, he never hit anything with it anyway.   Now maybe you can concentrate on your navigatin'*.

The bomber was equipped with vented Tokyo Tanks and was capable of carrying a heavier load, the crew chief, Charlie Wilcox,   told them.   Therefore she's not quite as fast as the earlier 'F's otherwise she was pretty much the same plane.   Since the flight was not mandatory and none of the gunners seemed interested in a new plane the crew consisted of the four officers and Dodge.   By regulation, the aircraft was forbidden to leave the ground without a radio operator and Quinn was nowhere to be found.   So Dodge grabbed the first radio man he could find and coerced him into a quick joy ride.   With Wilcox's blessing they fired up the engines and took off.

Hollis had filed a flight plan with the Squadron office which consisted of a direct flight to the coast at Felixstowe and a turn south to Clacton-on-Sea and a turn back to base.   It would probably take no more than an hour and a half and he would have them home for lunch. Wilcox had the armorer load the chin turret with several hundred rounds to give Sully a chance to learn how to use it.

For Hollis it was great fun.   He hedge-hopped all the way to Felixstowe never taking the plane above a couple of hundred feet.   He buzzed a train and people on the ground, nearly knocking a farmer off his combine and causing his draft horse to rear.   He was flying with reckless abandon, taking the plane around church steeples like a slalom skier.   The countryside was a green blur beneath the bomber.   The plane had not yet been painted with Group or Squadron markings so Hollis felt no need to worry about being disciplined as he was well below the minimum altitude for flying.   He noticed Leo's head snapping around as he looked out the window at the sights flashing past.   Down below, he imagined H-y holding on for dear life, cursing his great view out the front of the plane.

When they were over the North Sea, Hollis told Sully to fire away.   The bomber shook with a satisfying recoil as two lines of tracer lashed out at the sea ahead of them raising hundreds of small white geysers.   As suddenly as it started the firing stopped.

"Bombardier to Dodge.   These guns jammed.   I pulled on the charging handles until my arms are about to break.   Come down and give me a hand."

Dodge, who stood between Hollis and Leo, unplugged his headset and climbed down into the nose.   A short time later the guns fired a short burst and quit.   Again they fired a long burst then abruptly stopped.

By the time they reached Clacton-on-Sea Sully had fired no more than about ten seconds worth of bursts.   Hollis climbed the plane to two thousand feet and let Leo fly it home.

"What's wrong with the guns?" he asked Dodge as he returned from the nose.

"There's a little assist motor that helps the gun feed.   It keeps jamming up at the end of the feed chute after he stops firing.   I think it's a design flaw in the motor.   It doesn't shut off for a few seconds and keeps pushing in rounds until they jam.   I'll tell Wilcox when we get back."

Hollis gave him a thumbs up.

Then Dodge yelled, "Sully wants **Cleopatra's Asp** back."

Hollis smiled and shook his head.

When they deplaned, Wilcox was there to greet them asking Hollis how she did.

"Nice airplane.   We had trouble with the chin turret though.   Talk to Dodge."

"What kind of trouble?"

"Feeder chute kept jamming."

After Wilcox turned to find Dodge, Leo came over, saying, "I feel kind of bad for Moe Jablonski."

Hollis turned and heard H-y telling a corporal, "Belinda.   Right up there under my windows.   B-E-L-I-N-D-A."

"Yes sir, I know how to spell it."

H-y was obviously excited, like a kid with a new toy.   The explanation for this emotion was completely lost on Hollis.   What was not was the fact that this new plane sat on Cassidy's old hardstand.

"What would you like to name her?" Wilcox asked.

"Well, the whole crew isn't here and nothing really comes to mind," Hollis replied.

"She's your airplane, Charlie.   She really belongs to you.   I'm just borrowing it once in a while. You name her."   He saw Wilcox break into a big smile.

"What are you grinning about?" Hollis asked.

"Cassidy would never let us name the plane.   He never said why.   We offered to let him or the crew pick a name way back in Texas, but he never did."   Wilcox reached into the pocket of his grease-stained leather jacket and pulled out a picture of a pin-up which had obviously spent a lot of time in his pocket creased by countless foldings and unfoldings.   It was a Varga ripped from an old <u>Esquire</u> of a smiling, demure young lady lying on her back, her long willowy legs extended skyward at an angle.   She wore only high heels.   "I'm going to call her **La Femme Fatale**."

"Nice," Hollis replied.

Staring up at the nose Sully turned to Hollis and asked, "I wonder why they gave us a new plane?"

Hollis glanced obliquely at Leo who returned the glance.

"Beats me."

"They like us," Leo responded.

Later that evening, Hollis wrote Jessie of his thrilling romp over the verdant English countryside.   He told her that they were stood down for a week and the boredom was stifling. He told her he was being groomed to lead the squadron.   Hardly anybody below the rank of captain ever leads a formation.   Now here he was,   First Lieutenant for less than a month and he was leading.   Jokingly, he speculated on how he would hold up under the strain of command. On paper it was a joke.   His heart and mind were still rife with doubt.

As Hollis stuffed the envelope, Leo came into the room, from where he did not know, undressed quickly and climbed into bed without saying a word.

Hollis smoked a cigarette and did the same.

Tuesday, September 21, 1943

For the past several nights there had been pre-mission activity, but no strikes had been launched.   Bad weather over the fields or the target, indecision.   It didn't matter.   People were getting edgy.   Hollis could see it in their faces and by the way they spoke.   Even the stand down had started to take its toll on the emotions.   The Squadron had received several new planes and three new crews as part of the relentless build up.   The rosters of the squadrons had been expanded from nine combat crews to twelve.   There were new faces, new names, new stories.   Hollis had not met them, but heard their names: Weldon, Balducci and Kehoe.   The planes were all new 'F's.   Fitted with Tokyo tanks but no chin turrets.   The last of the breed. The Fortresses now being turned out from Douglas, Vega and Boeing were all fitted with chin turrets and designated 'G' models.

Hollis sat at the desk after breakfast and read an old copy of <u>Time</u> magazine.   Leo reclined on his bed to reread his mail.   The door flew open and H-y walked into the room and sat on Hollis's bed.   He had a large grin on his face.

"What's so funny?" Leo asked.

"I'm off the crew."

Leo sat up.   "What?"

"I've been taken off the crew.   They're making me a lead navigator.   I move over to Group this afternoon.   I got some special talent."

"What is it?" Hollis asked.

"Don't give me any of your bullshit, Hollis.   I'm going to be the Assistant Group Navigator.   They're going to work me into the lead position."

"How odd," Leo added.

H-y came to his feet saying, "Well, I just wanted you guys to know."   He extended his hand to Leo.   "It's been great flying with you, Leo"   Leo shook his hand.   H-y turned to Hollis, "You, too, John."

Hollis came to his feet hoping his utter astonishment did not reveal itself.

"I guess congratulations are in order," Hollis said.   "Good luck to you, H-y.   See you around."

"Sure thing."   With that, he turned and walked out of the room.

After they heard the door at the end of the hall slam closed, Leo turned to Hollis and said, "I have no faith that we will win this war when they make the likes of Howard Elias Smith lead navigator of a whole bombardment group."

Hollis knew H-y had been made an assistant to the Group navigator, Sudberry.   Hollis thought that was effectively shelving him. He recalled his conversation with Rager and Farrell. Perhaps they had perceived some tell-tale sign in his expression when they began discussing the role of the navigator in the lead ship and deduced leaving H-y on the crew was a distinct liability. He would probably never know.   "That's a surprise."

"I'll say," Leo said.   "Sully used to tell me he was never sure if H-y knew where we were half the time.   He's gotten us lost at least twice.   We were surprised you didn't boot him off the crew after we got lost over Kansas.   The crew couldn't decide whether to admire your loyalty or curse your stupidity.

"Sully would say that by the end of a flight he would have pencils and maps and his calculator strewn all over the nose.   He'd get this confused look on his face and hit Sully in the back with a pencil to get his attention so he could help him look for some checkpoint.   If it weren't for Darky we'd still be looking for Ridgewell.   Not a real confidence-builder."

Hollis felt both embarrassed and relieved.   "I wonder who they will give us now?"

"Won't really matter, he can't be worse than what we've had to put up with all this time."

"I guess I dropped the ball on this."

"No real harm done.   We're going to be leading the Squadron, maybe these people aren't as dumb as we think."   He looked at his watch.   "We better get going.   We've got an intelligence lecture in half an hour."

"Given any thought as to what his special talent might be?"

After dinner, with Leo in tow, Hollis headed for the Officer's Club.   No alert was on so the place was crowded.   Hollis found Sully at the bar.

"You hear the news?"

"I helped him pack," Sully responded.   "Things are looking up.   Now, hopefully, I won't have to listen to him fart and stink up the nose.   If he threw one more pencil at my head I was going to kill him with it.   He was so proud of that big gun pokin' out his window.   The son of a bitch hardly ever fired it.   I think he was scared of it.   He didn't want links and hot shells falling all over his maps.   I had to push him out of the way to fire the damned thing.   Can't say as I'm sorry to see the guy leave.   He couldn't find his own dick with both hands.   He knew how to get chicks, though."

Hollis looked around the room.   There were many unfamiliar faces.   Ransahoff sat in the corner and appeared to be giving the straight poop to three new pilots.   Probably Weldon, Balducci and Kehoe.   Hollis tried to figure out who was who.

He saw Selkirk standing alone at the end of the bar.   He was about to go over to him when he heard someone call his name, "You Hollis?"

Hollis turned and saw a short, stocky Lieutenant, a stubby cigar protruding tersely from the corner of his mouth.   He was in need of a shave.

"Yeah, I'm Hollis."

The man extended his hand.   "I'm Cobb, your new navigator."   He pulled the cigar from his mouth, a tenuous string of saliva stretched back momentarily to his lip, and he placed it in an ashtray.   Hollis studied it.   It looked like a wet, brown turd.

Chapter Thirty-seven   **Nantes**

Thursday, September 23, 1943

"Wake up, Lieutenant."

"Beamis?" Hollis asked, awakened from sound sleep.

"Yes sir.   You need to get up."

"I thought we were stood down?"

"Yes sir, they are, but you're not.   They want you over at Group in half an hour."

"Why?"

"Dress warm."

"What time is it?"

"Zero Zero thirty."

"Jesus Christ," he muttered as he threw the blankets back and flipped his feet to the floor. "This has got to be some sort of mistake."

"You Lieutenant John Hollis?"

"Don't fuck with me, Beamis."

"Then it's no mistake.   You got half an hour."

Leo started to get up.   Beamis turned to him and said, "Go back to sleep sir.   You ain't goin' nowhere today."

In the dark he could see Leo resume his former position.

Hollis gathered his toiletries and cursed softly stepping into the cold night.   He shivered against the chill as he walked alone on the cinder path, his booted feet making the only sound he heard.

He entered the latrine praying for hot water and wondering what they had in store for him.   Whatever it was couldn't be good.

He doubted Beamis would light up the water heater for one lone shaver and he was right, the water was cold near to freezing which only added to his discomfort.   He slept better when he went to bed knowing he would not get awakened for a mission.   So it was a rude surprise to find himself splashing water on his face at twelve thirty in the morning.   He calculated he had been asleep for no more than two hours when Beamis walked in.

He heard a commotion and looked around to see Selkirk stumble in and urinate into the trough.   He was drunk.

When he was finished, Selkirk walked over to the sink and splashed water in his face then pulled up the front of his olive-drab tee shirt to wipe it off.   He noticed Hollis standing at the sink, shaving soap on his face.

"Where are you going?" he mumbled, his body swaying slightly.

"Don't know."

"See ya," he said as he turned to leave.

"You're drunk."

"Who are you, my mother?" he said as he stumbled back into the night.

Hollis was surprised.   Why didn't he just piss in the bushes like everybody else? Maybe he was too drunk to recall the alternative.

Hollis quickly dressed and headed for Group.   He looked up at the sky as he rode his bike.   No stars.

When he arrived at the Operations building he stepped into a brightly lit room with teletype machines clattering and cigarette and pipe smoke clouding the air.   He saw H-y over in the corner figuring something out on a map.   His hat was cocked back on his head and his legs were crossed Indian-style as he sat on the table absorbed in whatever task Assistant Group Navigatin' required.

Hollis walked over to Begay who was looking at a clipboard.   Duckworth, in flying clothes, stood beside him.   He was likely the Bangmaster.

"Major, Hollis reporting as ordered."

"Huh?   Oh, good.   Hollis you're flying copilot with the low squadron lead."   He looked at his watch.   "Go get some breakfast.   Briefing is at 0200."

Without acknowledgment he was about to leave when he turned and asked, "Who am I flying with?"

Begay looked at the clipboard and said, "Lemaster."

The Combat Mess was practically deserted when he arrived.   It was only a little past one. Typical military snafu to wake somebody up an hour before it was necessary. There was considerable activity by the cooks.   Food, today it was powdered eggs and bacon, was already being set out, an indication that soon the early arrivals would start shuffling in.

Hollis walked down the line pushing his tray along and watched as the amorphous, offensive gray-yellow lump was ladled heavily onto it by one of the cooks.   "Good morning, Lieutenant."

Hollis looked up and saw a smiling corporal who seemed genuinely interested that Hollis have a good morning.

"Good morning," Hollis said, trying to return the smile.

"Good luck."

"Thanks."   Hollis took his tray and a small glass of juice and a steaming mug of coffee to a table and sat.   He spread a layer of catsup onto the eggs in hopes this might enliven or otherwise modify their taste, but he had no real desire to eat them, his stomach, as usual, knotted tight as a fist.   As he sipped the coffee, careful not to burn his tongue, he tried to recall who Lemaster was.   A captain, one of the originals in the 534th.   That was about it.   He wasn't even sure he would recognize him when he walked in.   He thought his first name might be Keith.

A few men sauntered into the Mess.   Then a few more.   Soon the place was filled.   As Hollis studied their faces he wondered what the target was.   Up early, might be big.   It was cloudy.   Maybe get scrubbed again.   For four out of the last six days, missions had been called off during various stages of preparation.   Perhaps that would happen today.

The room grew noisy and rather than sit with unfamiliar faces Hollis emptied the contents of his tray into the garbage can and left.   Outside he heard his name again.   He turned to look, recognizing Scorch Alexander in the dark.

"They put you in one of the lead ships?" he asked.

"Yeah.   I'm flying with Lemaster."   Hollis lit a cigarette.

"I know him.   He's a good man.   Cavannaro lets him lead all the time."

"You?"

"Yeah.   I'm riding shotgun with Bonner."

Hollis didn't feel like conversing so he wished him luck and walked off toward the briefing room, sucking in smoke as he walked.

Duckworth took the stage and began.   "I'm today's Bangmaster.   Our target--"   there was a hush "is Nantes.   The U-boat tender on the River Loire.   The same target as last week."

"I guess this means we didn't hit it," was whispered from the crowd.

"Probably won't today neither," came a response.

Hollis listened as the details were given.   He forced himself to pay close attention.   In the unlikely event Lemaster got hurt, he would be leading the squadron.   Even so, the briefing had a numbing quality to it that made paying attention a chore.   Nantes would be a long haul, as it had been before.   Escort part of the way, much of the trip over water.   Maybe this wouldn't be so bad.   It would be his tenth mission.   They all counted regardless of which seat he was in. It would knock his count out of synch with the rest of the crew, but he didn't care.   He studied H-y standing against the wall.   He wasn't dressed for flying.   He looked bored, too.

In the Equipment Room, he sought out Lemaster and found him.   Lemaster acted like he knew who Hollis was, that they had been friends for a long time.   Where this familiarity came from Hollis did not know.

Lemaster had a large smile and cheerful demeanor.   He didn't seem scared at all.   He told Hollis that he would tell him everything he needed to know to steer a squadron.   Did he remember how to be a copilot?

Hollis nodded, not sure if he was kidding, and said, yes, he remembered.

The Fortress was as old as **Cleopatra's Asp**.   It had seen some fighting, too.   The name on the nose was ***der kriegsbringer*** in bold red letters.   Aptly named, Hollis thought.

Lemaster introduced Hollis to the crew.   They listened intently as he told them of the mission and reminded them of their tasks.   It looked like a good crew.   When he finished, he turned to Hollis and told him to pass out the escape kits.

"Son of a bitch!   I forgot 'em."

"You're the copilot today, maybe you better go get them."

Hollis looked around and saw an empty jeep idling at the next hardstand.   He ran to it clumsily clomping in the grass in his flying boots.   He commandeered the vehicle and tore off down the perimeter strip toward the Headquarters block, thoughtless to the possibility he might plow into something in the dark.   Fortunately, he didn't have too far to go.   He signed for the kits, gathered them up in a small satchel and for good measure grabbed a fist-full of Hershey Bars, tossing them in too, and raced back to the hardstand.   Hollis handed a kit to each crewman, saying as Leo always did, "I want it back, I want it back, I want it back," as it left his hand.   The one remaining he tucked into his pant leg pocket and zipped it shut.   To make amends for his stupidity, he handed out the candy bars with a smile and an 'eat up.'

"Hey," someone yelled from the dark, "did you take my jeep?"

"Yeah," Hollis yelled back.   "It's sitting right here.   Sorry.   I had to borrow it."   The voice sounded familiar.   It was Van Patten.

Van Patten gave Hollis a stern glance, but did not say anything.   He got into his jeep and drove off.

"Sorry," Hollis said again knowing Van Patten could not hear him.

The crew didn't converse much, huddling together under the wing trying to stay warm. Hollis joined their periphery and smoked.   He was embarrassed that he had forgotten the escape kits and then unwittingly stole the CO's jeep to retrieve them.

"Stations," Lemaster announced.   The men came to their feet and walked to the back edge of the hardstand and, standing shoulder to shoulder, urinated simultaneously.   Hollis joined them, not wanting to be the odd man out.   As he headed toward the nose he walked away a short distance and for good measure, heaved his stomach contents into the grass.

Hollis settled into the copilot's seat and adjusted it to his liking.   Not wanting to make any more rookie mistakes, Hollis took the laminated card and carefully called off each item just like he demanded from Leo.   It was still dark and he kept the flashlight beam as shrouded with his hand as he could so as not to ruin anybody's night vision.

Soon the engines were running.   The hot blue glow of the exhausts lit up across the field casting an eerie incandescence beneath each wing.

"Green flare," the engineer said.   All eyes in the cockpit turned in the direction of the tower.   The two green flares seemed extraordinarily brilliant in the dark.   They cast their own light back onto the tower until they returned to earth and bounced onto the grass of the infield, burning themselves down to small green cinders.

"Brakes."

"Brakes off," Hollis replied, releasing the handle.   Lemaster inched the bomber forward slowly in staggering fashion to test the brakes and follow the flashlight waved by the crew chief guiding the plane onto the perimeter strip.   Lemaster kept his head out the window keeping a wary eye on the edge of the perimeter strip, steering the bomber along by brakes and outboard engines.   Hollis did the same out his window.

Across the field, landing lights flicked on and off as the bombers felt their way along in the dark.   When all had lined up waiting, the controllers held the planes a little longer than planned.   Waiting, perhaps for weather to clear or the ceiling to rise a bit more.

Eventually, take off began.   Lemaster took *der kreigsbringer* up into the overcast and circled the buncher.   It was a dark cloud.   Dawn should be breaking soon, Hollis thought. *Not soon enough.*   He felt panic start to seize him.   Lemaster looked cool, too cool, knowing that in this black abyss lurked seventeen other bombers all swimming around the same beacon in some sort of random Brownian fashion.

Suddenly, red and green wingtip lights appeared out of the murk coming right at them. Hollis instinctively braced for the collision which was just an instant away.   Lemaster slammed the throttles to the stops and pushed the nose down in a futile effort to avoid the lights and the wingspan they defined, cursing as he did.   The crash never came.   They flew right past the lights as if the plane had evaporated into thin air.   How could this be? Hollis asked.   It was coming right for us!   Hollis was sure he had shit his pants again.   The revelation of his survival in such a circumstance defied explanation.   With the oncoming plane that close, how could they have missed?

"Flares!" Lemaster yelled trying to put the bomber back on an even keel.   He started yelling into the command channel, "Bangmaster! Stop firing green and red!   Stop firing green and red!   Repeat, Bangmaster, stop firing green and red flares!"

Had those lights belonged to a Fortress they would have been dead.   Hollis wiggled his bottom against the seat feeling for something warm and fresh, relieved to feel nothing.   Even his colon had not had time to react.

"Jesus, that was close!" he yelled at Lemaster.

"Sons of bitches should have known better."   He looked over at Hollis.   In the dark cockpit, illuminated only by the glow of the dials, Hollis could see him shaking his head.   They saw another red and green flare drift past, probably already fired, descending from above, but no others.

Within a few minutes they were above the clouds, popping up into a starlit sky as clear and beautiful as any Hollis could recall seeing.   A thin rim of light, the approaching dawn, glowed in the east.   Nine thousand feet.   Nearly twice as high as predicted.   Hollis looked for the other planes.   He saw yellow-yellow flares arc into the night, rising in a perfect parabola above the Bangmaster.   The other bombers had their navigation lights turned on full.   Hollis counted perhaps eight or nine planes.   There should have been twelve, the lead and high squadrons.

"Fire green-yellow," Lemaster told his engineer.   Hollis watched as he took a flare gun, opened it, dropping in a cartridge and placing it into the fitting in the roof beside the turret.   He fired the gun with a loud 'POP'.   Lemaster made a bee-line for his position below and behind the lead squadron.

The bombardier appeared in the hatchway on his way to pull his pins.   He yelled, "I sure hope this God-damned ship is worth it.   We oughta let the Limeys sink it.   They got the *Bismarck* didn't they?"   Hollis gave him a thumbs up.   Lemaster seemed too preoccupied to notice their little exchange.

Lemaster rubber-necked one way then the other.   "Pilot to crew, keep a sharp eye. We're missing a bunch of planes.   They could be milling around here almost anyplace."

Hollis tapped Lemaster on the arm and pointed over the right wing.   They had at least picked up their right wingman.   Lemaster pointed over his left shoulder and Hollis could see the left wingman had taken his position, also.   They had to catch up to him.   Lemaster's proper position was slightly behind and below the left wingman of the lead ship of the lead squadron. In the burgeoning light, Hollis could see Lemaster lean forward, his face almost touching the windshield, and ease his way up into his assigned place in space, jockeying the throttles and kicking rudder.

"Copilot to crew, ten thousand feet.   Go on oxygen."   Hollis pulled his mask on and adjusted the rubber to fit his face.   He turned on the valve and watched the indicator blink at him confirming the life-sustaining flow of the gas.   He looked over at Lemaster who seemed to be completely absorbed with attaining his position.   After a few moments, Hollis tapped him gently on the arm and pointed to his oxygen mask.   Lemaster patted the wheel, the signal for Hollis to take over, and Keith pulled on his mask and plugged it in.   Lemaster must have decided to let Hollis fly for a while because he did not take back the controls.   Hollis kept his angle off the left wingman of the lead.   Lemaster started looking around.

"Pilot to tail.   Did we pick up anybody?"

"Tail.   No, it's just the three of us."

Lemaster glanced at his watch.   "Pilot to navigator.   How much longer till we have to depart for rendezvous?"

"Navigator.   Three minutes, Keith or we'll miss it."

Lemaster yelled to Hollis above the throbbing engine noise, "If they don't join us by departure time, I'm gonna latch onto the lead squadron.   Low squadron of the low group.   I ain't gonna stick out here like a sore thumb.   You'll have to learn how to fly low lead some other day."

Hollis nodded.   He didn't want to stick out like a sore thumb either.

"One minute, Pilot."

"Pilot to tail, anybody?"

"Negative.   It's just us, Cap."

Lemaster tapped Hollis's arm.   He then pushed the throttles forward and pulled back on the yoke.   The three planes rose in unison and Lemaster parked them behind and above the lead squadron as a third element of three planes.

Duckworth fired another yellow-yellow flare and turned north for Wing rendezvous.

"Tail to pilot, two more planes popped up through the clouds.   One turned around and headed in the opposite direction.   Probably lost.   The other must have spotted us because he's turning inside and beating feet to catch us."

Hollis figured the first pilot either was lost as he had said, or figured he couldn't catch up or just decided to call it quits for the day, his nerves frayed raw by the harrowing climb.   He would orbit until he was sure everybody had left and go back down into the cloud gingerly feeling his way back to the field.   Hollis envied him.

Hollis wished he had had one last cigarette before they went on oxygen.   The fact that Sully wasn't there had allowed the opportunity to pass unnoticed.

Lemaster held his position loosely above and behind Duckworth's lead squadron through wing assembly.   When they turned toward their run across the Channel he pulled in tighter. Hollis admired his ability to effortlessly hold his place as Duckworth weaved in and out through the turns.

The sun rose in the east shining in through the side window and they flew south-south east toward France.   Their route was nearly identical to the course taken a week earlier to the same place.   This probably reduced the guesswork for the Germans, Hollis thought.   As he looked down at the shimmering water of the dark Channel, he imagined the sirens going off in Nantes already.   *Take your time, though*, the Germans said, *they'll be a while yet.*

"Navigator to copilot, get Keith for me."

Hollis tapped Lemaster on the arm and pointed to his earphones.

"Rendezvous time with the escort, Keith.   I don't see 'em."

Lemaster swiveled around in his seat looking behind and up and past Hollis, "Me neither. Pilot to crew anybody see the escort?"

The silence on the interphone confirmed the negative.

"OK, keep your eyes peeled.   We're coast-in in twenty minutes.   Pilot to tail, anything back there?"

"England and an empty sky, Cap."

"We got away with an easy one last time.   We may not be so lucky today.   Stay on your toes."   Lemaster switched back to VHF.

"Navigator to crew, OK to fire."   ***der kriegsbringer*** shook with the simultaneous recoil of its guns, the cockpit filled with the familiar, reassuring smell of burnt cordite.

The trip proved quiet.   Perhaps the Germans were giving them another free pass. There was the usual random flak bursts sent up seemingly to annoy and distract rather than kill.

Halfway to the IP the Wing leader took the formation down to 18,000 feet to slip under a cloud bank. They would stay there, it was announced, and not try to climb back up to their original altitude. Maybe, Hollis thought, the lower altitude might have the added benefit of improving their aim. As the formation approached the IP, a few Me-109s were sighted, but none came close enough to shoot or be shot at. They may have tangled with somebody else, but it was not obvious anybody was in a serious fight.

The wing took interval at the IP and turned to the right toward the target. Hollis looked down and could make out submarines and ships in the port. Bombs away at 0820. It was all very neat. Clean. They turned at the rally and crossed the Brittany peninsula. It was an easy mission. Hollis wondered if they hit the damned ship. If one God-damned ship was worth all of this effort.

Lemaster brought the plane in for a perfect landing. No one said anything as they deplaned and headed for interrogation. Hollis collected the escape kits and returned them to the satchel. They were very business-like, matter-of-fact, as if they had just made a cross-country trip from Ardmore to Galveston instead of occupied Europe.

After they were finished debriefing which lasted no more than a few minutes, Hollis turned to leave expecting Lemaster to say something to him but he did not. *Nice flying with you, Hollis* or *Thanks for joining us*, as if Hollis had a choice. But no, they all dispersed without a word.

Hollis had been very nearly killed today by a red and green flare. It was casually mentioned to the debriefing officer. Had Lemaster stalled the bomber in an effort to avoid the flares it would have been nearly impossible for him to recover the overloaded airplane, sending them in a precipitous dive earthward. Maybe such violent evasive maneuvers could have sheared off a wing or separated the tail or the sudden change in altitude dropped them into the path of another, real, Fortress. Regardless, it was no easy mission. People die on milk runs. Hollis took solace that he had completed his tenth mission. It was a mixed triumph.

As they left interrogation, they were told to return to their quarters and be prepared to go out for another mission that might be laid on for the afternoon.

He ate lunch at the Combat Mess rather that scarf down the soggy bologna sandwiches the Red Cross girls were passing out. They must have been serious about the second mission because as he left the briefing room he became aware that no one was passing out combat rations.

Back in the room, Hollis took off his jacket and boots but stayed dressed in his flying clothes, stretched out on the bed and fell asleep. Leo was gone. He slept light, his brain refusing to let him relax too much in anticipation of another call so when Leo shuffled into the room he awakened immediately. He was dressed for flying.

"Where've you been?" he asked Leo.

"I got to lead the squadron."

"What are you talking about?"

"Ransahoff took the new guys up for the red paint treatment and he climbed into the top turret to do his yelling. That left me flying the lead plane."

Leo looked rather proud of himself.

"I don't know what you're so worried about. It wasn't so hard."

Hollis nodded but thought to himself, *Where was the rest of the Group, you ninny?*

Even the dumbest goose could lead a gaggle if everybody is behind him.
        "Who else went?"
        "Spats flew number four.   Weldon, Baldini, Kehoe and Powell.   Where'd you go?"
        "I flew copilot for the low squadron lead.   It was easy."
        "Hit anything?"
        "Yeah, we blasted the bejesus out of that U-boat tender again."
        "Looks like we both had a good day."
        "They told us they might be sending us up again this afternoon."
        "I doubt it.   Ransahoff told us to relax.   We go back on ops tomorrow."
        "You might, but apparently I already am."
        Hollis watched as Leo changed out of his flying clothes and into his Class A.
        "Where the hell are you going?"
        "Long division."

Chapter Thirty-eight   **Emden**

Friday, September 24, 1943

The instant the door opened Hollis knew it was business as usual.

"Where to today, Beamis?"

"Schikelgruber's summer home.   Eight five-hundred pounders, twenty-four hundred gallons."

"Shit," Leo muttered as he threw back the covers.

"Germany, huh?"

"You didn't hear it from me."

Beamis had hot water running and Hollis surveyed the crowd at the latrine.   Spats, Powell, Selkirk, Watanabe.   The squadron's most experienced crews.   Weldon and Kehoe were there, too, riding shotgun, no doubt.

Hollis's suspicion that it was a big mission was confirmed by the smell of fresh eggs wafting from the Mess.   Mission eggs.   They don't waste fresh eggs on a milk run.

At briefing, it got worse.   Van Patten was the Bangmaster.   He stepped up to center stage and pulled back the curtain.   All eyes went to the most westward point by reflex. "Frankfurt."

A great moan arose from the multitude.   Hollis watched Selkirk's reaction.   He sat emotionless, staring, as they all did, at the damned map.

"Our target is the Vereinitgte Deutsche Metallwerke A. G. propeller factory at Hedderheim.   The First Wing will be last in the Division.   Our Division will lead.   We will be lead Group of the Wing.   532nd will be high squadron, 534th low and I will lead in the 535th. Major."

Hollis had forced himself to eat the eggs; fresh eggs, after all, were hard to come by.   He now regretted that decision.   Hollis saw Rager nonchalantly light a cigarette as he stood in the corner with the rest of the Group staff.   Where do such men get their balls?   It was unnatural and unbecoming to show such aplomb in the face of death.

Hollis stared at the mission board, Ransahoff would lead, he would fly second in the new chin-turreted "F", Watanabe in the number three.   Selkirk number four with Spats and Powell on either side.

Hollis snapped back to mental attention when he heard Gorton say something about a serious fight on penetration and withdrawal.   Several heavy bomber missions into Germany had been planned and alerted for the past two weeks, but they'd been canceled or scrubbed.   The Germans are well-rested and they're pissed, he said.   They're itching for a fight.

The lights went off and the projector beamed aerial recon photos of the target onto the screen.   Hollis found it hard to concentrate on the rest of the briefing.   He caught himself glimpsing repeatedly at Selkirk who sat quietly on the bench.   Perhaps he might go to pieces any second, Hollis thought.   He might jump up and scream he wasn't going and no one could make him.   But he did not.   Instead, he licked his lips once or twice and stared without blinking, the glow from the projector putting the features of his face in *bas-relief.*

When the lights came on, the weather officer told them the conditions at takeoff and landing should be OK, but the weather at the target was iffy.   Five-tenths cloud, but they thought they could bomb through it.

Finally, Begay took the stage and presented the details of takeoff, assembly, routes and timings.   When he was done, Van Patten stood up, gave the time hack and said, "Navigators and bombardiers report to their briefings.   Good luck and good bombing. Protestants to the front, Catholics to the rear."

"Ten-hut!"

They shuffled to their feet more because they were tired of sitting than out of respect and the entourage walked briskly down the aisle.

Hollis left the room, Leo in tow, heading to the equipment room to beat the rush.

At the hardstand, Hollis walked over to Wilcox and wished him a good morning, looking up at the nose of the bomber.   **La Femme** had been painted on along with a rough outline of the girl's picture.   **Fatale** had not yet been applied.   "Not quite done, eh?"

"No.   So be careful.   Don't put any holes in her."

"I'll try not to."

Wilcox smiled, "I'm sure you will."

A truck rolled up and Sully and Cobb climbed down over the tailgate and strolled over to the plane.   Cobb had the stub of a cigar protruding from the corner of his mouth.   He looked up at the nose to see what Hollis and Wilcox were looking at and said, "Who the fuck is 'Belinda?'"

Hollis turned to him, "Girlfriend of H-y Smith."

Cobb mumbled something and threw his briefcase up through the hatch and climbed in. After a moment, he poked his head out of the hatch and called to Hollis.

"Hey, Hollis, give this back to him."   He handed down Belinda's cheesecake snapshot and disappeared back into the nose.

Hollis gathered the crew together and told them of their target and expected opposition. Hollis suspected they already had a good idea of what was going on by the reaction Hulse had witnessed from outside the briefing room.   They looked concerned.   More worried than he had seen them in a while.   He couldn't think of anything pithy to say that might alleviate their fears, Schweinfurt and Stuttgart still fresh in their minds.   He was as scared as they were assured nothing he could say would make any difference.   But he tried anyway.

When he was done they huddled under the wing against the morning chill and said little, inconsequential pre-mission chat fueled by jitters.

Hollis walked behind the tail and urinated into the grass.   He looked at the plane to the right, where he saw Powell talking to his crew.   On the other side, Watanabe and his crew were emptying their bladders as a group into the weeds, much as he had done with Lemaster the day before.   Finished, he returned to his crew and, glancing at his watch, announced, "Stations." The crew pulled themselves to their feet, gathered their equipment and clothing and, performing whatever rituals they felt obliged to complete, climbed into the plane.

Knowing Wilcox was watching him, but not caring, Hollis walked over to the grass again and heaved so violently he thought he might have snapped some innard during a spasm of regurgitation.   He wiped his chin and climbed into the plane.

The bomber was heavy and it took a long take off roll to get airborne.   They climbed slowly upward, circling the field behind Ransahoff.   They were high squadron and the ascent was uneventful.   Ransahoff had them tucked in expertly, Hollis paying closer attention to what

Ransahoff was doing than he had before, knowing one day soon it would be his turn.   Provided, of course, he lived through the day.

After about an hour, the squadrons tucked neatly into group formation, Van Patten turned toward Wing rendezvous over Bedford.   They were to climb to twelve thousand by the time they reached Bedford and turn for departure at Cromer.   Passing through eight thousand feet, Sully came up to pull his pins.   He smoked with Hollis, but said nothing.   He looked frightened, too.   Sully performed his task quickly and returned to the nose.   Hollis told Dodge to pull the Tokyos when something caught his eye.   He saw two flares arcing up from the lead squadron.   Two more flares, red, popped upward a moment later.   Leo tapped him on the arm and pointed to his headphone.   Hollis reached down and turned his jackbox to intercom.

"Radio to pilot."

"Pilot, go ahead Quinn."

"Goonchild announced a recall."

"Why?"

"Didn't say, Lieutenant.   They told us to be alert to a recall if weather over the target got worse.   I guess that's what happened."

Hollis watched as Van Patten, Rager actually, turned the Group in a large, flat, half-circle back toward whence they had come.

A few minutes later, Sully returned to replace the pins since they were prohibited from landing with live bombs on board.   This time he looked angry.   No one, even himself, Hollis conceded, liked a recall once the mission was launched.   It resulted in so much wasted emotion, fear, anxiety.   For naught.

Hollis's next concern was to bring the heavily loaded Fortress back to the ground without blowing out a tire and careening across the field.   He had never landed a plane so heavily loaded.   Fortresses always arrive home at or close to their empty weight after a mission.   They were easy to land when they were empty.

Rager brought them back to the field, slowly descending to about five thousand feet by several large flat orbits.   The low squadron peeled off one by one and stretched out in line astern before turning back to final approach.   Hollis allowed himself to loosen his position off Ransahoff for safety's sake and watched the first few planes land.   He didn't see any problems, but even at this distance he could tell they were coming down hard by the large blue puffs of tire smoke which billowed from under each wing.

One more orbit and Rager landed at the head of the lead squadron.   After a few more minutes they were all down without apparent incident.

At last, Ransahoff brought the high squadron around and Hollis quickly adjusted the power settings for landing and lowered the gear.   Watanabe peeled off first, then Ransahoff. He could feel the sweat running down his cheeks as he kept his eye on **The Flying Dutchman**. Ransahoff appeared to be coming in a little faster and lower than usual, figuring he would use the whole runway and keep his airspeed up to give him an increased margin of safety above stalling speed.   He checked the airspeed, one-forty.

"One third flaps," he called to Leo.

Leo reached for the toggle and replied, "One third flaps."

The bomber hit some turbulence as Hollis turned left onto short final.

"Call airspeed."

"One thirty," Leo responded.

Hollis inched the throttles forward a bit.

"One thirty-five."

Hollis backed off the throttles as he was too high turning onto final.   He felt the plane sag toward the runway, too quickly he thought, and inched back on some power.   The bomber started to rise.   He worried the plane might porpoise its way down to the runway, terrified to back off too much power and allow the heavy plane to stall and yet too fast, too high, or both, to bring the bomber gently to the runway.   It was, after all, a bet.

"One twenty-five."

As the ground came up toward him, Hollis lined up the nose of **La Femme** with the center of the runway, crabbing slightly into a mild crosswind.

"One twenty."

Too high and too fast!

The threshold came up at him, sliding quickly beneath the nose of the bomber.   He was over the runway.

"One fifteen."

Hollis felt he was low enough to gently flare the plane down onto the concrete.   He cringed mightily as he did, waiting for the bang and slewing that indicated a blowout. The sidewalls would bulge beyond their resilience as the weight of the bomber came down hard on the tires and, in an instant, he would lose control of the plane and skitter off the runway at over a hundred miles an hour careening across the grass toward the bombers taxiing on the perimeter strip.

He held his breath as the tires smacked the runway with a satisfying chirp-chirp.   He waited for a bounce hoping the tires would take a second impact, but there was none.   He pulled back the throttles to idle.   The plane was going too fast, its momentum too great.   In the milliseconds required for calculation, he decided to ease the control column forward putting the weight of the bomber on its main gear and gingerly touch the brakes.   They squealed in protest ready to melt down by the speed.   Quickly, however, the plane slowed, its tail wheel settling back to the runway.   The roll out was uncomplicated and Hollis turned **La Femme** onto the perimeter strip without fanfare, sure that nobody except perhaps Noah Dodge realized what had just happened.

As they deplaned, the bomb loaders were already preparing to remove the ordinance only to be reloaded later that night should the order come.   So much wasted effort.   So much needless risk.

"Came in kinda fast, didn't we, Sport?" Sully said as they waited for the truck.   Hollis ignored him.

With no mission there was no debriefing, so the crowd in the equipment room was huge and noisy.   There was a lot of griping about the recall.   Most seemed outwardly frustrated, but Hollis thought this was really a manifestation of relief, or was it reprieve?

Hollis took the view that Frankfurt would be there tomorrow and the next day and they would see it soon enough.   They all knew that, too.   He left the Operations block and caught the shuttle back to the squadron area.   He rode back with Cobb and Leo.   Powell and Watanabe were on, too.   No one said much.

When they returned to the room, there was mail laying on their beds and Hollis watched

Leo as he ripped into his.   Leo smiled as he read the two letters, but his eyes did not linger long on the pages.   He replaced them into their envelopes and changed quickly.   He opened his foot locker and stuffed a fistful of Milky Way bars into his jacket pocket.   As he was about to leave, Hollis turned to him and said, "More long division?"

"Fractions.   They're a bitch."   He left without further comment.

Leo never really behaved in what Hollis would consider a normal way, but even for him, his recent behavior was strangely different.   Hollis thought maybe, instead of fractions, what he was really after was poking Mrs. Thomas.   It was totally out of character for Leo to do such a thing, repeatedly and proudly proclaiming his celibacy while he was away from his beloved Christie.   This was exactly the reason he felt this possibility so likely.   He would think of a clever way to glean this information from him, expecting Leo to be guileless and forthright in his pronouncement.

Hollis read with delight the letters from Jessie and his folks.   Chatty without much genuine news.   It was always a boost to his morale to get a scented letter regardless of what it said.

He napped, ate dinner and went to the Club.   No alert was on, but rumor circulated that a large practice mission was planned for tomorrow.   Hollis had two drinks, read a dog-eared <u>Life</u> magazine and listened to the Nine O'clock News from the BBC emitted by the large radio near the bar.

Leo returned late in the evening.   Hollis did not feel compelled to engage him in conversation.

Saturday, September 25, 1943

Beamis told Hollis and Leo they were to report to briefing at 0900.
"Practice?" Hollis asked.
"Yep," was all he would say.

They were putting up three full squadrons as the room was filled.   Van Patten was in flying gear as was Gleason and all three squadron COs.   Van Patten seemed relaxed as he began the briefing.

"Gentleman, today we are going to participate in a practice mission designed to assess our ability to bomb using radar.   A practice mission was held two days ago and flaws in signaling and bomb release were uncovered.   Today, as part of the First Division, we will again be attempting to bomb off signal flares dropped by lead aircraft equipped with radar.   The principles of the technique are unimportant and I won't go into them.   Suffice it to say, the ability to identify the bomb release signal *is* and that is what we are going to test today.

"Our order of battle will be the Forty-first Wing, Fortieth and the First.   Radar planes will fly with the lead Wing.   We will be high group, 91st will lead, 351st low.

"Major Begay will run through routes and timings.   As always, bomb release will be on the Group's lead aircraft."

Sully leaned over to Hollis and whispered, "We can't hit things when we can see 'em. How do they expect this is gonna work out?"

After the briefing, Ransahoff saw Leo and said to him, "Go back to bed Wychulis, Hollis is leading the Squadron today and I'm his copilot."   Ransahoff turned to Hollis and grinned. Leo gave Ransahoff an exaggerated 'thumbs up', winked at Hollis and walked away whistling. Hollis thought it might have been "Follow the Yellow Brick Road."   The 532nd was low squadron.

Hollis settled into the left seat of **Cleopatra's Asp** and soon had the fans turning.   He led the procession of bombers around the perimeter strip until he had arrived at the end of the runway.   The flight control officer held take off for nearly twenty minutes for reasons unknown, but soon Cavannaro, leading the high squadron, tore down the runway and left the ground effortlessly.

Ransahoff watched Hollis closely, much to Hollis's annoyance.   It was like a check ride with Butch Mullen.   Hollis figured he was long past such scrutiny.   So, in retaliation, whenever possible he would tell Ransahoff to do things the copilot should do a few moments before he might actually be expected to do it.   Ransahoff seemed unmoved, dutifully executing whatever task Hollis gave him.

During assembly and the subsequent climb toward wing rendezvous, Hollis kept his station off Van Patten's left wingman.   It was more work than he had thought it would be and found himself leaning forward repeatedly much as Lemaster had.   It was awkward and tiring. He acquitted himself well, he thought, for Ransahoff said very little and offered no suggestions.

The three wings came together over Cromer, but the First arrived early and had to swing out over the sea in a large circle to fall in line astern of the Fortieth.   Hollis, on the far outside of the turn had to run the speed up in order to keep his place.   He could see that he was losing ground, falling further behind.   He caught a glimpse of Ransahoff shaking his head, his mask hose flopping back and forth contemptuously against his chest.   The turn, which took five minutes, left Hollis and the low squadron clawing to catch up and regain its place.   Finally, as the wing straightened out to head north, Hollis had them in position, but it was a struggle and he was not happy with himself.

By convention, there would be a six mile separation between wings, the procession twelve miles long.   In the clear, bright sunlight Hollis could make out the wing ahead of them, dots against the sky, and beyond, the lead wing.

At the IP, the lead plane of the wing opened its bomb bay and fired red flares and each group took interval.   Hollis anticipated the turn and kept them close, close enough that only minor adjustments in power were required to reestablish his position, admonishing himself all the while that he should never have let them get out of position in the first place.

Since they were the last group over the supposed target, they looked for the signal, smoke marker bombs and parachute flares, dropped by the lead group, replenished by each subsequent group.   When they arrived at the bomb release line, there was nothing.   The flares and marking smoke trails had drifted away or otherwise dispersed by turbulence, rendering the effort pointless.   Finally, well beyond the 'bombs away' point, Van Patten's bomber fired off two red flares and they saw the yellow practice bombs drop from his bomb bay.   The rest of the group's bombers followed suit.

It was a wasted exercise and everybody, from Van Patten to the tail gunner in the last plane of the bomber stream knew it.

At the rally, they reassembled the wing and turned for home, no more ready to participate in radar bombing than they had when they had taken off.

After landing, as they deplaned, Ransahoff gave Hollis some pointers and told him he was now qualified to lead the Squadron.

The next day, Hollis led the Squadron on a raid on an airframe assembly plant at Meulon. Just as they crossed the French coast however, they were recalled, bad weather over the target. No credit was given for the mission, despite the fact that enemy-held territory had been penetrated and some flak had been fired at them. One B-17 blew out a tire on landing and skidded crazily down the runway, angling one way then the other, a shower of sparks from the wheel rim on the concrete as the rubber tire disintegrated. This caused the remaining planes aloft to continue their orbit until the disabled plane had been hauled off the runway. No one had the stomach to try and land their loaded bombers on either of the shorter runways.

Monday, September 27, 1943

"Up and at 'em, Lieutenants. Breakfast at 0300. Briefing at 0400."
"Where to today, Beamis?"
"Light load, but expect a warm greeting. Briefing 0400."
When Beamis had left Leo said through a yawn, "I wish he would just wake us up and leave. I'm getting tired of his stupid riddles."
"Then stop asking him."
At the latrine, Hollis looked for Ransahoff but did not see him. Hollis thought he might be leading the Squadron again. He counted pilots, Watanabe, Selkirk, Fissano, Weldon and Spats. That meant he was leading, almost for sure.
Would they let him lead to Germany? Sure, why wouldn't they? It was just another target on a map.
At briefing, Gleason was the Bangmaster, but Van Patten started the talking. Sure enough, the mission board had Hollis leading the high squadron in **Cleopatra's Asp**.
"Gentlemen, the best defense Germany has against our bombing is cloud cover. Today we will be inaugurating our first mission using radar bombing--"
"Great," Sully said sarcastically.
"--our target, Emden." Van Patten pulled back the curtain and followed the red line to the northern coast of Germany. "Most of the German shipping has been shifted from port facilities in Hamburg and Rotterdam to Emden, here." He tapped the board with the pool cue. "Emden sits on an estuary that should make its radar image very clear. We will be bombing the docks and port facilities. Radar should allow us to bomb through any cloud cover and will therefore expand our operations regardless of weather at the target. If this works as expected, the pace of our missions will increase and the war will be shortened because nowhere will be safe."
"Does he expect us to believe this?" whispered Sully.
"Sully, shut the fuck up," Hollis whispered back.
"As those of you know who flew on the practice mission two days ago, we had trouble spotting the bomb release point, and other bombardiers complained that they did not see the flares or the smoke markers. In order to aid in this, bomb release will also be marked by a VHF signal from the lead aircraft. If, of course, we find the target clear, bombing will be visual.
"Our Thunderbolts have had their range extended by auxiliary drop tanks. We should

be escorted all the way to and from the target.   If the Germans come up for a fight they're gonna get one.   Colonel Gleason."

"Morning, Gen'lemen, I'm the Bangmaster for today's historic sortee."

After the briefing, Hollis rose to leave figuring that it might not be so bad.   No milk run, they were headed for the Fatherland, but they would be fully escorted, over water for all but a short time, and the German fighter pilots had a reputation for being unwilling to climb into an overcast to engage.

As he stepped from the Nissen hut he saw Rizzo, who was obviously agitated and looking for him.

"Rizzo, shouldn't you be out at the plane?"

"I just wanted you to know I had nothing to do with it."

"What are you talking about?"

"Them niggers beat up Augie last night and I didn't have anything to do with it.   I told him to leave them alone but he just wouldn't so they beat the shit out of him."

"Calm down.   What happened?"

"That ordinance captain came around last night.   He was dressed like a corporal and he had a gunner's cap pulled way down over his face, but I knew who he was.   He asked if I knew Augie Reese and I said yes and he tells me there's a guy over in his hut who knows Augie from Mississippi and he wants him to come over.   I tell Augie and he goes off into the woods behind the hut and they kicked the livin' shit out of him."

"Is he alright?"

"I don't know.   He looked hurt pretty bad.   He broke his knuckle and I think they broke his rib.   We could hear him all night moaning."

"Where is he?"

"At the plane.   We told him to go to the hospital but he told us to go fuck ourselves. He thinks we're in on it somehow, especially me."

"Are you?"

"No, sir.   I told you I wasn't."

"OK, go on out to the plane.   I'll be there soon."

When Hollis entered the equipment room, Leo asked, "What was that all about?"

"A couple of those Negro boys gave Augie a whipping last night?"

"Is he hurt?"

"Rizzo says he is."

"We need another waist gunner."

"Apparently, Augie is at the plane ready to fly."

"Jesus Christ, I warned him.   After that business in London I took him aside and told him he was gonna get into trouble one of these days.   How did this happen?"

Hollis thought of the captain.   If he was found to be responsible for the beating of a noncommissioned officer by the Inspector General he risked twenty years hard time in Leavenworth.   Just so a couple of Negroes could beat the snot out of a stupid hillbilly.   "I don't know any details."

Hollis gathered his stuff and tossed the duffle bag into the back of a shuttle which took him down to the dispersal area.   On the ride out he pondered what to do.   He would see how badly Augie was hurt then decide.

At **Cleopatra's Asp**, he walked over to the crew but did not see Augie.   They were quite upset.   Did they feel implicated?   Were they?   Did it matter?   Were they afraid he might die?   He was pretty sure they were not agitated by the upcoming ride to Germany.

"Where's Augie?"

Dodge pointed to a dark lump in the grass behind the plane.   Hollis took Moe's flashlight and walked over to the boy.

Augie sat Indian-style, legs crossed, hunched over, his head in his hands.   One of the hands was heavily bandaged.   Hollis shone the light in his face and could see a huge purple swelling around his right eye, the eye so puffy Hollis could barely make out a blood-shot eyeball between the slit of his lids.   His nose had dried blood caked around the perimeter of his left nostril and his lip was cut, the bright red blood glistened in the light.   His cheek was swollen and Hollis wondered if his mask would conform to it or his goggles would fit over his face.

Mustering all his sympathy, Hollis said, "Jesus Christ, Augie, you can't fly like this." Hollis gently lifted his chin so he could look face to face.   But Augie slapped his hand away.

"Don't touch me.   I can fly just like the rest of you bastards."

"Go to the hospital."

"Fuck you.   I'm flyin'."

"I don't think your mask will fit.   Your face is all swollen.   Come on, Augie, for Christ's sake go to the hospital."

Augie let his head fall back into his hands, "Leave me alone."

Hollis stared at the pathetic scene before him, got up and walked away.   It would be a fitting end to have the son of a bitch die of anoxia at twenty-five thousand feet because his oxygen mask would not form a seal around his fucked up face.

Rizzo walked over quickly, "I didn't know them niggers was gonna beat him up like that. Not that he didn't have it coming.   But--"

"Don't worry about it, Bobby."

"Honest sir, I didn't know that was going to happen."

Dodge walked over and pulled Hollis to one side.   "Get him off the crew.   We don't want him flying with us anymore.   Nobody likes him and he's picked fights with Hulse and Mollica and he's picked fights with them colored boys.   They don't trust him."

"OK," Hollis said softly. "In the meantime, he flies today."

"They might just toss him into the sea."

"No.   They won't do that."

Hollis turned to Moe, who had eased his way into the conversation, "Is she ready?"

"Ready as she'll ever be."

"Stations, Noah."

He watched as Augie struggled to his feet and pull on his helmet.   Hollis turned to Hulse and said, "Keep an eye on him.   If he looks like he's getting into trouble call me."

"Yes sir."

Hollis climbed in realizing he had been so distracted by the business with Augie that he had failed to smoke his last cigarette and vomit.

When the engines were running, he pulled **Cleopatra's Asp** onto the perimeter strip and stopped just beyond the entrance to the side branch.   As soon as the other planes of the Squadron fell into line he guided the procession around to the end of the runway.   Since he was leading the high squadron, **Cleopatra's Asp** would be the first plane off.   All eyes would be on him.   They would follow him up.

Cleopatra's Asp performed perfectly, like a thoroughbred from a starting gate, lifting from the ground with ease.   Hollis flew the orbit upward turning back around the field as he climbed.   He looked down at the takeoff and saw a plane leave the ground, he knew not who, trailing smoke, indicating whoever it was had lost an engine.   He watched as the plane veered off to the right and leave the flight pattern.   He lost sight of the plane and the smoke.   Whoever it was would have to wait until the group take off was completed before attempting a return to the field.   At least there was no big explosion to light up the morning.   Flying was such a precarious business.

Being the last wing in the bomber stream of the First Division, they were carrying incendiaries in order to make the rubble burn and Sully had no pins to pull.   He came up for a smoke anyway, but Hollis was too busy to converse and after they were done smoking he returned to the nose without comment.   Cobb was very precise with his information, businesslike, without that vague hint of uncertainty, a far cry from H-y's way of doing things.   It was a welcome change.

He watched as Gleason inched forward and took the lead.   As leader of the high squadron, Hollis was third in command of the group.   Should Gleason and his deputy no longer carry on he was to fly down and take over the lead squadron as the Bangmaster.   Hollis thought this unlikely.

Nonetheless, he made sure Cobb stayed on top of things while he listened to the command channel.   He had told Sully   and Leo to keep an eye on Augie's voice during the oxygen checks.   If he failed to respond appropriately they were to tell Hulse to check on him.   Hollis was still worried Augie's face mask would not conform to his bludgeoned face and he would become anoxic.

Hollis switched to the intercom, "Pilot to left waist. "

"Left waist."

"How's the right waist?"

"He's asleep on the floor.   He told me to wake him if we see any Germans.   I nudge him every few minutes with my boot.   He seems OK, sir."

"Roger, left waist."

Maybe for everybody's sake and the good of the war effort, the best solution would be if Augie *did* die of anoxia.   Then again, if he did there would probably be a court martial for allowing Augie to fly in the first place, needlessly and callously risking his life.   Hollis could have ordered him not to fly.   He *was* the aircraft commander.   There would be unbelievable hell to pay if they had to abort a mission for a personnel failure, especially since said failure was predictable before the engines were even started.   Hollis felt angry that he allowed Augie to put him in such a fix.

"Keep an eye on him."   Hollis switched back to VHF.

The 381st joined the other two groups to form the First Wing.   The assembly went well and the wing turned for Cromer where the bomber stream would form and head northeast over the sea towards Germany.

Hollis watched the escort, several neat squadrons of Thunderbolts in finger-four formation, pass overhead flying toward the bombers in the van.   Each fighter had the unmistakable white stripes on the empennage and cylindrical belly tanks slung beneath each centerline.   Little Friends.   They were faster and could therefore take off later and simply climb to rendezvous altitude and overtake the bombers as they departed England.   Hollis watched them disappear from view winging their way toward the lead wings where they would most likely be needed first.

He envied of them.   They were an elite bunch, unencumbered by the travails of a crew, supreme warriors like the Knights of Old.   Good doing battle with Evil.

As they approached the enemy coast, having doglegged right twice to angle in on the IP, cloud cover below became ten-tenths and Hollis knew they were strictly at the mercy of the radar operators and their gadgets.   He had little faith that they would hit anything.   It was all a big experiment.   There was the unmistakable sound of confusion over the command channel as the lead wings neared the target.

Leo tapped his arm and raised his gloved hand, the fingers outstretched, the signal for five minutes to the IP.   Hollis grew more nervous and sat upright watching Gleason's bomber for the turn.   As high group he would turn inside after the lead group became uncovered and assume line-astern behind the lead, the low group swinging in after the 381st fell in train.   Red flares started popping up from the lead group indicating the primary target was to be bombed, Gleason lowered his bomb bay doors and fired flares of his own, the signal that the IP had been reached.   Hollis had no problem following Gleason's lead.

As Gleason settled the Group in behind the lead, Hollis edged the Squadron in a little closer to tighten the bomb pattern.   Regardless of what they were about to hit, at least they would hit it good.

Black smudges of flak flew past and new bursts erupted all around them.   The Germans were firing up through the clouds, radar against radar, neither attacker or defender seeing what they were trying to hit.   Modern warfare.   A burst came close and rocked **Cleopatra's Asp** but there was no damage immediately apparent.   Then another, much closer.   Hollis wondered, as he steeled himself against the explosions, whose radar was better?

Preoccupied by the flak and keeping tight against Gleason, it was a surprise to feel the unmistakable shutter of **Cleopatra's Asp** as the bomb load fell free.   Instinctively, Hollis adjusted the trim and resumed steady flight.   He could hear and feel the bomb bay doors grind shut.   The flak suddenly ended and they were in clear sky once again.

Leo tapped his arm and pointed to his headphones.   Hollis reached down to the jack box. "Bombardier to pilot."

"Go ahead, bombardier."

"You see a smoke marker?"

"No, bombardier."

"I have no idea what we dropped on.   If I didn't see any signal, I'm sure the lead bomber didn't either."

"OK, bombardier."

"Can you kill fish with incendiaries?"

The Germans down below must be apoplectic with laughter and derision.   That the stupid Americans would put their faith in a bunch of vacuum tubes.

Hollis switched back to command and led the Squadron toward the rally point.   It was Hollis's eleventh mission.

Withdrawal was as uneventful and boring as the penetration.   The only excitement, if one could call it that, was the way Gleason broke for home after re-crossing the coast.   He banked sharply and slid down toward Ridgewell like he was flying a fighter.   It took everyone by surprise and Hollis thought it was an unnecessary show of bravado as the fancy flying was not meant for a full group and there could have been a collision.   People die on milk runs.

On the hardstand, Hollis watched Augie get down out of the plane without assistance. His lip had been bleeding and his chin was wet with blood.   He would need stitches.   There was dried blood caked under his helmet from a reopened scalp laceration.   Hollis told him to report to the hospital instead of going to interrogation.   *You slept most of the way*, he could have added, and wouldn't have much to tell the intelligence people anyway.

Hollis watched as Hulse took Augie's gun out of the plane after removing his own and laid them on the tarp beside the waist.   They would be collected later by the armorers.

Moe came over and asked how it had gone.   He had no knowledge of the mission or the radar so Hollis simply said that everything had gone fine.

"We had a little excitement after you left."

"Yeah, what?"

Some guy from one of the other squadrons lost an engine on takeoff and when he came back to land, came in too fast on three engines and had his landing gear collapse.   Made a hell of a mess.   Nobody was hurt but Van Patten was really pissed.   He was out there trying to get the damned thing up on jacks so they could tow it clear of the runway."

"Who was it?"

"Scorch Alexander."

After the interrogation, which lasted only a few minutes, made notable only by Sully walking up to any bombardier he could find asking *what did we hit?   Anybody know what we hit?*   Hollis sought out Ransahoff.   As Hollis approached, Ransahoff said, "Well, it sounds like everything went OK."

"I want Augie Reese off my crew."

Ransahoff was taken aback.   "Why?"

"He's disrupting the harmony of the crew and I want him out."

Ransahoff probably knew there was no arguing so, after a moment he said, "OK."

"I'd prefer if he were transferred out of the Squadron."

"OK.   May I ask why?'

"He just doesn't fit in and nobody likes him."

"We're not running some sort of popularity contest here, Hollis.   He's a good gunner."

"It's my prerogative as aircraft commander."

"OK."

Back in the room, Hollis turned to Leo and said, "Augie's off the crew."

"Good," was all he said.

Leo sat on the chair rubbing his neck so Hollis asked him the burning question, "Hey Leo, you screwing Ian's mother?"

ChapterThirty-nine   **Emden, again**

Perhaps the best defense against the bombs remained clouds because nobody was sure anything had been hit except Mother Earth or the water.   When the clusters of incendiaries disappeared into the thick, white under cast, nobody knew where they had ended up.   Sad, disappointing, but true.   The RAF practiced area bombing, figuring, perhaps correctly, that a bomb falling on anything in Germany was money well spent while the Army Air Force preached the virtue of and adhered to the method of precision bombing.   He wondered if anybody could tell the difference.

Leo had said nothing to Hollis after posing his question.   Leo looked at him acknowledging that he had heard something arise from Hollis's mouth, but went about his undressing as if Hollis wasn't even in the room.

Later that day, no flying list was published on the Squadron bulletin board outside Headquarters so it was assumed no alert had been posted.   This surprised them because the weather seemed as if it would remain decent for a few more days.   Everybody seemed relaxed. Hollis grabbed his coat to round up Leo, Cobb and Sully   to see if they wanted to pedal over to the White Horse when the base provost, some captain, stepped into the room.

"What happened to Sergeant Reese?"

"I don't know."

"Sure you do and I intend to find out."

"All I know is he showed up for the mission in the state he was in.   How that happened is unknown to me."

"He was put into the hospital.   He may be there a week.   He was beat up pretty bad and you don't know how he came to be in that condition?"

"No, Captain.   I do not.   Sergeant Reese is not the most endearing character I've ever met.   He's picked fights with a lot of people around here.   It's your guess who might have settled a score with him."

Frustrated he left saying, "If it turns out he was in a fight and must be off operations as a result, he will be charged with bad time and have to make up the days he missed at the end of his term of enlistment."

"I'm sure he will be very upset."

Hollis heard the door close behind him.

Dodge later told Hollis that Augie's stuff had been removed from the hut.

Hollis could not locate Leo Wychulis.   He had vanished again.   This reinforced the notion Hollis maintained that he was having some unseemly affair with that little English boy's mother.   That this might happen to Leo, that he would succumb to temptation like some mere mortal, was surprising and a bit disappointing.   Leo may be an egg-head, but he was a virtuous one.   What Leo did with his life was not Hollis's business, he told himself.   Hollis also recalled how much in love he was with Jessie Snowden, transfixed by fear and loneliness even proposing marriage to her, yet this did not deter his libidinous energy from seeking carnal knowledge of Penelope Halliday as if it might be the last fuck he would ever have.   After all, don't you know there's a war on?   Virtue fell victim to the exigencies of life and death and the imperative of circulating hormones.   It was understandable.   Regrettable, reprehensible perhaps, but understandable.

Hollis caught up with Cobb and Sully and they pedaled the path toward the road at the end of the field which lead to the White Horse.   Cobb lit a fresh panatela and the smoke roiled around his head as he rode.   Sully was uncharacteristically quiet, pensive.

"What's wrong?" Hollis asked.

"Nothing."

"Sully got a telegram that his father's sick," Cobb said.

"Shut up, Cobb.   Do I know you?   Do you know me well enough to tell other people about my life?"

"Sully...come on boys, let's not squabble."

"They're afraid he has cancer," Cobb added.

Hollis came to a halt.   "Jeez, Sully, I'm very sorry to hear this."

The others stopped also and for the first time Hollis could see the distress on Sully's face. So caught up had Hollis been on rationalizing fornication when they met up, he had failed to notice any sign in Sully's demeanor.

It seemed different this time.   On missions Sully expressed his fear by anger and cynicism, rarely ever looking scared or frightened.   In the late afternoon, this day in September, he looked genuinely afraid.

"What do they know?"

Sully appeared on the verge of tears.   "They didn't saying much.   How much can you say in a telegram?   They're going to operate on him."

"That's all you know?"

"Yeah," he said softly, bowing his head and brushing something from his cheek.

Cobb looked at Hollis, uncertainty etched on his face, as he moved the cigar from one corner of his mouth to the other with his tongue.

"Come on.   We're going to get to the bottom of this right now."   Hollis turned his bike around and pedaled briskly in the direction of Headquarters.   Knowing without looking, he could sense Sully and Cobb following.

Hollis hadn't always seen eye-to-eye with Sully, he had been a mutineer, but he was in pain and this struck a nerve of vulnerability in Hollis releasing a sensation of brotherhood he had not experienced in a long time.

When Sully caught up to Hollis he asked, "Where are we headed?"

"To see the Chaplain."

"I don't need to talk to a God-damned Sky Pilot."

"Knock it off, Sully, don't you know when someone's trying to help you," Hollis replied.

"I'm telling you, Hollis," Sully said harshly as he stopped his bike, "I've never needed to cry to no chaplain and I'm not starting now."

"Calm down, Sully.   Okay, we'll just go over to the Club and have a beer and drink to your father's good health."

"Come on, Sully, that sounds like a good idea," Cobb added.

They rode their bikes to the Club and dropped them to the ground amidst several dozen others.   The Club was crowded and noisy.   After they'd purchased a beer, Hollis turned to them and said he needed to get some cigarettes and that he would be right back.   He walked out into the street and ran toward the Chaplain's office in the Headquarters block.

As he arrived he found Chaplain Brown leaving his office.

"Hi, Lieutenant.   I was just leaving."

"Sorry to bother you, sir, but, I have a dilemma and I was hoping you might be able to help."

The Chaplain studied Hollis carefully for a moment and said, "Don't tell me you need more food?"

"No, sir, this is not *my* problem.   Of course *that* one wasn't really mine either.   It's my bombardier, Lieutenant Sullivan.   His father's having surgery.   They think he has cancer and I was wondering if you might be able to find out anything."

If the Chaplain was annoyed by the sudden intrusion on whatever plans he might have had, he did not show it.   Instead, he invited Hollis into his office and told him to have a seat.

"I really appreciate this, sir," Hollis said, just in case the Chaplain was particularly good at hiding annoyance.   The Chaplain took off his tunic and rolled up his sleeves.   He picked up the phone and tapped the cradle a couple of times.   Hollis lit a cigarette as the Chaplain pulled a file from a drawer and ran through the list of names.   Hollis wondered what the list was for.

"Hello?"   He was silent for a moment and said it again, "Hello?   Is this the operator?...Good, this is Chaplain Brown.   I have a priority call...Yeah, yeah, I know.   They're *all* priority calls.   Would you please connect me with the overseas operator?...Yes, I'll hold thank you."   He looked up at Hollis and asked, "What is his name?"

"Lieutenant Nathan Bedford Forrest Sullivan of Front Royal, Virginia."

The Chaplain scanned his list.   When he came upon the name he rolled his eyes slightly and smiled at Hollis.   "Yes, operator, thank you.   I need to be connected to a phone number in Front Royal, Virginia... Yes...It is an emergency, yes...OK, I'll hold."   He looked at Hollis and said, "This may take a while.   Where's Lieutenant Sullivan?"

"He's at the Club.   He doesn't know I'm here."

After almost an hour of being repeatedly disconnected and retracing his steps a half dozen times and, between the two of them smoking nearly a pack of Chesterfields, Brown finally asked, "Mrs. Sullivan?   Is this the wife of Mr. Robert E. Lee Sullivan?...Yes, this is England calling...How are you?"

Hollis bolted from the office and ran back to the Club as fast as his feet would propel him.   He arrived at the Club breathless and ran up to Sully, standing at the bar, his head resting on his hand.   Hollis grabbed him by the arm, "Sully, run over to the Chaplain's office.   Your mom is on the phone!"

Sully, a look of disbelief on his face, ran from the Club.

Cobb looked at Hollis and withdrew the cigar from his mouth, "I figured it was taking an awful long time for those cigarettes."

Hollis smiled smugly at Cobb and said, "I didn't do anything Sully couldn't have done for himself if he weren't such a God-damned hard-ass."

A half hour later Sully returned, beaming excitedly from ear to ear.

"Well?" Cobb asked, as if somehow he was entitled to know.

"He's fine.   They operated this morning.   I couldn't hear every word, but I think my mother said he didn't have cancer but had some problem 'diverticulitis' or something.   He should be OK."   He turned to Hollis and said, "Thanks."

"Don't mention it.   And I mean that."   Hollis took his beer and raised the glass toward the sky.   "Here's to your father and his speedy recovery."   He drank down the pint and slid the empty across the bar.   "Buy me another one."

As Sully handed him the beer he said, "If you think this means I'm suddenly going to be your best friend, Jack, forget it."

Hollis smiled through the wafting smoke and said, "Your gratitude is duly noted."   He hoisted the pint to his lips and drank down the warm liquid, contented that nothing had changed between him and his bombardier.   A short time later, Selkirk and others came into the Club having drank dry the White Horse and any other pub they could find.

Spats slapped Hollis on the back and launched into yet another rendition of how he had come to marry into the Van Hazen peanut oil fortune.   He and Selkirk, Fissano and Weldon were all thoroughly inebriated.   They were loud but no louder than any of the other revelers from the Group who had gathered in the Club.

Eventually, Watanabe, Baldini, Barbieri, DeBerg and Robertshaw strolled in until it seemed as if the entire Squadron had spontaneously convened a social.   Barbieri tried to endear himself to the pilots, including himself in conversations, but he was ignored.   No one liked him.

There was no mention of Sully's father or his brush with diverticulitis, whatever the hell that was.

For the next three days the Group was alerted, but no missions were flown.   On the thirtieth day of the month they were briefed for Emden again prompting Sully to whisper, "I guess we did such a good job of hittin' it the first time they want us to do it again."

Hollis whispered back gratuitously, "Follow-on raids are important to insure destruction of critical targets."

"I notice we ain't been back to Schweinfurt."

They picked up a stand-in right waist gunner named Otis Maybry, a tall, lanky fellow from New Mexico.   Much too tall, Hollis thought, to fly a whole mission hunched over at the waist, banging butts with Hulse.

By stations, the rain started coming down hard.   They sat in the silent **Cleopatra's Asp** and listened as it drummed down on the aluminum skin.   Finally a red flare arced from the tower.   They deplaned, Hollis again wondering how many people would be alive tonight in Germany because it was raining in England.

On October first, it continued to rain steadily.

Tensions started building again.   The repeated alerts with no missions allowed frustrations to build.   They kept Leo close to the base.   He seemed to have lost his happy-go-lucky demeanor.   He laid around more than usual.   The only bright spot occurring when the mail orderly delivered another perfumed letter, his first in nearly a week.   Perhaps that's what was on his mind, Hollis thought.   No news from the home front.   Perhaps the bad weather had kept the transatlantic mail flights pinned down.   Maybe the mail orderly liked to hold onto Leo's letters in order to fill the base post office with their exotic aroma.

Leo tore into the envelope and read the contents voraciously.   Hollis watched Leo's face grow red.   Leo got up and left, letter in hand, mesmerized by the contents.   Probably went to go wank Little Leo.

He returned about ten minutes later and handed the letter to Hollis who was keenly aware of his copilot's generosity.   Hollis lifted the envelope to his nose and savored the fragrance.

He then carefully took the single page from its embrace.   Hollis read the letter and felt himself stir inside his trousers.

"Can I borrow this?"

When Hollis returned he gave the letter reluctantly, but gratefully to Leo whose grin was even more salacious.

"She's something, ain't she?"

"Jesus, Leo, where the hell did you find that woman?"

"Would you believe she was a virgin when I married her?"

"Not after reading that I wouldn't.   You must thank her for me and thank you for letting me borrow it."

"You're welcome."   Leo grew pensive, the smile leaving his face.

"Leo, sometimes I think you must be the luckiest son of a bitch who ever lived.   You think she might write me a perfumed letter sometime?"

"Doubt it, son.   Find your own."

Hollis thought of Jessie and his consuming passion for her and figured he had.

Saturday, October 2, 1943

As soon as Hollis checked in and stepped inside the briefing room he looked, as he always did, at the mission board.   The 532nd was low squadron and he was leading. Curiously, he saw Otho's name in the number four slot.   Had to be either a mistake or a milk run.   Sure enough as the Group was called to order, Otho Barbieri took a seat on the bench with the rest of the Squadron's pilots.   Hollis realized quickly that he was not the only one to notice.   Selkirk would be flying number two, Spats three, Kehoe and Baldini, five and six, respectively.

Buckley Bonner took the stage and pulled back the curtain, "Gentlemen, it's Emden, again."

There was, as there had been the day before, a happy hoot from the crowd.   Sully leaned toward Hollis's ear and said, "First Emden was such an easy dish, I guess Otho thinks he can get in an easy one."

Bonner continued, "This will be a Pathfinder mission.   We will be high group with a full escort for penetration and withdrawal.   The order of battle will be the Forty-first, Fortieth and the First.   The mission will be identical to that briefed the other day but for those of you who were not included last time we will take it from the top.   Major."

At the plane, they were flying **Cleopatra's Asp**, they met their permanent replacement right waist gunner, a quiet kid named MacFadden.   He was from Down East Maine and, when he spoke, had an almost impenetrable accent.   He smile broadly, but didn't have much to say.

Otho was flying pilot with DeBerg's crew, DeBerg in the right seat.   DeBerg's copilot, who had shown up for the briefing was royally pissed and didn't hesitate to let everybody know of his displeasure.   He even went to Ransahoff and came about as close to chargeable insubordination as anyone could recall.   It was quite obvious he did not want to be separated from his crew or, perhaps most revealing, miss another 'easy dish'.

Finally, Ransahoff relented and told him he could go as the eleventh man, but he would not get credit unless he performed some function vital to the mission.   Otho, to somehow make amends for the dislocation, produced a Leica camera and told the copilot he was the official photographer for the Squadron this day. Ransahoff was placated and the copilot would be given credit.   Assuming, of course, the pictures turned out.

As they sat around waiting for stations, a delay which stretched to nearly two hours, Hollis noticed a difference in the crew.   They were more talkative, warmer.   Instead of huddling in twos or threes they all sat together under the wing and chatted.   Even Moe noticed. He strolled over to Hollis and said, "Everybody seems more relaxed since you got rid of that bum Reese."

"I guess that explains it," said Hollis offhandedly.

Take off and assembly went without hitch.   As the bomber stream exited over splasher five at Cromer, Hollis called up Mollica, "Pilot to tail, how's number four?"

"Tail to pilot.   He needs to take more lessons.   He's got 'em strung out behind a good four hundred yards.   They're stickin' out like a sore thumb.   If we get jumped they're gonna be the first to go.   Number five and six don't know whether to stick with him or pull up where they're supposed to."

Hollis switched to the VHF.   "Afghan M-Mary tuck it in!   Pull it in!"

Leo tapped his arm and Hollis switched back to interphone.   "Tail to pilot.   Whatever you said got somebody's attention, five and six just left him."

"Roger, tail, keep me advised."

"Roger, sir."

The route took them east-north-east toward some imaginary point over the North Sea where they would make a shallow dog-leg to the right followed in twenty-three minutes by another dog-leg toward the IP at the Dutch town of Veendam.

They were to be at their bombing altitude of 24,000 feet by the first checkpoint.   That was the rendezvous for the escort.   By the time they reached the turn, Hollis could see squadrons of P-47s flying parallel and above, each fighter painting the sky with a large ribbon of white, condensed engine vapor.

The Third Division had already proceeded the First and some of their condensation trails had not dissipated making visibility difficult.

"Pilot to tail, are we leaving contrails?"

"Yes sir, big ones.   I can barely see the second element."

Dumb son of a bitch doesn't have the sense to climb out of them.   "Afghan leader to M-Mary.   Climb above our trails.   Add fifty.   Acknowledge."

The static and the jamming was growing intense, but Hollis could make out a 'roger' from Barbieri.

Leo tapped him.

"Navigator to pilot, we're right on schedule.   Turn toward IP in five minutes."

"Roger, Cobb."

"Right waist to pilot."

"Go ahead, waist."

"Sir, we just lost number five.   He feathered an engine and banked toward home."

"Roger, Mac.   Pilot to navigator, Kehoe aborted."

"Noted, pilot."

The escorts disappeared, headed for the van.   Before Hollis could switch back to the command channel Dodge came over the interphone.   "Top turret to pilot."

"Go ahead, Noah."

"Sir, we've got a strange B-17 off our port wing.   He's too far out of the bomber stream to be one of ours."

Hollis looked to the left and spotted a lone Fortress about a half mile away flying parallel to the bomber stream.   "Navigator, fix your binoculars on that guy.   Does he have any markings?"

"Navigator to pilot.   I don't see any group markings.   I wonder what he's doing out there?"

"Maybe he's a fighter director."

"Maybe he's part of the low group," Cobb suggested.

"Too high to belong to them.   They're way down there, strung out to hell and back."

"Left waist to pilot, I can barely see him for all these contrails, still you want me to send a few tracers his way?   I doubt if I can reach him but he might get the message."

"What message is that Hulse?   Don't waste the ammo.   Besides, what if he *is* one of ours?"

"Then he shouldn't be there," Noah added.

Hollis had a sinking feeling.   What if he was a fighter director?   The escort was miles ahead by now.   Maybe they were going to go to work on the ass-end of the formation.   The three groups had a lot of new guys flying and the formations could hardly be called that. Maybe he was radioing that very assessment to the ground controllers right now.

"Keep your eyes peeled, crew.   Stay on the ball.   I have no idea what that guy's up to, but keep your eyes on him."

Hollis tucked the Squadron in tighter, nudging them a little closer to the lead.   Poor Otho.   He may have picked a bad day to be one of the guys.

Down below, as expected the cloud cover was ten-tenths.   The Germans, they had been told, were poor instrument flyers and may be reluctant to climb into solid cloud to engage, especially this far out over water.   If they homed in on the interloper, he could shepherd them along.   That had to be it.   He was a fighter director.

Hollis watched the contrails up ahead make a long flat curve to the right and head for the Dutch coast.   It was a short run from there to the IP.

From where Hollis sat, low squadron of the high group, he could see the lead group very clearly and he watched them turn, Bonner quickly following suit.

"Coast-in in five minutes."

From the coast to Veendam was ten minutes flying time.

"Bandits!   Nine o'clock low!"

Hollis snapped his head around to see a group of probably a dozen fighters, mere black gnat-like specks against the blinding white undercast.

"Where's our escort?" Sully asked.

"Home having tea by now," Cobb said.

"Knock off the chatter.   Stay alert."

Hollis tried to avoid watching the Germans, instead forcing himself to concentrate on keeping his place in formation.   He jockeyed the throttles a little and watched Leo exercise the turbos for the thousandth time.   He could feel himself start to perspire heavily.

He stole a glance downward but they were gone.

"Where'd they go?"

"Ran up ahead, pilot," Dodge said.   "And we were ripe for the pickin's."

"We're not home yet."

"Navigator to pilot, I hope those guys know where we are 'cause I can't see a thing down there."

Hollis stole another glance away from Bonner's wingman and saw nothing below but gleaming clouds, like fresh snow in bright sunlight.

"IP five minutes."

Up ahead Hollis could see the IP for it was marked by the wide sweeping curls of contrails toward the east.   They rode closer.   Hollis wondered what kind of radar image Veendam gave off.

"IP."

Simultaneous with this pronouncement he could see red flares arc from the lead plane of the wing and Bonner's B-17.   The bomb bay doors cranked open and Hollis adjusted his speed slightly to compensate.

"Ball to bombardier, bomb bay doors open."

"Roger, Ball."

Hollis watched the lead group bank toward the left and level off, Bonner turning onto a converging course as soon as they were uncovered.   The low group passed beneath them, their turn just commencing.   In trail, Hollis could no longer make out the lead ship of the wing as it followed the broad white path defined by the engine vapor of hundreds of preceding bombers. Large barrage-type flak bursts staining the pristine whiteness of the clouds and contrails like large clumps of black pepper.

Even so, he saw the flares pop skyward and the smoke marker bombs arcing downward from the belly of the lead plane signifying the bomb release line.   As the 381st passed over the smoke, two white puffs suspended at the origin of two long white lines, he saw the bombs appear from the bottom of Bonner's plane and an instant later **Cleopatra's Asp** shuttered with the release of her own burden.

"Radio to bombardier, bomb bay clear."

"Roger, Radio."

Hollis could hear the bomb bay doors close and **Cleopatra's Asp** was restored to clean flight.   Bonner pulled them around toward the Rally Point over Norderney Island off the German coast and settled them back into wing formation.

Hollis couldn't help but wonder what it was like to look up at the clouds and see tiny black specks emerge from them guided by two long smoke trails.   Could they follow the path of the marker bombs to the ground and see them reaching down, like the long fingers of Death, toward those about to be destroyed?

Hollis saw the P-47s, bringing up the rear, curve lazily one way then the other, pulling white streamers behind them like stunt planes at an airshow.   They dipped their wings in salute and passed overhead.

The course home was a direct line back to Cromer skirting the northern edge of the Frisian Islands so they were still within   interceptor range.   Hollis looked around for the renegade B-17 but did not see it.   The flight home was without incident.

Back on the ground, Hollis wanted to make sure he and Cobb gave very specific details about the suspect Fortress.   Others had seen it, too.   The interrogating officers gave no hint as to what they thought the B-17 might be.   Cobb plotted the course of the mystery plane from the time he was first seen until they lost sight of him not long after crossing the Dutch coast.   The intelligence officer was most appreciative.

Hollis noticed the elaborate recounting Otho gave of his experience on the mission which, on the whole, had been pretty unremarkable.

Back in the room, Hollis found mail on his bed.   A letter from Jessie and two from his folks.   He tore into Jessie's letter and out fell a folded newspaper clipping.   He read the letter.

Dear John,
I hope you are well.   I miss you terribly.
I read this article in the paper and sent it
to you.   I want you to know how proud I am
of you.   I, we, all share the hopes and
dreams of a better tomorrow and it will be
because of selfless acts such as yours that
will guarantee it.   I love you.   I miss you.
You are always in my thoughts.

Jessie

Hollis unfolded the clipping.   It was an article from the local newspaper entitled "Local Boy Dogfights Nazi with His B-17."

"Lieutenant John Hollis of 104 Eddystone Avenue, Chester, engaged a German Junkers 88 in a dogfight over the English Channel as he returned from a bombing mission to Stuttgart. The marauding Nazi was about to shoot down a crippled Fort when Hollis flew his B-17 to the rescue, shooting down the Ju88 with his belly guns moments before the German was about to send the crippled bomber he was stalking into the sea.

"Hollis was eager to share credit with his ball turret gunner, Sergeant Robert Rizzo, of Brooklyn, New York, who actually did the shooting but it was Hollis's quick thinking that brought down the German fighter, saving the crew of the crippled Fort from a certain death.

"For his action, Lieutenant Hollis has been recommended for the Distinguished Flying Cross by Eighth Air Force Bomber Command."

Hollis could scarcely believe his eyes.

He opened one letter, from his father, and the other, from his mother, each containing the same newspaper article, each with a congratulatory note.   His father spoke of his pride in his son.   His mother admonished him to be more careful.

Funny, he did not feel like a boy anymore. He was embarrassed, stunned that something he was essentially shamed into doing had resulted in the nomination for a medal.   If he were to receive the award it would diminish, not enhance the reputations and the acts of those who had legitimately earned it.

Still in flying clothes Hollis went to Squadron headquarters to confront Ransahoff.   He wasn't there.   Otho was, however, and he beamed from ear to ear.   This irritated Hollis.

"First mission to Germany, Otho?"

"Yeah."

"You're lucky you're not dead."

The smile left Otho's face.   "What do you mean?"

"You were all over the place up there.   The Germans could have spotted your sloppy flying a mile away.   If they had seen you, you'd have been the first to go.   Without realizing it you jeopardized the lives of everybody who flew with you.   So I wouldn't be quite so self-congratulatory.   You were graced by a milk run, next time you won't be so lucky.   Where's Ransahoff?"

Otho hung his head down and, rather than feel pity, Hollis laughed at him.   "Where's Ransahoff?"

No sooner had the question left his mouth Ransahoff came through the door laughing with Selkirk and Nevtushenko.

"Hollis!" he said.

"Can I speak with you privately."

Ransahoff looked at the sullen Barbieri and the smile left his face.   "Sure.   Step into my office.   What's the matter, you want to sack another crewmember?"

Hollis pulled the door shut behind him and retrieved the newspaper article from his pocket.   Ransahoff read it and a slight, barely perceptible smile set upon his lips.

"Says here I've been put up for the DFC."

Ransahoff folded the clipping and handed it back, "Well, don't get your hopes up.   Just because you're up for it doesn't mean you're going to get it."

"I don't deserve it.   Rizzo shot down that 88."

"Don't fret, we all get things we don't deserve."

"Who put me up to this?"

"You mean 'for' this, don't you?"

"Don't fuck with me, Dutch, you know what I mean."

"Their group commander was so grateful you saved that crew, he called our group commander and told him he thought you deserved the DFC.   Their group commander wrote it up and submitted it.   If it were up to me or Van Patten we'd have court-martialed you for leaving formation like that."

"What formation?   There were planes all over the place.   Most of 'em out of gas."

"You don't get it, do you?"

"No.   I'm beginning to think *you* don't."

"You know, Hollis, I used to think your naiveté was, in a way, refreshing.   Now, I find you annoying.   How did Otho make out?"

"He had trouble keeping his position but he did okay otherwise.   Why?"

"He looks a little down-trodden."

"He'll be OK.   He just needs a little more experience and maybe the red paint treatment."   Sniveling little cretin, Hollis thought, he's just as chickenshit as the rest of them.

When he walked out of Ransahoff's office Otho, Spats and Selkirk were having a good laugh.   Hollis's prevailing sense of paranoia made him wonder if they were laughing at him.

DFC?   That's a laugh.   Har-dee-har!

Selkirk must have been rejuvenated by two easy missions to Germany, his spirit somehow revitalized, his sense of foreboding softened for he appeared the same ebullient person he had been before as he joked with his comrades.

Hollis eased into the conversation when Otho's phone rang.   No one seemed to notice Barbieri answer but Hollis did.   He observed Otho nodding and saying 'yes sir' several times. He hung up and pulled a sheet of paper from his drawer.   Hollis watched as he made a short list. He got up from his desk and walked into Ransahoff's office.   Hollis heard him say, "Here's the roster for tomorrow's mission."

No one else heard him.   Spats and Selkirk continued to laugh.

Hollis felt the ice cold grip of fear encircle his heart.   As had happened once before, something Otho said had triggered an overpowering fear.   He noticed he still held the clipping in his hand.   He placed it in his pocket and walked out the door.   His hands started shaking. He could hear them still joking as the door closed behind him, their laughs mocking his fear.

He had the largest mission count of all the pilots in the Squadron, surpassing Selkirk and even Watanabe who had been around the longest.   He was second only to Ransahoff, who, until recently, had flown almost every mission the 532nd had participated in.   Statistically, with experience the odds of survival improved.   But this did not comfort him.   With each passing day, he felt, his time was running out.

He stepped into the alley and threw up.

Book III

Bombing

It's going to happen to me.   It's only a matter of time...

Chapter Forty   **The Brethren**

    The mission list had his name on it.   There would be no letup save for the exigencies of the weather that was fickle enough to drive even the most stout-hearted mad.   They had been lucky, too lucky for their own good, Hollis thought.   The missions had been easy, each a milk run, for practically a month.   Stuttgart was the last big raid and the Group had not lost a plane to enemy action since.   If Selkirk and Nevtushenko and their ilk had grown complacent, overconfident, he hadn't.   He was not so foolhardy to think this would suddenly be easy.   But there was no use talking to them.   They simply did not understand.   Maybe Selkirk did, he had two brushes with death, that would take the full measure of any man, and had suffered a depression which left him withdrawn and drinking heavily.   Even so, he now seemed his old self.   Spontaneously recovered by factor or factors unknown.
    But things were about to change.   Like an old man feels the coming storm in his arthritic joints, so did Hollis feel the burgeoning tumult that more bombing would bring.   The Germans

had let them have a free ride lately.   They weren't stupid.   They were biding their time. Resting.   Growing stronger.

Hollis wrote a letter to Jessie, telling her yet one more time that he would be careful and that he loved her.   He promised he would come home to her soon and they could finish what they had started.   But as the words made it onto the page they rang hollow, like the mocking laughter he had heard in the Squadron office.

He wrote to his parents and told them, by rearranging the words, basically the same thing. It was now the evening of October second and he had flown his thirteenth mission, or 12B as everyone liked to call Number Thirteen.   God willing and the creek don't rise, he would be home by Thanksgiving.   Certainly Christmas.   Provided, of course, the weather cooperated. But as he wrote it he thought any happy ending was too remote and unlikely to contemplate. But the words would make his mother happy, at least for the time being.

Hollis went to bed early.

It was a cloudy day. The sun was up there somewhere, why else could she see the flowers swaying gently on their long stems by the warm easy breeze?   She just hoped it wouldn't rain. She hated the rain.   It kept her from going outside and running around the meadows picking the pretty wild flowers which was her favorite thing to do.   She looked up hoping the sun would shine through the clouds and make them melt away to blue skies.

She was about to look away when something caught her eye.   Way up high in the clouds two white streaks appeared.   She could see them clearly and her gaze became fixed on them. Each streak had a small blue thing at its end coming straight for her.   They were joined by other, darker things.   She knew there were more than *funf* because that was as high as she knew how to count.   Whatever the things were they would soon be in her bedroom.   The whole sky was filled with dark things coming down, like rocks falling from the clouds, all headed right for her...

"Lieutenant?"

"Where to today, Beamis?"

"Don't know, but expect a hot reception."

"I *hate* that," Leo said as Beamis moved on.

Powell, Selkirk, Spats, Baldini and DeBerg and their officers were all jammed into the washroom trying to shave at once.   Mercifully, the water was warm and everyone shaved quickly.   There was a cacophony of bowels being evacuated and the washroom smelled damp of body odor, after-shave and flatus.   Hollis felt suddenly claustrophobic and departed before he had finished shaving.   After a few minutes most of the throng had left and he returned to complete his task.

He missed the first shuttle run to the Combat Mess and stayed long in his room dressing. He would probably be too late when he arrived at breakfast to have more than just a cup of coffee and some juice.   That was OK, he thought, he wasn't hungry anyway.

The briefing room was packed.   Maybe they were sending up a fourth squadron.   A maximum effort.   He could see Rager dressed for flying, standing, as he always did, nonchalantly, arms crossed and a sleepy look on his face, at the side of the stage.   Ransahoff was leading the Squadron, Hollis number two.   Van Patten was the Bangmaster.   The Group was leading the wing.

"The target for today is Kassel."   The red line went deep into Germany, almost halfway to Berlin.   A great groan and soft swearing resulted.   The gunners outside would be scurrying to deliver the bad news.

It started, was all Hollis could think.

Major Gorton took the stage.   "Gentlemen, I have the duty to inform you that based on our intelligence estimates, the *Jagdverbande*--the German fighter force--has increased its strength in Northwestern Europe to specifically counteract the threat from Allied, but mostly American, daylight heavy bombers.   It was estimated that in April of this year the *Luftwaffe* had on hand 300 single-engined day fighters in this Theater.   By withdrawing units from other fronts and expanding the *Jagd Gruppen* already in place, we now estimate that number to be eight hundred.   In addition, *Zerstorer Geschwader*, twin-engined bomber destroyers, number close to a hundred.   We believe the rogue B-17s seen by some of the crews on our last mission were captured Fortresses being used as fighter directors."

A pall settled over the crowd, a hush so silent one could hear hearts beating.

"Our escort will follow us to the limits of their endurance and you will be unescorted from the German border on."   Gorton let that little fact sink in.

"Our target, then, is--"

Hollis did not hear another word.   He stared at the images from the conical projector, he heard the words but nothing registered within his numbed brain.   He did not look around, he did not see the other faces.   His own suffering was all he could handle.

There was an eerie quiet in the equipment room save for the banging of lockers, the tinkling of parachute harnesses and the occasional swear word.

At the plane, **La Femme Fatale**, Hollis reiterated to the crew what he had heard.   They looked as stunned as he felt.   He told them of the target, an industrial plant in the city of Kassel, but he was weak on the details for he could not recall them and it didn't make any difference to them, anyway.

Quinn tried to stir up some conversation. No one was interested.

Hollis looked at his watch and was about to announce stations when a red-red flare poked into the sky.   The mission was off.   Probably weather over the target.

Everyone seemed relieved.   They all knew they would be headed back to Germany, they were all glad today was not the day.

A short time after Hollis awakened from a nap, Leo came into the room and told him that an announcement had been made over the Tannoy that all flying personnel were to present themselves in Class A's in parade formation at 1600 on the tarmac in front of the south hanger at the technical site.

What for?

Didn't say.

Hollis looked at his watch.   He had an hour.   He was about to doze off again when Selkirk appeared in his dress uniform.

"What's all this about?" he asked Selkirk.

"I don't know.   Some sort of ceremony or something is my guess.   Maybe they've come to their senses and have decided to send me home and this is some sort of sendoff."

"Fat chance."

"You know, Jack, me boy, I was about to say that since you started leadin' the Squadron

344

you'd lost your sense of humor until I reminded myself that you never really had one."

"You didn't have to come here.   If I want abuse I can always get that from Sully."

"Come on, get dressed.   It's clear over the other side of the field."

"I know where the tech site is."

"Get dressed."

"You think I'll be missed if I don't go?"

"If not, I'll report you."

Hollis dressed, the first time he had been in his Class A's since London.   He hoped whatever was going on would be over quickly.   The bane of any military organization was its recurring, ritual need to celebrate things.   Amidst chaos there was always the parade.

The flying personnel of all four squadrons as well as key members of the ground echelon stood at attention in the afternoon sun.   Van Patten, Gleason, Begay and the four squadron COs stood on the opposite side of a solitary microphone poised in the middle of the tarmac.   Beside Van Patten stood a general, someone Hollis did not recognize.

Van Patten stepped up to the microphone and began to speak.   "Gentlemen, we are privileged to have with us today, General Robert Williams, Commanding, First Bombardment Division.   He will say a few words and we will present the medals to be awarded today. General."

Williams was stocky and short, similar to Cobb, Hollis thought, except a lot older.   He wore glasses but from where Hollis stood it looked as if his eyes were not both aimed in the same direction.

"At ease, gentlemen.   I would like to congratulate you on completing your first three months of combat.   Your record has been an impressive one--" Hollis thought he was being particularly generous, damning them with faint praise--"and members of your Group have distinguished themselves in combat.   Beyond the growing pains experienced by all groups entering combat, the 381st has matured into a fine Group with strong leadership, establishing a tradition of excellence that will carry us through to victory.   I am here today, along with your commanding officers, to recognize those achievements.   When Colonel Gleason calls your name report front and center."

Williams turned the microphone over to Gleason.   It was the first time Hollis could ever remember seeing Gleason in anything other than his ubiquitous gunner's cap.

"Captain Bernard S. Rager."

Barney Rager snapped to attention and marched sharply to   Williams and Van Patten. He saluted and shook hands with both men.   Standing ram-rod straight, a vastly different pose from his relaxed slouch at briefing, Williams pinned the Silver Star on the left breast of Rager's blouse.

Gleason then read the citation which described his leadership of the Group on the Schweinfurt raid, *despite being blinded and critically wounded by enemy action.   While steadfastly guiding his bomber over the target, his perseverance and coolness under fire resulted in the Group's placing its bombs on target.*

As Hollis listened, he remembered that Sully told him they missed the target at Schweinfurt.

Williams next gave out three Distinguished Flying Crosses.   One to a pilot who saved his crew and his aircraft on the Hamburg raid in July, a navigator who, though severely wounded, put out a fire in the nose, toggled the bombs for his dead bombardier and provided first aid for his copilot, also on the Schweinfurt raid.   The third DFC went to a radio operator who had pulled his dying ball turret gunner from the ball and climbed in, proceeding to shoot down three German fighters, also over Schweinfurt.

"Lieutenant John Hollis."

Hollis was taken completely by surprise, so surprised that he almost failed to acknowledge his name thinking some mistake had been made.   Flustered, he snapped to attention and marched to the General.

He had been awarded the DFC for quick action in saving the lives on the crippled Fort returning from Stuttgart just as the newspaper clipping had said.   The citation sounded so heroic Hollis was certain they were talking about somebody else.

He looked at Williams, his one good eye focusing on Hollis's chest as he pinned the medal onto his tunic.   The other eye was Government Issue, no doubt, for it was looking somewhere over Hollis's right shoulder.   Then he remembered the story.   Williams had lost his eye observing the Blitz for the AAF.   Legend had it he could fly a B-17 better with one eye than most pilots could with two.

Hollis was embarrassed.   After the citation was read, which ended with the gratuitous comment that his actions reflected the finest traditions of the Air Force, Hollis assumed his place beside the radio operator.   There was that word again, tradition.   How many died on the altar of tradition?   It was the skeleton upon which the flesh of a military organization was supported.

Another DFC was awarded to Lieutenant Stanford Eisenberg, in his absence, for actions which saved the lives of his fellow squadron mates, Selkirk, in action over Hamburg.   Good old Stan.   Leaving formation was, to hear Ransahoff tell it, a court martial offense.   Yet their military code of honor could not turn their backs on bravery, no matter how inadvertent or undisciplined the act was.

Several Distinguished Service Medals were awarded for meritorious achievement. Some for the actions following the bomb loading accident early-on which killed over twenty men, the growing pains, Williams mentioned.   One of the recipients was the Negro ordinance sergeant who defused several bombs in the burning hulk of a Fortress.

Deserved or not, Hollis was now an unwitting, reluctant member of an exclusive, sacred fraternity.   He was a warrior.   He was one of the Brethren. It was amazing what a little piece of metal and some painted ribbon could bestow.

After the ceremony, the assembled were dismissed and the recipients had a drink with Williams and Van Patten.   One drink.   There was an alert on.

Hollis returned to the room, took the medal from his uniform and placed it in the rectangular box.   He pinned the ribbon on the chest of his blouse beside his Air Medal.   He wasn't sure he deserved it, but he would wear it anyway.   Leo, Sully and Selkirk entered the room.

"Royalty now," Sully said.

"Knock it off, Sully.   I was as surprised by this as you were."

"No," Selkirk said, "I think he deserves the medal.   Congratulations."   Selkirk shook Hollis's hand.   "What you did is no different than what Stan did.   He got a medal, too.   He saved my ass."

Hollis looked over at Leo who had a slight grin on his face but said nothing.   Hollis figured that was about as much as he would get from him.

They went to dinner and returned to the Squadron bulletin board to look at the mission roster for tomorrow.   Ransahoff, Nevtushenko, Powell, Robertshaw, DeBerg, Kehoe and Baldini.   Hollis noticed there were seven crews, one of them probably a spare, and that his name was not on the list.

When Hollis returned to the room Otho was there to tell him his crew had been given a forty-eight hour pass.   He explained that it was standard issue for crews that have arrived at the halfway point of their tour.   It had nothing to do with the DFC, he went on to explain.

Even so, Leo said after Barbieri left, the DFC didn't hurt.

Hollis was packed and ready to turn in when there was a knock on the door.   "Come in."

Barney Rager stepped into the room out of breath.   "Hey Hollis, I understand you got a forty-eight hour pass."

"Yeah, why?"

"You plannin' on going to London?"

"Yeah, why?"

"Hightower is sick.   I think there's something wrong with his ass.   Hemorrhoids or something and I can't wangle a pass so you've got to do me a favor."

"Yeah, like what?"

"I want you to meet a woman in London and escort her to some function at the U.S. Embassy tomorrow afternoon."

The blonde!

"Her name is Molly and she will meet you at the entrance of the Savoy at two o'clock."

"Sure, I think I can do that.   Two o'clock, you say?"

"Right, her name is Molly.   She's tall and blonde.   I really appreciate it.   I owe you."

"Sure."

Chapter Forty-one   **Molly**

Hollis was awakened by the sound of shuffling in the hall.   He checked the time, more out of habit than because he really desired to know, 0330, and returned to sleep.   He planned to awaken at seven, shit, shower and shave and catch the shuttle to Great Yeldham by eight.   The Toonerville Trolley was scheduled to depart for London at 9:05.   Liverpool Station by 11:30 or so, get a room at the Savoy or Dorchester and still have plenty of time to get to meet Molly by two.   This allowed him plenty of margin for bad weather, delays, problems at assembly...

Without need for alarm clock, Hollis was awake before seven.   Leo and Sully had decided to spend their pass in Cambridge and the truck to and from there left several times a day, so they slept in.   Cobb had not accumulated enough missions to go so he was ineligible. Hollis would be flying solo on this trip.

His stroll down the path to the washroom was a leisurely one.   He could hear the engines start across the field and wondered where they were going.   The slowly rising thunder reverberated among the trees around the communal site.   He could make out changes in pitch as the rpms were exercised, props feathered and mag checks were performed in a random, surrealistic symphony.   He wondered again where they were headed.   He wished them well, but was glad he was not one of them.

He admonished himself to stop thinking about them, he had decided that for the next forty-eight hours he would not think about or discuss the bombing with anyone.   He planned to get a little drunk, go to the Windmill or the Washington Club on Curzon Street and eat as much steak and fried chicken as his stomach would allow.   No Aussies, no trips down to the Underground.   He wanted to get this little business with Rager's girlfriend out of the way and relax.   Maybe take in some of the sights he missed last trip, a couple hour-long hot baths.

As he dressed, he listened to the bombers roar into the sky and waited for the sound to disappear.   Hard as he tried, he could not ignore the sound or its meaning, wondering yet again where they were going and what was about to happen to them.

He put on his trench coat, tossed the musette bag over his shoulder, wished Leo a fond *adieu* and left.

The run to Great Yeldham was right on time.   He arrived at the station at eight-thirty, purchased his ticket, taking a seat on the bench.   The platform was nearly deserted.   He expect to run into some of the crew or see some familiar face to keep him company but he was alone. How odd, he thought, that he would be the only one going to London.   Perhaps the crew didn't have the good time in London they had expected and decided, as Leo and Sully had, to go somewhere else.   No matter.   Today, they were not his concern.

The train was late.   Very late.   By ten o'clock not a single train had passed through the station.   Finally, Hollis went to the purchasing agent and asked, "What gives?"

"Problems on the line.   Patience, Yank.   Should be here soon."

Hollis resumed his seat, pulled a paperback, Tate and Bishop's <u>American Harvest</u>, from his musette and started reading.   He glanced at his watch repeatedly until another hour had passed.   He smoked and read, afraid he might finish the book before the damned train came.

"You know, I could have walked to London by now," he told the agent.   Hollis was trying to be polite, but he was wasting time.   The agent reiterated, *problems on the line, should be soon.*

Almost unnoticed was the appearance of several men from the base, none of whom he knew.   Some were flyers, others not.   A slowly enlarging congregation of locals occupied the station as well.   At this rate, Hollis thought, he would not get to London before one.   If Molly got stood up, through no fault of his own, Rager would be steamed.   No one wants to keep a beautiful woman waiting, even if she does belong to someone else.   A knockout on the arm beat a chest full of Air Medals and DFCs any day of the week.

Hollis thought of his DFC.   Surely those poor bastards would have died had he not moved **Cleopatra's Asp** to their rescue so Rizzo could fire at that Junkers.   He didn't feel like a hero.   Yet he wore the same ribbon as those who truly were.   He vowed that he would not think about this stuff and he was mad at himself for breaking his promise.

The shrill whistle of the Toonerville sounded and Hollis felt relieved to finally be on his way.

The train was packed to the gills.   The fact that it was late had allowed large crowds of passengers to accumulate at stations up the line and when the train finally came it was apparent to Hollis that he would be lucky to squeeze onto it.   How uncharacteristic it was for one of their trains to be so late, he thought.   The Brits were an odd people but it was a matter of national pride that their trains ran on time.

On a deadline and not to be deterred, Hollis wedged himself into the coach amidst people already standing in the aisle.   He figured he was entitled since he had been waiting the longest. He glanced back at the door over which was a sign, "If danger seems imminent lie on the floor." If danger was imminent, they would have no choice but to face it standing up.   He did not relish the idea of standing all the way to London but he was on a mission.

Hollis noticed a Tommie, his plaid tam-o-shanter cocked jauntily on his head, his tin helmet strapped to his knapsack, sleeping in the standing position, his body supported as the coach rocked back and forth unevenly on the rails, by an obese old woman and several GIs.

'Imminent danger.'   He had been in no imminent danger when he won the DFC.   Save for running out of gas and plummeting into the sea.   The Ju-88 was no threat to him.   It was not like he charged a machine gun nest or took out a dozen tanks with a bazooka and a .45.   His accomplishment was mostly the result of being in the right place at the right time and the pleading of his copilot.   Most of the time, as they reached the coast, Rizzo was already out of the ball turret.   So it was good fortune or circumstance which had resulted in those lives being saved and the consequent DFC, not some blind, impulsive charge with fixed bayonets.   He knew, if he thought about it long enough, that he would cheapen the Medal and what it represented.   He tried again not to think about it.

Now Rager, there was a genuine hero.   Guiding the Group over the target, his vision blurred by his own blood, his hand punctured by flak, so painful he had trouble gripping the control column, holding the bomber steady until the Group's bombs rained down on, well, somewhere in the vicinity of Schweinfurt.

Perhaps Noah Dodge should have gotten a medal.   Straddling the gaping bomb bay, the plane repeatedly jolted by flak, a hot piece of shrapnel in his thigh *-Boy, Noah, that musta hurt-* cranking up the bomb bay doors so they could gain the speed necessary to rejoin the safety of the Group.

Any rate, when he walks into that reception -at the Embassy, of all places- and they see the DFC on his blouse no one will know how hard or easy it was to come by.

What in the hell was he doing going to the U.S. Embassy, for Christ's sake?   He was just a lowly First Lieutenant in your average bomb group.   There were thousands of them all over England.   What was the protocol for this?   He had been given a brief lecture during officer training on military social etiquette but, as with many other things, it was just so much chickenshit and was largely ignored.

The train made several stops, discharging some and adding more until Hollis was certain that, if the locomotive took a curve too quickly, the whole train would hurtle off the rails into the woods.

The agonizing two and a half hours on his feet, which had been stepped on repeatedly, finally ended and the train pulled into the cavernous Liverpool Station.   He stepped onto the platform and went to the NAAFI kiosk and drank a hot cup of tea.   Reinvigorated, and not a little apprehensive, he headed off to the Savoy.

Hollis wanted to be courteous but not excessively warm. Pleasant, but not fawning. This woman was the girlfriend of a colleague and he had a fiancé waiting patiently in Pennsylvania.   He cautioned himself not to let the moment or the alcohol get the better of him. Besides it was just a stupid reception, how long would that last?   He'd drop her off like the gentleman he was and go his own way.

Hollis stepped out of the cab in front of the Savoy at precisely two o'clock.   He had fretted he might be late but was pleased that he was not.   Sure enough, standing in the same location she had been the last time he saw her was the fetching young blonde named Molly. She stood in front of the sandbags stacked against the facade, her small purse held by both hands in front of her, a medium-brimmed hat pulled down over her forehead, her golden hair draped onto her shoulders.

"You must me Molly."

"Yes, and you must be John Hollis."

"Yes, nice to meet you."   He extended his hand which she shook.   He worried that was some sort of social gaffe.   A gentleman never shook a woman's hand until she offered it.   But then again there was a war on.

"I was afraid I might be late."

"No," she said, her voice deep, slightly gravelly and   American, "you were right on time."

Hollis could tell in an instant that this was a sophisticated woman.   "I understand I am to escort you to the Embassy for a cocktail party."

"Yes, I hope this imposition doesn't interfere with any plans you may have made. Barney had hoped to make it, but I think he was detained."

"Yes, detained.   Interesting way of putting it."

"The reception doesn't begin until four, oh, I'm sorry, for you military types, sixteen hundred, so we have some time to kill would you like some lunch or tea?"

"Actually, I'm famished.   I had some tea after I got off the train to tide me over but yes, I would like something to eat."

"Good, my treat.   I know a nice little cafe close by.   We can eat there and catch a cab to the Embassy."

"Sounds peachy."

They started walking down the street and she wrapped her arm around his, Hollis figured, to be cordial.

"So tell me," Hollis asked, "what is a nice girl like you doing in a place like this?"

"I work at the Embassy.   I've been here nearly a year.   I'm the secretary to the secretary to Ambassador Winant."

"Sounds interesting."

"Oh, it is.   I've met and talked with just about everybody except Roosevelt himself.   I even met Eleanor.   I met Andrews before he was killed and Eisenhower, Churchill, all of them."

"They give you any idea when the war will end?"

"No.   But I hope it will be soon.   Then things can get back to normal."

"What did you do before the war?"

"I was a history major at Rutgers.   And you?"

"I was waiting to start medical school.   I graduated from Swarthmore in June of '41 and was working to save money to start school at Jefferson Medical College in the fall of '42 when the damned war started."

"Drafted?"

"No, my number was about to be called so I joined the Cadets.   I wanted to be the master of my own destiny.   Becoming an officer and pilot seemed the best way to do it.   I read all the comic books growing up, 'Flying Aces' that sort of thing.   It seemed like the natural thing to do."

"Ah, here we are."   She stepped into a small cafe, very narrow but deep, dark wood paneling and a long bar on one wall and small booths lining the other.   She waved to the bartender and he waved back.   He raised an eyebrow when he realized that it was not Barney Rager she had her arm around.   She guided him to a booth and a waitress came by almost immediately.

Hollis looked over the menu.   Slim pickings, really.   He was about to order and egg and Spam sandwich when Molly grabbed his arm across the table and said, "We'll each have a 'Special' and some tea."

Hollis glanced at his watch, yeah it was late enough, "Make mine a gin and tonic."

"Very good," she said as she nodded and left.

"What, pray-tell, is a 'Special'?"

"Corned beef on rye with Swiss cheese and a hollandaise dressing."

"Corned beef?   I thought there was a shortage of the stuff."

"There is, so after you eat it forget it.   I think they get it on the black market."

"Interesting, even, dare-I-say, exciting.   I've never eaten black market food."

"You learn to make do.   There is a war on, you know."   She winked at Hollis and they shared a laugh.

They ate their corned beef sandwiches and chatted.   Hollis specifically avoided any mention of her relationship with Barney.   She never brought it up and he never asked.

She told stories of life at the Embassy, dropping names occasionally.   Being a secretary to a secretary allowed her to know a great deal and she seemed to enjoy talking about it. Nothing secret or anything a spy would want to know.   Gossip, mostly.   Hollis displayed polite interest, asking questions from time to time, but after his second gin and tonic he just smiled and nodded.

She was very pretty.   Not as pretty as Christie Mellon or even Jessie Snowden, Hollis thought, but a bright, engaging smile, soft features, big green eyes demonstrating a warmth and familiarity toward Hollis that he found difficult to explain for such short notice.   She touched his arm to make a point once or twice but even that seemed natural and not some come on.

She looked at the time, "Goodness, it's almost four.   We need to get going."

She paid the bill and they left.   He hailed a cab and off they went.   When they arrived at the Embassy, Hollis noticed it was guarded by British and American Military Police and a contingent of Marines in dress blues.   Hollis showed his AGO card and was allowed in.

He stepped into a large reception room filled with smoke and the smell of fresh cut flowers.   There was laughter and small groups of officers and civilians chatting amiably.

He looked around, puny, but fascinated to be in the presence of so many powerful and important people.   A woman came over to them and was introduced as Molly's boss.   She whispered something in Molly's ear and this caused Molly to frown and say softly, "I don't know."

"Know what?"

"Nothing," she smiled.   "Remember, I said I didn't know."   She then leaned to Hollis's ear and whispered.   "Smile a lot, don't drink too much, don't ask any questions and only speak when you are spoken to."

He wondered if they could smell the residue of gasoline recently used to dry clean his Class As.

Like a juvenile in a room full of adults, Hollis felt chastened.   "OK."   He got separated from Molly who went to talk to some Brits.   He had another gin and tonic but nursed it until the ice was almost melted.   The novelty and excitement was rapidly supplanted by boredom.   His 'date' had left him and he felt more akin to the butler serving drinks than he did to anybody else. Admirals and generals strolled past giving him the same notice they would give a potted plant. Eaker, Spaatz.   To them the DFC meant nothing.   He even caught a fleeting glimpse of Winnie chatting with Ike.   Hollis pondered with some amusement, if the Germans wanted to alter the outcome of the war in one fell swoop all they had to do was blow up this place.   He lit a cigarette and ordered another drink.

"Hollis."

Hollis turned to the direction his name had been called and saw General Williams. Williams walked over and shook his hand.   "Nice work."

He didn't know which eye to look into so he stared at the bridge of his glasses and said, "Thank you, sir."

Williams moved on, drink in hand.   The tough life of the General staff.   Then he remembered that Williams was in the lead plane over Schweinfurt and he took back his thought.

He glanced around the room and made eye contact with Molly who winked at him.   He raised his glass to her and smiled.   *Now what kind of signal was that?* he wondered.

His sense of duty to Molly and, indirectly to Barney, restrained him from getting drunk for the alcohol flowed by like a river on great silver trays of mixed drinks.   After almost two hours of patiently smiling and nodding and wondering where Molly had gone, Hollis noticed the crowd started to thin, an indication that things might be winding down.

"Hi."

He turned to see Molly's smiling face.

"Hi."

"Bored?"

"Now I know how a potted plant feels."

She feigned hurt.

"Hey, I was only kidding.   I've enjoyed every minute of it.   Wouldn't have missed it for the world.   Beats hell out of driving a Fortress around any day."

She took his hand and held it for a moment trying to figure out if he was being sarcastic or just rude.

"I'm serious.   Nothing beats State Department booze."

She could not conceal her disappointment at Hollis's response.

"Come on, Molly, let's go somewhere and get a steak and go dancing, maybe drink too much and have more fun than we should."

She studied him for a moment, recovered her smile and said, "Sure, why not?"

As Hollis retrieved their coats and his musette bag he said, "Really, Molly.   I had a nice time.   I even met a general or two.   I hope I was a decent escort.   I hope I didn't embarrass you.   My impulse to mingle with the elite was successfully suppressed and I smiled a lot."

Molly's boss came over to them as they approached the door and extended her hand. "Lieutenant Hollis, it was a pleasure to meet you.   I'm sorry I didn't get a chance to talk to you. I was preoccupied with things, as you may have been able to tell."

"Yes, busy place."

"Please stop by again.   When you see Barney tell him we all said 'hello'.   He's quite a character."

"I'll say."

They left and stepped into the night.   Molly took his arm again.   "I'm sorry," she said softly.

"For what?"

"Wasting your afternoon."

"Don't be silly.   If nothing else it was interesting.   How many lowly lieutenants get a chance to hob-nob with the Supreme Allied Command?"

"Now you're patronizing me," she said, smiling at him.

"Yes.   Absolutely.   I'm just trying to stay in your good graces.   Besides, who wouldn't want a pretty lady like you on his arm?"

"Am I making you uncomfortable?"

"No, not at all.   Why should you?"

"Listen, John, if you have other plans, please tell me."

"If I did I would, but I do not."

"You're under no obligation to escort me any further that this stupid party."

"Now stop, Molly.   I had fun, really.   Let's say we just drop it and have a good time. Where shall we eat?"

"Are you hungry already?"

"Famished."

"Then let's go to the Grosvenor House.   It's right around the block.   We can eat at Willow Run."

"Great."

She steered them in the right direction and fell silent.   Hollis looked around as they walked and saluting to scores of officers walking up and down both sides of the street.   He figured by the time they reached the Grosvenor House, he had saluted more than in all the time since arriving in England.

Soon they were escorted to a table in a huge room nicknamed "Willow Run" after the immense Ford assembly line in Detroit where they turned out B-24s.   Hollis estimated there were two or three hundred officers and enlisted men seated around the room and it only seemed half-full.

They both ordered drinks and stared at the menu.   The Grosvenor House had been appropriated by the U.S. Military for housing officers and personnel attached to ETO headquarters which explained the menu, right out of the good old USA.   Fried chicken and dumplings.   Porterhouse steak.   Pork chops.   And absolutely nothing derived, disguised or mixed with Spam.   They were quiet until the drinks arrived.

"You're not very happy, are you?"

The question caught him off guard.   "What's to be happy about?"

"That was a stupid question.   I'm sorry."

"That's OK."   He smiled at her as a flash of whimsy occurred to him.

"What's so funny?"

"Nothing it's just that Barney's plane is named **Miss Sheila II** and for some reason I thought that was you."

She reached across the table and grasped his hand laughing.   "That's my real name. My little brother couldn't say Sheila when he was little so he called me Molly.   Some sort of speech impediment. He's been calling me that ever since."

"Oh, I understand.   I don't know your last name."

"Roberts."

Hollis sipped his drink.   "So what's your little brother doing these days?"

"You know him."

"I do?   What's his name?"

"Barney."

Hollis was stunned, "Barney is your *brother*?"

"Yes.   For as long as I can remember."   She giggled, understanding for the first time that some sort of inadvertent joke had been played on Hollis.

"So he named his plane after you?   But your name is Roberts."

"Yes, I was married.   My husband flew Liberators.   He was killed over St. Omer last October.   His plane was named **Miss Sheila**.   Barney and my husband were best friends. Barney named his plane after my husband's plane."

"You're his *sister*.   I saw you two the last time I was in London.   We all assumed you were his girlfriend or wife."

"Does that change things?"

"It certainly explains a few things, yes."   He saw her bow her head slightly as if seized by an irrepressible remembrance.   "I'm sorry about your husband."

She raised her head and smiled politely, her face glowing in the candlelight.   "Matt was assigned to the 93rd Group and was sent here.   We were married just before they shipped out. When we found out where he was going I dropped out of school.   Daddy is some bigwig in the New Jersey Democratic party so he was able to call in some favors and got me a job with the

State Department and got me sent here.   Matt was dead before I ever saw him again.   Barney was flying P-38s and was about to be shipped overseas, his squadron ended up in Guadalcanal. When he heard Matt was killed he got Daddy to arrange a transfer to a heavy bomber group that was being sent to England so Barney could be close to me.   He was sent to Texas, transitioned into Seventeens and came over with the 381st.   The rest is history."

"Well that explains a lot, too.   Everyone thought the way Barney flew he should have been a fighter pilot.   You think Daddy could get me transferred back to a training command somewhere?"

She looked at him wistfully, saying, "I'll ask."   She slowly sipped her drink.   "I can't shake the image in my mind of Matt's body lying among the people he was sent to kill.   I don't know what happened to him or where he rests.   Did they find him?   Did they give him a decent burial?"

Hollis was overwhelmed by her sorrow and her vulnerability.   Hollis was only twenty-four.   His experience with widows was limited.   What should one say?   Should he try to comfort, search for some sympathetic word and risk saying something inappropriate or trite, no matter how well-intentioned or should he express his empathy by saying nothing at all? Questions with no answers.   She'll probably spend the rest of her life and never know what became of her husband.

The waiter, an elderly Englishman, stepped up to the table to take their order, saw their expressions and turned away.

Molly wiped a tear from her cheek and looked up at Hollis, her eyes glistening with moisture.   "I'm sorry."

"You say that a lot.   For what?"

"You're on leave, you see this stuff all the time.   You don't need to be hearing it from me."

"Don't be silly."   He looked across the table at her face and thought he saw Jessie. They looked alike, Hollis thought.   Too much alike for his comfort.

"What's the matter?"

"Nothing."

"Do you have a girlfriend back home?   Oh, that's a silly question.   A good looking guy like you, probably has a dozen girls all waiting impatiently for the next day's mail."

"No, actually, I'm engaged, sort of."

"What do you mean, 'sort of'?"

"After the Schweinfurt deal I wrote her a letter and asked her to marry me.   I never have found out the answer.   I am missing a letter which, I think, contained her answer.   She's been writing me acting as if the answer was yes and that we are engaged, but no official confirmation and I haven't figured out a way to tactfully re-pose the question."

"Now that's some dilemma," she said coyly.   "Is she a member of the 'Always in My Heart Club'?"

"I guess she is."

"So are you engaged or not?"

"I guess I am.   But a moment ago, I almost wished I were not."

She raised her glass in salute and downed it.

"I think I would like another."   She said and swiveling in her seat, added, "I wonder where that waiter got to?   I'm starving."

"That was a great meal," he said.

"And the company was pretty terrific.   You're funny.   This was one of the best times I've had since I can't remember how long."

"The pleasure was all mine.   I thought the company was pretty terrific, too."

"Why, thank you."

Hollis wasn't sure what his next step should be, if any.   "What would you say to going out to a club and maybe doing some dancing?"

She thought for a minute and then cocked her head, "Sure, why not?   No harm in that."

"Where would you like to go?"

"You pick."

"Want to go to the Washington Club?"

"Sure, great place.   It's close by and they have a great band."

"Come on.   Time's a-wastin'."   Hollis paid the bill and they left.

After a short walk, they arrived at the Washington Club.   As they entered and checked their coats, Hollis could immediately tell that the band was very talented.   They were busy into a rendition of "Caribbean Clipper" which made the nerves in his feet twitch.   The last time he danced to this tune was with Jessie at a USO dance in Philly before shipping out.

Hollis muscled his way through the crowd, mostly officers and their dates, Molly gripping his hand in tow, until he found, as if by miracle, a vacant table.

"Sit tight," he yelled above the music and the crowd noise, "I'll get us some drinks."

She smiled and waved.

When Hollis returned with two gin and tonics, a lovely brunette stepped up the microphone and spoke, "Now, here's one I'm sure you'll remember."   She turned to the conductor and said, "OK, fellas, one, two," and the band, in response to the whiplash of the baton, launched into "Six Lessons of Madame La Zonga."

This caused Molly to erupt with laughter.   "My God, it's been a while since I've heard that!"

The brunette dove into the lyrics, swaying to the Latin beat of the song, doing her very best Helen O'Connell, which Hollis thought, was pretty darned good.   Hollis watched Molly still giggling, clapping her hands together lightly, and when the brunette arrived at the line, Molly sang, in perfect harmony, "And say, by the way, if you're sure it's OK, if Madame likes you, the lessons are free."   Hollis marveled at Molly's enthusiasm for the song, which he only vaguely remembered, and when the song returned to the line a second time she sang the words with even more bravado than she had the first.   Now Hollis, suddenly flushed with life and good cheer, laughed as did everyone near them.   When the song finished the crowd, led by Molly, erupted with applause.   And for a brief, shining moment everyone was happy and there was no war.

There was so much about Molly that reminded him of Jessie.   Molly would be an easy woman to fall for, Hollis thought.   As he danced with her, felt her against him, he knew that he was sliding and he must be strong.   Fidelity and virtue were important to him.   And, except for that one time, his only lover since Jessie had been his right hand. Very occasionally, his left.

They danced to "Tangerine," "All of Me," and "Brazil," the brunette continuing her Helen

O'Connell, until Molly asked if this show was being dedicated to Jimmy Dorsey.   They drank, a little too much, Hollis thought, and talked and danced until ten o'clock when the orchestra played their last song, "Moonlight Serenade."   Hollis held Molly close to him.   She was a little drunk and had lost some of the light quality to her step.   She became a little clumsy, but it would have been hard to notice the way they were jostled on the packed dance floor.

They left as the band played "God Save the King."   Stepping into the dark street, Hollis recalled how unsettling he found the blackout.   He looked up and, in the starlight, he could make out the dark hulks of the barrage balloons which he hardly noticed during the day, loomed large and ominous in the dark, clustered above the Embassy, a can't miss aiming point for any German with a bomb and a bombsight.   Surely, the Brits were up tonight.   What was it like in the pitch-black night, hurtling toward earth, in the dark, cluttered hulk of a bomber, clawing for the exits?

He lit a cigarette and they started walking, to what destination, Hollis wasn't sure.   He considered suggesting that they go find another club, but figured Molly had had enough revelry for one night.

"Where are you staying?" she asked him.

"No place yet.   I was afraid I'd be late meeting you so I didn't get checked in anywhere."

She tightened her embrace around his arm.   "I live close by, you can stay with me if you'd like.   The couch isn't very big, but it's quite comfortable.   You've been such a gentleman, pinch hitting on such short notice, it's the least I could do.   I'll get up and make you a nice breakfast."

Hollis contemplated the issue and said, "Sure, why not?   I'd like that."

They walked in silence.   There was traffic noise and the sounds of people nearby but for a moment, Hollis thought, they might as well be alone in the Universe.

"Is she pretty?"

"Beautiful."

"Do you love her?"

"Yes, very much."

For the rest of their journey nothing further was said.

They arrived at her flat, not far from the Embassy.   Hollis placed his musette bag and coat on a chair, stripping off his tunic and tie, while she gathered a sheet and blankets for him. The room was lit by only a single table lamp.   There were two rooms, her bedroom and the combination, sitting room, kitchen and eating area, a small table and two chairs up against the window, covered by a black curtain.   There was a Philco radio, a stuffed chair and the divan, a narrow affair but long enough to stretch out in.   She turned on the radio and offered him a drink.   He declined.   They sat on the divan and talked.   The BBC played some Glenn Miller tunes and she reminisced about how she and Barney and Matt had piled into a car one Saturday night and drove over to the Glen Island Casino on Long Island to see him play.   Matt was a big Miller fan, had all his records.

Hollis placed his arm around her more out of friendship and shared loneliness than affection.   She nestled against his shoulder much as Jessie had so long ago.   The irony was not lost on him when the next selection on the radio was "Long Ago and Far Away."   She started to snore softly.

The war had produced countless life-altering surprises, crossroads from which there would be no retreat.   This was only the most recent.   Here he found himself, engaged to a most beautiful girl, someone he had spent his whole youth adoring, yet in his arms he found the warm, delightfully attractive widow of a fallen comrade and the sister of one of the best pilots in England.   He wondered about cosmic justice and actions unseen and unrecorded.   Did the war, this ugly stain on the face of humanity, with all its exigencies and imperatives, justify actions which at another time and place he would never even contemplate?   It was a ruthless combination, hormones and privation.   He could feel her chest gently rise and fall under his arm.   He sat for a long time listening to the music, reckoning.   He wanted to do the right thing, he just wasn't sure what that was.

Finally, he lifted her in his arms and carried her into the bedroom.   He placed her on the bed, the smooth white skin of her thighs exposed above the tops of her stockings.   He took off her shoes and pulled her dress down over her lithe legs and covered her with the satin comforter. He bent down and gently stroked the hair from her face.   She reached up and placed her arms around his neck and kissed him on the lips.   He kissed her back despite the fact he couldn't be sure if she was kissing him or Matt.

"Good night, Molly."

"Good night, John."

Hollis awakened to the smell and sizzle of bacon in the pan, the room awash with warm, brilliant sunlight.   He flipped off the blanket and stood up realizing suddenly as he did so the unmistakable distension in his boxer shorts by a piss hard-on.

"Good morning," Molly said.   "Do you have to pee or are you just glad to see me?"

Hollis smiled sheepishly as he covered himself.

"It's down the hall."

He grabbed his pants and pulled them on quickly to save himself any further embarrassment.

"I suggest you hurry before Mrs. Ferguson gets in there, she'll smell up the loo for an hour."

"Right-o," Hollis said as he trotted down the hall.   When he returned Molly was busy frying eggs, a rare commodity in England, Hollis thought, wondering how she came to have them.   He finished   dressing and sat down at the table, looking down at the activity on the street.

"We call these mission eggs.   They usually give us square eggs, that powdered crap. They only serve these when they expect a bad deal."

"Yes, I know.   Barney won't eat them."

As she placed a plate of toast in front of him, he noticed that she was dressed.   "You have to work?"

"Yes, of course.   What are your plans today?"

"I don't know.   I thought I might see some sights.   Buy a couple newspapers and sit in the park and read them.   You know, find out how the war's going."

"Can I expect to see you here when I return this evening?"

"Sure, if you don't mind the company."

"Why would I mind?"

"I don't want to be an imposition."

"No.   I enjoyed having a man around, even if it was you."   She smiled at him and winked.

Hollis dove into the eggs and bacon, lavishing his palate with fine tasting coffee all of which, he took great pleasure in noting, would not be regurgitated onto the grass in a few hours. "This is a great breakfast.   Thanks."

"You're welcome."   She gathered her coat and purse and was about to leave when she turned to him and said, "There's a spare key on the table by the couch.   I'll see you later."   She closed the door behind her.

After breakfast, he cleaned up after himself and washed up, unfortunately, just after Mrs. Ferguson's olfactory blitzkrieg .   He dressed and stepped out into the bright morning sun.   He walked down the street and purchased a <u>Daily Mirror</u> and a <u>Times</u> and strolled over to Hyde Park.   He found a bench in the warm sun and started reading.   Naples was occupied by the British Army's King's Dragoon Guards.   The port is heavily damaged.   Units of the U.S. Army troops established a line on the Volturno River.   Ike and Badoglio signed the Italian surrender documents on the Royal Navy battleship *Nelson*.   Perhaps that was the inciting event for the reception.   So things seemed to be going well in Italy.   Finschafen in New Guinea was taken by Australians.   Japanese forces were being withdrawn from Kolombangara in the Solomons. So progress was being made in the Southwest Pacific.   The Russians established a bridgehead over the Dnieper south of Kiev.   So the Russians were doing OK.   Frankfurt was bombed by Flying Fortresses of the Eighth U.S. Army Air Forces.   Twelve B-17s were lost.   Over seventy enemy aircraft were claimed as destroyed.   Twelve Forts.   One hundred and twenty men. Hollis wondered how many of them he knew.   His breakfast didn't feel so welcome in his stomach anymore.   He folded the newspapers and threw them in the nearest trash-bin.   He looked up at the sky.   There were a few broken clouds.   He wondered where they had gone today.

He walked deeper into the park.   Babies were being wheeled around in carriages. Couples were stretched out on blankets or newspapers sunbathing or necking.   He didn't go far when he saw the first antiaircraft gun manned by a sleepy, bored RAF gun crew.   Then another. He studied them.   Sandbags were piled around the emplacements, their dishpan helmets back on their heads.   One's ears covered with a headset, a talker's mike protruding from the front of his chest like some rude appendage.

"Gentlemen in England now abed
Shall think themselves accurs'd they were not here
And hold their manhood's cheap."

He felt the almost irresistible desire to tear off his uniform and run away.   There was no escaping the war.   He wanted to put as much distance between him and the war as possible, but there was no place to run.   And he would be naked when he got there.

On the Serpentine he saw couples in rowboats, stared at them for a moment and vowed to redeem at least part of the afternoon.   He turned and strode briskly to the Embassy getting as far as the receptionist's desk.

"May I see Mrs. Roberts?"

"May I ask who you are?"

"Lieutenant Hollis."

The receptionist dialed a number and spoke on the phone for a moment.   "Mrs. Roberts will be right out."

"Thanks."   Hollis waited patiently.

"John?"

Hollis was glad to see Molly appear as if out of nowhere.

"Molly, take the day off."

"I can't just walk out.   I have work to do."

"Please."

She looked long and hard at Hollis and said, "Wait here.   I'll see what I can do."   She disappeared only to return a few minutes later, smiling.

"I'm off.   Now what do you have in mind?"

"Let's go rent a rowboat."

"A rowboat?"

Molly and Hollis arrived back at her apartment exhausted, but happy.   They rowed around the Serpentine for what seemed like hours, talking and not talking.   They ate fish and chips and walked to the British Museum.   As they walked, she pointed at the various statues of historical Britons. Gladstone, Disraeli, Florence Nightingale, Robert Clive, Horatio Nelson. The Angel of Christian Charity, Eros, in Piccadilly Circus. First statue in the world made of aluminum, she said. He had to take her word for it that it was there.   It was all boarded up to prevent German bombs from destroying it. She went on to explain that even though a distant relative had fought with Washington during the Revolution, she had become something of an Anglophile. Hollis could not understand the attraction. Dinner and dancing at a night club. Hollis could not recall having such a good time.   His mind was devoid of thoughts of flying and combat.   He even suppressed his anxiety about the darkened city.   They talked for a brief time then she bade him good night and they retired.   Hollis had no thought about making love to her.

Hollis had to catch the train back to Great Yeldham so he could be back by noon when his pass expired.   He was up before six.   He washed and made some coffee while Molly slept. At a little before seven he quietly entered her bedroom and sat on the side of her bed.   It was enough to cause her to stir.

"Good morning," he said softly.

"Mmmm," she murmured as she stretched, "Good morning to you, sir."

"I made some coffee."

"Do you have time for breakfast?"

"No, I must go soon."

She sat up and hugged him.   He could feel the soft, unrestrained mounds of her breasts press against him through her nightshirt.   He hugged her back, holding her warm body to his, his nostrils filled with her aromas.

"Thank you for a great time," she said.

"Thank *you*, Molly."

"We should have made love, you know."

"I know."

He released her and she pulled away to look at him.   "Your girlfriend is one very lucky girl."

"I suppose," he said smiling at her.

"If she should change her mind, give me a call."

"You'll be the first."

"You be careful, John Hollis.   I don't think I could bear to have my heart broken twice."

Hollis looked at her for a moment not sure what she had meant.   Rather than explore such uncertain ground he hugged her again and got up.

"I must go."

"Call, if you get a chance."

"I will."

"Give my best to Barney when you see him."

"I will."

"Keep an eye on him for me, would you?"

"Sure."   Hollis could see a thin rim of moisture below her eyes and he turned and left before things became even more complicated.

He stepped out into the street in a hard rain.   He flagged a cab, "Liverpool Station," he said to the cabbie.   As he was about to close the door behind him he looked up at her window. The blackout curtain was drawn back and he saw her smiling down at him.   She gave him a small wave.   He smiled, waved back and closed the door.

The trains were running more reliably and at precisely eight- oh-five the train pulled out of Liverpool Station.   Hollis watched the rain-soaked countryside slide past on his way to Great Yeldham.   It was a ride marked by profound and mixed emotion.   It was fitting that the rain streaked the window so he had trouble making out details.   Images were blurred, unclear.

He stepped into the room and found Leo writing a letter.

"Made it back OK, I see."

"Oh, hi, Jack.   How was London?"

"Great."

"You?"

"Had a good time in Cambridge, but I didn't stay long.   We worked on decimals yesterday."

"And how is Ian?"

"Fine."

"And Ian's mother?"

"Fine, as well."   Hollis noted Leo's response was unassuming.   Was he fucking this woman? he asked himself.   If he were, would Leo ever come clean?   Why should he?

As Hollis unpacked the toiletries from his kit, Selkirk came by.   "You missed a tough one the day you left.   We went to Frankfurt to bomb that stupid propeller factory."

"Yeah?"

"They got Mike Watanabe."

Chapter Forty-two   **Quinn**

"What happened?"

"We were rolling off the target when he lost an engine.   Flak, I think.   They couldn't keep up and fell back.   There was no one to cover him and he tried to drop back into a following group.   He never made it."

"Anybody make it out?"

"They were on fire, went into a flat spin.   There were two chutes.   Then the wing came off.   They were pinned inside.   We watched it go all the way down."

Selkirk became silent, stood perfectly still as his gaze focused on middle distance and, without saying anything else, walked away.

A short time later, Quinn poked his head into the room.

"Lieutenant, I came by to tell you I'm getting married and I want you to be my best man."

"You're joking?"

"No sir."

"Jesus Christ, Quinn.   What the hell's the matter with you?   We're not supposed to marry these people."

Quinn's smile vanished from his face.

Hollis felt his heart sink.   "Quinn, weren't you paying attention?   They don't want us marrying these people.   It's against regulations."

"No, it ain't.   I checked.   You need the CO's permission, is all."

"And you have to wait two months."

"We thought of that.   Penny wants to get preggers.   That way they can't stop us from getting married and probly won't make us wait."

"Mike, that's a very foolish thing to do.   I would advise against it.   It will only bring disgrace to her and her family.   It's only going to cause a lot of heartache for the two of you and her family and it's no guarantee that this little ploy of yours will work."

"Our minds are made up, Lieutenant.   I want you to be our best man.   Will you?"

"Of course, did you get permission yet?"

"I was hopin' you might be able to help us on this matter.   I mean you did such a good job with getting them some grub after Augie ate 'em out of house and home."

"Who have you talked to?"

"I went to the Major and he told us to go to the Chaplain who has to screen all requests. If the Chaplain says it's okay Penny then has to meet with the Colonel.   If he says it's okay, we have to wait two months.   I was hopin' we could get past the two month wait.   I'm thinking you might be able to help us out in this regard."

"I don't think it'll work.   Rules are rules, and as perverse as some of them are, there is a subtle logic to them that makes them inviolate."   He looked Quinn in the eye, "In other words, they don't like making exceptions."

"I'm not sure I understood what you just said, but I think the Chaplain likes you and maybe he might make an exception."

"That may be, but I'm not the one requesting the exception."

"Huh?"

He thought of Penelope and her eager mouth and the heaven in which this young boy now found himself.   It was enough to make Hollis want to go jerk off thinking about his semen rimming her lips and the way she revived his penis like some lurid Nightingale.   He thought of Molly, so recently caressed, warm and soft in her bed.   And Jessie.   He had stood the test and been redeemed.

"You thinking, Lieutenant?"

"What?   Yeah, OK, let's go see the Chaplain."

Hollis slipped off his tunic and climbed into his leather jacket.   He bid Leo goodbye and rode off to the Chaplain's office, Quinn pedaling along behind.

Quinn kept saying, over and over, how much he appreciated Hollis going with him until finally Hollis told him to shut up.   Hollis wondered why he kept getting involved in all of these irritating little personal problems.   He had troubles enough of his own without hearing about and getting caught up in the matters of others.   Did he have a kind face?   He thought not. He scowled far more than he smiled.   Did he exude that quality of human kindness that people in desperate circumstances seek out?   No, he didn't really care about everybody's niggling little affairs and if he somehow, inadvertently, gave some indication that he did, he hoped in the future he might be able to conceal it.   He could hear engine noises echoing from the field as he pedaled.   He was glad the rain had slackened to an intermittent mist.   If it poured now like it had earlier, he might have told Quinn to shove it.   He looked up at the clouds.   They were dark and menacing, roiling over the earth in a quickly moving front.   When they arrived at the Chaplain's office the mist had turned to a heavy drizzle.

Chaplain Brown rolled his eyes when he saw Hollis with another poor soul in tow.

"Lieutenant Hollis.   Congratulations on the DFC.   What can I do for you now?"

"Sir, this is Staff Sergeant Mike Quinn.   He's our radio operator, and a damned good one, I might add.   He's here to seek permission to marry this delightful young lady from Great Yeldham.   He asked me to come along on his behalf since you and I have become such good friends."

The Chaplain looked stunned and Hollis fought the urge to break down laughing.

"That's OK, Sergeant Quinn, you can speak for yourself.   It wasn't necessary to have Lieutenant Hollis here to do your bidding for you."

"In that case may I go, sir?"

"Absolutely not, Lieutenant.   Sergeant Quinn, have a seat.   Lieutenant Hollis, step into my office."

Hollis took a seat across from the Chaplain, the same seat he had taken twice before.

"You know, John, every time you come to me it's to facilitate the remedy to a problem. If you sought the Lord's Council as much as you seek mine, you might find the inner peace you so desperately yearn for."

"Thanks, sir.   Things not going well in the Sin Theater of Operations?   I don't mean to be flippant.   What you say is right.   Now, what do you think of Quinn's dilemma?"

"Rules are rules.   This is the Army, you know."

"We, should I say Quinn, were hoping the rules could be over-ruled."

The Chaplain sighed demonstrably.   "This is the fifth request I've had this month.   The reason they have to pass through me is that I've been given direct orders to discourage these marriages.   The Army, in its infinite wisdom, doesn't want a lot of these kids shipping home war brides.   The woman-folk back home will take great umbrage to the thought of the flower of its youth seeking connubial bliss in the arms of a bunch of foreigners, no matter how well-intentioned and innocent these unions might appear.   These people need to be investigated, she will be required to have an interview with the Colonel and there is a mandatory two month wait. After all of that, they often find that they aren't so earnest after all."

"Sir, they want her to get pregnant as a way of getting around the wait.   Does that sound pretty earnest to you?"

"Two months."

"Sir, he could be dead by then."

"All the more reason for them to wait.   If it's true love they'll survive the wait.   Who is this woman, anyway?"

"She's the daughter of the family you liberated the vittles for a while back."

"So you know this girl?"

"Yes sir, I've had experience with her, yes."

"What does that mean?"

"I've met her.   She's really quite charming.   You'd like her."

"Don't patronize me, Lieutenant.   God has not made the person I could not find reason to like."

Hollis almost blurted out *Hitler, maybe?*   "Yes sir.   I meant no disrespect.   Now about that waiting period."

"Two months.   Tell him."

"With all due respect, sir.   You tell him."   Hollis got up and walked out.   "Go on in Quinn.   He needs to talk to you."

Hollis was ashamed of himself, he could not imagine being so spontaneously insolent to a man he admired so.   He would go in and apologize after Quinn was finished getting his lecture. He sat in the outer office waiting, humbled by his own unbridled arrogance and cynicism.

Twenty minutes later, the door opened and Hollis stood.   The Chaplain walked out, his arm around Quinn's shoulder.   Quinn was smiling.

"Sir, I uh..." Hollis stammered.

"Lieutenant, you take good care of this young man.   He says you are going to be his best man.   I told Sergeant Quinn he had made an excellent choice.   Come back in two months and I'd be honored to perform the ceremony."

"Thank you, sir,   Quinn said.

"Yeah, thank you, sir," Hollis added.

They turned and left.   Outside Hollis turned to Quinn, "No, huh?"

"No.   He told me I had his permission to appeal to the squadron CO, ground exec and then the air exec and finally the Colonel.   But he said no one got the waiting period waived. Irregardless."

"Too bad.   We tried."

"He wants me to bring Penelope by to meet with him."

"That's a start."

"Yeah, he said I could get a spot instructing at the Replacement Center after our tour is up.   He'd see to it.   That way we can be with each other for the duration."

"That will be nice."

It started raining heavily.

Back in the room he was greeted by Leo sitting on his bed running his fingers between his toes liberating sock lint.

"How come you aren't working on trigonometry or something?"

"No passes.   Must be an alert coming.   How'd you make out?"

"Two months.   No exceptions."

"Aw, that's too bad.   At least you tried."

"It was crazy to even try.   The Army and its ridiculous rules."

"You never know.   The Lord works in mysterious ways."

"Bullshit, Leo.   They can pick a boy out of his life, train him to be a killer, send him off to die in war and he can't even marry the woman of his choice?   This is democracy?"

"You hit on the operative word: 'boy.'"

"Ahh, that's a bunch of crap and you know it."

"Perhaps you're right.   Even so, Rosey the Riveter might not feel quite so punctilious in her war work if she found out her high school sweetheart has fallen for some Limey cupcake."

"Leo, once again, your profound insight humbles me."

"As well it should."

Sully poked his head in, "I just ran into H-y at the PX.   An Advanced Warning just came in.   We're alerted for tomorrow.   Want to get some chow?"

As they returned from the Combat Mess increased activity around the base became apparent.   Trucks passed.   Engines coughed to life.   Long faces abounded.   Before returning to their rooms they passed the bulletin board to check the names.   Ransahoff, Hollis, Selkirk, Nevtushenko, Weldon and DeBerg.

Hollis sat at the desk and wrote a letter to Jessie.   In it he talked of the recent travails of Sully and his father's illness and Quinn's abortive attempt to expedite his marriage to this delightful little English lass.   He told her that soon they would be stepping up operations. Tensions had been increasing along with the griping about the inactivity.   He told her he had returned from London earlier in the day, but made no mention of Molly.   Oh, and the newspaper was correct, I was awarded the DFC for that little 'incident' with the German fighter. He had witnessed greater acts of bravery than his that had gone unnoticed.   He was not deserving and felt as if the award should have rightfully been bestowed upon Rizzo, the man who actually pulled the trigger.

Outside the rain intensified yet again.   It drummed in a steady rhythm against the blacked out window.   Perhaps the rain would do in the mission and they would waste yet another day on the ground.   He signed off, numbered the letter, Number 51, and folded it carefully into the envelope.   He closed it and put on his raincoat.   He wanted to walk it over to the base post office and drop it off.   He was surprised by his need to do this.   He easily could have left it at the mail drop at the Squadron duty room but there was some compelling reason to take it over which he felt unobliged to ignore.   So he pulled his hat down tight on his head, lifted the collar high on his raincoat and, dodging the puddles he could see and cursing the ones he did not avoid, he walked the mile or so to the post office.

He stopped at the Officer's Club for a Coke.   He found Barney Rager sitting on the couch by the fireplace talking to Chief Begay.

"Hi, Barney."

Rager turned to Hollis and suddenly beamed.   "Hello, old buddy!   I see you met my sister."

"Yes.   She's a heck of a gal."

"I called her this morning.   She was quite smitten with you, too."

"Smitten might be too strong a word."

"Not to hear her tell it.   She hopes you'll come back and see her again sometime."

"I'd like that."

"Chief, you know Hollis, don't you?"

"Yeah, by reputation," Begay said.   Hollis realized he had never once formally met or spoken to Begay.   He wondered what reputation he was alluding to.

"Major," Hollis nodded respectfully.   "We're on for tomorrow?"

"Yeah, the Group has been alerted."

"I guess you don't know where we're going?"

"No, they don't even know, I'd bet," Begay said. "Even if I did I wouldn't tell you."

Hollis smiled at him and said, "I know that.   Just thought I'd ask."

"Give her a call sometime, John.   I'm sure she'd like to hear from you."

"Sure thing, Barney.   Good night."

"'night, Hollis."

"See ya, Major."

"Yeah, good night, Hollis."

Hollis drank his Coke and left, braving the rain once again.

Thursday, October 7, 1943

"Lieutenant," Beamis said.   "Breakfast at oh-four hundred.   Briefing at oh-four thirty."

"Where to, Beamis?"

"Don't know, sir.   Expect a warm reception.   You'll have plenty of company."

"You know, I'm *really* getting tired of that," Leo said, his voice cracking with residual sleep, after Beamis departed.

"You say that every morning and nothing ever changes, Leo.   If you don't want him to answer my question, tell him to stop."

Regardless of what Beamis said or how annoyed Leo became, they all looked for signs and the signs had not been good.   Like reading tea leaves or animal entrails they each imparted their own significance to an observation or activity.   The engines were being run up with unusual intensity the night before as Hollis had returned to the room.   Even the rain could not dim the sounds of thundering engines, the ground crews working even though cold and drenched to the bone.   They were going somewhere bad today, Hollis knew it.

There was considerable commotion in the washroom.   They all seemed excited, nervous.   Perhaps they had seen the signs too and arrived at the same conclusion Hollis had.

They found mission eggs for breakfast.   As they settled in to eat, or not eat as the case may be, a pall fell over the crews.

"Ten-hut!"   The officers came to their feet and stood while Van Patten and his entourage strode up the aisle, some reassured to find that only Cavannaro and Ransahoff were in flight clothes.   The target couldn't be that important if they were sending Cavannaro as Bangmaster, Hollis figured.   The mission board showed him leading, Ransahoff high, with Hollis as second, and the 535th as the low squadron.   Spats was number three, Selkirk number four, DeBerg five and Weldon six.

Hollis looked around the room waiting for Cavannaro to take the stage.   There was nobody left from the original Squadron, but Ransahoff and his crew, except for a gunner who came down with Chicken pox and missed a bunch of missions.   Otho was an original with the Group, but had started out with another Squadron.

Ransahoff had refused to let his crew ride without him, the squadron CO's prerogative, Hollis thought.   They had led a charmed life, flying only when Ransahoff did, and hadn't suffered so much as a contusion for all the missions they had flown.   Ransahoff had promised them they would stay together and all finish at the same time as long as he was in a position to see to it.   He made that promise on the day the crew first came together in Texas and had kept it.

"Seats.   Good morning, gentlemen.   I'm the Bangmaster for today's mission.   Our target is Bremen.   The First and Forty-first Wings will be striking the Deutsche shipyard and dry docks about three miles north of the city.   The Fortieth will hit the Flugzeugbau aircraft factory here.   The Third Division will hit the center of the city proper.   The Second Division will form a diversion and hit the U-boat yards at Vegesack.

"Division routes will be different in a three-pronged effort to disperse fighter reaction." He took the pointer and followed the route the First Division would take.   "Our departure will be at Cromer and proceed almost due east through Holland with a dogleg at Assen here, to the IP at Wildehaussen.   A seventy degree turn toward the target.   A ninety degree turn to the rally point and the route almost straight out to Cromer.   Bombing altitude will be twenty-seven thousand feet.   High enough, we hope, to neutralize the effect of flak which we know to be very concentrated around the target."   *We hope?*

"Major."

Gorton took the stage and began.   "Let me first tell you about the expected German reaction.   There are approximately three hundred flak guns, 88's and 105's concentrated in and around Bremen."   More moans.   "Obviously not all of them can be brought to bear at once. Fast, high-flying RAF Mosquitoes will be flying in right ahead of the Division lead using a new invention which the Brits call Carpet, a radio device to jam German Wurzburg radars.   In addition, planes in the lead Bomb Wing, us, will be carrying boxes of thin foil strips, called chaff or Window, cut at the length of the German radar wavelength released to jam the gun-laying radars over the target.   Waist gunners will be told to throw out the chaff as the target is approached.   It is our belief that Carpet and Window, combined with our altitude will neutralize the flak."   *Our belief?*   A lot of men are going to die today, Hollis thought.   He felt nausea sweep over him.   He swallowed back the need to throw up.   From the expressions on the faces of others nearby, most felt the same.

"There are five hundred fighters concentrated within striking distance of Northwest Germany.   Our escort will be with us to the limits of their endurance.   Lights."

"Why does he keep saying 'us'?   He ain't going," Sully whispered.

The only question was the weather along the route.   It would probably be OK, they thought.   They should know before takeoff.

At the plane, Hollis went over the details of the mission with the crew.   They listened intently.   The newcomer, MacFadden, asked a question, which shocked everyone, for nobody had ever asked a question before.   After Hollis answered, they sat around beneath the wing and waited.

It had stopped raining and the broken clouds seemed to pose no problem for takeoff and assembly.   Wilcox had **La Femme Fatale** ready to go.   When the time came Hollis had the engines fired up and the procession began.   They were held at the end of the runway an inordinately long time until the red flares arced into the sky.   The mission was scrubbed.   Even above the engine noise Hollis could hear Sully cry "Shit, mother fucking shit!"   Leo shook his head and they guided **La Femme Fatale** back to its hardstand.

Hollis was frustrated and angry as they all were.   Climbing down from the plane he could hear them swearing.   There was no relief at the postponement as had been the case before.   They were pissed.   Hollis knew they would be going there tomorrow or the next day.

"Hey Lieutenant."   Hollis turned to see Quinn waving at him.   "I didn't get to thank you for going to the Chaplain with me yesterday.   I really appreciated it.   Next time I get to see Penny I'll be sure to tell her how we tried and that we'll have to wait.

"I think that's best."

Back at the room Hollis fell fast asleep and did not awaken until supper.

Chapter Forty-three   **Bremen**

Friday, October 8, 1943

"Wake up, Lieutenant."

"Where to, Beamis?"

Beamis whispered, unusual.   "Sir, you need to report to Group Ops in flight gear.   I think you have the weather flight today."

"What time is it?"

"Oh-five thirty.   You better get a move on, sir.   You've only got half an hour to get dressed and get over there.   If you hurry you may be able to grab a cup of coffee."

Hollis felt suddenly elated.   His name had been on the mission list for today.   The fact that he drew the weather flight probably meant he was now off the list.

Each group, on a rotating basis, sent up a Fortress to fly above the fields of the Division to take meteorological measurements for takeoff and assembly.   These findings were then reported to the crews at briefing.   The problem was, Hollis knew, the minute the weather flights from each Division popped up on the German long-range radar, they were tipped off about the subsequent mission.

Hollis drank a cup of coffee quickly from the pot brewing at the Operations room.   It felt good on his stomach, easing the chill of the dark morning.

Begay gave him the flight plan.   The navigator was there as well as the assistant weather officer, Perry Solomon, who looked particularly uncomfortable in flight clothes.   If one gained contemptuous confidence by the fear manifested by others this poor sap exuded enough fear to embolden the whole Group.   If anybody ever wanted to be some other place at that particular moment, it was this little guy with glasses and a clipboard.   Hollis happened to notice H-y in the corner, also in flight clothes, preoccupied by a large map and a Weems plotter.   Begay told him the rest of the crew would be at the plane.   Darby was the copilot.

It was simple.   Climb to 5000 feet and proceed from Ridgewell to Kings Cliffe to Bedford and back again and spiral up to 25,000 feet and orbit for half an hour.   The weather observer would do the rest.   Winds aloft, outside air temp, barometric pressures, *et cetera*. The observer would then broadcast his report to Division headquarters to be teletyped to the group weather offices in time for briefing.   It was strictly a taxi job.

How much trouble could he get into on a weather flight?   The sky would be dark and empty, save for the RAF who were all to the north and east, if they had been up at all.

Report back to Ops when you get back, Begay told him.

He was driven out to the Group's hack, an old 'F' stripped of guns and armor, now used for non-combat purposes.   The navigator, who fell fast asleep, and the weather observer rode in the back of the truck.

"Ever fly one of these before?"

"Yes, I went up with that crazy-man Eisenberg.   He scared the shit out of me.   No monkey business, OK?   I get airsick real easy."

"No sharp turns?"

"Yeah, real slow and level."
"You know how to use an oxygen mask?"
"Yes."
"Dress warm?"
"Yes.   I've done this before."
"Fine."
Hollis saw the mechanics pulling the big canvas covers from the engines of the planes they rode past.

He had nearly forgotten how well a B-17 handled and how easy it would climb when it was empty.   Besides Darby, the observer and the navigator, they took a radio operator and an engineer.   They were defenseless against intruders, but the Brits handled them pretty well, if there were any.   It was unlikely they would encounter one this close to daylight anyway.   He felt funny flying with a strange crew, like they had not been formally introduced, but the navigator's orders were crisp and sure and the flight was easy.

They broke through the overcast at 6000 feet, it had been predicted to be about a thousand.   Hollis quickly glanced at the wings.   Starlight reflected a dull sheen on the wings and cowling--rime ice.   Hollis had Darby adjust the intercoolers and carburetor heat.   As they flew higher, it sublimated off in the drier air above 10,000 feet.   There was no moon.   As always he found the stars breathtaking.   Hollis could not remember a time when he could see so many stars.   A million of them.   Each with a story.   He figured he could see to the end of the galaxy, perhaps the universe.   He was humbled by his sudden spiritual musing.   He felt small and irrelevant.   He allowed his mind to wander.   He thought of Molly and this surprised him.   Why had not Jessie been the first person to enter his thought?   He felt a little guilty.   For a brief, wonderful few hours she was a surrogate, reminding him of what was important and what he lived for.   Beyond a kiss and a few appreciative hugs Jessie's trust had not been violated.   Molly was probably snug and warm in her bed, dreaming of Glenn Miller and "Six Lessons with Madame La Zonga," high school dances and having her breasts caressed in a rumble seat by an appreciative Matt Roberts.

He kept the turns gentle so as not to induce vomiting and made sure the oxygen flowed into the observer without interruption.   At twenty-five thousand feet he orbited the Fortress for thirty minutes as directed.   He could see his long contrail curling behind like the phosphorescent wake of a speedboat on a midnight cruise.   Hollis made sure the radio messages had been sent and acknowledged before heading back to Ridgewell in a slow, gradual descent.

Within a couple of minutes of the ETA on his flight plan, Hollis placed the wheels of the tired, old B-17 back onto the runway.   He knew he would land before the Group took off, but he at least expected their engines to be turning.   That was OK, he would be back in bed before they even got number one turned over.

Begay was at the hardstand to greet them.   He yelled at Hollis to get in.   Hollis signed the Form 1A, tossed the clipboard to the sleepy-eyed engineer and climbed into the jeep.

"Home, James," he said to Begay.
"Briefing."
"Briefing?"
"Yeah, you're flying."

"Flying?   Son of a bitch, I had the weather flight, doesn't that entitle me to go back to bed?"

"Not today."

"Shit, Chief.   Where are we going?"

"Bremen.   Same as yesterday."

Hollis leaned over the side of the jeep and vomited.

"Jesus, Hollis.   You alright?"

"No."

"Maybe you better get your stomach checked."

"No.   What I need is my head examined.   I volunteered for this."   He wiped the side of his cheek.

When they arrived in front of the briefing room Hollis got out of the jeep and entered.   It was a little before nine.   He checked in at the desk and walked down the aisle until he found Leo, Sully and Cobb sitting in their usual locations.   He glanced at the formation board.   Just like yesterday, Number two in the high squadron.

"Glad you could join us," Leo said.

"Trust me, boys, the weather will be fine.   Dress warm it's forty-five below at twenty-five angels."   In the moments before the briefing was to begin Hollis looked around the room. He noticed H-y once again, this time standing at the side of the stage with Rager and Sudbury and Pilaccio.   H-y was dressed for flying and looked very distressed.   "Jeez, look at H-y. What do you think has him so upset?   They must have him flying combat again."

"I heard he just got a 'Dear John' letter from Belinda," Leo said.

"Which would you rather have, a 'Dear John' letter or flying combat?"

"Flying combat with you?   I'll take the 'Dear John' letter." Sully said.   Cobb and Leo started laughing.

"Ten-hut!"

Begay was right.   Bremen.   The entire briefing was a carbon copy of the one the day before.   Everything was the same.   Ominous and the same.

Hollis tried to pay close attention, but was distracted by his burgeoning fear.   They were low group in the van, Purple Heart Corner.   They were going to catch it today.   His mind became dulled by dread and would not focus.

Hollis had no need to go to the equipment room as he had all of his necessary paraphernalia in his hands from the weather flight.   So he stood outside and smoked cigarettes. The sun had come up and the overcast had thinned enough to see small stretches of blue.   There would be no difficulty with assembly and the weather to, from and over the target had improved significantly.   Barring an act of God, weren't they *all* Acts of God?, or engine malfunction they would be seeing Bremen this afternoon.

The Red Cross Clubmobile was parked nearby, its engine running, releasing large clouds of vapor from the exhaust, and the Red Cross girls were handing out sandwiches and donuts to the crews as they made their way to the waiting trucks.   Hollis walked over and asked for a cup of tea.   The plain-looking young girl smiled down from the counter cut in the side of the bus and said, "Sure thing, Lieutenant.   Would you like milk or sugar?"

"Black."

She handed the cup down to him and he lifted the steaming liquid to his lips.   He sipped it with a loud slurp to cool its passage over his lips.   He looked up and thanked the young lady who smiled back.   It was not gratuitous or patronizing it was just the smile of a sweet, innocent girl trying to help who, at that moment in time, was as radiant and beautiful as any woman alive.

"Good luck."

Hollis waved back, his mouth full of tea, but her attentions had been directed elsewhere and she did not see him.   She should be back in Keokuk or Raleigh getting ready for school, not here, not doing this.   He wanted to make a point of thanking her, but she was handing out donuts to the throng of eager hands, smiling with each delivery, giving back as best she knew how.

Hollis turned to find his crew when he saw Otho, none too pleased to be dressed for flying.   Otho should be back in bed, as was his custom on tough missions, not suited up.   This was worthy of comment.

"Hey, Otho, where ya' going?"

Otho looked at Hollis and said, "DeBerg's copilot is sick, a head cold or something and I'm filling in."

"This will put another notch on your pistol."

"Yeah."   He walked toward the waiting truck.

Good, Hollis thought, the son of a bitch needs to join the rest of us.   It was his war, too.

Finally Cobb finished with his navigator's briefing, tapped Hollis on the shoulder and guided him toward their truck.   They rode out to **La Femme Fatale** in silence.   Even Sully had no room for conversation.   Maybe the thought of looking down at all those flak guns firing up at him was sinking in.   He often commented that, perched up there in the nose, he had the best view in the house.   He could see everything.   The fighters climbing up, the flak guns flashing, the bombs from the preceding groups hitting the ground.   Smoke.   Fire.   Fortresses rolling in. He was more remote than Hollis had seen him before.   He was very upset about the previous day's aborted mission.   Maybe the waiting had gotten to him, too.   Maybe he shared in his friend H-y's grief over the departure of the beloved Belinda.   In any case, he was not the same. Had something happened in Cambridge?   Did Hollis really care?

Leo reached into the satchel containing the escape kits and pulled out a rosary.

"When did you become Catholic?" Hollis asked him.

"I'm not.   I thought I saw something in the bottom of this bag when I put these kits in here.   I hope the guy who owns this doesn't need it today."

Hollis was sorry he had drunk the tea.

Wilcox greeted them as they climbed over the tailgate.   "Mornin', sirs."

"Morning," Hollis replied.   "Ready?"

"As she'll ever be."

"Good."   Hollis gathered the crew around and told them what most already knew, that they were going to Bremen and today they would probably get to see it.   He could sense their apprehension, it was on their faces.   He looked at Quinn, but he did not return the gaze, his mind locked in thought elsewhere.   Probably recalling the look on Penelope's face the last time she came, Hollis thought.

Leo handed out the escape kits and passed around some Hershey Bars and gum.

Hollis placed his gear by the nose and walked over to the edge of the woods which separated the hardstand from its neighbors.   Through the leafless trees he could see **Cleopatra's**

Asp and, beyond, **Celina**.   Weldon and DeBerg.   He lit his pre-stations smoke and then another.   At precisely eleven fifteen he emptied his bladder, vomited his tea and called for stations.

Hollis placed the chute pack beneath his seat in the same place he always did, settled into the seat and adjusted its position.   He connected his headphones and mike and started the checklist.   After a few idle minutes they saw the green flare arc above the trees that blocked their view of the tower and Hollis leaned out the side window and yelled, "Clear!"   Leo did the same.

Wilcox gave Hollis a 'thumbs-up' then crouched to look under the bomber.

Hollis stuck his left hand out the window and put up his index finger.   This was the second time today he had done this.   "Start one!"

Leo depressed the 'start' toggle, the high-pitched whine of the fuel booster pump now joined by the noise of the inertial starter.   He pumped on the primer several hard strokes and Hollis watched the first tentative revolutions of the big propeller.   "Mesh one!"

The engine caught right away and the twirling black blades became a blur and Hollis moved the mixture lever to 'auto-rich'.   **La Femme Fatale** shook suddenly with the life of its newly-awakened engine.   It was a good, strong engine.   They would need good strong engines today.

Within a few minutes all engines were running smoothly.   Hollis, Leo and Dodge completed the run-ups and engine checks without problem.   The procession began.   Hollis would lead the way out of the cluster of hardstands, falling in behind Ransahoff as they turned onto the perimeter strip.   Ransahoff would be the first plane up.   Hollis second.

At the end of the runway, they waited.   No red flare today.   Hollis could see the Aldis lamp in the hands of the flight control officer wink at Ransahoff and an instant later **La Femme Fatale** shook with the propeller blast from Ransahoff's roaring engines.   Hollis watched as all but the tail of **The Flying Dutchman** disappeared from view beyond the gentle undulation of the runway as he inched **La Femme Fatale** forward.   Soon the plane reappeared and left the ground.   The lamp winked at **La Femme Fatale** and Hollis stood hard on the brakes, advancing the throttles forward to the stops.   The roar was deafening.   He glanced at the manifold pressure and released the brakes.   **La Femme Fatale** leaped forward and charged down the runway.   They were good engines.   **La Femme Fatale** bounced heavily at first but lifted into the air, taking flight without apparent effort.

Hollis felt the reassuring thump of the wheels as they entered their wells and listened as the engines retracting the flaps completed their task.   **La Femme Fatale** was a good airplane, maybe the best one Boeing ever built, and Wilcox took good care of her.   She was responsive, sported beautiful artwork, he just didn't care for her name.

Ransahoff took his position and Hollis pulled in alongside.   There was no need for pyrotechnics, visibility was perfect.   Spats took position on Ransahoff's other side.   As they started a gentle orbit Hollis could make out the others, Selkirk, DeBerg and Weldon as they joined the formation.   Further back he spotted Cavannaro, the Bangmaster, with H-y, no doubt nervous as a cat in a dog pound, tucked out of sight in the nose.

When Group assembly was complete, Cavannaro led them to wing rendezvous over Splasher Sixteen at Brampton.   There he found the 91st in a shallow right hand orbit, the 351st tucked high and behind, and Cavannaro flew them straight toward the two groups in a collision course save for the difference in altitude, passing directly under them into perfect position in an expert display of airmanship.   The 91st continued another revolution, the wing complete, waiting for the two following wings to show up.   More by timing than actual appearance, the leader of the 91st made his final turn and headed for Cromer.

Sully appeared in the hatchway and, saying nothing, handed Hollis a smoke.   When he was done he tapped Hollis on the thigh and climbed up into the cockpit on his journey to the bomb bay.   When he was done he returned to the nose, again, without comment.   Unusual, Hollis thought, not for Sully to make some comment in passing.

And they were off, the high afternoon sun blazing into the windows of the cockpit. Hollis loosened Jessie's scarf, long since stained by sweat and oils from his neck and hair, slightly, but not too much, it would be freezing cold soon enough.

As the massive formation turned for the coast they started a gentle climb.   They had to be at 17,000 feet at coast-out and 27,000 feet by the time they went coast-in at Den Helder, threading the needle between Texel and the Dutch peninsula.   The escort would pick them up halfway across the North Sea.

Sully did an oxygen check and Leo exercised the turbos.   Until coast-out it was just flying.   Hollis watched as a bomber from the low squadron dropped away, then one from the 91st, then one from Cavannaro's squadron.   He saw the spare fill in, receiving an unwelcome invitation to the party.   Hollis wondered who the poor bastard was that had suddenly found himself answering the call to arms.

"Navigator to crew.   Coast-out."

Hollis glanced down as the English coast passed inexorably below them.   He moved in a little closer to Ransahoff.   Suddenly **La Femme Fatale** rattled in response to the guns being test-fired into the sea below.   He knew to expect it but it startled him nonetheless, reassuring to feel.

"Pilot to tail, everybody with us?"

"Tail.   Yes sir, we're all together."

On they plodded.

"Navigator to pilot.   Escort should be here any minute."

Hollis looked around.   Nothing.   He tucked his scarf back in tight against his neck and pushed the muffler up over it.   It was getting cold.   They passed through twenty-one thousand feet.

Leo tapped his arm and pointed up through the overhead glass.   There he could see the thin, elegant condensation trail left by the hot exhaust of the escort.   He could see sunlight glint off their surfaces as they passed out ahead and weaved their way to and fro, hungry birds of prey, eager for a fight.   Little Friends who would throw themselves without thought or hesitation at anyone who dared to attack their Big Friends.   It was there that this war would be won, Hollis knew.   For it was there that the German spirit would be broken, the day they knew beyond any doubt that they could no longer defend themselves.

"Pilot to crew, escort has arrived.   Keep your eyes peeled.   Things are gonna happen fast today.   Stay on the ball."

"Navigator to pilot, just a quick thought.   Do you think we oughta paint over Belinda's name?"

Hollis smiled behind his mask and said, "Keep the lines open, Navigator.   This line is for official business only."

Cobb keyed his mike and laughed.

On they flew.

"Twenty-seven thousand feet, bundle up boys," Hollis said.   He pulled the mask away from his face slightly and the puddle of drool cascaded down onto the front of his Mae West and froze solid.

"Navigator to crew.   Coast-in."

Hollis could make out the Zuider Zee shimmering in the high sun.

"Flak, twelve o'clock level."

Hollis looked ahead and saw the first puffs of German resistance.   This was nothing compared to what lay ahead, he knew.   These coastal gunners were more of a greeting than a material threat.   If they hit anything it would be a lucky shot.

On they flew, contrails spewing from every engine.   Hearts beat faster.   Breathing quickened.   Mouths dried.

"Navigator to pilot, turn at Assen in five minutes.   A shallow ten degree turn to the right."

"There they go."

Hollis quickly glanced upward, he could see the P-47s, in unison and to a man, dip their wings and turn for home.   The 91st passed through their contrails.   The Little Friends could do nothing more.

"Here they come!"

"Aw Jesus!"

The sky ahead was filled with German fighters.   Great flocks of them.   Today would be the day, Hollis thought, his sphincter tightening in hopes he would not defecate.

"Call them out!" he yelled knowing nobody needed to be told.

"Focke-Wulfs twelve o'clock level, coming up--fast!"

They didn't even wait.   They threw themselves at the bombers before they even finished climbing.   The chin and top turrets exploded with return fire.   There was cursing.   Rapid breathing in keyed mikes.

"Oh, Mother of God, they got DeBerg!"

Chapter Forty-four   **Hell, Frozen Over**

Hollis snapped his head around and caught sight of DeBerg, his left wing engulfed in flames, the propellers absurdly clawing the air in front of the burning engines.   The bomber, half of which was now a flaming torch, seemed to fly on for a few seconds, as if impervious to the blaze that consumed it, then rolled onto its side and plunged.   The left wing separated in a huge explosion which sent a thousand pieces of flaming wreckage earthward.

Hollis looked to the front.   He could see a bomber in the 91st break apart before his eyes, torn to shreds by the impact and explosion of dozens of cannon shells from a string of FWs that careened by immune to the intersecting lines of tracers sent to stop them.   Hatches flew off and two bodies tumbled out.   The plane went into a steep climb, with no live hand remaining on the controls and stalled.   In agonizing slow motion, it nosed over and flew straight down narrowly missing two of its mates.

He saw more fighters climbing in the distance, eager to get at the formation. A B-17 from the low squadron drifted away from the formation trailing a thin line of black smoke from an engine.   The impact from the first assault stunned the formation like a boxer meeting an unexpected blow.   The sudden viciousness of the massed attack had its desired effect.   Wings rose and dipped, planes dodged one way or the other as pilots jinked in an effort to avoid being hit by the hailstorm of fire.   No one called out fighters, there hadn't been enough time to react. Even over Schweinfurt Hollis had never seen such concentrated violence as had been delivered upon the three groups.

In a few brutal seconds, the first wave had passed.   Gone.   The air in front momentarily empty.   They would be back.   He felt the blood leave his hands as he clenched his fists around the control column.   He looked around to see the *Staffeln* off to the left complete its climb and turn in.   Perhaps two dozen new fighters were about to join the fray.   All those in the bombers could do was watch and wait.   At the end of the next few moments more men would be dead.

"Twelve o'clock level, boys.   Here they come!"

The fighters settled into level flight, their noses and wings flashing.   One could not help but admire their balls and the desperation they must feel in their hearts to confront the oncoming bomber and their bristling guns.   They were not defending the Reich, they were protecting their mothers and their wives and their children. This was not about ideology.   **La Femme Fatale** erupted again with the firing of its guns. In the face to face duel of nerves and steel between the bombers and the fighters; one fighter exploded but two more bombers went down.   The second attack lasted only fifteen seconds.   More bombers were scattered and seemed to stagger along, dazed by the ferocity of the assault.   One more pass like that, Hollis knew and the formation might cease to exist.

"Keep the hot lead in their eyes, boys!" Sully called out.   "No tellin' when this is gonna end."

"Nine o'clock low coming up," Hulse said.

"Six o'clock high, Dodge!   They're diving on us!"   Mollica.

Hollis heard and felt the top turret blasting at the Germans.   He could feel the impact of shells striking **La Femme Fatale**.   He looked at one wing then the other, whipping his head around so quickly the mask nearly separated from his face.   He looked at Ransahoff who was also taking hits on the wings and tail surfaces.   The top turret on **The Flying Dutchman** spun around to confront the attackers coming down from above.   Ransahoff zigged one way and back the other in an attempt to avoid the hellish rain.   All he succeeded in doing was throw off the aim of the top turret gunner and the radio operator who Hollis could plainly see swinging his gun back and forth spraying fire at whatever was coming his way.   Then in a blur almost too quick to register within the brain the Germans dove past and were gone.

"They're coming around again," Rizzo announced.   "That first group is climbing back up.   Three o'clock low.   Must be fifty of 'em."

Hollis looked out the window beyond Leo and could easily make out the fighters, like ducks rising from a pond, tantalizingly close, but still out of effective range of defensive fire, as they leisurely completed the recovery of altitude.   They seemed to break into two groups of about twenty planes the first group started to turn in while the second group continued on ahead of the bombers, flying a parallel track, to form a second wave.

Dodge came on the interphone, "Sully, they're coming around from one o'clock.   The second group will probably come in from eleven o'clock, be ready.   Rizzo they'll be coming your way."   Hollis marveled at how calm his voice sounded, matter-of-fact, as if he were announcing the arrival of a train.   It was incongruous, unnerving.

"I got 'em, Dodge.   They're going after the lead group."   And they did.   Hollis watched with stunned fascination as the first wave tore into the 91st with reckless abandon.

Another Fortress left the formation, pieces of its skin shredding back into the slipstream, spewing bodies from hatches in the nose and tail.   The plane fell off on a wing and dropped.   Dodge and Rizzo tried to hit them as they dove down to the right, but they were too far away.

This is what it must have been like at the OK Corral, Hollis mused. An odd distraction to his crushing concentration. Odd that his brain found time for a stray, irrelevant thought amid the shattering carnage.

"Watch the ammo," Hollis said. "We're not even halfway to the IP yet."

"Second wave, ten o'clock high coming after us!" Sully yelled.

They hit the low squadron and Hollis saw the shells strike home on another Fortress.   A large section of the rudder broke off and disappeared into the contrail.   The bomber held on, seeming to close in even tighter, like a wounded animal nuzzling closer to the herd.   Another B-17 in the lead squadron was not so lucky.   Its left outboard engine ignited and the pilot pushed it over into a steep dive in an effort to blow out the fire.   Regardless, he was finished.   The Group had now lost, by Hollis's count, three bombers.   No more than five, six minutes at the most had transpired since the P-47s had dipped their wings and dragged their contrails home.   It was a slaughter.   Beyond comprehension.   Like the Charge of General Pickett.

Just as suddenly, they were gone.   But they would be back.

Hollis took stock.   "Sully, an oxygen check." The place he started first when he needed to right himself.

Quickly, the entire crew was accounted for.   All four engines were running, the controls were OK.   He checked the wings, nothing venting out.   "Dodge, how's she look?"

"You got some skin ripped off the wings and tail but she's fine."   She's fine.   How many pilots could say that?

"Eight o'clock level.   I got some twin-engine jobs coming around.   May be settin' up to fire rockets," Mollica said calmly.

"Three o'clock low, coming up.   A dozen of 'em.   Watch it," MacFadden said.

"Rockets!"

Hollis cringed.

"Jesus, he hit one of the lead squadron dead on!"

Hollis looked down at the lead squadron, but could not see the plane for his engines.   He looked back over the left wing and saw the flaming wreckage scattered about the sky.

"Tore the tail right off," Rizzo said, almost as an afterthought.   That was four.

"Here they come.   Twelve o'clock level." Dodge.

Hollis looked ahead and could see the fighters MacFadden had spotted lift their wings and turn in for yet another head-on attack.

They came in by twos and threes this time, picking away at the lead and low squadrons. This time, mercifully, no one fell.

"Navigator to pilot.   IP five minutes."

Hollis looked around.   The sky was crisscrossed by white vapors trails and smoke. Attacks broke down into runs by ones and twos.   He watched with exquisite clarity the shells strike a Fortress in the lead squadron.   The waist gunner fell away from his gun as if pushed aside by a mighty hand.   But the bomber held on.

"Flak 10 o'clock."

Hollis looked toward the target.   There was a large amount of smoke on the ground and a huge black cloud over the city.   Had it already been bombed?   Not possible.   The First Wing was leading the attack.   The Third Division was due after they bombed, not before.   His eyes were drawn to the black cloud.   He had never seen anything like it before.   What could it be?   Flak.   The black flak smudges had coalesced into a cloud over the city.   It was the coalescence of hundreds, thousands of black flak smudges.

"There's your target," Sully said.

Why were they doing that?   Filling empty sky with flak bursts?   He could now plainly see more bursts, a dozen at a time added to the cloud.   Why such a profligate waste of artillery?   Was it to give them pause?   Give them a few more minutes to think it over?   Perhaps pick another target?

For a moment it seemed as if they were doing exactly that.   They kept heading east while the target passed to the north.   Surely this would be the day reason would prevail over dedication.

Surely this is madness.   *Please don't turn.   Jesus Christ, Most Merciful God in Heaven, don't turn.*

"IP."

Please, Sweet Mother of God, don't go to that place.

Red flares streaked from the back of the wing leader.   Red flares fired from the Bangmaster.   His bomb bay doors opened.   A moment later, Hollis could hear and feel **La Femme Fatale**'s bomb bay open.

No.   The wingtips lifted high above the horizon as the planes entered the bomb run. The groups pulled apart and the bombers up ahead wheeled in a huge turn to the left, heading straight toward the patch of sky filled with black smoke like obedient lambs to the slaughter. The 351st and 381st took interval and turned.   As he banked the plane to the left Hollis thought of Jessie.   Surely, he would never see her again.   He was sad.   He was bearing down on a place no one should ever have to visit during life: Hell.   Tears welled in his eyes and froze to the rim of his mask as he saw them complete their turn and head with dogged determination toward the target, Bremen.

What had he been told?   No man should be forced to fight in a war he could not explain?

Surely, men would not do such things if they did not love it so.

His heart was in his throat, he could barely breath.   Never in his life had he been so afraid. Not even Schweinfurt.

The lead group, bomb bay doors extended, drove straight in as if on parade, nothing, no act of man, could stop them.

He saw Ransahoff tuck in closer to Cavannaro's squadron to make the bomb pattern tighter.   The rest of the Group closed in, too.   This was why they were here.

Hollis eased **La Femme Fatale** so close to **The Flying Dutchman** their wings nearly overlapped.   If he died in the next few moments at least his bombs would go where they belonged.   What else could he do?   Run away?   Hide?

WHOMP!   WHOMP!   WHOMP!   The flak explosions erupted about them and jostled **La Femme Fatale** and the other planes simultaneously.   Most of the time one couldn't hear the bursts unless they were very close.   Hollis could hear them by the dozen.   **La Femme Fatale** rattled with the impact of shrapnel, shaken with each burst until Hollis feared the plane may be concussed out of existence.

Barrage bursts, ten to twenty flak explosions erupting simultaneously in a confined piece of sky, shook the bombers. The sky was nearly obscured with the stuff, chaff floated by like millions of strips of tinsel, sparkling in the sun.

"They got **Cleopatra's Asp**!"

Jesus!

WHOMP! The force of the blast nearly ripped the wheel from his hands.

"Christ! A big piece of us just flew off!" Mollica yelled. The controls felt sluggish for a moment, but Hollis knew he still had control.

Hollis watched as the bombs left the Bangmaster and a split second later **La Femme Fatale** lifted with the release of her own load. Suddenly Cavannaro took a direct hit. The plane simply disintegrated. H-y was in that plane.

The Deputy lead continued on for the necessary seconds required for the cameras to record the strike. Then he dipped his wing sharply and dove off the target racing toward the Rally Point and out of the maelstrom.

Leo turned to look beseechingly at Hollis. Hollis just shook his head.

They got out of the flak as the gunners turned their attention to the bombers following. Hollis tried to look back and see what was left of Cavannaro's plane, but any trace was gone.

The groups reassembled and made another right turn southeast. As they did, Hollis could see the following wings running the gauntlet each group in line astern heading for an uncertain future.

"Me-109s, nine o'clock high coming down. Dodge stay on 'em." It was Hulse.

"Boy, we really clobbered that place. They won't be making any of them U-boats for a while," Rizzo said.

"Dodge."

"I got 'em."

Hollis could see the fighters flying parallel to gain altitude before turning in on the bombers. They each made a wing-over and barrel-rolled downward at the 381st. **La Femme Fatale** shivered with recoil of her guns.

"They musta hit Selkirk, he's feathered an engine." Mollica.

Hollis looked back, but could not see him. "Where is he?"

"He's staying with us."

"Keep an eye on him, Tail. If he starts to fall back let me know."

For the moment, the Germans were gone. They still had all of Holland to cross and Hollis understood that things were by no means over. The respite, nonetheless, allowed the planes to tuck in and regain some semblance of a formation. It also allowed a brief moment to reflect. The Group had lost six or seven bombers, sixty or seventy men, one of them the Squadron leader and Bangmaster, two from his own squadron, one of them his original plane, **Cleopatra's Asp**. Otho. H-y. Happy-go-lucky DeBerg. Weldon. It had been a deadly afternoon.

Now Mickey Selkirk was in trouble yet again. Hollis vowed not to let anything happen to him. He removed his glove and picked off the frozen pellets of sweat from his forehead.

Hollis was startled by more firing and shouts through the intercom. Two fighters raced past his window diving just in front of Ransahoff. He turned to look for Selkirk and found him hugging the space between and behind Spats and Ransahoff.   His number four engine was feathered, the prop hanging motionless on the engine.

"Pilot to navigator.   How far to the coast?"

"We're still in Germany.   We should be crossing into Holland in about three or four minutes.   Then it's another forty minutes to the coast."

When he checked on Selkirk again he had fallen back, unable to keep up the rapid pace being set by the leaders.   They were simply leaving him behind.   In the distance four fighters flew a parallel course ready, it seemed, to pick off the likes of Mickey or anybody else struggling to get home.   The entire bomber stream was behind them.   There would be plenty for them to do.

Hollis made a crucial decision.   He did not know the extent of **La Femme Fatale**'s damage.   The engines were good and he had control of the plane.   The following wing was too far back for Selkirk to drift back into.   He would soon find himself in No Man's Land, a long way from the coast.

"Pilot to crew, we're going to cover Selkirk."   Hollis expected some protest over the intercom but it was silent.

"Pilot to tail, Mollica where is he?"

"He's fallin' back a-ways, lost some altitude, too.   Those bastards are lickin' their chops."

Hollis pushed the throttle forward, climbing up and away from Ransahoff.   He banked the plane to the right until he was clear then cut back on the throttle diving slightly down in an effort to close the distance between **La Femme Fatale** and Selkirk.

"I don't see him."

"He's about five hundred yards behind.   He's losing altitude fast."

Hollis slowed even more and weaving back and forth to delay **La Femme Fatale**'s forward progress.

"Fighters coming in!   Three o'clock level."

La Femme Fatale shivered in response, the cordite stinging his eyes.   He took his gloved-hand and wiped his eyes.   The tiny, frozen shards came off his eyebrows onto his fingers.

Ransahoff and Nevtushenko faded into the distance along with the rest of the wing.   He had entered No Man's Land.   Selkirk was just off his left wing.   The fighters swept by hitting both planes.   They set up for a stern attack.   It dawned on Hollis what a terrible mistake he had made.   They might all be killed by a foolish attempt at bravery.

Hollis switched to the command channel, "Mickey, get her down on the deck, fast!"

Selkirk immediately dropped the nose and, picking up speed quickly, dove for the ground.   Hollis followed suit, the planes now side-by-side.   The ground came up fast.   He looked up to see the huge lumbering formation of the Forty-first Wing.

More firing.   Two Bf-110s circled around.   *Zoresters*, twin- engine fighters assigned the task of mopping up stragglers while the single-engine fighters continued to do battle with the main force.   The 110s were not as agile and easier to defend against.

"Left waist to radio.   I'm out of ammo, bring some back."

"I don't have much left, but I'll bring back what I have."

"Here they come.   Six o'clock level."

La Femme Fatale shook from the rattle of Mollica's guns.   Soon Dodge joined in, arcing shells past **La Femme Fatale**'s tail to hit the pursuers.

"Mother fuck!   I hit one!" Mollica shouted.

"Selkirk's lost his second engine.   He ain't gonna make it," Hulse announced, the tone of his voice matter-of-fact.

Hollis could see him feather his number three, smoke emerging from the cowling.   *Shit,* Hollis thought, *he isn't going to make it.   Dammit!*

It was difficult flying a Fortress on two engines, it took consummate skill when both engines were out on the same wing.   Butch Mullen showed him how.   He wondered if Selkirk knew.   Hollis could tell Selkirk was struggling.   They passed through ten thousand feet and Hollis ripped off his mask allowing the cold air to hit his wet face and the drool spilled onto his Mae West and jacket.

Two single-engine fighters appeared and Sully called them out.   Dodge fired at them even though they were still out of range in an attempt to discourage them.   It did not.   They barreled in after Selkirk and scored more hits.   Selkirk's plane sagged down in a shallow dive. Hollis was convinced he would run out of air before he cleared the coast and his asinine gesture would be for naught.

The countryside started coming up quickly.   They passed over the Zuider Zee at about five thousand feet, still in a gentle dive.   Finally, at about two thousand feet, Selkirk leveled off. As they approached the polders of West Friesland Hollis could make out a dozen windmills and canals.

"Any fighters?" Hollis asked, sensing salvation with each passing minute.

"Waist to pilot.   Don't see any."   MacFadden said.   "Maybe they think we ain't gonna make it anyway."

"Tail to pilot.   I think I see two back there, but I'm not sure they see us."

"Keep an eye on 'em."

"Navigator to pilot.   Coast-out in about three minutes."

Hollis leaned forward in his seat, but could not make out the sea in the haze.   Selkirk kept losing altitude.   He was now down to about seventeen hundred feet.   They still had a large body of water to cross.   Hollis could make out the dunes of the Dutch coast and a few windmills then in an instant it was all behind him and all he could see was dark green sea.

"Coast out."

Hollis could see smoke coming from the feathered inboard engine.   Either he hadn't gotten the fire out or it had reignited.   Either way, he was down to thirteen hundred feet.

"Navigator, how far to land?"

There was a pause.   "About a hundred miles now."   About forty minutes flying time at the speed Selkirk was going.

Leo, his oxygen mask dangling against his face, turned to Hollis and yelled, "He ain't gonna make it."

Hollis nodded.   He felt Dodge's presence behind him.   "How are we doing?"

"We're OK.   They're not."

There was a sudden line of tracers past the nose.

"Jesus!   Where the hell did that come from?"

"We got two E-boats.   They're following us out.   Must smell blood in the water," Sully said.

"Where are they?"

"We just passed over them.   They must be doin' twenty-five, thirty knots."

Hollis pushed the throttles forward and banked sharply in a one hundred eighty degree turn.

"What the fuck are you doin'?" Sully   asked.

"Going fishin'.   Guns armed?"

"Always."

"Fire away at the bastards."   Hollis saw the two German patrol boats plowing through the waves and placed **La Femme Fatale** as close to the water as he dared.   Two lines of tracer rose to greet them but they were wide, no doubt thrown off by the pitching of the boats in the rough water.   Sully's guns opened up and Hollis could barely make out over **La Femme Fatale**'s long nose and astrodome the rising plumes as the shells struck the water and walked right into the boats.   They suddenly darted away from each other in an effort to avoid the fire Sully directed their way.   Hollis flew right over them, low enough to nearly clip their masts as they bobbed in their own wake.   When he was safely beyond the boats, he turned around and flew past them again, Sully firing away until his guns suddenly stopped.

"That's it.   I'm out of ammo."

"That's OK, Sully.   I think they got the message."   Hollis sought out the lingering trail of smoke from Selkirk's plane and found it.   In no time he was alongside again.   He throttled back.

"How far, Navigator?"

"Seventy miles."

Selkirk was under a thousand feet.

"Local boy duels E-boats trying to save his squadron mates.   Wins second DFC."

"Knock it off, Sully.   Radio, call Air-Sea Rescue and tell them he's going in."

"He's already contacted them, Lieutenant.   They acknowledged."

Leo tapped his arm and touched his ear.   Hollis switched to command channel.

"Jack, we're going in.   Thanks for everything," Selkirk said.   "See you around."

"Stay dry."

"Roger."

Hollis switched back, not taking his eyes off Mickey Selkirk.

"Quinn, keep giving ASR fixes."

"No need.   They're on it."

"Anybody see 'em?"

  There was no answer.

"How far?"

"Sixty miles."

Smack in the middle of the North Sea.   They'd be a needle in a haystack.

Hollis switched back to VHF.   "Keep her up as long as you can, Old Boy.   England's just over that hill."

"Roger."

With all those holes, when it hit the water it would sink fast.   The sea was rough.   They probably only stood a fifty-fifty chance of surviving the landing on the water under the best of circumstances.   With two engines out, he had little control and no margin for error.

They were now down to less than five hundred feet. *Turn it into the wind*, Mullen had said. *Settle it onto the water. Smack tail first and it will pitch the nose right into the water.*

Hollis checked the direction of the waves and the spray ripped from the whitecap. "The wind is from your ten o'clock, Mickey."

There was no response.

The bomber lowered itself ever closer to the water.

"We're going in. Full flaps! BRACE!" Then the transmission was cut off. The bomber slowed and Selkirk crabbed ever so slightly to his left to confront the wind. Hollis pulled up parallel to it and throttled back as much as he dared. The B-17 made contact with the sea in a huge cascading explosion of white water which nearly enveloped the plane and Hollis was past them as they appeared to stop dead in the water. Two propellers flew off with pieces of cowling. Hollis reflexly gunned the engines and put the plane into a steep banking orbit to see. The Fortress settled onto the water and a huge shower of ocean splashed down onto it. For an agonizing moment there was no movement. The plane quickly settled nose first into the water, tail starting to rise.

"Okay, guys time to get out." Cobb said softly.

Suddenly, the two yellow dinghies deployed from the roof alongside the bomb bay. Men started climbing out through the open radio hatch. Two. Then two more. The first two out gathered up the rubber rafts and pulled the other to the side of the plane. The second two lifted a limp body out of the hatch. That was five.

"Quinn!"

"I got ASR on the phone. They're on the way."

Six. They lowered the limp crewman to the raft and they stayed to help pull more of the crew out of the plane which, in the brief thirty seconds or so since it had stopped in the water, was sinking fast. The wings were under, the tail lifting at an increasing angle.

Seven. Eight. "Come on, Jesus, get out!" Hollis said.

Nine.

Ten. The last one out, Hollis suspected the lanky Selkirk, seemed to nonchalantly step off the top of the fuselage and into the rubber raft. A moment later only the tail was visible above the water. Then it was gone leaving only two fragile, bobbing yellow rafts, a gasoline slick and some bubbles.

"I count ten."

"Me, too," Hulse said.

Hollis gunned the engines again and buzzed the rafts. He could plainly see Selkirk waving.

"Quinn?"

"I got 'em a fix, sir. They got help coming. They said be patient, they got other clients in the water."

Leo tapped Hollis's arm. "You better not fuck around anymore. I just got a fuel warning light on number one."

"Dodge, go back there and transfer some into one."

"We gotta go."

Hollis came in for a last pass and rocked his wings. He turned for home.

"How far, Navigator?"

"Sixty miles, just like before."

Hollis wondered if they would make it.   They passed over a Royal Navy cutter bouncing roughly in the swells heading straight for Selkirk and his party.

"We'll be alright," Hollis reassured Leo, even though he was not certain that was true.

Hollis leaned out the mixture and throttled back slightly.

In about twenty minutes, they passed over the English coast at Lowestoft.   Cobb gave him a heading for Ridgewell.   In another twenty minutes, they would be on the ground.   They were almost an hour and a half overdue.

Hollis requested landing instructions.   As he approached the field he could see a Fortress off to the infield apparently the result of a ground loop.   He settled **La Femme Fatale** onto the concrete with ease and finished the rollout.   He slowed the plane and turned it onto the perimeter strip.

They taxied past the empty hardstand where **Cleopatra's Asp** had once stood.   He could see Moe Jablonski standing in the middle of the concrete pad, his hands in his pockets waiting for an arrival that would never come.

He parked **La Femme Fatale** guided to a halt by the pleasantly astonished Wilcox.

They got out and surveyed the damage to **La Femme Fatale**.   The big piece of airplane Mollica had seen fly past his head was a section of nacelle from the number two engine.   It left the inner workings of the engine exposed like the internal organs of some dissected metallic beast.   A cannon shell had struck the blade of number four propeller placing a perfectly round hole through it.   There were several dozen holes and punctures. There were two holes through the center of Quinn's seat big enough to pass a finger through.   He was manning his gun at the time.   Hollis looked up at the nose and saw Belinda's name stenciled below the navigator's window.   While they were waiting for the truck, MacFadden quit counting at a hundred. Wilcox looked forlorn, not just because of the damage that had been done to his charge but also because of the full night's worth of work he had ahead of him to get her ready for tomorrow, if that were possible.   Hollis could see the squadron and group engineering officers already surveying the damage.

A jeep pulled onto the hardstand screeching to a halt.   Ransahoff.

"Hollis, you're trying my patience."

Hollis ignored him.   He signed the Form 1A and handed to Wilcox.

"And?"

"They all made it into the dinghies.   When we left them there was a PT boat racing to pick them up."

"Hollis, get in."

"No, thanks.   I'll ride in with my crew."

"Then get over to interrogation right away.   I think there's still some people over there to hear your side of the story."

"Another bad day, eh Dutch?"

"Yeah, we took a beating."

In the truck, nobody would look at him.   Did they hate him?   Did they loathe him? Did they despise the air he breathed because he had unnecessarily risked their lives today?   It was a stupid, foolish thing he did.   Against all regulations and common sense.   All the fears they harbored about him were confirmed, that, at the crucial moment he could not be trusted.

What was his motivation?   How could he be so terrified that he risked paralysis from panic and in the next moment expose himself and his crew to such danger?   How could he be so cautious and yet so bold and stupid?

He knew.   Molly would know.   If he survived the war, unlikely as this seemed, and Selkirk had died he would be forever haunted by the unanswerable question: had he done everything possible to save his friend?   And Eisenberg didn't even like Mickey.

"You know this is getting to be a habit with you," Sully said.

He felt like Stan Laurel confronted by a reproving Oliver Hardy.   The image made him smile despite himself.   He started laughing.   This caused nine surprised looks.   Soon they were laughing, too, and Hollis was sure no one could explain why.

At interrogation, he was handed a peanut butter and jelly sandwich and a cup of coffee by the same Red Cross girl that had given him tea earlier.   She smiled, but he was sure no hint of recognition passed her memory.   He ate the sandwich and chased it down with two combat rations of scotch.

A few Intelligence officers sat around waiting for any late arrivals.   There were a few lingering men talking loudly, wild-eyed, close to the fine edge of hysteria, their surging adrenaline would not let them come down, combat rations having no effect.

They were the last crew the intelligence officers talked with.   Instead of one, there were three listening as Hollis recounted the mission.   He compared the ferocity of the initial attack to that of the Schweinfurt mission.   He noticed two of the officers nodding as he said that.   The initial attack was devastating and they accomplished their goal, to disrupt the formation enough to scatter some of the planes for the next wave to pick off.   They all agreed they had never seen anything like it.

"Did the Carpet work?"

"Couldn't prove it by us," Hollis said.   "We lost three planes to flak hits within seconds of each other."

MacFadden turned to Hollis, seemingly embarrassed, and said, "You know, sir.   I plumb forgot to toss our chaff out the window.   I hope that didn't matter."

Rizzo said he saw the bombs hit the target and, from where he sat, it looked like a perfect strike.   One of the intelligence officers said that it was.

"Thank you, gentlemen," he said.   "Go get some chow."

Sully got up and asked, "How many did we lose today?"

"You know I'm not supposed to tell you that."

"How many?"

"Seven."

Dodge got up and said, "For a while there I was convinced Hell had finally frozen over."

Chapter Forty-five   **Selkirk**

After interrogation, they went to chow.   The two shots of scotch left Hollis with a warm glow which eased his ambiguity a bit.   There was little discussed among the four officers who found themselves alone in the Mess.   Hollis could not tell whether they were angry or relieved. Perhaps both.   What was the line between selfless bravery and unconscionable stupidity?   It wasn't just his life at stake.   Maybe they knew and weren't telling him.

On their way back to quarters, they ran into Nevtushenko.   "Rough one, huh?"

"I'll say," Hollis replied.   They walked in silence for a while, the only sound they made was the crunch of gravel under their boots.

Finally, Nevtushenko asked, "Did you hear about Scorch?"

"Alexander?"

"Yeah.   He led the low squadron today.   After interrogation he went back to his hut, put on his Class A's and walked into the woods and blew his brains out."

Hollis was stunned.   His mind became a tempest of emotion.   At first that struck Hollis as a very cowardly act, that Alexander would rather blow his own brains out than run the gauntlet one more time.   As he walked, locked in his thoughts, he wondered what could strangle his soul to the point where the only option was to take his own life?   The more he thought about it, trying to discern meaning, the more he came to the realization that it must have been a very courageous act and that Scorch would rather stare down the barrel of his own service automatic than face the unbridled terror of death in a bomber.   Hollis wondered what must have gone through his mind as he thought about his choices.   What was his last thought just before his finger squeezed down on the trigger discharging a single round into his brain?   What were his last thoughts?   His wife, his kids?   Was it his country or his crew?   Did he feel guilt over the loss of his squadron mates?   Or was it relief--an escape from the grip of terror--or did he finally wrest control of his life from forces over which he had no control, committing the ultimate act of self-interest simply by ending it?   To him the shame and humiliation of death at his own hand must have been less than the fear or the grip of terror that he was forced to endure daily.   He would not let his friends down by not going.   He simply took himself out of the picture.

"Gee, poor Scorch," Sully murmured.

By the time they were back in the room it was past eight.   Hollis changed out of his flight clothes, slipped on a fresh pair of long johns for warmth, and sat down to write a letter, but his mind was too rattled by excitement and agitation to focus on words and paper.

Leo must have sensed his emotional turmoil and suggested he pull out some of those records he was hiding and play some music.

"What records?"

"Those records in that ammo box you've got stuffed behind your footlocker."

"Jesus, I forgot about them.   They belonged to Cassidy."

"Play something."

Hollis pulled his footlocker to one side and lifted the heavy wooden box out from under his cot.   They had accumulated some dust.   He pulled the Victrola out as well.   He carefully placed the phonograph on the desk and plugged it in.   He shuffled carefully through the records until he found one he liked, Duke Ellington's "Mood Indigo."   After that he played Harry James' "You Made Me Love You."   By the time he played Jimmie Lunceford's "My Blue Heaven" they had acquired several visitors.   Spats and his copilot, Ransahoff's navigator, Sully and Cobb. Nobody said anything.   They just lost themselves in the music and their thoughts.   The room filled with smoke.   Were it not for the gentle music it might have seemed like a wake.   There were no requests, they seemed happy just to let Hollis pick the selections. A bottle of whiskey materialized and was passed around.   Each took a communional swig.

A little before ten, Spats got up saying he was going to turn in and left.   They all followed his cue and, thanking Hollis, took their leave.

A short time later, as Hollis was getting undressed, Selkirk appeared at the door.

"Boy, am I glad to see you.   You OK?"

"Yeah.   Thanks for saving us.   They had us.   I don't think we'd have made it without you.   Your guys beat those Gerries back pretty good."

"Yeah, it was close."   Hollis noticed that Selkirk was still dressed in his flying clothes. He looked beat.   His eyes were so sunken into their sockets they looked blackened as if he had been in a fight.   He had a cut on the back of his hand and he trembled slightly.   There was blood on his sleeve.   "You got back pretty fast."

"Yeah, Gleason flew down to pick us up.   Hollis, I'm not flying anymore.   I'm gonna go tell the Colonel.   Will you go with me?"

"Don't you think you better tell Ransahoff first?"

"No, he'll just try to talk me out of it."

"Why don't you sleep on it?"

"Can't.   I'm on the list for tomorrow."

Hollis knew the policy.   Like a rider tossed from a horse, putting them right back in the saddle was considered the best therapy, the best thing you could do for them.   This was asking too much of Mickey Selkirk.   He looked finished.   And taking someone off operations for a rest and a chance at rehabilitation frequently didn't work.   Once a man was broken there was little chance for recovery.

Hollis knew this was a terrible mistake but dressed anyway.   As they walked Selkirk started talking.

"If God wants to kill me why doesn't he just do it?   Why must He insist on torturing me? I'm done with this.   I have a wife and kids.   I never should have volunteered for this in the first place.   A Selkirk has ridden to the sound of the guns in every war since Concord.   I've done my part.   I can't do anymore."

Hollis was encouraged.   This was a lucid decision of a rational man, not like Alexander, who weighed the odds and found they were no longer in his favor.   They were not in anybody's favor, really.   Selkirk's just seemed worse.   "Maybe you just need a rest."

As they walked, they could hear planes circling overhead, landing.   Replacements.

When they arrived at Group headquarters they were told Van Patten was busy and could they come back tomorrow?   No, Selkirk said.   I just got fished out of the North Sea.   This isn't going to wait.

OK.   Wait here.

Hollis noticed Ransahoff talking to Gleason and Begay.   They were huddled over a map with Sudbury and Pillacio.   Imparting significance to this meant that Ransahoff was tomorrow's Bangmaster.

OK, Lieutenant, you can go in.

Hollis preferred to wait outside while Selkirk went into the office and closed the door. Van Patten saw him before the door closed. Hollis suddenly feared two MPs would appear and put him in shackles and cart him off to the stockade for violation of group integrity. Perhaps that would be a good thing, Hollis thought.

Selkirk was in with the Colonel for what seemed like ages, but was probably not more than twenty minutes. In that period of time the energy left his muscles and the exhaustion and whiskey hit him. His arms ached, his chest hurt and he felt that he probably would not be able to make the walk back to the room.

The door came open and Selkirk's appearance was unchanged. The Colonel had his arm around his shoulder. Selkirk stood with Hollis while Van Patten went to a phone and made a call.

"What's going on?"

"The Colonel said he understood how ditching today might have really upset me. It would make anyone think twice about going out again, he said. He's calling Clevenger to put me in the hospital tonight. He's going to give me a sedative and tomorrow he's sending me and the crew to London for a seventy-two hour pass."

So much for getting back in the saddle.

Selkirk put out his hand. "Thanks for saving us, Stan. I'll see you later."

Hollis shook Selkirk's hand and watched as Van Patten guided him back into his office. Van Patten turned to Hollis and said, "Get some rest, you're going out tomorrow."

Chapter Forty-Six   **Anklam**

Saturday, October 9, 1943

Hollis heard the door close. He figured he had only been asleep a few hours and it was a fitful sleep at that, his brain preoccupied by a nebulous dream about flak and water.   It was after eleven when he finally climbed into bed, exhausted, physically and emotionally, quite disturbed by the mental collapse of his friend, Mickey Selkirk.   He heard the approach of steps to his door and it opened.   Beamis tried to shield the beam of his flashlight as he came to Hollis and tapped him on the shoulder.

"Wake up, sir.   You and Lieutenant Cobb and Lieutenant Sullivan need to get over to Group.   You're the Deputy."

"I'm awake."

"You got just enough time to wash up and grab a cup of coffee."

"What time is it?"

"Oh-two thirty."

"Where to today, Beamis?"

He whispered, "I think this could be the big one.   You're going a long way.   Nobody's going who ain't got Tokyos or bomb bay tanks."

"Berlin?"

"I'm only speculatin'."

Leo sat up in bed, "We're going to Berlin?"

"No.   I'm just speculatin' and you didn't hear it from me.   You can go back to sleep, sir. You don't need to get up for another hour."

In the washroom, Hollis found Cobb and Sully shaving.   They looked very tired and more than a little annoyed at having to get up before everybody else.   Hollis didn't say anything.

Hollis emptied his bladder and started washing up.   After a few moments Sully turned to him and said, "Well, Horatio, where are they sending us today?"

"How would I know?"

"Don't tell me Beamis didn't say anything."

"No, he was speculatin', alright."

"For Christ's Sake, Jack," Cobb said, his annoyance obvious, "what did he say?"

"Berlin."

"Fuck you, Berlin," Sully said.

"Really?" Cobb said, disbelieving.

"He didn't come right out and say it.   I don't believe him anyway.   There is no possible way Van Patten would ever let Ransahoff lead the Group to Berlin without him.   Him and Gleason and the Chief would climb all over each other to be the Bangmaster on that deal.   It ain't Berlin."

"How do we know Van Patten ain't the Bangmaster?" Sully asked.

Hollis had to admit to the possibility.   Now he was even more worried.

"I'd like to know how the fuck we got chosen to be Deputy.   After that stunt yesterday, I'm surprised they didn't bust you right there on the hardstand."

"Me either," Hollis admitted.

Cobb washed the shaving soap from his face and said, "One thing's for sure.   I don't ever want to go back to Bremen again."

"Me neither," Hollis mumbled as he rinsed the last of the toothpaste from his mouth.

"Or Schweinfurt," Sully added.

"Me neither," Cobb said.   "And I never even went there."

"In fact, I'd be perfectly contented if the most hazardous thing they made me do was sit around and smell Cobb's rotten stogies."

"No chance, asshole," Cobb replied as he lifted the stub from the shelf above the trough, placing it back into his mouth.

As they left the washroom, Sully turned to Hollis, "You know that Seventeen we saw ground-looped?"

"Yeah."

"That was **Tinker Toy**.   The pilot had his head blown off at the shoulders.   They said it was the worst mess they'd ever seen."

"Why are you telling me this, you dumb fuck?"

"Some gunner took his glove off and put his hand out into the slipstream until his fingers froze."

"Sully, please.   If you don't shut up, I'll have you shot."

"Somebody told me Clevenger said he's probably going to lose his hand."

"Cobb, get him to shut up."

"Let me get my .45."

"You know, Jack, I can remember not long ago when you would be so scared before a mission you could hardly carry on a conversation.   What's come over you?   You are the last person I would have thought might duke it out with a German fighter or leave the safety of a formation to cover anybody who wasn't a blood relative.   Maybe even then. Now here you are Deputy Bangmaster.   What's come over you?"

"I don't know...I honestly don't.   Maybe I've just grown numb to it.   Maybe we're already dead and just don't know it yet."

"Both of you shut the fuck up," Cobb said.   "I mean it.   I'll shoot the fuckin' both of ya'."   Cobb took the cigar from his mouth and hurled it into the woods.   "You guys are really pissin' me off."

They finished dressing and reconvened at the Squadron office.   Being Deputy entitled him to a jeep, Hollis thought, and in the middle of the night, with everybody's attentions directed elsewhere he simply got in and started it.   As he drove them over to the Combat Mess, it dawned on him that this was Otho's jeep.   They ate quickly and headed for Group.   It was now three A.M.

They entered the Operations Room where Van Patten was talking to Ransahoff.   Begay and Gleason huddled with Sudbury and Pillacio along with Ransahoff's navigator and bombardier by the large wall map of Northwestern Europe.   Hollis could see the long red yarn stretch from Cromer over the North Sea to Denmark to a target in Northeastern Germany.   Sully saw it, too.   "Jesus Christ, we're in for it today."

Hollis stepped up to Van Patten unsure of what kind of greeting he might receive, "Colonel."

"Ah, good morning, gentleman.   Our target for today is the Arado aircraft assembly plant in Anklam.   Major Ransahoff will go over the details of the mission with you.   I'll chat with you again before briefing."   He then placed his arm around Hollis and took him to one side.   Van Patten looked Hollis square in the eye and said softly, "I have no doubt your actions saved Lieutenant Selkirk and his crew.   Stop trying to be a hero.   Don't ever leave a formation again.   I mean it.   I will not have this discussion with you again.   Understood?"

"Yes sir," Hollis replied, the lump in his throat nearly prevented the words from leaving his lips.   *Anybody ever tell you about the geese, you West Point asshole?*

He returned to Ransahoff who was already in discussion with Cobb and Sully. Ransahoff directed them to be briefed by Sudbury and Pillacio.   Ransahoff turned to Hollis saying, "Congratulations" and held out his hand.

"For what?"   Ransahoff dropped something into Hollis's outstretched palm.

"You made captain."   Hollis looked at his palm.   There was a pair of captain's bars. "Come by the Squadron office when you get back and sign the papers."

"I don't want to be a captain."

Ransahoff looked annoyed, "Hollis don't make me give you another lecture on the necessity for discipline in a military organization.   Put 'em on.   They were hardly used."

"Did you get any sleep?"

"Enough."

"You look beat."

"Thanks for your concern," Ransahoff said sarcastically, "but I'd be more worried about this mission than my health, if I were you."

"You give me no end of reasons to dislike you."

"I appreciate that, Hollis, I truly do.   Now, here's the plan."   He took out flimsies and handed them to him.   One was the formation board.   Bomber call.   Routes and timings. Hollis perused the list.   Kehoe was number three, Spats number four, Robertshaw five and Baldini six.   The 534th would be high, 533rd low.   Ninety-first low group. Three-fifty-first will lead.

"Our task force will be in the van, 41st will lead, our wing will follow.   We will be the diversionary force for the rest of the three Divisions which will continue east.   Two wings will hit the Focke-Wulf plant at Marienburg in East Prussia, another two will hit the port facilities at Gdynia and another the ship yard at Danzig.   The Germans think this is beyond our range and, for that reason, there should be little or no flak in the target area.   Therefore, the mission will be flown at a slow climb until we reach the Frisian Islands where we will be at our bombing altitude, 12,000 feet.   The thinking is that the Germans will have so much trouble trying to figure out what we're up to that the fighter opposition should be, at best, confused and limited, or, at worst, confused and strong.

"Hopefully, this will be a long, dull mission."

"You think?"

"Sure, Captain.   They got Bremen right, didn't they?"

"At least we won't need oxygen or freeze our asses off."

"There is that.   Did you eat?"

After they left their briefing, Sully mockingly tried to click the heels of his boots together and saluted, saying, "Jarwohl, Mein Kapitan."

It was obvious to Hollis that he had been bestowed a dubious honor.   He knew, without being told, that when Ransahoff placed the captain's bars in his hand, he was second in command of the squadron, something he never could have envisioned two months ago.   Nor aspired to. The mere accomplishment of having survived at all had left him the ranking officer after Ransahoff.   Selkirk, apparently, didn't count.

Sully said, "The thought of you having any kind of command authority leaves me absolutely speechless."

"Let's get to the briefing."

He waited for Leo at the door of the briefing room.   He led him to the front of the room where the important people stood during the briefing.   Hollis could not resist the inflation to his ego.   Against all expectations, instead of being busted back to Second Lieutenant for yesterday's shenanigans, he had been promoted and stood before his peers as a *bona fide* combat leader.   Wouldn't his mother be proud?   Such were the vagaries of total war.   It also reinforced his long-held belief that decisions made by military organizations frequently defied logic, the benefit of experience or ordinary common sense.

Hollis watched the officers shuffle in, so many unfamiliar faces, all wondering about what he already knew.   He fought the desire to be smug.

At precisely five AM, the adjutant called the group to attention.   The entourage took their seats and Ransahoff began.   "Good morning, Gentleman.   I'm the Bangmaster for today's sortee.   You will be interested to know that the RAF hit Bremen last night, adding to the damage we inflicted on the same target yesterday.   Today we might be having a little fun." He pulled the curtain back and was greeted by gasps and groans.   "Our target is the Arado Flugzeugwerke aircraft component factory in Anklam.   They manufacture parts for FW-190s. We will be part of a larger force attacking targets at Marienburg, Danzig and Gdynia and serve as a large diversionary force with two combat bomb wings assigned to our target.   He doesn't think we can strike a target that far.   Because there are few if any flak batteries at the target our bombing altitude will be 12,000 feet.   That means no oxygen and we won't be freezing our asses off.   Further, S2 believes that the different routes, lower than expected altitude and timings will upset and divide the interceptor force so we expect opposition to be light.   One other item of some interest is the fact that Anklam is the training facility for new German fighter pilots."   This elicited some snickers from the crowd.

"All aircraft will have 2780 gallons of gas.   We will be at maximum weight.   Climb out slowly.   Keep mixtures lean and rpm low."   Ransahoff went on to describe, in exquisite detail, the rest of the mission.

The Squadron had received one new F and two new Gs, one of which sat where **Cleopatra's Asp** had stood only the day before.   It was the one Hollis and his crew would be flying.

He greeted Moe warmly.   Moe seemed glad to see him.

"They flew it in yesterday afternoon.   I went over it with a fine-toothed comb.   She's a good airplane.   She'll serve you well."

"Thanks, Moe.   You'll need to pick a name."   Hollis looked over the plane quickly. He noticed the manufacturer, in this case Vega, had restored the two cheek guns to the nose compartment.   H-y would have been happy.   Dodge got a newer, high-profile turret and the gun positions of the radio operator and the waist gunners were enclosed by windows.   The frigid gale they had to endure roaring through the middle of the plane, which had resulted in countless cases of frostbite, was eliminated.   The best news for Hollis and Leo was an electronic control for the superchargers instead of the hydraulic controls which tended to freeze up becoming dangerously problematic at high altitude.   Hollis found himself hoping they would get to keep this plane.

Hollis said, "Gather 'round," quickly enlightened the crew to the mission, adding at the end, "We're the Deputy today.   On the bomb run nobody gets on the intercom but the navigator, the bombardier or me.   They say we shouldn't see much flak at the altitude we'll be flying at today.   They have predicted a milk run.   But we've been surprised by bad information before, so stay sharp.   Any questions?"

"Yes sir," MacFadden said.   "Is it okay if we take some extra ammunition?"

Hollis said, "Yeah, stow it forward.   Keep the weight out of the tail."   Hollis nodded and tucked away his escape kit, tied his shoes to his parachute harness and climbed aboard the new, as yet unnamed, bomber.   He and Sully calibrated the autopilot and the Norden Bombsight.

Not everyone expected a milk-run, Hollis certainly did not.   Sure enough, a six by six pulled up to the hardstand dispensing extra ammunition to the anxious gunners.   They believed the Germans were too clever to be fooled, and if they were, they would recognize their error and seek retribution with a vengeance.

When they were satisfied, tasks completed, Hollis and Sully deplaned and grabbed a smoke.

Sully said, "You know, Jack, as long as you looked and acted as scared as I felt, I knew you wouldn't do anything stupid and we'd be OK.   Now you're starting to worry me."

"You just make sure the bombs are on the target, Sully.   I'll take care of the rest."   When had it changed?   When had he become a warrior?

Hollis sat by himself, on the grass beyond the wing, smoking his last cigarette.   He could not stop thinking about Mickey.   He and Selkirk, so much alike when they first met, had taken such divergent courses.   Selkirk was at or near cracking.   Hollis acknowledged his terror and overcame it by inner forces he neither understood nor recognized.   The terror had consumed Selkirk like some virulent disease.   Too many close scrapes.   Was it luck?   Was it pre-ordained?   Were they witnessing The Divine Hand ruthlessly toying with them, playing some game of chance with their lives, to see how it turned out?   Had he experienced the same close shaves Selkirk had perhaps Hollis would be in the same shape as Mickey.   Or worse. Alexander

The one thing Hollis admired most was physical courage, the one thing he most lacked, or did he?   He always went.   Like Milo and Stan, Gruver, Barney, Dutch, Watanabe, Lemaster, Cassidy, DeBerg.   It was an impressive list.   Maybe he could see it in others but was incapable of recognizing it in himself.   How could this be?   It was a thin line which divided the weak from the strong.   But you knew it when you saw it.   Combat failure.   Shell shock. Entwhistle.   Scorch Alexander.   Brubaker.   Now Selkirk.

Poor Selkirk.   Probably still sound asleep from the shot Clevenger had given him.   He was supposed to report directly to Clevenger when he returned from London to be reexamined. Hollis wondered what Clevenger might find.   Mickey was a broken man.   He hoped they recognized that fact and took pity on him.   Were they capable of pity?   Was the word even in their lexicon?

Hollis looked at his crew.   Combat veterans.   Their toughness surprised even him. They knew they were part of an elite organization.   The fear they shared with their fellows established a bond that was nearly unbreakable.   It transcended patriotism and propaganda. And the shame of not going was far greater to them than any fear of mutilation or fiery death. It was contained within their soul.   It was called Honor.   *If it be a sin to covet honor/I am the most offending soul alive...those now abed/Shall think themselves accurse'd they were not here/And hold their manhoods cheap.*   Twas ever thus.

His heart swelled with pride that they could see fit to count him among them.   He looked inside and found what he thought he was missing. Where it had been all along.   He snubbed out his cigarette in the dirt.

Oh-seven thirty.   Stations.

Chapter Forty-seven   **The Deputy**

Hollis advanced the outboard throttles then backed off, the brakes squealing as he applied them.   He waited for a moment then repeated the process advancing along the perimeter strip, nose to tail, in stop-start-stop fashion.   He shut down the inboards to conserve gas. He could see out of the corner of his vision the high squadron take off.   It was slower than usual because each bomber paused long enough to have its tanks topped off by two fuel bowsers on each side of the runway threshold.

Finally, Dutch Ransahoff turned the **Flying Dutchman** onto the runway.   One mechanic connected a static line to the ground while two others scurried up onto the wing dragging fuel lines.   The process took a minute or two as Hollis re-fired the two engines..   When they were clear, the Flying Officer gave the light, Ransahoff gunned the engines and sped off.   Leaning Moe's Fortress into the wind blast just erupting from Dutch's engines, Hollis guided the B-17 around and watched as the fueling crew repeated their task.

"Lock tail wheel."

"Tail wheel locked.   Gyros."

"Gyros set."

The mechanic on the left wing, his head bowed into the wind behind the propellers, looked right at Hollis and gave a small wave as he scurried back down the ladder dragging the gasoline hose behind him.   Hollis inched the throttle to 1500 RPM.

"Generators," Leo called.

Hollis reached down and made sure they were on.   "On."

Hollis advanced the throttles to the stops and watched the manifold pressure needles climb, while he stood on the brakes.   "Brakes."

Leo reached up and released the parking brake.   When the needles touched forty-six inches he eased off the pedals and the bomber surged forward, tentatively at first, but gaining momentum quickly.   With the extra weight Hollis expected a longer than usual take off run. He was not disappointed.   The bomber left the ground with less than five hundred feet of runway to spare, causing Leo to once again brace himself for the crash he knew was an instant away.

With the wheels up, Hollis kept the climb slow, orbiting only a few hundred feet off the ground until he pulled up alongside Ransahoff.   Ransahoff led them around again, maintaining five hundred feet until the low squadron tacked on, one by one.

Group assembly complete Ransahoff turned the Group for Wing assembly, climbing one thousand three hundred feet.   A short time later, he met with the other two groups, assuming high position and the Wing turned for coast-out at Cromer.

Hollis glanced at his watch.   Nine thirty-five.   Right on time.   They fell in line behind the leading combat wing and headed out over the North Sea at an altitude they all found uncomfortably low.   They could make out the white caps clearly, the rising sun shimmering on the dark water.   The Task Force Commander, General Travis, set the pace for the climb, one hundred feet per minute, to conserve fuel.   Hollis made sure his mixture was lean and his rpms low.   He saw a bomber abort from the lead group then one from the low.

Sully appeared on the flight deck, but instead of sitting on the edge of the hatchway, climbed all the way up and stood behind Hollis pointing up and to the left.

Hollis saw a string of dark planes, Lancasters, heading on the opposite course, done for the night.

"Pilot to Turret, Dodge pull the Tokyos."

Sully lit a cigarette and handed it to Hollis.   "Long ride."

Hollis nodded and took a long drag, the harsh smoke filling his lungs.

A moment later, Dodge leaned around Sully in the cramped space in front of his turret and gave Hollis the thumbs-up sign.   He returned to his turret.

"Navigator to crew, fire away."

The new bomber shook with the recoil of its guns.

Sully finished his smoke, gave Hollis a wave and left to pull his pins.   When he finished he tapped Hollis on the leg, as he always did, and returned to the nose.

"Navigator to pilot.   Escort should be here by now.   See 'em?"

Hollis looked around.   "Negative."   It made little sense to have the escort follow them. It was unlikely the Germans would contest the approach of the bombers this far out to sea.

He let Leo fly for a while.   All he had to do was stay close to Ransahoff.   How hard could that be?   He reached into his flight suit for another pack of cigarettes and felt something unfamiliar.   He retrieved it.   It was the picture of Belinda.   He looked at it for a moment, examined her fetching over-the-shoulder smile, her demure pose, rubbed his gloved thumb over her face and placed it back where he had found it.   He thought of H-y, blown to pieces yesterday over Bremen.   He felt the fear grip his heart and wondered what it was like, being blown to pieces.

They passed five thousand feet, halfway to the Danish coast and Travis increased the rate of climb so they would be at 12,500 feet by the time they reached Denmark.

"Navigator to pilot. Coast-in Denmark in twenty minutes. Will be turning to heading 90 degrees in ten minutes."

"Roger, navigator."

Flat sea in all directions. Over the horizon was Denmark. There were German day and night fighters stationed there. Why would anyone suppose this would be a milk run, Hollis wondered.

The formation droned on. Soon Hollis could make out the Danish coast, a dark, thin rim of land. It was ten-twenty.

"Coast-in ten minutes," Cobb announced.

"Pilot to crew. Stay alert." Hollis reached down and turned on the autopilot.

"Right waist. I think I see fighters at three o'clock level."

"Too far for escort. Keep an eye on them, Mac," Hollis said.

Hollis leaned over Leo to see if he could make out the planes, but could not see anything.

Up ahead, a smoky trail spiraled downward. A casualty from the leading wing. The sky was crystal clear, not even the hint of haze over the sea. He could barely make out the planes up ahead. Black dots. They were in a fight.

Hollis checked the three o'clock again. Nothing.

The formation droned on. Leo's lips were moving. He was singing. Hollis had never seen Leo in combat without the lower half of his face concealed behind the bulky oxygen mask. He could not make out the tune above the engine noise which was a constant thunder in the ears.

Hollis looked down and saw the green-brown coast of Denmark pass beneath his wings, faster it seemed because they were lower.

"Hitlerites, twelve o'clock level!" Ransahoff's voice blasted into Hollis's headphones. "Close it up, we're gonna to get hit!"

Instinctively, Hollis eased the bomber in toward the **Flying Dutchman**. Suddenly a line of tracers shot out from Ransahoff's plane. A split-second later the guns in the nose and top turret of his plane erupted with fire as two twin-engine Me-210s bored in on Ransahoff. The nearest German banked onto a wing and flew over the **Flying Dutchman**. Hollis could make out the green splotches of paint on the gray surfaces of the wings and fuselage as it flashed past his window. In the instant before it passed, he could see the German pilot's helmeted head through his canopy. Dodge blasted away at the German.

Dodge must have yelled into the intercom for Leo snapped his head around to look back over the right wing. Leo broke into a grin and yelled, "Dodge chopped his tail off!"

Two more Me-210s raced past after making a pass at the lead group. Nobody was hit but the bombers weaved in and out from the encounter.

The Fortress shook again, this time it was the tail and ball turrets answering fire. The battle lasted for a few minutes. One Fortress from the low squadron dove away from the formation, an engine on fire, in an effort to get back out to sea. Quickly, the sky was empty save for the three groups, the sky clean, the smoke long left behind dissipating into nothingness. Hollis looked around. From his vantage point, except for the one plane in the low squadron, the Group appeared intact. He wondered how much longer it would stay that way.

Leo tapped Hollis and pointed back over the left wing.

Hollis looked out his side window and saw a half dozen Me-109s climbing upward in loose formation.   They passed out of sight beneath the left wing and reappeared as they leveled off.   They were tantalizingly close.   They knew the range to the closest bombers, the low group, and stayed just outside of it trying to draw fire.   The gunners down there displayed remarkable discipline for no tracers reached out for the Germans.   The gunners knew they still had a long way to go, extra ammo or not.   Hollis kept a wary eye on the Germans and scanned the sky ahead for trouble.

Hollis felt a jolt and more firing.   Had they been hit?   He looked around quickly at one wing then the other.   The engines were fine.   An Me-110, a night-fighter, for it was painted entirely in black, banked in at the high squadron and dove away.   Hollis switched to intercom, "What was that?   Are we hit?"

"Pilot this is tail, a rocket went off below us.   I don't think it hit us.   We got some FWs back there with rocket launchers under their wings.   They look too scared to close in before they fire which is fine with me."

"You keep an eye on 'em, Tail.   If they get itchy tell me."

"Roger."

Hollis switched back to VHF, looked at Ransahoff and closed in.   He looked for the 'escorting' Messerschmitt's and they were gone.   They must have grown impatient and flew on ahead.   They would be back very soon.   The bomber shook with intermittent short bursts but it seemed as if there was no active attacks for the time being.

The formation crossed over the Danish peninsula and out over the archipelago south of Copenhagen.   A few bomb bay doors opened and the extra fuel tanks those planes were carrying were dropped.   Empty.   Just so much extra weight.   Ransahoff's doors opened and he kicked out his tank, too.

Up ahead, he saw the return of the Me-109s.   They were coming head on, their wings and noses blinking with machine gun and cannon fire.   The lead group took hits.   The bomber shook with return fire and quickly the fighters turned belly up and dove down, putting as much distance between them and the bombers as fast as they could. Leo tapped his arm and pointed to his headphones.   Hollis switched to intercom.   "Navigator to pilot.   Our next checkpoint is in five minutes and we will make a forty-five degree turn to the right for our run to the IP at Neubrandenburg."

"Roger."

Before he could switch back to VHF, he heard Sully yell, "Fighters coming in twelve o'clock level!"

Hollis saw the black dots, a dozen or more, banking sharply for a run at the wing.   They were coming right at him.   "Hold your fire, Dodge," Hollis muttered.   "Still too far."

They closed quickly and the bomber shook yet again as Sully and Dodge opened up. Hollis cringed down behind the instrument panel and, for a moment, closed his eyes.   This might be it.   He could tell when they had passed because the tenor of the return fire changed and stopped.

"They got Ransahoff!" Leo yelled.

Hollis bolted upward in his seat and could see black smoke pouring out from the nacelle of Ransahoff's right outboard engine.   He watched with stunned fascination as Ransahoff's copilot stared at the burning engine.   The propeller stopped spinning and feathered motionless into the wind.   The engine continued to smoke and Ransahoff slowed appreciably causing everybody to throttle back abruptly to keep from over-running him.   Another group of fighters flew by smelling the blood of a burning engine and Ransahoff's plane took more hits.   *He's finished, that poor son of a bitch.*

Ransahoff lowered his landing gear.

"Ransahoff's surrendering!" Leo screamed.

Hollis could not tear his eyes away from the burning **Flying Dutchman**, expecting any second that it might blow up.

"No he's not.   He's passing the lead to us."

Hollis wagged his wings and Ransahoff's copilot gave a small wave.   Ransahoff tipped the **Flying Dutchman** into a steep diving left bank, raising his undercarriage as he fell away from the formation, dragging the long ribbon of smoke behind him.

Hollis got on the intercom and said, calmly, "Take a good look at Ransahoff.   I fear this is the last we shall ever see him."

The **Flying Dutchman** salvoed its bomb load and disappeared behind them.

"Maybe he's heading for Sweden."

"I hope he makes it, poor bastard."

For a moment, the fear which gripped Hollis's heart like a vice left him replaced by a profound sadness.   Hollis eased his Fortress into the spot Ransahoff had vacated.

"That makes you the Bangmaster," Sully said.

Hollis banged Leo's arm and yelled for him to monitor the VHF while he stayed on the intercom.

The formation made a sweeping turn over the Baltic Sea and headed for Germany.

"Navigator, how far to the IP?"

"Seventeen minutes."

Hollis checked the autopilot again to make sure he had turned it on and it had warmed up. They were over Mecklenburg Bay heading on a course the Germans were to suppose would take them to Berlin.

"Coast-in in five minutes," Cobb said.

This close to the German capital Hollis expected a fearsome air battle, but, for the moment, the sky was devoid of German fighters.   Hollis's mind started to race making mental calculations.   They would still consume fuel between here and the IP, changing the weight. He would wait until they were closer before adjusting the autopilot.

Back in the old days, Hollis knew, strike photos showed bombs scattered hither and yon. When the bombs failed to strike the intended mean point of impact it was invariably the fault of the bombardier, the pilot or both.   Hollis vowed that if the Group's bombs didn't hit the target today, he would be certain it had been through no fault of his.

Under ideal circumstances, wing-tip to wing-tip in combat box formation, a group laid a swath of bombs 1800 feet wide traveling at three hundred feet per second.   A second or two difference in bomb release could make the difference between success and complete failure.   At the IP, the group would tuck into the tightest formation possible to make a compact bomb pattern.   Today, the turn would be nearly 90 degrees, a little sharper than usual.   A lot was riding on Sully, too.   Today would be his moment of truth.

"Coast-in."

"After the turn, give me a level as quickly as you can," Sully said.

Cobb came on the intercom, "Jack, six minutes after the IP make a sharp left turn to the Rally Point.   It's CAVU, we should have no trouble spotting the IP or the aiming point."

"Roger.   Dodge, red flares at the IP."

"Yes sir."

There was a considerable volume of flak thrown up to the right as they passed over the coast.   It was in the direction of Rostock.   None of it was close enough to cause concern.   The lack of opposition was disquieting.   Perhaps the dopes at S2 were right.   For once. Since the Germans always hit the formations harder on penetration than withdrawal maybe this wouldn't turn out so bad.

"IP ten minutes."

Hollis looked at the Group, swiveling back and forth in his seat.   They all looked intact. He noticed Robertshaw had pulled into the number two position.

Hollis carefully trimmed the plane and set the indicated airspeed at precisely 165 mph. He reached down and engaged the autopilot.   He turned the aileron centering knob until the tell-tale light at the top of the console extinguished.   He did the same for the rudder, then the elevator.   He trimmed the autopilot, centering the PDI and turned the sensitivity to high.   This would allow the autopilot to correct even the slightest deviation.   When they commenced the bomb run at the IP, Sully's bombsight would fly the plane through the autopilot Hollis now had ready to go.   He set the ratio, disengaged the autopilot and resumed control of the plane.   Any deviation, acceleration or deceleration in speed or attitude would throw off the bombsight. Evasive action was out of the question.   Fortunately, there should be little or no flak at the target which might tempt him to fly erratically.   The fighters had gone and it did not appear as if they were about to return.   This should be as good as he could possibly make it.

"IP, five minutes," Cobb announced.

"Quinn, turn on the strike camera."

"Roger."

The minutes dragged by.

"I've got the IP," Sully said, very business-like.

Hollis could not believe how numb his ass had become.   He arched his back in an effort to look down beyond the nose to spot Neubrandenburg, but he could not see it.

"IP, one minute."

"Bomb bay doors coming open," Sully said.   Hollis could hear the rush of air and sense the slowing of the bomber.

"Dodge."

"Got 'em."

"Bomb bay doors open," Rizzo said.

Hollis tightened his grip on the wheel and advanced the throttles forward to resume 165 mph.

"IP."

Hollis could feel his heart pounding in his chest.

Chapter Forty-eight   **Bangmaster**

Hollis heard the report of the flare gun and watched the lead group swing into its turn to commence the run at the target.   He waited until they were uncovered and eased in some rudder for the turn to guide his own group around.   He hardly touched the aileron.   He wanted a nice flat turn that everyone could handle.

He switched quickly to the VHF, "Tuck it in, we came a long way."   He snapped the control back to intercom.   He leveled the wings at exactly 12,000 feet, checked the airspeed advancing the power a tiny bit to resume 165 and locked the throttles.   He re-trimmed the plane, but it needed virtually no adjustment.   Ignoring earth's horizon and his senses, he checked the artificial horizon, rate of climb and turn and bank indicator in rapid succession.   He checked the airspeed one more time and took his hands off the wheel.   The bomber flew perfectly, trimmed to fly straight and level without need of human guidance.

"There's your level."

"Roger."

Hollis waited, fingertips on the controls while Sully leveled the bubbles on the bombsight gyroscope.   A few moments later, "Got it" spoken so softly he barely heard it.   Hollis reached down to the autopilot and engaged it.   "PDI's centered.   It's your airplane."

"Roger," again barely audible.

Hollis kept his hand an inch off the wheel ready to over-ride the autopilot if there was trouble.   From this point until bomb release, which would occur automatically the instant the cross hairs in the bombsight came together, the plane was being controlled by the coordinated action of the Norden bombsight and the plane's C-1 autopilot. Any deviation in any parameter, regardless of how slight would foil the effort. The plane jerked slightly in response to adjustments made by Sully, who, hunched over the sight, fed little corrections into its computer by turning the knobs.

Hollis sensed bomb release was just moments away. He barely noticed the flak puffs floating past the window. He realized this was the first bomb run he had made using the bombsight/autopilot since phase training some four months ago.

A little longer...

Come on, Sully...

The wheel made little jerks, twitches...first one way then the other.

Any time now...

WHOMP! The bomber was jolted.

"Shit!" Sully yelled.

"We're hit!" screamed into his headphones.

He looked over at number three and saw gray smoke pouring out from beneath the cowl flaps. Streamers of flame licked back onto the nacelle.

Instantly, powered by reflex, Leo reached for the fuel cut-off and the throttle. But before his hands reached the controls Hollis slapped them away. He put his hand on Leo's chest and pushed him back into his seat. Leo looked out at the burning engine and back at Hollis, his eyes ablaze with sheer terror. Hollis watched the IAS. Still 165. The engine was still putting out power.

"It's OK. We'll be alright," Hollis yelled to a disbelieving Leo. With almost clinical detachment, Hollis wondered how long it would take for the flames to burn through the firewall and reach the internal regions of the wing, the fuel tanks and lines. If that happened the wing would erupt like a volcano and that would be the end.

The temptation to cut the engine and feather the prop was nearly overpowering. Leo's eyes bulged with horror as he stared helplessly at the flames. But Hollis didn't want to do anything that might ruin the minute corrections Sully was making as they approached the release line. He knew all eyes were on his bomb bay.

Any second...

Hollis could feel the sudden vibration of the bombs releasing from their shackles, the intervalometer casting loose each missile in rapid, predetermined sequence.

"Bombs away."

The moment the vibration stopped Hollis shouted, "Now!" He pushed the throttles forward on the three good engines while Leo hit the fuel cut-off switch. Hollis pushed the rpm lever to high, his hand then moved quickly to the throttle of the number three engine shoving it forward to the stop to scavenge the remaining gasoline from the line. Leo pressed the feather button and held it until the propeller blades turned their sharp edges into the wind and stopped rotating, hanging still on the engine while flames lapped the wing behind it. Hollis cut the generator and pulled the voltage regulator. Now there was nothing else to do but wait. Leo would have reached for the CO_2 fire extinguisher if they had one. The fire extinguisher system was felt to be ineffective for fighting engine fires and was removed on order of the Air Corps to save the weight.

Hollis watched the burning engine with a tortured silence.   Knowing death might be but a scant second or two away.   *God, make the flames stop.*

Dodge had come down from the turret, a concerned frown on his face, nearly pushing Leo out of his seat to inspect the engine.   He looked at the controls as if double checking the pilots.   He and Hollis exchanged glances, but no words were spoken.   None were needed.

Hollis hoped the dive toward the RP would blow out the fire.   If not he would have the crew bail out.

"We'll be alright," he told Dodge and Leo, but they knew he was lying.   *God, please fix this, I beg You.   I've killed my crew.*

"Wow!   You really hit it Sully!   They'll be cooking a little Weiner schnitzel today! Hot damn!" Rizzo shouted.

They got their pictures.   Hollis yelled, "Hang on" nosing the bomber into a diving turn to the left toward the Rally Point.   He felt the centrifugal force push him into his seat as he watched the airspeed climb, hoping everyone behind him would keep up, complete in the knowledge of what it was he was trying to do.   He kept the flames visible in the corner of his eye.   He noticed Leo reaching for his parachute, snapping the shackles onto the harness on the front of his chest.

"Bomb bay empty," Quinn said.

A moment later, Rizzo came on the intercom, "Bomb bay doors closed."

"Pilot to tail, they still with us?"

"You took 'em by surprise but they're catching up."

"We got any stragglers?"

"Couple in the high squadron are back aways, but they should catch us, too, cutting to the inside.   And the low squadron is right behind us."

Hollis leveled off at 11,000 feet and throttled back.   He banked one way then the next in shallow 'S' turns to allow the group to reform and anybody straggling to catch up.   Hollis could see the lead group, a little ahead and a thousand feet below, finishing its turn at the Rally. Hollis advanced the throttles, eased back on the control column and turned in behind the lead group.   Within a few minutes they had tacked on in perfect position.

"Fire's out," MacFadden said.

Dodge said into his ear.   "Call me if you need me.   I'm going to take a nap."

Hollis gave him the finger and Dodge climbed back into the turret.   Hollis looked at the engine and saw little wisps of gray smoke slip from beneath the cowls, but for all practical purposes the fire was, indeed, out.   He adjusted the power settings and settled into the long ride home.   Unfortunately, they were falling behind as the wing leader picked up the pace.   The loss of the engine had slowed them and, as the leader, the entire Group with him.

They had a long way to go.   He had a choice.   He could turn the lead over to Lemaster, leading the high squadron, who was next in command, reduce the power and try to limp home on the three good engines or he could flog them a little harder and try to keep the lead.   Even though they were not under attack, this was by no means over.   If he left the sanctuary of the formation, the Germans would seek him out and finish him as an afterthought.   Much as they had probably done to Ransahoff. If, in his effort to save himself, he put the rest of the group in jeopardy, he would be guilty of the most egregious cowardice.   Wasn't this the very same choice Ransahoff had made not twenty minutes earlier?   *Poor bastard.*

They were new engines.   If he burned them up trying to keep up so be it.   New or not, what if they gave out midway across the North Sea?   Who would be there to snatch them from the freezing water?   He eased forward on the throttles and increased the rpm slightly.   He would take his chances continuing the lead and do his best to try to stay with the wing.   The bomb load was gone.   Half the fuel had been consumed.   They just might make it.   If he fell behind, though, he would call to Lemaster to take over.   He wondered how close they were to Sweden?

Hollis would swear to whatever oath God should choose if He would see His way fit to just get them home.   He eyed the cylinder head temperatures.   The needles moved upward slightly.

He took stock.   He had led the Group to the target and bombed it successfully.   They had endured the battle on the way in.   Hopefully, they would get back without further opposition.   It was a long shot.

As they neared Rostock, where they would exit Germany, the sky was filled with floating black clouds of flak fired at the preceding wing.   In a few moments, it would be their turn.

"Fighters, nine o'clock low, coming up," Hulse said.

"Me-410s, twelve o'clock high!" Dodge shouted.

Hollis switched to the VHF.   "Close it up," he said around the lump in his throat. "We're gonna get hit!"

The bomber rattled and shook with return fire.   He could feel distinctly the plane being struck.

No sooner had the lead group entered the flak zone, when Hollis saw a Fortress in its high squadron take a direct hit, its tail flying off like a toy torn apart by a monstrous child.   The impact knocked the front part of the plane onto its back and it dropped straight toward the ground trailing smoky debris behind it.

The fighters pressed home their attacks despite the heavy flak that pocked the sky in all directions.   The bomber was tossed around violently by near misses.   Some close enough to hear above the engine noise.   Hollis kept up with the lead group even as the wing leader in the lead ship sped up even more.

This may be a big mistake, Hollis thought.   Not only would they lose us, he would leave behind others in his attempt to escape, for there were stragglers, falling behind like wounded animals from   a stampeding herd.   Even planes from the leading wing were drifting backward seeking refuge where they could find it.

When they were coast-out and beyond the flak at Rostock, the Germans threw themselves at the formations with renewed abandon.   All semblance of coordinated attack was gone.   It became a free-for-all.

"Jesus, pull up!   Pull up!" Mollica screamed.

Hollis yanked back on the control column until the yoke was   pressed against his abdomen.   Leo slammed the three good throttles forward.   An instant later, a slender exhaust trail from a rocket passed beneath the bomber, expending itself harmlessly in front of the Group, the spent missile tumbling end-over-end earthward.

"More Rockets!   Mother of God they hit Baldini!   Blew him right out of the sky."   As Hollis struggled to level the bomber he snapped his head around, but all he could see was cascading debris.

"God help us," Mollica muttered.

"FW coming straight in!   Twelve o'clock high!" Sully yelled.

Dodge opened up as did Sully, four steady streams of yellow and red tracers reaching out for the marauding German.   He had closed to within range and started firing at them.   Hollis could feel the plane shake as cannon shells raked the bomber.   He gripped the wheel and wagged one way then the other, but it was no use.   The impacts continued.   Quickly, the German flashed past, the damage done.

"Check in, God-damn it!"

"Nose OK, " Cobb said

"Phew, that was close!" Sully said.

"Top turret, OK.   He hit our wing pretty good."

Hollis looked out at the left wing and the leading edge had been badly mauled.   Large holes, aluminum skin peeled back, dotted the upper surface of the wing.

"Waist OK."

"Tail OK."

"Rizzo!   Quinn!"   As he said it, he could sense the ball turret firing.   "Quinn!   Pilot to radio!"

Nothing.

"Hulse check Quinn."

"I see him.   He's down."

God, not Quinn.   Please God.

"He's OK, he slipped on the shells and pulled his headset out of the jack."

"Son of a bitch is coming around again.   He's flying out past the high squadron, Dodge," MacFadden said.   "He must see our feathered engine and think we're easy pickin's."

Hollis turned to look, but could not see.

"They got one from the low squadron.   They're bailing out.   Come on you guys," Rizzo said.

Hollis had memorized the formation board.   It was Jones.

Ransahoff, Baldini, Jones, Legg.   Who was next?   *Us?*

They kept coming.   Singly and in pairs.   109s, 190s, twin-engine 110s, 210s and 410s.   Nightfighters.   Ju-88s lobbing rockets.   He checked on Kehoe and Robertshaw to either side.   They were tucked in close   He could not see Spats.

"Pilot to tail, see Spats?"

"He's in the slot.   They hit him pretty bad, but all four are running.   We got somebody from the low squadron, I think, fading back.   Looks like he's had it."

"Can you tell who it is?"

"No, sir."

They were being decimated.

"Navigator to pilot, we're over Denmark."

"Pilot to crew, how's the damage?"

"Six o'clock high, Dodge, get him!"

The turret opened fire with a sustained burst.   As jarring as the sound from his turret was, it was always reassuring to hear and feel Dodge's guns.

Hollis checked the oil and cylinder head temperatures.   They had crept dangerously high.   The engines could not sustain this punishment much longer.   He had no choice but to open the cowl flaps.   This would add drag and slow them down for sure.

"Pilot, this is Tail, we burned through the fabric on the starboard elevator.   All I see is ribs and a few shreds."

"Radio to pilot.   I got lots of holes.   They took out some of my transmitters.   The IFF transmitter is blown to pieces.   I got vacuum tubes and wires all over the place."

"Navigator to pilot.   We got all sorts of ventilation down here but everything else is just peachy."

Hollis could feel the ball turret firing again.

"Anybody hurt?"

"I bruised my ass when I slipped," Quinn said.

"Three o'clock high.   Two one-tens coming after us."

Hollis snapped his head to look, but could not see them.

"Come on, Dodge, lead 'em for Christ's Sakes."

The turret swung around as the two twin-engine night fighters dove past the lead squadron.

"Pilot to crew.   We're gonna burn up these engines soon.   We can't keep up.   I'm going to turn over the lead to Lemaster and see if we can get down onto the deck and scoot home."

"Navigator to pilot.   We should be over water soon.   Another five, six minutes max."

"Roger."

Hulse came on the intercom, "Sir, there's a small group of three or four planes making up their own little formation of stragglers on our eight o'clock low.   Maybe we can join 'em."

Hollis switched to VHF.   "Midget leader, this is Afghan G-George."

"Midget leader, go ahead, G-George."

"Take it, Keith.   I'm burning up.   Acknowledge."

"Roger, G for George.   I'll be down."

Hollis put the bomber into a gentle dive to clear the formation and watched as Keith Lemaster pulled away from the high squadron and into the lead slot.

Hollis knew they were in trouble now; joining the flock of cripples Hulse had spotted might offer only limited respite.   It would only cluster the wounded and make it easier for the Germans to knock them off, one by one in rapid succession.   He saw his group pull away. There was little else he could do.   He eased into the little formation, now numbering five aircraft, nearly a full squadron, and took an outside position.   Glancing at the tail markings, Hollis saw   one each from the 91st and the 351st, one from the 303rd, the lead group of the Anklam task force and one from the 379th.   The last two had drifted back through No Man's Land between the two wings and had managed to survive, a feat in itself.   All five planes either had one, or in one case two, engines out or serious structural damage that rendered them incapable of keeping up.   From the looks of it the *Luftwaffe* had had a field day.   He wondered how the other wings had made out.   If they had been the diversionary force, they had truly suffered because of it.   *More like sacrificial lambs*, Hollis thought.   There was one satisfying note.   Hollis felt pretty certain they had hit the target square on.   He was proud of Sully and intended to tell him so, if he lived.

"Fighters nine o'clock level.   Out of range," Hulse said.   "Sizing us up."

"Keep an eye peeled, left waist.   We still have a long way to go."   They passed over the western Danish coast at 1230.   They had four more hours, at least, of flying time left.   All of it over water, most of it fortunately, out of comfortable range of the German fighters.   But they were not out of danger yet.

"Here they come.   Ten o'clock high."

Hollis watched the fighters enter a steep bank at the apex of their climb and swoop down on the five hapless bombers.   Lines of tracers, Dodge's included, reached out to the Me-109s and the four fighters peeled away in different directions.   One of the cripples had been hit.   He started trailing smoke from an engine.   He feathered it quickly and now there were two planes with two engines out.   Hollis could clearly see ammo belts, boxes and machine guns tossed out the waist windows in an effort to lighten the ship.   They would now be relying exclusively on the protection afforded by the rest of the formation, an unsavory situation indeed.

The Me-109s, probably dissatisfied over the meager results of their attack, one engine knocked out and nobody finished off, came up from behind.   Hollis could sense Mollica's tail guns firing.   Suddenly, he squealed into the interphone, "I'm out of ammo, Hulse, drag some back here."

"I'm almost out, too."

"Quinn?"

"I got one box left.   I'm on my way."

Hollis checked the engine gauges.   The slower pace had allowed the engine temperatures to cool off some.   Finally the 303rd Fortress wagged its wings and turned back toward Denmark, two engines and all hope gone.   The last Hollis saw of him he had lowered his landing gear as the Me-109s approached.   Maybe he would take some of the fighters back with him as an armed guard.   Perhaps that had been the pilot's intention.   If it was, he deserved a medal.   They would probably never know.   Two Messerschmitts came back for another pass, but it was not pressed home and they departed, out of ammo, fuel or both having gained, perhaps, some grudging respect for their American adversaries.

In the distance, Hollis could make out two Ju-88s flying a parallel path with the four remaining bombers.   They did not close in for attack, figuring, Hollis suspected, that the four bombers were too badly shot up to make it and were, therefore, not worth the risk of engaging. Maybe they were right.

"Dodge, transfer fuel out of number three to number four."

"Yes sir."

Leo tapped Hollis's arm.   Hollis switched to VHF.

"Hey, G for George, this is Nightjar N-Nan.   Do you read me?"

"Roger, this is George.   Go ahead, N-Nan."

"My navigator's dead and my pilot is badly wounded.   Can you guide me back?"

"Affirmative, N-Nan.   Kimbolton is on the way."

"Roger."

Hollis looked back at N-Nan.   The aluminum skin of the nose had been peeled back as if by a giant can-opener leaving a gaping hole Hollis could see into.   They had a large panel ripped from the outer wing, but still had three engines running.   If the copilot kept his wits about him, with a little help he could make it back.

Hollis surveyed the other three planes.   The one with only two engines was drifting back.   The other two slowed down to keep the struggling cripple within reach so Hollis was obliged to do the same.   They were barely making 135 indicated.

"Navigator to pilot.   I think we're beyond effective range and I don't see those two Ju-88s anymore.   We may be in the clear."

"OK, Cobb."

The little formation droned on in a slow descent.   At this speed they were still a good two hours from coast-in at Cromer.

"Turret to crew.   Look up."

Hollis peered out the ceiling window above his head.   He tapped Leo and pointed up. There were bombers stretched across the sky, flying a similar course several thousand feet higher.   B-17s and B-24s in loose groups passing as if in parade above them, easily doing 170 or better, anxious to get home for supper.

Hollis let Leo fly most of the way.

"Ball to pilot."

"Go ahead, Bobby."

"Sir, I just noticed the wheel on the right looks flat.   It's kinda sagging and it might be shredded.   I can't tell.   Better get a good look at it when you drop the wheels."

"Thanks, Bobby."

"Can I come up now?"

"Yes."

Sully appeared in the hatchway and handed Leo and Hollis sandwiches wrapped in waxed paper.   Hollis ate the soggy Spam sandwich and chasing it with a cup of coffee and a Milky Way.   Leo did the same.   Dodge stood behind them, sharing in the bounty.   The crew started chatting on the intercom, but Hollis told them to knock it off.

Hollis lit a cigarette and passed it to Sully.   "When you go back down, take a look at the right wheel and see if it looks shot up," he shouted.   Sully gave him the thumbs-up, finished the smoke and returned to the nose.   He reappeared in the hatchway below a few moments later, looked up at Hollis and gave a thumbs-down.   Hollis nodded.

Hollis got on the VHF and talked to the copilot flying N for Nan.   He seemed to be doing OK.   He told Hollis he had never landed a Fortress with one engine out.   Hollis gave him some pointers, more to reinforce his confidence than instruct on technique.   But Hollis had troubles of his own.   He had one engine out and a flat main wheel.   Butch never told him about that combination.   Butch drank a lot.   Maybe he just forgot to mention it.   Hollis would tell the copilot in which general direction his home field, Kimbolton, could be found and wish him well.

"Hey, Lieutenant, er-I mean Captain.   That number one engine looks like its throwing oil."

Hollis checked the gauge before he looked at the engine.   Oil pressure was down, but still OK.   Sure enough the dark, viscous fluid ran back in a thin slick from the cowling, painting the upper surface of the wing.

"Let her go," Dodge said.   "We can feather it with the standpipe oil if we have to."

After a few more anxious minutes, the oil pressure finally fell to a critical level and, rather than letting the engine seize, destroy the crankcase and spin the propeller off into space, Hollis shut down the engine and feathered the prop.   Now they could barely make 120.   This close to England the three pilots and one copilot agreed they should not hold back for their weakest member and head for home on their own.

"Pilot to crew, toss out everything not bolted down."

The effect of losing the extra weight was negligible.   Soon they were alone.   The copilot flying N-Nan thanked Hollis and said he would land at the first decent field he could find and forget Kimbolton.   Hollis told him that was a wise idea.   He hoped the boy would make it.

He thought of Leo sitting not two feet away and wondered if he would demonstrate such poise.   He also found it curious that he would think of the copilot as a boy.   He might be the same age or, as in Leo's case, older.   Yet he thought of him as a boy.   How odd.

After a time, Hollis could make out England on the horizon.   They would cross the coast further south as Cobb had given Hollis a more direct route back to Ridgewell.   Hollis ran through the steps for a two-engine landing and tried to factor in the wheel being flat.   Such a combination of circumstances would have sent Butch screaming for another bourbon.   His standard answer for such unusual exigencies, ones that taxed his mind too severely, was, "I doubt you'd get that far" or "I don't think it'll fly like that" or "Hit the silk, pal, you're done for the day." *Thanks, Butch.*

They passed over Lowestoft and suddenly found themselves escorted by two Spit IXs. The IFF transmitter was gone and the RAF was taking no chances on an intruder slipping in. Hollis waved and they departed after a few minutes.

As they passed over familiar territory, Stowmarket, Hollis called, "Quinn, get me Watchdog."

"Right, Lieutenant."   After a moment, "I got 'em."

Hollis switched to the channel.   "Watchdog this is Afghan G for George.   Coming in with two out and a flat tire.   Will need crosswind final.   Request landing instructions."

"Roger, Afghan G-George.   Use runway one zero for right flat, two eight for left. Wind is from the north at ten knots with gusts to fifteen.   Altimeter twenty-nine ninety-one. Do you need red flares?"

"Negative, Watchdog.   ETA ten minutes."

"Roger, G-George.   Welcome back."

Hollis went through the calculus one more time.   With the right tire out he should keep the wind on his left to turn the big tail into the good tire.   With a tire out he needed a normal glide with full flaps.   Make contact with the good tire first, hold elevator full back after touchdown, brake with the good wheel, use the outboard engine on the side of the flat to counteract the tendency to ground loop.   Fortunately, the outboard engine on the affected side was OK.

Now, with two engines out, he needed an approach speed at one thirty and a constant rate of descent, keep wheels up until shallow turn off base leg onto final, keep flaps one half until over runway then full.   *Then bend over and kiss your sorry ass Good-bye*, Butch might add, just before he became apoplectic.

Hollis saw the field and spotted runway ten.   He would make a shallow turn over the hamlet of Ashen and lower the gear on the base leg, then half flaps and add power to keep up the airspeed.   Dodge confirmed the tire had been shredded but the gear was down OK.

Over the runway threshold, he had Leo drop full flaps and felt the bomber sink toward the runway.   He added more power to the good engines and side-slipped just slightly to put the good wheel down first.   It hit the concrete with a loud chirp.   He leveled the bomber onto the runway and the bad tire made contact.   There was a loud screeching noise and Hollis pushed the number four throttle forward as soon as he felt they were about to ground loop.   The bomber straightened out and the horrible screeching sound was accompanied by the loud slap of rubber strips ripped from the disintegrating tire smacking against the undersurface of the wing and a shower of sparks as the rim cut into the concrete.   Hollis cut the left inboard and they coasted to a halt.   Crash trucks pulled up to foam down the wheel, but it was all anticlimax.   Butch would have been proud, astonished, even speechless, but proud, nonetheless.

Hollis and the crew deplaned, inspecting the plane that at sunrise had been in the virginal state.   Now, it was a beat-up old mistress, raped and violated and now abandoned in the middle of the runway.   Hulse and MacFadden dutifully counted holes.   It would take Moe several hours of pulling off panels and dissecting the innards to see how much damage she had really sustained.   The right elevator was burnt through, whatever had hit the number three engine, a lucky flak hit, Hollis supposed, had torn up the tire.

"Long fucking ride," Sully said, rubbing his bottom as he walked over to Hollis.   Sully looked up at the blackened engine, but seemed disinterested.

Rizzo strode up to him.   "Lieutenant Sully, I followed your bombs all the way down.   You clobbered that place dead-on."

"Yeah, that's what I saw, too."   Sully seemed pleased with himself, Hollis thought.

A few moments later, a truck came by and the crew gathered its gear and climbed in.   After such an ordeal, they seemed pleased with themselves, too.

As they rode down the perimeter strip toward headquarters, Hollis was confronted with a sight that, at first, he did not believe.   Burnt, battered, but unbowed sat the **Flying Dutchman** on its hardstand.

"I'll be damned," he said.   "That son of a bitch Ransahoff made it.   I thought he was a goner, I really did."

Leo looked at Hollis and said, "I thought the same thing about us, you bastard.   Why didn't you let me put that fire out?   We nearly bought it."

Hollis, sizing up his copilot for he had never seen him this angry, said, "You're absolutely right, Leo.   I should have just said 'fuck it' to the whole bomb run and put out the fire."

All eyes fell on Leo Wychulis.   As harrowing an experience as it might have been for everybody else, it was now apparent that Leo had suffered unspeakable terror in silence, too scared to even sing, watching that flaming engine only a foot or two from where he sat.   Leo bent forward and placed his head in his hands.

They went to the briefing room and found Gorton and two colleagues seated at a table.

"Well, who have we here?   Late, yet again, Captain Hollis?"

"Mind if I stand, Major, my ass is still numb?"

A bottle of Johnny Walker sat on the table next to a map of the route and blow-ups of the pre-bombed target.   Cobb delivered a fist-full of glasses and the bottle was passed around.   Leo still appeared withdrawn and did not participate, choosing instead to sit and listen, more, Hollis thought, to his inner demons than the interrogation.

Ransahoff walked up and said, "I heard you made it back.   Hollis, this is getting to be a bad habit with you."

"Well, I guess congratulations are in order all the way around.   We gave you up for dead."

"Or Swedish," Sully added.

Lemaster walked over and shook Hollis's hand.   "I gotta tell you, Hollis, you're one of the coolest sons-a-bitches I ever saw."

"What are you talking about?   My knees are still shaking."

"In the middle of a bomb run you make an editorial comment about the length of the trip."

"I have no idea what you're talking about."

"'Fuck it, we came a long way.'"

Hollis smiled, "No, I said, 'Tuck it in, we've come a long way.'"

"Either way, you did good today," Lemaster said and walked away.   High praise from one of the group's better pilots.

"Don't get too full of yourself, Hollis," Gorton said.   "We haven't seen the strike photos yet."

Van Patten walked over and shook Hollis's hand also.   "Nice job making it back."   He turned to Ransahoff and said, "Your squadron is stood down for three days."

Hollis and the crew described the mission in detail, which by Hollis's account had lasted nearly twelve hours from take-off.

Back in the room, Hollis tried to make small talk, but Leo would have none of it.

"Say, Leo, do you at least want to go get a drink?"

"No, I'm tired.   I intend to take a shit and go to bed."

"OK, I'll see you later."

At the Club, Hollis found Ransahoff and Gleason in conversation.   Since he had been the Deputy and Bangmaster, and now a Captain, he felt entitled to join the conversation.

"How many did we lose today?"

Gleason said, "Three.   Baldini, Jones and Legg.   We fared better than the other two. They lost five a piece.   The Anklam force got hit pretty bad."

"And the rest?"

"The other two task forces didn't get bounced near as bad as we did."

"I guess the diversion worked."

"I would say so, yes."

Hollis downed his second double and was feeling a little light-headed when a corporal from headquarters walked over to Ransahoff and told him to report to Group.

Gleason said, "I guess that's it for me, too.   Goodnight, Hollis."

"Good night, sir."   Hollis finished his drink and left, driving his newly-acquired jeep back to Pilot's House still wound up, his raw nerves only partially dulled by the alcohol.

He found Leo fast asleep.   It was well after eleven.   Hollis figured he had no more than four hours sleep in three days and yet he was not sleepy.   The electricity coursing through his veins would not let him rest.   He sat at the desk and pulled out stationary to write Jessie when there was a soft knock on the door.

It was Sully.   "You are going to find this hard to believe."

"Try me."

"They want you and me over at Group."

"Jesus, it's close to midnight."

"That was an order."

"Alright," Hollis said, straightening his tie and pulling on his leather jacket, "let's go find out what they want.   Whatever it is, they're pissing me off."

Hollis drove Sully over to the Headquarters block and stepped into Operations.   The alcohol still clouded his brain and he hoped he would not say anything stupid.

Van Patten stood over a table holding a sheath of papers with one hand and his chin with the other.   He motioned Hollis and Sully to join him.   He dropped the sheath, which contained photos, onto the table.   "I thought you two might like to see these."

Sully and Hollis took the pictures and spread them out on the table.   They were strike photos.   Hollis could see the bombs as they left the plane and followed them downward with each frame to impact.

"They're yours."

Hollis stared at the photos, his vision still imprecise from the scotch.   He said nothing, but handed the photos back to Van Patten.   Sully exchanged glances with Hollis, the expression on the bombardier's face clearly reflecting the uncertainty about whether they were being shown good news or bad.

"Here."   Van Patten handed each a sheet of paper.

Hollis started to read the words, his eyes improving their focus with each sentence.

Assuming leadership of the Group during a fierce engagement with enemy air forces, Lieutenant John Hollis conducted an expert and accurate bomb run despite sustaining damage to his aircraft, causing his bomber to lose an engine during the critical moments leading up to 'bombs away'.   Despite aggressive enemy attack, Lieutenant Hollis continued leading the Group away from the target area until damage to his aircraft made his continued role as leader untenable.   Displaying leadership and coolness under fire, Lieutenant Hollis acquitted himself in the finest traditions of the Army Air Forces.   He is hereby recommended for the

Distinguished Flying Cross.

(Signed)
Brock Van Patten, Colonel, USAAF
381st Bombardment Group (Heavy), Commanding

"I wanted to court martial you after that Ju-88 incident, but Major Ransahoff talked me out of it.   I don't think what you did deserved the DFC then, but that poor bastard's group CO thought otherwise.   This one you deserve.   You too, Lieutenant Sullivan.   That was one first-class piece of bombing."

Sully looked genuinely humbled.   "I was only doing my job, Colonel.   It's what I was trained to do.   No more, no less."

"Even so, you put more bombs within a thousand yards of the intended MPI today than this group has seen in a while.   You two look tired.   Go get some rest."

Hollis and Sully drew to attention and saluted.   Van Patten returned their salute and they left.

As he rode back, Sully said, "Moe told Dodge we're going to need four new engines."

Hollis was locked in thought.   Less than two months ago he could barely summon the courage to fly the plane off the ground and today he lead the entire Group to and successfully bombed a target just ninety miles from Berlin.   If this doesn't shorten the war, what would?

He wondered if the Colonel knew he had made captain?

Hollis sat down to write Jessie a letter.   He didn't think it would clear the censors, but he wrote it anyway.

My Darling Jessie, I hope you are well.   I am fine.   I made captain this morning.   The reasons for this are unknown to me. Things have been very hectic around here.   I flew number 14 today. It was a very long ride.   Nearly twelve hours in the saddle.   My ass is still numb. We almost lost Dutch Ransahoff today.   He was hit about ten minutes before we reached the target.   He couldn't keep up and rather than slow us down he turned the lead of the Group over to me.   I was the Bangmaster.   I took the Group   right into the target.   We really pasted the place. Sully's up for a DFC and I've been recommended for my second.

Dutch and the Colonel were real proud of us.   I went from goat to hero in a day. There's an alert on for tomorrow, but somebody else will be flying.   My Squadron has been stood down for three days.   We're supposed to pick up some replacements.   We've lost four crews.   Watanabe, the last of the 'originals', DeBerg, Weldon and Baldini.   DeBerg was a good man.   Everybody liked him.   He never complained.   He came with Spats and Robertshaw.   Weldon was so new nobody really knew him very well.   Today we lost Baldini. We nearly lost Ransahoff and we only made it home on a wing and a prayer.   We've lost a third of our squadron strength in less than a week.   They keep sending us new planes but they are of no value unless we have crews to fly them.

So much has happened in just two months.   It seems like years since we stepped off the truck ourselves.

I must go now.   I can hardly hold this pen in my hand I'm so tired.   I'll write tomorrow. All my love, John.

P.S.   Please don't worry.   I'm not taking any chances. I miss you.

Chapter Forty-nine   The Devil and His Mother

Sunday, October 10, 1943

"Come on, Hollis, wake up," the voice whispered.

"Huh?"   Hollis was seized by disbelief.   He had gone to bed the night before as exhausted as he could ever recall being and had slept well under the aegis of a stand down which had originated from the lips of Van Patten himself.

"Wake up."

"Dutch?"

"Come on, we've got work to do."

"What the fuck are you talking about?   We're stood down."

"Get up."

"You're out of your mind.   I'm not getting up."

"That's an order."

Hollis felt his disbelief give way suddenly to anger.   "Get the hell out of here, Ransahoff.   I'm not getting out of this bed for anybody.   Draw up charges if you want.   I'm not budging."

"Come on, Hollis.   Get up."

Hollis could barely contain himself.   He flipped his legs out from under the blankets and sat facing Ransahoff, his hostility barely controlled.

"What the fuck do you want?" Hollis asked, no longer trying to keep his voice down in deference to the sleeping Leo.   "And what the fuck time is it?"

"Six-thirty.   You've got to come with me.   We have work to do."

"I can't believe this.   What work?   We're stood down."

Ransahoff noticed Leo turning over in his bed, aroused, at least subliminally, by the amplitude of the voices so he whispered, "I know.   You're the new Operations Officer."

It was as if he had been doused with ice water.   "You can't be serious?"

"Very.   They're putting up a mission today and we're going over to briefing."

"I can't believe this."

"Bitch on your own time, pal.   If you want to eat you better get dressed."   Ransahoff turned and, as he left the room, said, "Meet me in the Squadron office in twenty minutes."

Hollis stepped into the office and saw Ransahoff dozing in his chair.   "I don't want to be Operations Officer."

Ransahoff bolted up in the chair and said, "What? Oh it's you."

"Get Selkirk to do it."

"He's a Section Eight.   You'll still fly missions, of course."

"Spats.   Get Spats to be Ops officer.   Now he has real leadership qualities."

Ransahoff shoved a piece of paper across his desk, "Sign at the bottom."

Hollis looked at the paper.   It was his promotion to captain.

"And if I don't?"

"I'll fucking shoot you.   Why must you give me such a hard row to hoe, Hollis?   This is total war."

Hollis signed the paper.

"Let's get some breakfast so we can get to the briefing."

They climbed into Ransahoff's jeep and drove over to the Combat Mess without comment.   Hollis contemplated the fix he now found himself in.   He had gone from a lowly second lieutenant, first pilot of a run-of-the-mill replacement crew in mid-August to a captain, second-in-command of a bomber squadron in mid-October.   He only wanted to do his twenty-five missions and go home.   Instead, with each passing day the complexities mounted.   This was lunacy. What had been simple was, for reasons he could not entirely explain, now hard. His universe had expanded beyond him and his crew.   It was insidious, this march toward command.   He had either been too clever or not clever enough.   He had become Otho.

Finally, as they pulled into the lot outside the Mess, Ransahoff said, "We're going to get replacements today.   Assuming the weather is decent over the next two days I want you to schedule a practice mission each day.   You have complete authority to do it any way you want. I'll even let you borrow my red paint.   Regardless, I want them ready to go by the end of the week.

"Spats, Robertshaw and Powell are the best pilots in the Squadron.   Use them wisely."

"And Mickey?"

"Mickey I don't know about.   Tell Begay what you plan to do and get it done."

"Do we have the planes?"

"Ask Tanner, he's the Squadron engineering officer.   He spends more time on the line than the crew chiefs do.   Let's eat."

Breakfast consisted to creamed-chipped beef on toast, canned grapefruit slices, strawberry jam and coffee.   There were three squadrons of officers all eating or not eating as the case went.   They looked scared.   Most of them were unfamiliar faces like those at the briefing yesterday.   He noticed Lemaster and saw Remington, who had joined the Group not long after the Hollis crew.   The Group had been badly treated by the Germans and the result was clearly visible on these faces.   They were contemplating their fates, calculating their odds.   No one, of course, knew where they were going today, but the smart money was on Germany for a third day.

Hollis had been the Squadron Ops Officer for all of half an hour and he already found himself scanning the pilots with clinical objectivity.   He knew how they felt, especially the new ones.   He had borne the same look, probably worse.

Ransahoff said little over breakfast.   For him this was not a learning experience; for Hollis, it was.

Gleason took the stage.   "G'morning, Gen'lemen.   I'm the Bangmaster for today's sortee."   He yanked back the curtain with characteristic flourish giving rise to a collective groan for the red yarn went into Germany.   "Our Target for today is Munster."

"Munster," Hollis muttered loud enough to cause Ransahoff to look at him.   Munster had a history.   Hollis racked his brain trying to remember, like a long-forgotten acquaintance whose name is heard afresh.

"Munster is a critical rail junction sitting astride the main lines connecting Germany's northern ports and the munitions and heavy industries of the Ruhr Valley.   If it's built here and has to go here"--Gleason pointed at the Ruhr and then to the coast--"it has to go through here.   But today is different, very different, from any military or industrial target we've attacked thus far.   Today we're going to hit the city itself, right smack in the center, where the people live.   We're going to bomb the homes of the people working in those railway yards.   You will disrupt their lives so completely that their morale will suffer and their will to work and support the Nazzis will be reduced."

Then, Gleason stopped.   Hollis at first did not know why.   Gleason placed the pointer behind his back, rocked back and forth in his boots and stared at the crowd.   Perhaps Old Ben was waiting for some protest, some exclamation of moral outrage.

Maybe they were too scared to notice; maybe they misunderstood.   Perhaps they were beyond caring what the target was.   They just stared back at Gleason waiting for him to continue.   Then again, maybe the choice of targets was just fine with them.

Regardless, Gleason smiled and resumed.

Ransahoff looked at Hollis again, "What're *you* smilin' at?"

"Stan would have liked this.   This target would have been right up his alley."

Now, maybe it was Ransahoff who didn't understand for he said nothing and returned his attention to the briefing.

"The Third Division will go in first, followed by the First fifteen minutes later.   The Fortieth Bomb Wing will lead the Division, followed by the First, then the Forty-first.   We should have full escort for the entire mission."

That news was met with an audible sigh of relief.

"The IP is Haltern, here.   Our secondary target is Hamm, located in the Ruhr Valley, here.   Our target of last resort is any industrial town in Germany.   Major."

Gorton took the stage.   "Lights."   The projector was turned on and the room dimmed. A reconnaissance photo of the target appeared on the screen.   "Our aiming point is this thousand-year old cathedral at the center of the city, here.   Our approach will be over the Aa Lake here.   Following the long axis of this body of water here will take you straight to the intended mean point of impact, right here.   The Zoo is here.   The star-shaped castle gardens are here.   This is the town hall.   Barracks here and here.   Water tower here and more barracks here."

"Hollis, what the hell are you laughing about now?" Ransahoff whispered.

"Do you have a sense of irony?"

"Sure, doesn't everybody?"

"Remind me later to tell you the story of Munster.   Interesting things happened there a long time ago."

"Why must you insist on intellectualizing every fucking thing?"

The rest of the briefing was fairly routine.   Begay gave the mission details.   Weather was next.   Instrument takeoff and landing, ceiling 500 feet, visibility 1000 yards, cloud tops four thousand feet.   The weather over the target should be CAVU.

At the conclusion, Van Patten got up and made his usual speech.   It all seemed so routine.   Were it not for the fear of the unknown and the unpredictable peril which loomed just over the horizon, Hollis thought, it would be easy to doze right through these little sessions. Hollis was uncertain why Ransahoff had made him sit through the briefing for a mission he was not assigned to fly.   Was he to attend every formal fucking function the Group had now that he was Squadron Ops?

Hollis held no particular skills, no distinguishing moral character which bestowed upon him the ability or where-with-all to lead men.   How had this happened?   Again, he reckoned, his ascendancy was through attrition not talent.   If Otho were alive today Hollis figured he would still be asleep.   The true leaders, the Van Pattens and Gleasons and Ransahoffs were easy to spot.   So were impostors.   The members of the Squadron would look at him and despair of one more foolhardy military decision.

"Ten-hut!"

Hollis who was already standing simply straightened up and brought his arms to his sides.

"Now," Ransahoff said, "what is so important about Munster?"

"Between marches around the Plain did you happen to study the Reformation?"

"I have vague recall of such things, yes."

"Do you recall the Siege of Munster?"

"No."

"In 1534, a religious zealot named King Jan took control of the city.   He was an anabaptist and converted the entire city to anabaptists, much to the dismay of the German

Catholics and Lutherans, who vowed to reclaim the city.   Surrender was demanded.   A siege ensued and, according to military custom of the time, once a surrender was demanded and refused, no quarter would be given if the place was retaken by force.   The Bishop hired a bunch of mercenaries to regain his stolen city and Philip of Hesse lent them two huge artillery pieces, named the Devil and his Mother.   They were so big and primitive they could only be fired five or six times a day.   They were used to bombard the city into submission.   It didn't work.

"The siege lasted a year and the anabaptists were defeated and a wholesale slaughter ensued.   All in the name of God.

"Doesn't this sound familiar?   The Third Division is the Devil and the First, His Mother?"

"Hollis, you have the power to awe.   No question about it," Ransahoff said sarcastically. "Let's go see when the replacements are due in."

Ransahoff and Hollis walked away from the briefing hut and climbed back into the jeep. Ransahoff drove over to Group headquarters and went in while Hollis sat in the idling jeep.   He watched the comings and goings of the headquarters staff, preparing to launch the mission, checking last minute details, scurrying around like ants at the mouth of an anthill.

They were going after civilians today.   This was the first time he was aware that the American bomber force had taken up the war against the ordinary German citizen.   It was prophetic, oddly fitting that they would select Munster as the inaugural effort to kill civilians, the site of so much calculated butchery in the name of God.

He was not surprised that no one had arisen to pronounce moral objection.   He simply had never thought about it.   As naive and stupid as that made him seem, he thought they were bombing factories, not people.   He lit a cigarette and watched as Gleason walked out of the Headquarters with his flight gear and a briefcase under his arm.

The premise of the American bombing was precision and, through precision, civilian casualties, while unavoidable, would be minimal.   Early during the war great pronouncements had been made declaring attacks on civilians as immoral and beneath the combatants. Churchill.   Roosevelt.   Maybe even Hitler.   Until today they had never been the target.   At least not by official sanction.   Killing was collateral to the primary goal of destroying factories. On this day the killing was primary.   Precision was an illusion, anyway.   To think otherwise was equally naive.   It was all area bombing.   The RAF was only being more honest about it.

Sure Hollis had seen the bombed out buildings in London, burned out shells that had once housed families.   He knew there were civilians under the bombs.   It disturbed him that this had never crossed his mind before.   Except perhaps in a nightmare.   In the process of becoming a warrior, did one automatically sacrifice one's humanity in the bargain?

As he sat in the jeep, he also wondered who had made such a decision.   It was oddly fitting that such a departure from doctrine would be over Munster; he just wondered if the person who decided it *would* be Munster today understood the irony.   Hollis felt he should have, but probably did not.   It was probably some bespectacled little functionary at Bomber Command who picked out a thousand year old church as an aiming point because it was easy to see not because of its symbolism.   If one cannot explain the war, one should not be compelled to fight in it.

Did they honestly believe that dropping bombs on a dictatorship would somehow be different than dropping them on a participatory democracy?   Did they expect the moral outrage at being bombed would be any different in Hamburg or Dusseldorf than it would be in Guernica, Nanking, London or Coventry or Brooklyn?

It was apparent to him for the first time that the bombing would cost more than lives and property.   Who would lay claim to moral indignation?   Who could? What group of persons, what politician could state that his people had suffered more? It is the victors that write the history.

Ransahoff got into the jeep and slammed the door shut behind him disrupting Hollis's musing.

"Hey Dutch, does it bother you that we're dropping bombs on those people as they are walking out of church?"

"No, should it?"   Ransahoff reached for the gear shifter and suddenly stopped, turned and stared at Hollis.   "Hollis, don't go getting soft on me, God-damnit.   They started this.   If we have to stoop to their level to give back as good as they gave, so be it.   So much the better. Perhaps when they sift through the corpses they will find some holier than others and there will be regret.   Perhaps that is the best we can expect.

"Hollis, you keep these moral qualms to yourself.   A sense of morality is not conducive to the effectiveness of military operations.   It gets in the way."

"You don't get it, do you?"

"Jesus Christ, Hollis, it's eight o'clock in the morning.   What the hell's the matter with you?"

"Do you believe in God?"

"Boy you've really fallen off the deep end, haven't you?   The mantle of command too much for you?   You're starting to worry me.   When you put the uniform on you made a pact that you would be willing to kill people.   The time and place and method was all that remained to be determined.   If you think that you didn't then you're not as smart as I think you are.   You think I'll lose any sleep if we bomb those people back to the Dark Ages?   We won't know who the moral high ground belongs to until this is over.   The winner will be standing on it.   Now I suggest you just do your job and quit thinking about this stuff.

"How many missions have you flown?"

"Fourteen."

"Fourteen.   You know you've flown more missions that I did when I took over the Squadron.   Now, all of a sudden you're having second thoughts about this?   You can't be serious?"

"No, it's just that this is the first time we've deliberately targeted women and children.   It was just never obvious to me until today."

"You know the difference between them and you, Hollis?"

"No."

"It bothers you.   I bet it gives them not a moment's pause.   You remain a mystery to me, Hollis.   You're probably one of the brightest persons I've ever met and yet you act like a fool.   Don't go getting a conscience on me.   This isn't about politics or morality.   It's about the preservation of civilization.   They're over there systematically wiping out a whole race of people.   If they win they'll be making all the rules.   If they decide they don't like people from Pennsylvania, you're next.

"Stop shaking your head."   Ransahoff let out the clutch and gunned the engine.

The replacements weren't due in until after lunch.   As Operations Officer, Hollis found mounds of paperwork that had to be done.   It came along with his ascendance to command. Otho may have been a bit of a martinet, along the lines of Entwhistle but, to his credit, he was very efficient at handling the paperwork.   Hollis expected great stacks of directives and reports that needed his attention, he was not disappointed.   He sat at Otho's desk in a tiny office separated from the main Squadron office by a partition.   He touched its metal surface and could almost feel Otho's presence.   Hollis never liked him.   He reminded himself that, before Otho, Ransahoff had sat here.   What was it, over a century ago?   It was here he would write the names on the mission roster, the List, and set in motion death and all manner of human heartache and suffering.   Such was the mantle of command.

After a while, he left the office and walked back to the room.   Take off had been delayed.   Hollis wasn't sure if this was because of the weather or a desire to let the hapless targets at least get out of church before the bombs fell.   Either way it didn't matter.   The result was the same.   What difference did the reason for the change make?   Morality versus meteorology.

Leo was gone.   Off tutoring little Ian on differential equations and sticking it to Mrs. Thomas.   Poor Mrs. Thomas.   As Leo drove his anxious member in and out, she would have to endure his bitching about how that fucker Hollis nearly got him killed yesterday, the flames just inches from his face.   *Poor Mrs. Thomas.*

Hollis lay on the bed, clasping his hands behind his head.   He looked up at the wall covered with pinups.   Pettys, Vargas and cheese-cake publicity shots.   Seductive poses mostly. There was the occasional exposed tuft of pubic hair on the more artistic ones culled from photography magazines.   He wondered who was the original owner of this fine gallery. Probably Milo Cody.   He had never met the man and here he was staring up at his sole remaining legacy.   Ransahoff had penciled in Milo's name, handed it to Entwhistle to approve and it was then given to the orderly to type up and pin to the bulletin board.

Helluva war.

Hollis stirred only briefly at the sound of planes leaving.

After lunch, three new crews were delivered by truck to the Squadron.   Gamble, Svoboda and Tedford.   They had gotten wind of Bremen and Anklam and the losses the 381st had sustained at those two places and the expressions on their faces betrayed their anxiety. Ransahoff took the officers aside and lectured them on the harsh realities of the war and their roles in it.   Hollis listened, half expecting an hour's rant.   Instead, Ransahoff was compassionate while being firm.   He wanted tight formations and no heroics.   Your purpose, your whole *raison d'etre*, he told them, was to put bombs on a target.   Hollis wondered how many understood what *raison d'etre* meant.   *Why must he intellectualize everything?*

Do not leave the formation unless you can no longer sustain flight.   Hollis, here, he told them, has left the formation twice and he's damned lucky to be here.

Selkirk is alive, thanks to people leaving the formation, it might be pointed out, Hollis thought.   *No heroics?   Bullshit.   If we win this war it will be the heroics that get the job done. What a fool.*

Hollis here, is our Squadron Operations Officer--*yeah, for what, all of six hours?*--and he will be scheduling a practice mission for the next two days.

When Ransahoff was finished he dismissed them recommending they get settled into their quarters. The Combat Mess usually opened for business about seventeen hundred. The food's not the best he's ever had, he added, but after a while you get used to it.

Ransahoff took Hollis back to the Squadron office and described the mechanisms by which he could execute a practice mission. Tanner walked in and handed Ransahoff a list of available aircraft. Get someone to take up 970, he told Ransahoff, it has two engines which need slow-timing. Ransahoff said nothing but smiled and pointed at Hollis. Tanner repeated what he just said.

Hollis ran through a list in his head. Who could he annoy the most? Spats? No, actually he had a rough couple of days. Powell. Hollis turned to the corporal and said, "Get Lieutenant Powell over here, dressed for flying."

"Yes sir."

His first official order. It was easy.

Half an hour later Powell walked into the Squadron office looking very annoyed. He said nothing.

"Pull together your copilot, engineer and radio operator and go out to Number 970 and take it up to slow time the engines. I've filed your flight plan with Group Ops. Steer clear of London and try to be back before the mission returns." Hollis looked at his watch. "They should be over the target about now so you'd better get going."

"My copilot is sick."

"Grab the first one you can find, then."

Powell turned and left. There was no semblance of military courtesy. Hollis had been one of them until that morning. Maybe Ransahoff should have gotten somebody from outside the Squadron to be Ops. Somebody they didn't know and for whom they might not garner such resentment. If familiarity breeds contempt, then Hollis had reason to expect it for he had not been universally liked by his peers. He had no interest in engaging in a popularity contest or extending himself to win their affections at this late date. They respected his handling of the mission yesterday, that had been communicated to him in various ways, but they still did not like him. *Too bad.*

Several hours later, Hollis and Ransahoff were down at the Squadron dispersal when Powell taxied 970 back toward the hardstand. Ransahoff looked at his watch. The Group was due back any minute. He and Hollis walked to the infield beyond the **Flying Dutchman** and waited. Soon the Group appeared flying low in a large orbit of the field. Hollis saw it first and tapped Ransahoff on the arm before pointing. A Fortress came in low over the runway, red flares popping upward from the radio hatch. As it settled onto the concrete, two more red flares arced skyward. No other planes signaled distress and the count showed they had all returned. A good day, then. One casualty.

One Fortress taxied past with a singed and feathered engine. Another had a chunk bitten out of the wingtip but that was all. Hollis watched as the crowd gathered by the B-17 that had fired the red flares. It pulled onto the closest hardstand and turned off the engines so the ambulance could get to it quickly.

As Hollis and Ransahoff returned to their conversation with the line chief, a jeep pulled up.   It was Clevenger.

"Hey Hollis," he called out.

"Yes sir?"

"That crazy hillbilly gunner of yours was our only casualty.   He's dead."

"Jesus."

"Want to ride out there?"

"Yes sir."   Hollis climbed into the jeep and Clevenger sped off.   He was flushed by foreboding that became nearly overpowering as the jeep drew closer to the B-17.   He envisioned his nightmare.   Brains, entrails, sinews.

When they arrived the body was being lifted from the ground, covered by a blanket, the only thing visible were Augie's booted feet.   The medics were talking to the other waist gunner who was covered in blood.   Hollis walked up to the waist door and looked in.   He could see a wide, dark pool of blood that ran from the upper waist down the rubber mat to the door.

"What happened?" he asked the gunner.

"Augie was killed by a piece of flak that came up through the floor.   I didn't even know he was hit.   He had this surprised look on his face and pulled his flak vest off.   When he did his guts spilled out.   He collapsed against the wall and tried to gather his guts up in his hands and push them back in.   He got confused and tried to stuff his oxygen hose in, too.   He was still alive while he watched his guts freeze.   I tried to cover him up with the electric blanket but the shock was too much, I guess.   He only lasted about five minutes.

"It just came right up through the floor and slit him open like a hog, crotch to breast bone. He looked so surprised."

Hollis returned his gaze to the inside of the bomber.   He looked at Augie's gun.   On the floor below where he would have stood was a jagged hole in the aluminum skin.   It was the only damage to the Fortress.   A mop and some sheet metal work and it would be good as new.

Hollis felt the sudden pang of guilt.   Had he not thrown Augie off the crew he would be alive right now.

No, now was not the time for self-recrimination.   Augie was disruptive to the crew.   He had to go.   Dodge said so.   Nothing happened today that was his fault.   Nothing.

Hollis skipped supper.   Instead, he went to the Officer's Club for a drink, the vision of an eviscerated Augie Reese swirling in his head.   He had one, then another.   He overheard Gleason talking about the mission.   The Third Division got creamed.   When the escort pulled away, they did not quite have the endurance to reach all the way to Munster, the German fighters pounced savagely.   The 100th Bomb Group lost all but one plane.   The 100th was nearly annihilated.   The other groups of the Third fared only slightly better.   The First Division was attacked also, but not nearly as ferociously.   The 381st, for a change, did fine.   Except, of course, for poor Augie.

Frankfurt, Bremen, Anklam and Munster.   Perhaps the final showdown was at hand. The next mission might be the one where nobody comes back.

He finished his third scotch and left.   When he arrived at the room he found Leo sitting on his bed.

"Oh," Hollis said, "you're back.   Where've you been?"

"You drunk?"

"Answer my question."

"Sines, cosines and tangents, that sort of thing."

"Didn't like it when the flames were licking your chin, did you?"

"You're drunk."

"My sobriety is not the issue."

"What is?"

"They killed Augie, today.   And they made me the *Operations Officer.*   I don't know which is worse."

"They killed Augie?   How?   When?"

"He was like a son to me."

"You hated him."

"Poor fucker got his guts ripped out by a stinkin' freak piece of flak.   Do you believe that?"

"That's too bad.   Stop crying.   These things happen.   This is war."

"I'm tired of hearing that."

Leo ignored him.

Hollis sat at the desk and pulled out a sheet of paper and began to write.

> *Dear Mr. and Mrs. Reese,*
> *I wanted to write you and let you know how bad we all*
> *feel about Augie.   He was a good gunner and a good man.*
> *The boys in the crew looked up to him.   We share your*
> *loss and he will not be forgotten.*
> *He was strong and brave and gentle.   He looked after the*
> *boys in the crew and they, and we, are all better for*
> *it.   You should be proud of your son.   He died a man*
> *among men, serving his country and his sacred honor.*
> *You have our sincerest condolences.*
>
> > *Sincerely,*
> > *John Hollis, Captain*
> > *Pilot and Operations officer*
> > *532nd Bomb Squadron*

He showed it to Leo and asked, "You think they'll buy it?"

"It's fine."

"When the folks in Dog Patch read this, or have it read to them as the case may be, they will think I'm talking about somebody else.   Some other Augie Reese."

Leo said, "After they read this, when they compare it to the letters they got from Augie, they're liable to think it was a different John Hollis that wrote it."

"Niggers of the World rejoice.   The Germans did one good thing today.   I need another drink.   Want one?"

"I think you've had plenty."

"One more."

"OK, here."   Leo reached into his foot locker and pulled out a bottle of Old Granddad.

He poured into the two canteen cups that sat on the desk and handed one to Hollis.

"How long have you been keeping that there?"

"I've been nursing this bottle along since I last saw Christie."

"Thanks.   Good Old Christie.   I miss her."

"Here's to Augie.   An imperfection in an imperfect world.   May he rest in peace."

"Here-here."   Hollis downed the bourbon, which on top of the scotch and an empty stomach, made a painful alchemy.   "Sorry about that 'flames under the chin' crack."

Leo sipped his drink and said quietly, "That's OK."

Hollis sat down and pulled out another sheet of paper.

"Dear Dad,

I had a bad day.   Augie Reese was killed while   flying   with   another crew.   He left a bloody mess in the plane.   As you may remember, Augie was our original right waist gunner.   I feel like it was something I could have prevented.   I had Augie removed from the crew a few weeks ago.   Mainly because I didn't like him.   No one did.   Maybe Quinn liked him a little.   Even at his best he was loud, vulgar and obnoxious.   I was hard on Augie sometimes.   I yelled at him a lot.   I hoped it might bring him into line a little.   It never did. He was involved in the beating of a Negro and himself was beaten up shortly thereafter. Sometimes I couldn't stand him.   No one could.   So I had him taken off the crew.   Now he's dead and I can't help but think if he was still on the crew he   would   be   alive   today. Sometimes he was funny and he kept the crew loose.   They needed that.   He also kept them on their toes and as long as you stay on your toes you might have a chance of making it.   There is no room here for laziness or carelessness.   When you stop paying attention you can get killed so quickly.   He was a good gunner.   I think he made the enlisted members of the crew better, too. I guess what I'm trying to say is that I feel bad he's dead and that I bullied him around before he died.   I also feel responsible that he's dead.   I feel so sorry. I wonder what he must have thought as he watched his blood leaking out from him, red at first but becoming dark and thick like oil, making a frozen puddle on the floor?

Don't tell Mom.   There are some things a mother probably doesn't need to know about her son.   Kiss her for me.   Tell her I'll be safe.   You are never far from my thoughts.

Love, John"

Hollis urinated on a bush and fell into bed.   The dream came quickly, as he knew it would.   Augie grabbed at his intestines as they slithered away like shiny, wet eels out of water. He looked for help, but there was no one there to fix what needed fixing.   A look of incredulity on his face.   The surprise.   *Why me?*   He watched the blood run in great streams onto the floor.   How *did* it feel to watch your life ooze away, holding your bowels and your oxygen hose in your hands, watching your own guts freeze?

The medic leaned out the waist window after looking at Augie.   "This one's dead."

Hollis stared at the dead gunner's face, the surprised look set for all eternity by rigor mortis.   The medics lifted Augie by the shoulders of his jacket and pant legs.   They maneuvered the body out of the waist hatch of the Fortress and the medic holding his shoulders slipped on the puddle of thawed blood on the rubber floor mat and Augie's head thumped loudly against the sill of the doorway.   Embarrassed and ashamed at the mishap he regained his footing and gently passed Augie's body out of the bomber where he was placed on a blanket which had been spread out on a litter.   They wrapped the blanket around the body and tucked the woolen shroud under him.   Augie's booted feet stuck out the end of the blanket as a reminder that there was a person under it.   They placed the litter onto the ambulance and drove off without haste.

Later that afternoon, the crew chief cleaned up the blood from the waist compartment. He wept softly as he did so.   By the time he was finished it was dark.   No trace of Augie remained.   The sheet-metal crew placed a small aluminum patch over the hole that the shrapnel had caused and riveted it into place.

Hollis turned to walk away and saw a white-haired man standing nearby.   He was dressed in dungarees and a checkered shirt, a rabbit gun at his side.

"Funny," the man said, "I didn't think I was going to die.   I wasn't mad at anybody although, in retrospect, I should've been.   I kept thinking, 'Look at all that blood.   What a mess.'   Somehow, I just didn't think I was going to die.   It was like falling asleep.   I was cold, very cold.   My only regret was that I didn't get to say 'Good-bye' to my Mother."

Hollis said, "Few of us will."   He watched the ambulance drive away down the perimeter strip and he was alone, except for the bomber.   He turned to the old man, saying, "I'm sorry, Augie."   But he was gone.

Chapter Fifty   **Funeral**

Monday, October 11, 1943

It was raining when Hollis awakened, the hangover causing his head to throb with each contraction of his heart.   He thanked God for the rain.   It was drumming steadily on the window and meant no practice mission.   Leo slept soundly.

There was a soft knock on the door, which against his taut, hypersensitive eardrums sounded like thunder, and Hollis said that whoever it was could come in.

Dodge poked his head around the door.   "Good morning, Lieutenant.   I understand they're going to bury Augie today."

"Did you tell the crew?"

"Yes sir, everybody knows.   I told them myself.   They're going to bury him at the American Military Cemetery at Cambridge.   The Chaplain said anybody that wants to attend should meet at his office at thirteen hundred."   Hollis looked at his watch.   Eight-thirty.

"OK, thanks."   Dodge turned to leave when Hollis said to him, "I made captain."

"Yes sir, I knew that."

Hollis pulled the covers up over his shoulder and sought sleep as relief from his painful brain.

A few moments later, Ransahoff burst into the room.   Hollis thought his skull might split open from the sound.

"Jesus, Dutch."

"Come on, Hollis, we've got work to do.   You're a member of the chain of command now.   Can't just laze around like you could before."

"It's raining."

"All the more reason to get a move on."

"Jesus, what a headache."

"Meet me in the office in half an hour."

"Yeah, OK."   Hollis flipped his legs to the floor and sat up, his head spinning.   Leo stirred and asked what was going on.

"Nothing.   The 'chain' of command has become a noose around my neck."

"Now that you're a big shot in the organization, does this mean you won't be flying with us?"

"I don't think so.   I think it's business as usual.   We fly the full twenty-five.   What happens to me after that is anybody's guess.   Hopefully, I get to go home just like the rest of you.   Then they can find some other sucker to do this."

"Did I hear Dodge say Augie's funeral is at thirteen hundred?"

"Yeah.   I think I'm going to be sick."   Hollis ran from the room and flung the door open just before he vomited onto the mud.   He was seized by the cold, clammy hand of alcohol's revenge as he retched several times, the rain beating down on his already sweat-soaked underwear.

"And top o' the morning to you, too, Captain."

Hollis looked up to see Spats Nevtushenko tipping his cap, the collar of his trench coat pulled up around his face.

"Fuck you, you God-damned Rooskie."

Spats chuckled and said, "This war is filled with so many grim realities and you're one of them."

Hollis returned to his room wiping his face off with a towel.   He took a cold shower, Beamis apparently unwilling or incapable of providing heated water.   The shower completed his return to sobriety.   Three APCs helped the headache.   When he stepped into the Squadron office he headed straight for the coffee, which, fortunately for him, was hot and freshly brewed.

"First sign of moral collapse is an inability to control one's use of and response to alcohol."

"Leave me alone, Dutch.   No lectures today, OK?"

"Yeah, sure."

"I need to be off the base for a while this afternoon."

"Sure.   In the meantime, get the word out that there will be an aircraft recognition lecture at thirteen hundred and an escape and evasion lecture to follow."

"OK."

"Then draw up a roster for a practice mission in case the weather clears."

"What, exactly, do *you* do around here?"

"I do all the thinkin'."

Hollis launched himself into his assigned tasks.   At eleven thirty he had lunch and returned to his room to change.   He dressed in his Class A uniform, pulled on his trench coat and drove his jeep over to the Chaplain's Office.

He found Dodge and Leo, also in Class As, standing under an eave while two six-bysixes idled on the street.   Hollis expected to see the whole crew waiting, perhaps even mourning, but there was no one else.   The Chaplain and his assistant ran from their office and motioned for Hollis, Leo and Dodge to join him.   He tucked his head down against the driving rain as he guided them into the second truck.   Hollis caught a glimpse of Augie's coffin on the floor of the lead truck and several Negro ordinance men sitting on the benches.   Augie arrived at the war in the back of a truck and he was leaving it the same way.

Promptly at thirteen hundred, the humble cortege drove away.   Hollis noticed it grow light out as if the rain might cease and the dark gray clouds might part to reveal the sun.   But it did not.   The rain moderated briefly, but did not stop and the dark gray cloud rolled back in, roiling close to the ground like the steam from some evil stew.   Hollis wondered what symbolism God had imparted on the brief meteorological respite.

Soon they were off the base.   Hollis, Leo and Dodge sat with their own thoughts, sitting in the back of the truck as it rocked back and forth on a million miles of bad road, the downpour a constant, course drum beat on the canvas roof.

When they arrived at the Cemetery, Hollis stepped down from the truck as the ordinance men, doubling as pall bearers and honor guard, gently removed the flag-draped coffin and carried it across the field to the end of a row of crosses.   A freshly dug, empty grave was next in line.   Many of the graves looked fresh, Hollis noted.   The Chaplain followed the coffin, his assistant holding an umbrella over the Chaplain's head.

Hollis watched as they lowered the coffin to the ground beside the grave.   Chaplain Brown placed his shawl around his neck and removed a small volume from his pocket.

"We are gathered here today, to place to rest the soul of Sergeant Augustine Reese who was killed in action yesterday.

"I would like to read from the first letter of Paul to the Corinthians:

"'When the corruptible frame takes on incorruptibility and the mortal immortality, then will the saying of Scripture be fulfilled: Death is swallowed up in victory.   O Death, where is your victory?   O Death, where is your sting?   The sting of death is sin, and sin gets its power from the law.   But thanks be to God who has given us the victory through our Lord Jesus Christ.   Be steadfast and persevering, my beloved brothers, fully engaged in the work of the Lord.   You know that your toil is not in vain when it is done in the Lord.   Amen.

"War makes good men better and bad men worse"--*where had he heard that before?* "In death we are all the same, equal before the eyes of God.   Augustine was not a man without faults, but he fought bravely and died a hero's death."

Hollis listened carefully.   Even in death, it was not possible for the Chaplain to say one good or redeeming thing about Augie Reese.   What a pity.   It was no hero's death.   He was gutted by a stray piece of hot metal.   And those poor Negroes were about to bury the man they most despised.   How odd. Maybe they were here just to make sure the bastard was really dead.

"Please join me in reciting the Twenty-third Psalm."   They all spoke together, including the Negro pallbearers, following the Chaplain's lead.

"The Lord is my shepherd;   I shall not want.

"He maketh me to lie down in green pastures.

"He leadeth me beside the still waters.

"He restoreth my soul.

"He leadeth me in the paths of righteousness for His Name's Sake.

"Yea, though I walk in the Valley of the Shadow of Death, I will fear no evil;
"For Thou art with me.
"Thy rod and thy staff they comfort me."
"Thou preparest a table before me in the presence of mine enemies."
"Thou anointest my head with oil; my cup runneth over.
"Surely goodness and mercy shall follow me all the days of my life.
"And I will dwell in the House of the Lord forever.   Amen.
"We commend this soul to the ground, secure in the knowledge of the Resurrection, the forgiveness of sins and life everlasting.   In the name of the Father, the Son and the Holy Spirit. Amen."

Hollis did something he hadn't done in years.   He crossed himself.   His eyes were wet but it was not from the rain.

The honor guard meticulously folded the flag and handed it to the chaplain.

They waited until Augie was lowered into the ground and left.   On the long ride back Hollis wondered if Mammy and Pappy Yokum would rock on their porch for hours listening to the sing-song of crickets in the soft, warm evening waiting for their son to come walking down the path, his duffle bag over a shoulder, his chest festooned with medals.   When would it dawn on them that Little Augie was never coming back?

Chapter Fifty-one   **Ransahoff**

Ransahoff was waiting when Hollis returned.   Hollis wasn't sure if it was grief, guilt or the oppressive amalgam of both that he felt.   It didn't matter, his heart was heavy and he didn't feel like dealing with Ransahoff.   So he ignored him.

"Hey," Ransahoff said, "you keep an eye on the weather.   If it's a clear day, you schedule that practice mission."

"Yes sir."

"I met the new crews.   Gave them the official poop."

"Good for you, Major.   Would you leave me alone."

They watched as Leo returned to the room.   Saying nothing, he turned and left. "Pythagorean Theorem," Hollis muttered.

"What?" Ransahoff asked.

"Nothing.   Listen, unless you have some pressing matter I need to address, I'd really like to be left alone.   I have a headache and I don't feel well.   I think I have a fever."

"Feeling a little low since your gunner bought it?"

"Yes, among other things.   Yes."

Ransahoff rubbed his chin.   "My condolences, Hollis.   You didn't kill him.   The Germans did."

"Yeah, I almost forgot."

Ransahoff left.   Hollis stripped out of his Class A uniform and climbed into bed.   He tried to nap, but sleep would not come to provide him escape.   He stared at the pictures on the wall and wondered why no one else came to the funeral.   He was saddened both by his own loss, however difficult to reconcile with the Augie he knew and despised, and the abrogation of any relationship Augie may have had with the crew or they with him.

How long before Leo defiled himself with Ian's mother?   Minutes?

God, he hated this.   He wished himself to be anywhere but here.   Robbie's jungle. Some mud hole in Italy.   The bilge of some obsolescent, foul-smelling warship.   Any place, but here.   Any time, but now.

He was startled when Ransahoff came in through the door and called his name.   Hollis had no idea how long he had been asleep.

"Come on, Hollis, let's go to the White Horse and have a couple beers."

"I don't want to."

"Come on.   I order you."

"What time is it?"

"Nineteen hundred."

"OK, give me a minute."

Hollis pulled himself from the bed.   His muscles didn't seem as strong as they had been before.   Perhaps it was the soundness of his sleep that had taken the tension from his body.   He could not recall dreaming.   Perhaps it had been the first really relaxing sleep he had experienced since Molly's couch.

Ransahoff watched while Hollis dressed.

"Still raining?"

"Nope, not a cloud in the sky.   I think you shouldn't have any trouble getting that mission in tomorrow."

"Group alerted?"

"Yeah."

"Will the weather hold?"

"Don't know."

"You driving?"

"Yeah."

With that, they climbed into Ransahoff's jeep and left the base.

When they arrived, they found Powell, Nevtushenko and Robertshaw sitting around an old, oaken table with several empty pints arrayed in front of them.

"Well, ten-hut," Spats said.   "If it ain't the supreme command."

Ransahoff pulled a chair over for himself and one for Hollis and made the three officers push around closer to each other.

"You sons of bitches better stay sober, Captain Hollis here is plannin' a practice mission with you guys tomorrow."

"You may be able to pull that crap with those rookies, but it don't mean shit to us," Spats said, his speech slightly slurred.   "You can take your practice missions and shove 'em."

"Listen, you stupid Rooskie, if I say fly you say how high, sir?" Hollis said.

"Kiss my ass."

Hollis could tell Ransahoff was taking delight in the badinage.   If camaraderie supported the health of a military institution, he was all for it.   Him and that other West Point asshole, Van Patten.   The Plain, where Duty, Honor and Country count for far more than compassion and forgiveness.

After several rounds, Powell and his buddies excused themselves and left, each providing mutual support and direction for the other two.

Ransahoff got them another drink.   Hollis hadn't seen Ransahoff drunk since the night he told off the Chief at the O Club after Schweinfurt.   Tonight, he was well on his way again.

"You know, Hollis, you were the first person I ever saw in this business who gave a fuck about what we're doing or at least ever said so."

"What do you mean?"

"If I had to pick somebody who felt uneasy about this bombing business I just knew it would be you.   You know what your problem is, Hollis?"

"No, but I bet you're going to tell me."

"You think too much."

"Yeah, and what with you supposed to be the one doing all the thinkin' around here."

"Fuck you, Hollis."

"Fuck you, Dutch."

"I didn't expect Brubaker to drop his wings on my desk like that.   But I did expect you to do that as soon as you got back from that Schweinfurt deal and you didn't.   I never saw anybody so shook up in my whole life as you.   I watch you stand there and puke before each mission.   But you still go.   You stuck your neck out twice.   I admire that.   You're one dumb fuck for doin' it but I admire it anyway.   You handled yourself well as the Bangmaster.   You hit that place dead on.   You gained my respect.   Don't go spoilin' it by getting a conscience."

"What's wrong with that?"

"It'll cause you to make a stupid mistake."   He sipped his drink.   "That and love."

Hollis merely nodded, uncertain if he agreed or even understood.

Ransahoff leaned in close, the smell of bitters on his breath nearly overpowering.   "I wanted to be a squadron commander since before I learned how to fly.   Now I am one.   But did I come by this exalted position because I am a skillful practitioner of my art or because I am courageous beyond the rational?   No.   I was the first warm body they could find when that chickenshit Entwhistle decided to go over the hill."

"You flatter yourself, you're not that warm."

"And I hate these fuckin' people."   He jerked his thumb in the direction of a group of farmers and their wives sitting around a long table drinking, smoking and laughing.   "They were pissed off we didn't jump into the war sooner and now they're just as pissed off we're here. They think we're a bunch of unchivalrous, uncouth ingrates.   They look at America as if it were still a colony, part of the Dominion like Canada or Australia.   The Limeys give the impression that the Americans are not worthy of being their allies.   It would be more considerate of us, I suppose, if we could retake the continent and liberate the World from Nazzi oppression from Greenland.   Bismarck said the Balkans were not worth the blood of a single Prussian grenadier. The same could be said for this place."

"According to my dad, the same could be said for France.   We can and will win the war, he said.   He's just sorry that we will have to liberate France to do it."

"Smart man, your father.   You say it bothers you to drop bombs on innocent women and children?   Look Hollis, innocent people are dying by the ton every minute, every second, maybe.   You're innocent, I'm innocent.   That gunner of yours was innocent.

"We didn't start this war, Hitler did.   Nothing could please me more than to see his head on a post in the center of Piccadilly Circus, but I'll tell you who the real villains are.   It's not Hitler.   Hitler is a madman and the world is filled with madmen.   But it's not every day a madman gets to rule a sovereign nation into world war.   Genghis Kahn.   Napoleon, maybe. No, I think the real villains are these people."   He jerked his thumb again.   "They had the chance to stop this a long time ago and didn't.   They were signally duplicitous in their failure. And every innocent life lost rests on their heads."

Hollis slapped the table, "That's exactly what my father said."

"He's a smart man, your dad."   He took a long gulp of his drink.   "You asked me if I believe in God, do you believe in God?"

"I don't know.   My mother raised me a devout Catholic.   She goes to mass every morning.   My father never bought into it.   He didn't resist my mother's efforts, but neither did he encourage them.   I fell from the fold in college.   Religion seemed superfluous and the source of so much trouble in the world.

"If there is a God, I believe that he is neither benevolent nor malevolent.   A benevolent God would not allow this to happen.   If God were malevolent how could one explain the beauty of a sunset or the warm, uncompromising love of a puppy or a child?   I believe God is neutral, passive and unengaged.   As we speak, He is probably sitting behind home plate sipping His beer from a bottle, hoping for at least nine good innings before the rain comes again.

"He, after all, gave man free will and war was what he did with it.   Man has a gift, a true capacity for evil.   When I look around at briefing and see the faces of the men around me I know that there is good in the world--man has the capacity for good, too, else why are we all here trying with our lives and our treasure to turn back evil?"

"Yeah.   Me neither."

"I just wish I knew now how this is all going to turn out.   As a biologist, I believe Darwinian logic applies to all things.   Even war...especially war.   War can be viewed as the sort of cataclysmic evolutionary event which occurs from time to time, a defining moment which, if the species is to survive, it must endure and overcome.   Prevail, like the bullfinches. With each war would come a better world, each one slightly better than the one that preceded it. One less encumbered by racism and hatred and suspicion.   And one day we might arrive at Utopia after all."

"You make that up?"

"No, I read it in a book."   They both laughed.

When they finished laughing, prolonged by alcohol, Hollis grew pensive.   "I just thought the bombing would bother me and it bothers me that it doesn't.   I figured I should feel guilt; in need of some sort of redemption or absolution.   I'm not sure I could kill somebody face to face, but bombing them is impersonal, easy."

"The question is killing a man.   Once you've made the decision that you are willing to do that, the method one chooses becomes immaterial to the original question."

"They teach you that at the Point?"

"No.   I read it in a book."

They laughed again.

"I just wonder," Hollis continued, "if the purpose of the Allies is to inflict defeat, unconditional defeat, I might add, and, at the same time, teach them a lesson, I wonder if the teacher is worthy of the lesson being taught and will anything be learned?"

"'Fuck no' on both counts.   This is not about our self-righteousness or their wickedness. It is about power. And power is about sex. If everybody in the world got laid on a regular basis there might be no war. But, if virtue is needed rather than power to defeat an evil enemy, nonetheless, power helps."

"You don't like me, do you?" Hollis asked.

"Nope.   You're a big pain in the ass.   Do you have any idea how much easier it would be to fight this war if all you smart-assed college kids stayed home and left the war to us professionals?   Would you like to buy me another beer?"

"No, sir.   I think you've had quite enough.   Besides I think they're closing.   Here he comes."   Hollis watched at the pub owner came over to them.

"Time, gentlemen."

"Thanks," Hollis said.   He looked at Ransahoff and could plainly see that he was drunk.

When they stepped out into the cool night air they found empty space where they had parked the jeep.

"Somebody stole the fuckin' jeep, God-dammit!"

Hollis couldn't believe it. Dark, empty street in all directions.   "I wonder if that fuckin' Russian did this?"

"Nevtushenko?"

"Yeah."

"Why do you think *he* did it?"

"He left us two bikes.   I know they all look alike but I'm pretty sure that one is his."

"The dirty bastards."

"Guess we better mount up.   Otherwise, it's a long walk."

Hollis grew concerned about the odds of Ransahoff making it back in one piece, for when he got onto the bike Ransahoff started pedaling in the wrong direction.   "Hey, stupid!   This way."

Ransahoff stopped the bike, dismounted and turned the bike around and got back on.   "I think I'm going to be sick."   A moment later Ransahoff vomited loudly onto the pavement, adding symbolism to his disdain.

"Come on, Dutch.   This way.   Let's go."   Ransahoff started pedaling.   Hollis wished he had his flashlight, but as they had driven over in the jeep there had been no need for one.   He was guided only partially by the white stripe painted on the edge of the pavement.   Riding so close to the edge he was struck in the face several times by low branches.   Finally he dismounted and figured the walk would be safer.   He turned to check if Ransahoff was behind him, but all he could see was empty night.   "Dammit," he muttered.   He could hear faint giggling.

"Dutch?"

Giggling.

Louder, "Hey Dutch?"

"Shut up, Hollis, you want to wake the neighbors?"

"Dutch, we're in the middle of the woods."

Ransahoff rode up, appearing out of the night like an vision.   His razor-sharp creased pants wet and grass-stained, his spit polished shoes scuffed.   Hollis noticed the front wheel was bent.   "I fell off."

"I only hope that's Spats's bike."

It went on like that for nearly an hour until they had found the cut through the fence. Hollis tried to warn Ransahoff about the flooded creek, which on a normal day could be stepped over, with the recent rains had swollen sufficiently to need a generous leap.   He heard splashing and "Fucking shit!"   More splashing.   "This water's cold."

"It would serve you right to drown in a damned puddle.   Now *that* would be symbolic," Hollis muttered to himself. "Come on Dutch, almost home."

Dutch followed him up the path, now both officers carrying their bikes on their arms. Ransahoff heaved the bicycle into the woods and shouted, "There!"

At last, Hollis delivered Ransahoff to his quarters and guided him in.   As Hollis turned to leave, Ransahoff said, "If you think this little bit of assistance you have rendered to me this evening will somehow endear you to me forever, you're wrong, you bonehead.   Forget it."

"Fuck you, Dutch."

"Good night to you, Hollis."

Hollis walked away leaving the bike on the ground.   "You never get used to it," Ransahoff said softly.

Hollis turned and asked, "What's that?"

"The flak."

Chapter Fifty-Two   **Selkirk**

Tuesday, October 12, 1943

The practice mission came off without a hitch.   The Group's mission was scrubbed in the planning stages and the three squadrons assigned for the mission flew practice also.   Hollis rode with Spats in the lead ship.   Robertshaw was number two, Powell number four and the three rookies filling in.   He had the bomb loaders place practice bombs in the planes and flew them to the bombing range out over the North Sea.   He even arranged for an interception by a flight of P-47s.   Hollis wondered if the new crews were as stunned by the sight of fighters closing in on them as he had been. The fighter guys did a good job. Even Hollis got anxious.

Hollis harangued them just as Ransahoff had done.   If they could be provided with the requisite skills they might gain a survival advantage.   It was his job to give them the benefit of his experience.   He hoped they would be fast learners.   He never thought he would get this far. If he could, perhaps they might also.   The Squadron would go back on operations on the 'morrow.   Selkirk would return and he would have eleven crews available, including Ransahoff's and his own.   Still short one for the full compliment.

The yelling over the VHF rang hollow in the earphones of the three veterans.   They had seen almost as much combat as Hollis and could easily have conducted the lesson themselves. He earnestly hoped the new guys paid attention.   Good formation was the key.   *If you can't fly a tight formation all else will not matter.*

On the flight back, Hollis raised the issue of the missing jeep.

"What jeep?" he asked above the roar of the engines.

"You stole our jeep last night, you son of a bitch, and we had to walk home with those two bikes you left us."

"I have no idea what you're talking about.   Is the Squadron short a jeep this morning?"

"No.   I found it parked outside the office."

"Then it ain't missin', is it?"

"Just admit to me you took it."

"Never, Captain.   I will never admit to a crime I did not commit."

"Then which one of you clowns took it?"

"It was either Robertshaw or Powell."

"They told me you took it."

"They're lying."

"Theft of government property is a court-martial offense."

"There was no theft involved.   We thought somebody left it there by accident."

"Are you nuts?"

"Yes.   You want to fly for a while?"

Hollis had them safely back on the ground just as the other three squadrons returned. When he entered the Squadron office to give some official report to Ransahoff, he was told the Squadron had been placed back on ops and had been alerted for the next day.   Make up the list, Ransahoff told him.

Hollis sat in his flight clothes staring at the sheet of paper.   Who would he send?   The

Squadron had to put up six and a spare.   What kind of mission would it be?   A milk run, maybe, or another Anklam or Bremen?   Should he include the rookies?   All or none?   They had to make their first flight sometime.   Selkirk would be back, should he send him?   One thing was certain, only Hollis and Ransahoff were 'qualified' to lead the Squadron.   Obviously, that raised another order of business.   He had to 'qualify' one or two more pilots to lead.   Who?   Spats was a good pilot, so was Robertshaw.   But, he knew nothing about their leadership qualities,   how they might react in a pinch.   Powell reminded him too much of himself and felt that, had he been in a position to choose otherwise, would not have picked himself to lead.   Perhaps, using that twisted logic, maybe Powell was the best choice.

He continued to stare at the blank sheet of paper.   No answers miraculously appearing in his brain.   Milk run or another Schweinfurt?

He picked up the pencil and wrote: Ransahoff, Nevtushenko, Fissano, Kehoe, Svoboda and Tedford.   Powell would be the spare.   There, it was done.   He took the sheet of paper and gave it to the clerk who immediately typed it.   As he watched he almost yanked the list out of the machine to change it, but decided to stay with his first choices.   It was a burdensome chore. He was deciding the fate of seventy people with little more to go on than impressions.   He had read the training evaluations on the three new crews and could find nothing that might distinguish one from the other.

The clerk pulled the list from the typewriter and handed it to Hollis.   After a moment's hesitation, he signed it.   He kept the original and placed the carbon copy out on the bulletin board.   The fates were sealed.   Regardless of what happened, he would get all the blame or all the credit, likely the former.   He didn't like this.   Had he seen this coming, that he might be the Operations Officer responsible for such matters, he might have chosen a different career path. Like Brubaker.

Later that evening, he sat in the office reading a week old <u>Yank</u>.   He avoided the room. He didn't want anybody to come squawking about the list.   Like any combat leader, he did not feel the need to justify his choices to the chosen.   He sat drinking coffee, his feet on the desk when Selkirk strolled in.

"I'm back."

Hollis dropped his feet to the floor and sat up, "Hiya Mickey, how are you feeling?"

Selkirk looked gaunt, his eyes dark, bloodshot and recessed into their sockets.

"I have to go see Clevenger.   I'll tell you how I feel after I see him."

"Good.   Glad you're back."

Selkirk acted as if he hadn't heard Hollis.   "You would not believe the jolt when that plane hit the water.   It was like flying into the side of a mountain."   Hollis watched as Selkirk undid his belt and dropped his pants.   There was a four inch wide purple stripe which ran from one hip to the other where his body had impacted against the seat belt.   His lower abdomen and privates were black and blue, surrounded by an odd shade of yellow-green.   "Huh, you made captain.   What are you bucking for, Generalissimo?"

Hollis snickered, his eyes still focused on the tremendous contusion as it disappeared into Selkirk's pants, "I got a special talent."

"You're nothing but a goldbrick, Hollis.   The only special talent you got is for whining."

"I can fly a plane."

"I'll give you that.   I thanked you once.   Don't make me do it again."   He turned and left saying, "I'll see you later."

An hour later, Clevenger walked into the office.   "Where's Ransahoff?"
"I don't know, sir."
"Find him."
"Yes sir."   Hollis walked over to Ransahoff's quarters where he found Ransahoff sitting on his bed, mending a shirt.
"Clevenger wants to see you."
"What for?"
"How should I know?   What am I, a mind-reader?"
Ransahoff pulled on the shirt he was mending and grabbed his cap and jacket and followed Hollis back to the office.
"Yes, Major, what can I do for you?"
Clevenger directed them into Ransahoff's office and shut the door.   "Selkirk shouldn't fly anymore.   It was foolhardy to send him to London.   He sat in his room drunk the whole time."
"He flies."
"Major, I don't think you understand."
"Yes, I do.   If he is physically capable of flying an airplane, he goes."
Hollis could tell that Clevenger was getting angry.   He seemed like the kind of person who was not used to being argued with.   "Don't force me to over-rule you."
"Then don't.   If you feel the need to ground him, do so.   Otherwise he flies.   I have a Squadron to put up and not enough crews.   I have my job, too.   He's been headed for a Section Eight ruling for a while now.   Ground him if you want.   If not, he gets treated no differently than anybody else."   He turned to Hollis, "Put him on the list."
Hollis said, almost sheepishly, "I already made up the list."
"Put him on the next one."
Hollis looked at Clevenger, an apology on his face, "Yes sir."
Clevenger continued, "Ransahoff, he's on a short tether.   All it's going to take is one more bad day to finish him off."   Clevenger turned and walked briskly from the office.
Hollis said, "Dutch, maybe we shouldn't send him.   Put him on the shelf for a while."
"Send him.   If we are alerted tomorrow night, put him on the list."
"Dutch--"
"That's an order."   The three most dreaded words in the language.   Poor Mickey. "You can't let emotion or sentiment get in the way, Hollis.   This is war.   When are you going to get that through your thick skull?"   He was about to leave when he turned, almost as an afterthought, "I have a Squadron to run, don't ever question one of my orders again."
Stung, Hollis felt he didn't understand his role if he was not able to add his input. Clearly, he was not a full partner in decision making.   More of a mid-level apparatchik.   It was no wonder everyone held him in such contempt.   Just like Otho.   He threw the pencil he was holding onto the desk causing it to flitter across the surface and fall to the floor.   The sad truth is, Hollis admitted grudgingly, Ransahoff was right.   Absolutely and unequivocally correct. When *was* he going to get it through his thick skull?

Wednesday, October 13, 1943

"The target for today is Emden.   The port facilities and warehouses," Begay said.   "We will be lead group."

Hollis scanned the officers and watched the faces of Tedford and Svoboda.   They looked so paralyzed by anxiety they were barely taking breath.   They were lucky without having the basis or knowledge to comprehend their good fortune.   They were going to a target in Germany, perhaps the only target in Germany, which might be considered a milk run.   The escort would be heavy, the expected opposition light.   Actual time spent in hostile airspace not more than fifteen minutes.   The only uncertainty was the weather.   It always was.   Assembly would be the problem.   Takeoff might be delayed, Begay told them.   If a break comes, be ready to fire up on short notice.

Hollis figured Ransahoff would be peeved he had to fly the mission.   Hollis cut him off quickly, however, and told him that, with his permission, of course, they would trade Squadron leads back and forth until he could get another lead crew trained.   Ransahoff concurred.   Hollis suggested Nevtushenko or Robertshaw.   Ransahoff said Nevtushenko and Powell.   Interesting, Hollis thought, Powell had not been on his list for all the reasons he previously identified.

Rager was flying lead today, Hollis would talk to him about assimilating Spats and Powell to the role of lead pilots when he got back.

An hour after takeoff, the planes returned.   Assembly was impossible.   The clouds were solid up to and beyond assembly altitude.   Bomber Command announced the recall and the planes, now scattered far and wide in the clouds, felt their way back down to earth through the soup.   It was a risky, harrowing business for the most experienced of pilots; it must have been torture for the rookies.   How they all made it back without crashing into each other in the murk was nothing short of miraculous.

Not long after the last bomber was down, it started raining.

Hollis sat in the office reading the status reports for available aircraft that Tanner and the line chief dropped off.   The three day stand-down, interrupted by only a brief practice flight had allowed repairs and scheduled maintenance on virtually all of the Squadron's B-17s.   They had twelve bombers, seven 'F's and five 'G's, all but two fitted with Tokyo tanks.

Ransahoff poked his head in and told Hollis to make the list.   The warning order just came in, he said.   We need to put up six and a spare.

Who should be the spare? Hollis wondered for the second day in a row.   Somebody with no experience to cast his fate with strangers or should it be somebody with experience who could take care of himself regardless of the situation?   One thing was sure: both he and Selkirk were on the list.   Spats, Powell, Fissano and Kehoe.   Svoboda would be the spare.   The list was typed and posted.   Hollis put himself number one, Powell number two, Fissano three, Selkirk four, Spats five and Kehoe six.   Hopefully it would be another milk run.   Some hapless airfield in Belgium or marshaling yard in France.

A short time later, Selkirk walked in, looking no better than he had the evening before.

"I see I'm on the list."

"Mickey, I had no choice.   You have to fly the missions just like everybody else."

"OK.   That's OK."   Without another word he left.   He came back a short time later with a vacant expression on his face.   "Hey Hollis, do me a favor."

"Sure, name it."

"If anything happens to me, you can have any of my stuff you want.   You got first dibs."

"Cut it out, Mickey.   Nothing's going to happen to you."

"Also, there's a group of letters and a couple of photos with a rubber band around them in the bottom of my foot locker.   If I don't come back, burn 'em.   Would you?'

"Mickey--"

Selkirk held his hand up to quell further protest.   "Please?"

"Sure."

Later, Hollis ran over to the Club for a beer before they closed the bar.   Everyone suspected an alert was imminent so the room was crowded with men trying to get in one last drink.   Promptly at nineteen hundred, the bar closed for alcohol and the place emptied out.

Hollis returned to his room and found Leo sitting on his bed, a vacant expression on his face.

"Hiya, Leo.   Hardly seen you the past couple of days.   Why do you think them black fellows volunteered for Augie's funeral?"

"They wanted to see for themselves that he was really and truly dead, I guess."

There was something very wrong with Leo Wychulis.   "So how's the square root of the hypotenuse?"

"Huh?   You know, a couple of weeks ago you asked me if I was, how did you put it?, 'screwing' Ian's mother.   At first, I wasn't sure I heard you right.   Then, I figured, coming out of your mouth I had, indeed, heard you correctly.

"I never laid a hand on the woman.   In the brief time I tried to be the boy's dad.   His real dad is somewhere in the boonies of Burma.   It was fun.   I want to be a real dad someday. He's a good kid.   Smart.   Looks after his mother while his father is gone.   He's an easy kid to like, Jack.   It's a good thing we all don't think with our loins as you seem to think most people do.   It was warm and cozy and far away from here.   It wasn't about 'screwing.'

"They're scared.   Ian doesn't know if he'll ever see his father again.   And she's not sure she'll ever see her husband again.   I just tried to help.   It was a mutual thing.   For once I may have gotten more than I gave."   Leo looked down at a piece of paper he held in his hand.   "We got mail."

Hollis felt a sinking feeling sweep over him.   Had Leo been the recipient of a 'Dear John,' or in this case, a 'Dear Leo' letter?

"Bad news?"

Leo became choked with emotion.   He looked up at Hollis and said, "Take me home. Make a left turn next time we go up and just keep going.   I want to see Christie one more time."

"I can't do that, you know that."   Hollis could see the tears running down Leo's fat cheeks.   "What happened?"

"Not a thing.   I miss my wife.   And she," he waved the letter to and fro, "misses me."

"Sorry, Leo, old pal.   If it was within my power to send you home I would do so this instant.   You know that."

Leo nodded.

"And if I had that kind of power, I'd be there right behind you."

Leo smiled, "I know."   He pointed to the desk.   "You got a letter, too."

Hollis turned and saw the envelope, pink, a Victory Red lipstick kiss on the back. Hollis looked at the number.   It was number sixteen.

"Son of a bitch!" Hollis yelled.   The long, lost letter, which Hollis had assumed was in a mail bag at the bottom of the ocean or some abandoned mail slot in Kiska, was held in his right hand.   He ripped it open.

> *Dear John,*
>
> *The answer to your question posed in your most recent correspondence is yes.   Unequivocally, undeniably and categorically YES!   My thirst for your love is unquenchable.   You are my first thought when I awake and my last thought when I go to sleep. My heart is empty without you.   I am incomplete without you.   I am but an empty shell.   How could I have been so blind, so unfeeling, for all those years?   It took a war.*
>
> *I love you now and always and forever.*
>
> *Jessie*

Chapter Fifty-three   **Going Back**

Thursday, October 14, 1943

Hollis fell asleep perplexed by mixed emotions.   He was elated by the letter from Jessie and the life-altering confirmation it announced, but he was also disturbed by Leo's change in personality.   Even at his worst, Leo had a certain resilience that now appeared exhausted.   For as long as Hollis had known him, he had never seen his copilot so morose.   Perhaps Leo was not as immune to the tumult that surrounded him as Hollis had suspected.   Maybe that little ersatz relationship he had cultivated with Ian and his mother had backfired.   Even without the requirement that he fuck Ian's mother whenever possible, emotional attachments were bound to develop.   Maybe he was feeling guilt, expending emotions toward people with whom he had no real bond, taking advantage of them in a most selfish way.   Maybe there was something in that letter from Christie that drove him off the end of the emotional precipice.   Maybe that little fire under his nose the other day had revealed his own mortality as he had never seen it before. Regardless, it was unsettling and he did not sleep well.

So it was that Hollis was awake instantly when the door at the end of the hall opened. There had been fog and rain in almost an unbroken pattern since Munster. Hollis, as Operations Officer, was at no particular advantage when it came to weather prognostications, so when he had gone to bed he predicted another scrubbed mission. If they did launch, he suspected it would be for another strike at Emden and wouldn't be so bad. It was their *modus* to keep launching strikes at a target until they hit it before moving on. In boxing, it was called telegraphing one's blows, a tell in poker.

The footsteps came right to his door and stopped. The door opened, the dark figure entered and stepped over to him.

"Captain?" he whispered.

"Yeah?"

"They want you at Group. You're leadin' the Squadron."

"What time is it?"

"Oh-four thirty."

"Where to, today, Beamis?"

"Don't know, sir. But, I'd bet you ain't gonna like it."

"OK, I'm up."

Hollis stood up, the cold, damp air gripped him like the fingers on the hand of a corpse. Beamis left quickly. Hollis dressed and headed for the latrine. The night was raw with a light rain. Once there, he found hot water with which to shave. Ransahoff walked in, already dressed, a scowl on his face.

"You don't look very happy," Hollis said to him.

"I'm not and soon you won't be either."

"What's that supposed to mean?"

"You'll find out soon enough." Ransahoff finished urinating into the trough and zipped up his pants.

"Where are we going?" Hollis asked, suddenly flushed with apprehension.

"Can't say. The Colonel said he would never send his men someplace he would not go to himself. I share that philosophy. Fortunately, it's not my turn to fly."

Hollis noticed a vacant expression descend on Ransahoff's countenance as he left, his mind seized, undoubtedly, by some intrusive thought. Hollis departed the latrine with a mounting sense of dread. Like a prophet trying to read meaning into every nuance, every subtlety of phrase or expression, Hollis was suddenly convinced this was going to be a day like no other.

Hollis returned to the room and finished dressing in the dark, trying not to disturb the slumbering Leo. He looked down at his friend and tried to sort out the emotional turmoil Leo must be feeling. Leo still desperately loved his wife, Christie, of that there could be no real doubt. Maybe he was in love with Ian's mother, also. How hard or easy might it have been for a lesser man to fall in love with Molly Williams?

Poor Leo, finding himself in a situation where cherubic charm and a feigned naiveté could not protect him.

Hollis was forced to turn on the light for he could not find Jessie's scarf. He had placed it, as he always did at the end of a mission, on a hook on the locker door. It was not there. With the light on, he noticed a letter addressed to Christie on the desk. Only Christ in His

Temptation could have been more enticed than Hollis was at that moment to open the envelope and read the letter.   Fortunately, he found the scarf.   It had fallen to the floor.   Hollis checked to make sure he had everything and departed, the contents of the letter a burning mystery in his brain.   He just prayed Leo hadn't done something hasty or irrational and there might yet be time to talk Leo out of whatever foolish choice he may have committed to paper.

He got into the jeep and drove to the Headquarters block.   He parked and walked into the Operations room.   His eyes fell upon Van Patten and Hollis's burgeoning sense of impending doom was confirmed.   Everyone was there, Lemaster, the replacement for the late Cavannaro, Duckworth, Bonner, Gleason and Begay all huddled around a map.   The only one missing was Ransahoff.   Lemaster and Van Patten were dressed for flying.   Hollis stepped up to the map and found the answer to his dread: Schweinfurt.   They were going back.

Hollis was suddenly whelmed by a sense of relief, as if his heart was unburdened.   He was oddly at peace, his fate sealed.   All that had gone before was but a prelude to this.   He would not live through the day.   He almost felt relief.

His senses sharpened and when he made his presence known to the Colonel, Hollis returned the nod.   Every word spoken, every gesture made stood out in sharp focus.   He heard a voice and turned to see Ransahoff had joined them, also dressed for flying.

"Good morning, Major," Van Patten said sarcastically, "glad you could join us."

"Yes sir, and a top of the morning to you, too, Colonel."   Ransahoff was his old self. No vacant expression.   Two West Pointers exchanging sharp remarks as only they could, everyone else was ineligible.   Like some secret handshake.

"What are you doing?" Hollis whispered to Ransahoff.   "I thought I was leading?"

"You are.   I'm riding shotgun with the Russian.   He's number two, today."

"Fine.   It's your Squadron."

Van Patten shot an annoyed glance at Hollis and continued.   They would be low group in the second wing.   The 532nd would be low squadron.   This should have caused Hollis to vomit violently the instant this information entered his skull, but it did not.   They were in the worst possible location in the next to the worst position in the whole affair.   Only the low squadron of the low group in the lead wing would fare worse today.   It was set.   There would be no reprieve.   Unless he pulled a gun and took himself out of the picture with messy finality like Scorch or admitted his cowardice and drop his wings onto the map like Brubaker, he would go, flying toward Judgment, obediently leading the Squadron to slaughter like a Judas Goat.

The Officer's meeting broke up.   Van Patten told them to go eat and reconvene at briefing, which was scheduled for oh-seven hundred.   Any questions?

Hollis ate quickly, the first time his stomach had allowed the consumption of food before a mission since he had arrived in England.   Mission eggs, bacon, coffee.   He wanted to get back to the room to write a hasty letter to Jessie.   As he left the Combat Mess the early arrivals were just starting to trickle in, their expressions etched with concern, confronted by the aroma and implication of fresh eggs.   He looked for familiar faces, but saw none.

In the room, he sat at the desk and pushed to one side the letter Leo had written.   He took a piece of stationary and wrote a short note to Jessie and one to his parents.   It was essentially the same letter to both.   He explained that the mission was important and his role in it was crucial.   He hoped they would understand that he had a job to do and, if this was the last communication they would receive from him, they should know that he died doing his duty.   In the letter to Jessie, he declared his deep, everlasting love and his eternal regret that there were things left unsaid and actions left undone.   Paraphrasing her, he pointed out that it had taken a war to bring them together, but it was also a war which prevented them from fulfilling their destiny, a hope and a future unlike any they could ever imagine.   He was sorry.   Very sorry.   She would be the last thing he would think of when his life ended and her name would remain on his lips for all time.

He spent a long moment staring at Leo's letter.   In the quiet isolation of the room, Leo was at breakfast by now, he could steal a glimpse at the contents of the thickened envelope and no one would be the wiser.   If they did not return, the letters to Jessie and his folks would be mailed in his absence, his last act, even after death.   So also would Leo's find its way into the mail bag and, for better or worse, its way back to Christie.   Would Leo's letter bring heartbreak or pain or final confirmation of eternal love and devotion?   It didn't matter to Hollis.   It was none of his business.   Fate would deal with Leo separately.   Christie, too.

He got up from the desk, making sure the three letters would be easy to find for whoever it was, Beamis or the Squadron adjutant, responsible for the final disposition of their personal effects.   He looked around the room.   There was nothing left for him to do.   No incriminating evidence or potentially embarrassing items.   Jessie's satin pillow cover still had the indentation of his head.   He felt sad that there was not more he could do in his final hours.   He looked at his watch.   Briefing was in ten minutes.

The fog was closing in as he drove to the briefing room.   He made the trip in less than three minutes, parking the jeep at the end of a long line of vehicles.   The officers shuffled in, each funneling through the door, pausing to show their AGO cards to the stern-looking MP.   Hollis looked for Hulse, standing with the   contingent of anxious, chain-smoking gunners, and gave him the customary wave.   Hulse acknowledged the greeting in silence, his expression grim.   He understood, Hollis knew, that today would be different even though Hulse would have no way, at this point, of knowing why.

Hollis checked in at the desk and walked to the front of the room, taking his position with the Group staff and mission leaders.   Sudbury, Pillaccio and Rager sat nearby.   They looked anxious even though they were not going today.   Hollis glanced at the mission board and saw that Ransahoff had, indeed, changed the order of things.   Nevtushenko was now the number two and Robertshaw was three.   Selkirk was four, Powell five and Fissano six.   Fate was a fickle mistress and Hollis wondered what destinies had been altered by Ransahoff's last minute stroke of eraser and pencil?   Hollis surveyed the officers as they took their seats, their voices hushed, the growing tension in the room palpable.

The assembled were called to attention and the instant they all saw Van Patten in flying clothes their fears were confirmed.   Hollis could make out heads shaking.   *No milk run today, boys. Sorry.*

How many silently prayed the rain and murk would not clear or something would break on their particular plane?   They all knew that if it was not today, it would be tomorrow or the next.   Eventually, it would be their turn.

Van Patten took the stage.   "Seats, Gentlemen."   He waited for a moment, went to the map and pulled back the curtain.   All eyes fell on the most eastward extent of the red yarn as it angled downward deeply into Germany.   "It's Schweinfurt again."   Moans filled the room as well as a few gasps, a sporadic curse.   Many had not been to Schweinfurt the first time, perhaps most, but they all knew of its significance.   Hollis searched the crowd looking at the place Selkirk usually sat, but could not see him.   The faces reflected shock, disbelief that after several tough missions they were now going after the toughest target any of them could imagine.

"As some of you know, especially those of you who went there the first time, the results of our first raid on Schweinfurt were less than hoped for at best and disappointing at worst.   The damage to ball bearing production was significant, but the Germans have managed to bring production back almost to pre-strike levels.   We have to go back to finish the job.   No platitudes today, Gentlemen.   If we hit it hard today we will cripple German war industry for some time to come.   If we do the job right we may never need to go back."

No one really believed him.   He said it sincerely, and may have actually believed it himself, but if so, he was the only one in the room who did.

"The three Bombardment Wings of the First Division, the lead 40th, middle 1st and the trailing 41st will head for the target along this route," Van Patten pointed on the map.   "The Third Division will follow a route thirty miles to the south, parallel to the First until here where they will turn south to here where they will turn east toward the target, arriving after the First Division has cleared the target area.   The Second Division will follow the route of the First.

"The Initial Point is here, the town of Wurzburg.   A right turn off the target to the Rally Point here.   Withdrawal will take a direct route out of Germany, almost due west, from the Rally and then northwest over France.

"Penetration and withdrawal support will be provided to the limits of their endurance.

"Our secondary target is the center of Schweinfurt city.   The tertiary target in case of clouds is Ludwigshafen, here.   The last resort target is the city area of Saarbrucken.

"We expect enemy opposition to be...brisk and determined.   We doubt they will engage until after our escort has turned back.   We expect flak to be accurate and concentrated over the Ruhr Valley.   Moderate over Wurzburg.   Intense and extremely accurate over the target. Major."

Gorton took the stage and smiled.   He might have been dour or stern as was sometimes the case, or flat and businesslike which was usually the case, but not today.   His smile was sympathetic.   Not patronizing, not unduly enthusiastic, just a warm smile.   He went over each detail with slow, deliberate clarity, making those points he wanted remembered, repetitive.   He described the target, the aiming points and prominent landmarks in exquisite detail.   *They want to hit this one badly, Gentlemen, make no mistake.*   The essentials, which were really only important to the lead bombardiers, were mentioned several times and the photographic images of the ball bearing plants viewed from every angle.   Before ending, he said, "Good luck today, Gentlemen.   Hit them hard."   No further mention was made of the fighter opposition. Detailed analysis of the locations of fighter bases and the types of aircraft and expected tactics was conspicuously absent.   Maybe the others were still too stunned to notice the omission, but Hollis did and it was unfortunate.   Anyone in the crowd man enough to fly this mission deserved to be told what to expect, regardless of whether the information was of any value to them or not.   Hollis was disappointed that they would think the psyches of these men too fragile to be told the truth, which, of course, they knew all too clearly.   Hollis knew that there were over a thousand enemy aircraft capable of intercepting and engaging the bombers along their route, most of them were single-engine fighters.   That was nearly three German planes for each bomber in the force.   Not good odds.   Why didn't they have the guts to say so?

Hollis looked at the officers sitting in the front row, studying each as if he was seeing them for the first time.   Begay sat reviewing his notes as if they contained a grocery list instead of checkpoints and timings for a bombing mission.   Gleason, ever the warrior was so anxious to go along he could barely sit still. The great mystery was why Van Patten had decided to lead this, of all missions?   And why Ransahoff?   He knew of the target when he visited the latrine, why him?   It was excessive.   Perhaps even foolhardy.   Such bravado in the face of peril might prove their undoing.   They might die today just to demonstrate, to anyone who cared to notice, that they were as brave as anybody else.   Braver, maybe. Stupid.   Insane.   It was like going over the top at the Somme into a hailstorm of machine gun fire just to prove a point, show them you were a better man.   They would not send their men to attack a place they would not go to themselves.   *Incredible.*

Suddenly, as if seen clearly, also for the first time, Hollis understood the meaning of leadership.   It was the warrior ethic.   No different for the bomber crews of the Eighth Army Air Force as it was for Pickett's rebels or the archers at Agincourt.   It was at the same time both glorious and depraved.   It was Clauswitzian, the will of the people exercised through the blood of its youth.   Simple.   Darwinian even.   Now, he understood.   The war was *not* just about him.

Begay took the stage and spoke in his aboriginal monotone.   Routes and timings.   Take off.   Assembly.   Checkpoints.   A grocery list.

Then the weather forecast, which, the briefing officer was quick to point out, stinks. They expected the murk to clear by takeoff, but the final decision to launch the mission will not be made until the very last minute.   The overcast should extend to only two to four thousand feet.   Above that altitude, there should be a solid undercast all the way to the coast.   From there on, from the Channel across the Continent, the conditions should be perfect.   The target CAVU.   The weather for the return could be problematic, a euphemism for a complete and utter guess.   Hollis was unconcerned and faintly amused for he did not expect to return, the weather forecast for landing became irrelevant. This was how the brain worked when you presaged your death.

Finally, Van Patten took the stage again.   He tried to look confident, even brash.   His blood was up.   There was fire in his eyes.   Anticipate the turns.   If anyone ahead gets out of formation, move up quickly.   Don't hesitate, it's your neck.   Conserve ammunition.   Don't let your gunners fire at fighters which are out of range.   Navigators and bombardiers stay for their briefings.   Good luck.   Good bombing.   Revenge time, boys.   Give the sons of bitches a lesson they will not soon forget.   Protestants to the front, Catholics to the rear.   Dismissed.

The Group was called to attention, but before they had taken their feet Van Patten energetically bounded from the stage and strode from the room as if impatient to run out and fire up the engines.   His were not the idle words of a battlefield commander safely bivouacked in the rear.   He was the Bangmaster.   He would be in the cockpit of the lead ship, the forward-most rebel, the lead archer.   Everybody knew it.   They would follow him wherever he might intend to take them.   Over the top.   Into whatever hailstorm of fire might be in store.   Hollis was surprised they did not stand up and cheer.   It was a privilege to be led into battle, even unto death, by such a man.   Out by the planes, the dramatics would be gone and the painful reality would sink in, Hollis knew.   Many, perhaps most, would not be sleeping in England tonight.

Hollis came to his feet as the entourage left the briefing room.   The murmurings and anxious discussion began even as the last of the officers made their way down the aisle.   He sought out Leo as the throng melted into a shuffling mob at the door.   Hollis could not locate him.   He found Sully and Cobb.   When they saw Hollis approach they stopped.

"Seen Leo?"

Sully looked around and said, "He was here a second ago."

"He alright?"

"Yeah, why?"

"He seemed a little upset last night.   I just wondered if everything was OK."

Cobb walked over to the table where the other navigators congregated to collect their maps and flimsies and go over the details of the mission.   Sully left for his own special briefing. Hollis walked past a collection of men kneeling on the floor as they took communion from the Chaplain's assistant.   The congregation seemed larger than usual.   There are no atheists in foxholes, Hollis was reminded.   He toyed with the idea of seeking absolution for himself, but the hypocrisy, even at this late hour, was too much to bear.   He would take his chances with God on the terms as they existed.

Hollis stepped from the room into the fog and felt a cool moisture cover his flesh, not dissimilar to the sensation he had felt earlier.   He was surrounded by a couple dozen other officers all heading for the equipment room yet he felt alone, detached and disconnected as if walking in his sleep.   Soon the cool moisture penetrated his body down to his marrow.   It was not unpleasant.   He was calmed.   Even though he could see the gravel path beneath his boots and hear the crunch of his weight on the damp cinders he felt weightless.   He smiled to himself and continued walking.   He was relieved, unburdened.   He knew what this meant even though he could not explain it.

In the equipment room, he gathered his gear, slipping the Mae West over his head and the parachute harness over each arm.   He looked for Leo but, again, did not see him.   The faces and voices that surrounded him were mostly tense, nervous.   But there were others that were determined, a few even confident, routine.   Hollis dropped his personal effects into the bag and handed them to the clerk.   He kept the picture of Jessie, its edges worn, the image slightly dulled by repeated proximity to his perspiration.   He picked up his bag and headed for the door, stepping once again into the foggy mist.   He paused for a moment to smoke a cigarette when he heard a voice behind him, the unmistakable accent of Mickey Selkirk.

Hollis turned toward him and said, "Hi, Mickey.   Rough one today, huh?"

Selkirk muttered something which, at first, Hollis could not make out.

"I confess to Almighty God...I confess to Almighty God."

Hollis could see that Mickey was shaking, tears ran down his cheeks.   In a low voice he said, "I can't remember the words.   God forgive me, I can't remember the words."   He squatted to the ground sobbing softly.   Hollis knelt down and placed his arm around Selkirk.

Hollis cradled Mickey's face in his hands and started speaking, "I confess to Almighty God..."

Selkirk raised his eyes to Hollis and he could see in them an unfathomable terror, terror, Hollis thought, not for what lay ahead but because he could not remember these most important words.

Hollis nodded and smiled gently, "I confess to Almighty God..."   He paused for a moment and Mickey joined him as they spoke in unison, "and to you, my brothers and sisters, that I have sinned through my own fault in my thoughts and in my words, in what I have done, and in what I have failed to do; and I ask Blessed Mary, ever virgin, all the angels and saints and you, my brothers and sisters, to pray for me to the Lord our God."   Hollis continued, speaking for the priest, "May almighty God have mercy on us, forgive us our sins, and bring us to everlasting life."   Selkirk looked at Hollis and smiled, they said, again in unison, "Amen."

They came to their feet and Hollis said, "Come with me."   As they turned to head back toward the briefing room Hollis saw Leo come up to him.   Hollis placed his arm around Selkirk and said to Leo, "Go ahead, Leo.   I'll be by directly."   Leo took Hollis's bag, nodded understanding and turned for the truck.

Hollis guided his friend back into the room as the bombardiers and navigators filed out. Selkirk was in no shape to fly a combat mission.   He looked for Ransahoff or Van Patten. Even Clevenger, but no one was around except for a few lingering staff officers and Pillaccio and Sudbury, neither one of whom was in a position to help him.   Hollis looked for the Chaplain, who for his purposes would fill the role of priest, perhaps see the emotional wreck Selkirk had become and intervene.   Hollis saw him standing in the corner of the huge Nissen Hut and led Selkirk to him.   Selkirk spoke, "Help me, please.   I'm scared."

"Before there can be peace in the world men must find peace within their soul.   It is natural to be scared, Michael.   Sit with me for a moment," he told Selkirk, nodding to Hollis as they sat on a bench.   The Chaplain placed his arm around Selkirk as a sympathetic parent might, trying to console a child during a severe storm.   "This morning I read from Leviticus. 'The Lord said to Moses, Speak to the whole Israelite community and tell them: Be holy, for I, the Lord, your God, am holy.   You shall not bear hatred for your brother in your heart. Though you may have to reprove your fellow man, do not incur sin because of him.   Take no revenge and cherish no grudge against your fellow man.   You shall love your neighbor as yourself.   I am the Lord.'"

Selkirk nodded.   Hollis wondered exactly how did Leviticus pertained to the repair of Selkirk's emotional collapse?   It was a big mistake putting the poor son of a bitch back on ops. Whoever made that decision would be duplicitous in whatever happened today.   Ransahoff. Clevenger.   Van Patten.   Himself.   All of them. The Chaplain chatted quietly with Selkirk for a moment then said, "Recite the Lord's Prayer with me."   He looked up at Hollis and asked, "Would you like to join us, Captain?"

Hollis nodded and the Chaplain began, The three men spoke softly.   When they concluded, he looked at Selkirk and said, "Go forth, Michael, safe in the knowledge that by the power of the Holy Spirit vengeance will give way to love, salvation will be yours and peace will come to all men and through Jesus Christ we will have eternal life.   God bless you and be with you on this day."

Selkirk thanked him and they left.

If Selkirk's troubled soul had been fortified, his shattered spirit strengthened, it was not possible for Hollis to tell.   His head was bowed and Hollis helped him collect his gear.   He then guided him to his jeep, and they drove out to the dispersal area.   No words were spoken. Hollis noticed Selkirk's hands no longer shook.   He dropped Selkirk off at his plane, watched him for a few moments as Selkirk approached his crew and drove off.   If he had the authority to intervene Hollis had forsaken it.   Selkirk's fate, like that of everyone else's was in the hands of the gods and whatever skill and guts one might muster.   What else could he have done?

Hollis pulled the jeep onto the muddy grass beside Moe's shack.   It had acquired a larger, taller chimney and black smoke billowed out to commingle with the fog.   The crew had gathered, as they always did, under the left wing.   Hollis noticed the B-17 had acquired a name and a cartoon on the nose like war paint.   **Goofy's Glider**.   A rendition of the Disney cartoon of Dippy the Goof flying a wooden contraption meant to resemble an aeroplane.   Hollis walked over to them and they came to their feet.   The only sound was that of the gasoline powered generator that putt-putted diligently beneath the nose providing juice through a small cable to the slumbering bomber.

"As you no doubt know by now," he said, "it's Schweinfurt.   We're going back."

Chapter Fifty-four   **One More Bad Day**

The crew sat around waiting for stations, speculating, none of them convinced the mission would be flown.   The fog had not lifted and an intermittent drizzle fell.   Hollis had no doubt, though.   Today they would go to Schweinfurt.   After chatting with Moe, he and Leo, who appeared the same as ever, made a cursory walk-around.   Hollis asked if the engines had, indeed, been replaced.   Moe assured him that they had.   They were so badly damaged, Moe said, as to be unreliable after anything but complete overhauls.   The bearings had been shot in two and the gears in the crank box nearly reduced to sawdust in one of the others.   He had been lucky they were still running when he made it back the other day.

Had they been slow-timed?

Of course, Moe said, half-insulted at the question.   Hollis tucked his head into the bomb bay.   There he found six one thousand pounders shackled to the racks above his head.   They had been 'chalked,' epithets added to their dull gray sides, messages from the ordinance crews.

"These should break a few balls," Sully said, coming up beside him.

"Yeah, put 'em where they count."

"Of course," Sully said, feigning insult much as Jablonski had.   "You get us there and I'll take care of the rest."

"Fine."

Hollis took Leo to one side and leaned with him against the jeep.   "Smoke?" Hollis asked, offering a cigarette to Leo.   He knew Leo rarely smoked so he was mildly surprised when Leo pulled the Chesterfield from the pack, tapped it on the dial of his watch to compact the tobacco and placed it in his mouth.

"Thanks."

"Everything OK?"

"Sure, why shouldn't it be?"

"You seemed a little preoccupied last night.   I thought perhaps you had been given some bad news or something."

"No.   No bad news."

"I was just curious.   I meant no insult when I made that crack about Ian's mother."

"OK.   I know you can't help yourself.   I've learned to live with it."   Leo half-smiled and took a long drag.   He wanted desperately to ask him about the letter.   But he resisted.   It would remain one of life's unanswered mysteries.   Minutes passed.   He looked at his watch.   Time for stations.

"I guess we better suit up and climb in."

Leo agreed.   They relieved themselves on the grass and returned to the crew, who, taking the cue from their pilot, had already started climbing into the bomber.   Hollis tucked in Jessie's silk scarf and climbed into the nose.   He took his seat and began the checklist.   A light drizzle spattered droplets on the windshield and Hollis kept the side window closed.   The checklist completed, they waited.

As low squadron, they would be the last planes off.   The takeoff plan had them taxiing all the way around to the other end of the field to take advantage of the prevailing breeze for takeoff.   It meant guiding the overloaded beasts around the perimeter track in the fog as it snaked its way around to the runway threshold.   A daunting task.

They waited and waited.   The mounting tension in cockpits must be almost unendurable, Hollis thought.   He, having achieved some inner, transcendent peace, was unaffected.   He hadn't even felt the need to vomit.   Clearly, the takeoff had been pushed back.   Maybe they were right, the mission would be scrubbed.   No, as the thought registered in his brain, a forked green flare rose from the shadowy form of the control tower, barely discernible in the fog and drizzle.

Hollis pulled his window back and yelled, "Clear!"   Leo did the same.   Hollis put the index finger of his left hand out the window and motioned a circle.

"Fuel booster pumps on."

"On."

"Start one."

Leo made the action.   "Mesh One," and Hollis watched the number one propeller start to rotate, jerking around blade by blade.

The engine kicked over and expelled a blue cloud of smoke as it came to life with a few tentative coughs.   He watched as the cowling rattled uncertainly with the first uneven detonations of the cylinders.   After a few moments, the engine settled into a steady, satisfying roar.   Soon all four engines were running with the same reassuring throb.   Hollis, Leo and Dodge put the engines through the run-ups and mag checks, confirming that everything was in good working order.   They waited, engines idling, until there was another green flare, the signal to taxi.   Moe, using two flashlights, guided Hollis onto the perimeter strip.   The fog, instead of lifting, thickened and Hollis could barely make out the taxiway more than a hundred yards ahead of him.   It is a slow, tedious trek around the perimeter strip.   Jockeying outboard throttles and brakes, with Leo watching the edge of the concrete, Hollis managed to deliver **Goofy's Glider** to the end of the runway, falling in behind the last plane of the lead squadron.   Hollis wondered how Selkirk was making out.   Did he sabotage another turbo supercharger?   Did he collapse on the hardstand in a convulsion of terror or simply become catatonic, incapable of another willful act?

They were held a long time at the end of the runway.   As if by command of Mars himself, the fog lifted a fraction and the runway appeared to stretch out before them, visible enough to allow instrument takeoff, but still well below that which might be considered, in any other circumstance, safe.

Finally, unseen by Hollis, the signal is given and the lead bomber of the high squadron started down the runway disappearing into the mist.   Then the second.   The third.   Slowly, Hollis inched **Goofy's Glider** forward toward the end of the runway.   When he turned the B-17, he quickly looked back to see who was behind him.   He counted six Fortresses.   They were all there.   He waited for the signal.   This would be the last time he would ever see this place, he thought.

The Aldis lamp flashed and Hollis stood on the brakes while he advanced the throttles full to the stops.   The mighty engines thundered and, at the right moment, Hollis eased off the brakes and Moe's bomber roared forward.   Leo kept them aligned with the runway while Hollis watched the instruments.   Dodge called out the airspeed.   It had become nearly routine.   Almost.   Hollis felt his heart start to pound with the bouncing of the heavily-laden bomber as it churned forward into the unseen wake turbulence of all the airplanes that had just preceded them. He could feel Leo's light pressure on the rudders as the plane passed fifty miles an hour and the tail became aerodynamically useful.

The takeoff run seemed to last too long.   Hollis resisted the intense need to look outside, but knew that to do so would be an unforgivable mistake.   They passed eighty.   The bouncing eased slightly as the forces of lift sucked at the wings.   Ninety.

"Red lights!"

One hundred.

Hollis felt the plane take its weight from the runway.   One-oh-five.   Hollis felt Dodge's hand atop his.   One ten.

Hollis gently eased back on the wheel.   They were airborne.   Leo retracted the landing gear.   Hollis kept the climb slow, gaining precious airspeed by keeping a flat trajectory off the ground, the needle on the climb indicator barely moving.   Slowly, the earth receded beneath them and, at the signal from Cobb, Hollis turned **Goofy's Glider** into a gentle left-hand turn until the needle on the radio compass pointed precisely ninety degrees left toward the buncher. Dodge climbed into his turret to keep an eye out for any other planes.   There were a lot of neophyte pilots in the Group, many, if not most, had no experience climbing into an overcast like this.   They could be foundering anywhere inside the cloud.   What a miserable turn of events that would be to die ignominiously in a collision instead of nobly at the hands of the enemy, Hollis thought, today of all days.

The top of the overcast was reported to be around four thousand feet at takeoff.   By the time they passed six thousand feet they were still in cloud so thick they could barely see their own wingtips.   There were some anxious moments when **Goofy's Glider** was buffeted by unseen turbulence, the sure sign of the recent close passage of another bomber.   Hollis suspected, as they passed through eight thousand feet, that many of the rookies might be on the verge of panic, caught in the gray limbo between heaven and earth, fearful they might never climb above the murk and terrified to go back down into it.   To their credit, however, there were no cries for help over the VHF.

Suddenly, a yellow-red flare appeared dead ahead, drifting down from above, and Hollis knew they were close.   A few moments later, the dark interior of the cloud brightened and they were above it, small residual wisps of cloud moving quickly past the window, the sunlight of the late morning blasting into the cockpit with blinding ferocity.   Hollis quickly put on his sunglasses and even then it took several moments to adjust his vision to the full daylight.   He immediately snapped his head from side to side looking for other planes.   For the moment they seemed alone.   He kept the turn and bank indicator fixed and checked the altitude, ten thousand, one hundred feet.

"Pilot to crew, ten thousand feet.   Go on oxygen."

Hollis waited for Leo to put on his mask and settle it onto his face, checking the flow before giving Hollis the 'thumbs up.'   Leo took control of the plane and Hollis waited for Sully to appear for their ritual smoke.   As if by telepathic signal, Sullivan appeared in the hatchway and gave Hollis a cigarette.   They drew heavily on them for they did not burn well this high, the oxygen available for the combustion of tobacco barely sufficient to keep them lit.   They enjoyed their cigarettes, nonetheless.   Hollis looked down at Sully, making eye contact.   Hollis smiled.   Sully smiled back and winked.   There was tacit, mutual understanding that today would be different.   Sully snubbed out the cigarette and climbed up onto the flight deck, making his way to the waiting pins.   Hollis removed his cap from his head and took his helmet from the canvas bag and pulled it onto his head, adjusted the goggles to rest across his forehead and placed the rubber oxygen mask carefully over his nose and lower face.   He plugged it in and checked the blinker to assure oxygen flow.   He tapped Leo on the arm and took control of the bomber.

A short time later, Sully returned to the nose and Hollis called for the crew to check in. He searched the sky for Van Patten.   He saw other planes flying at various altitudes, all in a flat counterclockwise turn but did not see Van Patten.   It was immediately apparent that there was no semblance of formation.   The planes were scattered about in total disarray.

"Pilot to crew.   Keep an eye out for the Bangmaster.   I do not see him.   We're not going anywhere until we do."

"Maybe we should call this off, then."

"Knock it off, Rizzo," Hollis said.   "Keep off the intercom."   It was a weak, half-hearted admonition.   They all knew it.   But Hollis was obliged to say it anyway.   They expected it from him.

"Tail to pilot, I spotted flares from a Fort at our eight o'clock level, flying on the opposite course."

Hollis snapped his head around and looked back over the wing.   The flares were dropping quickly, but appeared to have come from a B-17 at the head of a loose gaggle of bombers flying on the opposite side of the huge circle.   They were at least two miles away and twice that distance beyond them in the turn.   Hollis hoped the rest of the low squadron was with him.   He wagged his wings and advanced the throttles, placing **Goofy's Glider** into a steep turn toward the receding bombers that Hollis knew was the formation he was trying to catch.   He looked inside the turn and saw The Russian and Robertshaw.   A short distance behind them Powell and Selkirk.   Fissano and Svoboda brought up the rear, each following Hollis's lead and turning inside the circle.   With any luck the squadron would come together quickly.   The high squadron and most of the lead were still strung out.   Van Patten 'S'ed back and forth to slow down the pace and allow compression of the trailing planes into the lead elements.   Regardless of how well assembly went from here on they were still way behind schedule.   The Group had not completely formed and they were due to depart for wing assembly already.

"Radio to pilot."

"Go ahead, radio."

"Sir, Bangmaster advised Goldrock that we are behind schedule and would rendezvous with them at Splasher Six.   Goldrock acknowledged."

"Thanks, Quinn."

The combination of Hollis pouring on the coal and Van Patten slowing down his forward progress by snaking back and forth brought the low squadron into formation.   The maneuvers worked for the rest of the scattered group, but not before another complete orbit had been made and more gasoline and time expended.   Advised that his flock had become properly assembled, Van Patten commenced a climbing turn toward Splasher Six near Scole.   It was the last checkpoint before coast-out at Orfordness.

They flew on, still in fairly loose formation, toward the southeast.   It was getting cold as they climbed, most of England obscured below by an unbroken layer of shimmering white clouds.

"Left waist to pilot, Lieutenant Powell just feathered an engine.   He dipped his wing and turned for home.   Looks like Lieutenant Svoboda's fillin' in."

"Roger, left waist."   Poor Svoboda.   Never flew a mission in his life and now, because of some mechanical failure on somebody else's plane, he found himself going to the most dreaded target any had ever faced.   He must be shitting in his pants, Hollis thought.   Poor son of a bitch.   Hollis turned as far as he could in his seat to locate Svoboda.   He was still out of position, but, hopefully, he would catch up and pull in tight.   As the outside, most rearward plane in the low squadron of the low group, he would probably be the first to fall.

Van Patten picked up the pace in an effort to make up time, but Hollis watched the clock closely and they would not reach Splasher Six before the wing was scheduled to depart.   Would the wing commander, Colonel Milton of the 91st, choose to depart without his missing group or continue to circle, throwing everything further behind in one huge snowball effect?   Or would he depart and leave Van Patten to his own devices?   No easy choice for Milton.

Should they depart, Van Patten would be confronted with   difficult choices: proceed along the route and try to rendezvous with the wing over the Channel and run the risk of finding himself alone on the brink of enemy territory or he could seek out any other formation and latch on for better or worse or he could abort the mission, flying an impromptu diversion or simply turn for home.   This latter was so unlikely as to be unthinkable.

Sure enough, Cobb reported they were over Scole and the sky was empty.

"Radio to pilot, Bangmaster told Goldrock he was going to proceed to Point Able."

"Roger."   Point Able was coast-in at Walcheren Island on the Dutch coast, making clear Van Patten's decision to proceed with the mission.   The Group continued the climb, angling not for Orfordness, but for Walcheren where, hopefully, they would intercept the main bomber stream and slip into place.

Off to the right, Hollis could make out a large formation heading south-south-east toward Clacton.   It was the Third Division.

"Radio to pilot.   Sir, I'm hearing all sorts of chatter on the command channel. Showboat can't find his low group and turned the lead over to Goldrock."

Hollis sorted this out in his head.   "Showboat" was the leader of the lead wing, the Fortieth.   His low group, which Hollis knew to be the 305th, hadn't shown up either.   There was a standing order that no wing would head into enemy territory with less than its three groups.   That meant two of the three wings were missing groups and, unless the errant groups showed up, would, by prescript, have to turn back.   Maybe the mission wasn't going to be completed after all.   It also meant that when Van Patten did show up, the First Wing would be leading the bomber stream, not be in the middle, like it was supposed to and the Fortieth would depart and leave the task force short all those guns.   The likelihood that any one of them would survive the day just went down even further.   Misfortune, ordinary bad luck, exacerbated by poor command decisions, were combining to make a bad situation into one which Hollis thought was rapidly becoming untenable.

Passing out over the Channel, Hollis could just make out the rim of the Continent.   To the left, he spotted the bomber stream.   One of the three wings seemed to be circling.   The lead wing had three groups.   Whoever they were, Hollis thought it was the First Wing, they had picked up a low group.   Maybe the other 'lost' low group had found a wing to join taking the place meant for the 381st.   Now what would Van Patten do?

At five minutes after one, at twenty-one thousand feet and climbing, as the leading First

Wing was about to cross over Walcheren, Van Patten slid the 381st into a position beside and slightly above the 351st, forming a second 'high' group.   The leading wing was now four groups strong.   Hollis could make out the tail markings on the 'new' low group.   It was the wayward 305th.   If their leader wanted to keep that position, Hollis, and probably everyone in the Group, was glad to let him have it.   Ironic, Hollis thought, of the four groups in the wing about to cross into the Netherlands, only one, the 305th, was actually where it was supposed to be: low group of the leading wing.   Because of the fortuitous mistake, of which they now found themselves inadvertent benefactors, the 532nd had gone from being in the worst possible location to probably the safest, inside, sandwiched between the high squadron of the high group and the lead squadron of an even higher group.   Maybe things wouldn't turn out so bad.   But, Hollis thought, a mission with this many things wrong with it at the outset, does not bode well.   Errors tend to compound, not cancel each other out.   But commanders, being who they are, were determined to seek out their target and do what they were sent to do, regardless of the obstacles placed before them.   Perhaps that was a good thing, Hollis thought.   If commanders had shied away from adversity they'd still be a colony of England.   *Perish the thought*, he smirked.

Then again, maybe Fate was just toying with them.   This was going to be a bad day, no matter how things developed.   Time would tell.   There would be signs.

"Escort, two o'clock high," Dodge announced.   Reassuring words.   Hollis strained to look, but could not see them.   He noticed a few scattered bursts from the coastal flak belt, but they were inconsequential.

"Bogies, twelve o'clock level," Sully said.   "Eight or ten of them."

Hollis looked dead ahead and could barely make out, blending with the horizon, several black dots in loose formation.   They grew larger as they approached head-on and, growing near, banked sharply downward in an effort to draw the P-47s away from the bombers. Acknowledging the challenge, four of the American fighters broke off to give chase, but the rest would not take the bait, to uncover the bombers, for other Germans were, no doubt, lurking nearby.   They maintained their back and forth weave above the bombers.   Patient, disciplined. They would be entangled soon enough.

The bombers passed over Walcheren and into the Netherlands.   The 305th stayed where it was and so did Van Patten.   The Germans returned a short time later, attempting the same ruse with the same result.   When they returned the third time they were clearly interested in inflicting damage to the formations, not just lead the escort off on a wild goose chase.   This time the P-47's had no choice but to respond and Hollis watched with grudging admiration as the American fighter pilots threw themselves into the fray.   In doing so, they had to drop their belly tanks to relieve themselves of the extra weight and drag.   That would cut short their range and they would be forced to chase the Germans all over the sky, using up more fuel.   With the P-47s engaged, a few fighters made passes at the bombers, but they were probably waiting until the fighters turned back at the limits of their range.   Then the real battle would begin in earnest.

A large dogfight ensued lasting no more than a few minutes, if that, and order was restored.   A few fighters wagged their wings in final salute and turned for home.   Slowly, those that remained had to leave also and the bombers were, briefly, alone.

"Bogies, twelve o'clock high!" Sully shouted.   "Jesus, there must be fifty of them. Good God, here they come."

Hollis watched with pristine clarity the first German Focke-Wulfs flip over into a dive and hurtle downward at the lead wing. Tracers arced out to greet them in a violent exchange of machine gun and cannon fire. A moment later, **Goofy's Glider** shook with return fire as the second and third waves came after the combined high groups. Almost immediately, Hollis could see bombers smoking. One from the low group fell, then another.

"Me-110's lining up for rocket attack, dead astern. Here they come!"

Hollis could see black lines of smoke plunge through the formation. One rocket struck a Fort in the lead group and the resulting explosion tore the bomber apart in a convulsion of flame and metal. More rockets passed through the formation and dropped away spent of fuel without hitting anything. But they had the desired effect. The low and lead groups were loosened and the Me-109s and FW-190s took advantage and savagely tore into them.

Hollis pulled his mask away and allowed the sweat and drool to escape his mask. They had been lucky so far. The two high groups had been unscathed. There was a lot of chatter over the intercom as fighters were called out and Forts in distress were identified.

Hollis looked at Leo and found him singing into his mask, rubber-necking from side to side, the oxygen hose flopping from side to side like the trunk of an apoplectic elephant.

With jarring suddenness, **Goofy's Glider** shuddered under the impact of exploding cannon shells. More return fire. It was a familiar, terrifying cacophony.

"We're hit! Tore some holes in the waist and the wing," Quinn yelled. "I think we're OK."

Hollis could see three holes in the left wing, metal torn open like a ruptured can, but no mist vented from the holes. A quick sniff of frigid air. No smell of gas.

"Crew check-in," Hollis demanded.

One by one, the crew reported in, everything and everybody was OK.

"Here they come again," MacFadden yelled. "Three o'clock level. Coming over, Dodge!" The bomber rattled and shook. Hollis saw the fighters zoom past and disappear below. A bomber fell from the 351st. It was under control, the crew bailed out.

"Count those chutes, ten o 'clock low!" Hollis yelled.

"Three...five...six. Two out the nose, eight. Nine, come on...there she goes."

The bomber rolled over and plunged toward earth.

The low group was getting it bad. They lost another. Then another Fortress left the formation and appeared to try for home.

A Fortress from the lead squadron was hit and started down. A bomber from the high squadron started smoking but seemed to hold on. Hollis figured that it would not for long.

This was the most intense air battle Hollis had ever seen. Even worse than Bremen or the first Schweinfurt. The sky was crisscrossed by smoke from burning engines and falling airplanes, the blue laced by tracers. Parachutes, white and brown, drifted down like leaves in an autumn breeze.

The fighters came in from all angles, singly and in pairs, firing wildly, barrel-rolling and split 's'ing downward away from the storm of lead sent out to thwart them. There was no coordination to the German attacks, it had degenerated into a free-for-all. A measure of the intensity of the battle was revealed to Hollis when he realized that the gunners had stopped calling out fighters on the interphone, there were targets everywhere. Nobody needed to be told where to shoot. **Goofy's Glider** vibrated like a shivering animal. It would be over soon, Hollis knew. There was nothing he could do to prevent it.

He pressed the intercom button on the wheel, "Watch the ammo, you guys.   We've still got a long way to go."   At least he had done something.   He reached down and felt for his parachute, fingering the pack, assuring himself it was where he had placed it in the unlikely chance he would live long enough to use it. Leo was watching him.

He felt detached, removed from this place of death and mayhem.   It was as if he had left his body and was floating weightless, unafraid, everything done by subcortical reflex, not requiring conscious thought or action.   He kept his eye on Van Patten,   determined to keep good formation to the end.   He heard sounds, but they were in the next room.   He felt things, but it was as if his body were padded by layers of cotton.

The words exploded in his head like a rifle shot.   "They got the new guy!"

Hollis turned to look at Svoboda.   His Fortress, **La Femme Fatale**, was on fire, pieces of it tearing loose and falling away.   The bomber nosed over and dove straight toward earth. The final impact was out of his view.

Hollis felt himself shaking.   He had come apart, he knew.   The numbness, the sense of detachment from what was happening around him, was the first sign of battle shock, the catatonia which would leave him a quivering, helpless blob of flesh at any moment, at even the most innocuous provocation.

Without warning, inexplicably, the lead elements of the wing turned left and the rest of the formation followed him.

"What the fuck's he doing?" Hollis yelled, almost annoyed, surprised his voice would work, equally astonished that he had maintained his place in formation when they turned.

"How should I know?" Cobb replied.   "He's left the briefed course, I can tell you that."

"Mollica, look behind and see if anybody's following us."

A few moments later, Mollica replied, "No sir.   Just us.   The wing behind us stayed on course."

Hollis exchanged glances with Leo.   If there was confusion in his mind, what was going on inside Van Patten's?

"Pilot to radio, anything?"

"No sir.   Just the usual jamming."   The bombers had refused a target before, but only because of weather, never by force of arms.   Perhaps today the Germans had succeeded in beating them back, defeating them.   Hollis was ashamed.   He could not countenance cowardice.   Not here, not now.

Again, without warning, the bombers turned south.   They found themselves over a large city, flak popping around them.

"Where are we, Cobb?"

"We're over Bonn.   Please, don't ask me why again."

"Why?"

"Because I don't want to talk to you anymore."

"No, why did he turn?"

"Couldn't have been to avoid the Jerries, they're still on us," Sully added.

The mystery, and Hollis's fear that he had witnessed an act of cowardice, was momentarily allayed when the formation wheeled again and resumed a south-easterly course. Hollis wondered where the other wings were.   This little detour had consumed time and gas, the following wings would have closed the distance.   Hollis did not see them.

The attacks resumed with terrible ferocity, the onslaught without end.   Twin-engine day fighters joined the attack, making passes just as the FWs and Messerschmitts had.   Hollis was certain no one would reach the target.   He looked down at the hapless low group.   There were only a few B-17s left.

Hollis heard laughing.

"Who is that?" Hollis asked.   "Bombardier, oxygen check."

Sully called out the positions.   Everyone answered but Mollica.   "Hulse, go back and check on Mollica."

"Yes sir."

Hollis envisioned Hulse negotiating the difficult passage into the tail.   Mollica was either hit or anoxic.

"Pilot, this is Hulse.   Mollica's passed out.   He came disconnected.   I got him hooked back up.   I'll stay with him 'til he comes around."

"OK."

Goofy's Glider shuddered and shook, taking more hits.   There would soon be nothing left of Moe's plane.

The leader made another turn, everybody dutifully followed suit.

"He's heading straight for Wurzburg," Cobb said.   Wurzburg was the IP.   "The Fortieth got ahead of us.   I can see 'em over to the right.   I think he's trying to take the lead again."

"How far to the IP?"

"Sixty miles.   With this visibility we should see it almost any minute."

"How far?"

A pause.   "Eight minutes."

"He's okay now, Lieutenant."

Hollis laughed.   Even if he were promoted to brigadier the crew would still refer to him as 'Lieutenant.'

"Mollica, you OK?"

"Yes sir.   I'm alright.   My plug came out.   Awful breezy back here.   Lotta holes."

The formation droned on, irrepressibly.   Hollis took a second to think of Jessie and Leo's letter.   So many unanswered questions, missed opportunities.

"They're going after Selkirk," Dodge yelled.   Hollis snapped his head around and felt a mixture of terror and fascination as the fighters came in line astern, seemingly singling out Selkirk's Fortress.   He was in awe of their airmanship and daring.   Hollis was transfixed by the scene unfolding before him as if played out in slow motion, yet lasted only a few seconds, 20mm shells exploded like flashbulbs across the nose of Selkirk's bomber.   The two panels of the windshield were suddenly covered with blood as if splashed with a bucket of red paint.   A moment later he watched as a hand, presumably Selkirk's, tried to wipe some of the red goo from the windshield.   An instant later there were two more small flashes, fleeting puffs of smoke and the windshields shattered inward revealing the cockpit to be a dark, macabre cave into which he could not see.   The B-17 held still for a moment then the left wing lifted and the Fortress fell off to the right.   It was the last time he saw it.   "Selkirk is going down," was announced.   Ten seconds.   No more.

"IP, five minutes."

Chapter Fifty-five   **Hollis**

Hollis looked at the clock above the windshield.   It was 1422.   The first attacks had occurred at 1330 and began in earnest about ten minutes later.   They had been under constant attack for about fifty minutes.   Hollis had lost count of how many bombers he had seen fall. His squadron alone had lost two.   The group one or two more.   Several had fallen from the 91st and 351st and the low group, the errant 305th, had been decimated.   And they had not yet reached the target.   When one group of Germans became exhausted they were replaced by fresh fighters, eager to extract their pound of flesh.

Hollis remained convinced he would not live through the day.   He had seen nothing which would give him reason to think otherwise.   He also began to think this would be the day on which, history would record, high-altitude, daylight, precision bombing had been defeated. How much damage can be inflicted on a target when only half the planes ever get there?   What future is there when the other half never makes it home?

Goofy's Glider was buffeted again and again.   Hollis wondered how long the plane might hold together.   It took, on average, between twenty and twenty-four twenty millimeter cannon hits to bring down a Flying Fortress.   Hollis figured they were getting close.   But all four engines were running and as long as no vital part was damaged and the bomber remained airworthy, they could keep their place and do what they came to do.   Hollis hoped they could at least get to put the bombs on the target before the end came as he was convinced it would. Selkirk knew.   Leo knows.   That was probably contained in the letter.   A final good bye.   A written kiss before parting for the last time.

"IP two minutes."

Hollis could see the city of Wurzburg dead ahead.   Off to the left he could make out Schweinfurt twenty-three miles northeast of the IP.

They had assumed the lead again from the Fortieth Wing.   They would be first over the ball bearing factories after all, just like last time.   *Dubious distinction*, Hollis thought.

"Radio to pilot."

"Go ahead radio."

"First of all, I'm out of ammo and I'm saving what's left here for the others.   Second, Goldrock told Rainbow and Buckshot he was going to turn short of the IP to allow the next wing to fall into trail.   He warned not to take too much interval and to keep the formation tight."

Hollis turned far around in his seat.   The two groups comprising the Fortieth Wing were close behind, the gap not more than a minute instead of the usual five.

"IP, one minute."

The German fighters continued their attacks.   Two FWs with their noses painted a black and white checkerboard pattern roared past hitting Spats's plane.   Hollis remembered Ransahoff was his copilot.   Ransahoff would never send his men to a place he would not go himself. Bully for him.   West Point.   Hollis, Ransahoff and Van Patten may be the only pilots to make both trips to Schweinfurt, another dubious honor.   Probably none of them would survive the day.   Nobody would be alive to say they had been there twice.   Once the Germans found out what the target was, their beloved ball bearing plants, hell would break loose and anybody who came out on the other side of the bomb run would meet a mighty gaggle of very pissed-off Hitlerites.

"IP."

Hollis took his eyes from Van Patten's B-17 long enough to see the bomb bay doors open on the lead ship of the wing and two red flares arc into the sky.   Its left wing dipped, entering a shallow bank to the northeast toward Schweinfurt.   Once The lead group was uncovered, the 351st turned, followed a few moments later by the 381st.   The wayward, decimated 305th simply turned with the lead group and held on for dear life.   The bomb run would last eight minutes.

Goofy's Glider rumbled with the opening of her bomb bay doors.   Hollis instinctively advanced the throttles.   The bombers rolled level as one and headed for the aiming point.   The fighters backed away.   They knew what was in store for the bombers and would give the flak wide berth.   They would be waiting at the end of the gauntlet.   Up ahead the flak started, small, silent puffs, dotting the sky.   The flak increased in intensity as the bombers drew near until it seemed as if the sky would turn black by the coalescence of the black, roiling smoke, dozens of new explosions each second.   No one, it seemed would come out at the other end. The Germans would be waiting and no one would emerge from the black cloud for them to attack.

Hollis turned to look at the formation to their rear and noted the closeness of the two groups of the Fortieth.   Several of their   planes were dragging a line of smoke behind them. Way back, Hollis could make out the last wing, the Forty-first, as it neared the IP.   Well beyond them, on a converging course, was the still-unseen Third Division.   Hollis wondered how they had fared.   Had the different course worked for them?

Hollis eased in close to Van Patten; the entire group noticeably tightened up as they drew closer to the target.   It would be a good bomb run.   Below the black cloud Hollis could plainly see Schweinfurt as it came closer with each passing second, growing bigger and bigger, flak cannon twinkling.

The bomb run seemed as if it would never end.   **Goofy's Glider** was knocked around and peppered by shrapnel.   A ship from the 351st caught fire, but held its place, the flames leaping back in the space behind the wing.   It would explode any second.   They passed over the bomb release line and Hollis saw the plane's load descend from its belly.

A few moments later, **Goofy's Glider** rattled and shook with the unleashing of its 1000 pounders.   The bomber rose with relief of its burden.   Hollis glanced at the place where the burning bomber had been.   Parachutes filled the sky, the burning Fortress was gone.

"Bombs away.   Let's get the hell out of here."

The bombers ahead made a diving turn to the right, like a flock of ducks suddenly diverted by the sound of a gunshot.   A few moments later the 381st followed suit, gaining speed in an effort to reach the Rally Point and regroup.

"Boy, we really clobbered the place this time," Rizzo said.

Van Patten put the 381st back where it had been, high and on the outside.   Hollis looked around briefly as he tried to regain his position off Van Patten's wingman.   Nevtushenko and Robertshaw were there.   He could not see Fissano.   The Group looked as if it had come through the gauntlet intact.   The Groups reformed the Wing at the Rally Point and made the big turn for home.

Dodge called out the returning fighters.   Hollis knew they would be back, he thought they would want to direct their attention to the bombers behind them that were yet to bomb. Now they just wanted retribution.   It would not be long in coming.

The air battle resumed.   It was not as savage as the battle had been on penetration, perhaps this was a good sign.   They would be out of Germany in another fifteen minutes. Maybe the battle would end over France and they just might make it home.   The German fighters attacked the lead and what was left of the low groups.   For the time being the two high groups were being spared.   The formation plodded onward.   Fortresses fell.   Cobb eventually announced that they had passed into France.   Hollis dared not let himself hope.

"Bogies, twelve o'clock high.   Here they come!"

Hollis snapped a glance upward and could see the fighters, fifteen or twenty breaking off to dive at the retreating bombers.   The top turret started firing.   They were still out of range. Hollis was about to say something to Dodge but felt such admonitions at this late stage were futile.   Hollis could feel the repeated impacts on **Goofy's Glider.**

"Hulse is hit!"

Hollis nearly leapt from his seat, his heart almost ceasing to beat.

"Aw, Jesus, he's hit bad!"

"Sully, get back there," Hollis yelled into the interphone.

Precious seconds seemed to pass waiting for Sully to appear.

"Sully?"

No answer.

"Cobb?"

Sully's dark hulk appeared in the crawlway below the flight deck and he struggled upward, one hand holding a bulky portable oxygen bottle, the other a first aid kit.

More firing as the battle continued unabated.

Hollis said a prayer that Hulse might be okay.   But there had been panic in MacFadden's voice, implying the worst.   Seconds dragged by.   Then minutes.

Finally, Sully reappeared.   There was blood on his gloves.   He shook his head, despair filled his eyes.

"He's dead," Sully yelled into Hollis's ear.   Leo, his eyes wide, turned away at the news. Sully returned to the nose.

Hollis was seized by the desire to give up.   He wanted to leave his seat, put on his chute and simply jump.   He had done all he could do.   He had no more to give.   He fingered the latch on his seat belt.

"109's coming around!" Mollica yelled.   "Get 'em!"

There was a sudden bang and Hollis saw a pair of goggles fly past his view.   He turned to look and saw Leo clutching his neck blood cascading between his lips, a look of utter surprise on his face.   Not pain, not fear.   Surprise.   An instant later, there was another loud bang and a red mist filled the cockpit.   The front of Leo's face exploded in a spray of blood and tissue.   He moved his hands to his face and held them there for a moment then slumped back in his seat.

"We're hit!   We're hit!" Rizzo yelled.   "Number One's on fire!"

Hollis could feel the warm liquid on his exposed temples.   He was covered with it.   It smeared Jessie's scarf.   He looked over at Leo and realized the only thing left of his head was some skull, scalp and an ear.   The rest was gone.   Hollis could not take his eyes off the dead copilot.   He could not move, his every muscle was locked tight.

He heard screaming in the headphones, but his mind would not let him discern the words. He finally removed his eyes from the corpse and looked out the windshield.   It was spattered with red polka-dots of various sizes and red smears of flesh.   Sinews covered the instruments. In a moment, they were frozen.   He looked at his gloved hands, they were covered with blood.

"Jesus Christ, we're on fire!   They must be dead!"   The words rang against his eardrums.   He snapped his head around and saw the left outboard engine engulfed in flames. He was surprised.   This was it.   He knew it was coming, but he was still surprised.   Like Leo. And Augie.   It was all happening in painful, astonishingly slow motion.   The flames wrapped around the wing in long, almost delicate bursts.   The propeller seemed to spin blade by blade. The yelling again distant, as if coming from the end of a long hall.

Hollis suddenly felt an electric charge run through his body.   He gripped the wheel with his right hand and reaching down with his left, toggled the bailout bell, pulling it several times before letting it ring continuously.   He said, calmly, he thought, so as not to raise a panic, "Bail out, bail out, bail out."

He reached across and, as fast as his hand could move, hit the fuel shut off valve and advanced the rpm.   He pushed the throttle to the stop then held the feather button.   He waited for the flames to miraculously resolve, but they did not.   They were inches away from the Tokyos, if not already enveloping them.   He stared at the burning engine.   It seemed remote, in the distance, as if it didn't even belong to his plane.   How would he die?   Would the explosion kill him?   Would he cook where he sat like Cahill?   Or would he die instantly on impact, like a bug on a windshield?

Sully appeared in the hatchway his eyes saucer-like above the rim of his mask at the sight of the blood.   He saw Leo's limp body the turbulence gently bouncing it in his seat.   He looked at Hollis, terror written in his eyes.   Hollis took his index finger and pointed downward several times vigorously, the signal to bail out.

Sully lingered for a moment.   The expression in his eyes going from terror to sorrow and he gave the thumbs up, tapping Hollis on the thigh with his bloody glove one last time.   He departed. A moment later, the nose hatch popped off with a gush of frigid air and light.   The light was blotted out twice in rapid succession and Hollis knew Cobb and Sully had left the plane.

Poor Leo.   Christie would never know what had become of her husband.   Where he had come to rest.   Would his final resting place be at the bottom of a smoking crater in the middle of nowhere, resting for all eternity among the people he tried to kill?   She might forever ask herself, as Molly surely will, was there enough of him left to give a decent burial or was he forever gone?   So much dust.   He would never again be with his beloved Christie.   Even if separated by six feet of earth.

Hollis waited until he was sure everyone had ample opportunity to leave, he shut off the alarm and pushed the nose over placing **Goofy's Glider** in a screaming dive.   He would try to blow out the fire.   Dead or alive, if Leo was ever to be reunited with Christie again this would be the only chance.   He watched the altimeter unwind like the second hand of a stop watch as **Goofy's Glider** hurtled, nearing the vertical, toward earth.   *Never put a Fortress in a near vertical dive*, Butch Mullen had said, *it will be the last thing you ever do.*

He didn't want to die and, for some inexplicable reason, felt his chances were better in the bomber than outside.

The airspeed crept close to 300 mph.   The wings were not designed to stay attached to the plane much above that speed.   He could see France rise up to greet him through the blood spattered windshield.   He glanced at the engine.   Smoke, but no flames.   It was now or never. With herculean effort Hollis pulled back on the control column.   It would not move, as if the control column were locked.   The force of the air over the control surfaces was more than he could overcome.   The end was near.   It was stupid.   He could have bailed out and left the two corpses to the hands of God, becoming a prisoner of war.   He didn't have to die by his own foolish choice, by his own hand.   He was amazed how the mind worked in such circumstances. Funny, he thought he might actually live forever.   *Pull hard*, Butch said.   *Keep pullin'.*

He tried one last time, hard as he knew how.   His gaze transfixed by approaching mother earth, out of the corner of his eye he saw Leo place his hand on the control and pull. Hollis closed his eyes, convinced if God was to choose, now was His time to do so.   Slowly, the wind screaming past the plane, the nose began to rise.   The G forces pushed him into his seat with the weight of a six men.   The world went gray as the blood drained from his brain, his arms pulling with all his might.   Would he know the impact when it came?   Did the brain, partially blacked-out, work that quickly?   As the plane began to level off and hurtle back skyward Hollis pushed the nose over into level flight.   *When all else fails, fly the fucking plane.*

He looked to see the left wing was still on.   The flames had not burned through and allowed it to separate.

He looked over at Leo.   The hand on the wheel belonged to Noah Dodge.

"Thanks!   I didn't think I was going to make it there for a second."

"Me either."

"How come you didn't jump?"

"I was waiting for you."

"You're a fool."

"No more'n you."

"You better get back in your turret.   We got a long way to go and they'll be after us soon."

Hollis and Dodge exchanged astonished glances when they heard firing from inside the Fortress.   It was the unmistakable rattle of the tail guns.   Hollis pressed the intercom, "Is anybody back there?"

"Tail to pilot.   Yes sir, it's me."   Mollica.   "I was just about to go when I heard the bailout alarm go off and I figured we weren't supposed to bail out any more.   I watched you put the plane into the dive and knew somebody was still at the controls so I thought I'd stick around. I saw the fire go out.   I didn't think you'd get us out of that dive."

"Me neither."

"You okay up there?"

"Yeah, Dodge is still here.   They got Lieutenant Wychulis.   What were you shooting at?"

"Some Me-110 prowling around back there.   I just wanted him to know I had my eye on him.   He left."

"Dodge, get up in the turret."

"You know the way home?"

"Yeah." Hollis raised his gloved index finger and pointed out the blood spattered window. "It's that a way."   Hollis was again drawn to Leo.   Dead.   That cosmic spark, that endowment of energy and awareness called life was gone.   Gone in an instant.   Vanished without a trace.

They were flying at no more than two thousand feet.   The warmer air rushing in from the nose hatch caused the frozen globs of what had been Leo's face and brain to melt, drawn downward by relentless gravity.   There was a piece of flesh clinging to the top of the throttle handle.   Hollis recognized it as a piece of lip.   He pulled the lip from its perch and placed it onto Leo's lap.   On the top of the ignition switches sat a partially collapsed eyeball looking indifferently back at Leo.

Hollis lowered the plane even further to the ground.   If they hedge-hopped and avoided flying near an airfield they might slip out of France un-noticed.   It was a long shot any way one looked at it.   Hollis figured they were north of Metz.   With Cobb gone, though, it was a guess. Hollis looked around for help, some wayward straggler who might have a navigator, but they were alone.   Empty sky above and France below.   Hollis figured if he flew a course west-north-west, roughly 300-310 degrees, eventually he would hit the Channel and England beyond. It was still a long shot.

They still had three good engines and the damage to **Goofy's Glider**, though extensive, did not affect the plane's ability to remain airborne.   If they could keep from getting jumped they stood a chance.

"Dodge, you in the turret?" Mollica asked.

"Yes."

"Three o'clock high.   I think I see two 109s.   I don't think they see us...wait I was wrong."

Dodge held his fire for an eternity, probably allowing them to think the Fortress was undefended.   Hollis turned to look.   Dodge hadn't even moved the turret toward them.

"They're gettin' real close, Dodge."

"I got 'em. Mollica."

Dodge swung the turret around and let fly a prolonged burst.

"Jesus, Dodge, I can't see.   Did you get him?"

"Yeah, nicked his buddy, too."

"Hot damn!   I see him now.   He just crashed into that forest!   Confirmed."

The lone Messerschmitt did not return.   But surely he would radio his pals and tell them of the crazy fat cow trying for the Channel.

On they flew.   Hollis kept track of time and airspeed and figured they were about fifty miles from the coast.   Suddenly an engine stopped.   Number three.   What had happened? The prop continued to windmill, but it was dead.

Hollis looked at the fuel gauges.   He could barely believe his eyes.   They were nearly out of gas.   He glanced at one wing then the other.   There were plenty of holes on both sides. It made sense that they had been losing fuel.   Hollis quickly pressed the feathering button.   To his dismay he saw smoke coming from the holes burned through the top of the wing behind number one.   They were still on fire.

"Dodge, Mollica, we got a problem.   We're nearly out of gas and the fire ain't out.   We lost a second engine and I don't think we can make it home.   I've got enough altitude.   I suggest you jump."

"How far are we from home?" Mollica asked.

"I figure another twenty, twenty-five minutes to the coast.   Depending on where we are, anywhere from half an hour to forty-five minutes to England."

Dodge appeared on the flight deck, ignoring Leo's body he leaned over to check the gauges.   He shrugged and yelled into Hollis's ear, "Let me see if I can transfer some fumes around.   We might could make it."

"Bail out.   You made one stupid choice already today, don't make another."

"What are you going to do?"

Hollis jerked his thumb at Leo.   "I'm taking him home."

Dodge yelled back, "I bet I can find us enough gas."

"Mollica.   I'm going to try and make it.   I suggest you hit the silk while you still can."

"What's Dodge going to do?"

"He's stayin'."

There was a pause.   "Me, too.   You got us this far."

"Are you sure?   We get out over the water and I have to set her down, ain't nobody going to find us."

"Nah, we'll make it."

Hollis, defying all reason and force of intellect, never felt so alive in his life.   It was as if he had lightning in his veins.   He was on the fine edge of mortality and he was in absolute command.   He sat up and looked beyond the bloody glass, trimming the plane, adjusting the mixture as lean as possible.   If there was any chance, he would take it.   He had, after all, gotten them this far.

Several minutes later, Dodge returned.   "I've done all I can.   Maybe she'll glide good." He smiled at Hollis.

The minutes dragged by, Hollis waited for the remaining engines to sputter and quit. There would be that awful silence.   Butch said *a B-17 don't glide well.*

Periodically, Hollis would force himself to look out the window at the smoke escaping from the wing.   It continued unabated.   The intensity of the moment brought him to the edge of euphoria.   He was invincible.   He was a warrior.   He had no fear of death.   Death was something he gave.

Hollis saw the thin rim of dark water.   The Channel.

"Last chance.   I suggest you jump."

"Think they'll be glad to see us, Lieutenant?"

"Yes, Sal.   They should be delighted.   Moe ain't gonna be none too happy."

The sea was calm, few whitecaps.   It would be easy to ditch.   They sank closer to the Channel.   The coast of France receded further and further behind.   Too late, now.   They could not bail out if they wanted to.   It was a long ride over cold, dark, empty water.

Hollis knew the arc of the propellers were only a few feet from the surface of the sea. When and if they reached the coast he was not sure they could climb above the dunes.   They were now flying on only one engine.

The number four engine quit.   The plane now being held in the air by only one engine. Hollis was barely breathing.   His heart was pounding in his chest, not from fear but from exhilaration.   He never felt so alive before.   Everything was crystal clear.   The ripples on the water, the vibration of the plane in his hands.   The smoke continued.   Up ahead, Hollis could barely make out the thin line on the horizon.   The Island.   England.

The End.

Epilogue

Sunday, January 30, 1983

Doctor John Hollis sat in his favorite leather chair overlooking Central Park, a fresh layer of snow covered the ground and clung to branches in fragile defiance.   He read the Sunday <u>New York Times</u>, section by section, a weekend ritual he had practiced for many years, until, by lunchtime, it had nearly exhausted his interest.   He went through the first section one last time when something in the obituaries caught his eye.   He studied the words: "Former SAC Commander dies."   He read the three inch long obituary: Retired Lt. Gen. Eugene P. Ransahoff died January 27th after a prolonged illness.   Ransahoff, an Air Force combat veteran of three wars, left a wife of 41 years, the former Helen Wicker of Nyack.   He is survived by his wife, four daughters and eleven grandchildren.

He stopped reading.   He knew the rest.   He was swept by sadness.   One of America's greatest warriors was gone.

He went to his library and pulled out an old tome, a small volume he hadn't touched in nearly forty years.   He returned to the window and began to read.

"When We Were Young" by Bedford Sullivan.

"My name is Nathan Bedford Forrest Sullivan, and, to the best of my recollection, this is what happened.

"They called me Sully.   I am the great-grandson of slave owners although I never admitted that to anyone.   I graduated *cum laude* in English from the University of Virginia.   I recently terminated my employment with the government of the United States of America.   I was a bombardier.

"I do not have a right leg.   When I finish committing this memoir to paper I think I shall kill myself as my hope and vitality were left behind with my limb

"John Hollis was the finest man I ever knew, but I did not like him.   He was a moody, humorless introvert, critical and demanding.   But he knew how to fly the plane and he took good care of us."

Sully never did kill himself.   The book won critical acclaim after the war.   To the best of Hollis's knowledge, Sully was still writing poems and short stories from his cottage in the Shenandoah.

After the war, they moved the remains of First Lieutenant Leo Wychulis to a cemetery on a hill overlooking Los Angeles.   His beloved Christie never remarried.

Hollis looked up from the page and returned his gaze to the snow.   Tears welled in his eyes, blurring his vision.   Ransahoff was right.   You never got used to flak.